Acknowledgement

A special thank you to Terri and Sue.
Your encouragement meant a lot to me.

Also to Mike, Justus, and Cathy
Thanks for putting up with all the craziness.

False Winter

Pamela R Calvin

By

Pamela R. Calvin

AmErica House
Baltimore

First printing

Cover Art by
Justus Calvin & Mike Calvin

ISBN: 1-58851-188-X
PUBLISHED BY AMERICA HOUSE BOOK PUBLISHERS
www.publishamerica.com
Baltimore

Printed in the United States of America

Chapter One

Wind howling from the north swirled around Kyla as she crouched on a stone ledge just below the crest of the hill. Every icy gust was a reminder of winter's reluctance to loosen its grasp on the land. Slamming into the trees on the ridge above her head with a sound like thunder, wave after frigid wave of wind rolled down the hill, the trees and grasses bending as it passed. She couldn't remember the last time she had seen the sun and had lost track of what day it was long ago, but it had to be late April or early May and the cold weather was still holding on with a vengeance.

Pulling her collar closer, Kyla tried to cut off another chilly blast of air. She was wearing every stitch of clothing she possessed - a hat and mittens, heavy denim jeans, and two shirts topped with a heavy sweater. On her feet she wore all the layers of socks she could and still manage to get her boots on. Over it all was a heavy woolen coat made for a large man. Holding her knees to her chest, her whole body fit under the coat. Inside her warm cocoon Kyla was comfortable enough, except for the wind from above and the frozen ground below.

Still, sitting on the cold hillside was not where Kyla wanted to be. Given a choice, she would have been in her cozy little hole with her hands warming above the fire. There was only one thing that could have brought her out into the frigid weather and that was hunger. She had no food. Her carefully rationed hoard was gone. Never, even in her wildest imagination, had she thought that she could have made her meager supply last as long as it did. When it started running low, she had tried to forage for food, but she didn't have the necessary skills required to live off the land, especially in the winter. Even if the weather improved and spring arrived tomorrow, it would be too late. Her choices were limited and Kyla was in the process of studying the only option available to her.

As she looked down at the valley, her gaze was riveted on the only source of food known to her, Cole Spring's farm. Only, it was no longer just a farm and the home of the Spring family. Perhaps the word fortress would have been a more accurate term. The farm had evolved over the last few months into an armed encampment, complete with a fence that encircled the farmhouse and surrounding buildings. During a time when the countryside for miles in every direction seemed totally devoid of all human activity, the farm had grown and new buildings erected in such a short time it seemed that they popped up overnight. Kyla had never seen anyone working on the buildings or the fence. During the months after the evacuations she had been too preoccupied with her own activities to care what was happening at the Springs' farm, but every time she had looked, there were more buildings and the fence enclosed more territory.

Once again Kyla went over her plan. She had been studying the farm for weeks, watching the sentries who walked the perimeter. There were always two men on patrol and they made their rounds at regular intervals. She had also noticed that the men on night watch had a bad habit of falling asleep. Hopefully, tonight would be one of those nights.

She would wait until it was dark before she made her move. There had been a truck full of men leave the farm shortly after daybreak and if they followed their usual routine, they would return just before nightfall. It would be too risky to try to cross the open fields and the road before they were back inside the fence. Even then she didn't plan on crossing over the road. Instead she would go under it.

From where she sat, she could slip into the cover of the brush and creep unseen down the hill. Using the trees and dense brush that grew next to the stream as cover, she planned to follow the frozen streambed and cross under the road by going through the corrugated metal tube the water flowed through. Then she would continue to follow the stream until it came to the southern end of the valley and Spring's farm where it ran close to the timber. That was there she planned to slip into the woods.

About a hundred yards into the woods was a grove of spruce growing so densely together that the limbs intertwined. It was the perfect place to cross the fence with the trees growing close on both sides. Climbing the trees would be easy enough. She had done it thousands of times when she was a child. The branches were evenly spaced along the trunk like the rungs in a ladder. The worst part would be forcing her way through the dead twigs that covered the trunk and branches. Dry and brittle, when they broke, the sharp ends penetrated even the thickest clothing, but it was preferable to trying to cross over the razor wire at the top of the fence. The tricky part would be crossing from one branch to another without crashing to the ground and she only had to do it twice, once to get in and then to get out.

Anyway that was her plan. It was at least a couple of hours until it would be dark enough to go. As she waited, Kyla tried to keep focused on the task she had set for herself and not let her mind wander but it was difficult. Her thoughts kept drifting back to that day, now more than a year ago, when her life had changed forever. Whether it was luck or fate, Kyla hadn't been at home when they came to evacuate the farms in her area.

The night before the evacuations there had been a terrible windstorm that had knocked down several trees and branches. It had also caused everyone in the area to loose electricity and telephone service. Since her husband had been called to active duty in the army a few months ago, all of the responsibilities of running the farm were hers. When one of the downed trees had fallen on the fence behind the barn, it was up to Kyla to do the repairs. She had just finished replacing a broken board on the fence and was chasing a cow that had escaped from its pen when she heard a truck pull into her driveway. Before she came out of the woods, Kyla saw the men in uniforms entering her house. There were several armed men standing outside the house as well. The intrusion into her home was unsettling and she decided to stay hidden until she knew what they were doing. Within a few minutes the men who had gone into her house came out and started searching the other buildings.

Kyla began backing away slowly as the searchers came closer to where she was hiding. Moving deeper into the woods, she kept her eyes glued on the men, fearful that they would see her. As soon as she was out of their sight, Kyla turned and began to run to warn her mother and father. Her memories of racing blindly through the trees, tripping and falling in her panic were as clear now as it had been a year ago. She couldn't count the times the scene had been repeated in her dreams. The sound of the truck rumbling down the road haunted her every night.

It had only been a mile to her parent's house, but there was no way she could have outrun the truck. By the time she topped the hill behind their house, it was too late. She was just in time to see her mother and father being loaded into the back of the truck with the other evacuees. For a brief moment, Kyla thought that she caught her father's eye as he sighted her standing at the edge of the woods. She was certain she saw him lower his head and shake it, almost imperceptibly, but she understood what he meant as clearly as if he had shouted the words, 'Stay away!'

The rest of that day she had stayed in the woods, hidden and out of sight of the road and the other homes in the area. Nor did she return to her house that night. Instead she went deep into the woods, past the pond behind her house where there was an old railroad bed that took her into the heart of the timber to a place her grandfather had shown her. It was the sight of an old town that had been abandoned long before he was a child. Nothing was left of it now, no buildings or even the rubble of their foundations only an old root cellar. The wooden door had rotted away a long time ago and a thick mat of vines hid the entrance. Pushing back the vines and cobwebs as she went, Kyla descended the stone steps. It was a familiar place. She had come here when she was a child and played in the cool dark cave with her cousins. It was full of pleasant memories and a refuge from the soldiers and their trucks. She spent that night sleeping on the dirt floor in the musty darkness. It was just the first of many lonely nights she spent there.

It would have been easy to stay in the cool dark cave and hide from the world, but then as now hunger had driven her out. In the first few days after the evacuations, Kyla had found it relatively easy to sneak out at night and gather supplies. Everything had happened so quickly no one had had time to gather their possessions and most doors had been left unlocked. She felt strange at first, going into the empty homes belonging to her neighbors and searching through their belongings. Picking the most isolated places and arriving just before dark, she watched for several hours, looking for any signs of activity, before deciding whether it was safe to enter or not. Owners or otherwise, she had to be absolutely sure that no one was waiting.

Kyla's greatest fear was that someone would become aware of her activities and start searching the woods for her. When she entered a house, she never broke into it. If there wasn't an open door or window, she would go on to another and she never took much, only a few items from each one. Canned goods she buried or hid near the homes where she gathered them. Blankets and perishable food she carried back to her hiding place deep in the woods. That was all she did the first few days

8

on her own. However, her foraging was curtailed sharply after a close run-in with the soldiers.

Actually, it was someone else they caught, but for Kyla the encounter had been way too close for her liking. Entering her chosen target that night had been easy enough. The back door was unlocked and she had gone right in. Everything seemed fine as she began searching the cupboards in the kitchen. After putting a few items into her gunnysack, Kyla had decided to check out the basement. When she reached the bottom of the basement steps, she heard a window opening and the sound of footsteps, moving softly and cautiously across the floor above her head. Quickly, she hurried to hide under the steps and crouching as small as possible, hid behind some boxes. There had been barely enough time to hide herself before she heard the sound of wood splintering, as the door to the house was forced open and then the scuffle of heavy, booted feet running across the floor. She had thought she would collapse with terror when the door to the basement flew open and someone started coming down the steps. Whoever it was stopped at the bottom step and flashed the beam of his flashlight around the room, but didn't search further than that. Although it had probably taken only a few seconds, it had seemed like an eternity before the man went back up the steps. Once the door closed, Kyla finally took a deep breath, but she was still afraid to move or risk making any sound. Even after she heard the footsteps leaving the house, Kyla remained where she was, hidden under the steps. It was nearly dawn before she slipped out one of the basement windows, but not without her sack full of food. After her close call, she had been afraid to enter the houses.

One of the items Kyla had found rummaging around in the empty homes was a small telescope. It was not much more than a child's toy, but she had found it useful in observing the next phase of activities, the systematic gathering of everything the citizens of the community had left behind. Tankers pulled into gas stations and emptied the underground tanks. Trucks were loaded with the contents of all the stores. Cars and other vehicles were loaded on transports and hauled away. Homes were searched and then boarded shut. Anything of value was packed up and moved away. Oddly enough, a significant portion of what was collected did not go far at all. The Spring farm was the destination for many items, which disappeared into the storage sheds that had obviously been built for that purpose. All contained inside the eighteen-foot security fence complete with razor wire on top and sentries patrolling the perimeter, it was a formidable place and there was nothing about it that said, "Welcome neighbor."

Still, that was what brought her here today. Right after the evacuations she had seen someone try to break into Spring's farm. He hadn't gotten within twenty feet of the wire before they shot him. Kyla didn't plan on ending up like him. Suspicion and caution had served her well up until now and she didn't plan on changing. Still, she wasn't too optimistic about her chances. She had to get inside the fence, find where the food was stored, and get back out with enough to make the whole effort worthwhile. It was probably no different than suicide, but her only other choice was death by starvation. It was just slower. So today, she watched and waited knowing that they were most likely watching her, too.

~ ~ ~

Everything had gone as Kyla planned, up to the point where one of the limbs had broken under her weight. She hadn't been able to stop her fall and now she was trapped in a tangle of broken branches hanging about fifteen feet above the ground. Every time she tried to move there was the sound of branches cracking and she would slip a little lower. Still, she was over the fence and hoping she could extract herself from her predicament without being discovered until she heard the sound of footsteps below. A bright beam of light searched through the trees and before long it came to rest on Kyla.

"Hey, Pop!" Someone called out. Kyla knew the voice. It belonged to Clovis Spring. When Kyla heard another set of footsteps approaching, Clovis said, "Look what we got up the tree."

Kyla tried to turn her head and see the second person, but all she could see was the bright light shining in her eyes. Thankfully, they hadn't fired first and asked questions later. For the moment she was still alive.

"Well, I guess you were right, boy." The low gruff voice belonged to Cole Spring. "It wasn't a big gray 'possum that you saw sneaking around on the bluffs today."

"Do you want me to shoot it down?" Clovis asked. His voice was almost gleeful as he made his offer.

"No, hold off for a minute," Cole answered. His voice was low, almost a growl as he added, "I think I know this one."

Kyla heard him move closer to the tree and tried to twist her body a little more so she could see the men on the ground. As soon as she moved, she began to fall, sliding from one branch to the next with branches snapping and breaking under her as she went. She finally ended up dangling just above their heads like a scarecrow on a pole. The only thing holding her up was a branch that was caught on the back of her coat. Now she was close enough to see their faces and they could see her clearly, too.

Cole moved closer and Kyla could see the look of recognition cross his face as he said, "Well, girl, unbutton that coat and you can drop the rest of the way." He turned and without looking back at Kyla added, "Or I can let Clovis shoot you down." Cole was done with the situation and having given Kyla her options, he was returning to the house.

He had given her no choice. Kyla hated to loose her coat, but she began to pull at the button at the top of the jacket and once it was loosened, she slipped out of the coat. She hit the ground on her hands and feet like a cat, but before she had a chance to stand up, Clovis placed his foot firmly on her seat and pushed her face first onto the ground. He had always been a bully when they were children, but now he was a bully with a gun.

"Hold still," he growled as she began to get up. "Just stay on your belly and get your arms above your head. I want to see your hands." Then holding his gun with one hand, he knelt with his knee in the middle of Kyla's back and began to search her using his free hand. It didn't take him long to find the hunting knife that she carried and a pocket knife that was tucked into her boot. They were the only items that she carried that could have been considered weapons, pitiful protection against men armed with guns. Still, Clovis continued to search or more accurately grope. Kyla knew that he wasn't looking for

11

weapons anymore and was seeking to confirm that he was searching a woman and not a boy; a cheap tactic that was another of Clovis' endearing characteristics.

When he finally stood, Kyla gasped for breath as his weight was lifted off her back. "Get up," he commanded and gave her a sharp kick in the ribs for emphasis. Kyla rose slowly, keeping a wary eye on him as she did. Once she was standing, Clovis began pushing her in the direction of the house using the barrel of the gun to prod her along. Kyla kept her eyes on the ground and let him guide her with a series of shoves and pushes. She was in no hurry to get to wherever he was taking her. Still, it didn't take long to get to the farmhouse, even with Kyla dragging her feet every step of the way.

As they came closer, Kyla could see the outline of the large two-story house. It was a familiar place. The Spring family had been her neighbors all her life and she had been to their home countless times. She had gone to school with both Clovis and his brother, Asa. All that made their current behavior even more bizarre. Even though she had seen the guards shoot the stranger, Cole and Clovis knew her. It didn't matter that she was sneaking over their fence in the middle of the night. Somewhere in the back of her mind, Kyla had been certain that they would be happy to see her, but there was nothing friendly about her welcome. When they got to the gravel driveway that led to the house, Cole Spring was waiting for them. Clovis gave her one last shove right at his father. Before she fell on top of Cole, Kyla managed to catch her balance, bringing her nose-to-nose with the older man.

Cole Spring was not a tall man, hardly as tall as Kyla who was not tall for a woman. He had a round belly and an obvious tilt to the left, like one leg was shorter than the other one. When he walked it looked like his body was rolling from side to side. As a young child when Kyla saw him walking, she thought that he looked comical, like a penguin, but there was nothing funny about him now. Cole had been studying her silently for several minutes before Clovis, impatient as always, got things rolling. "Are we gonna stand out here in the cold all night?" he asked, his voice whining and demanding at the same time.

Not impressed, Cole snarled, "Shut your, yap. I'm thinking." It was only a few moments longer before he snapped his order to Clovis. "Lock her in the shed. I'll decide what to do with her in the morning."

With that said, he wheeled his body around. Kyla watched him limp toward the house and saw the light as he opened the door to go inside. It was warm and inviting and then it was gone.

Which left her alone with Clovis, who was still fuming at having been told to shut up. He let out his frustrations on Kyla by slamming into her and shoving her in the direction of the shed. She almost ended up face down on the ground again, but managed to catch herself with her hands and at the same time move far enough away to be out of reach of the second blow aimed in her direction. Once on her feet, she hurried to keep out of Clovis' way as he stalked angrily behind her. She would have gone right into the shed, if she hadn't had to stop at the door and wait for Clovis to unlock it.

After the door was open, he grabbed Kyla by the scruff of her neck and pushed her inside. With his free hand he reached out and flicked the light switch. Kyla was amazed. They had electricity, one of those modern conveniences that she had taken for granted. As she blinked and shaded her eyes against the bright light, Kyla saw Clovis' gun propped up on the wall just outside the door, but as soon as the thought popped into her mind, she dropped it. There was no way that she could reach it before Clovis and Kyla didn't want to give him any reason to strike her again. Still, she wouldn't stop looking for a way to escape. In her estimation, her efforts hadn't been completely unsuccessful. She was alive and inside the fence. There had to be a way out. As her eyes adjusted to the light she scanned the room and her gaze came to rest on Clovis.

He had never been what she or anybody else would call a handsome man with a heavy brow and jaw that gave him a sullen and brooding look, which suited his disposition. At least he had always been presentable, but in the months since Kyla had last seen him his appearance had definitely gone to hell. He was wearing a coat that was way too small for a man of his size and girth, making him look awkward and gangly with his arms bare well above his wrists and the fabric stretched tight across his chest. Worst of all was his hair. It looked like a drunken barber had cut it with hedge clippers. His thick black hair was clipped so short in places that she could see his scalp. What hair was left was cut in varying lengths and stuck out in wild disarray. That was all topped off with a long scraggly beard that hung down to his chest. Clovis was one crazy looking son of a bitch.

"What the hell are you staring at?" he bellowed as he released Kyla and slammed the door shut.

Kyla had been staring, gawking actually. As soon as she realized that she had been standing with her mouth open, she clamped it shut and moved a step away from Clovis. When he reached into his pocket and produced a pair of handcuffs, she was visibly startled. Clovis laughed at her reaction, obviously enjoying Kyla's distress. "Did you think we were going to leave you out here and trust you not to take off? You're not the first guest we've had," he said as he grabbed her right arm and snapped the cuff tightly on her wrist. Then pulling her to the back of the shed, he attached the other cuff to the metal leg of the workbench that was built into the wall. Once she was secured, Clovis went to the door and turned off the light as he went out.

Alone now, Kyla felt the awful reality of her situation descending on her like the darkness. She sank to her knees, wanting to cry, but she was too exhausted both mentally and physically. Sneaking into the farm to get food and supplies had taken every last bit of strength that Kyla had possessed. Foolhardy as her plan now seemed, it had been the only thing that had kept her on her feet the past few days. Even as tired and distraught as she was, Kyla finally felt the cold and her need to survive crept back into her mind. She knew she needed to do something or she would freeze without her coat. The shed was protection from the wind, not the cold and Kyla was shivering as she began to feel around on the top of the bench behind her. For a workbench it was disappointingly uncluttered and she couldn't find anything within reach. When searching the top proved unsuccessful, she began groping around in the darkness under the bench, her hands searching for anything that she could use. At first all she felt were some large metal containers, probably paint cans, but when Kyla stretched out as far as she could reach, the tips of her fingers brushed something that felt promising.

She was barely able to touch it, but it felt like a canvas drop cloth, a little stiff and definitely not warm like a blanket, but it was better than nothing. Time and time again, Kyla tried to snag the edge with her fingers, but no matter how hard she tried, they always slid off. Then working her fingers along the edge and curling the tips under the fold, she finally found a small tear. With a little pressure from her finger, she was able to make the hole larger and work her fingertip inside and drag it toward her. After a few tries she had pulled the canvas out far enough that she could grab it with her hand. As she jerked it free, several cans clattered to the floor.

Quickly, Kyla grabbed the piece of canvas and wrapped it around her shoulders, all the while watching the door waiting for Cole or Clovis to come and investigate. They had to hear the noise, but no one came and after awhile, Kyla was able to relax a little. They knew that she couldn't escape the handcuffs. All she could do now was wait for Cole's decision in the morning, but Kyla had already decided that she wasn't going to give up on trying to escape. If an opportunity arose, she planned on jumping on it with both feet. They wouldn't find her napping, Kyla thought to herself as she laid her head on the floor. That was the last thing that she remembered that night.

It seemed as if only a few moments had passed before she was awakened by what was becoming Clovis' all too familiar greeting, a kick in the ribs. It was still dark outside and he was carrying a flashlight and shining it in her face. Kyla held up her hand to keep the light out of her eyes and squinted, trying to see what he was doing. The sight of Clovis looking as wild and crazy as the night before made her wish he had only been one of the nightmares that had plagued her while she was sleeping. She stood up and faced him defiantly, even though she knew she didn't stand a chance against a man of his size. When Clovis set the light on the workbench, she could see that he had a paper bag in his hands. She lost a little of her bristle when he took a small roll out of the bag and gave it to her. Without wasting time to say thank you, Kyla wolfed down the hard, dry bread. When it was gone, Kyla looked up and Clovis was pouring steaming liquid from his thermos into a cup and then handed it to her. It was dark and hot and smelled like coffee, but when Kyla took a sip it was so bitter she could hardly drink it.

When Kyla looked at Clovis again, he was grinning smugly. There was something more disconcerting about Clovis smiling than when he was glaring at her. She could only wonder what was going through his mind as he stood staring at her and fingering something in his coat pocket. When he took his hand out of his pocket, Kyla could see that Clovis was holding a small stone that looked like a pearl in the palm of his hand. He thrust his hands back into his pockets and fidgeted nervously for a few seconds before he said, "Kyla Wallace?" and peered at her with curiosity.

Kyla didn't answer. There was nothing that she wanted to say to the man standing before her. Through her whole ordeal she hadn't uttered a word and had allowed them to herd her into the shed and lock her up like some dumb animal, but from somewhere, five little words of civility came to mind. "Thank you for the food," Kyla muttered, saying the words so softly they could barely be heard. After so many months without speaking to anyone, the sound of her voice sounded strange.

"Ha," Clovis snorted with satisfaction. "It is you! Pop said it was, but I couldn't believe it." He glared at her for a moment and said, "We figured that you were dead like the rest of your family." Kyla snapped to attention, she had suspected they were dead, but hearing Clovis speak her worst fears was unsettling and she remained silent. Not that her reaction mattered to Clovis, he was moving closer to Kyla and stopped right in front of her. "I don't know why Pop didn't let me shoot you last night. That's what we usually do when we catch a trespasser," he said. Much taller than Kyla, he was looking at the top of her head when he said, "I guess the old man had his reasons." Then Clovis took her chin in one hand and forced her to look up at his face. As he studied her thoughtfully, "As I recall you don't look half bad when you're cleaned up."

When he began to squeeze her jaw and cheek, Kyla finally found her voice and she began pleading, "Stop, Clovis, you're hurting me. We've known each other for years, please stop."

He only grinned and leaned closer, pinning her against the workbench. "Well, things are different now, aren't they?" he said with a laugh. "We run things around here now." Before she could protest again, Clovis' mouth was on hers, kissing her. Kyla began trying to push him away with her free hand, but he just brushed her arm aside like it was nothing and held her by the wrist. His free hand was busy working its way under the layers of clothing that she wore. When Clovis found bare skin and touched her breast, Kyla did the only thing

16

that she could to fight back. She bit his lip as hard as she could. When Clovis jumped back cursing, Kyla could taste his blood in her mouth.

Kyla saw the look of shock on Clovis' face as he touched his lip. Then he looked at his fingers and saw the blood and his expression changed to rage. "You fucking bitch," he snarled and struck her squarely against the jaw. Kyla had seen it coming, but couldn't get out of the way. As she felt the jolt from the blow, her knees buckled and the room began to swim around her. She was fighting to stay conscious and was only marginally aware of Clovis hoisting her up and slamming her down on the workbench, still cursing and tearing at her clothes. She floundered around with her free hand searching for anything that she could use as a weapon, something to throw, anything. When her hand found the shelf above her head, she grabbed it and tried to pull away from Clovis. The only thing that she accomplished was to pull the shelf and everything on it clattering down on her head with a racket that was loud enough to wake the dead.

Only a few moments later Kyla heard the door bang open and then the lights went on. "What the hell do you think you're doing?" It was Cole's voice bellowing angrily as he pulled Clovis off of Kyla and began dragging his huge son out of the door by the scruff of his neck. The light went off again and the door slammed shut, but Kyla could still hear him shouting at Clovis as they went. "I told you to leave her alone. Who knows what kind of vermin she's carrying."

Kyla laid where she was, stunned and in shock. After a few moments, she carefully shook herself free from the pile of junk that had fallen on her head. As she sat up, dangling her legs over the side of the workbench, she felt her jaw. It was already beginning to swell. Her optimism was running low, as her situation grew less promising with every hour that passed. Even if she did escape, she couldn't go back to living like she had been and staying at the farm was an alternative that she didn't want to think about right now. Alive her prospects were bleak and death was beginning to look more promising. Slipping off the bench and onto the floor, Kyla gathered up the canvas cloth and wrapped it around her shoulders again. She didn't try to straighten her clothes. It would have taken more effort than she was willing to give. All she could do was stare blankly at the door and wait.

17

A few minutes later when Kyla heard the doorknob turning again, she jumped to her feet expecting the worst. Someone entered the room and turned on the light. "Oh, god," he gasped, "I'm so sorry. I am so sorry about Clovis." This time it was Asa, the younger brother, carrying a tray and he sounded truly apologetic. All of a sudden in the middle of the madness, here was someone showing Kyla some kindness.

Asa was a younger version of his father, only without the round belly or the limp. His light brown hair was neatly trimmed and his clothes were clean and pressed. He was staring at Kyla and suddenly remembered the reason that he had come. "I'm sorry," he apologized again and set the tray on the workbench beside Kyla. "I was supposed to bring your breakfast. Pop told Clovis to stay away." As he mentioned Clovis, he looked nervously at the floor. "It's just, well," he hesitated as he searched for the words. "It just that Clovis doesn't always think straight any more. You know, like he's not right in the head."

He stopped abruptly when he saw Kyla staring at him blankly. She wasn't sure what Asa expected her to say. Nor did she know what to think about the sudden change in attitude. Asa was treating her like a guest who had been treated badly and deserved some explanation. Cole and Clovis had left her without a doubt that they considered her a prisoner. Kyla remained silent and watched him uneasily.

Asa smiled weakly and looked at the tray of food that was sitting untouched. "Don't you want to eat?" he asked as he motioned toward the tray.

Kyla hadn't thought about the tray of food. The roll had been more than she had eaten at one time in days. Her eyes widened in amazement when she looked at the food Asa brought. It truly was breakfast with bacon, eggs, toast, juice and milk. She greedily grabbed the glass of orange juice and as she poured the golden liquid into her mouth, Kyla thought she would cry with ecstasy. Next the bacon and toast disappeared. The eggs presented a problem. When she tried to eat using her left hand, they kept falling off the fork. Not wanting to waste on precious morsel, Kyla quickly put the fork down and began eating with her free hand.

Asa watched her devouring the food and was wondering when she had eaten last. "Listen," he said, "I'll take off the handcuffs if you promise not to try to run away."

18

It was another surprise. "Thanks," Kyla answered gratefully as she chewed. She wasn't going to stop stuffing food into her mouth until everything was gone. As he reached past her to unlock the handcuffs, Kyla noticed the scent of soap and shampoo. Suddenly, she wished that Asa wasn't standing so close. This time it was shame and not fear that she felt. Kyla could only imagine what he must have been thinking about the way she smelled. Bathing hadn't been high on her list of priorities lately.

Once her hands were free she picked up the plate and began shoveling what remained of the eggs into her mouth. Looking at Asa while she ate, Kyla decided that she would keep her promise to him. While she was with Asa, she wouldn't try to escape. Like a stray puppy, she pinned her hopes and loyalty on the only person to show her any kindness. He had given her a little hope for her future. When she picked up the glass of milk, Asa removed the tray, now filled with empty dishes, and set it on the counter beside the door. Kyla tasted the milk. It was powdered, but she wasn't disappointed. While she sipped the cold liquid, Asa was talking.

"Kyla Wallace, it certainly is a surprise to see you," he said thoughtfully. "You're definitely not what we were expecting. But let me assure you, you've been the main topic of conversation since last night." He was laughing softly at his private joke as he went to the door and opened it. He brought a bundle in from outside and closed the door again. Then walking toward her, he continued, "Anyway, you'll be happy to know that I won the argument." Kyla continued to sip the milk and wonder what argument Asa had won. Hopefully, it was the one where they decided not to shoot her.

Asa looked her over from head to foot and said as considerately as possible, "Pop is worried about lice and fleas." At that point he cleared his voice before adding, "Clovis wanted to dunk you in sheep dip." For a moment Asa smiled weakly at the joke, but remembering Kyla's recent experience, he added quickly, "We managed a compromise. Pop says that you can come in and use the bath to clean up." Kyla's head came up and she looked at Asa. He certainly had her attention now. "But first we have to burn your clothes and cut off your hair." The last part he added hastily then looked at Kyla wondering what her reaction would be.

19

Kyla drank the last of the milk and set the glass down as she said, "Whatever you say." If the price of a bath and fresh clothing was a shaved head then she was willing to pay. It wasn't as if she had any choice in the matter anyway. She looked to Asa and waited for his directions.

Asa grabbed a small step stool that was leaning against the wall and set it on the floor near Kyla. "Sit here," he said as he took a pair of scissors from the bundle that he had set on the counter. Kyla, still wrapped in her canvas cloak, sat with her back to him. Immediately, he started cutting her hair and the long chestnut brown tresses began falling to the floor. As he worked on her, he was talking. "It seems so strange to see someone I knew from before," he trailed off. Before what? It really hadn't been that long, only a matter of months. He cut off another handful of hair and as it fell, he continued, "Before the evacuations. The only people we see now are the ones Manjohnah sends to help Pop guard the area against looters. Except I haven't seen any looters, not for a long time. At first there were a few now and then, but you're the first person we've seen from outside the compound in months. Except for Manjohnah's men, that is."

He said the name Manjohnah, like he was someone that she should know, but before now Kyla had never heard the name. "Who is Manjohnah?" she asked. "Is he part of the military or the government?"

"Where have you been living, in a hole?" he said incredulously. Asa was looking thoughtfully at the back of Kyla's head and he chose his words carefully when he answered. "Manjohnah? Let's just say he's the man, the big man. He's bigger than the military or the government. Understand?" Kyla nodded, but she didn't understand what he meant. Asa set the scissors down and began shaving off what hair was left with an electric razor and continued his story of his new life on the farm. "It's the men that Manjohnah sends here that I don't like. They're a strange bunch and most of them are just plain nuts! When Clovis started hanging out with them that's when he started to change. They're the ones who took his clothes and made him wear that get up he has now. And they're mean. They beat him up when he tried to wear something else. Did you see what they did to his hair? Pop won't do anything. He says Clovis has to stand up for himself. Me, I just stay as far away from them as I can." He stopped talking for a moment and

20

when Kyla still didn't speak, he said, "I'm sorry. After what Clovis did, I guess you're not interested in his problems. I know I've been rambling on, but it's just good to see a familiar face. Since Mom died, I haven't really had anyone to talk to. Pop keeps to himself and Clovis," he paused and added, "Well, you know about Clovis."

"I'm sorry about your mother, Asa," Kyla said truthfully. Margaret Spring had been a good woman and had always been nice to her.

"Well that's it," Asa announced as he turned off the clippers and set them down. When Kyla looked at the pile of hair on the floor, the practice of shaving the prisoner's head before execution came to mind. She stood and turned to look at Asa, still wondering what they had in mind after she was allowed her bath.

"Now if you'll take off your clothes, we can get you inside," Asa said as he handed her a blanket. Then being the perfect gentleman, he turned and walked to the door keeping his back to Kyla.

She undressed quickly. When she was finished and had the blanket wrapped tightly around her body, Kyla went to Asa and said, "I'm ready."

Asa looked her over, and then pointed to her feet. "Those boots have to go, too." Can't run without boots, Kyla thought as she kicked them off. "And the socks," Asa added. "Vermin, you know." Obediently, Kyla bent down and peeled off the socks. Finally satisfied, Asa opened the door and began walking to the house.

Now barefoot and naked under the blanket, Kyla followed close behind him as they walked across the frozen ground and up the walkway that led to the back door of the house. They entered through the mudroom and Kyla waited for Asa to open the door that led to the kitchen. When he did the warmth and the smells of breakfast wafted through the door. Thankfully, there was no one in the kitchen and Kyla could enjoy the homey smells as they passed quickly through the room. She didn't see anyone in any of the rooms they passed as Asa led her down the hallway and up the stairs to the second floor. While they walked toward the bathroom at the end of the hall, Asa was giving her instructions. "I left a towel for you inside and some clean clothes. You can use the tub, but not the shower. Only fill the tub a quarter of the way full, Pop doesn't want to waste any water. And believe me, he'll know if you do. Take all the time you want. I'll be waiting out here."

When they came to the door to the bathroom, Kyla looked at Asa before she went inside. "What happens after that?" was all she asked.

"You don't have to go back to the shed. Pop says that you can stay in there until he gets back tonight," he answered and pointed to the room at the end of the hall.

"Thank you, Asa. At least you've been kind," Kyla said gratefully. It was Asa's turn to be uncomfortable and he looked down at the floor, avoiding her eyes. She didn't wait for him to answer and went into the bathroom and locked the door behind her. For a few minutes at least, she would be free of them. When she turned and looked around the room, Kyla thought that she was truly in heaven. The first thing she did was to use the toilet. It wasn't on Asa's list of things that she was allowed to do, but what else could they do to her. They even had toilet paper. What a luxury! She was careful to use as little as possible. Cole most likely knew the exact number of sheets left on the roll.

As she went to the tub, Kyla caught sight of her reflection in the mirror and stopped to stare. It wasn't the lack of hair that she found shocking. It was the sight of the hollow faced skeleton staring back at her in the reflection. No wonder Clovis didn't recognized her. She wouldn't have known herself either and could only wonder how Cole had known who she was. Kyla smiled when she thought about Asa saying that it was good to see a familiar face. There was nothing familiar about her face at all. It was difficult to stop staring, but the thought of a hot bath brought her back to reality.

Kneeling by the tub, she put the stopper in the drain and turned on the water. It was pure pleasure watching the steam rise from the clear, clean water pouring into the tub. Once it was exactly one quarter full, Kyla turned off the water and dropped the blanket. She slipped carefully into the hot, almost scalding water and quickly went about the business of soaping and scrubbing and rinsing every bit of dirt from every inch of her body. All too soon the water began to cool and as it was now a dark muddy brown, reluctantly, Kyla decided it was time to get out of the water. As she began to dry herself, she looked at the clothes Asa had left for her and picked up the thermal underwear. They were ladies with little blue flowers. No doubt they had belonged to his mother. They were a little large, but they would do fine. Next she put on the denim jeans and those were way too big. Even after she put on the flannel shirt and tucked it in, the jeans were ready to fall every time she moved. There was also a pair of socks, but that was it, no shoes or a belt to hold up the pants.

After she was dressed, Kyla began to look around the room. There was nowhere to go except to the room at the end of the hall and Asa had told her to take her time. Carefully and quietly, she began to search the cupboards under the sink. There was nothing unexpected. Towels, soap all the usual items that you would find in a bathroom. When she found a small piece of soap, she put it in her pocket. Maybe such a small item wouldn't be missed. Just why she took it, Kyla wasn't sure. Soap was just another one of the little luxuries that she had taken for granted and now she missed them. She looked in the medicine cabinet behind the mirror. There weren't any razors, nothing sharp that could be used as a weapon. Cole was no fool; surely he would have had Asa clear everything out before she was allowed in the room. When she saw the toothpaste, Kyla put some on her finger and rubbed it around inside her mouth. Not a very effective toothbrush, but it did taste good. She looked once more around the room and deciding that there wasn't anything else worth snooping through, went to the door and unlocked it. When she stepped out, Asa was waiting just as he had promised.

"I'm ready now," she said and without waiting for Asa to lead the way, walked directly to the room that he had indicated earlier. At the doorway, Kyla turned abruptly and looked directly into Asa's eyes. He had been very forthcoming with information up to now and she had one question that she needed him to answer. "What's going to happen to me now?"

Asa pushed the door open and when Kyla went inside, he said, "I don't know its up to Pop," and began to shut the door.

Kyla caught the door with her hand before it was completely closed and still staring directly into Asa's eyes, she asked, "Can't you help me?" Desperation filled her voice and she watched his face for some sign of hope, but Asa just stared at her blankly and shut the door. Only when the door was closed completely and she heard the bolt slide into place, did Kyla look away. Despite the kindness that Asa had shown her, she felt an overwhelming sense of frustration. Everything she had seen in this house was a reminder of her life before the evacuations and she felt cheated. Why should Cole Spring and his family be allowed to continue with their existence as if nothing had happened, while she, on the other hand, had been living in a hole in the ground like an animal? It was not right or fair, but Kyla was certainly in no position to change her circumstances, and the thought of staying with Cole's family as a way to change them, was not appealing either.

As she looked around the room, Kyla's thoughts went back to thinking of a way out. The room was empty except for a cot with a bare mattress, just like a prison cell. There was one window that had a piece of green corrugated plastic nailed over it on the outside. It did let in a little light, which gave the whole room a greenish glow. As Kyla lay down on the cot with her head next to the window, she saw a tiny nail hole in the green plastic covering. Excited by her discovery, she jumped up on the cot and tried to open the window. She couldn't get the sash to budge, no matter how hard she pushed on it. Remembering the little piece of soap in her pocket, she rubbed some of it on the window jam. Then putting all of her strength into her next push, she was able to open the window far enough to fit her hand through the opening.

Laying on the cot and looking out the tiny hole, Kyla couldn't see anything. As she sat up on the bed, she was wishing that she still had her pocketknife. It was then that she thought about the cot. Bouncing up and down, she smiled as she realized that it had springs. Kyla lifted the mattress and unhooked one of them. Then using end of the metal spring, she began to chip away at the tiny hole and before long it was the size of a penny. She was afraid to make it any larger for fear that someone on the outside might see it. Still, it was big enough. Now when she lay on the bed and looked out, Kyla could see a small portion of the compound at the end of the road just inside the gate.

She watched all day, but there wasn't much to see. Occasionally someone would pass into view. Where they were going or what they were doing, she never could see for sure, but everyone she saw was carrying a weapon. It wasn't until late in the day when a truck rolled into her line of view. It was a large troop transport like the ones used in the evacuations and Kyla had heard it rumbling down the road long before she saw it. Just the sight of the truck was unnerving and she was certain that it had come for her. Suddenly, there was a flurry of commotion as the truck stopped and Kyla saw men wearing gray uniforms pouring out. They formed lines and marched down the road and out of her view. Kyla couldn't be certain, but judging by their uniforms and disciplined conduct, these men didn't appear to be part of Cole's regular crew. They were definitely reinforcements, but for what? She certainly wasn't worth that much effort. As she remembered what Asa had told her earlier, that she wasn't what they had expected, it made her wonder what it was that had Cole so nervous.

Kyla watched through her tiny peephole the rest of the day, only stopping when it was too dark to see. She was lying on her back staring into the darkness when she heard the sound of footsteps coming down the hall. Quickly, she sat up on the edge of the bed and faced the door, wondering whom it would be this time. She was thankful to see that it was Asa again. Wordlessly, he motioned for her to follow, as he turned and hurried down the stairs. He waited for Kyla to catch up before knocking on the door at the bottom of the steps. She heard the muffled response from within and Asa opened the door. Giving her a firm nudge in the direction of the doorway, Asa guided her inside and shut the door behind her, which left Kyla standing just inside.

She waited without speaking, staring at Cole Spring's back. He was standing at the far end of the room, arranging the logs in fireplace with the end of the poker. When he didn't turn or acknowledge her presence in any way, Kyla began looking around the room. It was a traditional study with wooden shelves lined with books, overstuffed chairs by the fire and a small desk in the corner by the window. All very nice and cozy, just as Kyla remembered the room. Nothing had changed about the house, but everything else had. She was not a neighbor here for a chat. It was Cole's game now and she didn't know the rules anymore.

Cole finally turned and looked at Kyla as he went to the desk and filled a glass with liquor from the bottle setting on it. "Go ahead and sit down," he said as he walked back to the fireplace. When Kyla didn't move, he took a drink from the glass and said, "Suit yourself." He turned his back to Kyla and set the glass on the mantle. Then picking up the poker he went to work on the fire again as he said, "You sure have presented me with a predicament, girl." His voice was agitated and he poked at the logs with a vengeance, causing the flames to rise with his anger. "You should have stayed where you were. We knew that you weren't picked up during the evacuations. Your name was never checked off the list." He looked at her out of the corner of his eye and added, "Then every once in awhile there would be a report of a female fitting your description. But I guess you had a good hiding place, because we never could find you." Kyla thought for a moment that the last was meant as a compliment, but she couldn't be sure.

He put down the poker and picked up the glass, emptying it this time before he turned and looked at her again. "Now here you are and that makes you my problem." Cole was studying Kyla. Even now he wasn't sure what to do with her. "I should thank you for showing me that little problem with the trees. The boys have been doing a little tree trimming today. We can't have branches hanging over the fence like that, can we?" he said delaying the real subject for a moment. He began to pace slowly in front of the fireplace. Until that moment, Kyla had never thought of Cole Spring as an old man, but his age was showing today and she could see that he looked tired.

"Sometimes there is a difference between doing what we want and doing what we must," Cole began slowly. Then walking to Kyla, he looked directly into her eyes and asked, "Can you understand that?" She nodded slowly. It was becoming all too clear where this conversation was heading.

Cole turned and went back to the fireplace, putting distance between himself and Kyla before he said, "I have to think of my sons. All that I have is this farm and it'll be theirs someday." As he went to refill his glass, he continued, "Clovis asked me to let you stay, but I don't think that's what you really want." Cole didn't look at her or wait for a reply, before adding, "You can't stay here. I just can't have a woman here with all these men. I don't need that kind of trouble." Cole looked at Kyla who was staring blankly at the fire. "You can't stay here and I can't let you go. The decision has been made for me. The only thing to do is what should have been done in the first place. You'll be sent to the evacuation centers up north with the others."

"Is that were my parents are?" Kyla asked desperately, "Do you know where they sent them?" For the first time since she had entered the room, she hoped that Cole might be able to do something for her. All she wanted was an answer to her question.

"Yes, I know where they were sent," Cole answered evasively, his answer short of being either the truth or a lie.

"But are they alive?" Kyla was pleading with him for any scrap of information. She watched him anxiously. If her family would be waiting, then the thought of going to the evacuation center would not be so bad.

Cole took another drink and said, "They're well taken care of." He stirred the fire absently, avoiding her eyes.

Suddenly, after having contained her emotions for so long, Kyla flew across the room to where Cole was standing. "A simple yes or no, are they alive?" she demanded angrily. She had nothing to loose if she made him angry.

Cole ignored her display of temper and answered flatly, "Yes, they are alive and they are being taken care of very well."

Kyla looked at him suspiciously. He had said it so easily, like he didn't care one way or another. He truly was a cold-hearted man. She eyed him contemptuously and asked, "When do I leave?"

"Tomorrow morning," he said with a flat emotionless voice, "and you'll spend the night in the lock-up in the barracks. No more special treatment." Finished with his distasteful task, Cole turned his back on Kyla and began attacking the logs with the poker as he bellowed, "Asa." Immediately, Asa came into the room and whisked Kyla out and up the steps.

Chapter Two

Asa brought Kyla her supper that night, a sandwich and water, nothing special, but for all she knew it could be her last meal. In the corner of the room was a small lamp or more accurately a flashlight in a box, which provided a dim light and only added to Kyla's feelings of gloom. A stay in the lock-up in the barracks with a bunch of men that Asa had said were worse than Clovis was not exactly a comforting thought. All too soon Kyla heard the bolt slide out and the door swung open.

It was not Asa or even Clovis or Cole this time, but a man she had never seen before and Kyla jumped to her feet, heart pounding. She couldn't help but stare at him as he ducked to enter the room. The man was huge and his girth matched his height. Kyla couldn't have reached even halfway around his waist. Nor could she make out his face. He had a bushy dark beard and wore his hat pulled low over his eyes. She noticed that he was not carrying a gun, but then he didn't have to carry one. His size was deterrent enough.

"Come here," he grunted gruffly. When Kyla didn't move, he simply put his hand on top of her head and moved her like she was a small, unruly child as he took a pair of handcuffs from his pocket. She stood limply while he snapped one loop of the handcuffs around her wrist and then the other around his own huge wrist. Then they were off. Walking with long strides, he pulled Kyla along as he went down the stairs then through the foyer and out the door.

Outside the darkness was complete. It was another cloudy and moon-less night. Her escort carried no flashlight or lantern and there were no yard lights overhead. Kyla stumbled often as they made their way down the steps and across the yard to the gravel road that ran just in front of the house. It was once a public road, but by fencing it off Cole had made it his private driveway, but there was no one left to complain. As they walked, her escort kept her at the very edge of the roadway. It was hard for Kyla keep her footing. The huge man was nearly dragging her and her feet kept slipping on the rocks at the edge of the road, causing her to slide down into the ditch. The fact that they had never returned her boots and she was walking in stocking feet didn't help matters. Apparently, she was not going to need boots or a coat where she was going. The insulated flannel of the shirt and the thermal underwear helped keep her warm, but she would certainly have liked a coat. Kyla was getting colder by the minute.

Absorbed by thoughts of her growing discomfort, she was suddenly brought back to reality when the man beside her fell forward dragging her down with him. Kyla thought that it served him right, tripping in the dark, after pulling her around like a rag doll. It wasn't until she heard a popping sound like fireworks, in the distance, that she realized what had happened. Her guard was not getting up. He had been shot. It was the opportunity she had been waiting for. Franticly, she searched his pockets until she found the key and unlocked the cuff around his wrist. Kyla didn't bother to waste time unlocking hers and shoved the key into her pocket. For just a moment she paused to look at the man lying dead beside her. Too bad he was so big, his coat and boots where of no use to her, but his hat she could use and she snatched it off his head. If they had not cut her hair, she thought angrily, her head would not have been so cold.

Kyla crouched at the side of the road trying to decide what to do next. There was the sound of sporadic gunfire all about the compound now. So far no one had missed them, but she was not going to wait until they did and she slid down into the ditch. Crossing the short distance between the ditch and a nearby building took all the nerve she had. As she crawled through the shadows to the first in the line of large storage sheds that ran along the road, she was certain someone would see her. Once across the open ground, she knelt in the narrow walkway between the first two buildings and looked back to the road where she had been. Someone was shouting and the sound of gunfire was much closer now. Kyla sat motionless when she heard footsteps coming down the road. Afraid to breathe as the sound of running men came closer, she hoped they would not see the dead man. From her vantage point, he was only a dark lump in the road, but she was sure whoever was coming would certainly find him and begin looking for her. To her relief they ran right by the motionless man and it seemed that she was forgotten for the moment.

The area between the buildings was pitch black but Kyla didn't dare stay where she was for long. There was a driveway at the other end of the building then another row of storage sheds all in perfect alignment with the first row. Beyond the second row was the pasture, several hundred yards of open ground, and then the fence. She didn't know how she was going to get over it, but she wasn't going to sit around waiting for them to lock her up again either. Creeping cautiously in the darkness between the buildings, Kyla kept an ear to the activities in the compound. It seemed that the shooting and shouting were behind her, which suited Kyla perfectly as she continued to head away from the sounds of the gunfire. When she reached the drive between the rows of buildings, she paused to listen. Hearing nothing she peered cautiously to the left and right like a good little girl before crossing the street, then flung herself across the open space and into the darkness of the walkway between the buildings on the other side. Once Kyla started running she was not about to stop. That is until she tripped over something in the pathway and fell hard onto her side.

Before she could move she felt someone grab her from behind. When Kyla felt the touch of cold steel against her throat, in the instant before the hand went over her mouth, she managed to squeal, "Oh, God, no! Please don't..." Whoever it was did not loosen their hold, but the knife was pulled back.

Very softly, audible only to her, she could hear the man cursing. "Damn, a woman? What the hell are you doing here?" Only he obviously didn't expect an answer since he was still holding his hand over her mouth.

So, he was puzzled. Kyla was, too. Everyone from the compound had to know about her. So was he from somewhere else? When the man loosened his hold on her mouth, she whispered urgently, "Please help me. I have to get out of here." Kyla knew what his answer would be before he uttered the words.

"I'm sorry but you're on your own there," he said and began to loosen his hold. There was only one way that Kyla could make him take her. In a heartbeat she took the open cuff dangling from her wrist and snapped it shut around his. He was furious and hissed angrily, "Listen sister, I'm not playing games here. Take it off!" The words were hardly out of his mouth when they heard the sound of gunfire behind them. It was much closer than it had been just moments earlier. It seemed he was caught. There was no time to argue with some stupid woman about keys to the damned handcuffs. Time was running short and he could get rid of her once he reached cover. Reaching down, the man picked up one of the bundles that Kyla had tripped over in the dark, shoved it into her arms, and picked up the others. There was nothing to do but make a run for the fence.

Kyla did her best to keep up with the man. He had to drag her every step of the way, all the while murmuring to himself, " I must be crazy." Before she knew it they were at the fence and then through it. There was no need to slow down. The wire had been cut. From the fence, it was only a few yards to the cover of the woods. Even after they reached the trees the man kept running, making his way deeper into the timber. When Kyla heard a rustling in the brush ahead of them, she could only wonder who would be waiting for them. So it was a relief when they came to a small clearing and she was able to make out the shadowy shapes in the woods ahead of them. He had horses waiting.

When the man stopped abruptly, Kyla stumbled into him from behind. He wasted no time and quickly deposited his bundles on the ground. "Now take off this handcuff," he growled as he took Kyla's bundle and put it with the others. She knew by the tone of his voice that she had best comply. Her goal had been accomplished. She was outside the fence. Quickly, Kyla unlocked both cuffs and put them and the key into her pocket. Once he was freed, the man moved quickly and loaded the bundles on one of the horses and mounted the other. Kyla was waiting for him to disappear into the woods. What happened next was not what she expected. He rode up to her and without a word held out his hand. As Kyla placed her hand in his, he pulled her up and onto the horse behind him. With a kick, the horse leapt to a gallop. Next thing Kyla knew they were weaving through the trees at full speed and she was clinging to the rider in front of her, trying desperately not to slide off. There was no time for a thank you or to even wonder why.

They rode without stopping until they reached the edge of the woods at the southern end of the valley. It was only two miles from the bluff where she had set out on her ill-fated plan the day before. There he slowed and began riding up and down a small area at the edge of the woods. Obviously, he was waiting for something. When they heard what sounded like a coyote yelping, he replied with a yowl of his own. Soon three other riders joined them. One of them brought his horse so close to theirs that Kyla legs were brushing against the other horse's rump.

"Marta's dead!" the rider said. His voice was filled with rage. Then he turned his gaze to Kyla. She didn't need to see him. Even in the darkness she could feel the glare directed at her. "Who's this?" he demanded. Both statement and question hurled out quickly.

With her arms still wrapped around his waist and her body pressed close to the rider in front, Kyla could feel his muscles tense as if he was ready to lash out, but was fighting the urge. His answer was just as terse. "I can't do anything about Marta. She knew the risk as well as anyone." He nudged his horse gently and moved away from the other rider. He had not answered the second question. "All we can do now is stick with the plan."

"So is this a part of the plan?" the other man demanded again as he pointed to Kyla. "Not the best time to pick up strays, now is it?"

"Listen Kurt. I am not going to waste time arguing," he said it in a level tone, no anger just facts. "We'll split up now like we planned. Everyone goes in a different direction and we meet back at the Settlement in three days." Then not waiting for discussion, he kicked his horse in the flanks. As it jumped forward, it brushed past the other horse, startling it. Holding on for dear life, Kyla looked back and saw the horse rear up and the surprised rider hit the ground. She pressed her face closer and tightened her grip. Aside from her fear of sliding off the horse, Kyla was experiencing an unfamiliar feeling. She actually felt safe with this man. There was no logical reason for her feeling secure about anything. She was holding onto a man that she knew nothing about as they galloped at full speed into the darkness. With every hoof beat, they were going further and further away from the valley, Spring's farm and her home.

They rode several miles that night, travelling cross-country and avoiding roads except to cross them. They continued at a steady pace, never stopping or back tracking even though the night was black as pitch. It must have been the same path the man used going to the farm. Every time they came to a fence the wire was already cut. After awhile Kyla lost track of the fences they passed through and the roads they crossed. Every once in awhile she recognized a familiar landmark and was able to tell that they were working their way to the west and just a little south of a small town which was about ten miles from Spring's farm. Kyla could see the dark shadows of the empty buildings as they rode past. Just the sight of them made her uneasy and she was relieved when they continued to ride to the south and did not enter the town itself. When they reached the public park at the southwestern corner of the town, he turned the horses and they rode through the old metal archway that was the entrance to the park.

The only sound was the soft clatter of the horses' hooves on the pavement as they followed the main drive through the picnic area and past the empty playground. At the far end where the paved roadway made its loop back to the main entrance was another road leading into the woods. That is where they turned and followed the narrow drive that wound around and up the hill. Kyla knew where they were going now. She had been to the park many times. At the top of the hill was a stone observation tower that resembled a round turret from some medieval castle. When they reached it, the man slid off the horse. After Kyla climbed down, he led the horses inside. Kyla stood in the doorway and watched him light a small lantern that gave off a weak glow, just enough to see. He gave the horses feed and water from one of the large canteens the packhorse was carrying, but did not take off the saddle or unload the bundles from the pack animal. They could leave at a moment's notice. After tying the reins to the metal stair rail, he took a bundle from the packhorse and climbed the steps to the second level. Kyla still hesitated at the doorway not sure if she should follow. The man stopped at the top of the steps. "Bring the light with you," was all he said. Kyla did as he asked and picked up the lantern. When she reached the top of the steps, he unrolled the sleeping bag and slipped inside. There was only one sleeping bag and Kyla was more than just a little uncomfortable at the thought of squeezing into it with a man she did not know.

He looked at her and said, "You don't have a coat or shoes. You can sleep with me or you can freeze. It really doesn't matter to me either way. Just turn off the light now." Then he lay down and closed his eyes. Kyla knew he was right. She walked to him and after turning out the light set it down on the floor. As she knelt beside him she said, "You saved my life tonight and I don't even know your name."

34

He rolled over and facing her, held the blanket up so she could climb in and said, "Fleet."

She lay next to him with her back against his chest. "Thank you," she said softly. "My name is Kyla."

"Well, Kyla," he said sleepily, "we'll see if you're still thanking me tomorrow." He lay back down and when his breathing became deep and slow, Kyla knew that Fleet was asleep. After that she could relax a little. Slowly, she drifted toward sleep. Warm and cozy now, a feeling of comfort was the last conscious thought she had. Tomorrow was something she had not even considered yet and she was too tired to worry about it now. Then as peacefully as a babe in its crib she fell asleep. At least she thought she did, because all too soon the sky began to grow gray in the east and the first light of dawn woke her from her slumber.

When she opened her eyes, Kyla realized that she was alone in the sleeping bag and could only wonder how Fleet had managed to slip out without waking her. She must have been sleeping very soundly. Reluctantly, she left the warmth of the down cocoon and after getting out, rolled it up into a bundle again. Kyla felt around for the lantern, but it was gone. Then picking up the sleeping bag, she made her way in the dim light to the stairs and went down to the first level where the horses were tied. Fleet was not there, so she went outside and began looking around the outside of the tower. When she heard a whistle from above, she saw Fleet. He was standing on the third level of the tower, the observation deck. Kyla went back inside and climbed the stairs to the top of the tower to join him.

There was a light wind from the northwest and it was just a little chilly. Kyla hugged herself and rubbed her arms for warmth. From the tower they had a clear view of the highway that ran from north to south just west of the town. Fleet was studying the road carefully, using a pair of binoculars. After a few moments Kyla asked, "Do you think anyone followed us?"

He didn't answer right away or give any indication that he had even heard what Kyla asked. Finally, he lowered the binoculars. "Don't know," he said, as he looked her over from head to foot. Kyla felt a little uneasy with the sharp look as Fleet made his assessment of her. "The question is, are we worth the trouble?" Kyla knew Fleet meant to say whether she was worth the trouble or not. Then without another word, he went back to watching the road.

Kyla watched, too. Only it was Fleet she was watching. She had not gotten a good look at him last night and she was studying him now. He was a very handsome man with a face that could be called pretty, but there was nothing feminine about him. The snuggly fit black tunic that he wore emphasized his muscular build. As he stood silently surveying the road in the distance, the wind was blowing his hair into his face. Shoulder length and a light burnished brown in color with streaks of blond, it was an unruly mass of curls that brushed his cheeks and forehead every time the wind blew. Fleet tried to keep his hair out of his face, smoothing it back with his free hand. Finally he lowered the binoculars and pulled his hair back, tying it with a leather cord at the nape of his neck. As he did, Fleet looked at Kyla and she was embarrassed by the fact that he had caught her staring. Still, she did not look away and returned his gaze, staring into his icy blue eyes. Fleet had to notice but he made no comment and considered her coldly, as if he was deciding what to do with her.

The only thing he said was, "We had better get going," and put the binoculars in the case he had hanging around his neck. Once he decided it was time to go, Fleet moved quickly. Taking the steps two at a time, he flew down both flights before Kyla had moved one step.

When Kyla got to the bottom floor, Fleet was unrolling the sleeping bag. He unzipped it and handed it to her. "Wrap this around your shoulders. It'll keep you warm." She took it and did as she was told. "Do you know how to ride? I don't think you're too heavy. Brownie can carry you, too," he said. When Kyla nodded, Fleet picked her up and put her on the packhorse. With a shove on her backside, she was seated. He then began to look through the pouches the packhorse carried until he found a pair of leather mittens lined with fur. Rather unceremoniously, he shoved them onto her feet saying, "These will have to do." After giving Kyla the reins to her horse, he mounted the other and with a flick of the reins, his long legged black stallion stepped out the doorway and they were off. Kyla nudged her horse forward and once outside, kicked her to a trot. She followed close behind Fleet as they retraced their path, riding down the hill and out of the park.

Once they passed through the archway at the entrance, Fleet began leading the way south. They continued in that direction for about a mile before coming to the river. There they turned and began following the river as it meandered in a generally western direction. When they reached a point where the bank was not too steep, Fleet led the way down. Riding along the river's edge, he kept his horse where the water met the frozen ground and the footing was better for the horses. Kyla stayed close, following his every move, hoping that the horse didn't step in the wrong place and fall through the ice. It was slow going and they rode without speaking.

When they rounded a sharp bend in the river, the highway and the bridge loomed before them. They had crossed several roads the night before when it had been dark. In the daylight using the river's bank for cover would hide them from some angles of view, but they were still easily visible from others. They listened when they came closer to the road for the sound of trucks roaring down the pavement to intercept them, but they came to the bridge and passed under it without incident. The only sounds were the horses' hooves crackling on the ice and the wind blowing over their heads.

After leaving the highway and the bridge behind they continued riding along the edge of ice. It was only a short distance before they rounded another sharp bend in the river and came to a place where the high riverbanks disappeared. Here the river widened and the adjacent field was level with the riverbed. At that point Fleet left the river and rode across the low ground. As she followed Kyla looked down. This area would surely have been a swamp and impossible to ride through if it hadn't been frozen. The earth was soft enough that even when it was frozen, the horses left light tracks as they passed. When she reached the gravel road, Kyla looked up and saw that Fleet had stopped and was waiting for her. She stopped Brownie next to his horse and asked, "What is it?" He had not paused to wait for her before.

Fleet smiled broadly and said, "I guess we weren't worth the trouble" Then looking back one last time in the direction of the bridge, kicked his horse to a trot and began riding down the road. Kyla kept her horse next to his as they rode side by side down the middle of the road. It seemed strange to Kyla. To ride openly without any attempt to conceal where they were going seemed unnatural. Hiding had become a way of life for her. Fleet certainly seemed at ease. "Your farmer friend, Mr. Spring, doesn't send anyone past the highway." He narrowed his eyes and looked directly at her and added, "At least he never has in the past." It seemed he was looking for some assurance from Kyla that her presence would not change that rule.

"I'm sure he was glad to be rid of me," Kyla said. The statement was probably true. She just hoped it would satisfy Fleet.

Fleet nodded and looked her over from head to toe. Whatever her story was, he'd bet it was a good one. The girl was a walking skeleton. Looking at Kyla, he realized that he should give her something to eat. Fleet had had other things on his mind that morning and hadn't thought of food until now. Reaching into the pouch that he kept hanging from his saddle, he took out a piece of dried meat. When he offered it, Kyla took it without a word and began eating. She hadn't asked for anything, but he knew she had to be hungry.

Fleet was relieved that everything had gone well so far. The highway was finally behind them. He could have ridden the rest of the way the night before, but the girl could barely hold on by the time they stopped. He still didn't know why he had taken her with him. Last night Kurt had been right when he said that it wasn't the best time to pick up strays, but it also was not the best time to leave anyone behind. If he had left her, it wouldn't have been alive. With that thought he looked at her again, wondering if she knew how close the decision had been for him.

Fleet said nothing directly to Kyla as they rode. Every few moments he would look at her and shake his head or murmur something too softly to be heard and then look away. It made Kyla terribly uneasy. Finally, he looked at Kyla and said, "That was a dirty trick, putting the cuffs on me like you did."

The statement caught Kyla off guard. Last night seemed like a lifetime ago. Everything that she had done was like a fuzzy memory from some strange nightmare. It had been a dirty trick, but it had been a risk for her, too. If he had decided to loose the time it would have taken to kill her and unlock the cuffs, Fleet would be free of her now. Any apology she could offer would not undo what she had done. She met his angry glare and looking directly into his eyes, said simply, "It was the only way I could make you take me with you."

Fleet knew what she said was true enough, so he asked the question that had been on his mind since she stumbled into him last night. "What were you doing running around in the dark with no coat or shoes?"

Right now Kyla wasn't sure how much she should tell Fleet. She could tell by the tone of his voice that he was suspicious of her and her motives. "I was trying to get out of the compound," Kyla answered with the obvious.

"So you left without a coat or shoes." Fleet was not going to let it go. "I put my life in danger to bring you with me, don't you think I deserve a little more in the way of an explanation?"

Kyla could tell he was serious, perhaps dangerously so. She looked down for a moment, a little shamed by her attempt to hide the truth of her situation and more than a little frightened of Fleet. She searched for the best way to explain. "I was a prisoner. The guard that was taking me to the lock-up was killed in the shooting."

Not waiting for her to tell the story Fleet interrupted, "Why were you a prisoner?"

"I was caught trying to sneak into the compound the night before. I tried to get over the fence by climbing a tree on one side and then crossing over to one on the other side, but the branches wouldn't hold me and I fell. They got me before I could get out of the tree," she explained.

"Why didn't they shoot you? That's what I hear Spring does with his prisoners." He looked at her closely and asked, "What makes you so special?"

"They knew me," Kyla answered simply. There was no point in hiding that fact.

Fleet let out a soft whistle. So that was it, old man Spring knew the girl and he had snatched his prisoner right out from under his nose. That put a whole new light on things. If the raid on the compound wasn't enough to rile the old snake, the fact that he had lost the girl wasn't going to help. The risk that they might be followed was more than he had thought. Still, he had to smile as he thought of Spring fuming over what had happened. That was at least a small compensation for the risk.

Kyla was relieved to see him smile again. For a moment she was sure that he had been upset by what she said about Cole Spring knowing her. After that they continued riding at an easy pace, always going west and south. There was little said except occasional directions from Fleet telling Kyla which way to go and when. Kyla said even less. There were a million questions that she wanted to ask. Where he was taking her was first on the list, but she was all too aware of her status as excess baggage. It would be easier for him if he did leave her behind and she wouldn't blame him. Finally, she worked up the courage to ask him the question, "Where are we going?" She asked with a soft, almost apologetic voice.

Fleet was a little surprised. This was first thing she had said for hours. He thought for a moment before answering not wanting to tell her more of his plans than necessary. Their immediate destination was all he was willing to reveal. "Tonight, I plan to stay with friends."

Kyla knew he was being evasive. He had no reason to confide in her. Without thinking she blurted out her next question, "Have you ever heard of Manjohnah?"

Fleet couldn't believe what she was asking. It was like asking someone if they had ever heard of Satan. "That is a man I wouldn't mention. It can get you killed just asking about him," he answered as he stared at her.

Despite his displeasure with her question, Fleet hadn't killed her. So Kyla persisted. "Do you know him?" she asked bluntly.

He was obviously agitated, but he answered anyway. "I know of him and I know what he's done. That's all anyone can say. Why do want to know about him?"

"Asa, one of Cole's sons, mentioned him. He said that Manjohnah had sent men to help them stop looters. I saw a truck load of them arrive yesterday." She stopped and looked at him before going on. Obviously, he was one of the looters.

What she said piqued is interest. Fleet wondered what else she had heard or possibly seen. He looked at her thoughtfully and said, "Well, it certainly is true about Cole Spring being in Manjohnah's pocket. Tell me, what else did Asa tell you?"

Kyla was happy that Fleet seemed genuinely interested in what she had said. Wanting to please him, she tried to remember the other things Asa had said. Then it came to her, it hadn't meant anything at the time, but now it made more sense. "He said that I wasn't what they were expecting."

The words hit him like a blow to the stomach. Cole Spring had been expecting something. Fleet could only wonder how he found out. Only a few people knew of their plans. People Fleet had known that he could trust. The only surprising thing now was that only Marta had died. He would have to wait until returning to the Settlement to see if the others were still in one piece. It was a miracle any of them had escaped with their lives.

He looked at Kyla now. She was a pitiful looking thing, but he had seen a lot of people just like her over the past months. There had been more of them in the beginning, coming out of their hiding places and gathering in small groups here and there about the countryside. Still, he had not seen anyone new in months. Judging by the little he knew, she had not been living at the farm. If she had been on her own for all this time, it was certainly a miracle that she was still alive. Even her question, asking where they were going, presented a problem. Fleet knew where he was going, but where she ended up was still in question. Whether there was a choice to be made or not, he would have little to say about it and Kyla would have even less say in the matter. The situation all depended on who was willing to take her in. The Settlement, where he was heading was the only place where anyone was welcome anytime. Maybe welcome was not the right word; actually anyone was allowed to try to survive there. No rules, no questions, you could come and go as you liked. The girl riding beside him would need more than a miracle if she went there. She had shown a little spark of spirit when she asked him about Manjohnah, but she'd have to fire that up to a full flame if she were going to survive at the Settlement.

Thinking of the Settlement brought back to mind Marta's death. There would be hell to pay with Sadie for that. He wanted to get back before Kurt and the others and tell Sadie himself. It was Sadie who had been against the plan from the beginning. Fleet wondered now if she had known that someone could not be trusted. He needed to get back before the others. That would mean changing his plans a little. Instead of meandering about the countryside for an extra day, tomorrow they would head directly for the Settlement. It would make them easier to intercept if anyone was looking for them, but he was willing to take that chance now. The desire to know who had betrayed them was foremost in Fleet's mind. He urged his horse to a faster pace and after travelling south and west all day he began to ride straight north. They were close to where he planned to stay that night and he wanted to arrive before dark.

~ ~ ~

It was late in the day. Kyla was tired and sore from riding. If she included the bumps and bruises from her attempt to break into Spring's farm and her scuffle with Clovis, she was more than ready to stop for a rest. Fleet had picked up the pace after turning north. Pressing the horses and keeping them going at a slow gallop most of the way, she could tell they were tiring, too. Still, it was nearly dark before Fleet stopped. It seemed that he had at last found the place where he was headed. To Kyla it looked like all the other patches of woods they had passed that day. She stopped her horse and waited quietly as Fleet rode slowly to the edge of the woods. When he stopped and motioned to her, she rode to where he was waiting. Without a word Fleet slid off his horse and began to lead it down the path. Kyla did as she had all day and followed where he led. It seemed darker with the trees surrounding them, their bare leafless branches forming a dense canopy over their heads. The only thing Kyla could see was the rump of Fleet's horse on the trail in front of her. When she heard a rustle in the underbrush ahead of them, Fleet and his horse stopped suddenly. She heard him call out, "Brother Fox, is that you?" Kyla wondered if it was some secret password.

Then a voice answered from the woods ahead of them. "Brother Fleet, I have been expecting you. But who is that with you?"

"She's a friend that I met along the way, Brother Fox," Fleet replied. The man hidden in the darkness hesitated only a moment before calling back, "If she's you friend, that's all I need to know. The Sisters will certainly be happy to met her."

Kyla could hear someone moving through the thick undergrowth, coming closer to where they were standing. Fleet turned around and moved closer to whisper, "Just relax and go with the flow. These people may seem a little strange, but they mean well. Besides, you might like meeting the Sisters." She didn't have to see his face to know he was grinning at her. She could tell by the tone of his voice that the idea of her meeting the 'Sisters' was amusing him.

They followed Brother Fox as he led the way along a trail that crisscrossed its way down a steep hill. In some places the trail was so narrow that it was all they could do to squeeze between the trees with the horses. Then suddenly they left the timber behind and were standing at the edge of a large clearing. It was dark, but Kyla was able to make out a small lake and on the far bank there were several small fires glowing like beacons in the darkness. Kyla was feeling a little uneasy as they rode around the edge of the lake making their way toward the fires. She had no idea what to expect given Fleet's advice not worry about how strange these people were, but the mention of the Sisters was promising. She would appreciate some female company.

When they reached the circle of fires Kyla noticed several low mounds just behind the fires. It wasn't until she saw the light from a door opening that she realized the mounds were earth shelters where these people lived; something similar to the root cellar where she had spent the winter only on a larger scale. Fleet dismounted and held his hand out and helped Kyla down from her horse. She stood beside him watching for some hint of what she should do next. Brother Fox motioned for them to follow while a young man who seemed to appear from nowhere took the reins of the horses. Before he led them away Fleet untied the bundles they had carried out of Spring's farm. He gave one to Kyla and they carried them into the earth shelter where Brother Fox had gone.

The entry was not very high and Fleet had to duck to enter. Once inside there was enough head room to allow him to stand, but the ceiling was very close to the top of his head and he had to remember to duck each time he came to one of the beams that supported the plank ceiling and the sod above that. The only source of light in the room was the fire burning at the far end of the room. It provided only a dim light and plenty of smoke. There was no chimney, only a hole above the fire where the smoke could escape. Very primitive, but it was warm and dry. For Kyla it was definitely an improvement over where she had been living. Then the door opened and a tall, dark haired woman entered the room. She was very attractive and dressed in a simple brown dress that swept across the floor as she went to Fleet and gave him a warm hug saying, "Brother Fleet, my arrow, has returned."

He grinned, obviously pleased with the warm greeting and returned her embrace. "Sister Samethia, it is always a pleasure to see you," Fleet said and gave her a peck on the cheek before turning his attention to the two other women who had entered just behind Sister Samethia. He lifted the younger girl and swung her around in a circle. "And you little Sister Eaglet, what trouble have you gotten into while I was away?" She laughed and pushed him away when he set her down.

It was the third woman who walked up to Fleet with hands on her hips and scolded, "Where are your manners, Brother Fleet? Are you going to let your friend stand alone by the fire and not introduce her."

"You're right, Sister Mischka. I must apologize," he said. "Sisters Samethia, Eaglet, and Mischka please meet Kyla, a new friend that I met just last night."

There was something about the three women as they stood together. Serenity and peace surrounded them like a halo. As they silently studied her, Kyla could feel her face flush red with embarrassment, suddenly aware of how ridiculous she had to look. She was still holding the sleeping bag around her shoulders and wearing mittens on her feet instead of shoes.

Sister Samethia saved her from the embarrassing silence. "You are welcome Sister Kyla. As a friend of our good friend Brother Fleet, you will always find shelter with us," She glided across the room with all the grace and bearing of a queen in her court and embraced her saying, "Welcome, Sister Kyla." Then the other Sisters each embraced her in turn, also greeting her by saying, "Welcome, Sister Kyla."

"I'm pleased to meet you and thank you for your warm welcome," Kyla responded, hoping her response would be acceptable. She wasn't sure what to say, but they seemed to like ceremony.

Brother Fox stood next to Fleet, watching without comment. Kyla had not gotten a good look at Brother Fox until now and she compared the men. They were both about the same age and height, but that is where any similarity between the two ended. Both men were very imposing in their own way. Fleet with his easy manner and Brother Fox with his grim expression that made Kyla wonder if he ever smiled. Fleet was fair skinned with blond hair that was a tangle of unruly curls. Brother Fox's skin was a golden brown and his hair was sleek and black. Fleet had a slim build, what Kyla would call long and lean. On the other hand Brother Fox was broader through the chest and shoulders. Fleet was dressed entirely in black and wore a heavy woolen coat over a tunic with a high collar. Brother Fox was wearing a shirt and trousers made from the same brown homespun material as the women's dresses and over that was a heavy vest made of leather and fur laced with rawhide strips. His boots went all the way to his knees and were turned down at the top. A light tan in color, they looked like they were made from buckskin.

Brother Fox did not greet Kyla or welcome her as the women had done. He turned to one of the younger women and said, "Sister Mischka, you and the little Sister take our guest and see to her needs." Kyla could tell by his voice and manner that he was used to giving orders. The Sisters' response was immediate as they came forward and each taking one of Kyla's arms whisked her out the door.

Fleet watched as they escorted Kyla out the door. He knew that the women would take good care of her. Then he turned to Brother Fox, anxious to get on with the business at hand. Kneeling on the floor, Fleet began unrolling the heavy canvas wrapping around one of the longer bundles. Brother Fox gave a small grunt of approval as the contents were revealed. There were two rifles in the bundle. Fleet gave the first one to Brother Fox and then the other to Sister Samethia. "It went well then?" Brother Fox asked as the held the gun to his shoulder and looked down the sight.

"Nothing comes without a price," Fleet answered thinking of Marta. He was not about to tell them that a woman had lost her life. It had been a high price indeed.

Brother Fox looked at his friend. He could tell by the tone of Fleet's voice that something was troubling him, but he would not ask what it was. "That's true enough. Still, I think the deal you made in exchange for the rifles was certainly more than fair. You and your friends keep the horses and we keep the weapons and ammunition." He looked at Sister Samethia and said, "These will give us some protection. We live too close to Spring's farm and his hired thugs will think twice before shooting if their targets start firing back."

"Why wait for them to come to you? When we start attacking and stop reacting, then we will have the advantage," Fleet said as he rose to his feet, "and with the horses you've given us we can move quickly."

"A few guns and you're ready to conquer the world." Brother Fox said as he bent over and placed the rifle back on the canvas lying on the floor. "You managed to get in and out of Cole's fortress and that alone will keep them on the alert for a long time to come." He crossed the room to stand next to Sister Samethia who had been standing silently, listening to the men.

"Don't be so critical of our friend Brother Fox," she said as she laid her rifle next to the other. "Brother Fleet is a warrior. A weapon that you have been more than willing to use when it suited your purpose." She gave Fleet one of her serene knowing smiles and continued, "As I am sure that Brother Fleet knows our strength lies in the fact that our enemy does not know where we are. Nor will he come looking unless we make it worth the effort"

Fleet did not see the fact that they had managed to stay hidden from their enemies as their strength. Instead their immobility was their greatest weakness. They may have plenty of horses, but they used them for herding. Fleet wanted to use them to take back what he could from people like Cole Spring, the ones who had profited from everyone else's misfortune. He had been hoping for the Family's continued support. Somehow he would have to convince them that they could not sit back and wait to see what would happen. Before he could make a reply to Sister Samethia's statement, a cold blast of wind from behind announced the arrival of two more members of the Family. Fleet knelt and quickly re-wrapped the rifles in their canvas covering.

"Brother Eldar," Sister Samethia called to the white haired man who walked with slightly stooped shoulders. "Please take these bundles and put them in Brother Fox's shelter," she ordered. To the other, a young red-haired youth, she said, "Brother Aquila, help him with the bundles then bring the meat to begin roasting for supper." The two men did as they had been told and disappeared again.

After they were gone Fleet changed the subject. "Where are the others? Are the old man and the boy the only ones here?"

46

"Some of them are north with the flock, but some of the men are scavenging." Scavenging was the Family's term for taking whatever they could find that wasn't nailed down. Of course, they often took things that were nailed down as well, but that took longer. If the taking needed some persuasion, well, that was when they needed Fleet. They also had some peculiar rules about what they would and wouldn't take, like leaving a pair of boots, but taking leather to make their own. Nor would they take even the smallest thing from the empty homes and buildings, things that could have made their lives easier. No beds, dishes, tools, or clothes, if they couldn't make it themselves, they didn't need it. Except for guns of course, Fleet thought wryly. Purists maybe, but stupid never.

Brother Fox moved closer to the fire and sat on one of the mats on the floor, making himself comfortable. Fleet did the same. Once he was sitting, fatigue hit him suddenly. He had been pushing himself for days, eating and sleeping little. Now that he had relaxed a little, he was not sure that he would be willing to get back up again for awhile. When Sister Samethia offered him a large earthenware cup filled with warm spiced wine, he was certain he would not. She filled a second cup and gave it to Brother Fox. Without looking at Fleet, Sister Samethia said, "Tell us about your new friend." She spoke with her usual calm self-assurance, but Fleet knew she was wary of anyone who was allowed into their homes.

"She was at the farm," he started, then paused slightly waiting for some response. When none came he continued. "She begged me to take her out. I couldn't leave her." Fleet didn't mention the handcuffs. Mercy need not always be voluntary.

"I can understand you dilemma," Sister Samethia said finally sitting to join them by the fire. "It was no place to leave a woman and from what I saw she was obviously not well treated."

Fleet took a long drink from the cup, draining it. A good bourbon was more to his liking, but the wine would do. He gave the cup to Sister Samethia. As she re-filled it he explained, "From what I gather she has been on her own since the beginning."

Brother Fox gave a snort of disbelief. "A tiny little thing like her? I find that hard to believe."

"I can believe it," Sister Samethia said with a certainty that neither Fleet nor Brother Fox were willing to challenge. "You can see it in her eyes. She's been alone for quite some time."

"Well you don't have to worry," Fleet said. "I plan to take her with me to the Settlement."

Both Sister Samethia and Brother Fox eyed him with disbelief. "You can't be serious!" Brother Fox was incredulous. "That place is a disgrace. Every one trades in pearls. I would not take a Sister there."

Fleet knew he was not talking about the kind of pearls that come from oysters. He meant the small round marbles that were found in the rubble of the cities. Most people thought they were a by-product of the blasts that had destroyed every population center of any real size, turning them into wastelands of pebbles and sand. No one knew who first discovered the unusual properties of the little white stones that shimmered in sun. Still, they did have a little bonus. When held in your hand they would begin to dissolve with the heat of your body. It didn't melt or crumble, just disappeared, but left behind a wonderful euphoric feeling. If you were sad, the pearls would make you happy. Hungry? With a pearl in your pocket you wouldn't care. It was a very powerful temptation for people living a miserable existence. If that had been the only effect it would have been great. Unfortunately, after the euphoria wore off then the violence began. There would always be a fight and it was not unusual for someone to end up dead. It didn't have to be that way, not if you were smart. Some crazy fools carried them constantly until they finally went off the deep end. Fleet had used the pearls in the past and he was not against using them in the future.

"Sadie's place is close by. She's taken in a lot of people. I'm sure she could go there," Fleet said hoping to allay their fears. He immediately wished he had not mentioned Sadie. Sister Samethia's face flushed with anger at the mention of her name. He didn't know why Sister Samethia had such a burning hatred of Sadie. Neither woman would say anything to him about what had passed between the two. If it weren't for the heated looks he received if he mentioned one of them to the other, there would be no reason to think that they had ever met. Fleet quickly added, "It's not like there is another choice, now is there?" They all knew the only choice was for them to take her into the Family.

"Some choices are made for us," Sister Samethia said coolly. It looked as if she was ready to explain when Brother Aquila returned, interrupting whatever she had planned to say. Brother Fox and Sister Samethia immediately turned the conversation to more earthy topics. The cabbage seeds had sprouted and a new lamb had been born that morning. Fleet was relieved with the change of topics. This was what he enjoyed about his visits with the Family. Their existence seemed uncluttered with the problems of the outside world. Fleet sipped his wine and smiled as the young Brother Aquila stepped past him and placed four rabbits skewered on a wooden spit across the fire. This is definitely what he enjoyed. Drink, good food, and a warm fire, it seemed that the Family had an idyllic life and he could not blame them for wanting to keep it that way.

~ ~ ~

Kyla had not been ready to be whisked away. She did not know what to expect from the two young women who almost lifted her off her feet going up the steps and escorted her out into the icy darkness. The fires that burned so brightly only a few minutes before had been extinguished. It was now quite dark, which made it easy to see the soft light glowing from the tiny crack at the top of the door in the next earth shelter. Sister Mischka opened it and in they went. Once inside Kyla saw that this shelter was identical in size and construction to the other, but here the smell of wood smoke mingled with the scent of the herbs and aromatic roots hanging from the ceiling beams. A man of Fleet or Brother Fox's stature would have had to stoop to walk across the room. But it was easy to see that no man lived here, there was a definite feminine feel to the place. The other shelter had no furnishings, just an empty room with straw mats on the floor. Here every inch of space was used, from the herbs hanging overhead, to the baskets lining the walls. On top of the straw mats were a variety of rugs of all shapes, colors and sizes.

They had barely stepped inside and closed the door before the two sisters went to work on Kyla. Sister Eaglet began by tugging at the sleeping bag. Kyla was a little surprised and clutched it tighter about her neck. At the same time Sister Mischka grabbed her hat and as she pulled it off, gasped, "Who did that to you?" She made it sound as if Kyla's shaved head was a personal insult to her, but Kyla had no chance to answer. Sister Eaglet freed the sleeping bag from her grip and tossed it aside while Sister Mischka let fly a few choice words for Fleet, implying that he was lacking in common sense and courtesy. By then Sister Eaglet had moved on to the task of removing the mittens from her feet, jerking them off so suddenly that Kyla nearly lost her balance. Once that was done the two of them stood back and looked her over. Apparently they were satisfied with the rest of her attire, since they didn't try to peel off any more layers.

Kyla studied them too. Everyone here was called Brother or Sister, but these two looked like they really were sisters. They both had the same heart shaped faces, blond hair and blue eyes. The younger one, Sister Eaglet, wore her hair in two long braids that reached nearly to her waist. Sister Mischka let hers fall in a cascade of loose curls over her shoulders. She could not be certain of their ages, but Sister Eaglet looked young, maybe in her teens and Sister Mischka was probably in her early twenties, about the same age as Kyla. "So, why did you shave your head?" Sister Mischka asked, her question blunt and to the point.

"I didn't do it. They did it at the farm. They said they were worried about lice," Kyla answered. She was not in the mood to discuss it further. So far she had not seen anything about these two that seemed friendly.

"No, they did it to humiliate you," Sister Mischka said contemptuously. "That's how they break your spirit. You're very lucky to have escaped." While Sister Mischka asked, "How did you get Brother Fleet to take you with him?" Sister Eaglet began searching in the baskets along the wall.

The questioning was making Kyla uncomfortable. She was certain the others were asking Fleet the same questions and they would surely compare answers later. "I escaped from my guard and ran into Fleet while I was trying to get out," Kyla answered tersely. She felt that the less said the better. There was no way to know if she could trust any of these people and she was getting good at telling parts of the truth. Judging by the look on Sister Mischka's face the answer had not satisfied her, but Kyla doubted any answer would.

Sister Eaglet reappeared with a huge smile on her face and an armful of clothes. The first thing she handed to Kyla was a pair of thick woolen stockings. As she took them Kyla could tell by the stitches that they were handmade, probably by Sister Eaglet. "I have no way to pay you. I can't take your things," Kyla said.

Sister Eaglet's smile suddenly disappeared. She was clearly dismayed by Kyla's mention of payment. "I am only giving you these things because I have them to give. You have no reason to feel that you owe me anything. You wouldn't survive for long dressed like you were."

Kyla nodded in silent agreement. The young girl was right. She needed stockings. The ones she had on were a little worse for wear and nothing to compare to a pair of woolen stockings when it came to warming the feet. Sister Eaglet smiled when Kyla sat on the floor and removed the soiled stockings and threw them in the pile with the sleeping bag and hat, and then pulled on the new stockings. While she was still seated Sister Eaglet handed her a pair of boots. These Kyla also took gratefully. She pulled them on and then stood and took a few steps. They felt like they had been made for her. The fit was perfect. The style of the boot was similar to Brother Fox's, hand stitched and made from the same soft and supple leather, but her boots only rose to mid-calf and not to the knees like his.

"Thank you Sister Eaglet. They are wonderful," Kyla had to fight to keep tears from welling up in her eyes. She did not want them to see her cry.

"When you receive a kindness you must pass it on to your Brothers and Sisters when they are in need," Sister Eaglet replied obviously pleased. "In the Family, we give freely to all."

"But I am not part of your family," Kyla said. Their definition of what made a family was definitely not the same as hers.

"We are all part of the Family," Sister Eaglet answered. There was a child-like simplicity in her belief. It was not a new concept. Most religions were based on a belief in the family of man. Kyla just didn't know which one these people followed or if they were just making up their own rules as they went. The latter seemed the most likely.

"You told us where you were yesterday, but where have you been living? The Family, the Settlement where Fleet stays, and Spring's men

51

are the only people we know of living in this area," Sister Mischka was back on task, determined to extract more information. Kyla was beginning to become a little annoyed with her blunt questions. At least Sister Eaglet was friendly.

"I lived by myself in a root cellar in the woods since the evacuations," Kyla answered simply.

"Alone? All that time?" Sister Mischka's voice and eyes were full of disbelief. Sister Eaglet's mouth gaped open too. Kyla felt a flush of embarrassment. They were staring at her like she had performed a miracle. Kyla didn't understand why they should find it so unbelievable. It had been no great accomplishment, just the act of survival.

As Sister Mischka looked at the thin woman standing before her, dressed in ill fitting men's clothing she believed at least that much of what she had said. She looked as if she was nearly starved. The rest of her story left much unsaid. Sister Mischka wondered what trick she had used to get Fleet to bring her along. Brother Fleet was well known for his impulsive behavior, but he was not foolish and Sister Mischka could think of nothing more foolhardy than picking up a stranger from inside Spring's compound. No matter how harmless and innocent the circumstances seemed. She knew Kyla was reluctant to tell them all that had happened just as Sister Mischka was reluctant to believe all that she said. It was the world of suspicion and mistrust in which they lived. That was why Sister Mischka was happy the Family had found her and Sister Eaglet. She could trust the Family and outside of the Family, she could trust Brother Fleet. On this one she would reserve judgement for now, time would tell. Once Sister Samethia had made her decision, then they would know.

Now it was Sister Mischka's turn to show concern about Kyla's clothing. "She needs a belt," she said turning to Sister Eaglet, "and a different hat." That sent Sister Eaglet off rummaging through baskets again.

"I don't mean to pry but I was wondering, are you and Sister Eaglet truly sisters?" Kyla asked, as she looked first at Sister Mischka and then at Sister Eaglet. "I know you call each other Brother and Sister, but you two look so much alike." Kyla was beginning to feel a little more comfortable. Perhaps she could get some information from them.

"We are all truly," and Sister Mischka emphasized the word 'truly', "Brothers and Sisters in the Family. But I know what you mean. Sister Eaglet and I have the same mother and father, but that was another life and another family. Sister Eaglet and I are very grateful that Sister Samethia found us and brought us into the Family. " Sister Mischka's answer was a bit prickly, but Kyla was actually getting used to her and took no offense to the tone and the mention of Sister Samethia aroused Kyla's curiosity. "How did she find you?" Kyla asked.

Sister Eaglet eagerly told Kyla the story as she bent down and began pulling a braided leather cord through the loops of Kyla's jeans. "We had been hiding in the woods for about a month after our area was evacuated when Sister Samethia found us. It was pouring down rain, so I guess we hadn't been watching, because it seemed like she just appeared out of nowhere." She stood up and tied the belt tightly, gathering the excess material of the oversized trousers around Kyla's thin waist. "I guess that will have to do," she said. "I could give you a dress, but if you want to wear pants, I don't think we have anything that will fit you any better than what you're wearing."

Kyla looked down at the trousers tied tightly around her waist at the top and tucked into her boots at the bottom, they looked quite baggy. All she needed was a little time, some scissors and a needle and thread and she could fix them, but right now she wanted Sister Eaglet to finish the story. "What happened then?" she asked.

Sister Eaglet smiled. In her mind the answer was simple and needed no further explanation but for Kyla's benefit she said, "She brought us here and taught us how to live from what the Mother provides."

Sister Mischka, apparently impatient with the conversation, interrupted them. "Try this on," she said and pushed a hat into Kyla's hands. Although she insisted that the hat she had been wearing would do just fine, the Sisters would hear nothing of it. They were in the process of having Kyla try on a variety of woolen knit and leather caps when Brother Aquila knocked at the door and announced that it was time for them to return to the meeting room. Luckily for Kyla she happened to be wearing one of the woolen caps at the time, because that is what she ended up wearing as they followed the young man back to the first earth shelter.

Kyla felt much more comfortable now that she was properly shod and the baggy jeans were held securely in place. She could walk with a confident stride instead of shuffling from place to place like a prisoner in shackles. When they entered the other shelter, Kyla was feeling less like an unwanted refugee and more of an equal to the others in the room. Her stomach growled in response to the smell of food cooking. The fact that she had been eating on a little more regular basis had also contributed to her growing feelings of strength and independence. Still, it was a relief to see that Fleet was still there. Stretched out on the floor on one of the mats by the fire, he looked quite relaxed. Sister Samethia motioned to them and indicated that they were to sit next to her, filling in the half circle around the hearth. Once they were seated Sister Samethia filled three more of the earthenware cups and gave one to each of them. When Kyla took a small sip and realized that it was wine, she smiled to herself. Apparently the Family did not disapprove of spirits. Most interesting of all was the food cooking on the fire. The roasting rabbits were crispy brown and the fire below crackled and hissed from the falling juices. Around the edges of the fire were some oddly shaped roots baking on the hot rocks.

She sat silently watching the people around her. On the far side of the fire, Fleet and Brother Fox were sitting close to each other, deep in some conversation. Kyla wished she could hear what they said. Their expressions were serious and twice she saw Brother Fox shake his head, which only made Fleet continue with even more persistence. There was an older man with thinning white hair standing near the fire who had not been introduced to Kyla yet. He was turning the meat on the spit and occasionally poking at the roots, checking to see if they were done. The young red haired boy sat down next to Sister Eaglet. They appeared to be about the same age. As they leaned close together whispering and giggling, Kyla could see that the boy was holding her hand and stroking it gently. It did not take a genius to guess what was going on between the two of them. Then there was Sister Samethia and Sister Mischka, who were busy discussing a recipe for some herbal mixture. The fact that no one was speaking to her was a relief. She was tired of answering questions and this was the first time in months that she had been able to do what she was now, sitting by a fire, drinking a cup of sweet wine, warm, relaxed and most of all safe. With the burden of fear gone, Kyla felt like a huge weight had been lifted from her body.

After a few minutes the man tending the fire bent down and speaking softly to Sister Samethia informed her that the dinner was ready. At that time she brought the gathering to attention by announcing, "Before we eat I have a gift for our honored guest, Brother Fleet." All conversation stopped except for Brother Fox who leaned even closer to whisper something to Fleet. Apparently he was the only person who was not required to snap to attention when Sister Samethia spoke. When Brother Fox finally turned his full attention to Sister Samethia, she rose and crossed the circle to kneel ceremoniously before Fleet, giving him a small packet of folded leather tied with a string.

Fleet waited until she rose and returned to her place. "Thank you," he said as he untied the string and opened the package to reveal a small arrow. He picked it up between his thumb and forefinger and looked at it more closely. It was meant to be a pin and although it was small and appeared to be delicate, it was made from one piece of tooled silver with the pin attached by the silver wire wrapped around the arrow to look like the banding that would hold the blade and fletching. As he admired the workmanship, Fleet asked, "Who made this? I'll have to thank him."

"It was Brother Treblki," Sister Eaglet blurted out. She received a glare from Sister Samethia. It was Sister Samethia's gift and her place to answer. Sister Eaglet ducked her head and looked down to avoid meeting her eyes. Fleet saw nothing wrong with Sister Eaglet speaking up. The Family was a little too concerned with rank and rules in his opinion. He liked the young girl. She had a little spirit left, but given enough time he was sure Sister Samethia would bring her in line.

"It's a fine gift, but I'm not sure what I've done to deserve to be honored," Fleet said. The Brothers and Sisters would never think of asking Sister Samethia such a question. If Sister Samethia said to honor the beetle in the corner, they would do it and never dream to ask why.

"It is meant to be a reminder of the last time we met. A reminder of what I told you," Sister Samethia answered. She was always patient with Fleet, tolerating his questions and treating him as an equal. Only Brother Fox was her equal within the Family, but she knew Fleet was special.

"You mean my reading?" Fleet's usual grinning demeanor erupted into a smile that nearly split his face in two. The rest of the Family said nothing, but they seemed uncomfortable with his response. Fleet continued, "Yes, I remember, but you have to understand something. I don't believe in all that fortune teller nonsense. I appreciate the gift and you can call me the arrow, if you like, but I just don't believe anyone can predict the future."

All tolerance aside, Sister Samethia was fuming. Fleet had crossed the line by questioning the very basis of their beliefs and the heart of the Family. He didn't believe what Sister Samethia had told him. Everyone in the Family knew how foolish that was, but Sister Samethia was not about to show that her feathers were ruffled. She smiled and responded with the self-assurance of a prophet, "What you believe is not important. You are the arrow that will pierce the heart of our enemy. That I know."

It was all too serious for Fleet. He laughed and drained his cup. Then held it out for a refill and bellowed, "Then fill my cup and we will drink to the death of our enemies!" That seemed to please Sister Samethia and ruffled feathers or not she rose and poured the wine.

"Kyla," Fleet said her name and suddenly all eyes were focused on her. She shifted uneasily, not really wanting to be a part of the conversation. "Pin this thing on me," he said casually as if talking to an old friend. Kyla felt a little embarrassed by the request. It was a rather intimate favor to ask and she was sure he knew some of the other women better. Sister Eaglet smiled at her and Sister Samethia looked indifferent, but Sister Mischka scowled sourly. Kyla wouldn't be surprised if she had something more than just a friendly interest in Fleet.

Kyla stood and went to kneel next to Fleet. Then taking the pin from his hand she began to fasten it to his tunic over his left breast. "No here," he said pointing to his shoulder. The tunic was made so it opened at the shoulder and had a standing collar. There were no buttons, only a long strip of cording that was threaded through a loop at the shoulder and tied. The cord had several dark beads threaded on the end and it hung down on his chest. It was at the point where the cord was tied to the loop that Fleet was pointing. Her hands trembled slightly and she felt a small tingle pass through her body as she slipped the fingers of one hand under his shirt and felt the smooth skin of his throat and shoulder. Fleet seemed to be enjoying her distress.

"Don't stick me," he said giving her a poke on the shoulder just as she began to push the pin into the fabric, causing her to flinch and prick her own finger instead. When she said, "Ouch," and stuck her finger in her mouth, everyone in the room began to laugh except Kyla. Fleet was having fun at her expense, it seemed, and without thinking she deliberately stuck him with the pin. When he jumped with a start, it started another round of laughter in the room. It was probably the best entertainment they'd had in days. Kyla snapped the pin closed and returned to her seat after giving Fleet a heated look. As she turned her back, Fleet rubbed the spot where she had stuck him. He had not expected that reaction from the meek and mild girl who had trailed silently behind him all day.

An awkward silence followed, no one seemed to know what to say next. Sister Samethia took things in hand by saying, "Brother Eldar will you please serve the food." From that moment on, all attention was turned to serving those seated around the fire. Brother Eldar divided the meat and roasted roots, which he explained were something like a wild carrot, into equal portions onto wooden platters that they passed down the line. There did not seem to be any deference to rank in the way they were served. Brother Fox was first because he was seated at the far end of the circle and Sister Samethia last, but no one began eating.

Sister Samethia rose and said, "Before we eat we must thank the Mother for all of her blessings." The others seated around the fire joined hands and lowered their heads. Samethia began the chant. At every pause those seated chimed in chorus, "Bless the Mother."

"The Earth is our mother. She gives us life."
"Bless the Mother."
The Earth is our Mother. She gives us food."
"Bless the Mother."
The Earth is our Mother. She gives us shelter."
"Bless the Mother."

"As Mother cares for her Family, so do we care for her."
"Bless the Mother."
"As Mother cares for her Family, so do we care for each other."
"Bless the Mother."
"So keep the Mother. So keep each other."
"Mother keep us in the end."

Once the blessing was said, there was silence except for the sounds of the meal being eaten. Their life was truly rustic. The food was served on wooden platters and there were no knifes or forks. So everyone ate with their hands, but Kyla didn't care. She thought it was a most wonderful meal. The roasted rabbit was excellent. She was not sure what had been used to flavor it, but some of the herbs in the other shelter surely had culinary uses.

Fleet watched as Kyla wolfed down the food on her platter. It would take some time for her to begin to regain some of the weight that she had lost. He hadn't had anything other than the dried deer meat to give to her earlier. He had also noticed the new boots and hat that she was wearing when she returned. Fleet knew the Sisters would be working on converting her or 'Bringing her to the Family' as they would say. A little kindness and charity spread in the proper thickness was their usual tool of persuasion. Not that it should make any difference to him one way or the other. It would be easier for him if she decided to stay. Still, he couldn't say that he liked the idea of leaving her with the Family either. He wondered if Kyla even knew there was another choice. Fleet hadn't mentioned the Settlement or Sadie yet. If anyone in the Family had, it would only be to tell her to never go there. He decided to get Kyla alone and tell her then shook his head at that thought. It had to be the wine. He was getting soft - soft in the head. Still a person should know what their options really were.

It wasn't long before every scrap of food had been devoured, every bone picked clean and the wine flask emptied and the evening gathering was over. Brother Aquila and Sister Eaglet gathered the platters and left. Sister Samethia stood and looking at Fleet said, "It's late and I'm sure that both you and your friend are tired. Please feel free to stay here or in the men's shelter. Sister Kyla, you can come with Sister Mischka and me."

Kyla looked at Fleet hoping to see some sign from him, but he was preoccupied with pushing a log deeper into the fire with the toe of his boot. It was obvious to Kyla that she was not on his mind. He couldn't have been less interested in where they took her but she was still uncomfortable with the thought of being separated from him. Worse yet was the thought that he planned to leave her with the Family. She wished that she'd had an opportunity to talk to Fleet without a Family member present. She had some questions she'd wanted to ask. Sister Mischka had mentioned a place called the Settlement where Fleet lived. From what she had seen of the Family, it was not the place for her. Their little group seemed happy enough, but Kyla wasn't sure she wanted to live the rest of her life jumping whenever Sister Samethia said to jump. She had just escaped from one prison and was not about to surrender her freedom for another no matter how pleasant it was. Kyla left with Sister Mischka and Sister Samethia without a word said between herself and Fleet.

They returned to the earth shelter where they had gone earlier and found Sister Eaglet was already there. Wearing only a thin shift, she was busy adding wood to the fire. It was much warmer in the room than it had been earlier and the fragrance of some herbal mixture simmering on the fire filled the air. The other two women where busy shedding their clothing until they too were wearing only their shifts. When they joined Sister Eaglet at the fire, Sister Mischka took over tending the fire while Sister Eaglet went to get one of the light shifts for Kyla. When she handed it to her, Kyla didn't bother arguing. Undressing quickly, she put it on and joined them by the fire.

Sister Samethia smiled, pleased by Kyla's quiet acceptance in joining their circle. "I think you will find the heat and the steam from the herbs soothing."

As she sat next to Sister Samethia, Kyla said, "I'd like to thank you for the kindness that you've shown me. The boots and stockings and the pin that you gave to Fleet all were handmade. Do you make everything that you wear and use?" Kyla asked. She was curious about the things that she had seen since her arrival.

"Of course they are," Sister Mischka leapt to the answer and bristled indignantly at Kyla's ignorance. With the wave of her hand Sister Samethia silenced any further comments that Sister Mischka might have wanted to make and she sat quietly while Sister Samethia explained, "I think what Sister Kyla meant to ask was, why we make most of the things we use." Sister Samethia looked directly at Sister Mischka who lowered her eyes and began to busy herself stirring the pot of herbs on the fire.

"Now I will tell you about our Family," Sister Samethia began. She paused and looked one last time at Sister Mischka. Then satisfied that she would not be interrupted, she continued with her story. "We make everything that we can, relearning many skills which have been lost over the generations, weaving, tanning, living off the land. Our Family is still young, still learning and some things we must scavenge from the abandoned towns. But we only take what we cannot yet make for ourselves - knives for hunting and tools for building, for example." 'And guns,' Kyla thought to herself. She was not so blind that she didn't know what was in the bundles that Fleet had brought to them. Still, she listened politely.

Sister Samethia turned to Sister Mischka again saying, "Sister Mischka has learned much about herbs and wild plants and their uses for medicines or food. We call our little Sister, Eaglet because she has become a hunter, like the eagle. A few months ago she would have gone to a store to buy meat. Now she has learned to hunt with a bow and to make snares. The rabbits that we ate for our supper tonight were ones that Sister Eaglet caught. We ate the meat and the skins will be made into clothing or other things that we need. Whatever the Mother gives us we use completely. It is a sin to waste her gifts." With that said Sister Samethia nodded to Sister Eaglet who began to ladle the hot liquid from the simmering pot of herbs into four small cups and pass them to the women kneeling at the fire.

Kyla looked at the liquid in her cup. It had a slightly yellow color and an earthy smell. When the others took a sip, Kyla followed their example. Whatever was in the cup, it didn't have much taste but it was warming. As Kyla sipped the tea, Sister Mischka gave a small bowl filled with a tiny amount of clear liquid to Samethia. Upon taking the bowl, Sister Samethia dipped her finger into the liquid twice and each time carefully let a tiny drop fall into one of her eyes before returning it to Sister Mischka. Then turning to Kyla, she said, "Please, put down your tea and give me your hands." Kyla did as Sister Samethia asked.

As she took Kyla's hands in hers Sister Samethia closed her eyes before continuing, "It is easy to see the things in the physical world that the Mother provides, food, water, and shelter but there is more to Her than what can be seen. Some things we must feel like the wind or love. Others act upon us without our knowledge like magnetic fields and gravity. You know of these things and accept them even though they cannot be seen. All we can see is the way they affect the physical world. There are forces that shape our destinies and those I can feel as surely as you can feel the wind."

When Samethia opened her eyes and looked at her, Kyla was surprised to see that her eyes now appeared completely black. She seemed distant somehow, and even though she was staring directly at her, Kyla didn't think she truly saw her now. Sister Mischka set another shallow bowl on the floor between them. Without a word, Sister Samethia released one of Kyla's hands and scooped up a small amount of the scented oil from the bowl into her hand. Then she began to firmly rub the mixture on Kyla's hands and wrists. "Mother knows us in the beginning and in the end. She knows the paths we must travel along the way." Sister Samethia continued the process, next massaging the aromatic oil onto Kyla's arms and shoulders. "She has blessed me with the ability to see parts of the paths and the people who walk them. Your path has brought you to the Family, but you will not stay and live as one of us." Kyla wasn't sure if it was the heat or exhaustion, but her head was swimming. Beads of perspiration covered her body as she felt the warmth from the fire more intensely now. A part of Kyla wanted to pull away from this strange woman and shut out the words, but the other part was rooted where she sat, mesmerized by what Sister Samethia was saying. As Kyla fought the urge to close her eyes and let sleep take her away, Sister Samethia was holding her head in her hands now and Kyla looked deep into her eyes. "You are tied to Fleet in some way. Your path and his wind together now." Samethia brought her face near to Kyla's and in a voice that was barely audible said, "Fleet needs you but you must beware. He is a danger to all those near to him. Like a whirlpool, he will draw you in. You must be strong to fight the tides that swirl around him."

Then finally she released Kyla and picked up the cup of tea that Kyla had set aside. "Finish this now. When you wake in the morning you'll feel refreshed and the aches will be gone from your body." The liquid had cooled and Kyla was able to drink what was left in one swallow. When sister Samethia released her, Kyla felt fatigue flooding through her body. Once her cup was empty, Sister Eaglet took her by the arm and helped Kyla to her feet. Like a sleepwalker Kyla let Sister Eaglet lead her to the far end of the room and help her into a soft bed that smelled of pine and cover her with blankets. Kyla's last memory before falling asleep was Sister Eaglet smiling and saying, "Good night Sister. Tomorrow will come soon enough."

Chapter Three

The sound that woke Kyla the next morning was barking dogs. She sat up suddenly and looked around the room. The fire still glowed in the corner, but it had burned low and provided only dim light. From what she could see, Kyla was alone in the room. She shivered as she threw back the covers. Not only did the fire provide less light, but also it was also much cooler than it had been the night before. Kyla found her clothes piled neatly beside her bed and dressed quickly. There were a few other items that had been left for her. First, there was a platter with two small biscuits and some dried fruit and a cup of water. Kyla ate quickly as she examined the coat that had been lying with her clothes and tried it on. It was made of furry, gray skins pieced together in crazy-quilt fashion. Kyla smiled as she wondered how many rabbits Sister Eaglet had snared to make the coat.

The next round of barking dogs and loud voices outside brought her back to attention. She grabbed the hat and mittens and put them on as she went out the door. It was pandemonium outside. Several riders on horseback were milling about in the clearing by the lake. Fleet and Brother Fox were standing in the middle talking to one of the riders. Kyla made straight for them. As she approached, Kyla was able to hear the rider talking to Fleet when he said, "We were about two miles north of there yesterday morning when they spotted us." Kyla stopped just a few paces behind Fleet and in the middle of the circle of riders. No one seemed to notice or care that she was there.

"Do you think they followed you here?" Brother Fox asked as he took the reins of the man's horse while he dismounted.

"No, we were careful," he answered as he slid of the horse. "But we had to leave the flock behind, so I sent the dogs to scatter them. It'll be too much trouble for Spring's men to gather them. That lazy lot wouldn't do anything that was real work."

One of the others, a red headed girl riding a black horse, spoke out. "They shot one of the dogs!"

Brother Fox turned to the girl and said, "You're all lucky it was just one of the dogs," and pushed the horse's reins back into the hands of his rider. "All of you, get the horses stabled and get those dogs quiet," he barked the orders like a general to his troops.

Jostled about in the flurry of activity that surrounded her, Kyla jumped as she felt a hand lay solidly on her shoulder. When she turned, she was relieved to see Sister Eaglet who took her by the arm and led her away from the crowd. "You had better come with me. You don't want to get in Brother Fox's way today. You can come with me while I do my morning chores." With that said, Sister Eaglet turned and led the way to the area behind the earth shelters. "These are the gardens," she said pointing to long rows of wooden boxes covered with glass. "Sister Samethia says we can raise vegetables in these cold frames even when it's winter." Kyla followed Sister Eaglet as she went to each of the little gardens, checking the condition of the little seedlings and watering them when she felt it was necessary. She told Kyla what was planted in each one, turnips, cabbage, peas, and many others, but the only thing that had sprouted so far was the cabbage and a few weeds.

"I'm glad I got the chance to talk to you," Sister Eaglet said when they came to the last one. She didn't say it, but Kyla could guess she meant that she was glad to have the chance to talk to Kyla alone. Sister Samethia and Brother Fox kept a firm hand on everyone in the Family.

"Thank you for the coat," Kyla said, "Is it one that you made?"

"Yes, I made it and you are welcome to it. I have another." Kyla could see the coat Sister Eaglet wore was just like the one they had given her. She smiled to herself at the thought of Sister Eaglet, the rabbit hunter and gardener. Surely, rabbits would not be plentiful enough near the shelters to be a nuisance once the garden was growing. Sister Eaglet looked around nervously; making sure that no one else was near before she pulled a long hunting knife in its leather case from under her coat. She pressed it into Kyla's hand, "Put this under your coat. You will need it if you go with Fleet to the Settlement."

Kyla took it gladly. Clovis had taken hers. It was one of the things that she knew she would need once she was on her own again. "Thank you again. It seems that I'm even deeper in your debt."

"You can repay me by staying alive and coming back some day," Sister Eaglet said. "I don't envy you at all. The Settlement can be a dangerous place."

"Have you been there?" Kyla asked, hoping for some useful information from Sister Eaglet.

64

"No, but I've heard the stories from the ones who have," she answered. Then leaning closer she whispered, "Whatever you do, if someone offers you some pearls, say no." She looked around again, "I am not supposed to know about them. Sister Samethia believes if you don't know about temptation it will be easier to resist, but I have heard her and Brother Fox talking about pearls and the harm that comes from using them."

This part of the conversation meant nothing to Kyla. She had no idea what Sister Eaglet was talking about, but she had no doubt the girl would not have mentioned 'pearls' if it weren't important. "What about you, Sister Eaglet. Will you stay here with the Family?" Kyla wasn't sure why she asked the question, but there was something about Eaglet that made Kyla think she had been born to fly free like her namesake the eagle.

Sister Eaglet smiled and answered as if she knew what Kyla was thinking, "This is my home. I wouldn't be here today if it wasn't for Sister Samethia. Besides, if Sister Samethia and Brother Fox give their permission, Brother Aquila and I will be married soon." Sister Eaglet's face positively glowed when she mentioned Brother Aquila, but the look faded quickly.

Kyla learned the reason soon enough when she heard someone approaching from behind. It was Sister Samethia, of course, the ever-vigilant keeper of the flock. "Sister Eaglet was showing me the gardens," Kyla said as Sister Samethia joined them. Only half a lie, she hoped that Sister Eaglet would not be in trouble and she certainly didn't mention the knife or the warning.

"Sister Eaglet, Brother Eldar is waiting for you to help with the cooking fires," Sister Samethia said as if reminding a forgetful child and Sister Eaglet obediently scurried on her way. Once she was gone Sister Samethia turned her attention to Kyla. "I must talk to you before you leave."

The memory of the ceremony the night before was coming back to her. "What was in the tea that you gave me last night?" Kyla asked. Whatever it had been, it worked as Samethia had promised. Kyla's aches and pains from riding all day, not to mention the bruises from her fall out of the tree were barely noticeable.

"That was nothing, only a little willow bark and some other herbs to give you comfort," Sister Samethia answered. "I need to speak to you about the Settlement."

Of course Sister Samethia would have some warning, for the first time since arriving Kyla was running out of patience. "I am not a child Sister Samethia. I am well aware of the dangers in the world."

"You have been isolated for so long and the world has changed." Of course Sister Samethia was not deterred. Kyla would have to listen to whatever it was that she had to say. Sister Samethia reached into the pocket of her coat. For a moment Kyla wondered if everyone in the camp would have something important to give her before she left. She was surprised when Sister Samethia held up the handcuffs that Kyla had been carrying. Until that moment, Kyla had not realized they were gone. She hadn't missed them when she dressed. "When you used these to attach yourself to Brother Fleet you began a bond that will last until one of you dies," Sister Samethia's proclamation was a solemn one.

Kyla reached out and took back the handcuffs. Fleet must have told them everything that had happened. "I only did what I had to do," she said. It was the only explanation she was willing to make.

"That is all anyone of us can say," Sister Samethia answered. Kyla wished that she would get to the point whatever it was. Sister Samethia looked into Kyla's eyes as she began her prophecy, "Brother Fleet did not tell me what happened at Spring's farm, Sister Kyla. It is part of what I saw and felt when I was with you last night. I know it is hard for someone outside the Family to believe, but what I tell you about your future is just as true as what I say about the past."

"Then tell me, what am I supposed to do? How am I tied to Fleet? I don't know anything more about him than I do about your Family or the Settlement." Sister Samethia was full of hints and pieces of fact but she was a little thin on real information.

"I can't tell you every step of your path. All I can give you is your general direction and who will walk with you. Fleet needs you to fulfill his destiny. Without you he cannot destroy our enemy." As usual Sister Samethia's answer was vague. "Even though you cannot stay with the Family, you will always be welcome here. If you ever need us, we will be here to help you."

"Thank you for everything that you have done for me, Sister Samethia," Kyla answered. She wasn't sure how to reply to her predictions. Instead she said, "I will always be grateful and I would like to come back someday."

"Brother Fleet will be wanting to leave soon," Sister Samethia smiled and continued, "He'll go to the Settlement from here. Since he'll be on horseback I've convinced Brother Fox to give you one of the horses, too."

"But why? That's too much, I can't take a horse," Kyla objected. She was already indebted to these people for the hospitality they had shown her.

"Our friend, Brother Fleet, is an unpredictable person. If you have your own mount, you can't be left behind," Sister Samethia's explanation was simple enough, but Kyla didn't think she would ever understand what the tall dark haired woman was thinking. "We should return to the others now," Sister Samethia announced abruptly as she turned and began walking back to the clearing by the lake.

Kyla followed, puzzling over what Sister Samethia had said. It was apparently important to Sister Samethia that when Fleet left, Kyla left with him. Important enough to give her a horse, the value of the gift wasn't lost on Kyla. Whatever it was that Fleet was destined to do, according to Sister Samethia, Kyla was destined to do it with him and she was doing everything in her power to keep them together. Either that or it was an overly elaborate plan to get rid of her, something that could have been accomplished without all the gifts. Still, Kyla was not unhappy about the outcome. With her new clothes, a good hunting knife, and miracle of miracles, a horse, she would be able to go where she wanted. If the Settlement turned out to be as bad as Sister Eaglet said there was nothing to keep her from leaving. She could go where she wanted. Kyla found it hard to believe that Spring's farm, the Family, and the mysterious and yet unseen Settlement were her only options. If there were three places where people lived in the area, then surely she could find more.

Fleet was standing outside the doorway of the Family's meeting house. He saw Kyla walking behind Sister Samethia as they came from the area behind the shelters where the gardens were located. There hadn't been an opportunity for him to speak to Kyla alone and Fleet could only wonder what the members of the Family had been telling her about him and the Settlement. Fleet could put up with all the nonsense from Sister Samethia about how he was the arrow that would kill their enemy. That is he tolerated it, when it was just the other Family members, but he didn't like her repeating the foolishness to others. He was certain Sister Samethia had done a reading for Kyla, too. She wouldn't miss an opportunity to perform her rituals. He watched Sister Samethia with some apprehension as the two women approached. There was no doubt in his mind that she would soon let him know what her plans for Kyla were.

"Good morning, Brother Fleet," Sister Samethia greeted him cheerfully. "I can smell rain on the wind this morning. It seems you will have a damp ride today."

"Good morning to you Sister Samethia, Kyla," he answered. Purposely, omitting the title 'Sister' when he said Kyla's name. No use making assumptions before the announcement was made. "I've traveled in worse." Talking about the weather seemed a safe enough subject. There was no hope that Sister Samethia would leave Kyla alone with him. He was sure she wouldn't want to take a chance on Fleet talking Kyla into leaving with him. The three stood silently for a moment before Fleet added, "Brother Fox has sent Brother Aquila to get my horse ready." He was uncomfortable with good-byes and would have preferred slipping out with no one knowing, but it was too late for that now. After what seemed like an eternity to Fleet, Brother Fox and Brother Aquila returned from the direction of the stables leading not one, but two horses. Fleet knew his deal had been for only one horse and wondered what Brother Fox and Sister Samethia had planned for him now.

As the two Brothers leading the horses joined them, Sister Samethia turned to Fleet. "Sister Kyla will be going with you," was all she said.

You could have knocked Fleet over with a feather, he was shocked, surprised to say the least. This turn of events was the last thing he had expected. The Family didn't usually let go of a likely convert without a fight. He looked at Sister Samethia with suspicion, knowing there would be no explanation from her. Around here, her word was law. Even though he had been against Kyla staying with the

Family, he had liked it better when it was his idea to take her along. Now that it was Sister Samethia telling him that Kyla was going, all he could do was wonder what she had planned. Fleet took the reins of the long legged black stallion he had been riding the day before and swung up into the saddle. "She's welcome to go wherever she wants, but I can't wait for her. If she wants to go with me then she'll have to keep up."

Taking him at his word, Kyla scrambled onto the horse that Brother Aquila was holding for her. It was the same shaggy mare called Brownie, which Fleet has used for his packhorse. It had no saddle, only a blanket thrown across its back, but Kyla didn't care. She had ridden bareback many times and wasn't about to let Fleet leave her behind. Kyla was more than willing to follow Fleet. For now Sister Samethia was right, her path and Fleet's would be the same. She had made sure of that. Before they could leave Sister Eaglet and Brother Eldar came hurrying out of the earth shelter behind them and gave them both a bag filled with dried meat and fruit and a flask filled with water. True to his word, Fleet did not wait for Kyla or the many words of last minute advice the Family was offering. He dug his heels into his horse's flank and it leapt to a gallop. With a shrug of apology to her hosts, Kyla did the same and followed Fleet as he rode around the shore of the lake. When they came to the narrow footpath, which Brother Fox had walked them through the night before, Fleet did not slow his pace at all. Instead, he turned his horse and they plunged headlong into the wooded trail at full speed.

Kyla was doing her best to keep up. The mare was no match in speed for Fleet's horse, but speed didn't matter on the narrow, winding trail and the sure-footed little Brownie was soon right behind the other horse. When they reached the other side of the woods, the horses emerged together. Fleet didn't stop. The only indication that he acknowledged Kyla's presence in any way was a slight turn of his head in her direction to see if she was still following before turning his horse and galloping over the open fields. Kyla followed. She still needed Fleet to show her the way to the Settlement and wasn't about to be left behind. It wasn't long before he was a good distance ahead of her. At times Kyla would loose sight of him completely, but Fleet always reappeared just ahead and always heading northwest, as straight as the arrow that Sister Samethia said he was. It became obvious that Fleet was allowing her to follow him. Kyla knew he could have lost her easily. There was no way her horse could have kept up. She didn't know why he was playing games with her. Perhaps he was angry with the Family for forcing him to take her along.

Fleet had kept a hard pace for many miles that morning. The last Kyla had seen of him was when he had disappeared over the rise of the hill that she and Brownie were now climbing. When they came to the top of the rise, she was surprised to see Fleet standing next to his horse waiting for her. "We need to stop and walk the horses," was all he said before turning and walking away.

Kyla slid to the ground and ran to catch up to him. "I am sorry to be such a burden to you. I promise that once we get to wherever it is you are going, I won't trouble you anymore." Fleet looked at her. His expression was not angry. He was smiling which frustrated Kyla even more. "You let me follow you. Why did you do that if you want to get rid of me?"

"Who said I want to get rid of you?" Fleet asked.

"Well, I just thought," Kyla began but he cut her off.

"That was your first mistake. If you want to know what I'm thinking just ask me," Fleet answered coolly.

He was an infuriating man. Just how was she supposed to ask Fleet anything when she hadn't had one opportunity to speak to him while they were with the Family? When they left he had done everything possible to keep his distance from her, but she would play the game by his rules. "Alright, Fleet, then tell me what are you thinking?" she asked. If he liked things simple and to the point, Kyla was more than willing to oblige.

Fleet turned to her a with a big grin and said, "I was just thinking how lucky you are. Twice now I could have left you behind and I didn't. I think you owe me big time, but that's just what I think."

"You're right," Kyla answered. "I owe you my life once and my freedom twice."

Fleet looked at her. She was serious about the last. "I don't know how you managed to wriggle through Sister Samethia's fingers, but I couldn't stand it there for long either."

"She told me I had to go." Kyla paused for a moment before adding, "Along with a bunch of other things about you and how I was supposed to be important to you somehow."

Fleet shook his head. So that was it, Sister Samethia and her blasted fortune telling. Now she had this one believing it and had sent her along to keep an eye on him. Well, he'd had enough of that nonsense. "I don't care what she told you," he said impatiently. "If you don't have enough sense to recognize bull-shit when you hear it, then I can't help you there."

Now it was Kyla's turn to laugh at Fleet. "What makes you think I can't? If you want to know what I think, then just ask," she said, using Fleet's own words.

He looked at her. She was not meek and mild anymore. Give a woman a new coat and shoes then throw in a horse to boot, and she starts acting as if she owns the world. If there was one thing he was learning about this one, it was that she had tenacity and he could not underestimate what she might be capable of doing. For the time being he would just have to accept her presence, it wouldn't be anything permanent. He was sure of that. Then like a woman, she soon began to shower him with a barrage of questions.

"How far is it to the Settlement," Kyla asked.

"If we keep going all day we'll reach it after nightfall," Fleet answered.

"What is it like there?" she asked.

Fleet wondered what she might have been told. "It's nothing like the Family's camp," he began. "Nobody cares who you were or where you came from. No questions, no rules, that's how I like it." He looked at Kyla and could tell by her expression that she wasn't satisfied and he continued. "I can't tell you how many people will be there because it varies from day to day. A few people live there all the time, but most people have a place nearby. The Settlement is more of a place to gather and trade than it is a place to live. After we stop at the Settlement, I'll take you to Sadie. She has a cabin and a greenhouse garden that puts those little cold frames the Family thinks are so wonderful to shame. I think you'd like it there." That explanation must have satisfied her, because now she changed the subject.

"Fleet, I want to find my husband and my family. Now that I have a horse and can travel, I think I could do it," Kyla said earnestly. "Do you know anything about where they took everybody? Cole said he was going to send me to join them."

He looked at her in disbelief. She might as well have announced she was going to fly to the moon. Fleet wasn't sure what to tell her, but the truth here would be the best thing. "You had better put that thought out of your head," he said with finality, meaning to end the subject.

"Why?" she pleaded, "Please, tell me what you know. Someone has to tell me."

Fleet could understand her desire to know, he just hoped she would understand his reluctance to talk about that particular subject. Hadn't he just told her that the reason he liked the Settlement was because no one asked you about the past? If someone had to explain these things to her, why did it have to be him? "It is considered rude to ask about the past, Kyla," he finally said. "No one wants to talk about what's gone, but I know that you need to know, too." Fleet was searching for the words, for the best way to tell her how foolish the idea of looking for her lost family was. "After we get to Sadie's house we'll have a Gathering. That's when we all tell our stories and you'll know as much as any of us do about what has happened. Do you understand?"

He looked at her as she pleaded, "I understand, but can't you tell me anything now? I have to know."

Fleet could hear the need in her voice and see it in her eyes. He remembered how it felt to be alone, without a clue. It was nothing he wanted to tell anyone, but she would hear his tale soon enough. "I can't speak for the others, but I can tell you my story. I hope you'll understand." Kyla considered him thoughtfully and wondered why he seemed to be apologizing before he began.

"I was in the service, in the Army," Fleet began cautiously. "Just a lowly private taking orders when all this began. The first clue any of us had that something was wrong was when they mobilized my unit and all the others on base to begin evacuating civilians living in the small towns and rural areas." Kyla's eyes grew wide as saucers, never in a million years would she have thought that Fleet had been involved in that side of the evacuations. Fleet however was not surprised. Hers was one of the milder reactions he had received. Most people wanted to kill him at the mere mention of his involvement. He continued his story. "They made an announcement before we left, telling us that surprise attacks had been made on all the cities in our area, reducing them to rubble and we were expecting an invasion to occur at anytime. We were told to pick up everyone and transport them to evacuation centers to the north where they would be safe. Once we made the first round of evacuations, they kept sending us back to look for stragglers."

So far his account of the events was the same as Kyla had experienced. Only this was the first she had heard of the cities being destroyed or an invasion. She could certainly understand why Fleet had been unwilling to talk about his past. In a way she felt sorry for him, he must feel badly about helping with the evacuations even if he had only been following orders. But Fleet wasn't paying any attention to her. Once he began his account, it absorbed all his attention. "That went on for weeks, and the invasion never came. When they announced that all non-essential personnel would be sent to the evacuation centers, I decided it was time to get out of there and find my family. So I stole one of the trucks and drove it north. I'd been to one of the centers dropping off evacuees, so I knew the way. Since I was driving one of the trucks they used for transports, no one bothered to stop me or they would have seen that my truck was empty."

When Fleet looked at her, Kyla could see the hurt and anger in his eyes as he said, "And guess what, my truck wasn't the only thing that was empty. When I got to the evacuation center, there wasn't anyone there. We had transported thousands of people to that location and they had just vanished. I walked around like I belonged there and no one seemed to care who I was or what I was doing. I kept looking in one empty building after another. It wasn't until I got to the far end of the compound that I saw men in gray uniforms loading people into railroad cars and this is the funny thing. The tracks led down into a mineshaft. They were taking them underground. There was no place for anyone to live down in that mine." Fleet shook his head as he thought about what he had seen. Looking at the sky, he sighed audibly and finished his tale. "Anyway, I had seen enough to know that it was time to leave. So I began walking south and I kept walking until I came to the Settlement and Sadie found me. Somehow, she forgave me for what I did and gave me a place to stay."

Kyla didn't know what to say. What Fleet had just told her was beyond belief. Everyone gone. Thousands, millions of people just vanishing into mines underground or into thin air, it was unimaginable. He obviously believed what he had told her to be the truth; Kyla didn't think he could have invented such an incredible lie. There had to be some reasonable explanation for what he had seen. Fleet watched the reaction on Kyla's face. He knew she didn't believe him, just like he didn't believe half of the stories that she would hear from the others. She would have to make up her own mind about what the truth was or was not. "You asked me," he said. "You insisted on knowing my story."

She certainly had asked for it. She didn't know why, but something told her it was Fleet who needed reassurance this time. "There's nothing to forgive, Fleet. You were just doing what you thought was right." She couldn't believe she was here with one of the men who turned her world upside down, one of the men who she thought of as evil, telling him he had only done what he though was right. It went against everything Kyla said she would do if she met one of the soldiers, but she knew what happened was not Fleet's fault.

Fleet laughed bitterly at Kyla's attempt to console him. "That's exactly the same thing Sadie said when I told her." He mounted his horse and said, "We'd better move along if we're going to arrive tonight." This time he started off at a slow gallop instead of a dead run. It was a more comfortable pace that both horses could keep. Kyla rode with him now but there was little conversation. About midday they stopped briefly to rest the horses and eat the meal that Sister Eaglet and Brother Eldar had sent with them. A fine mist of rain had begun falling when they started on their way again. Fleet's mood was quiet and sullen, fitting the gray weather. Kyla would certainly remember not to bring up the subject of evacuations or finding her family to Fleet again, but she was not going to forget about it either.

~ ~ ~

Kyla didn't know how far they had ridden that day. It had been a long and cold and certainly unpleasant journey. She was thankful for the coat the Family had given her because the parts of her body it covered were dry. Her legs were wet from the rain falling from above and from the blanket that was soaked with rain and the horse's sweat from below. Fleet seemed not to notice the soggy weather at all and rode on and on, well after the sun was gone.

Once it was dark, they stopped riding across country and took to the roads. They were following what had been a major highway, riding the horses in the gravel shoulder at the side the pavement. Fleet seemed to be very sure of himself as he rode openly right through the center of one small town after another. Finally they left the main highway and followed a much narrower paved road that led south. With the sudden change in direction Kyla began to wonder if they were near the place called the Settlement. When they came to yet another town even smaller than the others, Fleet slowed his horse to a walk. It was only four short blocks from one side of the town to the other. The last one was occupied by a large, single story building. In the darkness Kyla could see playground equipment beside it. This must have been the elementary school. At the end of the block with the school, the paved road turned to the east. Fleet continued riding straight, still heading south on a road that was overgrown with weeds, but there was a trail that was plainly visible and they followed it up and down the hills.

Kyla felt a knot growing in her stomach. She knew they were close now and Fleet had not been full of information or advice. The conversation earlier this morning had soured his mood and he had stayed that way. It was only a short time after leaving the town before Kyla thought she could see lights on the next hillside. Fleet led the way down the hill, turned his horse and began riding down a narrow path toward the light. When they came to a small bridge he stopped. Kyla couldn't see anything and wondered why they were waiting.

When two armed men popped up out of the darkness like trolls from under the bridge she got her answer. "Pay the toll or go away," one of them shouted in the darkness. The other added, "Horse meat for supper tonight." Neither one of them had a lantern. All she could see were two shadowy figures planted in the rode before them. Fleet didn't say a word. Instead he took out his lantern and lit it. Once the little light was glowing, her perception of the scene changed a little. The two men with guns were really boys with sticks. When they saw Fleet, both turned and ran into the darkness.

Kyla urged her horse closer to Fleet. "Is that why you stopped? For those two?" Kyla asked.

"No, I stopped for them," he said pointing to two small lights bobbing through the darkness and coming closer. "Those two are always hiding under the bridge, hoping they'll catch someone greener than they are and scare them into giving them something."

'Greener than they are', Kyla knew Fleet meant her. Lesson number one, don't let your fear get the better of you. She would have to be on her toes around here, Kyla thought to herself, as she waited nervously to see who was on the official greeting committee. Whoever it was, they were in no hurry. It took them forever to cross what looked like a very short distance. Finally, two men who really were armed stopped just at the edge of the bridge. She waited for Fleet to greet them, but he remained silent.

They were not dressed in black like Fleet. Their clothing was rather shabby looking and dotted with patches. Both men had long shaggy hair and beards. There was nothing pleasant about either man. As they stood staring silently back at Fleet, Kyla got the impression that these men were not exactly thrilled to see him. Finally, the taller of the two spoke. "Well, if it isn't the lord of the manor come home again," he said sarcastically. "And you brought some of that Family trash that you like to hang out with."

"Okay, Lipsky," Fleet said impatiently, "I stopped at the checkpoint. Now let me pass and I'll be on my way."

Lipsky, Kyla wondered if that was his real name or one he'd earned. If Fleet had to go through all this just to get into the Settlement, she wondered if it was worth it. Hopefully, the men would step aside as Fleet had asked.

The one called Lipsky pointed at Kyla and said, "You can go on if you want, but this one isn't welcome here."

Fleet slapped his horse with the reins and it jumped forward almost knocking both men to the ground. "It's not your place to decide who goes in and who doesn't." Then leaning low in the saddle he brought his face close to the other man and said, "If you have a problem with that you know where to find me. Come after you've been relieved here and we'll talk." Then turning to Kyla he said, "Come on."

She rode quickly after Fleet, not daring to look back. Lesson number two, she wasn't sure what lesson number two was. This was nothing like the warm reception from the Family. It appeared Fleet was well know but for what? 'The lord of the manor' is what Lipsky had called him. Fleet kept his lantern lit and it cast a pale glow around them as they rode forward. After a short distance the road began to rise sharply and the horses breathed harder beneath them as they labored up the steep incline. When they reached the top Fleet jumped down off of his horse and motioned for Kyla to do the same. "Let me lead your horse, too," he said as he reached out for the reins. "They're more likely to leave it alone if they think it belongs to me." Then he gave her the only advice he could, "Just be careful and you'll be alright. The less you say to anyone the better off you'll be. Don't mention the Family, the evacuations, and whatever you do don't bring up Manjohnah or old man Spring. Is that clear?" Kyla nodded solemnly. She had seen enough already to know to keep her mouth shut.

Kyla looked around the clearing at the top of the hill. It looked like it had been a picnic area and tonight there were fires burning in all the fire pits. Around each fire was a group of people huddled close for warmth and everywhere was the hum of conversation. No one paid them any attention as they passed by. They might as well have been invisible. Fleet was heading to the lone structure, a long wooden shelter house. The sound of the raucous laughter and shouting could be heard coming from within. When they came to the last fire in front of the shelter house, Fleet apparently saw someone he knew. "Hey, Rollo, come here," he shouted.

A short man with long black hair looked up and smiled at the sight of Fleet. He came over and slapping him warmly on the back said, "Fleet, old buddy, how's it going?"

"Pretty good, Rollo, but I need you to do something for me," Fleet said.

"Anything you want, old buddy, just name it," Rollo answered. He had his arm around Fleet's shoulder now and was hanging there using Fleet for support. It was obvious that Fleet's buddy was quite intoxicated.

As he extricated himself from the man's grasp Fleet handed him the reins to the horses. "Watch these for me," he said. When Fleet gave the reins to Rollo the man looked up with surprise. It was like he had just noticed the two large animals standing behind Fleet. Kyla would have laughed if he hadn't been so pitiful.

"Horses," Rollo said in disbelief. "Where on earth did you get horses?"

"Don't worry about that now, I'll tell you all about it tomorrow," Fleet said. He knew Rollo would probably not even remember seeing him tomorrow. "I have to go inside for awhile, just watch the horses and I'll make it worth your while." Rollo was still staring and Fleet actually had to wave his hand in front of his face to get his attention. "Hey, Rollo, did you hear what I said?"

"Yeah, I heard what you said. Sure, I'll watch your horses, but it better be worth it," Rollo said as he walked away leading the horses with him.

Kyla leaned close to Fleet and whispered, "That man is drunk. How can you trust him?"

Fleet laughed and said, "They're all drunk, but Rollo never passes out. If anyone tries to take the horses, I'll know about it." With that said Fleet pushed the door to the shelter house open and they stepped into bedlam.

The room was filled with people standing shoulder to shoulder. Despite the cold outside, the room was uncomfortably warm and the air thick with smoke from a fireplace at the far end of the room. Kyla tried to stay close to Fleet but he was soon swallowed up in the crowd. Truly on her own now, she made her way to the corner and stood with her back against the wall watching the people. Fleet was standing with a group of people near the fire and seemed quite at home, laughing and talking. Someone gave him a bottle and he drank from it deeply before passing it on. Kyla noticed that there were several bottles being passed around the crowd. When one was finally passed to her she took it and smelled what was inside. It had an odor that was reminiscent of lighter fluid. After taking a cautious sip, she was sure that was at least one of the ingredients in the vile brew and quickly passed it on.

After awhile, Kyla began to relax. It wasn't as bad as she had expected. No one had bothered her. As a matter of fact, no one had even seemed to notice her at all, which suited Kyla just fine. She worked her way along the wall until she came to a stone ledge near the fire. It was quite warm and Kyla slipped off her coat and rolling it into a ball, sat on it. It made a good cushion, but the heat and a soft seat were not the only reasons Kyla had taken off the coat. No one else in the room was wearing anything like it and after the reaction of the man at the bridge, there was no reason to take unnecessary chances. Once her coat was off, she blended in with the rest of the crowd. Everyone was wearing a variety of coats, sweaters, flannels, and assorted thermal wear, some were less shabby than others. There were even a few men dressed like Fleet scattered around the room and Kyla wondered at the meaning of the uniform.

So Kyla began to take stock, watching the people wearing black tunics with special interest. Excluding Fleet, she had seen four of them in the room. The one standing closest to her was poised casually with his back against the stone wall of the fireplace talking to a woman. Tall, with a muscular build, he had a pleasant face and no beard. As she took a closer look, she began to wonder if he was old enough to have a beard. He couldn't be much older than eighteen. From the conversation, she gathered that he was called Moon. The woman did not impress Kyla at all. She was pretty enough, very pretty. With her shirt unbuttoned nearly all the way, she was showing as much skin as possible without undressing completely. Her hands were on his shoulders, as she pressed her body next to his she wriggled and giggled telling him everything she could do for him if only he came outside. It was obvious that Moon was enjoying the attention, but he wasn't exactly jumping at the invitation either. After awhile the girl tired of wasting her efforts on the unresponsive Moon and moved on to another man, with the show over Kyla turned her attention elsewhere.

A black man sitting at a nearby table was also dressed in a black tunic. He was a bull of man with a thick neck and broad shoulders. Kyla watched as he examined a very long knife, holding it up in front of his face and turning the blade in his hands, his eyes flashing with approval at the glint of light on the polished metal of the knife. His round face lit up in a huge smile as he said something to the man next to him and plunged the blade into the wooden table, much to the delight of his companions who laughed and pounded the table in approval. The whole procedure was repeated with each person who picked up one of the knives. Some comment or joke followed with a round of laughter. Everyone in the group seemed to be thoroughly involved in the activity and having a great time. She watched until the man in the black tunic returned her gaze. He had caught her staring at them. Kyla lowered her eyes and turned her head. She would have to be a little less obvious in the future.

When she looked up her eyes came to rest on Fleet. Something about that made Kyla shift uncomfortably. She had been purposely ignoring him. He certainly had forgotten about her the second his foot was inside the door. Still, he was sitting with two other people in black tunics and since she had already decided to look them all over, the fact that Fleet was sitting with them shouldn't matter. It made her angry that he had her thinking like some silly girl whose prom date had left her at the door. He was nothing to her and she was nothing to him. Any other ideas were foolish. Still, she didn't want him to catch her watching him. Shifting her position slightly, she leaned back against the wall a little more. That put a group of people standing just to her left between her and Fleet and his friends. Then without turning her head to look at them directly, Kyla watched out of the corner of her eye.

There were four people besides Fleet who were sitting at the table. They were behaving like everyone else, joking, laughing, and drinking, just having a good time. From her position against the wall, Kyla could not see all of them at the same time. If she leaned forward a little, she could see Fleet and the man sitting to his right. He seemed a little older than most of the people in the group, but certainly not as old as the white haired Brother Eldar. Suddenly, it struck Kyla that it was odd how she hadn't seen any children and so far only three people that were older than fifty and that included Cole Spring. Right now the older man was talking and the other four were listening. Kyla leaned back and looked at the others at the table. Seated on the opposite end of the table facing Fleet was another of the men wearing a black tunic. He had long chestnut brown hair that hung to his shoulders and the beginnings of a beard and looked even younger than the fellow named Moon did. He seemed quite at ease and very confident of himself as he leaned back and balanced his chair precariously on two legs with his feet resting on the end of the bench.

Seated on the bench next to him was a man dressed in a camouflage jacket. All Kyla could see was his back. She couldn't tell anything about him other than the fact that he was about average in height with short black hair. Between the man in camouflage and Fleet was the second person at the table wearing a black tunic and the only woman Kyla saw in the room who was wearing the uniform. Like the man next to her, Kyla hadn't seen her face but the woman certainly had aroused her curiosity.

Kyla stood and wondered what to do with her coat. She wanted her hands free, so she tied the belt around her waist and let it hang like a bulky skirt made of fur. As she started to inch her way through the crowd she passed close to the table where the black man in the tunic was sitting with his friends. He scrutinized her closely as she approached. When his eyes shifted to look at her boots, Kyla suddenly realized why he was watching her. She had put Sister Eaglet's knife in her boot and the top of it stuck out just a little. Her first thought was that she should have hidden it better, but she had seen plenty of knives in plain view all around the room and a few people had rifles. If she was carrying a weapon openly, so much the better, she would have to convince everyone from the start that she was up to whatever they could dish out. It took all the courage she could muster, but Kyla returned the man's gaze without blinking. He had seemed to be a pleasant sort of fellow when she was watching him joking with his friends. Even though his expression was neutral, he continued to watch Kyla until she disappeared into the crowd behind him. Kyla didn't know what he might be thinking about her, but all she really cared about was the fact that he had stayed where he was. Pleasant or not he could squash her like a bug if he wanted.

What anyone in the room might think of her was not what concerned Kyla right now. What she really wanted was to get a look at the woman in the black tunic, but she was having a little trouble getting to the other side of the room. Tables and benches crowded close together filled the center of the room and the spaces between the tables were filled with people like her trying to get from one place to another. The end result was a crush of bodies trying to squeeze past each other in an impossibly small space. As she pushed her way past a tight knot of people huddled between one of the tables she saw what looked like a small white marble fall to the floor. A man wearing a thick sweater and fur cap bent down and picked it up with a furtive look around to see who might be watching. It made her think of what Sister Eaglet had said about pearls, but even the subject of pearls was not going to sidetrack Kyla now. She was finally across the room and trying to work herself into a position to get a good look without being right on top of Fleet's table. The only open spot she could find was against the wall. When she stood on the tips of her toes, she could just barely see above the heads of the people sitting on top of the table in front of her. Even on this side of the room Kyla could only catch small glimpses of the woman. There were just too many people in the way.

Fleet had been watching Kyla since the beginning. He had lost track of her in the crowd when they first came in, but when he saw her standing in the far corner he left her alone. That seemed to be what she wanted. Still he kept an eye on where she was. He had seen her sitting on the stone ledge next to Moon and the girl called Cissy. Now she had moved to the other side of the room and was behind a group of people sitting on top of one of the tables. As long as she didn't decide to go outside without him he wasn't worried about Kyla.

There had been no word of the others who had been with him at the raid on the farm, but that was what he had hoped. If they did as planned, they would begin arrive sometime tomorrow. Fleet leaned close to the woman next to him. There was a commotion at the other end of the room and the voices were so loud that he had to shout to be heard above the din. "What's Sadie been like?"

He didn't have to elaborate. She knew exactly what he meant. "Let's just say it's been a little stormy while you were gone," she shouted back. Fleet nodded, it was what he expected. He looked at the woman seated next to him. She stood only a little over five feet tall and was a bundle of nervous energy. Her dark brown hair was cut short and tight, little curls covered her head. He liked Riley and since she was one of the women living in the cabin with Sadie, she was a good source of information when he wanted to know how the wind was blowing.

Finally the voices behind them became so loud Fleet had to turn to see what the noise was about. At first all he could see was a circle of men at the back of the room, but when they lifted Cissy up onto the table it wasn't long before it became apparent to everyone that she was at the center of the commotion. She was smiling as she turned in a slow circle holding out her hand to each man within reach. Fleet wondered how many pearls she would earn for tonight's performance. Watching Cissy strip for pearls was a regular attraction and one he always enjoyed. Once her hands were full she stuffed her payment in the small leather bag that was hanging around her neck. It was the only thing she wouldn't take off. Some of the men had started clapping and stomping their feet. It wasn't music but Cissy began her swaying dance to the rhythm that they played for her. She shed her shirt quickly and when a man with a bushy beard held out a pearl she took it and deposited it with the others. Then taking his head in her hands pressed his face between her breasts before standing up again. That brought a flurry of hands pushing toward her, all wanting to pay for their turn. Fleet shook his head. He didn't mind watching, but he wasn't about to pay for the privilege. Fleet turned for a moment to pick up the bottle of moonshine. As he took a drink he could see that everyone at the table was absorbed in the spectacle before them, everyone except Riley. She was looking behind him.

Kyla saw them lift the girl up onto the table. Every eye in the room was on her as she finally began to shimmy and shake out of the jeans she was wearing. Everyone except Kyla and the woman sitting next to Fleet. The crowd had shifted, so she could finally get a good look. The dark haired woman seemed to be looking at something on the other side of the room. Kyla stepped up on the bench in front of her to see what had caught the other woman's attention. When Kyla saw Lipksy, the ill-tempered fellow from the bridge, entering with two other men through the door at the far end of the shelter house, she was immediately on her guard. Lipsky looked around the crowded room for a minute before he zeroed in on his target. With a nod in Fleet's direction from him, the three men began slicing their way through the crowd. Without thinking Kyla started toward Fleet taking the most direct route available, stepping from the top of one table to the next. The only reaction from the people seated there was to shout, "Get out of the way!" Kyla didn't pay any attention to them. She was watching Lipsky. When Fleet reached out to take a drink from the bottle sitting at his table she saw Lipsky reach into his coat and take a gun out of his shoulder holster. Kyla shouted to Fleet but her voice was lost in the noise from the clapping and stomping. At the same time Kyla shouted her warning, she saw the woman next to Fleet begin to stand. She had seen Lipsky reaching for the gun, too.

When Fleet saw Riley's eyes look first at him and then just over his shoulder, he knew someone was right behind him. Even without the look from her, he had felt the arrival of the men behind him as they pushed through the crowd. At the same time Riley began to stand, Fleet spun around to stand and face them just in time to see Kyla, with a hunting knife in her hand, jump off the table next to the men. She landed on Lipsky's shoulder and he shook her off easily but not before she sliced the back of his hand with her knife. He didn't drop the gun, but she had diverted his attention for the split second that it took for Fleet to turn and face his attacker. The others at the table were on their feet in the next second. When the black man in the tunic and young Moon joined Fleet, the battle lines were drawn. The room began to grow quiet as the crowd realized there was a confrontation brewing. A good fight was entertaining, too. One of the men behind Lipsky grabbed Kyla and pulled her up off the floor.

Fleet looked at the gun in Lipsky's hand. The cut on the back of his hand wasn't very deep but blood was streaming from it and dripping on the floor. He looked at Kyla next. She was standing with her knife still in hand and her jaw set defiantly. Lipsky's buddy was holding her wrist just above the knife but hadn't taken it away from her. Who would have believed she had it in her? Fleet needed to get control of the situation. "Let her go," he ordered sharply. The man holding Kyla released her and Fleet reached out and pulled her over to stand next to him. Kyla continued staring fiercely at Lipsky with her knife still clutched in her hand so tightly that her knuckles had turned white. Then to Lipsky, Fleet said calmly, "Put your gun away." He knew that the man wasn't going to use it if he hadn't already. Lipsky looked at his buddies and seeing that he wasn't getting any support from them, reluctantly put his gun back in the holster. Once the gun was out of sight the crowd lost interest and the murmur of voices returned, but there had been no fight and Cissy was gone so the entertainment was over and the mood in the room seemed subdued.

Lipsky was not subdued. He was simmering at a slow boil. "It's not over with me and you, Fleet."

Fleet was rapidly loosing his patience with the man, "What the hell are you talking about? I'm getting tired of this crap from you."

"Well, I'm tired of all of your people and your black shirt bull shit. What makes you so special, you and that woman Sadie? Everyone here knows she's got all kinds of fuel, food, and who knows what else hoarded in her cellars," he said sourly.

"I don't want to fight with you Lipsky," Fleet said coolly. "And if you ever think to shoot me in the back again just remember, I have a lot of friends. You'll be number one on my list of people for them to kill if I should have an accident." As he looked at the scrawny little man, Fleet shook his head. Lipsky was a bitter man. He wished Sadie had left him to freeze in the snow, but she had brought him back and fed him and given him a place to stay. It wasn't until she caught him stealing that she had asked him to leave the dormitory at the farm. Then she had asked him to be the crossing guard at the bridge despite Fleet's objections that he was untrustworthy and just plain mean. Sadie thought it would make him feel like an important part of the community. What community, Fleet had wondered, would want this nasty little man who wasn't the least bit appreciative of what Sadie had done for him.

The two men who had followed Lipsky into the room melted into the crowd leaving their friend standing alone. He bristled one last time and pointed to Kyla using the hand she had slashed, the dripping blood adding symbolically to his words, "I won't forget about you either, Sister." With that last threat delivered he whirled around and pushed his way through the crowd.

Kyla stayed rooted to the spot where she stood. All of her attention was focused on Lipsky's back as he made a hasty retreat. It wasn't until Fleet clapped her on the back and said, "You can put that thing away now Sister," that she suddenly remembered herself. She looked down at the knife and seeing the blood on the blade wiped it off quickly on her pants leg and slipped it back into her boot. Her mind was racing. She still couldn't believe what she had done. Everything had happened too quickly. Kyla didn't even remember taking the knife out of her boot. When she stood up, the group of people surrounding her and Fleet began to press in closer. The older man was pushing Fleet toward the door near the fireplace. At the same time the woman with the black tunic had taken hold of Kyla by the elbow and was whispering in her ear, "It's not safe to stay any longer tonight. Come with me." Kyla started to go the direction that Fleet was going, but the girl kept urging her toward the other door. Thinking they were to meet outside, Kyla followed her.

It took awhile to get through the crowd, and by the time they stepped outside Fleet and the others were nowhere to be seen. Kyla pulled on her coat and mittens and looked to the woman standing with her. Kyla wished she had just held onto Fleet. She was still buzzing from a rush of adrenaline and wanted to talk to him about what had happened. As she looked around Kyla noticed that most of the fires had died down and there was not a soul to be seen. One soul in particular was not to be seen. Rollo was nowhere around and the horses were gone, too. Things were not looking good for Kyla right now.

"Come on," the woman said as she pulled the hood of her long black cloak closer around her face. She turned and began to walk quickly across the open ground to a narrow foot trail that took them back down the hill. The woman leading the way knew every twist and rut in the trail and never faltered once even though it was dark. Kyla however stumbled after her every step of the way hoping that it was not a mistake to trust this woman. All she knew about her was that she had been sitting with Fleet. "Where are we going?" Kyla asked.

"I'm taking you to Sadie's. It's about a half a mile from here," she answered without turning. "There's a place where you can stay tonight." So on they went, down the hill and then following the trail across the dam at the end of the lake.

Kyla hadn't noticed the lake when she arrived with Fleet and if she hadn't become too turned around in the dark, the bridge was at the far side. Once they reached the other side of the lake, the trail turned. From that point, it followed a fence row and before long they reached their destination. Kyla couldn't make out much. In the dark it looked like any other farm. There were several large buildings clustered together. Not nearly as many as there were at Spring's farm and there was no fence either.

The woman took her to one of the smaller buildings and knocked on the door. While they waited for a response she explained to Kyla,

"This is the women's dormitory. You can stay here as long as you need."

A woman carrying a flashlight answered the door. She had obviously been awakened, but didn't seem surprised to have someone knocking at this late hour. Before going inside Kyla turned to her guide and asked, "What's your name?"

"Everyone calls me Riley," she said. "I'll see you in the morning. Good night, Sister." Then she turned and hurried off toward one of the other buildings before Kyla had a chance to say another word.

The woman with the flashlight held the door open, waiting for Kyla to enter. "Hurry up, you're letting in the cold," she said impatiently. Once Kyla was inside she closed the door and led her down the middle of a row of cots filled with sleeping women. When they came to an empty one near the end, she stopped and motioned to Kyla, indicating that this one was for her. Then going to a shelf at the foot of the cot, she pulled down a blanket and handed it to Kyla. With that done she took the flashlight and shuffled back to the other end of the room, put out the light and lay down on the cot next to the door.

Kyla didn't lie down immediately. She stood without moving for a few moments, trying to get a feel for the place in the dark. She didn't know how many women were there, more than a dozen, but probably less than twenty. As she listened to the breathing, snoring, and rustling, she suddenly felt overwhelmed by the sounds of humanity in the darkness. Kyla had been riding an emotional whirlwind and this was where she had landed tonight. In the last three days her world had been turned upside down and inside out. Everything she thought she knew was gone and everything she had seen and done had gone beyond her wildest imagination. She had actually stabbed a man. Kyla just couldn't get the picture out of her mind. Lipsky had threatened her and she believed he was not the type of man to forget. She had barely arrived at the Settlement and already had made an enemy, not a very good record for her first night here.

Her other choice was to go back to the Family. She smiled to herself in the darkness and finally sat down on the cot. Everyone here thought she was one of the Sisters. It was the only amusing thing that had happened that day. The more Kyla thought about it the more she liked the idea. Let them continue thinking she was a Sister, especially since they seemed to be afraid of the Family. It couldn't hurt to let them think she had dangerous friends. In a way it gave her a sense of belonging somewhere. Right now she truly felt like she was drifting and needed something to hold on to. The Family could serve as her emotional anchor for now.

Kyla thought back to the previous evening as she took off her boots. She didn't leave them on the floor next to the cot. Something told her they might not be there in the morning if she did. Instead she put them at the end of the bed where she could feel them with her feet, but not before taking the knife out. She left her coat on, too. It was not overly warm in the building and she still felt the cold. As she lay down and pulled the blanket over her, Kyla slipped the knife under her pillow and with the handle of the blade in her grasp, her thoughts turned to Sister Eaglet. She wondered if Sister Eaglet would have been surprised by the use Kyla had made of her gift tonight. Kyla thought about the Family sitting around the fire in the meeting room eating, talking, and laughing and wondered if the Sisters had tea at the fire in their shelter every night or if that had just been for her benefit. The Sisters had probably been asleep for hours. Last night she hadn't wanted to stay; now she found herself thinking fondly of her short visit with them and thinking of returning. Well, she had wanted her freedom and she now that she had it, Kyla still wasn't sure what she was going to do.

Chapter Four

Day three and Kyla was awakened by a loud banging that must have been the signal to rise because the woman sleeping next to the door got up and turned on a light switch. One single bulb in the center of the room came on. It was a dim light, but Kyla was impressed. They had electricity, too. As soon as the light came on, everyone in the room climbed out of their cots and dressed in silence. Kyla sat up and slipped her knife back into her boot then pulled up the cuff to cover it completely. Today she didn't want it to show. Watching the other women as they folded their blankets and put them on the shelves, Kyla followed their example and did the same with hers. There was a definite routine that they were following and Kyla fell in line and followed them out the door and to the building next door. The door was open and when she looked inside Kyla could see that it was the lavatory with two toilets in the corner and a large washbasin with a spigot. Kyla stood in line with the rest waiting for her turn to wash and use the toilet. Counting the number of women in front of her, Kyla understood now why everyone had been in such a hurry to get up and out the door.

There were thirteen people in front of her and two behind. Counting herself that made sixteen. She took note of each one, wanting to remember them all. First in line was a tall woman with white, blond hair that hung in long wispy locks around her face. She had been near the door and first in line. Next came a short, stocky girl with black hair in braids. Just behind them was the woman who had met her at the door last night. She still looked half-asleep and was leaning against the wall. Her short brown hair was sticking up wildly and she took out a comb and began to straighten the unruly mess while she waited. After her was the youngest girl she had seen yet, thirteen maybe, but definitely not a small child. She was a beautiful girl with coffee brown skin and long black hair plaited into dozens of braids. A woman with frizzy hair that was copper penny red followed the young girl and after her a tall woman with a solid, block-like build with blond hair hanging in one thick braid down the middle of her back. That made up the first six into the building. The rest waited in a line outside.

Number seven was standing in the doorway holding the door open with one foot on the inside ready to jump when her turn came. She had short dark hair and flashed a smile at Kyla when she caught her looking at her then gestured comically with her thumb, indicating that she wanted those who were already inside, out. Kyla smiled. Hers was the first friendly face she had seen that morning. When the short black haired woman emerged. The woman standing at the door smiled at Kyla again before disappearing inside.

Kyla looked at the next woman standing at the doorway and was surprised to see someone who she recognized from the night before. It was the woman named Cissy who had danced on the table, but looking at her today no one would have guessed that she was the same woman. She looked like everyone else waiting in line, tired, cold, and hungry. Number nine and ten were standing as far away from Cissy as possible and still maintain their place in line. It was easy to see the dislike between the women. Number ten was brushing number nine's bushy brown hair and then brought the whole mess under control by braiding it. Then they traded places and number ten was in front while nine brushed and braided her hair. When the tall blond woman came out and Cissy went in, number nine pushed past number ten to take her place at the doorway. It was plain to see how deeply their friendship went.

Luckily for number nine and ten two people came out at the same time and they could go in together, allowing their friendship to remain intact for awhile longer. The line was moving much quicker now because right after nine and ten went in the red head and the tall blond woman came out. They were the last of the first six women inside and with their departure the next two women slipped inside and that put Kyla in the doorway. She watched the women walking away from the wash shed to see where they went next. It was a ragged line, but they were all heading for another building across the yard. The soft light glowing through the windows was the only thing that made it visible through the trees.

Then it was her turn when the smiling girl with the impish grin jumped out and gave her a shove through the door. "Next!" she said. Then laughing at her prank, she danced off in the direction of the lights with a wave.

Once inside Kyla looked at the others in the room. Three women were standing at a table, each one with a basin full of water and washing themselves. There was an empty basin that no one was using on the table. Kyla picked it up and filled it with water from the only spigot in the room, the one in the washtub. She wasn't terribly surprised to find there was no hot water. Taking the tub of water back to the table, Kyla found an unoccupied space and started washing. She didn't have a washrag or towel but she did have a piece of soap. Searching deep in her pockets, she found it still intact. Kyla broke off a small piece and put the rest back in her pocket. She took off her hat and coat, then loosened her clothing and began to wash as thoroughly as possible under the circumstances. Since she was without a towel, she used the over-sized shirt to dry her face. When she brought it close to her nose, Kyla realized that no matter how thoroughly she washed, until she had a change of clothes she was going to stink like a wet horse in the rain. Once she had finished washing, she put her hat and coat back on then emptied the basin in the sink and returned it to the table. After that, she still had to wait in line to use the toilet.

When Kyla left the wash building there was no one else waiting to go inside. Walking toward the building beyond the trees, she followed the path the others had taken. Once she came through the trees, Kyla saw the line of men coming from the opposite direction. It made sense that if there was a woman's dormitory there would be one for men, too. As she approached the building with the lights shining through the windows, the smell of breakfast cooking was all the explanation she needed about her destination. Separate dormitories and a common eating place, so far all seemed very neat and proper, nothing like the gathering on the hill last night.

As she entered the door to the dining hall the first thing she noticed was the fact that there were many more men in the room than there were women. The second thing she noticed was there wasn't a single person wearing a black tunic in the dining hall. Everything was very orderly and Kyla followed the people entering just before her as they got into the serving line. The line move quickly and it wasn't long before Kyla had her breakfast. It was only a bowl of sticky oatmeal, a rather disappointing gray mush that didn't offer much other than to fill an empty stomach. She was given a cup of hot black coffee and that was all. Next Kyla had to find a place to sit and was relieved to see the friendly dark haired girl wave at her and motion to the seat next to her.

Before Kyla could sit down and take a bite the woman began talking. "I saw you come in late last night. My name's Carleen," she said and held her hand out to Kyla.

Kyla shook her hand and said, "I'm Kyla." She took the empty seat next to Carleen and cautiously took a bite of the oatmeal. It had no taste at all. Still, a couple of days ago she would have jumped at the chance to eat it. She took a sip of the coffee to wash it down. Nice and hot, at least the coffee was good.

Carleen laughed and said, "The food here isn't the best but you get used to it."

The two women seated across from Kyla and Carleen were the ones Kyla had seen braiding each other's hair outside the wash building. The one with brown hair who Kyla had counted as number nine commented sourly, "From what I hear about the Family, it's probably better than the dog meat you're used to eating." Kyla ignored them both and returned to eating the oatmeal.

Carleen had plenty to say. "That was about the dumbest thing I ever heard, Rachel. You know less about what the Family does or doesn't eat than Zoë does." She pointed to number ten. The one called Zoë smiled slyly and looked at her friend. Apparently she appreciated Carleen implying that she was the smarter of the two, even if it was a left-handed compliment. "Not to mention ill mannered and rude," Carleen added sharply.

Kyla finally had to cut in. She didn't need Carleen making anymore enemies for her than she already had. "Rachel and Zoë, please don't worry. I didn't take offense to anything you said and you are right about one thing. The Family certainly doesn't serve anything like this." That was true, but she didn't add that what they did eat was certainly not dog and a thousand times better than tasteless oatmeal. The other two seemed vindicated in some way and were happy enough to ignore Kyla from that point on.

Carleen looked at her and said, "So it is true. You came here from the Family."

The subject matter was getting stickier than the oatmeal. Kyla was relieved when a man in a black tunic entered the room and began calling for silence. Everyone seated at the tables turned to look at him. He was not one of the men Kyla had seen the night before. "If there is anyone new who needs a work assignment come with me now," he announced loudly and went outside. Two men near the door stood and followed him. Kyla hesitated for a moment but when Carleen smiled and motioned toward the door with a tilt of her head, she got up, too. The looks she got from Rachel and Zoë let Kyla know that they thought she was ignorant for waiting so long.

She hurried out the door and had to run to catch up with the man in black who took note of her late arrival by frowning at her. It was light now and Kyla was able to see the layout of the place. The women's dormitory and wash building were in a clearing just beyond the trees behind her and what had to be the men's dormitory was situated at the far edge of the farmyard to the left. On the right were several long buildings, which had to be the greenhouses Fleet mentioned; only they didn't have any windows. The man was leading them toward a large log cabin at the center of all the buildings. When they reached the walkway leading to the front entry of the cabin they stopped. The two men standing with her appeared to be just as scrawny and malnourished as Kyla. The man in the black tunic was looking them all over with a critical eye, as if wondering what he was going to do with such a pitiful lot.

It was not long before a group of people, who were all dressed in black tunics, emerged from the front door of the cabin. Kyla saw a few familiar faces as they appeared. Moon was one of the first ones out the door along with the broad shouldered black man. When Kyla saw Fleet walking out the door with a tall dark haired woman, her heart leapt at the sight of him. He appeared to be arguing with the woman. When he caught sight of Kyla standing at the end of the walk, he stopped in mid-sentence then pointed at her and called out in an agitated voice, "It's you!" He began walking toward her, taking long strides that covered the short distance quickly.

Fleet nodded to the man in charge of the new arrivals and grabbed Kyla by the arm, dragging her unceremoniously to the side. "Where did you disappear to last night?" he demanded.

The tall woman with whom Fleet had been arguing joined them and asked, "Who is this, Fleet?"

"This is the woman I told you about," Fleet answered still holding Kyla's arm firmly in his grasp.

Kyla wonder what he had told her because the woman frowned and eyed her critically. There was something about her that made Kyla feel uneasy. For one thing she was dressed in a rather unusual manner. The color was still black, but she was not wearing a tunic. She wore a long black skirt that swept the ground when she walked. A long, black cord was twisted tightly and wrapped around her waist several times to make her belt. Despite the cold her mid-riff was bared and she wore a tight fitting bodice with a scooped neckline and long sleeves. Even if her clothing had been the same, her regal bearing would have been enough to distinguish her from the rest and she was beautiful. Probably the most beautiful and exotic woman Kyla had ever seen. She had raven black hair that fell in thick waves over her shoulders. Her skin was a smooth bronze color and her slightly tilted eyes gave her a somewhat oriental appearance but there was something about her that made Kyla think of her as the queen of some ancient Mesopotamian empire.

She smiled. "So we owe you thanks for saving Fleet's life, Sister." There was a certain amount of condescension in her voice that made her gratitude sound a little less than sincere.

"I didn't do anything," Kyla protested weakly. "Fleet didn't need me."

"Probably not," she agreed, "but still we appreciate the act." Well, at least that statement had truthful ring to it, Kyla thought. "Fleet has asked me to make a place for you in the cabin," she added.

Kyla had no doubt that the offer was an honor that she should not refuse. "I am very grateful for you kind offer," Kyla answered stiffly wondering if it was something that she should be happy about or not.

The tall woman turned to the black man and said, "Armand, will you please show our new friend to her room?"

The tall dark haired women acted surprised when Fleet took Kyla by the hand and began pulling her away saying, "Let me show her." Without waiting for a response, he whisked Kyla away from the group almost dragging her up the steps and into the house. Once they were alone he turned and looked at her. "You certainly are full of surprises aren't you," he said with a large grin. "I guess you can say that you saved my life last night."

"I barely scratched him," Kyla protested. In her opinion her attempt to stop Lipsky had been feeble at best.

"Well, it was a good diversionary tactic," he complimented her. "But let me give you some advice, if you ever try something like that again, as small as you are, you need to use all your bodyweight to drive the blade in far enough to do any real damage." Fleet discussed the topic as casually as someone commenting on the best way to throw a ball would. He then turned and began walking down the hall and Kyla hurried after him.

"Who was the woman in the dress?" Kyla guessed that she was the one everyone called Sadie, but she wanted Fleet to confirm the fact.

"That's Sadie. This is her house," he gestured with his hands. "The story is that her great-great-grandfather built it. He was some kind of nut who was preparing for the end of the world. Under this cabin are cellars big enough to store food for an army. Well, nothing happened in his lifetime and his children used this place as a vacation campground for kids for years and after that it sat empty until Sadie moved here. Lucky for us that the old man was ahead of his time." They had come to the end of a long hallway and Fleet opened the last door and let Kyla go in before him. It was a small room and the only furniture was a small bed against one wall and a tiny night table with three drawers. After he entered Fleet closed the door and sat casually on the bed while Kyla stood stiffly by the door.

"They all think I'm a member of the Family," Kyla said trying to sound as casual as Fleet was acting. Why should the sight of Fleet sitting on the bed be so unnerving?

"So let them," he said. "It won't hurt to let people think you have the Family behind you. I wouldn't tell anyone that you aren't."

"Not even Sadie?" Kyla asked only because Sadie seemed to be the person in charge and now she would be living in her house. Kyla felt it would be best to start off with no secrets.

Fleet thought for a moment before answering, "No, not even Sadie." He didn't know why he had told her that. He trusted Sadie with his life, but something told him this misunderstanding was best left alone. The only ones who knew how Kyla had persuaded Fleet to bring her along where Kyla and himself, Fleet wanted to keep it that way. He went on to the next subject. "I've asked Sadie to let you join us."

Kyla was puzzled. She was here wasn't she? "What do you mean?"

He gestured to his uniform and said, "We call ourselves 'The Guard'. Altogether, there are twelve of us," Fleet answered. He should have said, 'there were twelve'. With Marta's death, there were only eleven now and they needed to replace her.

"Why would you want me?" Kyla was stunned. She knew nothing about what it meant to be a member of the Guard other than it seemed to come with a certain amount of privilege.

Fleet absently fingered the arrow pin at his shoulder as he thought how he wanted to answer. "There are a couple of reasons. Last night you showed everyone that you have the courage to jump into the middle of dangerous situation when you're needed. Watching each other's back is a big part of the job." Fleet paused slightly before adding, "Besides, I'm beginning to think you are one of the luckiest people that I have ever met. I'm hoping that if I keep you around some of it will rub off on me." He laughed after he said it. He didn't believe in fortune telling like Sister Samethia, but he did believe in luck.

Kyla stood staring at him in disbelief. She wasn't brave. How much courage had it taken to hide in a root cellar for a year? If it was an honor to be chosen, she wasn't sure that it was one she wanted. "I don't think I can do it, Fleet," she said doubtfully. Kyla wished that she could be as confident in her abilities as Fleet seemed to be.

Suddenly, Fleet's expression changed and his smile was gone. He had been very pleased with the arrangements that he had made for Kyla and had expected her to be thrilled. Hesitation or refusal from her was not in his plans. "You can and you will," he answered flatly. The thought of her saying no after he had recommended her was not an option. "You can't turn Sadie down once she offers. It would be an insult," he said in no uncertain terms. Although he always made the choice of who would become a member the Guard, Sadie had the official duty of asking them to join. There was nothing for him to discuss with Kyla. The deal was done and she would find out soon enough that it was really the best option available.

With that said Fleet stood and opened the door to leave. "One more thing," he added, "I'll have someone bring you a change of clothes." She was looking at him now with her eyes still wide with surprise. "Don't worry." Fleet laughed. He knew what she was thinking. "You won't get to wear black until your initiation tomorrow night" As he stepped out the door and started walking down the hall with his usual long strides, he called back, "I'll come back after you've had a chance to change."

Kyla closed the door and sat on the cot or more accurately collapsed on the cot. Suddenly her knees were too weak to hold her. She was having a little trouble accepting this new twist on her situation. The dormitory life would have been acceptable to her for the time being at least and unearned privilege was something that made her nervous, especially in a community filled with so many who had so little. That was only half of her conflict, the other half was thrilled. The idea of staying close to Fleet was giving her a flurry of emotions that she was having a little trouble dealing with. She wanted to jump up and twirl around the room with glee, but her legs were still too wobbly.

Before long there was a knock at the door, when Kyla opened it there was a large stocky woman wearing an apron standing at the door holding a neatly folded stack of clothing. She took them and after thanking the woman closed the door. Without loosing a minute, Kyla began shedding the clothes that she had worn for the two days she and Fleet had been riding. As she started to put on her clean clothes she thought about Fleet, he had definitely had a change since last night. He had looked very nice in his freshly laundered clothes and with his face scrubbed and shaved. His scent was still in the room, soap and leather mingled. Kyla would have liked a bath, but the change of clothes was enough for now. Her mind suddenly jumped back, thinking of her last bath and clothing change. Cole Spring and his farm seemed very far away right now.

She pulled her boots back on and stood. There was no mirror in the room but she knew these clothes looked much better than the ones she had been wearing. For one thing they were the proper size. The denim jeans were a little loose because she was so thin, but the thermal underwear helped fill in the difference. Then there was a bulky sweater with a gray tweedy color. As she looked around she had to ask herself if this wasn't what she had wanted, a warm bed in a house and all the amenities that went with having a real home. So why did she feel so nervous and ill at ease? She hoped Fleet would return soon. Kyla didn't want to be alone right now. Then she heard another knock at the door. She opened it expecting to see Fleet and was just a little disappointed to see that it was the woman in the apron again.

The woman looked her over from head to toe before saying what she had come to tell her. " I have a message for you from Sadie." She paused and with a slight arch of annoyance to her eyebrows she continued, "She said to tell you that Fleet will be busy the rest of the day and you are to help me in the kitchen and the laundry today." She looked past Kyla to the clothing piled on the floor and said, "You can start with that mess behind you." With that said, she spun on her heels and walked briskly down the hall. Kyla gathered up the clothes and hurried after her. She was a little disappointed that Fleet had not returned, but staying here and helping with laundry sounded like something she could do to be useful. She wasn't so sure she could say the same about what Fleet had planned for her.

~ ~ ~

After leaving Kyla, Fleet was feeling pretty good about the way things were going. The others had helped when they told Sadie about the way Kyla had jumped Lipsky when he pulled his gun on him. It had been easier than telling her about Marta. He had done that in private just before they went to breakfast this morning and Sadie hadn't said a word. When he stepped out of the hallway and turned to go out the front door, Fleet stopped dead in his tracks.

Sadie was standing in the foyer waiting for him. "I need to speak to you now," she said and walked into the room next to the front door.

Fleet didn't jump to follow. He waited until she had disappeared into the room before casually sauntering across the open space between him and the doorway where Sadie had disappeared. She was already seated in a high-backed armchair in the opposite corner facing the door. Fleet entered and stood just inside the door meeting her cool stare with one of his own. The room was the library with shelves on three walls filled with hundreds of books on every subject imaginable. The fourth wall held a large window with an arched top. There was no curtain and it faced the front of the house. Anyone standing outside could easily see who was in the library.

"Shut the door Fleet," Sadie's voice was firm. Fleet complied silently. Being called into the library with Sadie was as close as she ever came to a public redressing of one of the Guard but never Fleet. He was fuming. "Please sit down," she said as she motioned graciously to a straight-backed chair next to her. Fleet stayed as he was, back straight, his feet set slightly apart, and his hands clasped behind his back waiting for Sadie to say what was on her mind.

Sadie smiled as she looked at Fleet. Stubborn and proud, he wouldn't bend like the others. She let him stand and simmer awhile longer before speaking. She lowered her head a little but not her eyes. Looking directly at Fleet, Sadie watched his reaction as she said, "I can't tell you how the news about Marta has upset me."

He tried to keep his face blank and impassive. He knew Sadie well enough to know when she was trying to get a rise out of him. It was just like her, too. She knew how he felt. Marta was just one more ghost that would haunt him the rest of his life. He felt bad enough, but Sadie wanted to twist the knife and watch him squirm. Fleet had been expecting that, but what really bothered him was her choice of venue. He chose not to respond.

Fleet's silence was a challenge to Sadie. If he were to continue to lead her Guard he would have to be reminded of who was in charge. "Especially since I tried to warn you against going," she added smoothly. Another twist, but still no response from Fleet. Sadie decided to change the subject. "This new girl, I'm not sure about your choice if she really is Family." Fleet's eyes flashed with anger when she brought up the subject of Kyla. Sadie had never turned down anyone that he chose. It was all Sadie could do to keep from smiling triumphantly when she saw his reaction.

"That has always been my decision to make," Fleet said stiffly, trying to control his anger. Sadie made the announcements, but the choice had always been his. He needed to make sure the people at his back were ones he could trust.

Sadie looked out the window. There was no crowd watching, but by now someone must have seen them and gossip was all these people had to do. By evening she wondered what stories they would be telling about her little conversation with Fleet. The opinion of his friends mattered more to Fleet than he would ever admit. What they would say would do more to bring his ego in check than any browbeating from her. Besides there were other ways to keep Fleet in check, Sadie knew his weaknesses as well as she did his strengths. When she looked back to Fleet, he had not moved an inch.

Maybe it was time to give him what he wanted. She wondered what he saw in that skinny little rat he had ridden in with. Lipsky had been there last night to give his report. He was a disgusting little man, but she could depend on him to keep her abreast of everybody's activities and she did mean everybody. Sadie couldn't let Fleet get too far out of hand and she knew he only told her what he wanted her to know. She smiled graciously as she said, "I have never questioned your recommendations before and I won't this time. But I do wonder about why." She stood and brushed against him as she went to the door and said in a low voice, "I'll see you tonight?" Question, command, and invitation, all rolled into one little phrase, she left Fleet standing at attention and not bothering to wait for a reply left the room. She knew he would come.

Fleet wasn't about to answer. Sadie was the most infuriating woman he had ever met. She humiliated him publicly, questioned his judgement, threatened his authority, and then had propositioned him on the way out the door. Worst of all he knew he would go. Besides everything else, Sadie was also the most desirable and exciting woman he had ever known. That thought brought a smile back to his face. There was at least some compensation for putting up with Sadie's moods. As Fleet came out of the library he caught a glimpse of Kyla disappearing into the kitchen. He had told her that he was coming back but right now he was relieved to see that she was occupied elsewhere. He wanted to think about what he was going to do when the others got back and gave their reports to Sadie. Whatever happened, he would make up with Sadie tonight. His mood lightened and he went outside just in time to see the first of the other riders come galloping up in front of the cabin. It was Kurt.

Fleet picked up his step and went to meet him. He took the horse's reins while Kurt jumped down. Brushing off the dust and horsehair clinging to his clothes, he looked at Fleet with his fresh clothing and said, "You must have made good time."

"Sadie knows about Marta. I told her," Fleet said quickly.

Kurt looked annoyed. "I was with her when she died," his voice was flat and he looked tired. "You haven't heard what happened either." Kurt was not quite as tall as Fleet, but he had the same lean build and stood as his equal in every way. He shook his head sadly before he went on. "It's a miracle that any of us got back. Have you seen Peach or Rod yet?"

"No, not yet," Fleet answered with a hopeful tone. They had all gone their separate ways that night and so far Fleet and Kurt were the only ones who had returned. "But tell me, what happened?" he asked.

"There were more men than we expected," Kurt answered. "I don't understand. I was with the scouts. I don't know where they were hiding them."

Fleet made a mental note. All of this was new to him, planning and carrying out a raid on an armed compound. He had sent his men to count the guards and watch the daily routine, but he had not left a man to continue the watch when they left for a day. Given what he had learned from Kyla, it had been a busy day. It was a costly mistake but not one he would make again. Given his current situation with Sadie, Fleet didn't want Kurt talk to her now. "Let's wait for the others to return and we'll all go to her together." Then Fleet clapped him on the shoulder and said, "Besides, you need a bath and a change of clothes. Then we'll see about breakfast." Fleet motioned to one of the men who worked the farm and gave the horse's reins to him. "Please take him to the stable with the others."

As the man led the horse away, Fleet began walking back to the house with Kurt, happy to have bought a little time. Besides, it would be better to have only one more confrontation with Sadie rather than three. There was not much to do now but wait for the others. Hopefully, it would be sooner rather than later. He wanted Sadie to have time to cool off before tonight, but not too cool. He smiled as he thought of her.

Kyla was in the laundry room scrubbing clothing in a large washtub. Although there was electricity, she was finding that washing clothing was not worth wasting the wattage when there were plenty of people around to do the work. Today it was her job. She had no need of a bath now, as she was soaked from the waist up from scrubbing, rinsing, and wringing what seemed to be a mountain of clothing. She thought she heard Fleet's voice and was hopeful that he had come to save her from the endless task that was facing her. She dropped what she had in her hands and reached the door just in time to see Fleet's back as he disappeared through the door into the foyer. Kyla heard the heavy footsteps of the woman with the apron before she saw her appear in the doorway.

Crossing her arms, she gave Kyla the evil eye, obviously annoyed by the fact that she had found her standing there doing nothing, instead of being up to her elbows in suds. She pushed past Kyla, picked up a stack of black clothing, and put a towel and washcloth on top of them. Shoving them into Kyla's hands, she said, "Kurt has returned and will be needing these." As she walked out the door, she continued her instructions, "Down the hallway, third door on the left, just before your room. You know the way."

Kyla didn't have to be told twice. Anything was better than all that laundry. The woman turned her back and started something frying on the stove. As Kyla hurried out the door, she heard the woman shout, "And get right back here. There's still laundry to do!"

When she stepped into the foyer Kyla looked around. This was the first time she had passed through the room alone. It was a grand entryway with a vaulted ceiling that rose the full two stories of the structure. Beams made from the trunks of huge trees supported the roof above. There were two hallways, one on either side leading to the rest of the house. She took the one to the right and knocked on the third door on the left and a man answered. Kyla's mouth fell open with shock when she saw who it was. It had been dark, but she knew this was the man Fleet had argued with that first night.

"It's you!" Kurt said putting her thoughts into words. He was as shocked as she was. Kyla almost dropped the clothing and towel as she pushed them into his hands. Then she spun around and walked down the hall, leaving him standing at the doorway, still wondering about what she was doing there. Kyla had double the reason to hustle back to the laundry room and loose herself in the washing. She was sent twice more to deliver fresh clothing and towels. Two more arrivals, Rod and

Peach, who turned out to be the other men who participated in the raid. Their reactions were similar to Kurt's. Kyla wanted to tell them all that her presence here was just as surprising to her as it was to them.

Other than that she worked in the laundry all morning. Kyla could smell dinner cooking and before long the woman with the apron announced that she needed her help setting the table for the noon meal. She led Kyla into the dining room where there was a broad table and two long benches. They were made from planks of wood polished smooth then waxed and buffed to give the wood a warm golden glow. Kyla was instructed to set the table for eleven with one place setting at each end where the only two chairs at the table were sitting. Then they carried in the food, roasted chicken, boiled potatoes, carrots, beans, bread, and butter. It was good food and plenty of it. She wondered what was being served in the dining hall to the others.

Kyla was in the kitchen filling the water pitchers when she heard the sound of voices as people began arriving for the meal. She pushed through the door with a pitcher in each hand and looked over the first arrivals. The large black man from last night was already seated. He looked at Kyla and smiled when she put the water pitcher down in front of him. The three men who had arrived that morning were there as well. Kurt was standing and talking to Rod who was already seated. Peach was sitting next to him with his back to the other two. She set the other pitcher down in front of him but he didn't look at her. The same dark mood that she had noticed earlier when she delivered his clothing was still with him. When Kyla looked up she saw Fleet enter the room and right behind him were Riley, Moon, and the young man with all the freckles. Fleet pulled out the chair and took his place at the end of the table. When he saw Kyla he smiled pleasantly and then went back to the conversation he had been having with the others. Kyla hustled back to the kitchen. There were two more water pitchers and who knew what else the cook would have for her to do. By the time she returned they were all seated, including the man handing out the work assignments that morning. Sadie entered last and took her seat at the end of the table opposite Fleet. Only one empty place setting remained. As she sat down the last water pitcher and began to leave, Kyla wondered who the tardy one might be.

Before she could leave Sadie called to her, "Kyla, please take your seat now." Then she turned to the stocky woman with the apron and said, "Thank you, Agatha." The cook started to the door, but not before she turned to look down her nose at Kyla and with an audible, "Humph!" and stalk out. All at the table noted her opinion. Kyla sat in the last empty spot next to Riley. She was in the middle of the five people seated on one side of the table while four sat on the other. Riley gave Kyla a smile of encouragement when she sat down.

"Where are Eddie and Dylan?" Fleet asked as he looked around the table.

Sadie took her napkin, shook it out and laid it on her lap before she answered. "I was worried. So I sent them out looking for you and the others two days ago." She said it casually, as if she had sent them to the store on an errand. Then dismissing the subject she picked up the basket filled with rolls, took one and passed it to her right, as she said, "Shall we begin?"

Kyla watched as everyone at the table began passing bowls and filling their plates. Not much was said. Nine men - all young men ranging in age from their late teens and twenties, were heaping food high on their plates and devouring it without a word of conversation. Kyla filled her plate and ate all that she wanted, but it was nothing compared to the massive quantities of bread and potatoes consumed by the men sitting at the table. She noticed that Fleet was not eating. His plate was full like everyone else's, but he was just picking at his food. Sadie noticed, too. "What's the matter Fleet? Is something wrong with your food?" she asked.

He picked up a piece of the chicken with his fork. "I'm just tired of chicken. They call it fowl for a reason." That brought a round of laughter from the others at the table. He continued to poke at the chicken. As Kyla watched him from the corner of her eye, she was convinced that the meal was not what was bothering him.

In less than fifteen minutes every scrap of food on the table was gone and Agatha returned from the kitchen and began to clear the dishes. Kyla watched as she did all the work herself and was feeling a little guilty. When she was done all eyes turned to Sadie. Once she had everyone's full attention, Sadie stood and walked to the spot behind Kyla and put her hands on her shoulders. "I think that it is time to introduce, Kyla, our newest addition to the Guard." There was some shifting and a little stirring of feet under the table, but everyone was silent. "She will be initiated at the Gathering tomorrow night." Then she left Kyla and began to go around the table, laying her hands on the shoulders of each person and saying their name so Kyla would know them all. First, there was Riley. Then she went to Kurt. Of course she knew Fleet, but Sadie put her hands on his shoulders and announced him like the rest. Next was the man with the work assignments, his name was James. The black man was next, Armand. Then there were Rod and Peach. Sadie crossed to the other side of the table and finished up with the last two. Moon on the end and the freckled Justin sitting next to her. Then as she sat in her chair again she added almost as an afterthought, "And of course, my name is Sadie." She was not finished though, "We are all saddened by the loss of our good friend Marta, but we are fortunate that Kyla is here to fill her place." The statement made everyone extremely uncomfortable. No one liked to be reminded that the only way to join the Guard was if one of them died. Their number was twelve and always would be.

Then before anything further could be said, Sadie dismissed them by saying, "I know all of you have work that needs to be done." Everyone rose and started walking toward the door and Kyla began to leave with the rest when Sadie called out, "Kurt, Peach, and Rod. Fleet and I need to talk to you. Kyla, you stay, too." The ones she named returned to the table with a few uneasy glances cast between them as they did. Everyone knew the unpleasant subject that was to be discussed.

Fleet was leaning back in his chair as far as possible with his legs stretched out in front. He gave every impression that he was at ease. Kyla and Kurt sat on opposite ends of the bench to his right and Peach and Rod sat across from them. Sadie had never moved from her seat at the other end of the table. She was studying them all as they settled back in their seats. "Why don't you each tell me what happened," she finally said. "Kurt you start."

Kurt looked first to Fleet who was still maintaining his relaxed attitude and then at Sadie. He was nothing like he had been that night at the farm. Tempers had cooled since then and today Kurt was calm, cool, and collected. He brushed his hand through his short black hair and began by saying, "We were badly outnumbered. That's all there was to it." Then as an afterthought, he added, "Fleet and I scouted the place for days. They must have brought in people at the last minute. That's the only explanation I can think of." That got Fleet's attention and he sat forward in his chair. Kurt had said the same thing that Fleet had been thinking. Only Fleet's information about reinforcements arriving that day came from Kyla and he wondered where Kurt was getting his information. Right now Fleet was suspicious of everyone.

Watching Fleet's reaction to what Kurt had said made Sadie decide to keep digging. She turned back to Kurt and said, "Tell me everything that you remember."

"There's really not that much to tell," Kurt began. "We were supposed to create a diversion on the north side of the compound while Fleet came in through the fence on the south. After we fired a few shots, they returned fire. We held our position for the time that Fleet had said it would take him to get in and out, fifteen minutes. But we couldn't get out; they had us pinned down. It was when we ran for the woods that Marta went down. I tried to go back for her but there was too much gunfire coming from inside the fences," He paused for a moment, looking down at the table. It was plain to see that it was difficult for him to give this part of the report. "She never knew what hit her." When he looked up, he continued, "Then we got on the horses and got the hell out of there. We met up with Fleet at the end of the valley and that's when I saw her." He pointed at Kyla. "She was riding double with Fleet."

That piece of information was news to Sadie. Fleet had failed to mention that he had picked the girl up at the farm. She knew he hadn't told her everything and decided that she would get to the bottom of the whole mess sooner or later. Better that it was sooner; Sadie decided it was Kyla's turn. "It seems I was correct when I asked you to stay. Kyla, please tell us where you fit into this story."

All attention turned to her now. Fleet's recommendation that she maintain the charade of being a member of the Family put her in a tricky position. She didn't want to lie, since all lies come out in the end. So she decided to start with part of the truth and begin her account with Spring's farm. "I was a prisoner at the farm. Fleet brought me out." Let

106

them fill in what they wanted, she thought. Fleet settled back in his chair, Kyla was doing all right.

"It seems Fleet did quite a lot in those fifteen minutes," Sadie said dryly. If Kyla wanted to be evasive, she was more than willing to wring the truth out of her.

"Fleet didn't help me escape. I got away from the guard thanks to these three here." Kyla looked at Kurt and finished, "It must have been a shot from you that killed my guard." Fleet nodded appreciatively. This just added to his belief that Kyla was lucky. She hadn't told him how she had escaped.

"That explains how you escaped but how did you and Fleet arrange all this in advance?" Sadie leveled her eyes at Fleet and said, "To my knowledge, it was never discussed."

"Nothing was arranged in advance, it just happened. I ran into Fleet in the dark," Kyla said. For every question that Sadie could ask, Kyla was ready with the answer, never straying from the truth, but never elaborating either.

Sadie's voice was full of suspicion when she said, "That still doesn't explain why he brought you with him. Fleet may be soft hearted but I've never known him to be stupid."

Kyla reached into her pocket and brought out the handcuffs. Dangling them from her finger now, she said, "He didn't have much choice when I handcuffed myself to him." The reaction around the table was immediate laughter. Even Sadie cracked a smile. Fleet was leaning forward in his chair holding his head in his hands. He couldn't believe that Kyla had told them about the handcuffs.

It had been a risk for Kyla to mention forcing Fleet to take her. One of two things could have happened. Either they would be angry that she had taken advantage of Fleet or they would think her actions were bold and daring. She was betting on the latter, since the Guard seemed to find those qualities admirable. Actually, neither explanation was true, since desperation had been the driving force behind her actions.

As the laughter died down Sadie looked at Kyla with a small and amused smile. Kyla had tricked Fleet and that would explain his reluctance to tell her the whole story. She would have to keep an eye on this young woman. Satisfied for the moment, Sadie turned to the next in line and said, "Rod, do you have anything that you would like to add?"

Rod stopped laughing and was suddenly serious. He was one of the older men, probably in his mid-twenties. He had dark brown hair that hung in loose strands around his face and a rather scruffy looking growth of beard that had not been shaved or trimmed that day. He tugged nervously at the collar of his tunic before answering. "Not really, Sadie. I think Kurt covered it pretty well."

Peach had been sitting at the table moping the whole time dinner was being served. Except for some half-hearted laughter when Kyla told them about the handcuffs, he had been silent the whole time. Slowly he turned to Sadie, his pale blue eyes showing the rage he had been struggling to control. Suddenly he came to life. Peach wasn't holding anything in anymore. "Don't you want to know what I think?" he said as soon as Rod had finished, never giving Sadie a chance to ask. "I think they were expecting us." He looked around the table. "I think somebody sold us out," he snarled and cast a suspicious look at the others seated at the table. Everyone except Sadie shifted uncomfortably.

Fleet hadn't said anything yet but it seemed that everyone had come to the same conclusion. The question now was who? Right now Fleet suspected everybody, except Sadie, of course, and Kyla. She couldn't have been involved but the idea that Kyla could have been planted as a spy crept into the back of his mind. He shook his head slowly. There were too many possibilities and he would sort through every last one of them. That would take some time and right now Sadie was looking at him, waiting to hear what he had to say. "There isn't any point in worrying about what happened," he said gravely. "All we can do is learn from our mistakes and make sure we never make the same ones again." He looked around the table, no one moved. Then as his eyes came to rest on Sadie, he said, "What worries me now is the fact that we have two other men unaccounted for." There was no response from her, not that he really expected any. Right now, he was angry with her for endangering the lives of two men for nothing.

The silence seemed to drag on forever. Kyla felt like she and the other three were being held hostage in a war of wills between Fleet and Sadie. It seemed that neither wanted to break the silence. Ignoring

Fleet's comment about the absent men, finally, Sadie said, "My concern is for everyone's safety. The fact that these three men all think that someone betrayed them is not a comforting thought." She looked at each person sitting at the table with a long, piercing stare before saying, "I shouldn't have to remind anyone sitting here that what was discussed here will not be repeated." She looked at Kyla again, like she needed a little more warning than the others did. "You may leave now. Fleet and I need to talk." Within moments they were up and jostling for position in the race to be first out the door. When the door slammed shut, Fleet rose and walked to the kitchen door and pushed it open a crack. Satisfied when he saw Agatha busy with the dishes, he perched on the edge of the table next to Sadie.

"What did you think?" he asked. He was not happy with Sadie's decision to send out Eddie and Dylan, but that would not change things between them. Fighting with Sadie over every decision was the usual. She was a strong willed woman and he respected her opinions.

"It could have been a coincidence, just unlucky timing," Sadie offered one option.

Fleet shook his head. "I have to go along with the others. I think they knew we were planning something."

"How can you be sure? You don't have any real information." Sadie stopped. As soon as she spoke the words, the realization came to her. "The girl, Kyla, she told you something?"

Fleet watched her eyes light up. Sadie was sharp. There wasn't much he could keep from her but that never stopped him from trying when it suited him. "She was on the inside. She saw the troops come in and one of them even told her they were expecting something."

Sadie looked very distressed. It was an emotion that she never showed in public and one that Fleet didn't see very often. He shared her concern. The people who had been involved in planning the raid had been limited to the members of the Guard and the Family. Every last one of them was someone that he thought he could trust with his life. Sadie put his thoughts into words, "There seems to be someone among us who can't be trusted. Let's just hope it was a foolish slip of the tongue and not a deliberate attempt to sabotage. We need to keep our eyes and ears open."

Fleet smiled. He was glad that they could agree on at least one subject. Then with all the delicacy he could muster, Fleet brought up the other subject that was on his mind. "When did Eddie and Dylan leave?"

"They left at nightfall, day before yesterday," Sadie answered.

So they had only been gone one full day, Fleet thought and then asked, "Were they on foot?" If so, they couldn't have gotten very far. Sadie had insisted that they stop using the trucks months ago. There was not enough fuel to waste on them and it was too dangerous to drive openly on the highway. That was why Fleet had wanted the horses, walking everywhere was impossible. Riding on horseback took long enough, but if he'd had to stay on foot he would have been a prisoner at the farm. Fleet couldn't have tolerated that.

"I let them take the light truck," she said as she looked down at her skirt and picked at some invisible piece of lint.

"You did what?" Fleet struggled not to raise his voice and stared at her in disbelief. How many times had they argued about using the truck only to have her change her mind now? If he lived a thousand lifetimes, he swore he would never understand why Sadie did the things she did. She was staring at him now with a hurt look like she couldn't understand why he was upset. "If they were in the truck, then they should be back by now." Fleet paced the length of the table, down then back to Sadie before announcing, "I'm going after them."

"And endanger more men for nothing?" Sadie knew that was Fleet's opinion of her actions. "I have every confidence in Eddie and Dylan's good sense and their ability to stay out of trouble." She set her jaw defiantly. "I told them to return tomorrow if they didn't find you. We should wait until tomorrow before deciding what to do." Fleet didn't know which bothered him more, when Sadie was wrong about something or when she was right. And she was right; he wanted to do the same thing she had done. Sending more people out to look for the ones who were looking was a self-defeating strategy. They would have to wait until tomorrow and hope they returned. If they didn't come back, well, then he would hope that it wasn't too late.

Kyla was last in the line as they made their hasty exit from the dining hall. Rod, Peach, and Kurt were on their way out the door when Riley caught her by the arm and said, "Sadie has asked me to show you around this afternoon. First thing we'll do is get you fitted for a uniform. I'd loan you one of mine but I don't think it would fit." The buxom young woman with the bushy black hair smiled broadly. She seemed to be a friendly, straightforward person. Kyla followed as Riley led the way down the hall on the opposite side of the cabin from where Kyla's room was located and opened the door across from the library. Sitting inside was the tall, broad-shouldered blond woman from the dormitory.

"This is Sara," Riley said as they entered. Then to Sara, she said, "Sadie said that you need to make a tunic for Kyla."

Sara's only reaction to the announcement was to raise her eyebrows slightly. Without a word she rose and began taking Kyla's measurements and writing them on a note pad. When she was done she sat back down at the table holding a sewing basket. Next to the table was an old treadle sewing machine. It was an amazing thing that something so old was being put to use again. Things had changed, but they were certainly not moving forward. Sara picked up a shirt that she'd been working on when they came in. As she picked up the needle and thread she said, "I should be able to take in some of Marta's clothes. I'll have them ready tomorrow." Her eyes returned to her work and Riley and Kyla might as well have not existed. Sara did not look at them again or say good-bye when they left.

Riley looked at Kyla after shutting the door behind them and said, "Don't worry about her. She's like that with everyone, even Sadie." Then as they headed back into the foyer Riley said, "Go get you coat and we'll take a look around the place."

Hurrying down the hall after her jacket, Kyla felt like a schoolgirl being dismissed for recess. She was looking forward to spending the afternoon with Riley as her guide. It only took a minute to grab her coat and meet Riley by the door. As they went outside, the first thing that Kyla noticed was the temperature. The weather was considerably milder than it had been for many days. The rain had been a good sign. It had been the first time in months that precipitation had fallen and was not of some frozen variety, which meant the temperature had been above freezing yesterday. Today it was a little bit warmer. Things were definitely looking up and Kyla's outlook was becoming rosier with every step.

As they walked side by side down the walk, Riley began to chatter. Her personality was so effervescent that the words seemed to bubble from her mouth. "You've seen the women's dormitory. The men's dormitory is on the other side of the farm." She pointed to indicate where. "Like putting the men and women on opposite sides would keep them apart." She laughed at her observation. Then one after the other she pointed out the other buildings. "That's the dining hall, but I guess you know that one. Wash rooms, one for the men and one for women. That's the dairy; at least we hope it will be one day. All we need are the cows. We have one Guernsey though," she said brightly. "We'll go down to the barn and you can see her." With that she changed direction slightly and kept pointing out buildings. "That's the tool shed. All the big equipment is in that big pole building over there," she indicated a long building with sheet metal siding. "We have tractors, planters, harvesters, everything you need to run a farm but the gas to run them. We use a little bit of gasoline to run the generators for a few hours each day. Most of the power goes to run the lights and heaters in the greenhouses. But we do everything that we can manually. Sadie's had everybody out looking for old tools and machines."

"Like the wash tub and wringer that's in the laundry?" Kyla asked. She'd had some first hand experience with doing things the old fashioned way.

Riley laughed. It was a deep hearty sound that seemed to fill her whole body. "I forgot you spent the morning with Agatha."

It was only a short walk to the barn. An old building painted red and with a gambrel roof, it was the traditional design. Riley opened the smaller door beside the large hanging door for the wagons. Having grown up on a farm the odor that greeted Kyla was a familiar one, hay and dust mingled with the smell of warm manure. Once inside Riley made for the stables that were lining one wall of the building. Kyla looked into the stables when they passed. She had counted four horses before she saw two that were familiar. Her shaggy brown mare and Fleet's black were the last two in the row. Riley saw her looking at them, "Fleet wanted the horses but I don't know where we will get the feed. Hayburners, that's what my uncle used to call them." She stopped at the last stall and looked at the cow munching her cud. "Now if you feed the cow, at least she gives you milk." Riley laughed at that. After walking from one end of the barn to the other, they had seen all that Riley wanted to show Kyla in the barn. Riley pushed on the hanging door at that end and slid it back making a crack wide enough for them to squeeze through, then pushed it back into place. Kyla didn't think she could have moved the door. It would have been too heavy for her to budge.

Once outside, the next building didn't need to be announced. The sound of cackling was quite evident and as they walked around to the other side of the building Kyla saw the large wire pen filled with chickens, dozens of them. Eggs and chicken would be on the menu quite often from what Kyla saw. Two men were busy working there, cleaning the coop and filling the feeders and water trough. These were the only people she had seen working around the farm. Counting Sara and Agatha at the cabin that made four, nothing near the number she had seen at the dining hall that morning. "Where's everybody else," Kyla asked.

"Most of the women are working in the green house. Some of the men are cutting wood. We burn a lot of wood. Then it takes just as many men to carry the wood back and stack it as it does to do the cutting," Riley answered as she began to change direction again. Making a loop around the chicken coop, they started walking back toward the house. "Some of them are working up the ground in some fields near here. When the weather breaks they'll start planting."

"I would think the horses would be a help with all of that," Kyla said.

"Well, they would. Except we don't have harnesses or wagons. But I suppose you're right. Next thing you know we'll all be out searching through old buildings looking for plows and furrows for horses to pull," she said thoughtfully. Riley seemed to be warming to the idea of horses, if they could contribute to the work being done at the farm.

They walked past the log house and went to the first in the row of long buildings just beyond it. At first she thought the buildings had black roofs, but when Riley told her that they were the greenhouses, Kyla saw that the windows were painted black. It was all very puzzling until they went inside and she saw the large luminescent panels hanging from the ceiling. Long and thin, they were like nothing Kyla had ever seen. With so many lights, she thought the room would be uncomfortably warm, but the air inside was just a little bit humid and cool. The large fans in the ceiling hummed along as they kept the air moving from one building to the next. Just beyond the building where they entered there was another identical building connected by a short walkway and beyond that was another walkway leading to yet another building. The first room was filled with large tubs nearly four feet tall with plants growing in them. Riley provided the explanation. "Potatoes," she said simply and dug into one of the tubs and uncovered a small tuber. They went into the next building where Kyla could see the two women she had met earlier that day. Rachel and Zoë were busy digging in one of the raised beds and planting some seeds. When they saw Riley with Kyla, they stood and looked at Kyla. Rachel smiled smugly, assuming that Kyla was coming to help with the work. The smile changed to shocked amazement and then green-eyed envy as Rachel realized that Riley was not just dropping her off.

Riley saw the two women staring at Kyla and ignored them as she continued talking to Kyla. "There are two workers assigned to each building. They're responsible for planting and caring for their crops. Everyone who stays in the dormitory and eats at the dining hall has to work for room and board." Then she began telling Kyla what was planted in each bed. "Carrots, peas, cabbage, cauliflower, and some other cool weather crops are in here. Our biggest problem is growing enough for everyone, but with the lights we have the capability to produce crops year round," Riley said leading the way into the next building.

"Troops are ready for inspection, Riley, ma'am." It was Carleen and the young girl with the long braids. They were both standing side-by-side saluting, but when she saw Kyla, Carleen forgot the joke. "Good lord girl, where did you get off to? I didn't see you at lunch."

Riley stopped and said, "Kyla was working in the house this morning."

Carleen grinned ear to ear and said, "Let me guess. Agatha had you slaving in the laundry."

"How did you know that?" Kyla asked.

Carleen grinned and answered, "Because your fingers are still wrinkled." When Kyla looked at her hands, both Carleen and the girl

114

burst out laughing. It was the girl who said, "Made you look." Carleen acted as much like a child as the girl was.

Even Riley was smiling. She winked and pulled one of the girl's braids and told Kyla, "This is Armand's sister, Ruth." Kyla looked at the girl. She could not see much resemblance between the two. Armand's build was big and broad. Ruth was a slender reed with delicate features and a heart shaped face.

"What do you think of our crop, Riley?" Ruth asked. "Carleen says the peas will be ready to pick in a day or two."

"They look really good, Ruth. Armand will be proud of you," Riley answered and gave the girl a warm smile and stroked her fondly across the shoulder.

As Riley started to leave with Kyla following, Carleen called out, "Kyla, will we see you tonight?" Kyla looked to Riley and was starting to answer, but Riley cut her off saying, "Kyla will be staying with us tonight." Carleen and Ruth both looked like they were stunned. As Riley walked away, Kyla turned to Carleen and whispered, "I'll try to get away later." Then she hurried after Riley who was already in the third building. The whole length of the last building was planted in red clover. When Kyla entered she heard a buzzing that wasn't from the fans. The room was full of bees. Riley walked quickly down a path through the center of the room to leave by the door on the far end. Kyla saw one wooden beehive set up next to one of the walls. "It was an experiment and so far it's worked. The bees keep everything pollinated, but you couldn't work in there if you're allergic to bee stings." They went through three other sets of buildings, each with two buildings devoted to crops in two different stages of development and one to the bees. There were men working in two of the buildings and women in two.

After touring the gardens Riley headed off on a different trail going away from the farm. It wasn't long before Kyla began to notice something familiar about the track they were taking. It was the same one they had followed the night before when Riley took her to the dormitory. They were heading back to the Settlement. Finally, Kyla would be able to get a good look at the place. Riley kept a steady commentary going as they walked. "I thought we should get a better look around the Settlement before night. There's usually not much going on there this time of day. Everyone in the Guard takes turns going to the shelter. There are usually four of us. We're supposed to keep people from fighting and killing each other if we can." Kyla didn't say anything. She was just a draftee. Riley seemed to know her doubts and said, "It's really not that bad. The men take care of most of the rough stuff, but they liked me and Marta to come along to take care of the women." She looked at Kyla, her big brown eyes almost apologetic. "Like I did with you." Then her smile was back as she said, "But you jumped right in the middle of things last night!"

"There wasn't anything brave about what I did last night. I know I wasn't thinking straight or I would have never done what I did," Kyla protested.

"Well, sometimes if you stop to think, then it's too late," Riley said in her usual straightforward manner. "That's one of the reasons we thought you would be a good addition to the Guard. You acted with your heart and kept your head."

"Anyway," Riley continued, "I was going to tell you about watching the Settlement. The main thing we do is head off trouble before it starts. We watch the people who are holding pearls the closest of all. You get so you know who they are because it's usually the same people. You can tell how much they've been using just by the way they act. The first stage is euphoria and if it stayed there we wouldn't have a problem. The problem is that after the good times are over the violent behavior begins. The ones who think the have to carry a pearl in their hand all the time, well they're just crazy. They usually end up killing themselves. We just try to keep them from taking anyone with them."

Kyla thought about the girl named Cissy and her bag full of pearls, "What about that girl last night? She had several handfuls that she put in that little bag."

To her surprise Riley laughed. "I guess I can let you in on a little secret. Cissy has a special job." Riley smiled knowingly, "With her help we can take dozens of pearls out of circulation every night."

"You've got to be kidding?" Kyla was incredulous. It seemed perverted to use her that way.

Riley looked at Kyla staring with her mouth hanging open. "I know what you're thinking. We didn't tell Cissy to strip. She was doing it anyway. She would do anything for a scrap of food. All we did was tell her that we would let her stay at the farm, free room and board. All she had to do was turn in as many pearls as she can collect in a night. We know she keeps a few but she turns in enough to make a difference. But just as soon as we think they're all gone, someone wanders in with a sack full that he picked up somewhere."

It was like everything else around here, just a little part of the twisted reality that was Kyla's world now. Cissy working for the Guard, stripping and then turning in her pearls seemed to fit somehow. When they reached the earthen embankment at the end of the lake, Kyla looked across the water. On the opposite side was a low block building and beyond that was the road and the bridge where she and Fleet had stopped. The hill was different from the others that were part of the rolling landscape where each ridge flowed into the next like the waves of the ocean. The steep sided hill where the Settlement was located stood apart from the others with a rounded top. It reminded Kyla of a scoop of ice cream.

As Kyla looked, Riley was telling her about the place. "The lake is fed by a natural spring. It's one of the few in this area. They say that people have been using the springs since the ice ages." As they walked along the path crossing the dam Kyla saw people walking along the edge of the lake. When they reached the part of the path that led to the top of the hill, Kyla noticed the tents and primitive shelters in the woods and people moving around them. That part of the Settlement had not been visible in the dark. Now she knew where the rest of the people had gone. Not everyone here was dependent on Sadie and her farm, at least not directly. When they reached the top of the hill and entered the clearing where the shelter-house was located, there were only a few people wandering around. As Riley had said there was really not much to see.

Riley looked around for a moment. No one gave them any more notice than to look at them once and then look away. "I told you there wouldn't be much going on. Most people are out scavenging for food and things to trade during the day. Some go further than others and are gone for days at a time. Every day is different, different people, different tents, different things traded, different fights." She looked around the clearing and said, "It looks like we'll have a full house tonight and probably tomorrow." Riley looked at Kyla and said, "They all try to be here when it's time for the Gathering. Sadie opens the doors of the cabin for anyone who wants to come. Everyone is welcomed into the cabin then." As they turned and started walking back Kyla was thinking about the Gathering. Fleet had mentioned it once. He said she would hear everyone's stories then. It was also to be the time of her initiation into the Guard. That thought made her extremely nervous. She was looking forward to learning more but at the same time dreading the initiation. The last four days had been full of eye opening experiences and tomorrow promised the same.

Chapter Five

The evening routine at the cabin was much more relaxed and informal. There was no gathering as a group for the evening meal. When Riley and Kyla returned, Agatha and Sara were gone and the cabin was deserted except for the two of them. As they went into the kitchen Riley explained, "We're all on our own in the evenings. Some of the Guard comes here to eat and sleep, others don't. It's up to the individual. I stay here all the time. My bedroom is near Sadie's." As they looked in the refrigerator for something to eat, Kyla was grateful that it was one of the things important enough to use their precious electricity to power it. Once they had eaten and Kyla left for her room, Riley went into the library and lit the candles on the old candelabra stand. She took a book off the seat and sat down. Not in Sadie's high backed armchair, but one of the ladder back chairs lined up against one wall. The light was none too bright but enough for her to see. But the book was just a pretense; she wanted to look like she was doing something other than sitting and waiting for Sadie.

She was thinking about Kyla. She seemed like a nice enough person but Riley wasn't comfortable with the quick decision to initiate Kyla as a member of the Guard. She had never seen anyone accepted so quickly. That was the curious thing, it was Fleet who usually wanted things to go slow, but this time he had been the one wanting to initiate her at the Gathering tomorrow night instead of waiting. There was no doubt in the minds of those who had seen Kyla jump on Lipsky that she had spunk, but that alone was not enough for Riley. But then it was not her decision to make, she reminded herself.

She had not waited long before Sadie appeared in the doorway carrying a small lantern. The bright flame of the lantern cast long dark shadows on the floor behind Sadie and dwarfed the pale light from the candles. "How did it go?" Sadie asked. There was no need for her to elaborate. Riley knew exactly what she meant.

"Okay, I guess," Riley answered as she closed the book and set it on the chair next to her. "I showed her around the farm and we walked to the Settlement to look around. Then we came back here and ate. She's in her room now."

"Did she say anything?" Sadie had not moved from the doorway.

"No, not really," Riley said. "She had some questions, but she didn't talk much otherwise." Riley had not pressed her for information, but she would have reported anything that Kyla said if she had volunteered anything. There was one rule Riley stuck to, don't ask about the past.

When the front door opened Sadie turned her head to see who it was. Riley didn't have to look. She recognized Fleet's voice. Sadie turned back to Riley and said, "You can sleep in your own room tonight." Then she left and took her light to the door. Riley could see Sadie and Fleet standing in the glow of the tiny lantern and then turn to walk side-by-side past the library door talking softly to each other.

It was no surprise to her that Sadie would not need her to guard her room tonight. She had Fleet to do the job. When Fleet was away, Sadie had Riley sleep on a cot in the entry room to her suite. It was Sadie's greatest fear that someone would come into her rooms while she was sleeping and harm her. Even though things seemed peaceful enough at the farm, Riley did not think Sadie's fears were ungrounded given the situation in the world at large. Well, at least she didn't have to worry about it tonight and she never had trouble sleeping. So, she picked up her book and lit another candle on a small stand and blowing out the ones on the candelabra, Riley went to her room.

Riley was not the only one who heard Fleet's voice. Kyla had heard him when he came in, too. She opened her door a tiny crack and peeked out. She watched while Fleet and Sadie walked arm in arm down the hall to the opposite end of the house. Then Riley came out of the library with a book in one hand and a candle in the other and disappeared in the same direction. When they were gone and the hall and foyer were dark, Kyla closed the door with a soft click. Kyla wasn't ready for sleep. The only decision for her to make was whether she was going to slip out the front door or the window in her room. She opted for the window thinking that the front door would probably be locked and she definitely wanted to get out and back in again without anyone knowing. Kyla put on her coat, opened the window and quietly climbed through it. The ground beneath her feet gave a telltale crackle as she landed outside. The noise seemed loud to Kyla, but she doubted that anyone heard it. Reaching down she picked up one of the sticks that had broken under her feet and used it to prop the window open a crack, then hurried as quickly as she could in the direction of the women's dormitory. She was disappointed to find that it was empty. Kyla had passed the dining hall on the way and now she turned around and went back. There were a few people there drinking coffee, but no one that she was looking for. She had wanted to find Carleen and talk to her. If she was going to live here, Kyla wanted to have friends outside of the Guard, too. If no one was at the farm, that only left one place. After hesitating for a moment, she started toward the path to the Settlement. There was no point in being shy. Tomorrow night everyone would know all about her, so why not do a little to help shape her own image. Tonight she was still Sister Kyla to everybody she met.

Even though it was Kyla's first time without a guide, she had already traveled this path three times and it was not hard to follow. Besides if she had lost her way, the lights from the fires on the hill at the Settlement were like beacons in the darkness. All she had to do was keep heading in that direction. When she finally reached the clearing at the top of the hill, the scene was exactly as it had been the night before, a dozen or more large bonfires with people huddled around each one. But tonight was different, Kyla had seen this place during the day and it had given her a whole new perspective on the place. Her only plan was to find Carleen and talk to her. So Kyla began walking from one fire to another looking over the faces of the people standing around each one.

Every once in awhile she saw somebody that she recognized. The first person that she recognized was Agatha, the cook from Sadie's cabin. Somehow the sight of Agatha wrapped in her parka and drinking some of that foul brew that Kyla had tasted last night, seemed out of character for the stern faced woman. Agatha saw Kyla staring at her and gave her a sharp look before turning back to the others in her circle. Kyla passed the group without a word, but she heard them explode in a buzz of whispers once she was walking away. It was easy to see the rumor mill was already at work. It was the same at every fire. They would look at her and as soon as Kyla was past, the whispering started.

Kyla walked in a large circle around the clearing and had checked every bonfire looking for Carleen without any luck. As she stood looking around and trying to decide what to do next she heard a rustling in the bushes behind her. Kyla whirled around expecting the worst and was relieved to see Carleen. "I heard you were up here wandering around all alone." She put her hands on her hips and continued, "I told them that couldn't be true because you weren't that stupid." Her tone was friendly enough, but Kyla knew when she was being scolded.

"I was looking for you," Kyla explained.

Carleen smiled and said, "Well, I'm glad to see you're a person who keeps their word." She was an attractive woman with smoky brown skin and black hair that was cut short and fell in soft waves around her face. Her face had delicate features and her nose turned up at the end and Kyla thought it made her look impish. When she laughed or smiled, which was often, her cheeks became round little apples with dimples and her eyes twinkled with mischief. "I was on my way to the shelter. You're welcome to come with me," Carleen said. Then she walked past Kyla without waiting for her to answer. It was either go to the shelter house or back to the farm. So Kyla turned and followed Carleen. Who knew, it might be an interesting evening.

The crowd in the shelter house was the same as last night, bodies crammed shoulder to shoulder. It was a wonder that no matter how crowded it seemed, there was always a way to fit more people inside. Carleen was in front, watching Kyla every inch of the way, making sure that she didn't loose her in the crowd. It didn't seem like she had any particular spot in mind. They were just moving from table to table with Carleen making some comment to someone everywhere they turned. Usually, just a greeting, but sometimes more. When they finally found a place next to the wall, Carleen took a seat and Kyla sat beside her. "It's best to sit with your back against the wall. No one can come up behind you that way." That was the first serious thing that Kyla had heard Carleen say. "Besides," she continued in her usual playful manner, "this way you get the whole picture."

Kyla craned her neck to see, but there were so many people standing between the tables and benches, that it was impossible to see to the other side of the room. She saw four men wearing black tunics in the crowd. Tonight she knew their names. Rod and Kurt were sitting together at a table near the fire. They had seen her come in with Carleen and Kyla could see them looking now.

Carleen saw them looking, too and commented wryly to Kyla, "Your new friends are watching."

Bold and brave, Kyla thought to herself and said, "Let them watch, I don't care." Then she looked around the room a little more and saw Justin and James. They were staring at Kyla, too and there was nothing particularly friendly about any of their expressions. No one had told her that she had to stay at the cabin and she had enough sense to stay out of trouble. She returned their glares with a smile. Finally, they all looked away. Kurt was shaking his head and shot one last look at Kyla that she took as a warning.

Carleen was watching and taking everything in. "You are quite the talk of the place," she said in a voice that only Kyla could hear.

"What do you mean?" Kyla fired back defensively. She had wondered what they were whispering when she walked by the bonfires.

Carleen smiled broadly. She was more than happy to fill Kyla in on some of the wild stories. "Well, let's see," she teased Kyla a little, "last night it started out that one of the Family members had been here and killed Lipsky." She looked at Kyla and said, "It would have been a blessing to everyone if that had been true." Then in a lighter tone she continued, "But when the bugger showed up this morning, he started his own rumor about how Fleet had paid someone to stab him in the back. Then when someone reminded everybody about how small you were, well, old Lipsky got a ribbing about that." She looked up for a moment like something funny had just popped into her mind and leaned over to Kyla saying, "They told him that Fleet must not think that Lipsky was much of a threat if he had sent someone as small as you after him." Carleen was laughing so hard at the end that she could hardly get the words out.

Kyla didn't think it was quite that hilarious. She looked at Carleen and said, "That doesn't sound too bad."

"Well, that's just the beginning." Carleen became a little more serious as she continued, "This is a small place. You can't even take a crap around here without someone being there to report on it." Colorful choice of words, Kyla thought but undoubtedly an accurate appraisal of the situation. "There were a lot of people who saw Fleet pulling you into the house. Fleet!" she said his name again for emphasis.

Kyla wasn't sure but she wondered if it was because of Sadie. She had seen them together tonight and what had Lipsky called him? 'The lord of the manor', well, there was nothing between her and Fleet and she told Carleen just that. Carleen gave Kyla a look of reserved acceptance at her denial, saying, "I'm just telling you what people are saying. Anyway, we heard that you ate the noon meal with the Guard and then had a private meeting with Sadie and Fleet."

"There were others there," Kyla interrupted. Carleen looked at her and it was Kyla's turn to smile. "I know, you're just telling me what you heard."

Nodding now, Carleen continued, "Anyway, I heard all of that at lunch in the dining hall." News certainly did travel fast. It was no wonder that Fleet had a security problem. She made a mental note to mention it to him tomorrow. "So, I wasn't too surprised to see you with Riley later. What did surprise me was when Sara told us that she was fitting you for a black tunic."

"That part is true," Kyla said watching her reaction.

Carleen gave a long whistle and settled back against the wall looking at Kyla a little differently than before, wondering what was going to happen to her new friend. She considered everyone her friend until something happened that would change her mind otherwise. Carleen was a warm, open person to everyone she met, but she was not a doormat either. If somebody took advantage of her easy-going personality, she was not above getting even. Kyla had done nothing to her personally and she had nothing to gain in begrudging Kyla the luck of landing at the top of the heap. It may be the top of the garbage heap, but the top was a whole lot better than being at the bottom where she was. Besides, it never hurt to have a friend in the Guard. "Well, anyway, there's one rumor I heard where people are saying that witch, Sister Samethia, cast a spell on Fleet making him forget about Sadie and take you into his bed instead." She smiled at Kyla's shocked expression and added, "There's a lot of women around here who would like to jump in the sack with Fleet and some of them who say they have." Carleen was hoping for something from Kyla, one way or the other, but when she didn't respond Carleen continued with the rumors. "The next rumor is that the Family is going to take over the Guard and next thing you know we'll all be wearing brown monks robes and calling each other Sister and Brother. But most of what's going around are different variations of the story that Sadie is out and you're in." Carleen laughed at Kyla's red-faced embarrassment.

Kyla wished Carleen would change the subject. "Do you know many people here?" she asked. Carleen nodded and grabbed one of the bottles being passed around. Then after taking a drink offered it to Kyla. The smell was the same as last night's offering. Kyla held up her hand and said, "No, thank you. It tastes bad. Besides don't you people believe in using cups? It would certainly be a lot more sanitary."

Carleen wiped her mouth with her sleeve and passed the bottle on to someone sitting next to them. "That doesn't bother me," she said. "I always figured that whatever they put in it was strong enough to kill any germs." She looked across the room at a group of men who had suddenly raised their voices. Kyla could see that the members of the Guard were looking, too. Carleen leaned closer and said quietly, "I think that bunch has pearls in their pockets." They watched as the argument began to escalate into a shoving match. "The one in the camouflage is named Tom." Kyla looked at him and wondered if he was the same man that had been with Fleet the night before. He was the same build as the man sitting at the table and his hair looked the same, but still it could have been anybody.

The man named Tom was arguing with the other three men. Carleen told Kyla that she didn't know their names but that they showed up at the Settlement every few weeks with items for trade. Kyla watched as Kurt and Rod began moving up behind the three men. When one of them pulled a knife out of the sheath at his waist, Kurt was there. As he locked the man's head in the crook of his arm, Rod grabbed hold of the hand holding the knife and forced him to drop it by twisting his arm back. Before the other two men could cause any trouble Justin and James joined them and with Tom the odds were now five to three.

The room had become quiet. Everyone was watching to see what would happen. It was Kurt who took charge and said, "The shows over," to the crowd. Then to the three men, he said, "I think it's time we all go outside and cool down." Turning to the man wearing the camouflage jacket, he said, "Tom, I think it would be best if you go home now."

As Tom exited through one door, Justin, James, and Rod escorted the three unruly visitors to the other door. Kurt looked at Kyla and made his way through the crowd to come and talk to her now. He stopped a few paces away and motioned for Kyla to come to him. With a quick look at Carleen, she went to where he was standing only to have Kurt grab her by the arm and drag her toward the door. Kyla stopped and tried to break his grasp. "Where do you think you're taking me?" she asked angrily. Kurt turned and looked at her but he didn't let go of her arm. He was squeezing so tightly that Kyla was sure she would have bruises in the shape of his fingers in the morning. "Can you loosen up on your hold a little and tell me what's wrong?" Somebody had to be sensible, Kyla thought to herself.

Kurt looked around and then leaned closer to Kyla, "We can't talk here. Come with me." He let go of her arm and added, "Please." With a look and nod to Carleen, Kyla turned and followed Kurt out the door. Once outside Kurt began to walk briskly away from the shelter house until he found a dark area behind some trees. That's where he finally stopped. "Have you seen what you came to see?" he asked impatiently.

If she were ever to be respected, then Kyla would have to stand up to these people. She decided to begin with Kurt. "I don't remember anyone telling me I wasn't free to come and go as I want." She tried to sound just as arrogant as he was acting.

"I don't want to be responsible if something happens to you," Kurt said, moving out of the shadow and into the soft light of a nearby fire. The expression on his face was deadly serious. Whenever she had seen him, he always wore the same worrisome look. Otherwise, he was a handsome man with a strong square jaw and chiseled features that seemed to fit his stone cold personality.

However, Kyla could see that he really was concerned and she tried to explain her actions to him. "I don't care what you or any of the rest say about me becoming a member of the Guard. The fact remains that I will be initiated tomorrow. Now, if these people see you treating me as someone who needs your protection, then how will I ever earn their respect? If I don't have their respect, how will I be able to help you and the rest keep the order?" She stopped for a moment. She could see by his expression that she had his attention now. "It's in your best interest," and she stressed the word 'your', "if they continue to think of

126

me as some crazy Sister who Fleet brought in to dispense punishment."
She stepped out into the light so he could see her face, see that she was
serious, too. "What do you think?"

Kurt looked at the feisty little woman standing in front of him. He
remembered the night he had seen her clinging to Fleet after the raid.
She'd been wearing different clothes then. He knew he would have
remembered the rabbit skin coat. Other than the coat, there was nothing
about her that made him think she was Family. He had gone with Fleet
to meet with the Family and had seen a lot of people, but he hadn't seen
Kyla or heard anyone mention a Sister Kyla. He usually trusted Fleet's
judgement, but he'd had a hard enough time with the fact that Fleet had
brought someone, unknown to the rest of the group, out of the farm
with him. Then there was his rush to make her a member of the Guard.
Kurt had heard the story about her saving Fleet's life, but knowing Fleet
and Lipsky the way he did, he knew that Fleet hadn't been in any real
danger. Lipsky was all show and no go. Kurt was wondering if there
wasn't some truth to the story about Samethia casting a spell on Fleet,
because he was certainly acting irrationally when it came to this
woman who was standing in front of him and asking what he thought.
The only thing that he could think of that would make a man act like
he had lost all common sense was love. The idea of Fleet being head
over heels in love with this skinny little thing and ending his
relationship with Sadie was preposterous. He looked at Kyla again. He
still hadn't answered her question, not anything that she could hear
anyway.

"I think you made your point," Kurt said and bowed rather
elegantly. "But I also think that it's late and you have a big day
tomorrow." He started to walk toward the path leading back to the
farm.

"Thank you, but I think I can find the way myself," Kyla said
sharply.

Kurt stopped dead in his tracks and looked back at her. "Have it
your way," he said and then turned and walked back to the shelter
house leaving Kyla alone.

She waited until he was gone before beginning her way toward
the path back to the farm. Tonight she was aware of the soft sounds
coming from the woods where the tents were set up. It was as if the air

was humming with the sounds of humanity. It seemed so strange to Kyla to be surrounded by so many people after having been alone so long. Since leaving her hiding place every day had brought something new and astounding. Tomorrow promised to be the same. Finally Kyla reached the farm and quietly crept back to the cabin. The window was still propped open like she had left it and she climbed back in without anyone seeing her. Everyone would know tomorrow where she had been, but right now all she wanted to do was sleep.

~ ~ ~

The next day was as busy as Kurt had said. Like her first day at the farm she heard the loud banging noise that signaled the time to rise. Only it was much louder at the cabin since that was where the sound originated. There was no trotting outside to the public washroom. The bathroom was in the house, but she still had to wait in line and the water was still cold. Kyla decided that tomorrow she would try to warm up some water on the stove in the kitchen. That is if Agatha would let her. After washing, Kyla found a fresh set of clothes lying on her bed when she returned to her room. She was relieved to see that it was not the black uniform that she had been promised. She could spend another day at least, looking like she was just plain old Kyla. Once she had changed, then it was time for breakfast with the rest of the Guard. There were still only ten present and Kyla could tell that the mood of the gathering was tense. No one mentioned the absent men by name, but it was easy to see that they were concerned. When breakfast was over Kyla spent the rest of the morning with Riley making her rounds.

Then it was back to the cabin for lunch. It was chicken again. Kyla could understand how Fleet might tire of eating chicken if that was all they ever had, but eating regularly was still something of a novelty for Kyla and she didn't care what was served. The two men still had not returned and still nothing was said. The meal was eaten quickly and everyone excused themselves before leaving to return to their duties. Kyla was walking with Riley and ready to go outside when Fleet called to Kyla from the library. Kyla turned to Riley, who said, "You can catch up with me later."

When Kyla stepped through the doorway to the library, Fleet said, "Shut the door and sit down." Although she had seen him twice today, this was the first time that he'd spoken to her. Fleet was sitting in one of the chairs lined up against one wall and there was a comfy looking armchair in the far corner. She started to head to that one, but Fleet said, "Not there. Sit over here," and motioned to one of the chairs next to him. Kyla was a little uncomfortable being alone with Fleet after seeing him with Sadie last night and then hearing all the rumors that were going around. She didn't want anyone to think that there was something going on between herself and Fleet, and the fact that this room had a window large enough that everyone outside could see inside, didn't help matters. Kyla felt like she was on exhibit in a showcase but she did as he asked and left an empty chair between them.

Fleet wasn't sure where to begin. His ears had been filled with rumors and reports on Kyla's little excursion all morning. First it had been Kurt after breakfast complaining that she had been to the Settlement alone last night. Then there were the rumors that were flying everywhere. Fleet got right down to business. "Kurt told me you were at the shelter house alone last night."

"I wasn't alone. I was with Carleen," Kyla answered defiantly.

He knew who she was talking about, the woman with the short, black hair who worked in the green houses. "Carleen is a nice enough person, but she's not one of the Guard." He looked at Kyla as he talked. She was still terribly thin, but she was not weak anymore. She definitely had her hackles up, but then Fleet didn't know any woman who liked having a man tell her what she could and could not do. "It's the rule, and we all follow it when we go up there at night."

"Well, no one told me," Kyla was not about to let Fleet chastise her. She had done nothing wrong. "I'll tell you the same thing I told Kurt last night. If you want me to be a member of the Guard then don't make me look helpless by fussing over me like I'm a child."

"That is not what I am trying to do. All I want is to explain how we do things," Fleet found her defensiveness irritating. "When we go to the Settlement at night, we always go in pairs whether you're on duty that night or just going for fun. It's safer that way, having someone to watch your back. There are enough people who would give you a beating, or worse, just for being one of the Guards. Not everybody appreciates us meddling in their good times." Fleet looked at her to see if he was getting his point across. Her expression had mellowed a little, but he could tell by the look on her face not to expect any apologies for anything that she did.

"I will try to be more careful in the future," she answered coolly.

Fleet wondered for a moment why Kyla was so touchy. Then he realized that she must have heard the rumors, too. He shifted in his chair wondering what he could say to her that wouldn't make the situation more uncomfortable. "The other thing you will have to get used to is having people talk about you." Fleet was pleased with that statement. Direct enough so she knew what he meant, but still skirting the issue.

Of course Fleet had heard the rumors, Kyla thought. "I don't care what anyone says," she said quickly, but the flush of embarrassment rising in her face belied her true feelings.

He looked at her and smiled. Her face was quite red and she was actually trembling a little. He wondered how she would look when she filled out around the face a little and her hair grew back. Even thin as a reed, she was still very pretty with big blue eyes that never left his face for a moment. She was like a fragile piece of china and there was something about her that he just couldn't define. He thought about the events over the last few days, about Kyla. Starting with her luck in escaping, the guard shot by a stray bullet. Then she had managed to get that blasted handcuff on his wrist, luck again. When they were outside the fence, when he should have left her, Fleet had reached out his hand to her. No matter how many times he asked himself why, he kept coming back to the same answer. He didn't know. It had just felt like the right thing to do. That was certainly a lucky break for Kyla. Then there was the Family. He should have insisted that she stayed there but he hadn't. He could have lost her and that little mare she was riding a hundred times over, but he didn't. And then there had been that first night at the Settlement, when she had jumped on that snake Lipsky sneaking up behind him. Followed by him insisting that Kyla should be the one to replace Marta. Fleet didn't want to admit it to himself, but he was something about this girl that seemed to be tugging at him. The rumor he had heard about Sister Samethia casting a spell over him came to mind. Except for the fact the fact that spells and the like were just plain nonsense, he might have been inclined to believe it.

He smiled now hoping that would lighten the mood a bit. "I wanted you to join the Guard because I can tell," he paused and changed what he was saying, "because I feel that you will be an asset to our group. Physical strength is not the only requirement for joining us. What I look for in a person is their strength of will and character. There is something about you that tells me you have that strength."

Kyla felt her anger leaving, but she was even more embarrassed now than before. "I don't know what you expect from me, but I intend do what I have always done. Last, night I wanted to go to the Settlement like all the others. I wanted them to see that I was just like them, no better, and no worse. If you think I am capable, then try to understand why I went. These people will have to accept me and respect me. That won't happen if they think the only reason I am in the Guard is because I'm your new lover."

Her statement was blunt and definitely to the point. Fleet laughed and said, "You don't have to make that sound so distasteful." He looked at her before continuing and said, "If that's the worst thing that is ever said about you then you won't have anything to worry about." He jumped to his feet and began pacing back and forth across the room. "Tonight at dusk Sadie will open up the foyer and the front room for the Gathering. Everyone is welcome to come and there is always a large crowd. Tonight it will be larger than usual, because everyone will be coming to get a look at you." He stopped in front of her and asked, "Are you up to it?" As she looked up at him and nodded, Fleet took her arm and pulled Kyla to her feet. He took off the hat that she was wearing and said, "Don't wear this tonight. When you walk in there tonight hold your head high. Nobody cares about your hair. Hell, tomorrow all the women will be shaving their heads to look like you!"

Kyla had to smile as she the thought of Rachel and Zoë cutting off their long braids. The smile on her face encouraged Fleet. "If you conduct yourself with pride and respect you will get the respect that you want from others." Fleet knew that the image one presented was as important as anything you did was. Probably more important, since most people never looked beyond what they could see. Besides the wheels were in motion, so to speak, and he didn't want to stop them even if he could. He looked at her one last time. Standing close like they were, she had to look up to meet his gaze. He began to raise his hand and reach out, it was an instinctive thing, wanting to touch and comfort her. But he was suddenly aware of how close they were standing, then stepping back, he lowered his arm and said, "I'll see you this evening."

As he opened the door to leave, Kyla had one question. "You said everyone tells their stories at the Gathering. Do I have to tell mine?" She was relieved when he smiled easily and said, "Only if you want to," then disappeared out the front door.

Kyla stood in the library watching Fleet stride down the walk and finally disappear from view. When she heard the door close, she whirled around to see Sadie standing behind her. When Fleet had asked her if she was ready, she had not been thinking about talking to Sadie. That was something she was definitely not ready for. She watched as Sadie strode regally across the room and seated herself as if on a throne, in the armchair that Fleet had steered Kyla away from. Kyla stood where she was, but turned to face Sadie. She had gotten a little taste of what she could expect yesterday and was steeling herself for a confrontation.

"I suppose Fleet was telling you about tonight," Sadie said. Her tone was pleasant enough, but Kyla was wary. There was something about this beautiful woman that seemed dangerous. Even though she carried no weapons, it was her bearing that gave the impression that she was as deadly as a rattlesnake coiled to strike.

"Yes," she answered. Then hoping to deflate any possible lectures she might have coming, Kyla added, "And he explained to me about the dangers of going to the Settlement alone."

"Fleet looks after everyone," was Sadie's only reply as she dismissed Kyla's confession as unimportant subject matter. She looked Kyla over head to foot. It was the first time she had seen her without that hideous hat, but she didn't look much better. Sadie had heard the rumors about Fleet and Kyla, too. She found the whole thing insulting. Just the thought that any man would prefer this hairless bag of bones to her was totally unbelievable. She decided to get right to the subject. "The behavior of the members of the Guard is Fleet's responsibility, not mine. It is also his choice to pick who will become a member of the

Guard." She gave Kyla a hard look, "That is the way it has always been. Still, I can't help wondering how you can split your loyalties between the Family and the Guard. It would seem that one philosophy contradicts the other."

"I don't see it that way. It seems to me that you believe in the same basic thing as the Family, peaceful co-existence with your fellow man," Kyla answered in a level tone. It would seem that Sadie was looking for some chink in her armor.

"I care a great deal for Fleet." Sadie paused slightly hoping for some reaction from Kyla. Just a little disappointed when Kyla stood unmoving, she continued, "I know how much the loyalty of his people means to him and I wouldn't want to see Fleet hurt when someone could only give a half-hearted effort."

"If that's what you're worried about then you can stop," Kyla tried to keep her tone just as low and arrogant as Sadie's was. If attitude was everything, she was going to spread it on thick. "My loyalty will always be with Fleet. He saved my life and I would do anything to keep him from harm." She spoke those words slowly and there could be no uncertainty in the fact that she meant it. Then looking at Sadie, Kyla thought to herself, and that means you.

Sadie's response was as sour as her face. "I'm so glad you put my mind at ease about that." She hadn't cared for the tone of Kyla's voice at all. She was not so dense that she couldn't recognize a thinly veiled inference that Kyla included her in the list of things that might do Fleet harm. Sadie smiled to herself at the thought. Yes, if anyone could do harm to Fleet, she could. But Sadie wouldn't do that, Fleet was much too useful. That was the trouble with Fleet bringing in an outsider like he had. This skinny girl didn't know who was in charge and it certainly wasn't Fleet, no matter what he thought. Sadie had given him everything that he had. Without her support he would be just like all the others, begging for food at her doorstep. Still, the girl seemed to care about Fleet and Sadie knew that she could use that to her advantage.

"Tonight at the Gathering you will be representing Fleet and the trust that we have all put in the members of the Guard, I hope you will be up to the challenge."

Kyla met Sadie's eyes and said, "I'm looking forward to it. I would like to hear the truth of what happened."

Sadie seemed to find that amusing and told Kyla, "It has been my experience that the truth is usually the last thing anybody wants to hear." With that said Sadie rose and sailed out the door leaving Kyla standing in the center of the room.

~ ~ ~

Kyla and Riley returned to the cabin about an hour before sunset. Even though Riley cooked something for them, Kyla was too nervous to eat. When she returned to her room and saw the black tunic and trousers that had been laid neatly across the bed, the reality of the situation hit her. It had been easy enough to go along with the whole unbelievable plan to make her a member of the Guard, now it was staring her in the face. Kyla was beginning to wonder if she really was up to the challenge, as Sadie had said. But it was too late to back out now, way too late. She picked up the tunic and looked at it. It was very well made. Sara was definitely a wonderful seamstress. The fabric was a good heavy weave and it looked like it would be warm enough on a cold day. She took off the sweater she was wearing and tried it on. When she threaded the long cord through the loop, she thought of that first night when Fleet had asked her to fasten the little arrow pin to his tunic. She had noticed several beads on the end of his cord, but there weren't any on hers.

The tunic fit well enough, but it was a little loose in places. She wondered if Sara had done that on purpose so she wouldn't have to fit it again once Kyla filled out a little more. If she kept eating the way she had, it wouldn't be long. Kyla smiled and thought about the comment that Armand had made about the amount of food that she could fit into her tiny body. She kicked off her boots and jeans and pulled on the trousers. They were made of the same fabric and had a drawstring at the waist. Kyla had a lot of loose cording to tuck inside her pants. She was glad to find that the pockets in the pants were good and deep. As Kyla folded the clothes that she had taken off and laid them on the nightstand, she took the handcuffs out of the pocket of the jeans and dropped them in her pocket. Not that she needed them. Kyla wouldn't admit to herself that she had just gotten used to feeling them in her pocket and had begun to think of them as her good luck charm. She put the tiny, fuzzy piece of soap in the other one for all the same reasons. Then she pulled on her boots and tucked the bottoms of her pants into the boots. The lighter brown of the boots contrasted sharply with the black uniform, but they were all Kyla had. Even if they had left new black boots for her, she would have worn the ones the Family had given her. Once she had positioned her knife in her boot so it could not be seen, she was ready. Kyla sat on the bed to wait for the knock on her door trying to look like she was ready for anything.

She didn't know how long she waited, but when the light outside had begun to fade from gray to black, the moment that Kyla had been awaiting finally arrived. She couldn't help herself and jumped when she heard the rapping on her door. Wondering who they would send to bring her to the meeting, she rose slowly and opened the door. It was Justin, the young man with the wild chestnut brown hair and freckles. He was carrying two small metal trays with a handle on one end and a small candle in the center. As he lit her candle with hers, he said, "I have come to take you to the Guard. I am the one to bring you, because I was the last initiate." Then he turned and led the way down the hall. Kyla followed and said, "Let the ceremony begin," under her breath. Apparently, Justin overheard and he turned and gave her a stern look as he put his finger to his lips, letting Kyla know that she was not to speak. There was a soft murmur of voices coming from the foyer and when they emerged from the end of the hallway Kyla could see that people were still coming in. Next she saw that the foyer had grown larger. The large wooden panels that had formed one wall had been removed and now the foyer became part of the great room.

The doorway to the great room had been closed and this was the first time Kyla had seen what was inside. If there had been any furniture, it had been removed with the panels. The floor of the room had two levels or three if you counted the fireplace that covered one entire wall with a stone hearth that was raised above the level of everything else. When one entered from the foyer, you were on the first level that formed a walkway twelve feet wide around the remaining three sides of the room. In the center of each wall were two wide steps down to the bottom level. People were sitting on the floor and steps, leaning against the wall, sitting on the edge of the first level and dangling their legs, they were everywhere and still coming. Justin was nudging her out in front of him now and guiding her toward the fireplace. The crowd parted to make way and Kyla looked up and saw the ladder back chairs from the library. There were twelve. In the center with six chairs on each side was Sadie's armchair, also from the library. Behind her chair was the soft glow of the fire, that and the candles that each person was holding were the only sources of light in the room. Kyla tried to remember what Fleet had told her. As she walked from one end of the hearth to the other, past the row of chairs to stand before the last one in the row, she held her head high and was relieved that she hadn't tripped over her own feet. When she turned to face the people assembled there, she realized that she was not alone and was just the beginning of the procession. Justin had followed her, then Riley, Peach, Moon, Rod, Armand, James all in order by what Kyla assumed was their rank in the Guard based on seniority. Each one took their place before one of the chairs leaving the three in the center empty along with one empty chair between Riley and Peach and another between Rod and Armand. Dylan and Eddie had not returned and their chairs would be empty tonight.

Kyla did not look at anyone in the crowd sitting on the floor. She was watching the entry, waiting for Fleet. As the last people settled in and the front door was closed, Kyla saw Sadie making her entrance from the hallway across the foyer followed by Fleet and Kurt walking side by side, like the queen and her honor guard. When Fleet saw Kyla looking at him, he touched his shoulder and smiled. She could see the small glint of silver and knew he was wearing the arrow pin. Only when Sadie had turned and had her honor guard in position, with Fleet at her right hand and Kurt at her left, did she bring the meeting to order. "Welcome to my home." She was playing the part of magnanimous hostess flawlessly. "I see so many familiar faces. To those of you who are new I will explain what we will do here tonight." She paused dramatically, it was her show and she had staged it magnificently. Ten men and women standing at attention and all dressed in black, with the fire behind them their shadows seemed huge and formidable as they stretched across the room and up the far wall. Sadie stood at the center, positively radiant with beauty and power. It was definitely the best show in town. "We time our Gathering to coincide with the cycles of the moon. We chose to meet on the first day of the new moon because it symbolizes our lives at a new beginning. We meet here and tell our stories to everyone who has never heard them before, so they can know and for those who have heard them before so they will remember. Only at the Gatherings do we speak of the world as it was. The rest of the time we live every day looking to the future." Sadie looked around the room and said, "If any would like to speak, please do so now." Then as Sadie seated herself, the Guard took their seats together in a way that symbolized their unity.

There was a murmuring in the room. No one stood for a long time, until finally Armand stood and motioned to Ruth who was sitting with the others. She scrambled up onto the hearth and stood beside her brother. "My name is Armand and this is my sister Ruth. We were in the basement of our parents' house when the city we lived in was destroyed." He paused and looked at Ruth before going on. "I don't know why we were chosen to live when everyone else died. People have asked me what kind of bomb it was that could turn an entire city to dust and sand. There was no burning, no heat, only a roar like the wind, but much louder. We heard the sound just before it passed over our house and then we could hear it disappear in the distance like something had rolled over us. Then it was cold, suddenly and intensely."

Ruth held up her hand and interjected, "I got frostbite." There was a lot of whispering after her comment.

Armand waited for the talking to stop before he went on. "We lived the best we could, scrounging around in the rubble for food and living in a tent. But it was impossible to live there, it was like being in the desert with sandstorms blowing in and burying everything every time there was a windy day. Then we were lucky enough to find a way into a grocery store and Ruth and I were hauling out loads of canned goods. It was like finding a gold mine. That didn't last too long though. We hadn't seen a soul for weeks, but as soon as we found a food supply, it was like we'd lit a signal fire. When a group of men threatened Ruth, we left and started walking. We walked for days before finding the Settlement." Armand slowly turned his head to see all who were gathered and finished by saying. "And that is our story."

After Armand, Fleet stood. "My name is Fleet and I was a private in the army. My orders were to help evacuate civilians. After the first round, we just kept going out again and again looking for the ones who had been missed." He stopped and grinned before saying, "I'm happy to see so many were missed." Then his expression became serious as he continued. "When I heard the rumor that the evacuations were completed and that all non-essential personnel would be sent to the evacuation centers, that was when I decided it was time to look for my wife and son. I went to the centers looking for people but they were gone. I knew of thousands of people that we had dropped off there and when I arrived at the evacuation center it was empty except for military personnel. I just kept going from one deserted building to the other. I didn't see anybody until I reached the opposite side of the camp and saw the soldiers loading people into railroad cars and sending trains loaded with people down into what looked like mine shafts. I knew there wasn't anywhere for that many people to live underground. That's when I left and I just kept walking south until Sadie found me. And that is my story." Fleet ended his tale and looked at the audience before sitting.

The next person to stand was in the audience. It was the man Kyla had seen with Fleet the first night at the shelter house. She remembered him because he was older than the others were. "My name is Frye. I was a captain in the army. My units were assigned to the evacuation project. I had seen the devastation of the cities and when my superiors ordered the evacuation of civilians to the centers up north, I had no reason to doubt that there was an invasion force coming. I just had no idea where it would be coming from. It wasn't until I saw a top-secret report that my superior left on his desk that I knew what they were expecting. To this day I don't know whether to believe the report or not, but I do believe that it was left in plain view on purpose and I was meant to read it. It gave the source of the attack and it was from no place on earth. The attack had come from space craft orbiting the earth." He looked to those seated with him. "I'm no deserter, my superiors deserted me. When I left the base, there was no one left who outranked me. It was beyond my authority to do so, but I did what I knew was right. I told every man left on that base to get out of there. Then I left, too. Tom here," he indicated the young man next to him.

138

"He came with me and eventually we ended up here like the rest of you. And that is my story."

At the mention of the attack coming from a source beyond the Earth, the room was alive with talking and a few shouted comments of disbelief. A man near the door rose and made his way slowly to the center of the room. He looked at Frye and said, "I believe you because I saw them." The whole room erupted in hoots and laughter at the man's words. Sadie's voice, calm and even, cut through the raucous commotion. "Quiet. Let the man speak." Immediately, the crowd was silent and the skinny, man with ragged, dirty clothes looked to Sadie and said, "Thank you, ma'am." Then he looked around at the others and said, "My name is Orin. I've never been here before, but I would like to tell you what I saw. I come from a place far to the north and I saw the creatures landing in the woods. They came from the sky in strange looking space ships. The only way I can describe them to you is to say they looked like giant birds, like a ring necked pheasant." There was an outburst of laughter, but it did not last long as Sadie glared unforgivingly at the offending parties. "Laugh if you like but it's true," Orin said. His voice sounded a little hurt. "The ships were huge with a small oval part at the front with a point at one end, like the head of a bird. The back of the craft was a larger oval connected to the front with a slender neck. It was brown in the back and the front part was a shimmering green and there was a red band on the neck separating the two colors. That's why I said it reminded me of a pheasant." There was no laughter. Everyone was listening, wanting to hear what he would say next. "Then I saw these things getting out of the space ships. Strange looking things with blocky shapes, like crystals. They looked like giants carved from ice only they were moving and glowing." He looked around one more time before he said, "I have been telling everyone that I meet my story. Most people think I'm crazy, but I know what I saw. Believe me or not, I know what I saw." Then as an afterthought he ended like the rest, "And that is my story."

It was not the usual procedure but Fleet asked the man a question. "You said that you have been telling your story to everyone that you meet. Tell me where they are. Have you found many places like our settlement?"

139

Orin looked at the man dressed in black standing before the fire; he could not make out his face at all. Still he looked at Fleet and said, "Not many, but I have found some. There are some places that are like armed fortresses and they won't let you in, not alive anyway. There is a big settlement in the ruins of a city to the west of here and I have been to others."

Sadie cut him off and said, "Thank you, Orin." Then in a larger voice said, "Is there anyone else who would like to speak tonight?" When no one spoke up, she stood and said, "Then we will move on to other business." She motioned to Kyla now. Kyla stood and began to carry her candle with her but Justin took it and set it on her chair. Empty handed she walked before the others to stand beside Sadie. As the two women stood facing one another, there was not a sound from those gathered in the room. This was what they had come to see, Sadie and Kyla together. Very quietly, so only Kyla could hear, Sadie said, "Turn and face them." As Kyla turned slowly to face those assembled, Sadie said, "All meet Kyla, member of the Guard." When she spoke those words the rest of the Guard rose from their chairs to stand with her. "Kyla do you swear to protect and serve humanity?" she asked.

"Yes, I do," Kyla answered. When she spoke her words seemed as if they came from somewhere far away. The only thing that Kyla could hear besides Sadie's voice was the sound of her heart pounding in her ears. Her mind was a million miles away, she was still thinking about what Frye and Orin had said. Their stories seemed to confirm each other's but both were just too much to believe. She had come to the Gathering hoping to learn something of the truth of what had happened, but all she had heard were wild tales about creatures from outer space. There had been little said that Kyla would call the truth. The words that Sadie had said earlier came to mind, something about the truth being the last thing anyone wanted to hear. Well, after tonight she would have to add to that and say that is was the last thing anyone wanted to believe. Vaguely, Kyla was aware of the ceremony that was continuing despite her wandering thoughts.

To the crowd Sadie was saying, "There is no rank in the Guard. Each member is equal to each other and to you. I am giving Kyla this white bead to symbolize the fact that she has not been tested. Once Kyla has proven herself to be worthy of the trust that has been placed with her then we will replace the white bead with black. Every time a member of the Guard performs beyond the call of duty, he or she earns a bead." Sadie threaded the white bead onto the end of the lacing on her tunic and tied a knot in the end to keep it from falling off.

Kyla stood quite still. Once Sadie had tied the bead in place and returned to her seat, the members of the Guard standing behind Kyla began clapping. Before long the room was filled with applause and cheers. When the noise quieted, Sadie ended the Gathering. "Is there anyone else with business for the Gathering?" Sadie surveyed those seated in the room carefully. Once she was satisfied that no one was going to answer, she said, "Then this Gathering is ended and all may depart." As Sadie rose to leave everyone in the audience stood and watched silently as she left the room again followed by Kurt and Fleet. Once they had disappeared out of sight down the hallway, everyone began making their way to the front door. The rest of the Guard continued to stand at attention until the last person was gone.

Without a word the Guard began to put everything back the way it had been before the Gathering. The chairs were returned to the library and the wooden panels that closed off the great room from the foyer were replaced. Before anyone could leave, Fleet and Kurt returned to the foyer with Sadie and announced that there was to be a meeting for everyone immediately.

Kyla followed the group as they went to the dining room. She took her place with the others on the benches at the table. She was almost a full member now and she fingered the white bead absently. After Sadie and Fleet had taken their places at the ends of the table, it was Fleet who took charge. "We are missing two of our members and Sadie and I are worried that something may have happened since they have not returned before the Gathering as they were told." He looked at everyone who was seated at the table as he said, "I know that all of you will want to go with me to look for them, but we can't leave the farm and the Settlement unguarded either." Kyla could see the anxious looks on the faces of the young men and Riley, too, wondering who Fleet would choose. Looking at James he said, "I need you here, James." It was hard to tell from his reaction whether he was disappointed or relieved. "Kurt I think you should go. If we end up back at Spring's farm, your knowledge of the place will be helpful. Rod and Peach, we'll give you a break this time you can stay here." Their expressions left no doubt in anyone's mind that they were relieved to be staying at home.

Fleet looked at the rest of the people sitting there before naming the last two. "Justin, I know you are a good rider, so I want you with me, too." Then he looked at Kyla, "I have a feeling your knowledge of the area around Spring's farm would be helpful. Kyla goes, too. With me that makes four, which is all we can take and still have two horses for Dylan and Eddie to ride." Fleet was doing his best to be positive about returning with both men alive, but nearly four days had passed since they left. Plenty of time for Spring and his men to have killed them and if they had been lucky enough to be captured alive like Kyla had, Fleet was sure Spring would waste no time before shipping them off.

There was no immediate response to his choices. Everyone, except Sadie of course, was staring at Fleet. Kyla had been initiated only a few minutes earlier. Usually an initiate's duties would be limited to the farm for awhile before being chosen to for more dangerous assignments. No one would voice their reservations about Fleet's choice, but words were not needed to make their feelings known. Fleet had expected their reaction and he knew Kurt especially would object to taking a woman after what had happened to Marta, but there was something that was telling him he would need her there. If there was one thing that Fleet was learning it was that he should trust his feelings concerning how Kyla could be of use to him and not spend so much time thinking about why he shouldn't. There would be no discussion and he continued by saying to the three that he had selected, "We leave tonight. Get your things together and meet me at the stables immediately." Fleet rose and walked out of the room without a word. Sadie waited until Fleet was out of sight before she stood and said, "God speed and good luck. I fear you will need both." Then she left the room following Fleet to their quarters at the other side of the house.

There was some murmuring from the Guard members as they began to rise and leave. Kurt gave Kyla a look that could have frozen water and left after Sadie. The others went to Justin and Kyla offering them their best wishes and good luck. Then they left the room leaving Justin and Kyla standing alone in the room. As Kyla looked at Justin she took note of the fact that he had only one black bead on the end of his tunic lacing. "Have you ever been chosen before?" Kyla asked.

Justin shook his head. Then straightening his stance and holding his head high, he said, "But I am ready." He strode confidently from the room and turned down the hallway to the Guards' sleeping quarters. Kyla followed him, the last one to leave the room, and walking with a little more uncertainty. Just as she thought she might be able to look forward to a little quiet monotony in her life, Fleet had thrown her a curve.

As Kyla entered her room and looked around there was not much there to gather. She took the thermal underwear with the blue flowers from the drawer in her nightstand, peeled off her clothes and put them on. As she dressed again, she smiled. No one had told her what she could wear under the black uniform. She put on her rabbit skin coat, picked up her hat and mittens, and left to join the others.

Chapter Six

By the time Kyla reached the stable the horses were saddled and Fleet and Kurt were already there. They were in the middle of a heated argument, but stopped abruptly when they saw Kyla. Kurt turned as she came closer and busied himself by checking the cinches on the saddles. Kyla found Brownie and was happy to see that they had found a saddle for her. She checked the cinches herself, even after Kurt had done it. She wasn't so sure that he might not have loosened hers on purpose, just to be rid of her. Still, she found everything in order. Angry as he was, he was apparently not a spiteful person.

When Justin arrived and immediately mounted a large, gray dappled gelding. Kurt tied the reins of two of the horses around their necks and attached long leads to their halters and handed them to Justin who tied those securely to a metal ring at the back of his saddle. That left the black horse that Fleet had been riding and a bay with a white face and one white sock for Kurt, Kyla had seen him riding the same horse that night after the raid at the farm. When Kurt mounted his horse, Kyla did the same. They were all ready, except Fleet. He was looking in the direction of the cabin. Finally, Sadie appeared out of the darkness, accompanied by Riley and Armand who were carrying several large leather pouches and bags filled with food, water, and other supplies. Armand gave each person one of the saddlebags while Riley was busy filling two burlap bags with oats and corn for the horses. Armand was tying the two extra leather pouches behind the saddles of the rider-less horses when Riley joined him and slung the two bags tied together across the saddle of one of the horses.

It seemed they were ready. Fleet met Sadie's eyes and walked past her into the darkness outside the barn. She followed and once they were out of the range of hearing Fleet stopped and said, "I didn't want anyone else to know where we're going." He had not forgotten about the betrayal of his last plan. Sadie moved in closer so Fleet could whisper, "They knew we would go to the Family to get the horses, so I'll go that direction first. If we don't find them on the way and if the Family hasn't seen them we'll go back to Spring's farm and take a look around there."

"Just be careful Fleet," she looked at him and touched his cheek. "I want you to come back to me alive."

He smiled, wanting to kiss her, but mindful of all the eyes watching them. Instead he took her hand from his cheek and holding it in his, kissed her fingers and said, "Don't worry. I want the same thing."

Sadie watched him walk away and then leap into the saddle. He was certainly something to watch. When Fleet left the barn and galloped down the road and into the darkness, the others followed without a question or comment. They would all follow him even if he led them down the path to certain death. Fleet had confidence and an absolute belief in his ability to perform any miracle. Apparently, it was contagious because every member of his Guard believed it, too. Well, if he could bring those two boys back alive it would be a miracle. When the sound of the horses had faded into the distance, Sadie began to walk back to the cabin. She could hear Riley scurrying to catch up. The girl would be back in her anteroom tonight with Fleet gone again.

Fleet didn't know how he was going to find the two men and the missing truck. There were hundreds of miles of roads between the Settlement and Spring's farm. Tonight they would follow the roads while it was dark, but in the daylight they would have to head for the cover of the woods and countryside. He kept a steady pace trying to keep on the move. Occasionally, Fleet would leave the main road to lead them down what he hoped would be a likely short cut, but every one proved fruitless. It wasn't until it grew light the next morning that he allowed them to rest the horses and themselves.

Fleet left the road and led them across an open field to the shelter of the trees and brush along the fence row. When they reached the fence Justin jumped down and handed the reins of his horse to Kyla. Then he took a pair of leather gloves and wire cutters out of one of the pouches on his saddle and began cutting the fencing and barbed wire at the top. Once he had cut through them all, he took a firm hold on the end of the wire and pulled it back to make an opening between the fences posts. Fleet kicked his horse forward through the opening, followed by Kurt and then Kyla leading the string of three horses and Justin on foot. Fleet dismounted and began to lead his horse toward a grove of walnut trees at the end of the field. The rest followed, leading

146

the horses as they went. Finally, Fleet tied his horse's reins to the fence as his only indication to them that it was the time to stop. After Kyla tied off Brownie's reins, she went to help Justin with the other two horses.

While they sat on the ground and ate a meal of bread and dried meat, nobody spoke. They were all equally aware of the fact that looking for the missing men was like searching for the proverbial needle in a haystack. It would be luck at work if they ever sighted them. The other thing adding to their silence was the fact that they were all exhausted from riding all night, they had all gone one full day without sleep. Given the time they had already traveled, Kyla knew that it would still be a few more hours before they reached the lake where the Family lived.

After they ate, Fleet announced that they could rest for awhile. Then he walked a short distance and after clearing the ground of old walnut shells, sat down, leaned back against the trunk of one of the bare branched black walnut trees and closed his eyes. Each person found a place to sit comfortably and rest. Kyla leaned against the fence. She was exhausted, but she didn't think she could get much rest sitting on the ground. However, as soon as Kyla shut her eyes, she drifted slowly off to sleep. Then all too soon, she was awakened by Fleet kicking her, none too gently, on the bottom of her feet. As she opened her eyes, she heard him saying, "I said its time to wake up!" Kyla opened her eyes and stood. Her back and legs were stiff and her butt sore from riding. She was still a little groggy, too. She walked a short distance from the men to stretch her legs and find a place where she could have a few moments of privacy. When she returned Fleet was standing next to Brownie.

Apparently, he had been waiting for her to return. "I need to talk with you," he said when she came close. Kyla noticed that he had not awakened the others yet. Fleet went to her horse and unfastened the rifle case that was part of the gear that each of them carried. "I know Justin and Kurt can shoot." He looked at her as he slid the rifle out of its case. "Have you ever fired a rifle?" Without waiting for her to answer, he continued, "The rest of us have semi-automatic weapons, but I thought you would be more comfortable with this." He handed her the gun. Kyla knew it was the type of rifle used for deer hunting complete with a scope. She had used one just like it when she used to go hunting with her father.

Fleet was still explaining the gun to her and Kyla waited patiently for him to finish. "This rifle can't fire as many rounds as the others, but it'll get the job done." He reached into one of the saddlebags and pulled out a handful of ammunition and showed Kyla how to load the shells into the gun and then pulled the bolt back and handed it to Kyla.

She took the gun and held it to her shoulder. It would have been a little more comfortable for her if the stock had been a bit shorter, but it was good enough. She closed one eye and checked out the scope. At the far end of the walnut grove she spotted a squirrel in one of the trees. "You see that squirrel over there?" Kyla pointed to where it was sitting. Fleet looked in the direction that she pointed. Then Kyla stepped away from the horses, lifted the gun to her shoulder, sighted on the squirrel and fired. As it jumped and fell to the ground, she said. "It's a little much for a squirrel, but it'll get the job done," then lowered the gun and ejected the spent round.

Kurt and Justin were awake now. Kurt lost no time in coming over to Kyla and saying, "Are you crazy? If there is anyone around, they know where we are now." Kyla ignored Kurt's comment and unloaded the rest of the shells from the rifle and dropped them in her pocket. When she put the rifle back in the case, she saw Fleet with his hand over his mouth trying to keep from laughing. Kurt just shook his head and walked away.

"Well, that's one less thing I have to worry about," Fleet said with an amused grin, watching Kurt walk away muttering something under his breath. "But there are two other things," he turned his attention back to Kyla. "We need to get you ready for working at night, and that white and gray rabbit skin just won't work." He could see she was bristling already and added quickly, "I'm not saying you can't wear it, just put this on over it." He tossed a small black bundle to Kyla. "Riley said you could use this." Kyla unrolled it and saw that it was Riley's black hooded cape, the same one she had worn that first night when she took Kyla to the farm. She rolled it up into a small bundle again and stuffed it into the one of the leather pouches. "And your boots, too." He pulled a small tin filled with black boot polish from his pocket and tossed it to her. "We have a few minutes before we leave, so you'd better get working on it." She was staring at him with a hurt look and he knew she liked the boots the way they were. "If it makes you feel any better, I had to do mine, too," Fleet said. Kyla looked at his boots, she hadn't noticed before but they were very similar to hers, only his were black. It seemed the Family was full of little boot-making elves. Then with a quick smile, he added, "Or if you prefer, I have some mittens."

Kyla watched Fleet as he walked away. A few hours of sleep and he was back to his good-natured self, joking and acting like they were on a campout not a race against time. "Everyone come over here, we need to talk," he said as he motioned to Kurt and Justin. Kyla brought her can of bootblack and sat on the ground next to Fleet. With one boot on and one boot off, she began rubbing the greasy black goo onto the leather with the only thing she had to do the job, her fingers. When the other two joined them Fleet said, "I didn't say anything about my plans to anyone. I didn't want a repeat of what happened last time." He looked at Kurt who nodded appreciatively. Both men agreed on one thing. Someone had told Cole Spring that they were planning a raid on his farm. "Sadie told everyone that Dylan and Eddie were to go to the Family first and that is where we'll go, too. If we don't find them there or on the way, maybe one of the Brothers or Sisters might have seen something. They have a lot of eyes and ears roaming around the country."

Kurt was watching Fleet. He knew him as well as anyone could. They had been friends before anyone ever thought of forming the Guard. Kurt had watched Fleet's back and pulled him out of the proverbial fire more than once and Fleet had done the same for him. If there was anyone that he would trust with his life it was Fleet. No matter how tight the situation, they had always managed to pull it off without anyone getting hurt until last time. He knew where Fleet was going. No one had to tell him least of all Fleet. "Then where do we go, Fleet?" Kurt said, not as a question, but as a challenge.

"We'll go back to Spring's farm. It's the only place to look," Fleet answered. He looked only at Kurt as he spoke. The other two might as well not have been there.

"You can't be thinking about going back inside?" Kurt argued. He spoke with a controlled tone, not letting the heat that you could see in his dark brown eyes and by the set of his square jaw, enter into his words. He was a dark smoldering contrast to Fleet's casual manner. "There is no way that I'll go along with that," he stated flatly.

Fleet looked at his friend. He liked Kurt because as usual he was the voice of caution and as usual he agreed with him. He had never intended to go back into the compound. He grinned as he thought about his plan. It was so simple that it had to work. "We don't go in, we wait for them to come out," he looked at Kurt and when he saw that stony face of his start to soften he went on. "They have to come out sometime and I have a feeling our friend Kyla here knows where they go and what they do better than they do."

Kyla had been busy with her boots and listening to what Fleet was saying, but it wasn't until she heard her name mentioned that she looked up at the two men standing above her. They were both staring at her. Fleet smiling with that self-satisfied look he always had and Kurt examining her with such a burning stare that Kyla was surprised she didn't see steam pouring out of his nostrils. Justin was looking at her, too, but he just shrugged and sat down cross-legged on the ground across from Kyla like he was settling in for a long discussion.

Kurt was interested though and he turned back to Fleet and said, "Tell, me what you had in mind." He stood in as casual a manner as Kyla had ever seen Kurt take, feet set slightly apart and arms crossed against his chest.

"We'll have to hope they're still at the farm," Fleet began. "If they are then we'll find a place to hijack their vehicle when they bring them out."

"That's if they're there and if they decide to send them to," Kurt paused and looked at the two on the ground before continuing in a hushed voice, "to Manjohnah." Saying the name obviously made him uncomfortable. "They might just shoot them right there at the compound."

"I know," Fleet answered, "there's a lot we have to find out before we decide what we will do, if we can do anything at all."

Kurt nodded satisfied for the moment. Their immediate plans would be to go to the Family's camp. That suited him fine. Fleet was right about the fact that if there was anything to be seen they would probably know about it. The Brothers and Sisters had gathered a rather large flock of sheep that they split up into many small flocks, each tended by a pair of Family members and their dogs. It seemed like they were everywhere if they wanted you to see them and nowhere if they didn't. He had another reason to want to talk to them, maybe he could find out something about Kyla, too. He knew Fleet well enough to sniff out a little white lie when he told one. In Kurt's opinion, it was best to know about all the weaknesses of the people whom you entrust with your life.

Fleet looked at Kyla who was putting on the second of her boots. She had darkened them but they weren't black. The polish by itself was not enough to make them a nice smooth color, but they certainly would not stand out in the dark anymore. As she stood, she handed the tin with the polish back to Fleet and said, "I need to wipe off my hands," and showed him her hands, the fingers now blacker than the boots were.

He took hold of her wrist and before she realized what he intended to do, Fleet wiped Kyla's greasy fingers on her own face. She became instantly angry with Fleet for playing such a childish prank. When Justin laughed she pounced on him, where he was still sitting on the ground and managed to smear some grease on his face before he jumped up and pushed her away. Kyla whirled around with her hands up, threatening to do the same to Fleet who was laughing, too. Fleet opened up the polish and dabbed some onto his finger and used it to make a black streak under each eye and said, "I think we all need some war paint."

When Fleet held the polish out to Kurt, he shook his head and said firmly, "I think it's time to be on our way." He turned still shaking his head, walked to his horse and began to untie the lead. All the time wondering why he continued to follow Fleet. He seemed to be nothing more than someone out for a few laughs and a good time, it was a good thing that Kurt knew the truth about the man behind the smiling face. Fleet wanted people to see him as a simple, friendly guy. People liked Fleet when he made them smile. They trusted him and liked to do little favors for him. He always said it was best to hit some one on their blind side and there were a lot of people who underestimated what Fleet was capable of doing.

Justin did not wipe the grease off his face, so Kyla left hers alone. She did try to wipe some of the black on her hands onto the ground, but not much came off that way. As she untied Brownie's reins and climbed into the saddle, Fleet jumped into the saddle and looked at Kyla and laughed again. She frowned back at him and began trying to wipe some more of the black shoe polish off on the blanket under the saddle. They had to wait for Justin to untie the extra horses and fasten their leads to the back of his saddle. Once Justin was astride his big dappled gray, Fleet started to lead them off at a slow walk through the walnut grove. When they reached the far side, Kyla saw the squirrel she had shot lying on the ground and shook her head. It was a waste to leave it, but she doubted Fleet would allow any fires for cooking or the time it would take either. And Kyla wasn't hungry enough to eat raw squirrel, not anymore. Just as they had all passed by the furry little mound, she stopped Brownie suddenly and jumped down to retrieve the dead squirrel. She quickly stuffed it in her pouch and once she was back in the saddle kicked Brownie to a trot and caught up to the others. They didn't say anything about her going back for the squirrel. Everybody understood why she couldn't leave it.

They traveled more slowly now. The roads in this area were set up in a neat grid-work of gravel roads running north to south and east to west, intersecting at every mile. It was hard to get lost if you knew where you were going. As they rode across the fields, they had to stop two or more times in every mile to cut the wires dividing the mile squares into a patchwork of fields. Some fields were pastures, others were filled with the rubbish from the last harvest, but most of them were just a tangle of weeds where no soil had been tilled in over a year. As they rode, the empty fields made Kyla think about how they seemed as lonesome and empty as the towns. It had been hundreds of years since the earth had lain quiet this long without the buzz of humans and machines digging and planting their crops in her fertile soil. Kyla had to smile at herself. She was beginning to think like Sister Samethia.

Every time they came to the next fence a different person took a turn cutting the wires. Fleet and Kurt had taken their turns, so when they came to the third fence when Justin started to dismount, Kyla jumped down first and said, "Let me use your gloves and wire cutters." Justin handed them to her without a word. They waited for her to cut through the wires. It was just her luck, she thought, to have gotten this particular piece of fence. It appeared the farmer had repaired an old fence by stringing new fencing on the same poles without removing the old wire. That meant she had not one, but two layers to cut through. It took her a little longer than it had the others, but Kyla was determined to convince them that she was up to doing anything they did. When she started to pull the fence back one of the pieces almost got away from her. Justin jumped down to help, but she had already firmed up her grip and pulled the wire out of the way. Seeing that his assistance wasn't needed Justin took Brownie's reins and led her through with his horse and the other two on the leads. After Fleet and Kurt rode through the opening that she had made Kyla let go of the wire and it sprang away from her and snapped back into place. Kyla pushed her way through the opening to the other side. Once she was back in the saddle she rode next to Justin and gave him back the leather gloves and wire cutters. "Thanks," was all she said.

Kurt and Fleet were riding together discussing their plans. So Kyla brought her horse next to Justin's and said, "How long have you been in the Guard."

"We've all been with Fleet since the beginning," he answered. "Marta was the first person we ever lost."

"What about the order when we walked into the Gathering? I thought that is was ranking in the order of seniority," Kyla asked.

"Well, in a way it was. Since we all were initiated together the ranking was in order by age," Justin explained. "At least it was."

Kyla looked at Justin. He was a pleasant looking young man with long chestnut brown hair that bushed out in an unruly mane. His eyes were about the same color as his hair and his darkly tanned skin didn't hide the freckles that covered his face but the grease that was still on his face almost did. Kyla was beginning to feel a little more at ease with her companions and the horseplay with the boot polish had done a lot to break the ice. She looked at him now and asked a question that had been on her mind since last night, "Had you heard those stories about the invasion coming from...." She paused and looked at him searching for a word that was better than the one that came to mind, "You know from outer space."

"I heard Captain Frye before. He tells the same story at every Gathering." Kyla watched him. He was speaking casually enough and seemed quite at ease as he swayed with the motion of the horse he was riding. "But that other guy, I'd never seen him before."

"So do you believe what they said?" Kyla asked. Captain Frye seemed to be a credible person. The other man, well, she wasn't too sure about him.

Justin laughed, "I believe that they believe it. But I would have to see those pheasant shaped space ships and ice giants myself before I could believe something like that."

They rode for a few hours cutting fences, crossing roads, and looking for any trace of their friends or the vehicle they had been driving. It hadn't been long before they came to a fence that had already been cut and then another. After that they began to look for the places that had been cut. It was obvious that someone had been through the area quite recently. It didn't take an expert tracker either to tell by the tracks and droppings left behind that it had been someone from the Family who had been there with their sheep. They began following the trail of openings. Moving at a faster pace now that they didn't have to stop and cut through each fence. They were anxious to catch up with whoever was making the trail. It wasn't long before Fleet sighted them with the binoculars. Two riders and a dozen sheep almost a mile away at that time but it wouldn't take long for the four Guards on horseback to close in on the shepherds with their flock. Before they overtook them Fleet slowed to a stop and said, "We can be pretty certain that it's the Family's sheep and the Brothers and Sisters up ahead, but before we all go charging in there let me go alone. They know me."

There was no argument, even from Kurt. They waited patiently as Fleet galloped across the field and over the hill into the next valley to the spot where they had seen the sheep only minutes earlier. While they waited Kurt was riding his bay gelding back and forth, letting the horse pace out his concern. Finally, Fleet reappeared at the top of the hill and motioned for them to join him. Once they were at the crest of the hill, he pointed to the stream winding its way off into the distance and the strip of trees surrounding it. "It took me awhile to find them. They heard us coming and were heading into cover with the sheep. I probably wouldn't have caught up with them if they hadn't recognized me. They would have left the sheep and kept riding. They're waiting for us now." Fleet kicked the black horse's flank and took off again with his little band of followers right at his heels.

They saw the man dressed in brown homespun and wearing a sheepskin vest waiting for them once they reached the stream. He was sitting astride a black and white pinto. It wasn't a big horse and his feet came close to touching the ground. There was no saddle on the horse, only a blanket like the Family had put on Brownie when they gave her to Kyla. The long legged Brother was holding a rifle across the horse's back and he greeted Fleet as he approached. "Hello, Brother Fleet." When he saw Kyla he looked a little surprised but added, "It is good to see you Sister Kyla."

Kyla looked at the man. He was not one of those who had been present during her short stay with the family, but he could have very easily been one of the riders who returned in the morning just before she and Fleet had left. Everyone must have noticed the new face, it was only logical that he could know her name, but she didn't know him.

Kurt was a little disappointed when the Brother greeted Kyla by name. He knew her, but when Kyla didn't answer the greeting, his suspicions crept back.

Fleet was not worried about formalities. He was after information. "Brother Treblki, we're looking for two of the Guard. We think they may have been heading to your camp."

Brother Treblki was not a man given to quick responses. He stroked his long bushy beard as he considered his answer. Kyla thought he had been spending too much time with the sheep. He was beginning to look a little woolly, just like them. Finally, he asked, "Little, tan colored pick-up?" Fleet nodded. Brother Treblki turned and looked over his shoulder at the woman who was with him. She was busy with the dogs trying to gather the sheep that had been driven into the trees. Satisfied that all was well behind him, he turned back to Fleet. As he took off his hat and wiped his brow with his sleeve, he said, "We saw it yesterday toward nightfall. The pick-up was heading north in the direction of where you live, Brother Fleet." He spat on the ground for emphasis, "Cole's men caught them. We heard the shooting and went to see what was up. Got there just in time to see them put two men dressed in black like you all into the back of their truck. Threw 'em in there like sacks of 'taters. I don't know if they were dead or hurt." He

155

looked at the four and finished his story. "Anyway, me and Sister Treblki went down there after they were gone. It looked like they had shot out the tires. After that the truck had gone out of control and it rolled over in the ditch. If they came out of that alive, they were lucky, but you can bet they were busted up pretty good."

Fleet was as grim faced as Kurt when he asked, "Where's the truck."

Brother Treblki pointed and said, "On a gravel road that runs north to south about two miles from here, due east."

Fleet, Kurt and Justin took off immediately. Before leaving Kyla reached into her saddlebag and took out the squirrel. She tossed it to Brother Treblki and said, "Maybe you can use this." Then with just a nudge from her knees Brownie galloped after the other horses. Kyla could hear Brother Treblki shout after her, "If we don't eat it the dogs will."

Once they reached the road Brother Treblki was talking about, it took them a few minutes to find the pick-up. Justin spotted it at the bottom of a deep ravine. It was too steep for the horses, so Fleet and Kurt climbed down the bank leaving Kyla and Justin on the roadway with the horses. They looked around inside the cab of the pick-up for a few minutes before climbing back up to the road.

Before the two men were able to get back on their horses, Justin asked, "Can you tell what happened?"

Kurt answered, "It looks like they did shoot out the tires like the Brother said. There were some bullet holes in the back of the cab, too. It's impossible to tell if they're still alive, but there's blood all over the dash and seat."

They all looked to Fleet waiting for some word from him. "We'll be able to get to Spring's' farm tonight," he said. His voice was surprisingly calm and unemotional. "I'm hoping Kyla knows someplace nearby where we can hide the horses. Then tomorrow we'll see what we can see." He looked at Kyla now. The grim smile that crossed her face was Kyla's answer to his question. "You have a place in mind?"

"I think I know something that might work for what you need." She tried to contain her excitement as she told them about her parent's farm. "I know a place that has a barn for the horses. It's close, only a mile away from Spring's place. Still, it'll be safe there since Cole's men never go to the other farms in the area anymore. Not since everything of value was taken out of them." She looked at Kurt and Fleet and added, "As long as they're not looking for us."

They all knew what she meant. Fleet considered it for a moment and said, "Cole knows our limitations. All of our news travels on horseback. Even if someone had ridden as fast as they could to tell us about Dylan and Eddie, they couldn't have arrived before we left," Justin, Kurt, and Kyla all nodded in agreement with his statement. "They won't be expecting us to get there by tonight. We'll be settled in before they start looking."

Kurt added, "Getting in is always the easiest part, it's getting out that worries me."

Fleet smiled and replied, "That's why I keep you around"

~ ~ ~

It had taken Fleet and Kyla almost two days to travel from Springs farm to the Settlement. By cutting out the extra time they had spent travelling south before going to the Family's camp, they were able to reach the farm in a much shorter time. Once they were close, Fleet let Kyla lead the group. They wound their way up hills and down valleys, always keeping close to the cover of the woods. Some of the paths she used were hardly more than rabbit trails, but once Kyla took over as guide they never saw a building. When they had to cross the roads she took them to places where there was good cover on both sides. So far it seemed that Fleet had been right in his hunch about Kyla. Anyone who had spent a year hiding in the woods had to know them like the back of their hand.

Finally, she brought them to a long farm lane that ran through the woods for almost a quarter mile. When they came out into a clearing at the top of the hill, it was finally possible to see the dark shadows of the house and outbuildings. "The barn's this way," Kyla said, pointing out the way in the dark. She led them the short distance before stopping and jumping down off her horse. She started to push open the barn door, but before she got it all the way open Kurt was there, helping move the heavy door. Only when they were all inside and had the door shut, did Fleet take out his lantern and light it.

157

Kurt looked around and nodded approvingly. "It's far enough away from the road that no one can see up here if they drive by."

"If you look out the window in the loft, you can see the road for a mile in either direction, further, with your binoculars," Kyla said.

"I think we can stay here without any problems for tonight at least," Fleet said. He started to loosen the cinches on his horse's saddle and he said to Justin and Kyla, "Let's take these off and give these guys a rest," speaking of the horses.

Kyla was in high spirits. She was home! Rubbing her horse on the nose she said, "I wish I had a carrot for you Brownie."

Fleet laughed and said, "You gave your horse a name?"

As she pulled off the saddle and laid it on the ground, Kyla said, "You're the one who called her Brownie."

"I called it Brownie, because it's brown," Fleet was teasing her. Even though he was tired Fleet still had the energy to joke with them.

Kyla decided to ignore his attempt to get a rise out of her and said, "I'll just have to name all of them."

"Well, you do what you want but I'll bet Riley has named them all by now. You can fight it out with her," Fleet said. "Now let's find some place for the horses."

"There aren't stables, but there is a stock pen over here," Kyla led Brownie to the gate and swung it open.

When Justin was done taking the saddle of the gray horse he'd been riding, he led it to the pen. As he walked past Kyla, he said, "Well, I've already got a name for this one. I like to call him Pain in the Ass or just shorten that to Bung Ho'." Kurt liked that and laughed. It was the first time Kyla had heard him actually laugh out loud. The closest Kurt ever came to laughter was a smirk or smile, never anything you could hear.

With a little help from Kyla, they were able to locate a bucket. Then just a few paces from the back entrance of the barn was an old hand pump. It had to be primed and it took a little elbow grease, but they finally got the water flowing. Kyla was grateful for the fact that her parents had always tried to keep this old pump in working order. This wasn't the first time in the last year that she had come here for water. It took awhile with only one bucket and six horses, but they were all finally able to drink their fill. While Kurt and Fleet had been helping Kyla with the pump, Justin had been up in the loft and found some hay. It was old, but it was dry. Justin pushed it down just as the other three came back inside. With four of them working together it was only a few minutes before the horse were watered and busy pulling at the bales of hay.

Finally, they could sit down. Fleet sent Justin back into the loft and had him push down four more bales of hay to use as seats. They ate a little of the food they had brought with them, but everyone was too tired to care about eating. Between bites of food Fleet was saying, "We'll take turns at watch tonight. Each person takes two hours watching outside. Everything seems to be going smoothly enough but I don't want to take any chances." He stood and began to walk outside. "I'll take the first watch. Kurt next, then Justin, Kyla you go last." As he paused at the door, he added, "You'd better get some sleep."

He didn't have to tell them twice. They hurried to find blankets in their bulging saddlebags. There was no thick down sleeping bag like the one Fleet had let Kyla use. Still a good heavy blanket was better than nothing. Kyla found a place that would be out of the draft from the door and lay down. It was cold and the floor was hard, but she had slept in worse places. Exhaustion was the key. Once your body was tired enough, sleep was not a problem. She woke up when Fleet came in to wake Kurt, then again when Kurt woke Justin, each one taking his turn at watch. Finally, it was Kyla's turn and Justin was shaking her. "It's your turn. Wake up." Kyla got to her feet quickly and pulled on the black cloak Riley had sent for her. When she pulled the hood up, Justin handed her the rifle he was carrying. "Just do me a favor, don't shoot your foot off," he said as he stumbled back to his blanket. Kyla smiled, that was the same thing Kurt said to Justin when he gave him the rifle.

When Kyla stepped outside of the barn she could tell that everything was covered with heavy dew. Not frost but dew, for the last few days the temperature had moderated a little. If it continued, then spring would not be far behind. As she walked in the darkness, she thought about what it had been like growing up here as a child. When you lived on a farm your life was tied to the seasons and spring had always been her favorite time of year. A philosopher would say it was a time of renewal and rebirth. Kyla had just appreciated the pure pleasure of the warm winds and the vibrant colors after a long winter of browns and gray. This year the winter had been especially long and harsh. Despite the less frigid temperatures, the endless cover of clouds still showed no signs of breaking up.

When the sky began glowing with a soft light in the east. Kyla checked the time. She still had another hour before it was time to wake the others. In a few minutes it was as light as it would get that morning. The clouds looked dark and churned with the promise of rain. When it started to sprinkle, Kyla decided to go inside. She opened the door quietly and tiptoed past the sleeping men. Very carefully, she looked in Fleet's saddlebag and found the binoculars. Then she climbed the ladder to the loft and went to the window and pushed it open. The dust flew and the hinges squeaked, but the old shutter opened easily enough. Then Kyla sat on the floor and propping her elbows on the window frame began to watch the road coming from Spring's farm. Even though she couldn't see the farm itself, there was only one way to leave and that route went right past this farm. She had not been there very long when she saw the dust cloud that signaled a vehicle was coming down the gravel road. She ran to the edge of the loft and shouted, "Someone's leaving the farm."

From below, she heard Kurt's voice. "What are you doing up there?" She could also hear them scrambling below to gather their gear.

"When it got light I came up here so I could watch the road," Kyla shouted back. She still had her eyes on the truck coming down the road.

"We can't get down to the road in time," Fleet said from below.

When she saw the truck stop and someone jump out to open the gate at the end of the lane, Kyla left the window and looked down at the three men, "Don't worry about that. They're getting ready to come up the lane."

Fleet's mind was racing. They only had a few seconds and he had to decide what to do. Quickly, he gave orders. "Kyla do you have that rifle with the scope?" He didn't wait for her to answer. "You stay up there in the loft. You're a good shot, use it if you have to." He started for the back door to the barn. "There's no time to try to move the horses. Let's just hope they stay quiet." Moving quickly the three men grabbed their weapons and ran out the door. Once they were outside, they had just enough time to disappear into the woods before the truck pulled into the circular drive of the farmyard.

From her vantage point in the loft Kyla could see the entire scene below. She stayed back from the window opening far enough so she couldn't be seen. Still, she kept a wary eye on the pick-up as it made a slow circle around the drive. For a moment it looked like they would just keep going, but the truck stopped and two men carrying rifles got out. Her hands were shaking so hard that Kyla was afraid she wouldn't be able to steady the gun if she had to, but once the men were outside and walking around, she kept one of them in the rifle sight all the time. It seemed like an eternity while the men walked the circle and looked at the buildings. It appeared they were ready to get in their truck, when one of the horses kicked the wall of the barn. Cursing the stupid animal, Kyla was certain the others hiding in the woods were, too. When the men walked to the barn and began to open the door, Kurt had to do something. He charged out of the woods roaring like a mad man. "Drop your weapon and get your hands up." Before they could raise their guns, Justin came running from the other side of the barn with a knife in his hand and plunged it into the ribs of the man closest to him. As he cried out and fell, the other man immediately dropped his gun and raised his hands.

Kyla dropped her rifle and flew down the ladder and out the door just in time to see Kurt standing with his foot on the man's back and the barrel of the rifle pressed to the back of his head. "Don't shoot him," she said frantically searching for the handcuffs in her pocket. By the time she managed to pull them out Fleet was there. He took them from Kyla and used them to bind the man's hands behind his back. It was then that Kyla realized who they had captured. It was Clovis. She was staring at him, her mouth hanging open like she had been stunned. Fleet was busy telling everybody what to do. "Kyla find somewhere to hide that truck." He turned and said, "Justin." It wasn't until he looked at the young man, that he realized that Justin was still standing over the body of the man he had just killed, staring at the knife in his hand. "Listen," Fleet spoke a little more firmly, "Justin, it was him or Kurt. You did what you had to." Finally, Justin's eyes met Fleet's as he said; "I need you to keep your head right now." Justin stooped and wiped the blade on the dead man's coat, then put it back in the sheath. Fleet had his attention and he continued with his orders. "Go down to the road and make sure the gate is closed. I don't want anyone to drive by and know they came in but never went out." Justin sprinted off in the direction of the gate. While Kurt kept the gun on their prisoner, Fleet began dragging the dead man into the woods. Kyla was looking for the keys to the truck but when she didn't find them in the ignition, she came back to search the men's pockets for the keys and started with the dead man first. Fleet waited while she emptied his pockets on the ground, but when she didn't find the keys Kyla knew that Clovis must have them. She picked up the items that she had thrown on the ground, a small leather pouch, a pocketknife and some pieces of paper that looked like trash and dumped it all into the pack of the pick-up. She didn't want to leave anything lying around.

Then she walked to Kurt and began searching through Clovis' pockets. It took him a moment, but finally a look of shock crossed Clovis' face. He almost said something, but decided it would be better if he kept quiet. As she pulled the keys from his jacket pocket, Kyla could tell that Clovis was frightened out of his wits. She smiled to herself as she walked away with the keys in her hand. She hoped he was pissing in his pants. It only took her a few minutes to put the truck in the garage and return to the barn. Fleet had finished his distasteful task and returned at the same time. They waited outside until Justin came back, panting from running all the way.

Once they were all standing together, Kurt removed the gun and kicked Clovis. "Get up and remember, I'm just looking for an excuse to shoot you." Slowly, Clovis stumbled to his feet and Fleet began pushing him toward the door. Kyla opened it and they went in.

Fleet held out his hand to Kyla and said, "Give me the key for the cuffs." She handed it to him, wondering what Fleet had in mind. "Keep the gun on him," he said to Kurt and shoved Clovis toward one of the huge wooden beams that formed the framework of the barn. With Kurt right beside him, rifle ready, Fleet unlocked one of the cuffs and said, "I want you to wrap your arms around this beam and kiss it for me." Clovis was frightened enough to take him literally and kissed the rough wood while Fleet snapped the cuff back on his wrist. Now that he was securely locked in place, Kurt lowered the gun and both he and Fleet backed away. Then the four went back outside, leaving Clovis alone inside the barn. The first thing Fleet said was, "Kyla get back up in that window and watch the road."

"Wait," she said urgently, "I know that man."

Fleet looked at her, trying to decide if he was surprised by her announcement or not. "Where did you leave the binoculars?" he asked suddenly.

"They're up by the window in the loft with my rifle," she answered. Why was he asking about the binoculars, when she had just told him that she knew their prisoner?

"Justin, you get up there and keep your eyes open." Justin jumped to do what he was told but not without a certain amount of disappointment at being sent to keep watch. He wanted to hear what Kyla had to say. Fleet looked at Kyla next and asked, "Who is he?"

"That's Clovis Spring, Cole Spring's oldest son," Kyla answered. She watched the look that passed between Fleet and Kurt. When they smiled at each other, she knew that Clovis' status had just changed from prisoner to possible hostage.

"What about the other one," Kurt asked, "did you know him?" Kyla shook her head. Kurt looked from her to Fleet and back again to Kyla. "Do you think old man Spring will want to make a deal to get his son back?"

It was Kyla's turn to smile. "You can bet on that," she said. "I can tell you that Clovis is scared shitless. It won't take much to make him think you're going to kill him and he would sell out his own brother if he thought it would save his skin. Just let me talk to him for a few minutes and I'll have him ready to tell you anything."

Fleet wondered what Kyla had in mind, but he was beginning to trust her judgement and had a feeling that whatever it was, he was going to like it. "Okay, but what do you want us to do?" Fleet asked.

"I think you'll get the idea quick enough," Kyla said and turned to go back into the barn. When they were back inside, she picked up the lantern and handed it to Kurt so he could light it. After it was burning they walked to Clovis and stood for a few minutes looking at him in the dim light. Fleet was waiting for Kyla to say something, but she just stared at the man. Glared at him, would have been a more accurate description. The man she called Clovis was trying to watch all three of them at once, but Fleet and Kurt had moved to stand close behind him and finally he was just watching Kyla.

"Aren't you going to say hello to an old friend?" Kyla asked sarcastically. When he didn't answer, Fleet cuffed him on the ear and said, "Answer the lady."

"What are you doing back here?" Clovis asked.

This time Kurt hit him from the other side saying, "Try something polite."

It was an effort for him, but Clovis managed to squeeze the words, "Hello, Kyla, it's nice to see you," through his clenched teeth.

Justin walked to the edge of the loft to see what was going on, but Fleet motioned him back to the window then smacked Clovis on the head and said, "That's better." He wasn't sure where Kyla was going with this, but so far she was doing all right.

"What's the matter Clovis? Don't you like my friends?" Kyla said with mock concern.

"Just tell them not to hurt me," Clovis pleaded with her now. His voice sounded as if he were about to cry. All he got for his request was another smack on the head from Kurt.

The feeling of this kind of power was new to Kyla, but she knew how to use her advantage with Clovis. She got as close as she could and whispered so only Clovis could hear, "Do you think they would like to hear about how you treated me when I was your prisoner?" She stepped back and watched his reaction. His eyes were wide with fear and he looked at Kyla, pleading desperately for her silence with his eyes. Her question had gotten the desired response. She decided it was time to let Clovis know what she wanted. "We're looking for some friends of ours. You can't miss them. They're dressed in black tunics just like us." Kyla stripped off the cloak and rabbit skin coat so he could see what she was wearing. She thought she saw a look of recognition cross his face, but he kept silent. It would take a little more persuasion for him to talk. Kurt was ready to hit him again, but Kyla held up her hand for him to hold off and she moved closer to Clovis again, but this time she made sure that Kurt and Fleet were able to hear. "I know you've seen them. I could tell by the look that you gave me when I asked. You had better tell me or I'll have to tell them."

164

Finally, Clovis seemed to find some spark of courage and said, "I don't know anything."

He had called her bluff and it was time for Kyla to let Clovis know that she was serious. She was the one who was holding the cards and the deck was stacked against Clovis this time. She looked at Clovis and then to Fleet and Kurt. It wasn't something she wanted to say but finally she looked at Clovis and stepped back. She wanted to be out of the way. "What do you think these two would think about rape?" The words had hardly left her mouth when both Fleet and Kurt began to pummel Clovis with their fists and he dropped to his knees from the beating. Next thing she knew, Kyla was behind Kurt and Fleet pulling at them and shouting for them to stop.

Once they heard her the two men stopped and stood back. Kyla looked up at them. She had counted on their spontaneous reaction, but just didn't want them to beat him too badly. Even Clovis didn't deserve that. She bent down and asked Clovis again, "Did you see our friends?" Clovis looked at her with his one good eye. The other was beginning to swell shut from a blow that had landed on the side of his face and he was bleeding from a cut on his lip. He gave her a hateful look but didn't answer. Just a little more persuasion, Kyla looked up at Fleet and he kicked him savagely. "I don't want to let them work on you again," Kyla said and turned her back. When she heard another kick make contact, and then another, it was all that Kyla could do to keep herself from begging them to stop. One more kick and Clovis began to wail, "Okay, I saw them. They're at the farm. Just make them stop!"

Immediately, Kurt and Fleet stopped. Kyla knelt beside Clovis who had sunk all the way to the floor. The only thing holding him up was the fact that he was handcuffed to the post. "Are you going to tell us everything?" Clovis nodded meekly. He was beaten physically and emotionally. Kyla looked up at Fleet and said, "Do you want to ask him some questions?"

Fleet grinned grimly and said, "You're doing just fine." He regarded the big man on the floor with disgust. If Kyla hadn't stopped him he would have still been pounding on that big pile of shit. He wished he could think of something worse to call him but there weren't any words to describe how he felt about the man. The thought of that huge man forcing himself on the tiny woman who was standing with them brought out a rage from deep inside that had been hard to rein in. Still, she had handled the man like a pro and she had used them with the same expert delicacy. He had no doubt that Kyla would get Clovis to tell them everything they needed to know. She was already busy asking him a string of questions and with an occasional nudge from him or Kurt the questioning proceeded with Clovis' full cooperation.

"There were two of them. Are they both still alive?" Kyla asked. Clovis nodded. "Are they hurt?"

Clovis was suddenly defensive. "We didn't do anything to them. They were hurt when their truck crashed," he answered in a voice that was almost a whimper.

"Don't lie to us. We saw the truck. Somebody shot it full of holes," Kurt said and delivered a kick for emphasis.

"Nobody shot them. One of them has a broken arm and the other one just has cuts and bruises," he cringed when he said that, waiting for another blow from his captors.

"Then they're still at the farm?" Kyla asked.

"Yes," Clovis answered, and offered some further information. "They're going to send them up north later today."

"What else can you tell us?" Kyla asked, hoping that he might have decided to be cooperative.

Clovis looked up at her and craned his neck to look at Fleet and Kurt standing over him and said, "Screw you all. You'll be joining your friends soon enough. When we don't come back, Pop will send someone out looking for us."

Kurt had had enough. He picked up his rifle and used the butt to hit Clovis over the head. That blow was hard enough to knock him into unconsciousness. Fleet looked at the man slumped in a heap on the floor and said, "Why did you do that?"

"I was tired of listening to that piece of scum," Kurt said as he began to walk away. "You can ask him some more questions when he wakes up."

Justin had walked back to the edge of the loft and was looking down at them. Fleet looked up at him again and said, "Get back to the window. We're coming up there." Then to Kurt and Kyla, he said, "We need to decide what we're going to do next." One by one they climbed the ladder to the loft and went to sit next to Justin who was back to watching the road through the binoculars.

Fleet studied their faces before saying, "We have two options. Either we try a hostage exchange or an ambush on the truck that brings them out."

"I don't know about a hostage exchange," Kurt said. "I can't imagine anyone wanting him back. Besides once we come out in the open to make a deal we've lost what small advantage we might have by catching them unprepared. If they're planning on moving them today, they won't be expecting any trouble from us if they still think we left the Settlement last night." Kurt paused for just a moment and said, "I think an ambush is our best chance."

"What do you think, Kyla?" Fleet asked her next.

It was the first time that he had asked her opinion. She gave the options some more thought before she said, "I have to agree with Kurt. I don't think we'll gain anything by trying to make a deal with Cole. If he's sending them up north then that means that Manjohnah knows he has prisoners to send. I don't think Cole will be willing to make him angry by loosing two more prisoners. He would find some way to break the deal if we tried to exchange prisoners."

"Justin, what about you," Fleet asked.

Justin lowered the binoculars long enough to say, "We can make a road block and try to ambush them, but we still have to get away hauling two injured men."

Kurt answered his concerns, "I've been giving that some thought." He lowered his voice just in case Clovis had regained consciousness and was listening to what they were discussing. "First we block the road. A small tree across the road will force them to stop. When they get out to move it, that's when we jump them. We'll use the pick-up that these two were driving to get away."

"Then they'll just track us down like they did Eddie and Dylan and we're right back where we started," Justin had become very negative concerning everything.

"You didn't let me finish," Kurt said. "We can disable their vehicle and leave it blocking the road, too. That ought to slow them down long enough so we can dump the pick-up in some ditch where they won't see it. Then we switch to the horses and ride across country while they're busy searching the roads for the pick-up."

There were no objections from Justin this time. Fleet clapped Kurt on the back and said, "I knew you would come up with a plan to get us out of here with our skins still intact."

It was Kyla who asked, "What are we going to do with Clovis?"

"We could shoot him," Kurt suggested. "That would be the easiest thing."

"It might seem easy, but that would make us just like them," Justin snapped suddenly. They all looked at him. It was very much out of character for the easy-going young man to react that way.

Fleet tried to reassure him by saying, "I have never killed anyone unless it was in self defense or in the defense of another. It's not something that any of us would do without reason." He looked around the circle and said, "We'll leave him here tied to the post and put a note in the pick-up to let them know where he is." Fleet smiled at Kurt and added, "They'll find him in plenty of time, unless Kurt hides the truck too well." Then as he stood and began to walk to the ladder, Fleet said, "I have some more questions for our friend Clovis. I just hope you didn't hit him too hard." He was still talking as he climbed down the ladder. "Justin, you stay on watch. Kurt, we need to get these horses saddled and ready to go. I don't want to be caught unprepared again. Get Kyla to help. Then the two of you need to find a spot for the ambush and a place to hide the horses and ditch the truck." When his feet hit the floor with a thump, he shouted, "Get moving. No telling how much time we have to get ready."

Kurt and Kyla worked as quickly as possible. Kyla carrying buckets of water for the horses and Kurt putting on the saddles and packing all the gear on them. Soon they were ready to go. When Kyla began to walk out the door with the half full bucket of water to empty it outside, Fleet stopped her and said, "Bring it here." When she handed it to Fleet, he immediately dumped the contents on Clovis' head ending his blissful incoherence. As Clovis sputtered and shook his head from shock at the rude awakening, his eyes widened with horror when he saw Kyla and Kurt leaving and realized that Fleet was staying with him. Apparently, Fleet had seen the look on Clovis' face, too. As they closed the door and stepped outside Kyla heard him say, "You want her to stay? You'll be praying for her to come back if you don't answer my questions."

Kurt let Kyla lead the way. She seemed to know this area extremely well. They followed a footpath that went across a field and past a small pond before leading into the woods behind the house. It wound around through the woods and finally came to a point where the path followed the road. In this part of the country the ground was quite rocky and the limestone that formed the backbone of the hills showed through where the soil was thin. Kyla took Kurt to a spot where they had cut into the side of the hill when they built the road, forming a sheer rock wall that rose nearly fifty feet over the roadbed below. Standing at the top of that cliff looking down, Kyla was telling Kurt why she had brought him to this spot. She pointed toward the direction they had come from saying, "The road goes past the farm and it runs straight as an arrow until you get to that S-curve right there. When you're driving down the road you can't see what's around the corner from either direction because of the hill being cut like it is and the trees on the other side. But Spring's men aren't worried about running into anybody on the road and usually don't slow down at all when they go around the curve. They won't see something in the road until they're right on top of it."

Kurt was very satisfied with her choice. The cliff provided a good advantage for them. One man with a rifle could keep a dozen men pinned down from up here. "You seem to know a lot about the area," he said.

"I ought to," she said. "I grew up on that farm we're staying at. I used to come here all the time to look for fossils in the rock." Kyla looked at Kurt. He was busy studying the road, his brows knotted thoughtfully. Even though he was dark and brooding, Kyla was beginning to appreciate this serious man as a friend and ally.

Kurt was looking for a path down to the road. When he started to work his way down the steep incline, Kyla followed him saying, "I want to tell you something." Kurt didn't stop, but kept climbing down, holding on to the roots and trunks of the scraggly trees and bushes attempting to grow on the bank, as he went. Kyla scrambled after him, occasionally slipping on the loose stones, but all the while talking and trying to get out what it was she wanted to tell him. "Fleet told me not to tell anyone, but I know I can trust you and I don't want to lie to you," she said breathlessly as she descended the steep hill. Kurt had reached the bottom and was waiting for her to join him. As Kyla jogged down the last few steps, she managed to spit out the words. "I'm not one of the Family."

Kurt gave her an appreciative smile. It was better that she had decided to tell him. "I figured that you weren't" Kurt didn't ask her why she had decided to confess her lie. He was waiting for her to tell the whole story without any prodding from him.

Kyla continued, "Everything else I told you is true, everything that I said in the meeting with Sadie. I thought I could sneak into Spring's farm and steal some food. I never got a foot on the ground inside before they caught me. I escaped when the guard was killed. Fleet brought me out. I went with him and we spent a night with the Family and other than that I have never had anything to do with the Family. But when everybody assumed that I was from the Family, well, Fleet said to let them think that I was." She had been talking a steady stream and suddenly realized that Kurt was staring at her with an amused look on his face.

"Don't worry," he said. "It's best that you told me. Secrets tend to grow until they're too big to keep hidden anymore." He turned his attention back to the job at hand. "Is there a place near here where you can see what's coming on the road?"

Kyla pointed to a huge maple tree at the bend in the road. "There used to be a tree house up there and you can see a good distance in both directions."

"Is that all you did as a child, spy on you neighbors?" Kurt asked with a good-natured laugh.

"There wasn't much else to do." Kyla answered as she shrugged. Her spirits were high, too. There was a part of her, more than just a small part that was exhilarated by having exacted some revenge on Clovis. Besides that, it seemed like there was a very good chance that they would be able to be able to save the missing men.

It seemed that Kurt was thinking about Clovis, too. When out of the blue he said, "You shouldn't have stopped us. When I think of that animal attacking you or any other woman...."

Kyla stopped him and confessed, "What I said wasn't the real truth. Clovis didn't rape me. He tore my clothing and beat me up in the process of trying, but Cole stopped him."

She expected Kurt would be angry about her half-truth, but he shook his head and said, "It doesn't matter." He looked over his shoulder in the direction of the farm. "I hope he gives Fleet plenty of reasons to keep pounding on him," he said and started walking down the road examining the cover on either side. As he walked he motioned to Kyla and said, "Come on. We still have to find a place to dump the pick up and hide the horses."

Kyla followed happily. A few days ago she had been alone in the world, starving and cold. Now, she was with friends, because after what they had been through together, she definitely thought of them as very good friends now. It was a wonderful feeling and she would enjoy it while it lasted. Soon enough it would be time to put everything on the line again. These boys played rough and one false move meant you didn't just loose the game you lost your life or someone else did.

It was about an hour after they left before they returned to the farm and found Fleet waiting for them, standing outside the barn and leaning against the side of the building. He and Kurt spoke at the same time, both saying, "What did you find out?" Then Kurt said, "You first," to Fleet.

"He was pretty cooperative. They're moving them this afternoon. They'll be using a troop transport truck with two guards in the cab and one in the back with the prisoners. That's three of them and four of us, not too bad." He paused for a moment before he finished, "When I started asking about who had tipped them off about our last raid, he wouldn't talk. I got the feeling that he might have know something, but there's someone that scares him more than we do." Fleet took a small scrap of paper out of his pocket and showed it to Kyla, "Does this mean anything to you?"

She looked at it and saw the words 'North by Northwest Road' scrawled on the crumbled piece of paper. "No," she said, "it doesn't ring any bells." She gave it to Kurt and he read what was written and then returned it to Fleet.

"He seemed pretty upset when I found it in his pocket, but he wouldn't say what it meant." Fleet looked at Kurt and said, "He's resting now, but we can wake him up with another bucket of water if you want to ask him some more questions." Kyla wasn't sure if he meant it or was joking. She wanted Clovis to get the beating that he deserved, but she was afraid that Fleet had already gone too far.

Kurt shook his head. "Leave him alone, we have enough to do if we're going to finish what we came here for," he said and began to fill Fleet in on what he and Kyla had been doing. "We found the perfect place," Kurt began.

Fleet stopped him by saying, "We need to get Justin down here." and went to the front of the barn and called for Justin. In the time it took for Fleet to walk back to where Kurt and Kyla were standing, Justin had raced down out of the loft and was rushing out the door with the binoculars hanging from the strap looped around his neck and the rifle strapped to his back. He was relieved to finally be given a break from watching the empty road.

They moved away from the barn and came to stand around the pump. Fleet started by saying, "They won't be bringing them out for awhile, and we can get by without anyone watching the road for a few minutes. We need to decide exactly what we're going to do. We can't leave any detail to chance."

With everyone there Kurt began to tell what he had in mind. "Just a little way from here Kyla showed me the perfect spot, a blind curve where we can block the road and they'll never see it until it's too late. There's a high rock ledge on one side. We can put a man up there." Then grinning at Kyla he said, "And there's a tree house right there at the corner that we can use to watch the road. So with snipers above them on both sides of the road, we should be able to keep them pinned down. The third man will be in the ditch. He'll be right there when they stop the truck. The fourth will be with the pick-up and the horses. We can hide them in a grove of trees near the top of a hill a little over a mile from here. If you're standing in the right spot, you'll be able to see the man at the top of the hill. We'll signal when they're coming. That should allow enough time to drive the truck back here to pick us up."

No one said anything for a few minutes. Everyone was thinking over what Kurt had laid out for them. Examining every detail and trying to anticipate any problems that might arise. Finally, Fleet said, "I only wish it was going to be dark. The light will help in one way. It's impossible to get a good shot at night without a night scope. But it'll make it easier for them to spot the pick-up after we dump it and us, too."

"Well, I can't help that," Kurt said. "I didn't choose the time." He turned to Fleet. "I'll take the place on the road." It was his plan and he would choose the most dangerous spot as his own.

"Then I'll take the spot at the top of the bank," Fleet said firmly.

Then both he and Kurt looked at Justin, but before he had a chance to speak, Kyla blurted out, "I'll take the look-out in the tree." All three men gave her a look that Kyla would have to call reserved approval, but no one tried to talk her out of it.

Justin looked most concerned of all when he said, "Then I guess I'll be watching the horses."

They spent the rest of that morning getting ready. Kurt took the pick-up out of the garage and cautiously drove to the end of the lane. This was the riskiest part of all, getting the truck to the spot where they had decided to stash it. If he met anyone on the road, it would be all over, but there hadn't been any traffic in or out of Spring's farm all morning since Clovis and the other man had left. Justin and Kyla left with the horses. Kyla riding Brownie and Justin with his gray horse that he had called Bung Ho' among other things the night before. Each of them had two other horses in tow now. Fleet was left at the farm to clean up and try to get any more information that Clovis might be willing to divulge.

Once it became clear to Clovis that they were moving out and planned to leave him behind he began to get desperate. Fleet had found some rope and was in the process of tying Clovis' wrists together with it so he could remove the handcuffs and return them to Kyla. He smiled when he thought about Kyla and the handcuffs. She had gotten a lot of use out of the things.

Clovis saw him smiling and figured that he meant to kill him. Tears started pouring down his face, "I'm sorry. Tell her I didn't mean it." He collapsed to his knees and began pleading, "Don't kill me. I won't tell anybody you were here. I'll stay here until dark."

Fleet looked at the man groveling in front of him. He was a big man, bigger than Fleet, and had a bushy beard and his black hair was a mess, short in places and long in others. He looked like he was half-crazy, wearing ill-fitting clothes and he acted like it, too. Fleet had taken a big leather bag full of pearls out of his pockets and wondered how long he had been using them. It was obvious that the man could get all he wanted and more. The bag he had was enough to keep the whole Settlement going for a day or more. He also wondered if Cole knew that his son had them or what they were doing to him. Using the pearls was no excuse for what he had done to Kyla, but it was one explanation of why it had happened. As much as Clovis disgusted Fleet, he also felt sorry for him. Fleet picked up his rifle by the strap and slung it over his shoulder. When he picked up the saddlebag that held the extra rounds of ammunition and began walking to the door, he didn't even look at Clovis as he said, "Don't worry. I'm not going to shoot you." As he stepped outside and began to follow the foot path that Kyla had shown him, Fleet could hear Clovis bellowing at the top of his lungs, "Don't leave me," over and over again until finally he was too far away to hear him anymore.

Chapter Seven

By noon they were all in place. When Kyla had climbed up into the tree, she found that most of the planks that made the tree house had rotted away, but there was a good spot for her to perch in the crook between the branches. There had been some discussion about whether she needed the binoculars or Justin. When Kyla finally got Fleet to climb up the tree and take a look for himself, he agreed that she didn't need them. She wouldn't be able to see something coming down the road any sooner with them, than she could without. The next problem had been something to use to block the road. They didn't have an axe to chop down a tree, so they had to find a piece of dead wood that was big enough to do the job. Finally, they found a large, partially rotted tree trunk. It was too heavy for them to carry, so they had to use the truck to move it. Fortunately, there was a rope in the back of the truck that they could use to pull the log out of the woods and drag it to the place for their ambush. They were taking a chance by blocking the road before they spotted the truck coming, but it was a gamble they were going to have to take. After the tree was across the road, Justin left with the truck. All they could do now was wait.

Finally, late in the afternoon Kyla saw the truck. There had been no dust cloud as it came up the road, the sprinkle of rain they'd had that morning had settled the dust so there had been no advance warning. Kyla stood and bracing herself against a large branch, she waved to Fleet. When he saw her signal, Fleet stood and waved his arms for a few moments. He couldn't see Justin and he prayed that the young man was watching and hadn't looked away at the wrong moment. Kyla was busy getting her rifle set in position in the tree. From his vantage point, Fleet could see Kurt lying in the ditch. He had seen the signal, too. This was the worst part. Planning and getting ready were important, but until the deed was done anything was possible.

Fleet lay on his belly looking at the road below. Before long he heard the truck coming up the road and could tell by the sound that it was the troop truck they had been waiting for and not another pick-up truck. Just as they had hoped, it came barreling around the turn at top speed. The driver was barely able to keep the truck under control as it skidded to a stop. They sat with the truck idling for a moment before the man on the passenger side jumped out. Fleet could see that he was carrying a rifle and was ready to use it. He kept the man in his sight, waiting for Kurt to make his move.

Kyla saw the man get out, but when he walked in front of the truck to look at the tree she lost sight of him. Her view was of the back of the vehicle. She watched through the scope, waiting for the guard to come out the back. Out of the corner of her eye, she could see Kurt moving cautiously, crawling through the weeds and up the side of the ditch.

Kurt couldn't see where the man was standing, but he knew only one had gotten out of the truck and had heard his footsteps as he went to look at the tree blocking the road. He needed to get to the driver first, to stop him from backing down the road. Then with all the courage he could muster, Kurt leapt up out of the ditch yelping and howling like a coyote. He jumped up on the running board on the passenger side of the truck and pointed his rifle through the window at the driver. "Don't move," he growled. When the man in front of the truck raised his gun and took aim on Kurt, Fleet rose to his feet, howling like a madman, too. The man standing in the road hesitated for only a split second distracted by Fleet's sudden appearance, but that was too long. One shot from Fleet and he fell in a heap on the ground. It was then that Justin appeared around the corner driving the pick up. It seemed that he didn't even wait for the truck to stop completely before he had the door open and was getting out. He had his rifle trained on the driver of the truck, too.

Kyla wasn't sure whether it was the gunfire or the sound of the other vehicle arriving that got the guard in the back to leave his place inside with the prisoners, but she saw him slip out and start to move in on Kurt from the side. She had him in her sight. Kyla squeezed the trigger and a split second later the guard fell as the bullet found its mark. Kyla felt a knot in her stomach and she fought the urge to vomit. She had shot a man and that was a long way from popping squirrels off the branch of a walnut tree. When she saw Fleet scrambling down the rocky slope, she put her mind back on the task at hand and began to climb down the tree as quickly as possible.

By the time she reached the truck, Fleet was helping Eddie and Dylan out of the truck and Justin was busy slashing the tires with his knife. When he saw the confused daze on Kyla's face, he knew what was wrong without asking. Before this morning, he had never killed a man either. He had talked about it, trained to do it, but it was something that he never wanted to do. He gave her a nudge in the direction of the truck and said, "It'll be okay. Just get in the truck." Then he went back to work on the tires. By the time Justin had made it around the truck, Eddie and Dylan were in the back of the pickup with Kyla. Fleet and Kurt had taken the driver to the back of the truck and used the handcuffs they had taken off Eddie and Dylan to keep him from going anywhere. Everyone moved as quickly as possible, because once the first shot had been fired, their time was limited. At the best they had five minutes before someone from the farm could be there. Fleet, Kurt, and Justin all jumped across the log at the same time and ran to the pick-up. Justin jumped in and started up the engine. As they pulled away and rounded the turn Kyla saw another troop truck stop just behind the first and men began streaming out of it. As they began to push the tree and the truck out of the way, she started pounding on the window of the cab yelling, "Faster, Justin, they're right behind us."

They traveled the next mile in seconds as the little truck sped down the road at top speed. Justin slammed on the brakes, skidding to a stop, when they reached the spot where the horses were hidden. Kurt and Fleet were yelling, "Go, go," but they didn't have to. Everyone was out of the truck in a heartbeat and running into the woods at the side of the road. Justin got out of the truck and began pushing it toward the other side of the road. Fleet and Kurt hurried to help and soon it was rolling down into the steep ditch and over the edge of the steam bank below. They were still running through the woods when they heard the truck roar by on the road behind them. When it kept going, they all gave a collective sigh of relief, but they knew that it could turn around and come back at any time.

When they emerged from the woods and began to scramble into their saddles, the horses seemed to sense the urgency of the people on their backs. When she climbed up on Brownie, the horse pranced impatiently. Fleet brought his horse close to hers and said, "You're the guide. Get us out of here without being seen."

Kyla wasn't exactly ready to be in charge of this part of the plan. She told Fleet the first thing that came to her mind, "That road leads south toward Springwood. If we go straight west back toward the farm, they should be miles away before they figure out that the truck's not in front of them anymore." She looked at him and added quickly, "It's the same way we came in last night."

"Sounds good to me. Let's get going," he said and slapped Brownie on the rump. The mare took off with Kyla and Fleet followed right behind her. Next were Dylan and Eddie, Kyla just didn't know which one was which. There had been no time for introductions. Justin and Kurt with their rifles still slung over their shoulders were bringing up the rear. Kyla put all of her concentration into the task at hand. She tried to keep them under cover as much as possible. They followed winding trails through the woods and kept close to the fence rows. Twice they heard the telltale rumble of troop trucks out looking for them. Once they had hidden in a wooded slough. The second time they were able to disappear out of sight over the rise of a hill, playing a deadly game of hide and seek.

Kyla's route had been direct enough, but they were not making very good time. Fleet was glad when it began to grow dark. He had been watching Kyla and could tell as they left Spring's farm further behind she was hesitating more and more often about where to lead them next. He finally called them to a halt in a narrow valley as far from any road as was possible. They could rest for a few minutes and he wanted to use the time to talk to Eddie and Dylan. Fleet had not dismounted, so everyone else stayed astride their horses and brought them in as close as possible to hear what Fleet had to say. "We should be able to stay here for a few minutes. Dylan, tell us what happened."

"We were on our way home," answered the man riding the bay mare. Dylan was a thin young man with a slight build and silky black hair and looked to be of oriental parentage, having light brown skin and almond shaped brown eyes. "We'd been driving around for a couple of days and hadn't seen a sign of anyone, not even one of the Brothers or Sisters with their sheep." He looked at Kyla who was wearing her rabbit skin coat when he spoke of the Family and wondered if she was one of the Sisters.

The other man, the one with the broken arm, had to be Eddie. His hair was a dark blond and it stuck out in disarray. He took up the story when Dylan paused. "They came up behind us and started shooting. We really didn't expect any trouble since we were west of the highway."

"I think they were waiting for us, sitting at an intersection with their lights off," Dylan added. "Because one minute we were alone and after we passed the corner they were right on our tail."

"You can be sure they'll go past the highway looking for us, too," Justin said watching nervously in the direction from which they had just come.

It was Kurt who said gruffly, "We haven't gotten there yet. We can worry about how far they'll follow after we get past it."

"But we do have to cross it if we're going get home," Fleet said. "The question is where." He was scratching his chin and thinking out loud, "The woods start to thin north of here. I don't want to go that way. Straight west we run into the town and there are too many roads that way. The only other choice is south, but we have to cross the river. Thanks to this thaw we've been having the ice won't hold the horses anymore and they'll be watching all the main roads and the bridges." From Fleet's commentary, it sounded like they were hemmed in especially if Cole Spring decided to mount an organized search.

"Do you think we should split up?" Kurt asked. That had worked for them last time.

Fleet was against the idea, "I want everybody together. Then we don't have to worry about someone else turning up missing." He was thinking. Trying to remember everything he had ever seen or heard about the surrounding countryside. "There is one bridge over the river they might miss. Especially if they still think we're in the truck." It was a place one of the Brothers had told him about. Fleet thought he knew where it was and hoped he could find it in the dark. "There's an old covered bridge about three miles south of here. It's sitting a few hundred yards from the new bridge they put in beside it. If we can get the horses across without any sound, I think we can cross the river there."

"Those guys have night vision goggles and infra red sensors," Eddie said. "Dylan and I saw them unloading the stuff from trucks when they were moving us out."

"It seems old man Spring has a good supplier," Kurt said.

The mention of the night vision goggles gave Fleet an idea. "Maybe I've been going at this from the wrong direction. We need to change the way we think," Fleet said. He was grinning now. Sometimes an idea would just seem so right that he just had to smile and he began to tell the others what he had in mind. "They have a lot of territory to cover. If they try what they usually do, they'll post a few men at key positions. I'll bet there won't be more than four in any location." He paused for a minute before finishing, letting them think about what he had said. "They're expecting us to be on the run, but what if we're not running? What if we take the offensive and attack them?"

Even though it was quite dark and hard to see, it was still possible to see the look of concern on Kurt's face and hear it in his voice. "You want to shoot your way back to the Settlement with them following us every step of the way?"

"I don't think it will come to that," Fleet said. There was however that little nagging doubt in the back of his mind. That was why he liked Kurt. He always gave a voice to the nagging doubt. Sometimes Fleet needed to hear the voice of reason. No matter how often he ignored it. "We'll wait and see what the situation is when we get there," he said, hoping it would satisfy Kurt.

Kurt wheeled his horse around and circled around the others until he came to Fleet. "I need to talk to you," he said and rode a few paces away from the others. Fleet followed him and brought his horse as close as possible to Kurt's mount. "Do you have any idea what you're proposing?" Kurt was incredulous. His understanding of their plan had been to rescue Dylan and Eddie and return everybody in one piece. "If what Eddie said is true, we'll be lucky if we get across the bridge without being seen let alone attack their position." Kurt's horse seemed to sense his rider's agitation and he pranced nervously as Kurt struggled to hold him in one place.

"I realize the risk, but either way, it's going to be a gamble. If they have night vision or infra-red scopes, we could be just as dead running away," Fleet answered. "Besides," he smiled now as he told Kurt his real reason, "if Cole has that kind of equipment, then we will just have to take it away from him, won't we?"

Kurt rolled his eyes and said, "I can't believe the way your mind works." He had to admit that Fleet had a point. His mind had been focused on one thing, getting home. Fleet was ready to conquer the world or at least his portion of it and drag Kurt with him all the way. What could he do? An argument between Fleet and himself at this time would not accomplish anything. "Let's just say I'll reserve judgement until we find out what is waiting for us."

"That's good enough for me." Then turning to the others Fleet said, "We'd better get moving." As he rode to lead the way, Kyla was relieved that she was no longer the guide and happily fell into line behind the others.

They rode a little more slowly than before. Eddie's news about the night vision equipment had everybody concerned. They were all nervous, especially since it seemed that Fleet was having difficulty finding the landmarks he was looking for in the dark. Twice they had to turn around and go back the way they had come. Eventually Fleet found what he had been searching for, an old stone barn. He turned and led them down the lane that ran past it. Behind the barn the rutted old lane went down a steep hill and ended at the bank of the river.

When they reached the river and there was no covered bridge, Kyla wondered if Fleet had taken another wrong turn in the dark, which was fine with her. She hoped that they were nowhere near the bridge and whoever might be waiting for them. The ambush and their close escape had been enough for her. She'd had something to keep her mind occupied while she was busy leading the way through the woods and sloughs west of Spring's farm, but once Fleet had taken over that job, all Kyla could think about was the man lying in the road, the one that she had shot. She didn't think she could make herself pull the trigger with a man in her sight again, not ever.

It was only the second night of the new moon and the darkness that surrounded them was complete. Besides, not even a full moon would show as more than a faint glow through the clouds. They huddled close together and it was difficult to see much of their surroundings. The trees crowded close to the road and the woods surrounding them were only a deeper shade of darkness. Fleet looked at each person, no one's face was visible, but he did not need to see them to guess what each had on his or her mind. Justin and Kyla both were thinking about the fact that they had killed somebody today and had no stomach to do it again. The two who had just escaped were

181

worried that they would end up right back where they had been. Then there was Kurt and he was thinking what he always did. He just wanted to get home with everybody in one piece. Still, Fleet knew that they would put body and soul on the line if he asked them and he would not ask them if he thought they would be able to get home any other way. He was certain that Cole Spring would not stop his men at the highway this time. Three prisoners snatched away from him in little more than a week should be reason enough for him to pursue them all the way back to the Settlement. Manjohnah was a man with no patience or mercy, with a man like that to answer to Cole would surely do anything that he could to stop them and Fleet planned to resist where he could. Fight and flight; that was his plan. Guerilla tactics were their best bet.

"I know you're all tired, but we're almost to the bridge," Fleet said in a hushed voice. "I can't tell you exactly what is waiting for us, but we can't run forever. If they have infra red scopes, there's a very good chance that they will spot us, but even with the scopes they have to be looking in the right place at the right time." He paused expecting someone to say something, but even Kurt remained silent. Fleet continued, "I want to use the horses as decoys. One of us leading the string of horses across the covered bridge would certainly give them something to look at."

Kurt couldn't remain silent anymore, "Don't you mean something to shoot at? It sounds risky to me."

"I never said it wouldn't be," Fleet answered. To the others he said, "I wouldn't ask any of you to risk your lives if I could see any other way. But if one rider leading five horses will be seen then what makes you think that six riders won't?" He waited, but the only answer he received was silence. "Are you with me then?" It was an uncomfortable coincidence when they all answered him by saying, "To the death."

The dubious honor of leading the horses across the bridge fell to Kyla. She had been the logical choice. The plan was to try to jump the men and overpower them. Even Eddie with his broken arm would be more help than she would be. The only task for which she was suited was the target. As Kyla waited in the darkness by the river, the others were on foot creeping through the woods on both sides of the river. Justin and Fleet had been the ones to make the precarious crossing to the other side. They had all heard the creaking and moaning sounds as the ice strained under their weight. Miraculously, they got across without being plunged into the ice-cold water. All Kyla could do was hope that when she made her move, she would time it right. If she went too soon and they weren't ready, it would be a disaster. If she waited too long they might be discovered before she arrived. 'Wait ten minutes,' Fleet had said, but how was she supposed to tell when ten minutes had passed when sitting alone in the darkness every second seemed to be an eternity.

Sister Samethia came to mind, her warning about Fleet and her prophecies for his destiny. She found herself wishing that she really did have a psychic connection with Fleet as Sister Samethia had implied. Perhaps then she would know exactly when he wanted her to make her move. The best that she could do was to use her own judgment and that told her it was time to go. Slowly, she started to make her way through the timber. There was no trail and she let Brownie pick the way around the trees and underbrush. Kyla made sure that she did not stray too far from the river. At one point the lead of one of the horses trailing behind had become tangled and Kyla had to get down and free them all. She rode lying close to Brownie's neck her face buried in her shaggy mane. Kurt had wanted all the horses to look like they were without riders. Just one more thing to keep them watching the decoy, every extra moment of indecision would be to their advantage.

When the string of horses left the cover of the trees behind them, Kyla felt as if someone was watching her every move. She kept the horses walking slowly in single file along the bank of the river, but not too close to the edge. The muffled sound of the water flowing far below told her that it would be a long way down if the bank gave way under the horses' weight. Looking upstream, it was impossible to see how far it was to the covered bridge and in the darkness her eyes played tricks on her. She would think that there was something ahead of her only to find nothing when she got there. Finally one of the shadows didn't disappear and the form of the old wooden bridge materialized out of the darkness.

She stopped the horses at the entry to the bridge and listened. There was nothing to be heard other than the horses breathing and occasionally stomping impatiently. Nothing had happened so far and that was what had her heart running wild. There was no point in delaying, she thought, and nudged Brownie forward. There was a step up onto the bridge and Brownie balked at going forward onto the wood decking, as did each horse in the line. The first thing that hit Kyla was the smell of decay and rotting wood. The planks were groaning under the weight of the horses and she had to keep urging Brownie on. Each step forward was becoming a battle of will between Kyla and the mare. She had been worried about someone using her for target practice now all she was worried about was whether of not she would make it to the other side. She thought it was all over when she heard the sharp crack of wood breaking and the horses squealing in terror behind her. The lead rope stayed firmly tied to Brownie's saddle, but all forward motion had stopped as the other five horses tried to back out of the bridge.

As Kyla struggled with the horses all hell was breaking loose on the outside, too. The air came alive with the sound of coyote howling and she knew that Fleet and the others had made their move. She was kicking the mule-stubborn mare trying to get her to move. When the gunfire started the mare gave a start and sprang forward dragging the others with her. Finally, the line was moving again and when a spray of bullets tore through the wooden bridge even the most stubborn of the horses was running. In seconds they were out the other side galloping through an open field. Kyla could hear the shouting ahead of her and kept riding in the direction of the voices, plowing right through the center of the ruckus with all six horses. She didn't see the others on the bridge until she flew by them. The next thing she knew two of Cole's men were running up the embankment on the other side of the road with their rifles raised and ready to fire. Kyla couldn't have stopped the horses from running directly into them even if she had wanted to do it. Brownie was at the head of a stampede and at this point Kyla was just along for the ride. The men fired as they saw the horses descending upon them, but it was too late for them to get out of the way. They fell and were trampled under the frightened beasts.

Kyla struggled to get Brownie under control and finally had her headed down the middle of the road. Gradually, she brought her from an all out gallop to a gentle trot and finally to a stop with the other horses following the mare's lead. Once the horses were under control, she heard the howling and shouting coming from behind her, this time mixed with an occasional victory cry. She recognized the voices and heard them call her name, shouting for her to come back.

Fleet was exhilarated. His plan had worked and the final and deciding factor in their favor had been Kyla and the horses trampling the two men who had come running up out of nowhere. He and Justin had crawled on their bellies through the weeds and tall grasses along the river until they were under the bridge. It had been nothing short of a miracle that they managed to get that close without being seen whether Cole's men had any night vision equipment or not. Once they were in place, they sat tight waiting for Kyla and the horses. Above their heads they had heard the footsteps of the men walking on the bridge. Two were walking directly above their heads and two more were at the other side. All was quiet and Fleet was wondering how close Kurt and the others had managed to get. When Kyla made her entrance, it was evident by the actions of the men overhead. All four sets of footsteps went to one side of the bridge and they heard their hushed whispers as they discussed what to think of the approaching horses. It wasn't until she actually went into the bridge and they heard the disturbance caused by the horses that they opened fire. At the sound of the gunfire everyone sprang to action. Fleet and Justin charged up the bank behind the men on their side of the bridge and were on top of them before they realized what was happening.

Fleet had his arm wrapped around the throat of the man he had taken and was trying to choke the breath out of him. All the while, the man was flailing wildly and firing his gun in every direction until Fleet forced him to the ground. Once the man was down and lying on top of his gun, Fleet had the advantage. He still had one arm around the mans neck bending him backwards until he heard the man gasping for air. When he stopped struggling Fleet let go. Not caring whether he was dead or unconscious, Fleet rolled him over and grabbed his gun. As he took it and looked up Fleet saw Justin struggling with the other man. They both had their hands on the man's weapon and Justin was loosing the battle. Fleet came up behind them and using the rifle in his hands like a club, hit the second man's skull with a resounding thud.

Fleet and Justin had just enough time to look to the other end of the bridge to see if Kurt and the others needed help before they heard the stampede of horses thundering toward them. When they turned to look, they saw the two men coming up the bank with their guns pointed directly at them. The shot came just as the horses flew across the road and over the men. As the horses headed up the road, Kurt and the others came running across the bridge, yelping and howling and shouting at Kyla. Once she reappeared out of the darkness with all six horses in tow it was time to get back to the business at hand.

There was no time for celebration and Fleet reminded them of that when he said, "Let's gather these men and see if anybody is still breathing." That brought everybody back to a somber silence and they scattered. Each one grabbing one of the motionless men, and dragging them into the woods. Kyla looked at each face, relieved that she did not know any of them but none were still alive. They had done their job with deadly efficiency. She had killed two of them herself. It didn't matter to her if it was planned or not. They were just as dead as if she had pulled the trigger. Three men in one day, eight men killed in all and Clovis abandoned to starve to death in the barn if nobody found him. They had racked up quite a tally in the last twenty-four hours.

Once the bodies were stashed out of sight of the road, Fleet turned his attention to the trucks parked at each end of the bridge blocking the road. He began rummaging through the cab of the closest one and found a flashlight under the seat, using that the rest of his search went quickly. They looked through both trucks and to Fleet's disappointment; found no night vision gear at all. What they did find was enough guns and ammunition for twenty men. It was more than the six men guarding the bridge would have needed. Fleet couldn't bring himself to leave it behind and they immediately began loading as much ammunition as possible into their saddlebags and pockets and everybody strapped a second rifle to their packs. Still, the horses were tired and nobody wanted to add too much more to their burden. Most of the cache, they carried to the covered bridge and pushed up under the decking, where it meet the bank. They covered it all with a tarp from the back of one of the trucks, hoping that someday they could come back for it. While the others were busy carrying cases of ammunition, Kyla and Eddie had been posted a little way from each end of the bridge, watching the road in both directions. It was not very long before they were finished hiding their captured booty. Only then did Fleet tell them what he had planned for the next step of their escape.

"We need to put some distance between us and this place," he said in a hushed voice. "The fact that they have so many supplies makes me think that there are more men coming. I only wish we had been able to question one of these men." That was the only regret that Fleet had concerning the men they had killed. "I have a place in mind where we can cross the highway. There's good cover on both sides of the road. I think it'll be our best bet." He paused and looked at all their faces. They were frightened and tired, ready for an end to the nightmare. As he walked to where the horses were tied, Fleet said, "We'll rest when we get to the south branch of the river. It's about a two hour ride from here." They all climbed wearily back onto their horses. Everyone knew that although they had won another battle, it would only fan the fires of revenge. Every victory for them was another reason for Cole Spring to keep sending more men after them. It seemed that it was only a matter of time before one or all of their party would be captured, wounded, or killed. The odds were definitely not in their favor.

So they continued to ride on through the night. Wandering through the fields and stopping to cut fences made for slow going. Occasionally, they would ride on the roads to gain a little time, but only for short distances. When at last they reached the south branch of the river, Fleet would not let them stop to rest until he found a place with enough cover for the six horses. Finally, he found a place that suited him and let them dismount. Before they had finished watering and feeding the horses, it was beginning to grow light in the east. No one spoke, as each found a spot to sit on the ground and as they had done the night before, took turns at watch. Despite the uneasiness that filled their minds, it had not been difficult for any of them to fall asleep.

Kyla's sleep was anything but restful. She was plagued by dreams filled with guns and death. Then she was riding in the darkness and when her horse disappeared, she was running. As she ran, she recognized the path and knew that it led home. Suddenly, she was at her parents' farm. Opening the door to the barn, she began looking for Clovis, calling out his name, but he was nowhere to be found. That was when she heard a voice. At first she could not see who it was. Kyla looked around the inside of the barn but it was becoming dark inside the barn, too dark to see. At the same time the light in the doorway became brighter, like a brilliant summer sun was shining outside. Forgetting about the voice, Kyla went to the door and found Sister Samethia standing in the sunlight waiting for her. "I told you that I would help you when you needed me," Sister Samethia said to Kyla. "But I killed a man today, three men," Kyla was crying, looking at Sister Samethia and the three dead men who had suddenly appeared on the ground next to her as if in evidence of the crimes that Kyla was confessing. "I warned you that Fleet was dangerous to all those around him. Death follows him whereever he goes," Sister Samethia said as she began walking away. "Don't go," Kyla pleaded, "you said that you would help me." Then Sister Samethia was gone, but Kyla could still hear her voice saying, "But I already have."

That was the last thing she remembered before being awakened by Justin. It was her turn for the watch. The young man had no comments to make to her this time before collapsing in a heap on the ground. She picked up the rifle that was lying on the ground beside her and looked up. The sun had climbed as high as it would that day, making it close to noon. Kyla took a little of the dry bread and meat from her pack and chewed it unenthusiastically as she walked around the sleeping men huddled in the underbrush. While they were sleeping Cole's men were still looking for them. It would only be a matter of when and where they encountered them again not if they did. She wondered if any of them would make it back to the Settlement.

When Kyla heard a crackling sound in the brush behind her. She brought her rifle to her shoulder ready to fire as she turned to see who it was. Relieved that it was only Fleet, she lowered the rifle. She could tell by his face that he was worried and wondered if he had slept at all. Kyla wanted to ask him what they were going to do, but judging by the look on his face, she wasn't sure that he knew either.

Fleet walked to where Kyla was standing. She was small, but she had as much courage as any of the men did. If it had been one of Cole's men instead of him, she would have fired without hesitation. He was sure of that. "How are you doing?" he asked.

What a question! Kyla wondered what she could say. She was tired and more frightened than she had ever been in her life. Instead she said, "I was having the strangest dream before Justin woke me. I saw Sister Samethia and when I asked her to help me, she said that she already had. The strange thing is that it was one of those dreams that seem so real. You know, like you can reach out and touch the other person." She stopped talking and looked at him. Fleet was staring at her with an agitated look on his face. Kyla was certain that he was upset with her for wasting his time with nonsense about dreams.

"Would you wake Kurt? I need to talk to him," Fleet said. Weariness was heavy in his voice. As Kyla hurried to do as he asked, Fleet watched her go. How could he tell her that he'd dreamt about Sister Samethia last night, too? In his dream he had asked her to send the Family and she had replied to him that she already had. It was only logical that both he and Kyla might be dreaming about Sister Samethia since they both knew her. Still, it was an eerie coincidence that the dreams were so similar.

Fleet turned to walk back in the direction from which he had come. It was a few moments before Kurt joined him. Even though he had been sleeping only seconds before, Kurt was completely alert and wondering what Fleet had in mind for today. All he could imagine was another day of sneaking from one wooded slough to the next. As long as they stayed in the area between the north and south branches of the river, they could stay under cover. The only problem was that the river flowed to the south and west while the Settlement was to the northwest. Already, they had traveled a long way south and every mile they went out of their way, added another to be traveled when they did turn north.

"Where do you plan to cross the main road?" Kurt asked when he finally caught up to Fleet.

Without stopping Fleet said, "Come up here and take a look. Then tell me what you think." He led the way up the rise to the top of the steep bluff that was the reason he had decided to rest in this spot. When they came to the top, he gave the binoculars to Kurt.

Looking through the glasses, he was surprised to find that they were less than two miles from the highway. He could see the gray ribbon of roadway for miles in both directions. It dipped up and down over the hills and into valleys, but he could make it out plainly. Before long he saw why Fleet had brought him up here. First he saw a pick-up appear at the top of one of the hills only to disappear again as it sped into the valley. Kurt watched it travel from the north until it disappeared to the south. A few moments later another truck appeared from the south and he watched until that one disappeared, too. He stood there for a few more minutes and two more trucks passed by on the road. When Kurt put down the binoculars, he turned to Fleet who was sitting cross-legged on the ground beside him. "How long has that been going on?"

"I've been up here watching since dawn. They've been driving up and down road the whole time," Fleet answered.

"You didn't sleep?" Kurt looked at his friend. There was no confident smile on his face. Today Fleet looked haggard and grim and Kurt was worried about him. There was no answer from Fleet, but Kurt had not expected one. He just hoped that Fleet had not finally pushed himself too far. Fleet would be of no use to any of them if he didn't get some rest. "Have you seen them send out anyone to search the side roads or any foot patrols?" Kurt asked.

"No," Fleet answered, "they seem to be concentrating their efforts on the highway."

Kurt knelt next to Fleet balancing on one knee. "We'll never make it across that road in the daylight."

Fleet nodded. He had been thinking the same thing himself. It helped to hear that Kurt agreed with him. "It's a risk to stay here so close to the road, but we can't move before it's dark again," Fleet said. He looked at Kurt before asking his next question. "Do you think Eddie was right about the night vision gear? The men at the bridge didn't have any."

That question had been plaguing Kurt, too. "He wouldn't have said it, if it wasn't true and I think he would recognize a night vision or infra red scope if he saw one. But I've been thinking about that, too. Eddie and Dylan were prisoners. They saw the scopes because Cole wanted them to see them. I'll bet they've got one or two, but I doubt they have enough for everybody."

"We'll go tonight then," Fleet said as he stood. "Once we're on the move I'm heading northwest from here, straight back to the Settlement." Kurt started to say something, but the look that Fleet gave him made him change his mind. Fleet smiled for the first time that morning, but it was not a pleasant one. "You were going to say that they'll follow us?" he asked wryly. Fleet stooped and picked up a small stone. "They can follow us all the way to hell for all I care," and for emphasis he flung the stone as far as he could off the top of the hill. When it landed with a dull thud below, Fleet said. "I'm going to try to get some sleep. Tell the others what we plan to do."

~ ~ ~

It had been a long day spent wondering and worrying. After Fleet and Kurt returned from the hilltop, Fleet tucked himself under one of the low hanging branches of a pine tree and pulled his blanket over his head. He finally was getting some sleep. Kurt had Kyla wake the others and he took them aside to explain their situation. The news had not been encouraging to say the least. They had tried to keep themselves busy. Feeding and watering the horses took only a short time. The rest of the day they took turns walking guard around the perimeter of their little bivouac and cleaning and loading their weapons.

Fleet had not slept long and he was awake and waiting for darkness with the rest of them. Once it began to grow dusk, he was the first to walk to his horse and begin to put on the saddle and prepare for the night ahead. There was nothing to be said and they all worked in silence. Before long all the horses were saddled and their gear tied in place. It wasn't quite dark when they finished. Standing in the failing light looking at each other, everybody's mood was somber.

"We'll all cross the road at the same time," Fleet said. "I don't want anyone trailing behind." He looked them over. Kurt's face was hard as stone. He would stand up to whatever was thrown at him. Eddie, with his tousled brown hair and equally disconcerted look on his face, was another matter. He could see the doubt in his eyes. Dylan was next to him. He was generally a quiet man and his expression was somber, but he was not one to turn from a fight. Justin was busy checking his rifle again, unloading and reloading over and over again. It was his way of preparing himself for the fight that they all expected. Last he looked at Kyla. The black hood of her cape covered her face. Even though things might not have gone quite as well without her, Fleet was sorry now that he had brought her along.

Kyla waited quietly. She was trying to steel herself for what lay ahead. Both rifles that she carried were loaded and ready to fire. There was no question in her mind that she would need to use them tonight. During the day she had come to a fatalistic decision. If things had gone differently that night at Cole's farm, if Fleet had not rescued her that night she would be dead now. If not dead, perhaps wishing that she was. The last few days had just delayed the inevitable. She was living in a brutal world now where it was a matter of kill or to be killed. If she was not up to the test then she would not live. It was simple and she was ready. When Fleet said to go, she would be right behind him.

They all stood with their horses awaiting a word from Fleet. When he looked up and said, "God help us," he mounted his long legged black stallion. "Time to get this over with."

Once they were all mounted, Kurt spoke. "We all know that there is a good chance that some of us may not make it back to the Settlement. We've been lucky so far." He lowered his head and raised his eyes to look at the riders. "But I intend to give them hell every step of the way," he spat the words out defiantly. When he raised his head again he opened his hand. Kyla saw that he was holding the tin of boot polish. He dipped his fingers into the grease and smeared it on his face. As he rubbed it on his skin he passed it around the circle and soon everybody's face was painted for battle. Then with one hand on the reins and the other on his weapon, Kurt raised his rifle above his head and let out a blood-curdling howl. There was no point in hiding any more. They all followed Kurt's example. Each person raising their rifle and as their war cry filled the air, they felt unity in their defiance. At that moment each person's survival would depend on the others. Fleet led the way not bothering to hide in the woods. Their main objective now was speed and the sooner they were across the road the better.

It didn't take long for them to come within sight of the highway. As they came closer they could hear a truck whiz by on the pavement ahead. The headlights of the vehicle were visible through the trees lining the road. After seeing it pass, they pressed the horses even harder. There were only a hundred yards remaining before they crossed the highway and everyone was hoping they would make it before the next truck appeared. All six horses were galloping at top speed when they reached the roadbed and scrambled up the bank. Kyla felt

Brownie's hoofs hit the pavement then out of the corner of her eye she saw the glow of headlights coming over the hill. In the next instant they were across the road, but it was too late. They were clearly visible in the lights of the oncoming vehicle. As they plunged down the slope on the other side, they were cut off from escaping into the woods by a fence running parallel to the road. No time to stop and cut the wires, Fleet turned his horse and led them away from the oncoming vehicle. When they saw lights coming from that direction, too, they knew they were trapped. Fleet's only choice was to turn to the west when they came to a narrow gravel road running that direction.

Fleet was watching for any break in the fencing, anything. The trucks were right behind them and when he heard them slow to turn, he shouted, "Off you horses. Let them run. We'll have to face them here!"

In a moment of mad panic, Kyla found the presence of mind to throw her saddlebags filled with ammunition into the ditch. Then grabbing both rifles, she swung her leg over Brownie's head and slid off her back. She shouted at the horse to frighten her off, but the mare had enough sense to run on her own. Kyla scrambled down into the ditch and finding her saddlebags, drug them with her. When she reached the bottom of the slope, a hand reached out and pulled her down. It was Dylan. He was on his belly and motioned for Kyla to lie on the ground, too. As she lay down next to him, Kyla looked to see what was behind them. The trees were close to the road, but there was a wire fence to get over first and there was not enough time for that now. She could hear the truck rumbling closer.

They were moving slowly up the road. Kyla couldn't see the trucks but she could see the lights. Very bright lights, they were searching the ditches and the woods with searchlights. She wondered how many men they had brought with them. Not that it mattered. There was no place to hide. Her only choice was to fight. She would not go back to Spring's farm as a prisoner again, especially, not after what they had done to Clovis. Kyla had made up her mind that she would die tonight.

Despite their effort to scatter the horses, two of them had stayed milling around in confusion just above the spot where Kyla and Dylan were hiding. The truck stopped. For a few seconds the only sound was the deep rumble of the engine idling, then they heard someone shouting, "Put down your weapons and come out with your hands up and we won't harm you." No one answered. The searchlights swept through the woods and into the ditch. The light fell only a few feet short of the place where Kyla and Dylan were hiding.

When Kyla heard the sound of men jumping out of the trucks, she looked at Dylan. He was up on his elbows with his rifle pointed up toward the road ready to fire. Following his example Kyla readied herself, too. There was nothing left to do except pray for a miracle. When one of the men walked to the edge of the roadway and looked down in their direction Kyla sighted on him and squeezed the trigger. Then the explosive sound of a gun being fired rang out in the night and the man fell to the ground, but it was not Kyla who had fired the shot. It had come from the woods behind them. After that the sound of gunfire filled the air. It was coming from both sides of the road. The men in the trucks, finding themselves caught on the high ground and in the crossfire, began to dive into the ditches right on top of Kyla and the others, who began firing as the men came their way. The whole nasty business was over in only a few minutes. When the last of Cole's men had fallen, the gunfire from the woods stopped.

Fleet leapt to his feet and ran up onto the roadway to the trucks still idling with their lights on. He shut off the engine and lights of the first one and was on his way to the next, when he saw Brother Fox at the edge of the woods climbing over the fence. He paused only a moment as he looked at him before going to the second truck and shutting it off, too. By then there was a flood of Family members climbing the fences on both sides of the road. He had hoped that they would receive some aid from the Family, but what had just happened was beyond his wildest hopes. Still stunned by what had happened, Fleet stood motionless in the middle of the road and waited for Brother Fox to come to him.

When Brother Fox stood before him Fleet embraced his friend and said, "I don't think I have ever been so happy to see anybody in my life." As he released Brother Fox from his grasp he asked, "How did you decide to come here?"

It was dark but Fleet could tell the usually somber Brother was smiling when he said, "Sister Samethia told us where to go."

Before Kyla could get up, the Family members coming over the fence were lifting her and Dylan to their feet. When Kyla looked at Dylan, she could tell that he was not sure if he was being rescued. Many of those who lived at the Settlement mistrusted the Family as much as they did Cole Spring's men, but Kyla was grinning from ear to ear. She leaned close to Dylan and said, "Don't worry." He looked at her and smiled weakly. When she heard a familiar voice calling her name, Kyla shook free of the hands on her arms and ran to find Sister Eaglet.

As the two hugged, Sister Eaglet said gleefully, "I hoped you would be here. Sister Samethia said that you would." Then she stepped back and looked at Kyla's clothing. Sister Eaglet said nothing about the fact that Kyla was now wearing a black tunic like Fleet's, but her surprised reaction was enough to convey her thoughts.

They were standing near Brother Fox and Fleet when Kurt came out of the ditch and said, "Justin's been shot." Immediately, the two men followed Kurt with Kyla and Sister Eaglet close behind them. One of the Brothers was kneeling beside Justin, when the others arrived he said, "He's alive. The bullet went right through his shoulder." Fleet knelt on the other side and said, "Justin, can you hear me?"

It was obvious that he could when he answered in an irritated voice, "Hell, yes, I can hear you. They shot me in my god-damned arm not my ears."

When Sister Eaglet arrived she began to push the men out of her way saying, "I need some light." Within seconds Brother Fox was holding a small lantern next to Justin's head and Sister Eaglet went to work. She opened the bag that was hanging at her waist and took out her knife. Justin's eyes grew wide as she flashed it near his face then used it to cut his clothing away from his shoulder. First she washed the wound with water, then taking a small wad of something that resembled green moss from one of the packets in her pouch, and she packed it into the wound to stop the bleeding. "Help him sit up," Sister Eaglet ordered.

"I don't need help," Justin said and pushed Fleet and Brother Fox away when they tried to help.

When he tried to lift himself up on his elbows and collapsed back onto the ground from the pain, Sister Eaglet scolded him, "You'll do as you're told. Now let them help you." None of the men argued with her as they lifted Justin and held him while Sister Eaglet washed and packed the exit wound in his back. Then she applied a poultice to both sides of the wound and wrapped his shoulder with a long piece of cloth. Once that was done, she took out a small flask and handed it to Justin. "Drink this," she ordered.

After he had taken a small sip, he grimaced and said, "This is worse than the moonshine they brew back at the Settlement."

Sister Eaglet glared at him and said, "Drink it all." He started to protest again, but the shock of being shot was beginning to wear off. After drinking the rest of Sister Eaglet's brew, he was more than ready to let the men lay him gently on the ground again. Sister Eaglet packed the rest of her supplies back into her pouch and stood up. She looked down at Justin and said, "You'll feel better soon."

Fleet turned to Brother Fox. Time was ticking away and it would not be long before someone missed the two trucks that had come after them. When he looked to where the trucks were sitting, Fleet could see that the Brothers and Sisters had been busy. The men and trucks had been stripped of weapons and ammunition. Looking in the other direction, Fleet could see one of the Brothers was riding toward them leading their horses. It was Brother Treblki, the shepherd that they had seen the morning after leaving the Settlement.

"They didn't get far," he said as he rode up with the horses in tow. He grinned sheepishly at Fleet and said, "I hope you don't mind me telling Brother Fox that I saw you."

"It was our luck in meeting you that day," Fleet said as he took the reins from Brother Treblki with one hand and shook the Brother's hand with the other. Then something else came to mind and Fleet asked, "Brother Treblki, you grew up in this area didn't you?"

"Lived here all my life," Brother Treblki answered simply.

He was thinking about the crumpled note in his pocket. "Have you ever heard of the North by Northwest Road?" Fleet asked.

"That's where your friends here had their accident," Brother Treblki answered. "That's what the old timers call it. It runs diagonal to all the other roads for a few miles. It's used as a shortcut when you're going northwest. I guess that's why your friends were using it. Why do you ask?"

"Enough, we can discuss this another time," Brother Fox said impatiently. "It's time to be gone. We need to get back to the camp."

"We won't be going with you," Fleet said. "We plan to head directly for the Settlement."

Sister Eaglet spoke up, "Your man won't make it that far. Our camp is much closer. He needs more care than I can give him here in the dark."

Fleet knew she was right. He hadn't wanted to leave anyone behind, but it seemed he had no choice. At least he knew Justin would receive the care he needed and he would probably be safer with the Family than with them. It was an easy choice for him to make. The hard part was convincing Justin that it was a good idea. Once Fleet told Justin what had been decided, he managed to stagger to his feet. "I can ride," he argued unconvincingly as he swayed and fell to one knee. "You will not leave me," he said. Then he looked at Sister Eaglet and in a slurred voice said, "What did you give me?" and fell the rest of the way to the ground.

Fleet looked at the rest of his party and said, "Mount up and get ready to go." Then to Brother Fox he said, "What are we going to do with him?" He nodded to Justin. "It's obvious he can't ride."

Sister Eaglet took the reins of the dappled gray horse saying, "This is his horse?" When Fleet nodded, Sister Eaglet scrambled onto the horse and sat on the pack behind the saddle. "Help me get him in the saddle and I'll hold him." Fleet and Brother Fox picked Justin up carefully and carried him to the horse. He was still conscious, but barely and rambling incoherently, insisting that he was fine. He even managed to voice his objection to the idea of Sister Eaglet riding with him. Still, with them pushing from behind and Sister Eaglet pulling from above they managed to get Justin seated on the saddle in front of her.

Brother Fox took the reins of the horse and began to lead them away. "We will take good care of your man Brother Fleet. Let the Mother keep you until our next meeting," he said as they followed the last of the Brothers into the woods.

"Let's get out of here," Eddie said when the last of the Family disappeared. He didn't have to ask twice. They were all more than happy to leave the place.

197

Once again they were on their way. The timely arrival of the Family had saved them from death or worse than death, from being taken prisoner. Kyla was grateful beyond words. As she followed Fleet, who was only a shadow on his black horse, she thought of her dream about Sister Samethia. It was hard not to believe in Sister Samethia's powers of prophecy and premonition when confronted with such an astounding coincidence. It was something you wanted to believe in.

Chapter Eight

Once again the highway seemed to be the point at which Cole abandoned the pursuit. Fleet was not sure why the man had given up so easily. He would not have stopped if their roles were reversed, especially when they had killed so many of his men. If they had found Clovis, Cole could add beating his son to their list of offenses. As they rode, he also wondered why Cole's men would go past the highway to lay in ambush for Dylan and Eddie who had done nothing to them. Something just didn't make any sense, it was as if someone had sent them for a purpose and the only purpose Fleet could imagine was to bring more men running to their rescue, which was exactly what he had done. Still, he was not sorry when they were able to ride the rest of the way to the Settlement without any further incidents.

It was late at night when they finally returned to the Settlement. They did not go over the bridge or check in with the guard, but went directly to the cabin. Before they arrived in front of the house, a crowd had already gathered waiting for them. When they left four nights earlier they had galloped down that same lane, but the group that returned was much more subdued and the horses were spent. Once they had dismounted, the horses were whisked away at a word from James. The five returning members of the Guard stood looking wearily toward the door to the cabin as Sadie and Riley came running out to meet them.

It was Sadie who asked, "Where is Justin?" She looked beautiful dressed in a flowing white gown with her black hair spilling over her shoulders in long ringlets of curls. Even though it was cold, it did not seem to bother her. She wore no robe or jacket.

"He's been shot," Fleet answered. He looked uneasily at the faces of the people pressing in around them. When they gasped in shock, he added quickly, "But he's alright." Fleet looked at Sadie and said wearily, "We're all exhausted. Can we go in and talk?"

Sadie acted like a forgetful hostess as she began fussing over them saying, "Yes, yes, don't stand here. Let's go in." Then to the crowd she added, "Please go back to bed now." Then like a worried mother hen, she began to urge her brood toward the door. Slowly, they walked the short distance to the cabin, Armand, James, Sadie, and Riley following behind them

Once inside Sadie closed the door and it shut with a soft click. She crossed the foyer and turned to face them. There was no joyous welcome for the five who returned. Sadie's tone was demanding, as she repeated the question. "Where is Justin? Has he been taken prisoner now?"

Kyla was listening to Sadie. Her head was buzzing from fatigue and lack of sleep, but something in the way she asked about Justin's whereabouts didn't seem right. It was a jumbled thought, just beyond the reach of her conscious mind.

It was Fleet who answered, "We left him with the Family."

Sadie's reaction was incredulous horror. "You did what?" she snapped.

Fleet was not in the mood for an argument with Sadie. "You heard me," he answered, well aware of her opinions of the Family and Sister Samethia in particular. Her hatred and distrust of the Brothers and Sisters was something that Fleet could not understand. The worst thing was that her opinion was usually contagious. If Sadie objected to something, then everyone at the Settlement objected to it, too. The people respected Sadie and followed her example.

"What were you thinking, leaving an injured man with those people. You can't treat infections with herbs and prayer. You should have brought him here where we could care for him properly." Sadie was furious and she continued her tirade, "They live like savages."

It was Kyla, not Fleet who cut her off. If Fleet would not stop Sadie, then she would. "We left him in very good hands." Sister Eaglet's hands to be exact. Anger was rising in her as fast as the color in her cheeks. "Justin could not have made the ride to the Settlement. The Family's camp was much closer." When Sadie's angry glare turned to Kyla, she stopped speaking abruptly. Setting her jaw, she frowned stubbornly back at the tall dark haired woman.

Kurt added to what Kyla had started to say by explaining, "If we had tried to bring Justin with us, we would not have made it home tonight and it would have been another day before he received any care at all." He looked wearily to Sadie and the other three standing with her. "If we send a rider to their camp tomorrow with medicine, it will get to him just as quickly as it would have with us dragging him along."

That seemed to satisfy Armand who said, "He is right. Making the long ride would do more harm than delaying the use of antibiotics for a day or two."

Riley finally did what Kyla had been expecting from the beginning. She came forward and embraced first Eddie and then Dylan and said, "We are so glad to see you back." Then turning to Sadie she smiled. "When Justin returns, we'll be twelve again."

Sadie was not satisfied and answered icily, "You mean if he returns." She whirled around angrily and stormed out, calling to Riley before exiting the room. "Riley, you will sleep in my anteroom tonight." That in itself was a surprise. Although Fleet had a room in the cabin, he never used it except for a place to store his belongings. When he was home, he always stayed with Sadie.

After Sadie left, Riley looked at Fleet and then lowered her eyes, embarrassed to see Fleet's surprised expression. It was a rejection that he had not anticipated. Then she sprang into action. "You must all be hungry. Come into the kitchen and I'll see what I can find for you to eat." As she bustled off through the door that led to the kitchen, the others followed. There was a small table in the kitchen and the ones who had just returned took five of the six chairs. Armand sat in the sixth, while James stood just behind him with his arms crossed over his chest. Riley was busy rattling around at the stove and soon she had some eggs frying in a pan. In a few minutes she brought them plates and served each of them a large portion of fried eggs and bread, nothing elaborate, but she had made enough to satisfy their hunger.

Once they were finished James said, "I know you're all tired, but I would like to know what happened."

Fleet, Kurt, Dylan, Eddie, and Kyla all looked at each other wondering the same thing, where to start. When Fleet let out a laugh, it spoke for them all. It was a relief to be home. When they all joined him in laughter, the other three gave them a puzzled look. As the laughter subsided, Fleet wiped a tear from the corner of his eyes and said, "How long do you have? It's a long story."

James stood tall behind Armand. He was a broad shouldered man, which suited his personality. He was responsible for running the

201

farm and managing the laborers. Although he never went with Fleet when he left the Settlement, it was not because he was afraid to go. James never left for any reason that was not related to maintaining the farm. In his opinion, Fleet wasted his energy running all over the countryside. Forays to Spring's farm and other places were a waste of time as far as James was concerned. Fleet's activities not only placed himself in jeopardy, but the lives of others were being risked needlessly. In a little over one week, a woman had died and a young man injured following him on these pointless excursions. James waited patiently for the laughter to stop. That was another thing he didn't understand. The five sitting at the table with Armand looked like they had been to hell and back and they were laughing about it. He shook his head and said, "I have all night."

Before Fleet could answer Armand spoke up. "James, it's late and they're tired. This can wait for morning. They can tell us at breakfast when everyone will be here." They all knew he meant that Sadie would be there. She always insisted on being with the Guard when there was a report to be made.

"He's right," Riley said as she began clearing the table. She would make sure there was no trace of their midnight meal left for Agatha to find in the morning. No one wanted to listen to the woman complaining. "You five get to bed. We'll clean this up," Riley said and shooed them toward the door. She did not have to ask them twice. They all rose and went wearily to their rooms. Once he was in the foyer, Fleet left them to walk down the hallway opposite from the one that led to the others' bedrooms.

He held himself stiffly, as he took long strides to quickly cross the room. There would be no welcome for his homecoming from Sadie tonight. A part of him was relieved. He was too tired for anything but sleep. Still, it bothered him when Sadie publicly announced when he was in her favor and when he was not. It was just one little irritation in a long list of things that were on his mind. First there had been the betrayal when they went to Spring's farm the first time and Marta had been killed. Then there was the abduction of Dylan and Eddie, because in Fleet's mind that is what it had been. Someone had told Cole Spring where they would be. It was becoming apparent to him that somebody at the Settlement was keeping Cole Spring informed of his activities.

In the morning he would begin asking about who had left the Settlement or arrived while they were gone. Fleet walked past the doorway to Sadie's room and paused only slightly, wondering if he should go in and try to talk to her. Then with a shake of his head, he walked by the door and opened the one next to hers.

It was cold and dark when he entered his room. No one knew when he would arrive; aside from the fact that he always spent his nights at home with Sadie, so there was no reason to start the fire in the room. Fleet lit the small lantern just inside the door. It cast a feeble light that barely reached into the next room. His apartment was not quite as large as Sadie's, but it was more than the simple sleeping quarters provided for the rest of the Guard. From the hallway he stepped into a small sitting room with a sofa and chair and then through the door that led to his bedroom. Picking up the lantern, Fleet went inside. The first thing he did was light the fire. The kindling and wood were in place and it wasn't long before the dry pine logs were crackling and its light and heat filled the room with the fire's warm glow.

As Fleet began to peel off his clothing he opened another door that led to his own private bathroom. The water in his was just as cold as everyone else's was. He may have had better quarters, but there were no extra luxuries like hot water. If Fleet wanted that he would have to wait for it to heat in the fire. First he washed his face and hands, trying to remove the remainder of the boot polish that he had smeared there. Then he soaped the rest of his body and rinsed and dried quickly. It was a relief to wash off three days of dirt and sweat.

He threw another log on the fire and slipped naked between the cool sheets of his large bed. As he stretched out on his back with his fingers clasped behind his head, Fleet watched the light from the fire flickering on the ceiling. Something about the soft light made him think of Sister Samethia, reminding him of the time she had done his reading. A smile of fond remembrance spread across his lips as he thought about that night. It had been pleasant enough, sitting with Sister Samethia while she was dressed in her thin shift. She was a beautiful woman and with the steam rising from the fire and the sweat from her body, the fabric had clung to her, revealing every curve of her body.

Then she had put the drops into her eyes. After that, the other women had left the shelter leaving them alone. Sister Samethia had asked him to remove his tunic and he knelt with her by the fire while she massaged his hands and then his arms and shoulders with scented oil. All the time she was talking to him, telling him about how she knew things that no other person could know. That she could see his future and knew his past. It had all been about how he would pierce the heart of his enemy. She told him that he would need help and like an arrow he was useless without the bow to propel him. That was where all the business about the arrow had begun, but that was not what had brought the smile to his face.

It had been what happened next. After she gave him a cupful of warm herbal tea to drink, he had kissed her. To his surprise she did not pull away and returned his kiss with another. Then using the scented oil Fleet had massaged Sister Samethia's hands, arms, and shoulders as she had done with him. Her eyes were still dilated and looked totally black when she had looked at him and said, "I must know all about you," then removed her shift, to sit naked before him. Although he was surprised by her seductive proposal, the sight of her firm round breasts and willing body was all the invitation that he needed. Sister Samethia had captured both his body and soul. Fleet had taken her into his arms and made love to her and the memory of his night with Sister Samethia brought him almost as much pleasure now, as she had then. He slipped off to sleep thinking about her and wondering about Justin. He was certain that once he felt better, Justin would enjoy his visit with the Family, especially if Sister Samethia favored him with a reading like his.

~ ~ ~

Kyla followed the others down the hallway to their rooms. She was pleased to see a clean set of clothes and a towel and washrag waiting for her on her bed. Unfortunately, she was not quick enough to be first into the bathroom that they all shared. So she lay on her bed waiting for the other three to take their turns. It was peaceful and safe in her room and Kyla was not anxious to leave it to go anywhere.

First in her thoughts was Justin. Kyla wondered how he was doing. He had to be all right. Sister Eaglet would not let him die. Something told her the young woman would not allow it. Then her thoughts turned to Clovis. Leaving him tied to the post in the barn had been a cruel thing to do. There was a good chance that they had not found where they ditched the truck. If they didn't find the truck, then they would not find the note. Despite what he had tried to do to her, Kyla knew he didn't deserve to die that way. No one did. That of course, wasn't the only thing that Kyla was sorry about. Shooting the man from the tree house where she had played as a child seemed like something that had happened a long time ago in some crazy nightmare. That ugly episode had been followed by the horses trampling the two men at the bridge. Then there had been the skirmish at the highway. With bullets flying from every direction it had not been possible to say who shot whom. Still, it didn't make her feel any better. There had been too many people killed. She had spent the last eight days reacting to one perilous situation after another and she was exhausted, mentally and physically. If she had led a sheltered life before now, she wanted it back.

Finally, when she heard the door to the bathroom slam shut followed by silence in the hallway Kyla slipped out her door and into the bathroom. She had taken off her dirty clothes and left them in her room and was wearing only the flannel shirt that Asa had given her. It was quite large and hung nearly to her knees and was more suitable for Kyla as a robe than it had been as a shirt. When she closed the door to the bathroom, she could see that the others had been tidy enough, but it was not pleasant being third in line to use the bathroom. The rug on the floor was already wet and the soap showed traces of the boot black that everybody had smeared on their faces and hands. She washed quickly and was returning to her room when she ran into Kurt coming from his room.

He was only wearing his trousers and seemed as surprised to see her, as she was embarrassed at being caught in the hall wearing nothing but her flannel shirt. If Kurt had been wearing his shirt she might not have been so flustered, but she found herself looking at his chest and shoulders. He had a very muscular build. With a body that was as hard and chiseled as the features on his face, he was a handsome man and Kyla couldn't help staring a little.

Kurt had forgotten about having a woman living next door. Riley and Marta had shared a room on the other side of the house. Fleet was the only man living in the east wing and until Kyla had been assigned the room next to his, only men lived in the west wing. From now on he would make sure that he was fully clothed before leaving his room and he would say something to Riley about getting Kyla a proper robe. He looked at her and the fact that she was staring made him shift nervously. Still, he was glad that he had met her alone. There was something that he wanted to say to her.

He regarded her fondly now. She was still little more than skin and bones and the last few days of hard riding and short rations had done nothing to improve her condition. Fleet should have left her at the Settlement. It would have been better for Kyla, but maybe not for them. He was certain that Clovis would not have been so quick to talk if she hadn't been there and her knowledge of the area had been invaluable. "I wanted to thank you," he said awkwardly. Kurt knew what he wanted to say to her, but was having trouble putting it into words.

If Kyla hadn't been staring at him before, she certainly was after Kurt said that. What on earth could he be thanking her for? It was Kurt who had been strong when Fleet and the rest of them needed him. If Fleet was the heart of the group, she was learning that Kurt had the strength of will that bound them together. She looked up and met his eyes. There was something warm and comforting about the way he was looking at her now.

When she didn't answer and only stared at him, her eyes opened wide with a questioning look, he said, "When Fleet first wanted you to join the Guard I was against it. But I should have trusted his judgement, Fleet has never been wrong before." Then with only a slight pause he added, "And he was right about you." Then with an uneasy nod he said, "Goodnight, I'll see you in the morning," and hurried down the hall to the kitchen where he had been heading when her ran into Kyla. Kurt had wanted to add that he would choose her over most of the men he knew if they ever were in another armed conflict like the one they had found themselves caught up in for the last three days. Kyla had proven herself to be a shrewd and resourceful person. He wondered how a woman as tiny and frail as she appeared had kept up with everything the men had done. She certainly was a stronger person than she looked.

When he reached the kitchen he took a teakettle full of steaming hot water off the stove and headed back to the bathroom. Kurt wanted to wash his hair and he could not bring himself to use cold water. He wished that Sadie allowed the use of electricity for the hot water heater. Either that or at least do something about heating it with fire. It was just one of those things that he needed in his life and he didn't think that wanting hot water to wash ones hair was unreasonable. Once his hair was washed and combed Kurt looked at his face in the mirror and rubbed the stubble of his beard. He looked a little rough with four days growth and decided that he might as well shave while he had the hot water. Once that was done he went back to his room.

It was cold in the room and when Kurt slipped off his trousers, he quickly climbed into bed and pulled the covers over his shoulders. He was thinking about Sadie. She had been unfair in her assessment of the situation. Leaving Justin with the family had been the only choice they had. When he thought of Justin swaying in the saddle with the little blond haired Sister riding behind him and keeping him from falling, it was a decision that Justin would thank them for and for more than one reason. Kurt rested peacefully that night. Everyone was home except Justin and he did not doubt the fact that he was being well cared for.

Sadie was the first one to rise the next morning, long before dawn. She walked into the anteroom and saw Riley sleeping there. The young woman did not wake when Sadie entered. There was not a doubt in Sadie's mind that if someone ever did break into her room that Riley would probably sleep through it. Sadie had no real expectations that Riley would ever provide much in the way of protection, but she slept better when she was not alone. As she stepped into the hall she fought the urge to go to Fleet's room, he would be rested by now. She smiled at the thought, but she would not go to him. She had been consistent too long. Fleet was permitted to share her room and he came to her when she wanted him. It would never be the other way. Sadie could not allow that.

She did not carry a light. There was no need for one. Sadie knew every inch of the house and grounds. She hurried out the door and into the darkness without bothering to put on a coat, still wearing the same white gown that she had worn when Fleet and the others arrived. She was easily visible in the darkness as she walked to the greenhouse nearest to the cabin and went inside. Lipsky was waiting for her. He was even more haggard and worn than usual. Sadie couldn't be certain, since she never really paid much attention to the way the man looked, but it seemed that his coat had some new holes and tears in it. "What did you find out?" she asked impatiently. Every moment she spent with the man was a trial.

"They went back to the farm just like you suspected," Lipsky looked at her nervously. She was beautiful, but he was afraid of what she could do to him if he made her angry. He couldn't count how many times Sadie told him that she would have the Guard kill him if he didn't do her spying. The irony was that usually he was spying on the Guard. It would do no good to confess. The Guard members all hated him as much as he hated them. Besides they would never believe him if it came to his word against Sadie's. They would kill him either way. Still, he knew things about Sadie that even Fleet did not know. Lipsky knew everything about everybody. For now that was what was keeping him alive.

"Well, get on with it," Sadie said. Lipsky was about as far beneath her as anyone could get and he knew that she wouldn't hesitate to have him killed. When Lipsky was no longer of any use to her, she would let Fleet do it. She hoped things didn't work out the other way around, she would be sorry to let Lipsky have Fleet. There were so many other things that Fleet could do for her and Lipsky's uses were limited.

"It seems Fleet and his friends did a lot of damage. They blocked the road a few miles from Spring's farm and rescued the two boys. Altogether, twelve men are dead and they left two wounded." Lipsky had saved the best for last, "They even kidnapped Spring's son. They beat him up and left him tied up in a barn somewhere."

Sadie had to smile at the thought of Cole Spring stewing over his precious son. She wondered if it had been the idiot named Clovis or that simpering coward, Asa. Sadie knew them all and had little respect for the farmer or his sons. He must be an inept idiot himself, if he let men riding horses get away, let alone twice in the span of only one week. "Did he go past the highway after them?" Sadie also knew the boundaries of the territory that Cole Spring patrolled.

"No," Lipsky answered. "They managed to ambush two of the trucks just off the main road, killed all the men but one."

Sadie had heard all she needed from Lipsky. Before she turned to go, she said, "Don't let anyone see you when you leave." Lipsky looked at her and opened his mouth to speak. When he hesitated, Sadie handed him a small leather bag that she was carrying in her hand. Of course, he wanted to be paid.

Lipsky loosened the drawstring and looked at the twelve luminescent pearls inside the bag. They were more valuable for barter than anything else. He wouldn't use them all himself, but he would trade them for food and other things.

Sadie was smiling when she walked back to the cabin. Twelve men dead and two wounded and there had been only six of them. That was one of the things about Fleet that she found exciting. She wanted a strong willed man who could fight and win. It was the winning that was important to Sadie. Fleet continued to amaze her and beat the odds. Even when the deck was stacked against him, Fleet had done the impossible or perhaps this time he'd had some help. Sadie was certain that the Family had done more than take in Justin when he was wounded. Sadie would bet on that. Fleet would probably tell her everything in the morning, but she liked to make sure. That's why she had Lipsky.

When Sadie slipped back into the front door and whisked through the foyer she was pleased that everyone was still asleep. She returned to her room and crept past Riley. The girl was useless as a guard, but she was loyal to a fault. That was one thing that Sadie counted on and always treated Riley well or as well as she did anybody that served her. It was Sadie's farm and she supported everyone through her generosity. Without her they would all be eating nuts and berries like those wild things that called themselves the Family. That is if they were lucky enough not to starve trying. Sadie would not let any of them forget that fact.

She slipped back into her room and waited for the sound of the morning wake up call. It somehow seemed appropriate that it was Agatha pounding on the side of an empty metal trash can that started everyone's day at this god-forsaken place. In that way she was like everybody else, wishing that she were someplace else. It was hard trying to feed everybody who came to the Settlement and she was growing weary of the task.

After Sadie had gone back into her bedroom, Riley turned over and looked at the door. She had been watching while Sadie slept for many months now. It was a job that she knew well enough to know to pretend that she was sleeping when Sadie slipped out and back into the room in the middle of the night. She never followed or asked where she went. That was Sadie's business and none of hers.

Kyla was awake early, too. She had heard the sound of the door opening the first time. When she waited, watching with her door open just a crack, it was Sadie that she saw slipping back into the house. Kyla was not surprised that Fleet and Sadie were lovers. They were the two most beautiful and powerful people in the Settlement and it just seemed like they belonged together. Still, from what Kyla had seen since her arrival a few days ago, Sadie demanded a high price for the honor of her company. Now Kyla wondered what she was up to, sneaking around at night wearing only her thin nightgown. Especially after she had made a point of letting everybody know that Fleet would not be sleeping in her room. If Sadie had another lover, it would not surprise Kyla. She seemed the type of woman who used people to her advantage and discarded them when she was finished.

There was nothing to do at this time in the morning. It was still dark outside and no one would be awake. Kyla decided to get dressed and take a walk before breakfast. If she sat alone in her room she would only dwell on the unpleasant circumstances of her trip back home. She dressed in her fresh black tunic and trousers and pulled on her boots. Kyla began to put on her rabbit skin coat but decided against it. She wanted to take her walk without attracting any attention. So she threw the black cloak over her shoulders and walked quietly to the door. Then after making sure that the door was unlocked, she stepped out into the chilly morning.

She had no real destination in mind. It was just chance that she decided to walk toward the greenhouses. Before she reached the corner of the cabin, Kyla saw someone leaving one of the greenhouses. Whoever it was looked around furtively before coming out of the doorway. She immediately moved closer to the side of the house to hide in the larger shadow of the cabin. Kyla could not imagine why anyone would be in the greenhouses at this time of night and wondered if he was the reason that Sadie had been outside. Her first thought was to go and get someone else, but who would she wake? Anyway, the man would be gone by the time she returned. She had her knife in her boot, but that was her only weapon. She had become accustomed to carrying a rifle the last three days and was wishing she had it now, despite the fact that a few hours earlier she would have sworn to never pick one up again. Still, Kyla didn't plan to confront the man. She just wanted to find out who it was.

She followed him quietly and cautiously. Whoever it was, he seemed to be trying to stay hidden, like he was expecting someone to follow him, which made Kyla wonder even more about what he had been doing. Before long they were at the lake. Instead of going across the dam and up the hill to the shelter house, the man took a narrow footpath that wound through a tangle of sumac growing in the low area beside the springs. Kyla stopped at the edge of the low bushes and watched as the man she was following crossed the open space to the low concrete block building that was used as the guard post. It wasn't until the door opened and the light from inside fell on the man's face that Kyla realized she had been following Lipsky. For a brief moment, he looked in her direction and she was certain that he had seen her. But when a voice from inside shouted, "Shut the door. You're letting the cold in," Lipsky turned and closed the door.

Kyla wondered why Lipsky had been at the greenhouse in the middle of the night. She dismissed the idea that Sadie had met with him. Kyla could not imagine Sadie having anything to do with someone like Lipsky. Still, he had as much right to be wandering around in the dark as she did. He worked at the guardhouse and distasteful as he was, Lipsky lived here, too. Still, there was something about his behavior that said he had been up to something. Kyla filed it away in her memory. A little piece to a puzzle and maybe some day she would see where it fit.

She made her way quietly back to the cabin and was coming in the door at the same time that she heard the sound of someone pounding on a metal drum; the signal that it was time to rise. Kyla was

211

already dressed and ready for breakfast. She met a sleepy eyed Dylan as he made the dash to be first to the bathroom. She let him pass by and went to her room to wait. That morning breakfast was a lively event. Everyone was home except Justin and since all except Sadie were confident that he would be returning soon, the mood was jubilant and Eddie and Dylan were bombarded with dozens of questions.

Sadie had not waited for them to finish eating before beginning her questioning. "Dylan, did you see anyone while you were driving around looking for Fleet and the others."

Dylan was still busy stuffing food into his mouth. He swallowed quickly and took a drink before answering. "Not a soul," he said and looked nervously to Eddie. "We didn't see one person until that truck pulled out on the road behind us. We were on our way home by then about twenty miles southeast of here."

Without waiting for Sadie to ask him what he thought, Eddie added his opinion anyway. "If Cole's men are going to start coming that close to the Settlement then I think Fleet is right in trying to arm the Family." He was ready to elaborate, but one look from Sadie and he decided that eating was a better use for his mouth at that moment.

"When I'm ready for your opinion Edward, I will ask for it," Sadie said as she regarded him harshly. The young men at the table were all in high spirits this morning. Fleet was back and victorious beyond all imagination. She needed to maintain her control, at least over who was speaking and on what subject. She did not need Eddie to tell her that he thought Fleet was right. At this moment they all thought Fleet was infallible. Sadie continued questioning Dylan. "How did they take you as prisoners?"

"Well, given the fact that they were armed with rifles and we weren't, it wasn't too difficult," Dylan answered sarcastically. He hadn't forgotten that it was Sadie who had sent them to look for Fleet in the first place. It was also Sadie who had insisted that they should not need guns if they stayed west of the highway. Then looking at Sadie, he remembered his place, and softened his tone a little. "They just shot at us until they blew out one of the tires and we lost control of the truck. After it rolled and crashed in the ditch, you could say we were pretty well subdued." So far he had covered what they already knew. At this point Dylan looked around the table before adding, "Then they took us to the farm."

Sadie had not cared for his tone when he answered. The young man was insolent as far as she was concerned, but she would deal with that later. "It looks like you received some medical attention. Who set Eddie's broken arm? And someone had to stitch up that cut on your head."

"Some young kid, I think it was one of Cole's sons." Reflexively, Dylan's hand went to the ragged looking gash on his head. As he touched it he said thoughtfully, "They didn't treat us badly, other than the fact that we were being held as prisoners."

Sadie looked at Eddie and said, "Would you like to tell us what you have to add, Eddie?"

Eddie looked at Sadie and then to Fleet before answering, "I don't know what they're doing at that farm, but they have enough men there for a small army." He had already tried to state his opinion and was determined to have his say in the matter. "What I wanted to say is that Fleet is right about Cole Spring. It's a mistake for us to sit here and think that he's going to leave us alone, because he's not. He sent his men after Dylan and me. How long is it going to be before he sends them to the Settlement?" There was a murmur of concern and agreement that went around the table when he asked his question.

So far Fleet had been sitting silently, enjoying the trouble Sadie seemed to be having with the two young men. He was pleased that both Dylan and Eddie seemed to have found the nerve to speak out honestly about what they thought. Before their latest excursion, they had always acted like awkward young boys when talking to Sadie. That was probably why she had decided to send them in the first place. She knew they would do whatever she said without question. Now they were speaking their minds like men. Somewhere along the way, they had both found some courage.

"Did you get a chance to talk to anyone or see anything while you were in there?" Fleet asked the question. He had already heard the answer but he wanted Sadie to hear it, too.

"I already told you about seeing the night vision equipment," Eddie answered. When he mentioned that Sadie shifted her position slightly, but said nothing. Eddie looked at her before continuing, just to make sure that he didn't interrupt her again. "Other than that they kept us in a storeroom without windows in the men's barracks. No one talked to us except when some old guy came and told us that they were sending us to some work camp up north."

"Was he short with a big round belly?" Kyla asked. She knew who they were talking about before Eddie and Dylan nodded in agreement. "That was Cole Spring. When I was there he told me that he was going to send me to join my family. Do you suppose that's where they sent everybody?" It wasn't just Sadie who was staring at Kyla when she had finished. Everyone at the table was. She had broken the unwritten rule. Nobody ever spoke about where the thousands of evacuees had gone. It was accepted that they were gone and in everyone else's mind, gone meant dead. No one ever spoke of going to join them. It just wasn't done.

The only thing to do was change the subject. Something that Kurt did quickly. "Eddie when you saw the night vision equipment, where were you then?" Everyone's eyes shifted away from Kyla. Everyone except Sadie, she continued to watch Kyla while Eddie talked. The girl was becoming a problem. Just one of the many little annoyances that were cropping up like weeds, since Fleet started his visits to Spring's farm.

"They walked us right past a truck that they were unloading when we first got to the farm. After that they kept us locked in the room," Eddie answered.

"Well, you're lucky Fleet was able to arrive in time to rescue you." Sadie looked at Fleet and said, "I still haven't heard how you did that."

There was something about the way Sadie asked that hit Fleet the wrong way. Almost like an accusation rather than a question. He wondered if she was still angry about last night. He should have gone to her room and tried to smooth things over with her, but it was too late now. Fleet would just have to make up with her tonight. "We had some luck in that." Fleet began slowly, looking for the right words. Whenever he talked to Sadie he chose his words carefully. "Kyla was a big help. She knew the area very well." He looked from Kyla to Sadie and began to tell their story.

"We didn't have much luck looking for Eddie and Dylan. It wasn't until we ran into one of the Brothers tending his sheep that we found out what happen. He told us where to find the truck and it didn't take too many guesses to know where they had been taken." Fleet took a deep breath and leaned forward, putting his elbows on the table. The eyes of those who had not been with them were riveted to his face, wanting to hear him tell how they had managed to rescue Dylan and Eddie when the odds had been against them. "We rode hard after that. We wanted to get there as soon as we could. Kyla showed us a place close to Spring's farm where we found a barn to hide the horses. We were surprised with a visit from two men from the farm just after dawn the next morning. Justin killed one of them, but we took the other as prisoner and questioned him."

Sadie interrupted his story, "I hope you treated him as well as Dylan and Eddie were treated. I would hate for us to be the ones to set a bad precedent on the treatment of prisoners." Kyla, Kurt, and Fleet all exchanged an uncomfortable look. It was all Sadie could do to keep a smile from her lips. The looks between the three guilty ones had been all the answer that she needed.

Kurt was the one who said, "That man got what he deserved." He did not explain his reasons. Kurt felt justified no matter what Sadie thought. There was a mixed reaction from the rest, but he didn't care.

Fleet also had little patience for the subject. "We did what we felt we had to do. Without the information that he gave us we couldn't have known when they planned on moving Eddie and Dylan." That was all the explanation he was going to give. Fleet continued with his story, saying, "We set up a roadblock. Two of us took positions above the road as snipers. One on the road to take out the driver and one to watch the horses and drive the truck to get away once we were done." He looked at Dylan and Eddie, "That was the easy part. After that we still had to get home." Fleet stopped and leaned back in his chair. His face had a thoughtful look and he continued, "We had two more confrontations with Cole's men. Once at a bridge crossing the north branch of the river and the last just after we crossed the highway."

"I don't know what those of you who weren't with us will think. I know Rod and Peach will understand. There is nothing brave or courageous about anything we did. We killed the men who were trying to stop us because it was our only option. Twice now in a short time I've asked you to go with me to Spring's farm. The first time for weapons for the Family, who I consider strong, allies. I am not sorry about that, because when we needed them most, the Brothers and Sisters were there to help us. We would not be here now, if I hadn't given them the weapons that they used in the ambush at the highway." Fleet looked at Sadie and the others. He did not add the fact that he still wondered how the Family knew the exact spot where they were heading. That was a secret that the Brothers and Sisters could keep. The fact that they had been there when he needed them was all Fleet cared about.

"The second time we went to bring our friends, Dylan and Eddie, back home. What we did to accomplish that was worth it. If I have started a war with Cole Spring, it's because I can't just sit here and wait for the day that he sends his men and guns to the Settlement and decides to send us all north or worse."

All eyes shifted to Sadie. It was Sadie who continually told them that the answer was peaceful co-existence. She had assured them that Spring and his men were not a threat. But just as surely as poking a stick into hornets' nest will get a reaction, Fleet's raid and subsequent rescue were sure to get a response from Cole Spring. Everyone was certain that Sadie's reaction would be immediate. They were all surprised when she said. "It seems that Fleet was right about Cole Spring. Fleet and I need to talk seriously about what is to be done in the future." Although her answer was nothing definite, it seemed to satisfy everyone. "You should all go now and see to your duties." She dismissed them summarily, but before any of the others could move to leave, Sadie was up and out the door. As everyone left the mood was light. Fleet and Sadie would decide what was best. They always did.

Fleet was the only one who stayed where he was. As he remained seated, alone at the table, he was thinking about Sadie's reserved acknowledgment of his success. It also galled him when Sadie tried to make it sound like he needed to speak to her before he made a decision. He did need to talk to Sadie, but it would not be about what he planned to do about Cole Spring.

216

As Kyla left the dining room, she wondered what she was supposed to do that day. As far as she knew, she had no duties. She went to Riley and said, "Do you mind if I go with you again today?"

The good-natured young woman shrugged and said, "Sure, if you want." They went to the barn first where Riley checked on her Guernsey cow and then looked at the horses. "They looked like you had almost run them to death last night," she said as she patted the bay mare that had come to the gate. "But they look better now," she said and turned to Kyla. "You should have rested them more."

Kyla wondered if Riley had any real idea of what they had been through. Her main concern seemed to be the treatment the animals had received. Still, Kyla knew that the animals were as important to Riley as any of the humans. The two women were still looking at the horses when Kurt entered the barn. When he saw them, he said, "Riley, you're just where I thought you might be." He looked at the horses and asked, "I need to go the Family's camp to check on Justin and take the antibiotics."

Riley put her hands on her hips and bristled back at Kurt, "You will have to wait until the horses have rested before you do or you can walk there yourself." However, as soon as Riley remembered why he needed to go, her attitude softened a little. Fortunately for Justin she cared as much about him as she did the animals and she said, "They should rest a little more before you go. Just promise me you won't push them too hard."

"I'll promise not to drive them too hard, if it can be helped," Kurt answered. He understood her concern. The horses were valuable to him, too, even if his reasons for wanting to keep them alive and useful were different than Riley's.

It had been mentioned the night before, but this was the first Kyla had heard about anyone planning to go back to the Family's camp to retrieve Justin. "Can I go with you?" Kyla couldn't believe that she was asking, but she did want to see Sister Samethia. She had some questions that she thought the Sister might be able to answer.

Kurt was a little surprised that she asked, too. He had planned to speak to Fleet about the two of them going. Kurt would have gone alone, but he had never been to the Family's camp and didn't know the exact location. The only times he had met with the Family it was always at some secret rendezvous. Fleet knew the location of the camp, but the possibility that Kyla knew it, too, was something that he had not considered. As he looked at her, Kurt decided against taking her and said, "You need rest more than the horses. If I take you then Riley will be scolding me about that, too."

"Kurt's right," Riley agreed. "You need to stay here. Your biggest concern should be getting to meals on time."

Kyla was relieved and disappointed at the same time. She would have liked to visit the Family again. "What am I supposed to do around here? I need to have something to do other than show up for meals."

"If you need to feel useful, then you can take your turn at the shelter house tonight," Kurt said. "When you see Armand at noon today, tell him that you're to go with them tonight." Then he turned to Riley and said, "It will just be Fleet and me going. What time do you suggest?"

Riley looked at him and then at the horses. It was a hard decision for her to make. "You can leave after lunch," she said hesitantly. Then she shook her finger at him and added, "Just promise that you will be careful."

"That I will do," Kurt answered. He was actually smiling. Kyla had rarely seen Kurt with any expression that wasn't serious.

As he turned to leave Kyla waited until Kurt had left the barn before saying, "Riley, I'll catch up to you later." Then Kyla ran out the door after Kurt. "Wait!" she shouted as she came out of the doorway. "I need to talk to you."

He turned and said, "I know you want to go, but I just can't allow it this time."

Kyla almost said something to him about using the word 'allow', but didn't. She had something more important to say. "That's not what I wanted. I need to tell you something."

Kurt was relieved. He had expected an argument from Kyla. Waiting for her to catch up, he asked, "What is it?"

Kyla took a quick look around to make sure nobody was standing nearby. There were two men walking by and she waited for them to pass before speaking. "I woke up early this morning, before dawn, when I heard someone in the foyer," she paused and lowered her voice.

"I saw Sadie coming back into the cabin wearing nothing but her nightgown."

"Is that all you wanted to tell me?" Kurt asked. "It's her house and farm. She can go where she wants." If Kyla was going to spy on Sadie, she was asking for trouble.

"I know that," Kyla said impatiently, "I didn't think anything about it either. Well, after that I knew I wouldn't get any sleep before it was time to get up, so I decided to go for a walk, too. As soon as I went outside I saw someone coming out of the greenhouse. He was acting funny like he was up to something, so I followed him." She stopped when Kurt gave her a sharp look. She knew what he was thinking and said, "I was careful. I just wanted to see who it was."

Kurt couldn't believe her. She was certainly one to keep her eyes and ears open to everything. He had to ask, "Well, tell me who it was."

"It was Lipsky," Kyla said his name in a whisper.

She shouldn't have bothered. "Lipsky?" Kurt almost shouted the name. Kyla was motioning for him to be quiet and he lowered his voice to a whisper, too. "Are you implying that Sadie and Lipsky..."Kurt couldn't finish. The idea of Sadie and Lipsky together was ridiculous.

"I know," Kyla said. "I know, it sounds crazy, but the more I think about it the more I wonder why both of them were outside at the same time." Kyla could see that she had Kurt thinking now.

He looked at her and said, "I'm not worried about Sadie, but I don't like the idea of Lipsky sneaking around here at night." Remembering Kyla's first encounter with Lipsky, he added, "Stay away from him. I don't trust him at all." Then putting his hand on her shoulder he said, "If you're worried about what you can do to be useful, you're already doing it. Just keep your eyes open and let me know what goes on while Fleet and I are gone."

Riley watched Kurt and Kyla talking and wondered what it was that they were whispering about. One thing was certain, Sadie did not know about Kurt's plan to go to the Family's camp or that he planned to leave immediately. She always kept Sadie informed of what was happening with the Guard. Fleet and Kurt in particular had a bad habit of taking off and forgetting to mention to Sadie that they were going. Riley knew that it was nothing that they did intentionally, but they were men. It was a matter of pride for them, and checking with a woman before leaving was just not one of the things that they would do. She wished that Fleet and Kurt were more like James. Like herself and Sadie, James had his priorities in the right place and that was here at the farm.

As Riley saw it, her primary loyalty was to Sadie. Besides her duties with the farm and being Sadie's eyes and ears in the Guard, Riley was the one who guarded her bedroom at night, a job that had fallen to her more often than usual in the last few days. But where Fleet and Kurt went and what they did was Sadie's concern. If they ran into Cole's men again, it would concern them all. After Kyla and Kurt moved on, Riley hurried back to the cabin to find Sadie.

~ ~ ~

For the first time since Kyla had run into Fleet in the darkness, he left without her. She had gotten used to having Fleet around and would miss him while he was gone. Added to that, was the fact that Kurt was going and Justin was already with the Family. She had become close to the three men and was feeling a little lonesome knowing that they would all be with the Family while she had to stay behind. When Kurt and Fleet left they made it clear that they would wait until Justin was well enough to travel and not to expect them back at the Settlement for several days. That meant that Kyla would be on her own again.

There had been some discussion with Sadie before they left. Kyla could not hear what was said, but she could tell that Sadie was not pleased. The whole episode ended with Sadie storming back into the cabin. Kyla received a scathing glare from Sadie, as she passed by the spot where Kyla was standing. That was when Kyla decided it was time to make herself scarce and the closest place to go was the greenhouse.

Kyla crossed the short distance and went inside. She had been through the greenhouse gardens with Riley a few times, but this was the first time she had come on her own. Kyla strolled at a leisurely pace through the first building, taking the time to look more closely at the gardens. With the exception of the potatoes planted in the tubs, the other gardens were in raised beds. The watering was done by a buried drip irrigation system, but what caught her attention were the long panels of lights. They provided a very bright light, like a sunny day in

July. It seemed that such a bright light would also give off a lot of heat, but it wasn't overly warm anywhere in the buildings. When Kyla reached out to touch one of the panels that were mounted on the wall, she was surprised to find that it actually felt cold when she touched it. Rachel was at work in the garden and saw Kyla touching the panels.

"'Don't do that," she said and went to where Kyla was standing. "You can damage the panel."

"What are they?" Kyla asked hoping Rachel could explain the mystery.

"They're light panels," Rachel answered with the obvious. Then taking Kyla by the arm, she guided her to the end of the row of panels. Kyla watched as Rachel touched the corner of the black metal frame holding them in position. At her touch a row of lighted symbols appeared along the edge of the frame. "These are the controls. If you want to know how to work them, I'll show you."

By then Zoë had seen Rachel talking to Kyla and stopped working. Zoë looked agitated when she shouted at Rachel, "What are you doing?" and stomped over to where they were standing. "Who told you that you could show her that?" she demanded angrily.

Rachel was hurt by her friend's accusing tone and defended her actions by saying, "She's one of the Guard."

"That's alright," Kyla said, "I don't need to know how they work. All I wanted to know is where they came from. I've never seen anything like them."

Zoë answered sharply, "I don't know. They've always been here as far as I know." She turned abruptly and went back to her task of thinning and transplanting the precious little seedlings growing in her garden.

Rachel watched her go then turned to Kyla and said, "Don't worry about her. I'll show you." Kyla watched as she pointed to the series of strange symbols. "We enter a code for each crop. By pressing the proper sequence of symbols we can set the day length, the intensity of light, everything to mimic an ideal growing season."

"How do you know which sequence of symbols to press?" Kyla asked. There were no letters or numbers from any alphabet she could recognize.

"Sadie knows them," Rachel answered and added proudly, "Once she let me enter the code."

Kyla could tell by the smile on Rachel's face that she considered it a great honor. Also, the deference that Rachel was showing her did not escape her attention. There was no doubt in Kyla's mind that Zoë's chilly attitude had the same origin. The fact that she was wearing a black tunic had changed everything for Kyla. People who ignored her when she first arrived now went out of their way to talk to her. Others who she had never seen went out of their way to avoid her. As she walked around the farm this morning, she had found that people reacted to her in one of two extremes. Kyla knew it would take time for people to accept her.

Worrying about what people might think of her was not on Kyla's mind when she left the greenhouse. She was thinking about the light panels. They seemed out of place with the rest of the farm. When everything else was moving backward, technologically speaking, the light panels were an amazing advance in technology. If she wanted to know more about the panels then the person to ask would be Sadie. Something that Kyla was not ready to do.

~ ~ ~

Armand crossed the foyer and went down the hall on his way to get Kyla before going to the Settlement. Usually, they would go in teams of four, but he still considered Kyla as too new to be counted. Armand had seen her attack on Lipsky the first night when Fleet had brought her to the Settlement. He wasn't sure if her actions had been brave or fool hardy, but it was hardly an effective blow. Still, from what he gathered, she had done well enough with Fleet and Kurt on their last trip to Spring's farm. At least Kurt's opinion seemed to have changed. Before they left Kurt had nothing positive to say about Kyla. That's why it was such a surprise to Armand that it was Kurt and not Fleet who had told him that she should be included in the regular rotation at the Settlement once Armand was satisfied that she was ready.

Everyone had their special duties in the Guard, but they were not assigned. They were earned. Armand had gained the respect of his fellow Guard members when it came to managing the volatile crowd at the shelter house and they deferred to his judgement. He was their unofficial general in the battle to keep some semblance of order in the Settlement. His good-natured smile and easy-going disposition meant that he was well liked by everybody. The fact that he was built like a bull and just as strong was another reason his fellows in the Guard appreciated his presence. Until Armand was satisfied that Kyla was ready, she would remain number five in the group.

When Kyla heard the knock on her door she was ready. She had been waiting since nightfall. With one last adjustment to the knife hidden in her boot, Kyla opened the door. When she saw Armand was the only one standing at the door she asked, "Where are the others." It was her understanding that Moon, Rod, and Peach would be going, too.

"They've gone ahead," he said as he started walking down the hall to the foyer with long forceful strides. Armand intentionally set a fast pace, forcing Kyla to hurry to keep up with him. "We'll catch up with them at the shelter house," he said as he opened the door and stepped out into the cold night air. As they walked toward the path that led to the Settlement Armand was talking. "All I want you to do tonight is observe what goes on." He looked at her with a warning scowl and said, "I don't want you jumping into the middle of anything tonight. Understand?" Kyla nodded at his obvious reference to her attack on Lipsky.

"The only advice I can give you is to get to know everybody. Be their friend. It's been my experience that a person is more likely to do what you ask and less likely to put a knife in your back if they like you," he said giving Kyla the best advice that he could. "You'll get to know them all soon enough. First, there are the bonfire people. A lot of them come from the farm and they don't like to mingle with the ones in the shelter house too often. Usually, we don't have much trouble from them."

Kyla thought about seeing Agatha at one of the fires that night when she had gone to the Settlement by herself. But she couldn't let her mind wander too far. Armand was still telling about the cliques at the Settlement. "Then you have the people who live at the Settlement. There are about thirty men and women who have set up permanent residence in the woods around the campground. That is if you can call tents and shanties permanent residences." Armand paused from his tutoring to look at Kyla. Once he saw that she was still watching and listening intently, he continued. "The third group are the ones who cause most of the problems. Most of them are scavengers. They spend all their time wandering around the countryside looking for anything that they can use for barter. That's what goes on at the shelter house most of the time and the most of the trading is done for food, weapons, liquor, and pearls."

"Early in the evening food is the big attraction. Even though Sadie will feed anyone who wants to help out at the farm, a lot of these people don't want to work. So they depend on a few hunters who keep everyone fed and if you have something for trade then you eat. The hunters spend all day out in the fields hunting for rabbit, squirrel, pheasant, quail, and if they're lucky even a deer. But they've been at it for so long that small game is pretty scarce around here and they have to go a little further everyday to find anything."

"Then we've got a couple of enterprising men who have a still somewhere. In a place where everybody knows what everybody else is doing, the location of their operation is the best-kept secret at the Settlement. Their other secret is what they put in the stuff. Every batch is different, guaranteed to get you drunk if it doesn't kill you first. With some of these people, I don't think they really care which. All they want to do is get stoned out of their minds and stay that way. In a way I can't blame them. What do they have to look forward to?"

"Another big item for trade are guns and knives. A lot of people have guns. The big problem for them is there is no ammunition for the guns, which is fortunate for us. So most people carry knives, and I mean the plural. Nobody stops at just one. So don't think that if someone drops their knife, that he is unarmed. Chances are he's got another." Kyla thought of her one and only knife tucked in her boot. The more Armand talked the more she worried that she would not be any help if there were trouble.

"Of course, that means that everyone needs to have something to trade. If they don't have anything then they steal it from someone else. We have some accomplished pickpockets in the Settlement. Others prefer to use strong-arm tactics and just take what they want. It doesn't matter, either way it always ends up in a fight."

All the time Armand was talking he was chugging along like a freight train, it was a wonder to Kyla that he had enough breath to speak. She was gasping for breath just trying to keep up with him. In no time they were walking on the trail across the dam. He stopped when they were half way across before discussing his next subject. "Then we have the pearl traders. They're regulars but they don't live here. They'll be gone for days and when they do come back, they're loaded with pearls to trade. You'll know them when you see them. They'll be the most popular people in the shelter house. Everyone wants to get their share and they'll trade anything." He stopped and looked at Kyla judging what her reaction was. Then he went on quickly, "But it's the nights when we have a pearl trader visiting that we have most of our trouble. There are always a few traded and used every night, but when the traders come there's plenty for everybody and things get a little crazy."

Kyla had listened to everything he had said without speaking. Now that they had stopped she had a question for Armand. "I have heard a lot about pearls, but I don't know anything about what they do. Have you ever used them?"

Armand did not pause before answering, "I'm no different than anyone else. I've tried pearls and know why they like using them. They make you feel great, like you could do anything. Everything tastes better, feels better, and for awhile you can feel content even if you are living in hell." He looked at her and added, "I can't tell you not to try them. I know you will do what you want, but I would strongly recommend that you don't. Once the euphoria fades, the down sets in. It seems to be different for men and women. Men get violent and the more they use the pearls the worse they get. I've seen men kill each other over a single pearl. The women get depressed. If they kill anyone, it's usually themselves." Then Armand was all business again and said, "But if you do, you do it on your own time. When you come to the shelter house dressed in black you are on duty and answer to me. Do you understand?"

Kyla looked at him, "Perfectly," was all she said.

After that Armand was silent as they walked the path leading up the hill to the shelter house. He was moving slowly now and would stop every once in awhile. Kyla could see that he was listening and looking at the shadowy forms of the tents and shanties in the woods. It seemed that they were all empty and dark. Still they stood for a few moments at each one until Armand was satisfied that all was well and they would go on to the next.

Before they reached the clearing, Kyla could see the glow from the bonfires on top of the hill above them. She was following Armand when they left the path through the trees and went to the group at the first bonfire. There was somebody that Kyla knew standing at the fire. It was Rollo, the man that Fleet had asked to watch their horses. He was standing with two other men.

"Hey, Rollo," Armand said in a deep and booming voice. It was impossible not to hear him. Still, Rollo continued staring at Kyla, ignoring Armand for the moment. All three men were staring at her, but Armand ignored that fact and started talking to Rollo. "I hope that your new batch is better than the one we had last night."

That got Rollo's attention. His eyes immediately went to Armand and he said, "I make a quality product and if you would stop drinking it there would be more for the rest of us." Rollo's friends seemed to appreciate his remark and laughed heartily.

Kyla was gathering by the conversation that Rollo was one of the enterprising moon-shiners that Armand had mentioned. Now that Armand had their attention Kyla looked at the three men. Rollo was a rather short man with a barrel-chest and stocky build. He was not a very pleasant looking man. His face was dirty and under the dirt his complexion was rough and deep pockmarks scarred his face. His dark brown hair looked a little shaggy, like he had tried to cut his own hair without the aid of a mirror. Most of that mess was covered by his cap, an old stained hunters cap with earflaps and a bill that had been bent and shaped so it curled at the edges.

The man standing next to him was talking now. He was about the same height as Rollo but much thinner. Kyla was relieved to see that he was much cleaner than Rollo was. He was a dark skinned man with dark brown eyes and black hair. He reached into his pocket and took out a stone. Holding it in his open hand he said, "I was down at the 'rock cut' today and found this."

Something about the stone looked familiar and Kyla asked, "Can I see it?" The man looked at her like he was shocked to see that she was still standing there.

Armand decided that it was time for introductions. "Rollo, Amit, and Wolf," he said and pointed to each man as he said their name. "You all know Kyla. You were at the Gathering the other night."

The man Armand named as Amit was holding the stone and gave it rather reluctantly to Kyla. She held it close to the fire so she could see it better. It was a small piece of chalky white limestone with a small snail shaped fossil imbedded in it. After looking it over Kyla returned it to the man and said, "I used to find those all the time when I was a kid. I found them at a hill near my home." Her last visit to the rocky hill came back to Kyla and she tried to shut the unpleasant memory out of her mind. Then she asked, "What is the 'rock cut'?"

Wolf answered. He was younger than the other two and a little taller. "It's about two miles from here at the rapids. It's called the 'rock cut' because the river has cut out a deep channel in the limestone. There are ledges that you can climb up and down like stairs to get to a wide rocky shelf almost a hundred feet wide that goes right to the water." He seemed to be feeling a little more comfortable and opened up a burlap bag that he had on the ground at his feet. Inside he had about half a dozen fish, "I caught them all today." He was obviously very pleased with his catch.

It was time to go when Armand announced abruptly, "We'll see you later." Kyla followed as he walked away. Once they were far enough that the men would not hear, he said, "I hope Wolf doesn't trade all his fish for moonshine."

There were a few other groups of people standing around fires, but Armand did not stop to speak to anyone else. Kyla looked at the faces of the people standing around the fire. She saw a few that were familiar but nobody that she knew by name. When they came to the shelter house Kyla saw a group of five people standing by the door. They were leaning casually against the wall and when they saw Armand approaching, began to cast furtive looks from one to the other. She recognized two of them. They were the boys who had been hiding under the bridge when she had first arrived at the Settlement but Kyla had never seen the other three. They were older and definitely more menacing than the boys were. One man in particular caught Kyla's attention. He was wearing a black cowboy hat pulled low over his eyes and a long black trench coat. Keeping his hands in his pockets, he was watching Armand very closely.

Armand did not take his eyes from the man when he said, "Zack, Norton, would you like to introduce me to your friends?" His tone was pleasant enough but his expression was deadly serious.

The taller of the two boys spoke up nervously, "They just got here. We were just telling them where they could get something to eat." The fact that both boys were now squirming nervously was proof enough that food was not all that was being discussed.

The man wearing the black hat drawled slowly, "Like I told the man at the bridge, we're just passing through. All we want is a place to spend the night." Something about his voice made him sound both weary and insolent at the same time. Then almost as an afterthought he added, "We don't want any trouble."

"Same here, my friend," Armand said and smiled warmly, but Kyla could see his eyes never moved from the man wearing the black hat. "You can call me Armand. What name do you go by?"

"My friends call me Slick," he answered and tipped his hat. The other two smirked when he said the name. "These are my friends," he said as he pointed to the men standing with him.

Armand was sizing up the man. So he wanted to be called Slick. Armand hadn't needed to hear the name to know that he was looking at trouble. The man was sure to have a pocket full of pearls and using them, too. When Armand looked at Slick, he knew that he was looking at the most dangerous kind of snake and it had just slithered into his path. Only this one had brought help and Armand did not like the odds. Even with four Guards, once the crowd got involved they would be at a definite disadvantage. As soon as they were inside he would send Peach back to the farm to get James and Dylan. He looked at Kyla and wished that he had left her in her room.

Kyla was watching all three wondering if they were just tired travelers or pearl traders. She was willing to bet on the latter. The man calling himself Slick was apparently the ringleader of the group and appropriately named from what she could see. If Kyla had to describe the other two, it would be to say they looked like hired henchmen. With the two large men standing at his left and right, Slick felt very sure of himself. Kyla followed Armand to the door. When she looked back at the man in the black hat, he was grinning at her. It made her feel like a chicken in the coop with the fox grinning through the gate. The fact that she was the chicken was not comforting.

Slick was curious about the big man and the skinny little woman following him. They were the oddest looking pair that he had seen in a long time. The man was as big as either of his bodyguards and dark as they came and the woman was about as skinny and pale white as anybody he had ever seen, especially with her head shaved like it was. Two more opposite people he could not imagine, but they were both dressed in the same black tunic. It could prove to be an interesting evening. He turned his attention back to the two boys. Before they had been interrupted, the two were telling them about the women who had just gone into the shelter. "What was that name you called those girls?" Slick asked, getting back to the subject.

The boy called Zack answered with a big grin on his face. "We call them pearl divers. You know, they'll go down for pearls." He looked at his friend sheepishly.

It was obvious that these two were only repeating rumors. They were both snickering like schoolboys. Still, they were useful source of information and he had a few other questions. "Who were those two that just went in?" he asked.

"They're members of the Guard," Zack answered eagerly. Most people ignored both him and Norton. He was enjoying the fact that someone was actually listening to what he had to say. "Armand is nice enough. I've never seen him get mean for no reason, but you better watch out if you make him mad."

"What about the other one, the woman?" Slick asked. He could see the big man being a guard but not the woman.

"She's new here," Zack said starting to answer but Norton interrupted.

"Her name's Kyla. Fleet brought her with him almost two weeks ago. We saw her the first night when they got here," Norton blurted it all out quickly. The words coming so fast that it was hard to understand him. "She's one of the Sisters from the Family. We think that's where the horses came from." Norton looked at Zack who was nodding vigorously in agreement.

The mention of horses pricked his interest. Now that would be something if he could get his hands on some horses. If there was one thing Slick hated, it was walking everywhere he went. He didn't have to ask any questions to keep these two talking. The black haired boy named Zack was telling another story now.

"You wouldn't believe it just looking at her but she nearly killed a man the first night she was here," Zack said. "She jumped right on top of the man and stabbed him with a knife." Now, it was Norton nodding as Zack talked.

He wasn't listening to Zack's story. Slick was thinking about horses. When he saw a young man dressed in a black uniform like Armand and Kyla slipping into the woods just beyond the shelter house, he asked, "Who's Fleet?"

"You won't see him tonight," Zack answered. "He left this afternoon with Kurt."

"Is he in the Guard, too?" Slick asked. He had been happy with the boys. So far they had been very helpful.

"Him and Kurt both," Norton volunteered. "There's twelve altogether."

Twelve men and two gone, meant ten were still here. Slick smiled and thought nine men. He could subtract one from their number if it included the skinny bald girl. Despite what the boys had said, Slick doubted that she was the dangerous character they made her out to be. "Do they come here every night?" Slick didn't ask the question he really wanted answered which was, how many are inside right now.

"Yeah, every night like clockwork," Zack answered. He was trying to imitate Slick's attitude but ended up sounding whiney. "Four of them come at sunset and don't leave until the fires go out."

Slick had heard all he needed from the two boys. He was ready to get rid of them and paying them off would be the quickest way. "Do you two have leather pouches?" Zack and Norton fumbled through their pockets and each one produced a small leather bag. They pulled open the drawstrings and held the empty bags out to Slick. "Put them down and come with me." Slick walked away from the building with the boys following at his heels. Once they were out of sight of the doorway, he reached into his coat and took a large leather bag from his inside pocket. Carefully, he dropped two pearls into each boy's sack and said, "One for each of you and two for the pearl divers." He laughed to himself as they took the pearls and made a beeline for the shelter. Four pearls were a small price for the information the boys had provided.

When Slick returned he took his two companions aside and laid out his plan for the evening. Slick was to go on with business which had brought them to the Settlement in the first place and that was trading pearls. He was certain the big man named Armand had sent someone to bring more help. He looked smart enough to anticipate trouble, but Slick had meant it when he said he didn't want any. He was there to get what he could from these people and he knew that they would be begging him to take everything they had for a few pearls. Still, he knew as well as anybody, how quickly things could get out of control once enough pearls were floating around the crowd. That was his plan. Tonight he could afford to be generous with his pearls. He wanted to create enough trouble to keep those black uniformed guards busy trying to keep everyone from killing each other. That was Slick's part. Create enough confusion that his friends could do a little old fashioned horse stealing. The way Slick figured it, the extra pearls would be worth it if they rode out of here instead of walking.

Once Armand and Kyla were inside the shelter house, he began making his way through the crowd to the fireplace at the front of the room where Moon and Peach were standing. It seemed like everyone made way for Armand and he walked easily through the crowd with Kyla following close on his heels. As soon as they reached the other two Armand took Peach aside and whispered something in his ear. When Armand turned back to where Kyla and Moon were waiting, Peach went the opposite direction, leaving the shelter house by the side door. Rod was there, too. When he saw Peach making his hasty exit, he started pushing his way through the crowd and joined them.

Armand did not want to spend a lot of time talking to the group. The fact that all four of them were now standing together was causing people to stare. He knew that they would be wondering what was being discussed and eavesdropping was a favorite pastime with these people. Armand spoke quickly, "I saw three men outside that need some watching; a real smart-ass, who calls himself Slick. He's wearing a black cowboy hat and black trench coat and has two big guys with him. One has a long scar on his left check and the other looked like someone tried to chew his ear off, you can't miss them. I sent Peach to get some more help. Now spread out and keep your eyes open. If we can keep the local trouble makers under control maybe we can keep things from getting too far out of hand."

When Kyla began to turn and look for a place to sit, Armand caught her arm and said, "Promise me that you will be careful and leave if things get ugly."

She looked at him and said, "I'll be careful," but she would not promise to leave.

Armand gave her a sharp look and said, "I was hoping for a quiet night but it seems that we will be busy after all." The words were hardly out of his mouth when he saw Zack and Norton tearing through the crowd. It seemed that Slick was done with them. Armand was still holding Kyla's arm and watching the two boys. They were always high-spirited but when they went directly to one of the women standing at the side door Armand knew what they were doing. When they left with her, Armand was fuming. Slick must have given the boys pearls. The woman wouldn't have gone with them if they didn't have pearls to pay for her services. It was always amazing to him when grown men gave something like that to boys as young as those two were. At the same time the boys were leaving by the side door, the object of Armand's irritation came in the other entrance.

Kyla saw Armand watching something behind her and twisted to see where he was looking. She watched as Slick swaggered in the door and found a spot to sit near the exit. The moment he sat down people began swarming to him. He might as well have had a sign that said, 'Pearls for Sale', but obviously it wasn't necessary. Armand had forgotten about her and released his hold on her arm. He was focused on Slick and his activities. When Armand began drifting slowly toward the crowd gathering around the stranger, Kyla began to look for a place where she could keep an eye on things and stay out of the way as Armand had requested. Then she saw the little old man from the Gathering, the one who had told the story about aliens from outer space. He was sitting alone in the corner near the side exit. Kyla started working her way through the crowd in that direction.

She had not thought about the little man since her trip back to Spring's farm. Maybe she could get some more information out of him. As Kyla got closer, it seemed that the man looked weary and when he saw her coming, he shifted uncomfortably. "Mind if I sit here?" Kyla asked. The man shrugged and made room on the bench. She sat next to him and was immediately struck by his odor, wondering when the man had bathed last. Even in a place like the shelter house that was brimming with unwashed bodies, the little man's odor stood out above the rest. He did not seem to be overly chatty, so for the time being Kyla watched the crowd.

All the activity was swirling around Slick. He was like a black hole sucking in all the energy in the room. There was a man sitting next to Slick showing him a knife but he was fighting a loosing battle for the man's attention. The woman on Slick's other side seemed to be presenting a more interesting trade. She had glued herself to Slick and was holding onto his arm and whispering in his ear. Kyla could see him laugh and take something out of his pocket and press it into the woman's hand. Once he had done that, she released her hold on his arm and sat back with a satisfied grin. Slick returned to his business with the others. Apparently, the woman could wait until later. There didn't seem to be anything that the man would not take in trade. Knives, food, clothing, sometimes Kyla could not even see what was being traded, but everyone seemed to be very satisfied. It seemed that Slick was not the shrewd trader that he appeared to be.

There was not much to see and she looked at the man sitting next to her. "I saw you the other night. Your name is Orin, isn't it?" He didn't answer and gave her a look that said he preferred to be left alone. Still, Kyla persisted, "I thought your story was very interesting. Where are you from?"

"Up north," he answered tersely.

"How long did you have to walk to get here?" Kyla asked. She wanted to get some kind of idea of how far north.

"I've been walking for months," he answered. "I don't have a home and I don't have anywhere to go. So I walk."

233

Kyla was wondering how to bring up the subject but there was no tactful way so she got right to the point. "Tell me more about what you saw up north.

Orin looked directly at her now and was quite agitated. "Listen lady, I'm tired of all of you giving me a hard time about what I said. It's all true, there are aliens that look like ice giants and they are busy up north building towers. Only they're not doing the building, they have people doing the work for them. You can believe me or not, but I'm leaving tomorrow and no one will have to bother with me anymore." Once he had his say, Orin got to his feet and found a seat on the other side of the room.

She was surprised by his reaction and could only wonder about what people had been saying or doing to the little man. Still, the parts about the towers and people building them, was something new. Kyla was still trying to piece together something in her mind, some explanation for what had happened to the world that she had known. The space alien part was a little much, but still she thought there were probably some parts of Orin's story that might be true. One thing seemed to be the same in everybody's story. People were being moved north. Fleet said the evacuees were taken to camps up north. Dylan and Eddie were told that they were being sent to work camps in the north. Add to that Orin's story about people building towers up north somewhere, leaving out the part about aliens and it would seem that there was something going on to the north.

It was then that Peach returned with James and Dylan. They did not come in but opened the side door and looked inside. When they saw Kyla they motioned for her to come outside. The first thing she saw when she stepped outside was that all three men were carrying rifles. All James said to her was, "Go get Armand."

Kyla hurried back inside and began searching for Armand in the crowd. It was not an easy task. Everybody seemed to be on their feet tonight and Kyla was caught in the movement of the flowing tide of bodies. It was a small building and Armand was a big man, but it still took Kyla a few moments to spot him standing with a group of men between the door and Slick. Kyla tried jumping up and waving at him to get his attention. All that got her was an angry shove from the man in front of her and a surly growl, "Get off my back." Kyla returned his glare and pushed past him and continued working her way toward where she had last seen Armand.

When she finally reached him, Kyla could see he was in a rather heated discussion with three men concerning a fourth man that was cowering behind him. Armand had not seen her yet, but Kyla was close enough to hear him say, "Your property has been returned, so let's all cool down."

One of the men was not satisfied, "I'm tired of that little sneak. Just let us take him outside for a few minutes and we'll teach him what happens to thieves."

When he tried to reach past Armand to grab the man, Armand caught him by the wrist and said, "He's not going anywhere with you." It was then that Kyla was finally able to catch his eye and got a cold glare from Armand for her efforts. Not wanting to get between Armand and the men, she motioned to get him to look toward the side door. Finally, he did look and said to the men, "He's leaving with me. So you might as well stay here."

Once he was in motion Armand moved quickly for such a large man, pushing the man who had been hiding behind him out the door. It was a little more difficult for Kyla to get through the crowd and by the time she got out the door, the thief was scurrying into the woods and Armand was at the side door talking to the other three. She arrived to hear part of what Armand was telling them.

"You three stay out here. I don't want anyone inside to see that you're carrying rifles. If we need you to break up the crowd, I'll call you then." As she walked up behind Armand, he stopped speaking and turned to see who it was. When he saw that it was only Kyla he continued, "What worries me is the fact that his two buddies have disappeared. I'm sure whatever they're up to is sure to be trouble for us." Armand found himself wishing that Fleet and Kurt had not left that afternoon. He could use two more men. Part of him wanted to send a couple of men after the missing strangers, but two of these young men would be no match for the brutes he had seen with Slick. His other problem was that he couldn't spare anyone at the shelter. Right now things were heating up inside. What Armand wanted to do was drag Slick and his bag of pearls out the door and show him to the road, but he knew that would start a riot. So they would do what they always did, and that was to ride out the storm.

As he started to go back inside, he gave one last order to the three men outside, "Don't let anyone else inside and if anyone comes out they don't go back in." Then he looked at Kyla who had been standing quietly off to the side. "Come here," he said gruffly. He was not in the mood for babysitting, but she was here and might as well make herself useful. He opened the door and pushed the man sitting on the window ledge right beside door off his seat and lifted Kyla up into his place. "You sit here and keep an eye on me. If I need James and the others, I'll signal you and don't waste time getting to the door. Just go out the window."

As Armand started to work his way through the crowd, Kyla took her knife out of her boot. She pretended that she was using it to nonchalantly clean the dirt from under her fingernails. What she was really doing was to try to appear armed and dangerous. Whether it was working or not, she couldn't tell but nobody bothered her. From her perch in the window she could see everything going on in the room. Rod was busy by the fireplace. He was holding onto a man brandishing a knife. Fortunately, someone in the crowd had helped him by restraining the other fellow involved in the fight. They were trying to move the men toward the door and disarm them as they went. Rod and the other man took their knives and then shoved the two troublemakers out the side door. Rod's helper handed him the knife that he had taken from the man that he was holding and disappeared back into the crowd.

When Rod saw Kyla sitting in the window next to the door he shoved the two knives at her and said, "Here, hide these somewhere." Kyla took the knives and looked at them briefly. They looked more like ice picks. She pushed them carefully into her boots, wishing that she had somewhere better to hide them. Rod was still looking at her after she stashed the knives. "What can you see from up there? I can't tell what's going on," he said.

"Armand's back by the front door and Moon's talking to a bunch of men over in the corner on the other side of the room," she answered and pointed in that direction.

"Does he need help?" Rod asked. He stretched on his toes and tried to see where she was pointing.

236

Kyla noted that he wasn't worried about Armand. They both knew Armand could take care of himself, but even though Moon was tall and stronger than most men were, he was young and inexperienced. "I can't tell what's going on. Moon's standing with his back in the corner."

"Damn kid," Rod cursed and pulled a man sitting on the bench in front of him off his seat, and then he stood on the bench to get a better look. He could barely see Moon. Three men who were regulars at the Settlement were arguing with him. Tom was with him, so at least there was someone in his corner. Rod didn't see any weapons, but decided to go check it out anyway. "Yell if you need me," he said and began pushing his way through the crowd telling everybody as he went that it was time for them to leave. It was no surprise when nobody listened.

So far there had been no major eruptions of fighting. A push here, a jostle there, all answered with another shove back to the offender. Slick was still there, but he was not busy anymore. It seemed his trading was done. He had a good seat with a bench near the wall and was leaning back with his legs stretched out on another bench in front of him. He had one arm around the woman, who had been there from the beginning. She was prettier than most of the women who stayed at the Settlement. At least she appeared to be cleaner and that helped her overall appearance. In the other hand he had a bottle of the local brew. She hadn't seen Rollo come in, but he didn't seem like the sort who would miss out on a good trade. There was no doubt in Kyla's mind that Slick was thoroughly enjoying the chaos that his pearls were causing. When Slick leaned over and whispered something into the girl's ear, she started to help him gather up the sacks full of junk that people had given him. Then they both began to make their way through the crowd toward the side door where she was sitting instead of the front door where Armand was busy moving people out the door.

Kyla watched Slick and the woman as they made their way through the crowd. It took them awhile because once people became aware of the fact that Slick was leaving, he was assailed every step of the way by requests for more trades for more pearls. He just smiled holding up his one empty hand and shaking his head every step of the way to the door. When Slick got to the door he paused a moment and looked up at Kyla.

"Why don't you come down from there? If you come outside, you can come with us. One of my friends might like you," he said. As he put his hand on the calf of Kyla's leg, Slick squeezed hard and gave her a quick jerk like he was trying to pull her off her perch. He laughed when Kyla flashed her knife in front of his face and let go saying, "Maybe next time." Then he pushed the other girl out the door in front of him and took one last look at the thin girl with the shaved head. He smiled at her and closed the door. Maybe the boys had been right about that one. She was flashing around a big hunting knife and had two others in her boot. Slick was pleased with the way things were going. He walked past the men with rifles standing outside the doors and smiled at them as he followed the girl. He had plenty of time to finish his business with her and be on his way to meet his friends. The boys in black would be busy for a long time.

Once their pearl trader was gone, the crowd was becoming more agitated by the minute and it was beginning to be a battle of the have and have not. Kyla could tell things were rapidly coming to a full boil, but she was waiting for some sign from Armand to call for the other three. She was trying to split her attention between what Armand was doing at the front door with Rod, Moon, and Tom who were being swallowed by the crowd in the opposite corner. Armand was still busy herding people out the door and Kyla began hoping that he was not just moving the fights outside where Dylan, James, and Peach would have to deal with them.

It was a shout from Rod in the corner that got things rolling. One of the men had pulled a knife and was threatening Moon. It only took a moment for the crowd to begin to fall back, giving wide berth to the man swinging the knife wildly back and forth. The man's friends had grabbed both Rod and Tom before they could help Moon. It was a one sided fight since Moon didn't have his knife. All he could do was try to stay away from the blade, which was impossible in the crowded room. Especially, since people in the crowd kept shoving him back toward the man every time he tried to back away from the blade.

Kyla pushed open the wooden shutter and sitting with one leg on each side of the wall called out to Dylan who was standing outside a few feet from the door. "Get in here quick."

Dylan shouted, "James," and pointed toward the building. Dylan ran to the door carrying a second rifle. As quickly as possible he slipped it off his shoulder and handed it to Kyla and said, "Use this if you have to." Then he began to try to get in the door, but the flow of bodies was now out the door and he couldn't get past them to go inside. Once the man who was fighting Moon started waving his knife around everybody had begun heading for the door. Apparently, James and Peach were having the same problem at the front door. Nobody was coming in.

Kyla had the rifle in her hands and knew what she had to do. Without waiting for a signal from Armand, she fired a shot over the heads of the crowd. It was instant pandemonium. Everyone began pushing toward the door, but Kyla had gotten the attention of the man who was in the process of cutting Moon to pieces. He was looking at her now. Moon was on the floor and Kyla had the man in her sight, "Drop the knife!" she yelled as loudly as she could. She knew that she would have to shoot if he moved and she kept him in her sight until Armand got to him. Once Armand had the man's knife and Rod and Tom were released, Kyla lowered the gun. Dylan was just outside the window and Kyla held his gun for him while he climbed onto the window ledge beside her.

Once Dylan was inside he took his rifle from Kyla and began to walk across the tops of the heavy wooden tables, his rifle in hand ready to fire if necessary. Kyla followed his example and the two of them provided the armed deterrent needed to clear the rest of the people out of the shelter. Armand and Rod got things moving in a little more orderly fashion, while James and Peach ended up staying on the outside and kept the crowd moving away from the building. Once the building was empty Dylan and Kyla each took a door and shut it. Then went to see how badly Moon had been hurt.

Luckily, most of the cuts were not deep, but there were several on his hands and arms that would need stitches. While Tom was busy tearing his shirt into strips to use as bandages, Armand was telling them what needed to be done. "Dylan," Armand said as he reached out and put one of his large hands on his shoulder, "you, James, and Peach stay here for awhile and make sure everybody goes home." Without a word Dylan nodded and trotted to the door. "Tom will you help Moon and Kyla get back to the farm?"

That made Kyla just a little hot, she had been the one who brought the situation under control with one shot from the rifle and didn't feel that she should be included in the same category as the wounded man, but she had agreed not to argue with Armand. At least not now, she would save her argument for a better time. Besides, it might be Tom and Moon who would need her assistance, she thought wryly.

"I don't need any help," Moon protested loudly and he stood to prove it. Once he was on his feet, he wobbled for just a moment before passing out decisively on the floor.

Rod poked him with the toe of his boot and said, "That kid never could stand the sight of his own blood."

As Tom pulled Moon to his feet, he complained, "Why is it always the big ones that you have to carry home?" Kyla followed them outside. Before they had gone out the door, she could hear Armand telling Rod, "You and I are going to find Slick and his friends and make sure they're gone in the morning."

It took awhile for Kyla and Tom to haul Moon down the hill. When they finally did make it to the bottom, Tom stopped and put Moon down on the ground and said, "I'm not going to carry that boy all the way back to the farm." When he began to walk away, Kyla thought for a moment that he was going to leave her to try to get Moon home by herself, but when she saw that he was just going to get some water from the lake she knew what he had in mind. Tom filled his hat with the icy cold water and climbed back up the bank to where Kyla was waiting. Then he dumped it all on Moon's face; who awakened immediately.

Tom pulled him back to his feet. Holding one of Moon's arms draped around his shoulder, he started Moon walking. When the young man started to go weak in the knees again, Tom growled, "Don't you pass out on me again or I'll leave your ass where you fall." It was only a few minutes before Moon was walking on his own, and by the time they reached the farm he was no longer woozy.

As soon as they came within sight of the farm Kyla knew something was wrong. It was late and everybody should have been asleep in the dormitories, but the farm was abuzz with activity. The electric yard lights were even turned on. The whole place was lit up like it was day. Everyone seemed to be heading toward the barn. So, Tom, Kyla, and Moon followed the crowd. Once they reached the barn they had to push their way through the crowd of people to get inside.

It was plain to see what had caused the commotion. Riley and Sadie were standing in the barn with rifles in hand. The two men who had come to the Settlement with Slick were both lying face down and dead on the floor in front of them. As they stood looking at each other, it was only a matter of who asked the question first. It was Tom who spoke up. "What happened here?"

Sadie straightened and faced Tom. "We caught them trying to steal the horses," she said defiantly. Like a tigress after her kill, Sadie was exhilarated. When she looked at Moon and saw the bandages, she asked, "What happened to you?"

Neither Moon or Tom knew who the two men were but Kyla did. "These two came to the Settlement with a pearl trader tonight. Armand and the others have been busy trying to keep things under control at the Settlement."

Sadie looked at Kyla contemptuously and retorted, "Well, they left the farm unguarded." Then she turned to one of the men gawking at the door and said, "You, get some help and get this mess cleaned up." As Sadie walked to the door, the crowd outside parted to let her and Riley pass. Kyla watched them go. No matter what Sadie had said, Kyla didn't believe that she really needed guarding. She seemed to be very capable of taking care of herself. Kyla watched as the men began to drag the two lifeless bodies out the barn door. It seemed Slick, true to his name, had managed to slip away.

Chapter Nine

It was an uneventful journey to the Family's camp. Fleet and Kurt arrived in a little less than two days easy riding from the Settlement. Riley would have been pleased to know that they had taken such a slow pace. The only reason to hurry was to take antibiotics to Justin, but for Fleet that had just been a convenient excuse to leave without telling anyone the real reason for the trip. He planned to return to the covered bridge where they had hidden the guns and ammunition. Hopefully, it would all still be there and Fleet could use them to trade for more horses. He wanted enough to put all twelve of the Guard on horseback.

It was midday when Fleet and Kurt arrived at the wooded glen where the Family lived. Fleet found the narrow path leading down the hill and led the way through the trees. They had not gone very far when a voice called out, "Stop where you are." A young man wearing a brown homespun shirt and lambskin coat stepped out from behind one of the trees. He was carrying one of the rifles that Fleet had brought with him on his last visit. Although Fleet didn't know him, he knew Fleet. "Brother Fleet," he called out, "Brother Fox said that you would be coming," and he began to lead the way to the camp. Fleet and Kurt both dismounted and led the horses along the narrow winding trail.

It was Kurt's first time at the camp. He was surprised when they emerged from the woods and he saw the row of earth shelters on the far side of the lake. It was a pleasant and peaceful setting. He watched for any sign of Justin as they walked around the lake and began to approach the buildings. Before they were all the way around, a woman wearing a long brown dress came out of one of the shelters. When she saw them coming, she went back into the building and returned with a tall man and another woman and they began walking to meet Fleet and Kurt.

Sister Samethia was the first to reach the visitors and embraced Fleet warmly, "Brother Fleet, I've been waiting for you." She smiled at him and was especially pleased to see that he was wearing the pin she had given him. "How is Sister Kyla?"

"She was well when we left," Fleet answered stiffly. The question made him uncomfortable. It wasn't his place to report on Kyla. Then motioning for Kurt to come forward, he said, "Sister Samethia, I would like you to meet my friend Kurt."

"Welcome, Brother Kurt," Samethia said with a warm smile. "Any friend of Brother Fleet is welcome."

Her greeting was quite formal, but her smile was genuine. In a way Sister Samethia reminded Kurt of Sadie, both women held themselves regally, like queens. Only Sister Samethia had a more earthy quality, where Sadie was cool and controlled. Sister Samethia was also quite beautiful, with long dark brown hair that fell in loose curls over her shoulders. Kurt found himself staring into her big green eyes as he stammered, "I am pleased to meet you Sister Samethia."

Sister Samethia was studying Fleet's friend. Brother Fox and the others had told her everything that happened the night she sent them to the crossroads to wait for Fleet and the others. They had reported everything about the men with Fleet and had described this one perfectly. He was not as tall as Fleet, but he was definitely built more solidly. Sister Samethia watched as Kurt nervously ran his fingers through his short black hair smoothing it back from his forehead. She returned his gaze, challenging him to look away first. When he lowered his lashes and looked to the ground like a bashful boy, Sister Samethia smiled with satisfaction.

As he watched the staring match between Kurt and Sister Samethia, Fleet could not help smiling. It was amusing to see the usually stone-faced Kurt, blushing like a schoolboy. It was all he could do to keep from laughing at his friend. Sister Samethia could do that to you, especially if you weren't expecting it. "How is your patient?" Fleet asked hoping to end Kurt's discomfort.

"Brother Justin is doing well," Sister Samethia turned her attention back to Fleet and answered in her most gracious voice. "Would you like to see him now?"

"Yes, we would," Kurt answered quickly. "Please take us now." It was a polite demand. Kurt was not going to let Sister Samethia think that all she could turn him to jelly by staring at him.

Turning to one of the young men behind her, Sister Samethia said, "Brother Wesley, will you take the horses and see that they are fed and stabled?" He nodded to Sister Samethia, but kept a wary eye on Fleet and Kurt as he led the horses away. Then to the young man who had met them on the path, she said, "Brother Wyatt, you can go back to your watch." Once they were gone and Sister Samethia was alone with Fleet and Kurt and she said, "Brother Fox is not here. We've had trouble with Cole's men since you passed through, but I expect him home tonight." Then with a slight nod to the men and said, "I will take you to Brother Justin now."

They followed as Sister Samethia led the way to one of the earth shelters. Fleet knew she was taking them into the women's sleeping quarters, and wondered if Justin knew how lucky he was to be allowed to stay in the quarters where the women lived. Then knowing Justin, he was certain that he did. When Fleet and Kurt entered the dimly lit building it was too dark to see at first, but Justin saw them immediately and shouted, "It's about time you got here. They won't give me my clothes."

He started to get up, pulling the blankets with him to cover himself in front of the women. Sister Eaglet was standing near the fire and when he got up she started scolding, "You still have a fever. Now lay down and do as you're told." If Justin had been smart, he would have done as she said. Instead he started to walk to meet Kurt and Fleet at the door. Sister Samethia stepped inside next and hot on her heels was Sister Mischka who pushed past the three standing just inside the doorway to get to Justin. She was kind enough to grab his good arm, and then pulled him none to gently back to the bed where he had been lying only moments before.

"If I were you I'd do what they say," Fleet advised as he ducked under one of the bundles of herbs hanging from the ceiling and walked to where Justin was standing. When Kurt came to stand next to Fleet, Justin finally allowed Sister Mischka to push him down onto the floor again, where he sat cross-legged, looking up at the others. Kurt and Fleet knelt beside the reluctant patient while Sister Samethia updated them on Justin's progress.

"We had to take Brother Justin's clothes so he would stay in bed," Sister Samethia said as she eyed Justin sternly. "Until this morning, he had a high fever and as soon as he was feeling a little better, he tried to sneak out."

Justin did not appreciate Sister Samethia talking about him like he was a child. "I'm fine," he argued, "and I've been laying around for three days now. I'm ready to go back to the Settlement with Fleet and Kurt."

Fleet clapped Justin on his good shoulder and said, "Well, don't worry about that. We won't be going back for a few days." As he stood, Fleet smiled broadly and said, "So just relax and enjoy yourself." He was thinking about giving Justin the packet of antibiotics that Sadie had sent for him, but there was apparently no need for them and it would have been an insult to the Sisters' belief in their herbal remedies to offer them. Fleet decided they were best kept in his pocket.

Kurt had to smile as he looked at Justin sitting on the floor with the two blond haired women standing guard over him. It was rather comical. The two girls were quite pretty and looked like they truly were sisters. The older Sister, who had drug Justin back to his bed, had her arms crossed and was glaring at him. The younger girl was standing next to her with a basin of water and towels. It looked like it was bath time. Justin was protesting as they began to leave, but Kurt could not imagine that it was all that unpleasant to have the young women fussing over him.

Justin was fuming when Kurt and Fleet left. Worst of all they were laughing about leaving him. He hadn't seen daylight for three days and was tired of sitting in the dark earth shelter. Both Sister Samethia and Sister Mischka had gone with them and he was glad of that. He hated the way Sister Samethia stared at him and it was Sister Mischka who pulled him down and sat on him that morning when he started to go out the door. As much as he hated to admit it to himself, she wouldn't have been able to stop him if he had been feeling stronger. That left him alone with Sister Eaglet, which was his only consolation after being left behind.

She knelt beside him and without a word began to take of the dressing on his shoulder. Justin watched her as she took off the gauze padding. He had been watching her a lot over the past three days. Justin vaguely remembered her being there after he was shot. There had been so many hands lifting and pushing him and everything that happened seemed a blur. One thing he did remember was riding with Sister Eaglet behind him, holding him in the saddle.

Nor did he remember being carried into the shelter, but when he did wake up Sister Eaglet was the first person that Justin saw. She was always there, washing him with cool water, giving him water and tea to drink, and doing everything for him. At times when he was awake, he had watched her through half closed eyes. It was comforting to see her in the room and he had memorized everything about her. From her blond hair, which she wore in two long braids, to her trusting blue eyes, he knew every inch of Sister Eaglet. When she was close, like she was now, Justin could smell her scent, it reminded him of flowers and spring. Her hands were small and delicate and her touch light as a feather as she washed his wounds. His contented reverie was interrupted when Sister Eaglet's sponge bathing began moving south. Justin pulled his blanket tighter around his waist. As he twisted around to face her, he growled, "I can wash myself."

Eaglet seemed surprised that he had objected and said unabashedly, "It's not like I haven't seen you naked."

Justin could feel the color rising in his cheeks. He wasn't sure which made him angrier, the fact that he was blushing or that she acted like seeing him naked was part of her job. To make matters worse, now she was laughing at him, too. Justin did not think it was funny at all. He was the one stuck in bed with no clothes and nowhere to go. He was relieved when Sister Eaglet decided not to continue trying to bathe him.

"I have to get out of here," Justin said as she started to put fresh dressings on his shoulder. "I can't stand being cooped up in here for another minute."

Sister Eaglet smiled at him. It was good to hear him complaining. Yesterday, Brother Justin hadn't felt well enough to put up a fight about anything. "You won't get strong unless you get some rest," she said and handed him a cup.

As Justin took a sip of the broth, he made a face and said, "I won't get any stronger if I don't get some real food," and set the cup on the floor. "Don't you have some meat?"

"I'll ask Sister Samethia if you can come to the evening meal tonight. I'm sure she'll agree if you stay in bed until then," Sister Eaglet said and began to rise.

Without thinking Justin reached out and took Sister Eaglet by the hand, keeping her from going. He wanted to tell her that she was the most beautiful girl that he had ever seen but he couldn't find the words. She was a bright and shining light in the darkness and he was drawn to her like a moth to a flame. Her eyes were questioning and Justin could see that she was waiting for him to say something. The only words that came to mind were, "You're not going, are you?"

When Justin reached out and took her by the hand, Sister Eaglet had felt a thrill pass through her body that she could not explain. "I'll be right here if you need anything," she said, but did not pull away. Brother Justin was a puzzle. She had known him only a few days, but Sister Eaglet could not imagine what it would be like when he left. Now that Brother Fleet and his friend had come, she knew that Justin would want to go with them and Sister Eaglet did not want to let him go. She looked deeply into his soft brown eyes and found herself drawing closer, wanting to ask him to stay, but at the same time she was afraid to hear his answer either way. When Justin released her hand and brushed his fingers gently across her face, Sister Eaglet jumped to her feet, spilling some of the water from the basin. The feelings that Justin stirred in Sister Eaglet were not something that she was ready to acknowledge.

Justin watched Sister Eaglet as she fled like a frightened rabbit. As he lay down, Justin was shaking his head with frustration. If that was how she wanted things, it was fine with him. Still, he turned onto his side so he could see her. She was sitting on the far side of the room and had picked up her sewing. Occasionally, she would look at him, then lower her eyes quickly and continue working furiously at her stitching.

Every time Eaglet looked up, she saw that Justin was still watching and it was hard for her to concentrate on her sewing. A part of her wished that she had not run away when he touched her, but she was torn. It was Brother Aquila that she loved and had promised to marry and the attraction that she felt for Justin was confusing. Her feelings for Brother Aquila had not changed, but when Justin touched her she felt a flutter in her heart and it was something that she could not ignore.

Finally, she heard him snoring softly. Now Sister Eaglet could look at Justin without him peering back at her. Once she was satisfied that he was soundly asleep, she crept quietly across the room and knelt beside him. Brushing his soft brown hair away from his face, she kissed him on the cheek and Justin stirred slightly in his slumber. For a moment she was afraid that she had awakened him, but his eyes remained closed. Sister Eaglet pulled the blanket over Justin's shoulders and went back to her sewing. If Justin was going to go anywhere, he needed a shirt. His black tunic was beyond repair.

~ ~ ~

Once the evening meal was over Brother Fox decided that at last he could relax and leaned back on his elbow. He had not been surprised to see Fleet had arrived to take his man home. This time he would make sure that Fleet did not go any further east than their camp. There had always been trouble with Cole Spring's men, but now they were searching for anyone on horseback. Family members were being followed and harassed on a daily basis. He had spent the three days since he had last seen Fleet talking to Brothers and Sisters who were being fired upon at every turn.

The safety of the Brothers and Sisters was his first priority. He had told everyone to begin moving the flocks west, but if they went too far in that direction, the people from the Settlement were a problem. Theft was a way of life with them and he could not afford to loose sheep anymore than he could men. The smaller the area into which they were squeezed, the harder it was becoming to stay hidden. If it had been up to Brother Fox alone he would have opted to take his chances with Sadie and the people from the Settlement, but Sister Samethia was adamant that they keep their distance.

As he thought of Sister Samethia, Brother Fox looked to where she was sitting, in her usual spot, opposite him in the half circle of people gathered around the fire. He smiled as he watched Sister Samethia with a personal satisfaction. She was like a precious jewel and the center of his life and the Family. He liked to watch her as she went about her business, the mother hen surrounded by all the chicks. Talking first to Brother Eldar and sending him on some errand and then conferring with Sister Mischka.

Earlier that evening Sister Samethia had mentioned something about Sister Eaglet and Fleet's young friend, Brother Justin. He had only half listened to her when she said it would be best to keep them apart, but during the meal he could see the stolen glances passing between the two. Not to mention the fact that Brother Aquila had spent the whole evening glaring at the new rival for Sister Eaglet's attention. That was the kind of thing that Sister Samethia kept her eye on. To Brother Fox it was not important; he had other things to worry about. The fact that the young men and women would take an interest in one another was inevitable and he did not have time to worry about such things. Besides he could not blame Brother Justin for showing an interest in Sister Eaglet. But if there was one thing about which Sister Samethia was consistent, it was her insistence that none of the young women have anything to do with the men from the Settlement or go there ever.

That was why it had surprised him when Sister Samethia had insisted that Sister Kyla go with Brother Fleet to the Settlement. He would have welcomed another pair of hands to help with the work. Still, if there was one thing he had learned in his time with Sister Samethia, it was to trust her judgement in such matters. She had an uncanny way of knowing things that she had no reason to know, the most recent example being the ambush at the highway. How she could have known when and where to send them was something that had no explanation. When Brother Fox asked how she knew, Sister Samethia said that she saw it in a dream.

Her unexplained ability to be in the right place at the right time was the secret to Sister Samethia's genius. One by one she had found them, bringing each one into her Family and spinning her web of enchantment about them all. Brother Fox was not immune to her charms and even though Sister Samethia was the love of his life, her body and soul belonged to the Family. Just seeing Fleet reminded him that no matter what he wanted, there was always a part of her that he could never totally possess. With Sister Samethia he had one choice and that was to accept the fact that the Mother was guiding her actions.

He had been watching Fleet and his friend, too. Fleet was, as usual, pleasant and charming. Tonight he had given most of his attention to Sister Mischka since Sister Eaglet was preoccupied. Fleet liked to spend his time teasing the young women. The fact that Brother Fleet spent so much time on pointless chatter was something that Brother Fox had never understood. On the other hand, his friend, Brother Kurt was quiet, speaking only when spoken to, and always polite. Still, Brother Fox could tell that he was listening and taking in everything that was said. Brother Kurt seemed to be a serious and thoughtful man, more in accordance with his own principles.

Fleet had been waiting for the meal to end and when he saw Brother Fox lean back and relax on his elbow. He began to extract himself from his conversation with Sister Mischka, who had been chattering on about herbs and farming. Fleet was listening to only half of what she said, but he did enjoy teasing her. She would always frown and scold him, but with one word from Fleet she melted into smiles again and went on with her story. She was busy telling him about a patch of dog-tooth violets nearby that had come into bloom when Fleet said, "Sister Mischka, I need to talk with Brother Fox if you will excuse me."

Sister Mischka looked at Brother Fox and then at Brother Fleet and with her lips pushed together in a pouting frown she said, "Yes, certainly." Her words were as short as her temper. Then she softened her tone just a little as she added, "But I will see you later?"

Fleet wasn't sure what she meant by later, but she seemed pleased when he said, "Of course, we won't be leaving for a few days." When Sister Mischka turned to speak to Sister Samethia, Fleet looked to Brother Fox wondering how to bring up the subject that was on his mind. There was no delicate way, so Fleet got right to the point. "I need more horses. I want enough so all my men can be mounted and some for reserve. I don't want to have to worry about fresh mounts anymore."

"The six that you have were more than we could spare," Brother Fox protested. "I think that six horses in trade for four rifles and some ammunition was more than generous." It was obvious by his answer that he was not anxious to discuss the matter. He looked at Fleet suspiciously and added, "And I don't want any more weapons if you have to go back to Spring's farm to get them. We are the ones dealing with the consequences since your second attack on the farm. Every time Spring's men see one of the Family, they fire on them and shoot our sheep." He was clearly angry with Fleet.

"I am sorry for that, but you know the reason why I went. If they hadn't attacked and taken my men, I wouldn't have gone to the farm a second time," Fleet said. Brother Fox was a hard man, but if there was one thing he understood, it was loyalty.

Brother Fox's expression was still one of disapproval, but he did nod. Only once and then it was only a slight movement, but he did acknowledge Fleet's responsibility to his men. Then picking up a stick that had fallen out of the fire, he said, "I know you well enough to know when you have something in mind. Tell me what it is, and I only hope that it won't put me into the fire." He tossed the stick that he was holding into the flames as if to emphasize the point. Whatever it was that Brother Fleet had planned, Brother Fox would make sure that the best interests of the Family were served before he agreed to anything.

"We have to go across the highway," Fleet began. When Brother Fox arched his eyebrows with disapproval, Fleet added quickly, "but nowhere near Spring's farm." Then looking to Kurt and back to Brother Fox again, Fleet went on quietly so only the three of them could hear. "We were able to confiscate and hide twenty rifles and hundreds of rounds of ammunition." When Brother Fox straightened suddenly, Fleet knew he had his attention.

"Twenty rifles would be enough for all the men," Brother Fox said. Then with a cautious look to Fleet, he added, "But what I said is true. I have already given you all the horses that I can."

"I want to know where you got your horses," Fleet said flatly. "I haven't seen any horses running loose. You had to get them somewhere. Tell me. Then Kurt and I will go after them ourselves." Fleet leaned back and waited for Brother Fox's response.

The proposition that Brother Fleet offered was tempting; enough rifles and ammunition for all of his men in exchange for the location of the stock farm. Brother Fox motioned to two young Brothers at the far end of the room to join them. As they knelt beside Brother Fox, he said, "Brother Fleet would like to know the location of the stock farm."

Both of the young Brothers stared at Brother Fox with their mouth open and a look of utter disbelief on their face. The taller one, Brother Wyatt shook his head and pushed his hair back behind his ears. "I don't think so," he answered with a derisive laugh and stared boldly at Fleet and Kurt.

Kurt had been sitting silently while Fleet told Brother Fox their plan and did not like the fact that the decision was being left to the young man. "I don't see what this boy has to do with anything."

Brother Wyatt looked down his long straight nose and considered Kurt arrogantly. "Brother Wesley and I are the only ones who know where the stock farm is."

Fleet looked at the two young men and said, "I find it hard to believe that these two brought back all of your horses by themselves?"

Brother Wesley grinned slyly at his friend. Then peering at the two men dressed in black tunics, he said, "If you want horses. You'll need a horse thief and we're the best you can get."

~ ~ ~

It was quite late when Fleet left the earth shelter to get some fresh air. The fire was growing low and it was quite smoky in the building. Brother Fox, Kurt, Justin, and the two self-proclaimed horse thieves, Brothers Wyatt and Wesley, were all still inside. They had spent the last hours discussing their plans for retrieving the hidden weapons and ammunition and for a raid on the stock farm. The two young Brothers insisted that the location of the farm remain a secret and had the audacity to insist that Fleet and Kurt go blindfolded. Fleet laughed to himself as he remembered Kurt's reaction. The boys had backed down when he started explaining how he would personally whip both of their arrogant asses if they even thought about anything so foolish. If there had been any doubt that Kurt was more than capable and willing to carry through with his threat, Fleet did not think that the Brothers would have backed down.

Fleet had wanted some time away from the others, a little time to himself to think things through before returning to go to sleep. The men from the Settlement were to sleep in the meeting room. It seemed that Justin was now well enough to leave the women's shelter. No doubt the decision had been hastened by the looks passing between Justin and Sister Eaglet. The young man had spent the entire evening mooning over her like some love struck puppy. It was just as well to keep them separated. The fact that Justin was wearing one of their homespun shirts made it look like he was thinking of joining the Family and one of the beautiful blond sisters would certainly be an enticement. Still, he didn't thing that Justin would make a very good shepherd.

It was then that he heard a soft rustling sound behind him. When he turned, Fleet was surprised to see Sister Mischka. She had left earlier with the other Sisters when they began discussing their plans. "Sister Mischka, is something wrong?" Fleet asked. Whatever it was that had brought her out at this time of night had to be important.

She stood close to Fleet looking up at him in the darkness. "I've been waiting for you." Sister Mischka stepped closer and said softly, "I'm relieved that you were not hurt when you went to Spring's farm." Sister Mischka was hesitant to say what was really on her mind. She had been relieved when he did not bring Sister Kyla. It had been an irritation to see Fleet with another woman, even if she was skinny and had a shaved head. Anyone taking even a few moments of Fleet's time was enough to make her jealous. Sister Mischka wanted to be the only one in Fleet's eyes, and tonight she had enjoyed his undivided attention.

Fleet was still wondering what she wanted when Sister Mischka suddenly threw her arms around his neck and kissed him on the lips. It was the last thing that he had expected. Taking hold of her arms, Fleet loosened her grasp and pushed her away. "Sister Mischka, I..." was all he was able to say before she looked at him with tears welling up in her eyes. Then she ran away and disappeared into the darkness. All Fleet could do was stare after her in a state of shock. He hadn't wanted to hurt her feelings. He truly cared for Sister Mischka and thought of both her and Sister Eaglet as his younger sisters. Shaking his head, Fleet continued his walk in the cold night air. Sister Mischka was only one more thing to plague his thoughts.

Foremost in his mind were their plans for tomorrow. The possibility that the guns had been found had to be considered. Then the question would be whether Cole Spring and his men had simply removed the weapons or were waiting for them to return for them. It was a deadly game of chess where Fleet tried desperately to anticipate Cole's next move. Only Fleet was playing the game blind and he could not afford to loose even one man.

Kurt and Brother Wyatt were to leave at daybreak to scout the bridge where they left the guns. If it was still being watched, they would have to wait for another day. They had planned that it would take six hours to ride the distance between the Family's camp and the covered bridge. That would leave a few hours of daylight for them to check out the area. Fleet would leave at mid-day with three extra horses to carry the boxes of ammunition and meet them after dark a mile south of the bridge. In addition to himself the young Brothers, Wesley, Wyatt, and Aquila would be going to help. Brother Fox was going, too, which was a surprise to Fleet. Usually, he preferred let Fleet take care of this sort of endeavor on his own. With the three young Brothers going, he felt he needed to be there to watch out for their welfare.

If everything went according to plan, the guns and ammunition would be recovered without anyone knowing they had even been there. Once they were back across the highway and west of Cole's boundary line, Brother Aquila would take the horses and guns back to the camp by himself. Then the rest would head south and go after the horses. The only information that Brothers Wesley and Wyatt were willing to divulge was the fact that their destination was three days ride to the south.

Fleet wondered if Manjohnah was responsible for the operation of the stock farm like he was at Cole's farm. It had been Manjohnah's network that was responsible for the wholesale looting that took place toward the end of the evacuations. While military units like his own were busy gathering the populations of hundreds of small towns, Manjohnah's men had followed behind them loading trucks full of anything they could find. Stores were stripped bare of anything of use and what hadn't been taken had been destroyed. It had been the same with livestock and it only made sense that Manjohnah had several locations were he stored his stolen hoard. Fleet's world was becoming larger, as he was realizing that Cole Spring's farm was most likely only one of many.

Fleet had walked to the end of the small collection of earth shelters. There were only four so it had been a short walk. Walking back now he passed the shelter that was Brother Fox's and Sister Samethia's, next were the men's sleeping quarters and then the women's. Fleet paused for a moment as he passed the women's shelter wondering if he should try to find Sister Mischka and smooth things over with her. Maybe if he mentioned what had happened to Sister Samethia, he wouldn't have to do anything, which was what Fleet preferred. Consoling young girls with crushes was not Fleet's strong point.

He had not been gone very long when he returned to the earth shelter where Brother Fox and the others were waiting. As Fleet opened the door to enter, he was met by Brother Fox and the other Brothers on their way out. Fleet waited outside and watched as the three younger men went to their sleeping quarters and disappeared inside.

Brother Fox remained behind. There was something on his mind that he wanted to say to Fleet away from the others. "I am concerned about going to the stock farm to the south, Brother Fleet." Brother Fox took a deep breath before adding, "I do not want the lives of those young men put in jeopardy."

Fleet could hear the tone of warning in Brother Fox's voice and answered, "I would go by myself if you could convince those young men to tell me the location of the farm." That had been his original plan. Fleet had no desire to take any of the Family members with him.

For Brother Fox the issue was not so clearly defined. "Nor do I need an enemy to my south in addition to the one to the east," Brother Fox said, getting to the heart of his dilemma. He should have added the one to the west, but Fleet's attachment to the Settlement and Sadie was something Brother Fox had not been able to change. He did not want to tell his friend that he considered him as much of a threat to the Family's safety as the others.

"Your two young Brother's assured us both that they could sneak in and steal as many horses as we need without any shots being fired," Fleet reminded him. He knew Brothers Wyatt and Wesley were embellishing their story a little, but if they truly were good horse rustlers then they would be able to do it. By definition, one could not be a good thief, if one is discovered in the act.

Brother Fox knew Fleet well enough to know that there was no way he could keep him from going south without them and looking for the stock farm himself. And knowing Fleet, he would be fortunate enough to find it. At least this way he would be there to keep an eye on Fleet. His only problem was the fact that Brother Wyatt and Brother Wesley were acting like obstinate mules. No matter what he said, they had refused to tell them where the farm was located and the only reason they refused was because they wanted to go with Fleet. Everyone had heard the stories about Fleet and his exploits from the Family members who participated in the ambush. They had also been talking to Brother Justin. It was hard for Brother Fox to keep young men's minds on farming and shepherding with the lure of adventure looming in their future.

Then there was the fact that Sister Samethia had chosen to retire with the women instead of listening to their plans. Brother Fox would not feel at ease with the plans they had made tonight until he had an opportunity to discuss them with Sister Samethia. He had come to rely heavily on her when deciding such things. Especially when it came to Fleet. Brother Fox needed to speak with her and perhaps he would speak with Brother Wesley and Brother Wyatt again in private. There had to be a way to change their minds and Brother Fox vowed to find it.

He regarded Brother Fleet as his equal, but their focuses were different. Brother Fox respected and liked the man, but at the same time he could not trust him completely. Fleet was driven by the desire for power and revenge. Brother Fox wanted the power as well, but he wanted to use it to protect and insulate his Family from the dangers in the world around them. Fleet would throw himself and anyone with him right into the path of destruction and fight it to the end. He tilted his head in a cautious nod to Fleet and said, "I'll see you in the morning. The Mother keep you until then."

Fleet smiled and returned the farewell with one of his own, "And don't let the bed bugs bite." Then Fleet disappeared into the shelter chuckling at his joke.

As he strode quickly across the camp, Brother Fox was shaking his head. Fleet was a puzzle to him. Maybe Sister Samethia would have some insights for him tonight. He smiled as he opened the door to their earth shelter and went inside. The fire was glowing warmly in the corner and Sister Samethia was kneeling next to the fire. When she saw Brother Fox, she poured some warm tea into a cup sitting on a mat next to the fire. She had been waiting for him. Brother Fox crossed the room and sat on one of the rugs next to the fire. It was a special rug for them. Sister Samethia had made it from the scraps of their old clothing when they had shed their old life for the new one that they now lived. It was, as Samethia had wanted it, a symbol of their metamorphosis.

As he removed his boots and leather jerkin, Brother Fox looked at Sister Samethia. From the waves of dark brown hair falling over her shoulders to the tips of her toes, which were peeking out from the end of the thin white shift that she wore under her dress, Sister Samethia was the most exquisite woman he had ever known. Her eyes were a hazel green and the iris of one eye had a fleck of brown that marred the smooth green color. It was most unusual and unless you were very close and very observant you would not see it. Brother Fox was close and he peered into her eyes, hoping to see what she saw. He was loosing himself in the pleasure of her scent and sight of her body beneath the revealing fabric of her shift, forgetting the questions that had been on his mind only a few moments ago.

Sister Samethia broke his reverie by saying, "What agreement have you come to with Brother Fleet?" She picked up the cup of tea and handed it to Brother Fox.

As he took the cup of tea and sipped it slowly, Brother Fox sat back a little. "Brother Kurt and Brother Wyatt will leave first thing in the morning to scout the area where Fleet and his men left the guns." He watched her carefully, gauging her reaction.

Sister Samethia only stared at the fire and poked the dying embers with a stick. "Brother Kurt is a good choice," she said rather absently.

When she did not elaborate, Brother Fox continued, "The rest of us will leave at midday."

Before Brother Fox could list the names Sister Samethia said, "You'll be taking Brother Wesley and Brother Aquila with you."

It was not a question, but a statement. The choices had been obvious, they were the only able bodied men available at the time. Brother Fox did not bother to acknowledge her statement, but said, "That will leave you and Sister Eaglet and Sister Mischka alone with only Brother Eldar." He worried about Sister Samethia, even though he knew her to be a very resourceful woman.

"Brother Justin will be here as well," Sister Samethia answered rather coolly.

Brother Fox knew he had ruffled her feathers a little but he didn't care. He would smooth them soon enough. As he watched her stirring the ashes he asked, "Tell me what you see, Samethia." It was an unusual thing for Brother Fox to drop her title, but at times when they were alone he liked to use her name. When said aloud it had a lyrical sound.

She did not look at him when she said, "This is not Fleet's time. If it were then Sister Kyla would be with him and the other."

Sister Samethia had told him of her visions concerning Brother Fleet and Sister Kyla. It was something that she found difficult to put into words and what she did tell him was impossible to understand. Brother Fox's interpretation was that during Sister Samethia's readings of both Brother Fleet and Sister Kyla, she had seen similar visions. What Brother Fox wondered about was the third person that Sister Samethia was waiting to find. She had told no one other than him about the full meaning of her visions. Not even Fleet or Kyla knew. Samethia used the example of a bow and arrow, Fleet of course was the arrow. What was needed for him to reach his mark was something to propel him. Samethia said that two people would accomplish that goal. One was the most unlikely choice, Sister Kyla, and the other was still unknown to Samethia. Brother Fox's question to her now was this. "Is Brother Kurt the one?"

"No," she said, "I'll know him when I meet him." Sister Samethia stood now and held her hand out to Brother Fox. As he took her hand and stood next to her, Sister Samethia pressed her body next to his and said, "It's late. We should go to bed. You need your rest before you leave tomorrow." Brother Fox smiled and let her lead him to their bed, but rest was the last thing on his mind.

~ ~ ~

The trip back to the covered bridge couldn't have gone more smoothly. There had been no sign of Cole Spring's men along the main highway. Nor did they see anyone after passing east of the boundary. Kurt and Brother Wyatt had scouted the area thoroughly before meeting Fleet and the others. They hadn't seen anything or anyone. When they went to the bridge there was no sign that anything had ever happened there and the guns were exactly as they had left them. It took awhile to load all the weapons and as much ammunition as the horses could carry. They were forced to leave four cases of ammunition behind, but Brother Fox knew the location now and someone would be sent for the rest once they returned to the camp. It was a personal triumph for Fleet and earned him the somewhat reserved approval of Brother Fox.

Once they were west of the highway again Brother Aquila headed back home with the packhorses trailing behind him. As he headed off on his own, he urged the horses to go faster, Brother Aquila had been anxious all the time they were away from the camp. Leaving Sister Eaglet alone with Justin was preying on his mind. Watching him hurry off, Fleet hoped he didn't try to go too fast and end up having to repack one of the horses when its load fell off.

At the insistence of Brother Fox they stayed at the crest of one of the higher ridges and watched with the binoculars until Brother Aquila finally disappeared out of sight. Only then did they begin their journey south. Every mile traveled was taking them further from Cole Spring's sphere of influence and by the end of the day they were riding openly on the gravel country roads. It seemed as if they were on a leisurely outing.

Brother Wyatt and Brother Wesley were in high spirits. They often rode ahead of the others looking for a landmark or road sign to guide them. It was nearly dark when they returned, horses galloping at full tilt from one of their forays. As they reined their horses to a halt, Brother Wesley shouted, "There's a rider following us."

Kurt and Fleet immediately began to reach for their weapons, but Brother Fox motioned for them to stop and said; "Spring's men don't ride horses." He looked at the young man and asked, "How far behind us?"

"He's only a half a mile back," Brother Wesley answered and pointed in the direction from which they had come, "on the other side of that ridge."

"Did you recognize the rider or the horse?" Kurt asked. He still had his hand on the stock of his rifle. Brother Fox's assurance that Spring's men didn't ride horses was not enough for him. Anyone following was potentially a threat and Kurt planned on being ready. When Brother Wesley shook his head Kurt said, "We're out in the open here. Let's ride to that stand of timber up ahead and wait to see who it is." There was no argument and they set their horses to a gallop and rode as quickly as possible to take cover. Once they had stopped, they did not have much time to wait. Whoever it was riding toward them was hot on their heels.

As the horse and rider suddenly appeared in view, Brother Fox recognized them immediately and hurried from the cover of the trees to flag them down. Once the rider saw him, she pulled firmly on the reins and brought speeding mount to a skidding halt then wheeled him around and trotted back to where Brother Fox was standing. She slid off the horse and stood in front of him with her hands on her hips.

Fleet was leading his horse and Brother Fox's from the woods. He had seen the Sister with Brother Fox only once before now. She had long red hair and instead of a dress, she was dressed in trousers and a shirt with lacing up the front and a lambskin coat like the men wore. Brother Fox had not said anything yet, but was staring at the young red headed woman with obvious agitation.

It was Brother Wesley who spoke first. "What are you doing here?" he said as he almost tripped over some branches in his hurry to get to her.

The girl whirled around and glared at Brother Wesley, "What made you think that you could leave me behind?"

Brother Wyatt looked down at her and said, "What made you think that you could come?" He had set his feet in a wide stance and with his arms crossed as he confronted her with his question.

She looked at Brother Wyatt and sneered contemptuously, "This doesn't concern you, Brother Wyatt. So I would recommend that you mind your own business."

Fleet was watching the whole exchange wondering when Brother Fox was going to get these three youngsters under control. Whatever reasons the girl would give for following them; it was all a waste of time. Finally Brother Fox said in a low voice, "What in the name of the Mother, do you think you are doing here?" His tone was as sharp as a knife.

The girl flinched only slightly. She stood tall and looked Brother Fox directly in the eyes, "My place is with Brother Wesley, where he goes, I go."

Brother Wesley was clearly embarrassed. He shifted uncomfortably as the other men stared at him as if the Sister's uninvited appearance was his fault. He looked at the redheaded Sister and said softly, "You shouldn't have come." He wanted to talk to her away from the others, but this was no time for private conversations.

Brother Fox was not so soft spoken when he reiterated Brother Wesley's statement. "Sister Alisma, you should not have come and you will go back now," he was nearly bellowing with anger before he had finished speaking.

Fleet was loosing patience with the whole situation. "Young lady, there is no reason for you to go any further."

"You can try to leave me behind, but I won't go back." She looked at each of them in turn, daring them to try.

Kurt shook his head. He was beginning to think all the Brothers and Sisters were stubborn and arguing with any of them was pointless. He mounted his horse and said so. "You are all mule headed and I am tired of wasting time. If the girl won't go, then she'll come with us. She might as well, the whole trip is turning into one big Family outing." He slapped his horse on the rump and galloped on ahead of them. Sister Alisma didn't wait for the others. She was back on her horse in a flash galloping after Kurt leaving the others to catch them both.

Chapter Ten

As the six riders continued their trip south, the hills were becoming steep and rocky and the land was more densely forested the further they went. Occasionally, they passed orchards where the trees were planted in rows on the slopes, but there was very little in the way of open fields or pastures. Day number two passed without incident as they rode up and down one steep hillside after another. Every mile they traveled was the same as the last, but about midday on the third, Brother Wyatt announced that they were only a few miles from the stock farm. "See that ridge," he said, pointing to a rocky hilltop about a mile away, "from there you can see the farm. It's in the valley on the other side."

Brother Wesley led the way up the winding trail and around the trees on his black and white pinto. He seemed quite at home on horseback, swaying as he rode and speaking casually about the farm. "They have the whole valley divided into pastures with cattle in some, horses in others, and sheep, too. It was easy enough to cut the fence and drive the horses out. There were so many, I doubt they ever noticed that any were missing."

"What about guards," Kurt asked. He was riding at the end of the line and had to raise his voice for Brother Wesley to hear him.

It was Brother Wyatt who answered. He turned to Kurt and said lightly, "What guards?" Apparently, it was some private joke between Brother Wesley and himself, because they were the only ones who thought it was funny.

Kurt found the light-hearted attitude of the two Brothers bothersome. He was not one to assume anything, "Just because you don't see anyone, doesn't mean that no one is watching," he said. From his position at the end of the line, Kurt had been evaluating the members of the party riding before him. First there was Brother Wesley who had a very easy-going personality. Sister Alisma had been chattering and teasing him since joining them, but she had never been able to get a rise out of him, no matter what she said. When Kurt looked at Brother Wesley, his first impression was that the shaggy haired young man was pre-occupied and not paying attention, but Kurt found that little escaped Brother Wesley's eye. His whole attitude was one of understated self-assurance. Kurt just hoped that he would be able to perform the miracles that he had promised.

Next in line was Brother Fox riding a high strung bay mare with four white socks. The horse and rider did not seem very well matched. The horse pranced nervously every time they came to a stop, while Brother Fox, on the other hand, was a hard and immovable object and reminded Kurt of statues he had seen of men on horseback. Still, he was growing to respect the man. Brother Fox and Kurt thought alike. Their main concern was the safety of the group and if that meant going home empty handed then that is what they would do.

Sister Alisma followed Brother Fox, her red hair tied in a long ponytail that was swinging back and forth with the movement of her horse. She was trying to move in front of Brother Fox to keep the place she had claimed since arriving and that was next to Brother Wesley, who seemed to be her only focus in life. It was as if he was the center of the universe and her life revolved around him. She kept kicking her little brown gelding with the appaloosa markings until he was almost on top of Brother Fox's mount. When Brother Fox turned and gave her a sharp look, warning her to back off, she finally pulled back on the reins and allowed him to stay between herself and Brother Wesley for the time being. Kurt hoped that she would not be an encumbrance when it came time to move quickly.

Fleet was fourth in line and was being unusually quiet. Kurt knew that he was going over all the possible scenarios in his mind. His pre-occupation was something Kurt had come to expect. Fleet was well aware of his responsibility for the men who followed him and the closer they came to the actual confrontation the more sullen and moody Fleet became.

Then there was Brother Wyatt. Kurt had already spent a little time with him alone when they were scouting the area around the covered bridge. He was tall and thin and at the age where a young man has attained his full height, but had yet to develop the musculature and build of a mature man. It appeared that he was trying to grow a beard, but all he was able to achieve was light fuzz along his jaw line and an almost imperceptible moustache. Kurt watched as Brother Wyatt guided his horse effortlessly between the trees, with the horse responding to the slightest pressure from the Brother's knees.

Just short of the crest of the hill, Brother Wesley stopped and slid off the back of his mount. "We'd better leave the horses here," he said as he tied his horse's reins to the trunk of a small sapling. Then without waiting for the others, he started to hike the short distance to the top on foot.

Fleet, Kurt and Brother Fox followed cautiously, while Sister Alisma and Brother Wyatt ran ahead. Fleet was hoping all their youthful enthusiasm could be harnessed and put to good use. When Fleet reached the top of the hill the three were already lying at the edge of a cliff looking at the valley that lay before them. Fleet took his binoculars from the case and chose a spot next to Sister Alisma. What he saw was not exactly what the Brothers had described.

The stock farm was there and it was a huge operation, filling the entire valley. As far as Fleet could see there were pastures with cattle and sheep, but no horses. At the far end of the valley, nearly five miles away, was a collection of buildings. Barely visible even with the binoculars, it appeared large enough to be a small town. Just beyond that was small ribbon of silver, it was the river that formed the southern border of the valley. Between the ridge and the river, it was all prime farming land, wide, flat and rich but it was not unguarded, as the Brothers had led him to believe. Fleet could see men on all-terrain vehicles in the pastures with the stock and others riding along the perimeter of the well-maintained fencing. He was irritated with the two Brothers. It appeared it would not be a simple venture as he had hoped and Fleet had come too far to go home with nothing.

Even without the binoculars Kurt and the others could see the men on all-terrain vehicles, too. See them and hear the roar as they passed near the bottom of the hill where they were hidden. Without a word spoken, they all withdrew to the spot where the horses were tied. It was only then that Fleet vented his frustration with the Brothers. "I should have know better than to trust the word of two boys who are still wet behind the ears," Fleet spat the words out angrily.

The insult was not lost on either of the young Brothers. Brother Wyatt pulled himself up to his full height, shoulders back, and looped his hair behind his ears, a gesture that always preceded some arrogant statement. "I am not a child," he said as he looked Fleet squarely in the eyes, "and you will not speak to me that way." His fists were clenched ready for whatever Fleet might do.

Brother Wesley's response was much the same. Although he was much smaller than Fleet he stood next to Brother Wyatt and with an obvious disrespect for Fleet added, "You are the one who wanted us to bring you here. It is not our fault that things have changed in the last six months." The two young men stood together, if Fleet acted against one then it became the concern of the other. When Sister Alisma joined them as well, it was three.

Kurt and Brother Fox were watching as the three squared off against Fleet. It wouldn't help matters if there were a brawl. Brother Fox stepped in between them and said, "We won't accomplish anything with accusations and fighting." He was looking directly at the three Family members. A word from Brother Fox was all it took for them to back down, even if it was somewhat unwillingly. In a way Brother Fox was relieved, surely Fleet would see now that there was no point in trying to steal anything. "I know Brother Wyatt and Brother Wesley told us everything accurately, but it has been six months. Things change, Brother Fleet. You have to admit it doesn't look very promising under these circumstances."

Fleet turned to Brother Fox; it was what he had expected from him. At the first sign of trouble, he was ready to head for home, but before Fleet could reply, Brother Wesley spoke the very words that he had wanted to say. "You're not thinking of going back! I am not leaving until we have done what we came to do." Smiling now Fleet looked at Brother Wyatt, Brother Wesley, and Sister Alisma. A moment before they had been ready to fight him over an insult, but now they were his allies in what was sure to be a battle of wills.

Kurt joined the argument on Brother Fox's side. "Even if we did manage to take some horses, how do you propose that we get away without the men on the ATV's chasing us down? They can follow anywhere we can ride."

Fleet had to hurry to answer before either of the two young men. "Why don't we take some time to look over their operation before we decide what is possible or not." His initial shock and anger were fading and Fleet was looking at the situation as he did any other. If you wanted something badly enough, a way could be found around even the most formidable obstacles. He watched Brother Fox and Kurt, knowing that if it were left up to them, they would be back up on the horses and heading home.

Brother Fox knew when to stand firm and when to bend. He would bend a little for now. As he looked at his young charges, he said, "There is no harm in looking, as long as everyone is careful and nobody does anything unless we all agree on it first." The last was directed at Fleet. Then Brother Fox headed back up the hill with Kurt following him. The group was officially divided.

As he scrutinized the Brothers, Fleet had several questions for them now that he had seen the stock farm. "Was the operation this big when you were here?"

"Yes," Brother Wyatt answered slowly and he eyed Fleet warily before adding, "It looks the same except for the men patrolling. That's new."

"It looks like a big spread, how far does it go to the east and west?" Fleet asked. He was trying to get them to fill in the blanks on what was beyond the view from the ridge.

As they began to realize that Fleet was still interested in the task that had brought them here, Brother Wesley and Brother Wyatt's mood lightened a little, but they both regarded Fleet with a certain amount of reservation as they had from the beginning. Brother Wyatt answered by saying, "We're at the center point here. They have stock scattered in pastures and pens for nearly ten miles in both directions." Then he added smartly, "At least that's how it was." He was not quite ready to forget Fleet's insult.

Fleet rubbed his chin thoughtfully before asking his next question, "You never did tell me how you plan to steal the horses."

Brother Wyatt looked at Brother Wesley and with a nod from him began to explain what they had done. "We looked for a pasture with horses along the north edge of the valley with a fence near the trees. After finding a spot we liked, Brother Wesley and I spent a day just watching the horses that we were after. We wanted to catch the lead horse. There's always one in every herd. We figured that if we were riding the horse that the others were used to following, then our job would be that much easier."

267

Brother Wesley cut in and said, "If you're on foot and you want to catch a horse then you have to think like one." Then as he shook his head a little to clear the hair from his eyes, he added with a sly grin, "And smell like one, too." When he saw Fleet looking at him, Brother Wesley added, "We rubbed horse manure all over our clothes to cover our scent."

Sister Alisma laughed, but cut it off short when Brother Wesley cast an irritated glance in her direction. She had to hold her hand to her mouth to hide her grin, but she couldn't fight the urge to jibe him just a little. "If it smells like horse shit, then it must be horse shit," she said in the most serious voice that she could manage.

Ignoring her comment, Brother Wesley continued, "We slipped into the herd at night and with Brother Wyatt's help I managed to get a rope on that black stallion that you're riding."

"You have got to be crazy," Fleet said incredulously. The black horse was difficult enough to put a saddle and bridle on when he was tied securely, he couldn't imagine how these two were lucky enough to catch him, let alone stay on him riding bare back.

Brother Wyatt took Fleet's comment as a compliment and said, "Crazy or not, we did it once and we can do it again."

Smiling now Fleet reached out and clapped them on their shoulders saying, "I'm beginning to believe you can, but unfortunately getting them out is the easy part. We have to do it so they don't know they've been robbed until it's too late."

Sister Alisma looked at the three men standing in front of her and with a confident smirk, stated what should have been obvious. "Well this time we don't have to do it on foot. We can ride in and after we have ropes on the ones we want, then we knock down the fence and drive the rest of the herd into the woods. They'll be busy rounding up the ones that we leave behind. By the time they're done counting heads and realize they're a few short, we can be long gone." Brother Wyatt looked irritated that Sister Alisma had said it first, but Brother Wesley nodded with approval. They looked to Fleet to see what he might have to say.

"There's only one thing you left out," Fleet said flatly. "What are we going to do about the patrols?" There was no answer from the threesome and he finished by saying, "We need to spend the rest of today and tomorrow watching. I need to know how many men there are. Where do they go when they not on patrol? I need information." Fleet looked up toward the top of the hill where Brother Fox and Kurt were waiting for him. "Wait here," he said. Then looking at the three young Family members he added, "Whatever happens, you remember that what I say goes. Do you understand?" He looked at each one in turn and added, "I can't have an argument where even a second's delay can cost someone their life."

They looked from one to the other. Fleet was asking them to follow his orders, knowing that was Brother Fox's prerogative. The three were torn, wanting to agree with Fleet, but unable to disregard their obligation to Brother Fox. Finally it was Brother Wyatt who broke the uncomfortable silence by saying, "We will be there to do what needs to be done, but Brother Fox is the only man that we answer to." He stood proudly in front of Fleet, speaking for himself and the other two nodding in agreement with what he said. Nothing could shake the foundation of their belief in the Family and Brother Fox. Argue and protest, though they might, they would never betray their commitment to the Family.

Their answer didn't surprise Fleet, but it did concern him. In a life or death situation it was usually best not to have men who were unsure about who was in charge. And Brother Fox or no Brother Fox, Fleet would be in charge. It was the only way he could accomplish his goals, but it would not be an easy task to convince Brother Fox of that fact. Fleet set off up the steep grade to find him.

Kurt was lying on his stomach studying the farm in the valley. Only a few of the fields were actually being used for pasture. The others were empty and once things warmed up a little, Kurt was sure they would be used for hay and grain production to provide feed for the livestock. As he calculated the amount of feed that it would take to keep all those animals alive and also the food below that was still on the hoof, enough food to keep everyone at the Settlement fat and happy, Kurt found himself shaking his head in frustration. It was not right that such abundant resources where being hoarded while so many people were near starvation. Dealing with these people directly and trying to trade honestly would have been preferable to stealing, but

Kurt knew it was dangerous to try and he could not deny the fact that he wanted to take what they needed as much as Fleet did.

When he heard footsteps on the loose rock behind him, Kurt turned and saw that Fleet had joined them at last. Fleet lay next to Kurt on the edge of the rock ledge and asked him the question that he always did. "What do you think?"

"I think I want a thick beef steak, cooked over the fire, charred on the outside and pink in the middle." Kurt knew that was not the answer that Fleet wanted, but this time he wanted to hear what Fleet had to say before he offered his opinion. "What did Brother Wyatt and Brother Wesley have to say?" he knew that Fleet would not have missed an opportunity to question them.

"This is just a part of their operation," Fleet said as he held the binoculars out to Kurt allowing him to look through them while they talked. "They said that the farm covers the whole valley and is stretched out over twenty miles."

"That's a lot of territory to keep patrolled," Brother Fox added his input to the discussion. Even he was finding it hard to resist the temptation that the stock farm presented. Stealing livestock seemed justified when there was no other way to survive. There was no justice in the world and that left Brother Fox to exact the penalties as he saw fit.

The fact that both Brother Fox and Kurt seemed receptive to discussion was encouraging. "I want to spend the rest of today scouting the area. We need to know where the herds are located if there are any," Fleet said. They needed more information before any definite plans could be made. "I thought we could split up into pairs and meet back here tonight. Then we'll decide what to do tomorrow."

"I will take Sister Alisma with me," Brother Fox announced quickly. It seemed that he felt she needed watching more than the other two did.

Kurt continued to study the valley through the binoculars and said, "It makes no difference to me," leaving the choice of which Brother went with him up to Fleet.

"Take Brother Wyatt with you," Fleet said leaving Brother Wesley to go with Fleet. Then Brother Fox, Kurt and Fleet walked back down the hill to tell the others what had been decided. The fact that they were being split up did not go over well, but one word of warning from Brother Fox was all it took to quell their younger companions' objections. It seemed that Brother Wyatt, Brother Wesley, and Sister Alisma were beginning to realize that the fun was over and the three older men were deadly serious. Fleet and Brother Wesley took the eastern half of the valley. While Kurt and Brother Wyatt were to scout to the west. Brother Fox decided that he and Sister Alisma would explore the area north of the farm looking for the best route to take when and if they left with their stolen horses.

By the time all six met again that evening the weather had changed drastically. A strong cold front with a strong northerly wind and rapidly dropping temperatures had moved in. As the wind whipped around them, all agreed that it would be better to spend the night somewhere else. They pulled their coats and hoods closer, trying to keep their exposure to the cold wind to a minimum, while Brother Fox led the way to a thick stand of cedars that he had seen earlier in the day. It took them several minutes to find the spot again and a lot of winding around patches of underbrush too dense for the horses to get through. When they found the cedar grove, Brother Fox led them into the heart of the trees. It made a good camping spot with the windbreak of trees to the north and a small clearing in the center of the grove that was big enough for them and the horses. After the horses were fed and tied off for the night, it was all they could do to huddle together wrapped in blankets shivering in the cold. The frigid wind seemed to sap every ounce of energy from their bodies, but there would be no fire and no one asked. It wasn't worth the little bit of comfort it would provide, if the flames and smoke revealed their location.

As Fleet sat on the cold ground, he shifted uncomfortably, trying to brush away the debris from the cedar trees blanketing the ground where he was sitting. There were sharp little needles and sticks poking him even through the thick fabric of his trousers. Fleet pulled the hood from his jacket down over his face until only a small space remained open and watched the others. When he looked at Brother Wesley, Fleet saw that he no longer had reservations about Sister Alisma's presence. The two were huddled together, with Brother Wesley leaning against the trunk of one of the larger cedars and Sister Alisma nestled with her back against his chest. With two blankets and double the body heat,

271

they were warmer than everyone else was. If it got much colder they would all be huddling together for warmth, but when Fleet thought about whom his partner might be, it was certain that Brother Wesley and Sister Alisma had certainly gotten the best deal.

Fleet wanted to hear what the others had found, but no one said much. If you wanted to speak and be heard, you had to uncover your face. Hopefully, Kurt and Brother Wyatt had found something. Fleet and Brother Wesley had ridden to the east and covered the entire northern border of the farm and hadn't seen one horse. There were several pastures with cattle. Many of those were filled with pregnant cows and several with their new calves. They had also seen sheep and lambs. There was an abundance of meat being produced here, but Fleet could only wonder whom it was for.

The guards had been everywhere. Brother Wesley and Fleet had to stop and take cover on several occasions when they rode too near the trail where the guards patrolled. They had seen a cluster of buildings near the eastern end of the valley that looked like a base camp for the guards. Fleet had counted five all terrain vehicles parked outside a large garage and several men who appeared to be off duty, walking around at their ease. All day the patrols had continued at regular intervals. One rider was barely out of sight before he could hear the sound of the next one approaching. The noisy engines were a blessing, since it made it impossible for them to approach without being heard well in advance.

There were too many unknown variables, too many things to consider. Fleet got to his feet and brushed the sharp cedar needles from his clothing. He loosened his hood enough to say, "Set a guard, I'll be back later." Then picking up his rifle and binoculars, he headed back to the ridge overlooking the farm. Fleet needed to see if the routine at night was the same as it was during the day. Besides, he couldn't rest with the cold and the wind, so he might as well do something useful.

As he made his way through the dense underbrush, Fleet heard the sound of coyotes howling in the distance. The sound sent a chill up his spine that had nothing to do with the cold. It was a mournful song of death and sorrow that mingled with the whistling wind. He released the safety on the rifle and made sure a round was loaded and ready in the chamber. Every shadow and movement had become ominous. Two-footed animals were not the only dangerous creatures that might be lurking in the darkness. When Fleet finally reached the top of the ridge, he found a place to sit beside a large tree. It provided him with a little shelter from the wind and something to lean against. As he wrapped his blanket around himself and settled in with his binoculars in one hand and holding his rifle propped against his shoulder, Fleet was thankful for one thing. There were no sharp cedar needles poking him.

Fleet watched the town at the far side of the valley for awhile; it was lit up like a carnival. The lights were so bright that the reflection could be seen on the clouds. Every once in awhile he saw a vehicle travelling one of the roads. It seemed that all the traffic was moving toward the town with none going the other direction. The patrols continued, but with a little less frequency. From his vantage point at the top of the hill, Fleet could see the headlights of the all-terrain vehicles as they made the circuit around the farm. The lights made it easy to see where occupied buildings were located and the exact route that the patrol followed. Despite the biting wind, taking up the watch again had been worthwhile.

As Fleet rose to return to the cedar grove where the others were waiting, he heard the coyote howling start again to the east. It had to be a large pack. There were so many distinct sets of yelping and yowling, all mingling like voices in some unholy choir. Before long the howling was coming from the west as well, as another pack announced their presence. Fortunately for Fleet, all the activity was below him on the valley floor. He would be hard pressed to defend himself against a large pack. Just as Fleet had decided that it was time to leave, he heard the sound of gunfire coming from the same direction as the howling. He watched the headlights began to converge on the area where he had heard the gunfire. When the shooting stopped, so had the howling and Fleet waited until they began riding their patrols again. Heading back down the hill, Fleet was thinking how it would be helpful if the coyotes made another appearance tomorrow night.

It took awhile for Fleet to find his way to the camp in the dark. When he returned Kurt was waiting for him. Standing just outside the grove of cedars with his rifle slung over his shoulder, he was rubbing his hands together and stomping his feet to keep warm. The wind had died down, but it was still bitterly cold. When Kurt heard the rustling in the undergrowth, he was immediately on the alert and brought his rifle into position ready to fire. Once he realized that it was Fleet, Kurt relaxed and slipped the rifle strap over his shoulder again. "I heard the howling and gunfire," he said simply. His concern was understood and there was no need to put it into words.

"There was a little excitement for the men on patrol tonight, but I wasn't close enough to see what happened," Fleet explained. "What did you and Brother Wyatt find out today?" he asked, changing the subject. "I didn't see any horses. Did you?"

"We saw a few in a field at the far end of the valley," Kurt answered and paused slightly before adding, "but they built a stable. Brother Wyatt said that was done after they were here last."

"You can be sure that the best stock is in there," Fleet said shaking his head. Things were becoming more complicated. He looked at Kurt and said, "We'll go there in the morning. I want to get a look at the stable before we decide what to do. I also want to check out the area where all the shooting was coming from, but right now I'm going to try to get some sleep."

Kurt didn't say anything as he left. Fleet was still focused on the horses. That is what he had come for and Kurt knew he would not be satisfied with anything else. Kurt, on the other hand, would be more than happy if all they took where some of the cattle. The idea of grabbing one of the calves and carrying it away with him on his horse had occurred to him more than once. And even though nothing had been said, Kurt was also certain that the stock farm had been the source for the Family's flock of sheep. Horses were not the only things of value to be found in the valley.

Tomorrow they would decide what to do. When night came it would be time to act or leave. Another day spent scouting the valley would have to be enough. He and Brother Wyatt had had too many close calls with the patrols for Kurt to feel at ease anywhere near the valley. Every hour they stayed increased the risk that they would be discovered. He knew that Brother Fox would agree, but it was Fleet who worried Kurt. Even if Brother Fox and the others left, Fleet would stay and try to take the horses on his own. No matter what, Kurt would not leave him.

Dawn arrived with the promise of stormy weather. The clouds were dark and churned violently with the northwest wind that had returned with a vengeance. As they ate their meager breakfast of dried meats and fruit, the mood in the camp was as gloomy as the weather. The cold and the uncomfortable blanket of twigs and needles on the ground had made it impossible for anyone to sleep. Brother Fox finally broke the silence by saying, "Can you smell the snow? I think we have a big storm coming."

Fleet looked at the disheartened group scattered around the clearing. Brother Wesley and Sister Alisma were still huddled together with Sister Alisma resting her head on his shoulder. Brother Wyatt was staring sullenly at them and everyone else. Kurt was wearing that stone-like face of his with his jaw set, but no matter how tired or worried he was, Fleet knew he could depend on him. He wasn't so sure about the others.

Fleet stood and turned to Brother Fox who regarded him with a look that carried as much chill as the wind, but Fleet choose to ignore his obvious disapproval and said, "We had better get moving if we are to do what we came to do before it snows."

When Fleet turned to saddle his horse, Brother Wyatt jumped to his feet and said, "Let me go with you." He didn't want to sit and do nothing. Besides, if there was going to be any action, he knew that Fleet would be at the center of it and that was where Brother Wyatt wanted to be.

Fleet looked at him only briefly before returning to his task and saying, "Get ready then." To the others he said, "We'll go and look over the spot where I heard the coyotes last night. After that we'll come back and all of us will take a look at the stable that Kurt and Brother Wyatt saw yesterday." No one answered. They all watched silently as Fleet and Brother Wyatt prepared to leave. When Fleet swung into his saddle, he added, "We'll be less than an hour. Be ready to leave when we get back." Then kicking his horse, Fleet rode the black stallion through the cedars with Brother Wyatt close at his heels.

Fleet was in a hurry and pushed his horse to go as fast as was possible through the dense woods. They had not gone very far before they found the results of the previous nights shooting. Apparently, Fleet had been closer to the coyotes and shooters than he had realized. There

275

were several carcasses lying on the ground less than a quarter mile from the ridge where he had been sitting. When Brother Wyatt saw them he jumped off his horse and immediately began skinning the coyotes. He looked briefly at Fleet wondering if he would need an explanation, but Fleet had been around the Family enough to know that it would go against everything he believed if Brother Wyatt left without the skins. To kill and leave the animals to waste was not permissible. As he waited for Brother Wyatt to complete his task Fleet rode around the area. He was surprised to find a dog lying among the coyotes and wondered if it had been part of the pack. Once Brother Wyatt had completed his task and had his four coyote skins and the one from the dog rolled and tied to the leather strap that he used to hold his horse's blanket in place, he stood looking at the carcasses.

Fleet could see that he was considering whether or not he should take the meat as well. Dog meat was not something that Fleet would eat unless it was a choice between that or starvation. "Leave them," he said. His time and patience were running out.

Brother Wyatt looked up at him and said, "It's such a waste." Shaking his head Brother Wyatt mounted his horse.

"Maybe not," Fleet said leading the way closer to the trail. "The pack is sure to come back and the carcasses will make sure of that." When Fleet looked at Brother Wyatt, he could see that the young man wasn't following his reasoning. "If the patrols are busy shooting coyotes, they will have less time to bother us," he explained.

Brother Wyatt grinned from ear to ear, as he understood what Fleet had in mind. "I think the Mother would approve. She will send Her pack tonight to help us. I'm sure of that." The Family's Mother would protect them and send her aid. Brother Wyatt believed that this time the aid would come in the form of coyotes.

The seeds that Sister Samethia planted in the young fertile minds of the Family members had grown and blossomed into a blind faith in the benevolence of the Mother. All Fleet had was a belief in two facts. A coyote would eat anything and would always return to a spot where the food was plentiful. As they rode he watched the ground for signs of blood, until he finally found what he was looking for. About twenty paces from the dirt path the patrols followed was all that remained of the victim of last night's feeding frenzy, a patch of blood on the ground and some scraps of hide. It had been one of the calves. Fleet doubted that it had taken very long for them to rip it to shreds. They must have been done before the men arrived with their guns or they would have found the dead coyotes closer to the kill. Fleet planned to use the same tactics that the pack did, striking quickly and disappearing into the woods. Only Fleet hoped that they would be smart enough to do it without being shot in the process.

When they heard the sound of the next patrol approaching Fleet and Brother Wyatt turned their mounts back to the woods. They stopped behind a pair of cedars. The dense foliage provided the best cover in the leafless forest and fortunately, they seemed to be abundant in the area. They waited until the roar of the engine had gone past their hiding place before they headed deeper into the woods. It had taken longer than Fleet planned and they met the others while riding back to their campsite.

It was Sister Alisma who gave the explanation. "We were worried when you took so long," she said once they reached Fleet and Brother Wyatt.

"That was my fault," Brother Wyatt answered and handed one of the pelts to Sister Alisma who was obviously pleased.

"I was wishing last night that I had a fur lining for my hood," she said. With a satisfied smile she tied the bundle behind her and said, "The Mother provides us with what we need."

Brother Fox was not in the mood for pleasantries. "Brother Kurt was telling me that they saw the horses to the west. We had better get moving if we're going to be ready before nightfall." It appeared that Brother Fox was still willing to consider going along with the plan, but it was obvious by his tone that he was still reserving judgement until he had seen the place for himself.

Kurt looked at Fleet and Brother Fox as they considered each other coolly. "Let's go then," he said and took the lead. He had the sinking feeling that his vote would be the deciding factor in whatever happened. A fact that would not have escaped Brother Fox either. Kurt did not like his position in the middle of the two men, both of whom were used to having things done their way and compromise could prove to be an elusive thing.

As they rode a fine mist began freezing on the trees and the ground as it fell. It was not a pleasant ride and there was very little conversation. Each member of the party was busy watching and listening to the sound of the patrols passing only a few hundred feet to their left and occasionally they had to scramble for cover. It was mid-morning when they arrived at the pasture where the horses were grazing. At this end of the valley the land was more level and there was no towering hill or ridge that they could use to observe the horses from above. That meant they would need to creep in close on foot to get a good look at things. It was decided, much to Sister Alisma's dissatisfaction that she would take the horses deeper into the woods and wait for them. Once Brother Fox was satisfied that Sister Alisma and the horses were situated in a safe but convenient location, the five men set out on foot to the edge of the woods.

The mist was now mixed with fat heavy snow that fell in clumps and before long the ground was covered with white. Fleet wanted to go over the fence and into the field with the horses. There were a few trees in the pasture that they could use for cover, but they couldn't risk leaving footprints that would be visible even to a man riding by at full speed. Fleet found the whole situation frustrating.

What plagued him most was the fact that he couldn't see enough of the pasture to know how many horses there were or get a good look at the large building that was being used as a stable. As he looked around, he noticed a tall pine growing nearby. "Come with me," he said to Kurt and began to creep cautiously in the direction of the tree. When they reached the base of the tree Fleet said, "Give me a boost."

Kurt clasped his hands and Fleet stepped into the cusp that his hands formed. Even with a leg up from Kurt, it was not enough to put Fleet within reach of the lowest branch. He ended up standing on Kurt's shoulders before he could reach it and pull himself up with Kurt pushing up on his feet to help him. The first branch was not high enough and Fleet reached up and pulled himself up onto the next two branches above his head. At that point he was as far up into the tree as he was going to get, the next branch was out of his reach. As Fleet straddled the branch and took out his binoculars, he was counting on the patrols keeping their eyes on the ground. In his black clothing, he stood out against the white snow cover, but as he looked down at the pasture, he decided that it was definitely worth the risk. He could see about two-dozen head huddled together in a low spot just beyond the fence. They had been hidden from view by a stand of trees between them and the fence. When he looked toward the barn, he could see only two men working around the building. One was using one of the all-terrain vehicles to pull a small wagon loaded with bales of hay and heading across the pasture to the place where the horses were gathered. The fact that he was taking the feed to the horses rather than the other way around was encouraging. It made it seem less likely that all the horses would be locked in the barn.

As he watched the building, he saw the other man who was probably cleaning the stalls inside. Every few minutes he would come out with a wheelbarrow and dump the contents into a heap near the barn and disappear inside only to return with another load. He watched until the man hauling the hay had dumped his load and returned to the barn. A few more horses appeared from the far side of the pasture when they realized it was feeding time, making the total thirty. Fleet was about to climb down when he saw one of the men lead a horse out of the barn. A striking white horse, it was quite high spirited and pulled at the rope while the man tried to hold it steady. Just as Fleet had predicted, the best stock was housed in the stable. It was as close as Fleet ever came to entertaining a whim, but he decided that he wanted that horse. The fact that he would have to go into the stable did not present a significant obstacle in his mind.

When he decided that it was time to leave his perch, Fleet's descent took less time than it had to climb up. He landed with a thud next to Kurt who was waiting for him. "What did you see?" Kurt asked as Fleet shook the snow off his hood.

"There are thirty horses about a hundred yards from the fence just on the other side of the ridge and those trees," Fleet said as he pointed toward the spot.

From where they were standing the ridge was not clearly visible. All Kurt could see were the trees that grew thick in that area. "If I can't see the horses from here neither can those guards on patrol," Kurt said thoughtfully.

Fleet smiled for the first time that day. It was if Kurt had read his mind. His friend was on the right track. "Let's go talk to Brother Fox.

It'll take both of us to convince him that it's worth a try." Fleet hurried quickly back to the spot where they had left the Brothers.

When they got there Brother Fox was alone. Fleet didn't inquire as to the whereabouts of the two young Brothers. It was Brother Fox's prerogative to send them on errands as he saw fit. "It looks promising," Fleet said. Even the fact that Brother Fox raised his eyebrow and gave him a skeptical look would not dampen Fleet's spirits now. "The horses are just past those trees over there. The weather is working to our advantage. They're all bunched together. Once we get over the fence, it should be easy enough to round up the ones we want without being seen."

Brother Fox did not appear to be swayed, but what Fleet was saying piqued his interest. "How many?" he asked.

"Thirty that I saw," Fleet was still smiling. He knew a compromise that he thought would be acceptable to Brother Fox. "Let me tell you what I want to do," he began, looking to both men and trying to gage their reaction as he spoke. "Once it's dark Kurt and I will go in after the horses. I don't want to cut the fence to get in. We'll have to get the horses to jump the fence."

Kurt jumped in at that point. "I have never tried that on my horse or any other for that matter. How can I be certain that he'll jump?" Kurt was not sure that was something that he wanted to try in the dark.

"I'm sure the black will jump. If you don't think yours can, then you'll ride one that will," Fleet answered just a little irritated with Kurt for balking at the idea. Then returning his attention to Brother Fox, he said, "Once we're over the fence, you and the Brothers can sweep our tracks to hide them. After we have the horses we want on leads we'll signal you. That's when I want you to pull down the fence." Fleet paused for a moment, as he heard one of the patrols approaching. They sat silently, waiting for it to pass. Then for one heart stopping moment they heard it slow just after passing by them. It was only a moment before it picked up speed again to go on its way, but it served as a reminder that they needed to be careful.

The next thing they knew Brother Wesley was crashing through the brush, coming from the direction where the all-terrain vehicle had slowed. He looked sheepishly at the three men as he said; "I thought he had me for a minute. I was laying right at the edge of the woods."

When the three men remained silent, he knelt next to Fleet and asked, "What are you planning?"

"Be quiet and you'll hear all you need to know," Brother Fox said gruffly. He knew Fleet's enthusiasm for taking risks would be contagious.

"I was just getting to what I wanted you to do," Fleet answered. He paused a moment before telling Brother Wesley, knowing what his reaction would be. "When Kurt and I have the horses, I want you and Brother Wyatt to put ropes on the fence poles and use the horses to pull the fence down."

Brother Wesley jumped to his feet. "I didn't come to pull down fences. Brother Wyatt and I are the ones who should go after the horses."

Fleet shook his head and said, "We wouldn't be here if it weren't for you and Brother Wyatt, but I can't allow you to risk your lives for horses. If anything goes wrong, you'll leave with Brother Fox."

"Brother Fleet is the one who should go after the horses." Brother Fox agreed whole-heartedly with that part of the plan. Then he frowned at Fleet as he added, "But we would not desert you or Brother Kurt." It was one thing to risk a life to gain property; it was another to do it to save the life of a friend.

Fleet paused as he nodded slightly in response to Brother Fox's promise. Then he continued, "Once the fence is down, we'll drive all the horses out with us. Then we can head north and leave the farm behind," Fleet finally finished laying out his strategy. He looked at Kurt who was nodding slowly. He had already voiced his reservations. It was Brother Fox who had to give his opinion, yes or no.

The fact that Fleet was staring at him did not hurry Brother Fox's deliberations. The plan was good enough, but there were so many things that could go wrong. Still, he had to give Fleet credit for knowing what it would take for him to give his blessing. Brother Wyatt and Brother Wesley would remain with him and there was no reason for Sister Alisma to get involved. She could wait for them at a safe distance. He stroked his chin thoughtfully and asked, "How many horses do you plan to take?"

Fleet smiled triumphantly, Brother Fox's approval was the last piece of his plan. When Brother Wyatt returned, they were ready to go

281

and went rejoin Sister Alisma. The white flakes were falling fast and furious now and swirled about them as they walked through the ever-deepening snow cover. It would be nice if they could find some shelter. A warm bed and a hot meal would be nice, but Fleet knew it would be several days before he could enjoy those simple pleasures again.

~ ~ ~

They spent the day trying to keep dry and discussing their plans over and over again. Exploring every detail and possible problem that could arise. Brother Wesley and Brother Wyatt were unenthusiastic about their roles, but they did suggest a good place to pull down the fence. It became dark quite early with the storm still upon them. By then, the snow was a foot deep. As soon as it was dark everyone was ready to go and get it over with, but Fleet wanted to wait until later, insisting that the patrols would be further apart. What he was waiting for, counting on actually was for the coyotes to return. He just hoped that the snow would not keep them away.

As the hours passed and there were still no coyotes, Fleet knew that they had to go. Already he had delayed too long. He and Kurt were mounted, ready to go. Fleet would go first riding his black stallion and Kurt would follow riding Brother Wyatt's horse. It was a broad-chested horse with short legs. He didn't look like he could get over the fence, but Brother Wyatt assured them that the horse would jump. That had renewed the argument that he should go with Fleet and not Kurt, but he could not sway the three older men.

As Kurt sat atop Brother Wyatt's horse he could feel the perspiration beading on his forehead despite the cold. He had never been afraid to try anything that Fleet suggested, but the idea of jumping the fence was not something that he wanted to try especially with a foot of snow on the ground. Brother Wyatt's horse had shied away from him when he first tried to put the saddle on his back. The Family members insisted on riding bareback with only blankets and there was no way Kurt was riding bareback and jumping the fence. It had taken Brother Wyatt's calming touch to hold the horse steady long enough to get the saddle on his back. Once it was cinched on tightly, he still did not release the horse, but stroked his nose and spoke to it softly. Kurt had

282

seen the way the horse responded to the slightest touch when Brother Wyatt was on his back, he only hoped it would do the same for him.

They were waiting for the next patrol. When they heard the sound of the engine, it was the signal for everyone to be ready. Standing next to the men on horseback were Brother Wesley and Brother Wyatt carrying pine branches. The guard passed them by like all the others and as soon as he was out of sight Fleet kicked his horse and galloped at an angle toward the fence. He was over the fence and had almost disappeared before Kurt made his move, following in the tracks that the black horse had left in the snow. It was as if the horse knew exactly what he wanted and they flew over the four-foot fence like it was nothing. When it came down on the other side, the horse lost it's footing and for a split second Kurt was certain that they was going to fall, but the sure-footed animal recovered quickly and they were following Fleet toward the grove of trees. Stopping short of the spot where the horses were huddled, they took out the ropes they had packed into their saddlebags and made their way slowly through the trees.

From what Fleet had seen the horses seemed quite docile and he didn't want to spook them by rushing in at a gallop. Hopefully, they could ride into the herd and slip ropes over the necks of the ones they wanted without too much trouble. Choosing which horses to take would be difficult. They had not been able to watch the horses to see which were the more spirited animals. In the darkness their choice would be guided by chance.

When they came out of the trees they saw the horses were still huddled together, rumps to the wind and covered with snow. A few lifted their heads to look when Fleet and Kurt rode near, but there was no alarm in their actions. It was as Fleet had hoped. They would not present a problem. Both Fleet and Kurt had managed to loop ropes around the necks of two of the horses when they heard the patrol pass by without slowing. The Brothers had apparently done a good job of covering their tracks. They worked as quickly as possible and soon had twelve horses roped and ready to go.

Then it was time for Fleet to let Kurt know about the rest of his plan. He rode over to Kurt and handed him the leads for the six horses that were following him and said, "There's one more that I want to get."

Kurt looked at the herd wondering which one Fleet meant. "Not there," Fleet said, "it's in the barn."

"Are you crazy?" Kurt asked incredulously. Everything was going well, it was the type of thing that Fleet would do. He always had to push things just as far as he could. Kurt thought he actually thrived on danger. "Let's go now," Kurt was pleading, but Fleet actually laughed when he wheeled his horse around and galloped toward the barn leaving Kurt simmering angrily.

It took less than a minute to reach the barn. Fleet knew no one was there. Brother Wesley had spent the afternoon up in the pine tree watching the pasture and had seen the men leave after their chores were done. As they came to the barn, Fleet pulled hard on the black's reins and he skidded to a stop in the snow. Fleet jumped off his back and pushed open the door to the barn. It was warm and dry inside. The smell of sweet clover hay and horses mingled together met Fleet as he entered the barn. Once inside he took out a small candle and matches that he had in the pocket of his jacket. He needed some light if he was going to find anything. Holding the tiny candle in his hand, he peered into the large stalls, looking at the horses and thinking about how they were living in better conditions than most of the people he knew. When he found the white horse, he opened the door to the stable and went inside.

Fortunately for Fleet, it was wearing a halter and was tied to a ring on the stable wall. The horse reared back when it saw Fleet approaching with the candle. As Fleet reached out to untie the rope with his free hand he was making low soothing sounds trying to calm the frightened animal. Once he had the rope untied and in his hand, Fleet began to lead the horse from the stall. It balked and pulled like a mule resisting his efforts, forcing Fleet to find a place for his candle. He let a few drops of wax fall on the wooden sill just outside the stable and pressed the candle onto the hot wax. It stuck and Fleet had both hands free. With his full attention on the horse, he was able to coax it forward.

Once they were outside the stall, a saddle lying on top of a bale of hay caught his attention. If he were going to take the horse it would need a saddle and bridle. He tied the horse's lead to a nearby post and hurriedly began trying to get the saddle on the horse. It turned out to be a battle of wills, but Fleet won out in the end and led the horse out into the snow where his horse was waiting. It was then that Fleet thought about the candle but decided there was no point in going back for it. With the horse and saddle missing, they wouldn't need the candle to know that he had been there.

As he rode back to where Kurt was waiting, Fleet heard the sound that he had been waiting for earlier. The coyotes were back and their howling, although they were far to the east, could be heard above the sound of the wind. All the pieces were falling into place and Fleet was quite pleased with the outcome thus far. Fleet had no real idea how long it had taken in the barn but by the look on Kurt's face he could tell that it had been too long.

Kurt eyed the horse, saddled and ready to ride and said sharply, "Are we ready?"

"As soon as the next patrol passes," Fleet said. The words were hardly spoken before they heard the roar of the engine approaching. Fleet took the leads for the six horses that he had given to Kurt earlier. As soon as the patrol went past, Fleet let out a howl that was as blood curdling as any that the coyotes could produce. Kurt answered with the same as they whipped and prodded the cold and unwilling herd of horses toward the place where Brother Wyatt and Brother Wesley were supposed to be bringing down the fence.

When they came over the rise dragging the horses behind them, Fleet could see the two Brothers untying their ropes from the fence and clearing the path for the horses. Once the herd was through the fence all the Family members came to meet them, with each one taking the leads for two of the horses from Kurt and Fleet. They moved quickly into the woods now with Brother Fox leading the way. As they wound through the trees in the darkness they could hear the sound of gunfire in the distance. The patrol was busy battling coyotes again just as Fleet had hoped.

They rode silently through the woods until they came to a dry streambed. It led to the northwest and it was wide and flat enough to allow them to ride the horses at a full gallop. The snow was still falling with the wind driving it into their faces, but they pressed on as hard as they could through the storm. They had traveled a little over a mile when Fleet looked back and saw a glow in the sky behind them. It was a fire. He shook his head and thought about the candle he had left in the barn. He had lit a bonfire big enough to bring every man for miles, but there was nothing to be done about it now. Another diversion or a flaming beacon to call attention to their theft, Fleet didn't know how it would turn out, but sometimes luck dealt him a winning hand or if he had been one of the Brothers he would have to believe that it was the work of the Mother.

They had traveled for several miles following the streambed. When Brother Fox was at last satisfied that no one was following, he slowed the pace and led the group onto a road that crossed the creek. It was much easier for the horses, who were nearly spent from pushing their way through the drifts that were three feet deep or more in places. The ditches on either side of the road were designed to keep the roadway clear of drifting snow. They had slowed to a walk and the horses trudged on with the snow swirling around their hooves as they went.

It was then that Fleet went to Brother Fox and said, "We have to find shelter." Brother Fox eyed him warily and Fleet added, "We need a place big enough for us and the horses." He knew how the Family felt about using the houses and buildings that were deserted, but it had become a matter of survival. Even though Fleet felt the same way, he was willing to use whatever was available when necessary. They had already passed one deserted farm with a large barn and they would surely pass another one soon.

With the snow blowing all around them it was difficult to see very far. When Fleet saw what looked like a driveway leading away from the main road, he left his horses with Brother Wesley and rode ahead to see if there was a building that they could use for shelter. It was like a thousand other small farms in the area with a house surrounded by several outbuildings and a large barn. Fleet rode back to the group waiting at the end of the lane and motioned for them to follow.

Once they were back to the farmyard, Fleet dismounted and began to try to pull one of the tall doors open. The snow had drifted against it and Fleet could only open the door a crack. Kurt handed the leads for the horses to Sister Alisma who was next to him and got down to help. Within moments all the men were pushing together while Sister Alisma held the horses. Fortunately for her, they were all too tired to move. There was no way she could have stopped them all if they had decided to run.

It took all five men to open the door enough to lead the horses inside, but once all were inside the simple fact that they were out of the wind made them feel warmer immediately. There first task was to light a fire. Dry, dusty straw was there in abundance, but wood was a problem, Brother Fox found a place where the wood planking inside the barn was broken and rotted and managed to kick some boards loose and break them into pieces. They hastily cleared the debris from a spot in the middle of the barn and using the straw to get things going, they piled the wood on top and soon had a small blaze going, which made the horses pull nervously at their leads. Now that they could see, the horses were quickly led away from the fire and into a stock pen at the far end of the barn.

With nineteen horses to tend, there was plenty to do before they could think about resting. While Brother Fox continued looking for anything that they could burn, the others began removing saddles, blankets, and bridles. Then used the blankets to try and brush away the snow that was caked on the horses' legs and bodies before hanging them across the fencing to dry. Feed was the next problem. They could not have carried enough for this many horses if they had wanted. Originally, they planned to let the horses graze on the dried grasses that were along the trail, but the snow had covered that food source. It was Brother Fox who found some ears of dried corn in one of the grain bins that he was breaking apart for firewood. It was old and a little moldy and some ears had been chewed in half by rats, but it was all they had. They carried it all to the pen where the horses waited and threw it on the floor. The horses ate without hesitation; corn was corn. Water wasn't a problem. All they had to do was fill the metal pails they found in the barn with snow and set them near the fire to melt. When they were finally done, they all fell exhausted next to the fire.

There was no celebration, no congratulations. Everyone was too tired and numb with the cold to move. They sat silently watching the flames dance as they consumed the dry wood, sending a thick gray cloud of smoke upward until it filled the rafters. Drafts of wind were blowing in through the cracks and swirling through the smoke filled barn. As they looked at each other, they could see the steam rising from their clothing as the fire dried them. One by one, everyone settled down by the fire and drifted off to sleep until only Brother Fox and Fleet were awake.

As he put another board onto the fire Brother Fleet thought back to the night when Fleet had first proposed his plan. That had been another fire and another night, but the memory brought a smile to his face. He looked Fleet in the eyes and said, "The Mother has smiled on you again, my friend."

Fleet regarded Brother Fox thoughtfully. He was a formidable friend, but one that he had come to trust as much as Kurt. He got to his feet and said, "We're not home yet. I think it would be best to have someone on watch just to be on the safe side." With that said he picked up his rifle and slung it over his shoulder. Then as he pulled on his gloves and pulled his hood over his head, Fleet stepped out into the cold again.

The snow had stopped falling, but there was still plenty blowing around. He waded through the drifts until he came to the south side of the barn where he was shielded from the wind blasting in from the north. Next to the wall there was an area that was clear of snow and Fleet went to stand there. As he leaned against the side of the barn, he looked up into the sky. The clouds were beginning to thin and he could see a halo of light glowing around the full moon. Then for a few glorious moments the clouds broke apart so he could see the moon. The light sparkled and cast a blue haze on the snow, it was beautiful and for just a moment he felt the power that Sister Samethia spoke of so passionately. The forces of nature were more deadly and wondrous than anything man could ever hope to create.

Chapter Eleven

Justin was standing outside of the men's quarters at the Family's camp, finally without his shadow. Brother Aquila had attached himself to Justin and refused to leave him for a moment. It was his way of assuring that Sister Eaglet and Justin could not have any private conversations. Still, Justin had managed to steal away for a few seconds earlier that day to whisper in Sister Eaglet's ear and had used the opportunity to ask her to meet him later. She had not answered one way or the other, but Justin knew she would come. Justin had been waiting for his opportunity to slip out without being seen. Even Brother Aquila had to sleep sometime and when Justin left, he was snoring loudly in his bed.

Justin rubbed his hands together to keep them warm and began walking along the path that had been cleared to the main earth shelter. The snow had stopped a few hours earlier, but the cold wind had not. No matter how cold it was Justin would not go back inside until he had seen Sister Eaglet, even if that meant going into the women's quarters to bring her out.

He did not have long to wait before Sister Eaglet appeared in the doorway of the women's shelter and hurried toward him. As she approached the snow was bathed in a soft glowing light. With an effort Justin tore his eyes from Eaglet, just in time to see the full moon shining overhead before the clouds closed in to cover it again. When he looked down Eaglet was standing there looking up at him. Without thinking Justin did what he had wanted to do since he had first laid eyes on Eaglet. He wrapped his arms around her and pulled her to him then kissed her with all the passion that had been building within him for days. This time she did not run from him, but after a moment wriggled out of his arms. Taking his hand, she said, "Follow me," leading him past the earth shelter and through the trees until they came to the primitive wooden shelter that housed the horses.

Just inside the door was a lantern, which Eaglet lit and then hung back on its hook. It was then that Justin could see that all she was wearing was her thin white shift with a blanket thrown over her shoulders as a shawl. He knew that she had to be freezing and quickly found some of the blankets that were there for the horses and threw them down on a pile of straw at the other side of the small stable. It was as far away from the door as they could get. Now he led Eaglet by the hand and as she sat on the bed that he had made for them Justin threw off his coat and kicked off his boots before sitting next to her. He couldn't believe that she had come and he reached out to stroke her cheek.

Eaglet moved closer and wrapped her blanket around them and began kissing him gently about his cheek and eyes. Justin had been all that she could think about. After he had moved in with the men, she had looked for every opportunity to be alone with him for a moment, but Brother Aquila had always been there. Although she still felt something for Brother Aquila, now that she was finally alone with Justin, Eaglet knew which man she wanted.

Justin took her in his arms and kissed her again. As he began to caress her, Eaglet shivered, but it was not from the cold. Gently, he laid her down on the blankets and pulled the other one over them creating a small pocket of warmth within. As he slipped his hands under her shift, Eaglet was untying the lacing on his shirt. Her skin felt soft and smooth to his touch and his fingers traced the curve of her hips and waist. When he touched her breast, he felt Eaglet tense and she pulled away from him. "What's wrong?" he asked softly and kissed her ear lobe tenderly. Then looking into her soft blue eyes, he began to loosen the braids in her hair until she was lying with a halo of golden hair surrounding her face and spilling over her breasts. Justin twirled one of the silken tresses between his fingers waiting for her answer.

As Eaglet looked into Justin's face, there was so much that she wanted to say, but the words failed her and all she could say was, "I've never." Then as she lowered her eyes she finished, "I've never made love to a man."

He lifted her chin bringing her eyes to meet his and he said, "And I've never loved any woman before you." When she smiled at him, Justin thought his heart would burst. What he said was true. Even though he had experienced the physical act before he had never truly felt love before he met Eaglet. Justin was drawn to her in a way that defied all reason. When he looked at Eaglet, he could see the love that she felt for him and said, "We don't have to do anything if you don't want to." Although Justin was more than ready, what he wanted from

Eaglet was more than just one night of passion. He would wait until he was certain that she wanted him as much as he desired her.

Her answer was to pull her shift over her head and drop it next to their bed of straw. When Justin looked at her firm round breasts and supple body, he could feel the blood pounding through his body as his pulse quickened just at the sight of her. Then she reached out to him and when she pushed the shirt that she had made for him off his shoulders, he let it fall. She was no longer a frightened girl unsure of herself, but a woman who wanted all that love had to offer and she waited for him now. He drew her close and as she felt Justin's bare skin touching hers, Eaglet lost herself in the sheer joy of feeling his body next to hers. She opened herself completely to him and for a few blissful minutes they lost themselves in their lovemaking. Once it was over, Justin lay contentedly on his back with Eaglet nestled on his shoulder.

There was nothing to say as they both continued to caress each other. Enjoying the feeling of closeness, neither one wanting to break the spell that they had woven around themselves. It was Eaglet who sat up suddenly and pulled her shift over her head. Justin pulled her back and kissed her again, not wanting her to leave.

"I have to go," Sister Eaglet said. It was hard for her to tear herself from Justin. "Sister Samethia will look for me if I'm gone to long." She could have made love to Justin all night, but she could not break from her responsibilities to the Family.

There was a part of Justin that wanted to beg her to stay, but he didn't. "I want you to go back to the Settlement with me," he said as he began dressing. It was what he wanted. For Justin it was the next step. He would take Eaglet with him when they left.

"I can't go there," she said in a tone that suggested that he was crazy for even suggesting such a thing. "I thought that you would stay with the Family."

"I am not a shepherd," his answer was full of anger. Her reaction had shocked and hurt him. Justin would never have thought that Eaglet would deny him anything, not now.

Eaglet looked at him with a puzzled expression. She could not understand his anger. "I can't leave the Family. I can't leave my sister."

It was the first time that Justin had heard Eaglet refer to Sister Mischka as a blood relative. The realization that she was being torn in two directions was slow in coming, but Justin understood her hesitation now. He stood and lifted Eaglet to her feet and kissed her one last time before he said, "We don't have to decide anything now. I love you and we will find a way to be together." Eaglet's warm smile was all the answer he needed. Reluctantly, he released her and said, "You had better go now," and watched as Eaglet hurried out the door. After she was gone, Justin watched the door hoping that she would return. It was a few moments before he moved, carefully putting the blankets back where he had found them, so no one but the horses would know they had been there.

It was the first thought he had given to the horses. When Eaglet was with him Justin was blinded to the rest of the world. When he saw his big gray roan staring at him, he smiled and slapped the horse on the rump and said, "You're right old boy. She's one sweet little filly." As Justin stepped out into the cold he was smiling.

When Brother Fox was away, Sister Samethia always slept with the other women. She had heard Sister Eaglet when she returned to the earth shelter just as she had heard her when she left. If Sister Samethia had wanted, she could have prevented Sister Eaglet from going, but there was no point in trying to keep her and Justin apart. Sister Samethia had been successful when Brother Aquila had been the object of Sister Eaglet's love, but Brother Justin was not Family and she did not have the influence over him that she held with the others. Still when love and passion entered the picture, she knew she could not control every aspect of the young Brothers' and Sisters' lives. Still, Sister Samethia had tried to delay the inevitable as long as she could. In their world where survival depended on hard work, there was no time for childhood. Sister Eaglet had assumed all the responsibilities of being a woman long ago. Now Sister Samethia was certain that Sister Eaglet was a woman in every interpretation of the meaning.

There would be problems with this match. Sister Samethia knew it as surely as she knew Sister Eaglet. Under no circumstances would she allow Sister Eaglet to go to the Settlement with Brother Justin. It had nothing to do with Brother Justin. Sister Samethia liked the young man and would welcome him into the Family; if that was his choice, but she was certain that he would not be willing to give up his life at the Settlement. Justin could not help being drawn to the life that Fleet offered the young man. In exchange for their loyalty, Fleet gave him power and a station in life that was privileged in comparison to others in the Settlement.

What this union would bring even Sister Samethia did not know. The Mother did not tell her all things in her visions. As she heard Sister Eaglet tossing restlessly in her bed, Sister Samethia smiled. It was a selfish thing to wish for, but she was hoping for a baby. Sister Samethia knew that she could never have children; the Mother had revealed that at the same time she had given her the visions of the Brothers and Sisters. They were her Family and she cared for them all like they were her flesh and blood. Sister Samethia wanted the Family to grow and prosper and children were a blessing that she prayed for every night. The resolve that Sister Eaglet would stay with the Family deepened in Sister Samethia's heart. Sadie would never allow a child to be conceived or born in the Settlement.

Sister Samethia had only met Sadie once. It had been only a few weeks after the evacuations and before she had gathered her Family. Sadie had seemed very generous with her invitation to join her, but the moment that she had touched her, Sister Samethia felt a shock run through her body. It was not like the readings that she normally had. When she laid her hands on somebody she always felt a little tremor. With some people the feelings were stronger. It seemed that the stronger the person's spirit was the stronger she felt their thoughts. To really loose herself in the other person's thoughts she had to create trance like state. Sister Samethia didn't fully understand her gift, and it was a different experience with every person.

She had always known about her strange ability and never dared speak of it. It wasn't until after the evacuations that she had what was either a dream or a vision, which started her on the path to her Family. She knew the Mother needed her to watch her children and keep them safe. Once she knew that the Mother was guiding her, she began to trust her hunches. Her first strong premonition had guided her to Brother Fox. He was living at the lake in a smaller version of the shelter that they used now. He was her first experience with a truly strong reading and she had seen her life twined with his. Without

Brother Fox's help and confidence in her abilities there would be no Family.

Then there had been Fleet's reading. Whatever, it was that was shaping Fleet's destiny; it had pulled her into the center of the storm with him. She knew that his essence was stronger than even he realized. A truly surprising reading had been Sister Kyla's. Small and quiet as she seemed, Sister Samethia had felt something from the moment she had walked through the door with Brother Fleet. Sister Kyla was fated to help Fleet realize his final glory and she would be with him in the end. The Mother had shown her that in her reading, but Sister Samethia had not seen enough to know how. Still, knowing that much had been enough for her to make sure that Sister Kyla left with Fleet.

No matter how strong the feeling had been with the others, what she felt at her meeting with Sadie was the most powerful encounter she had ever experienced and she would never forget the day. It was shortly after she had met Brother Fox. Sister Samethia had been trying to construct a snare for pheasants when she looked up and saw Sadie walking across the field toward her. There didn't seem to be anything unusual about her except for her outlandish dress. Even though it was a chilly day she wore no coat, only a short blouse that left her midriff bare. When Sister Samethia politely refused Sadie's offer to leave with her, that was when Sadie had touched Sister Samethia's arm. Instantly Sister Samethia's mind had been flooded with images. It was hard to comprehend what had flashed through her mind, but she had seen cold and ice that was coming. There was nothing but the promise of death in her touch and Sister Samethia had pulled away quickly before the flood of emotions overwhelmed her. Sadie had eyed her warily before turning to walk back in the direction from which she had come and called out, "You are welcome to change your mind." It seemed that Sadie was laughing although Sister Samethia heard no laughter. She wondered if Sadie knew what she had experienced, but that would have been impossible. Still, Sister Samethia had never been able to shake the feeling that Sadie had read her thoughts, too.

Thoughts of Sadie and the Settlement brought Fleet and the others to mind. They had been gone for five nights. Two or three more and they would be home again. That gave her two or three days to decide what to do about Brother Justin and Sister Eaglet. Until then she was sure that Brother Aquila would continue to dog Brother Justin's every step, but he had already lost the prize. She felt sorry for the young man for he was truly in love with Sister Eaglet, but Brother Justin was stronger in heart and spirit and truly was the better man.

Suddenly, she heard a commotion outside. The angry tone of the voices was clear but the words were muffled. Sister Samethia did not need to go outside to know who it was. When Sister Mischka leaped out of her bed and started out the door to see what was happening, Sister Samethia said, "Stay where you are. They'll work it out on their own."

Sister Mischka mumbled something under her breath as she returned to her bed. Before lying down again she looked at Sister Eaglet who had not even stirred when they heard the fighting. She thought it was odd that Sister Eaglet seemed to show no interest in what was happening outside, but only shrugged her shoulders and lay back down, pulling the covers over herself.

Once Sister Mischka had lain down Sister Eaglet pulled the blanket up over her head and pressed her hands over her ears. She knew what the commotion was about and was ashamed to be the cause of the disharmony. It was the very thing that she had been dreading.

Brother Aquila had awakened to find that Brother Justin was not in the shelter. Dressing quickly, he had stepped out of the men's quarters just in time to see Sister Eaglet disappear inside the women's. She was wearing nothing but her undergarments and a blanket. When he saw Brother Justin striding toward him, he had met him half way to the men's shelter. "What have you and Sister Eaglet been doing?" he spit the words like a venomous accusation.

Justin regarded him coolly and tried to step past Brother Aquila as he said, "That is none of your business."

Brother Aquila stepped with him and would not allow him pass. "It is my business. Sister Eaglet and I have made plans to marry." The thin young man's face was as red as his hair as the rage that he felt toward this unwelcome outsider grew to the point where Brother Aquila thought he would explode. Which is exactly what he did when Justin laughed derisively and pushed him out of his way. Brother Aquila jumped on Justin's back and before long they were both rolling in the snow with Brother Aquila on top. When Brother Aquila hit the wound on Justin's shoulder the fight was over. Once he saw that Justin's shoulder was bleeding, Brother Aquila stopped his attack and stood over Justin who was still lying in the snow holding his shoulder. Brother Aquila had made his point. He was not the weak little puppy that Brother Justin had thought he was. It was Brother Aquila's turn to laugh as he said the one thing that he knew would hurt Justin more than any blow he could deliver, "You'll be gone soon enough and Sister Eaglet will stay here with me." Then he turned and walked back to the men's quarters leaving Justin to pick himself up off the ground.

As he stood and brushed off the snow, Justin was angry more than anything else. Angry that he had let Brother Aquila get the better of him and because what he said was true. If he could not convince Sister Eaglet to leave with him, then Brother Aquila would do whatever he could to return to his former place as the object of her love and affection. He looked at the blood that was now staining his shirt. It looked worse than it was, but his shoulder was throbbing again. Justin had no desire to return to the men's shelter and the women's was off limits. The only place left was the large shelter the Family used for their meals. As Justin turned and headed toward it, he made a promise to himself that he would spend the next three days doing whatever it took to ensure that he would always be first in Sister Eaglet's heart and mind, no matter how much distance came between them.

The next morning when Sister Eaglet found Justin sleeping in the main shelter and saw the blood on his shirt, she immediately began fussing over him. Normally, Justin would have protested, but when Brother Aquila walked in right after Sister Eaglet, he let her pull off his shirt and examine his shoulder. He had already decided that he was going to spend all of his time with Sister Eaglet. If Brother Aquila wanted to follow, then Justin would let him.

The others were beginning to arrive for the morning meal. Brother Eldar was the next one to come into the shelter. He was ready to start cooking breakfast and instructed Brother Aquila to tend to the fire. As Brother Aquila started adding wood to the fire that had burned down until only the embers remained, he glared at Justin who grinned back at him. When Sister Eaglet scurried out the door to get the medicines to wash Justin's wound she almost knocked down Sister Mischka and Sister Samethia on their way in the door.

Sister Mischka looked at Justin sitting on the floor naked from the waist up and then at Brother Aquila. The tension between the two was unmistakable. She swept past Justin and eyed him coolly, "Good morning, Brother Justin." She had not made up her mind about the young man that Sister Eaglet was so smitten with. Personally, she did not see the attraction. Brother Justin was not very tall and she did not find him especially handsome. He had wiry brown hair and freckles that covered his entire body. Next to Brother Fleet he seemed puny. When she thought of Brother Fleet, her embarrassment of the other night came back to her. Even though he had not responded to her advances, he was still in her thoughts every minute. She would compare every man to him and no one could ever measure up to her idyllic version of Brother Fleet. Sister Mischka sat down next to Brother Aquila and began staring at Brother Justin, too. As soon as she had the chance, she would have a talk with Sister Eaglet.

A few moments later Sister Eaglet returned with her smelly salve and for once Brother Justin didn't complain when she put it on his shoulder. Once she had finished with his shoulder Sister Eaglet looked at the dark stain on the brown homespun shirt. "It will never come out," she said.

"Don't worry about it," Justin said as he took it out of her hands and pulled it on quickly. It was too cold to sit for long without a shirt. Besides, Justin had made his point.

Then she turned to Brother Aquila. "What did you think you were doing last night? Brother Justin's shoulder hasn't had time to heal completely." Brother Aquila did not answer, but he did finally look away, turning his attention to the fire and helping Brother Eldar who was making fried bread using a large piece of metal for his skillet.

"I'm fine," Justin said as Sister Eaglet sat next to him. He had wanted to add that it would take more than Brother Aquila jumping on his back and pushing him into the snow to stop him, but he was not going to taunt the other young man. He did take Sister Eaglet's hand in his as they sat together. At first she was a little surprised, but understood what Justin intended. There was no point in hiding their feelings when everyone in the little community already knew.

Sister Samethia was watching the two young men closely. There was still a good deal of ill will between them, but it seemed that tempers were under control this morning. She still intended to make sure that Brother Justin and Sister Eaglet were chaperoned from now on. At least until she had managed to resolve the dilemma their relationship had created.

No one spoke much as they ate their meal of cornbread and dried fruits. Once breakfast was over, Brother Justin left the shelter with Sister Eaglet right behind him. Only seconds later Sister Mischka rushed out following them both. The way she flew out the door made Justin think that Sister Samethia must have pushed her after them. As the two young women followed him down the path scooped in the snow Justin turned to them and said, "If you will excuse me Sisters, there are a few things that I can take care of on my own." As he began to walk toward the area where the outhouse was located, Justin shook his head. He had two more days of this to get through without loosing his temper.

The next two days were a trial of Justin's patience. Although he spent all of his time with Sister Eaglet, there was always someone else around. He tried to take the intrusions with good grace. Even Brother Eldar had taken a turn at following them around. It would have been easy to loose the old man, as slowly as he moved, but Justin did not want to cause him any embarrassment. It was important for them to accept the fact that he was going to stay with Eaglet regardless of anything they did. Still, it was not all that bad, because he was with Eaglet. He had helped her with her chores, carrying the water for the gardens, even trying his hand at spinning wool and sewing. His thread that he spun did not hold together and his stitches were uneven, but he didn't care. Justin was doing whatever he could to spend time with her.

It was the morning of the third day when an opportunity to be alone with Sister Eaglet finally presented itself. Justin had gone to the lake to fill the water buckets for Sister Eaglet. When he returned to the gardens, he noticed that Sister Mischka was nowhere to be seen. He dropped the buckets and grabbing Sister Eaglet by the hand said, "Come on." Without even so much as a look over her shoulder, Sister Eaglet pulled up the hem of her skirt with her free hand and they began to run toward the woods.

"Slow, down," she said breathlessly as he pulled her down the path behind the shelters that led to the woods. Still, Justin kept running. Eaglet was wondering if he intended to run all the way to the Settlement with her. Once they were through the stand of trees, they came to the place where several large rock ledges jutted out of the hillside. It was there that Justin finally stopped.

The weather had warmed the day before and the snow was melting and dripping down the rocks. Justin peeled off his coat and threw it down on one of the stone ledges and then lifted Sister Eaglet up and set her on his coat. She was about to tell him to put his coat back on before it got wet, but she never got the chance. Justin kissed her before she could say a word. Now that they were alone there was only one thing on their minds and in their hearts. Sister Eaglet was busy loosening his shirt and trousers and as he lifted her skirt above her thighs, she wrapped her legs around him and whispered, "Make love to me." There was no time for caresses and conversation, as they both felt the urgency of their love. Once their passions were satisfied, Justin smoothed Sister Eaglet's clothing and sank to his knees, burying his head in her lap. He knew their time was running short. Fleet would be returning soon and he would have to go. Justin still wanted Sister Eaglet to leave with him. As she lovingly stroked his hair, Justin felt a pain in his chest and stomach so strongly that he moaned, "Oh god, how can I ever leave you?" The sound of someone approaching through the trees behind them brought Justin and Sister Eaglet to their feet.

Sister Samethia looked at the two young lovers and said, "Sister Eaglet, I believe you still have some work to do." With a look to Justin, Sister Eaglet turned and ran up the path, leaving him alone with Sister Samethia.

Justin slowly began to straighten his clothing, tucking in his shirt and fastening his trousers. He met Sister Samethia's gaze without blinking. They had done nothing wrong and Justin felt no shame, only irritation that no one seemed to respect their privacy. As Justin picked up his coat and pushed his arms into the sleeves, he started to walk past Sister Samethia. Before he could pass, she laid her hand on his shoulder and said, "I need to talk to you Brother Justin." He stepped back, forcing her to release him. Justin had been expecting Sister Samethia to corner him for a 'talk' long before now.

Sister Samethia opened her hands and gestured toward the rock where Sister Eaglet had been sitting when she arrived. "Is that what you want for Sister Eaglet? I thought you had more respect for her than this."

Justin was furious. "I have nothing but love and respect for Eaglet. You and the others have forced us to sneak around like this."

It was plain to Sister Samethia that he was thinking with his heart and not his head. "No one has forced you to do anything," she said, her voice calm and even. "What I would like to know is what you plan to do." She looked at the young man waiting for his answer.

"I want to take Sister Eaglet with me," Justin answered flatly.

"To the Settlement?" Sister Samethia was trying to guide Brother Justin to the decision that she wanted him to make.

"Yes, to the Settlement." Justin was not backing down. The only reason he was even willing to talk to Sister Samethia was out of his respect for Sister Eaglet.

"And where will you live?" Sister Samethia asked. This time Justin remained silent. It was what she had expected, neither one of them had thought beyond their physical desire to be together.

The question caught Justin off guard. He stayed in the cabin with the rest of the Guard. Sadie's rules allowed for no one but members of the Guard to sleep in her house. Even Armand's younger sister was not allowed to live in the cabin. Still, Justin knew there were other options. "We will find some place to stay," he said confidently not wanting Sister Samethia to think that she had won the argument so easily.

"You can stay here with us. The Family would welcome you Brother Justin." Sister Samethia's offer was real. This stubborn young man was beginning to earn her respect.

"I am a soldier, not a shepherd," Justin answered quickly. The role that the Guard played in keeping order at the Settlement was important and he was proud to be part of it.

Sister Samethia nodded thoughtfully. It was the answer that she had expected. Her next question brought her closer to the conclusion of her questions for Brother Justin. "And you will be there to assure her safety?"

"Of course," Justin could not believe that Sister Samethia could have any doubts concerning his devotion to Sister Eaglet. "I would rather die than let anyone touch her."

"When Fleet needs you to go with him, who will assure Sister Eaglet's safety?" Justin was visibly troubled by her question. He had an image in his mind of some of the shady characters that frequented the Settlement and Sister Eaglet did not seem to fit. It would be like dropping an angel into the pits of hell. Sister Samethia had made her point and it had pierced Justin right through the heart. He had no answer to her question and he looked at her as he anguished over the choices.

Brother Justin was not a fool. He truly loved Sister Eaglet and could understand her concerns. Still, she was not blind or heartless. For the last few days, she had racked her brains for some compromise that would be acceptable to all concerned. Now Sister Samethia was ready to offer Brother Justin her terms. "No matter what happens, you can see it is best if Sister Eaglet remains here with the Family," she began. She was speaking softly now, trying to let Brother Justin know that she only had their best interest at heart. Slowly and with an obviously pained look, Brother Justin nodded. "Sister Eaglet needs someone willing to make a commitment to her."

To that Justin responded, "That is what I want to do."

"You will always be welcome here with us, even if you don't join the Family," Sister Samethia said.

"I don't understand what you mean," Justin said impatiently. He had already told her that he had obligations at the Settlement.

Hoping that she was doing the right thing, Sister Samethia continued. "Does a soldier have to take his wife into battle with him?" Sister Samethia did not use the word battle lightly. She had heard enough stories about the fighting at the Settlement to know that Fleet and the others were at war every day, fighting for some semblance of order.

When he heard the word wife, Justin jumped at the bone that she had tossed out to him. He would agree to anything if it would assure his place with Sister Eaglet. "Are you giving me permission to marry Sister Eaglet?" Justin could not believe that he was actually asking Sister Samethia for her blessing, but if he had to get down on his knees and beg, Justin was ready to do it. Still, he had some suspicions about Sister Samethia's offer and wanted to make sure of the terms of their agreement. "You will allow us to be married and live together as man and wife?"

Sister Samethia nodded and added, "As long as Sister Eaglet continues to live here where she will be safe."

"Thank you, Sister Samethia," Justin said. It was not what he wanted, but it was a compromise he was willing to take. Justin looked at Sister Samethia and for the first time spoke to her as a friend. "The day that I was shot was the luckiest day of my life. If that hadn't happened, I would never have met Sister Eaglet."

Sister Samethia had the same thought, only she wondered if it had been fortunate or not. "Brother Fox and Fleet should be back today." She could have added that he would be leaving tomorrow, but left that part out. Instead she said, "We can have the ceremony tonight. There is just one thing I was wondering. Have you asked Sister Eaglet?"

Justin looked at her for a moment before starting toward the gardens. He made a point of walking until he was out of Sister Samethia's sight. Then he flew down the path to find Sister Eaglet. Of course, he had not asked her. There had never been a chance to discuss any plans, but he knew what her answer would be. If Fleet did return today, Justin would convince him to remain another day at least.

As Sister Samethia had promised Fleet and Brother Fox did arrive shortly after midday. When they rode into the camp with the string of horses, there were already signs that a celebration was in the making. Wood had been piled to form six large bonfires and Brother Eldar was busy roasting the lamb they had slaughtered for the feasting. At first Fleet thought it was to welcome them home.

Justin came running from the direction of the stables. "We made room for more horses," Justin said as he met them. Then he added, "but not for this many." He had expected six at the most, but he counted thirteen. One was a beautiful white mare with a saddle trimmed with silver. "She's a beauty," he said as he stroked her neck and walked beside them while they rode to the stable.

"I see you were expecting us," Fleet said to Justin. He smiled and gestured toward the fire where the lamb was roasting on a spit.

Justin grinned from ear to ear and burst out laughing. "This isn't for you." He was not sure how to tell them. The whole idea that it was his wedding was still unbelievable. So he just blurted it out. "I'm getting married."

Fleet stopped short and looked at Justin, "What did you say?" he asked with disbelief. They hadn't been gone that long.

The others had all stopped and were staring at Justin who repeated, "Sister Eaglet and I are getting married tonight."

There was a long pause before Fleet finally said, "Congratulations, to you and Sister Eaglet." He tried to make it sound as genuinely heartfelt as he could, but was not sure what to think. Justin and Sister Eaglet had known each other for less than two weeks. He regarded Justin suspiciously, wondering what had been going on while they were gone.

It was then that Sister Samethia emerged from the women's quarters and came to greet them. "Brother Fox, I'm glad to see everyone has returned safely." She looked directly at Sister Alisma as she stressed the word everyone. Then looking at the horses she said, "I see that you were successful. The Mother has been generous."

Fleet smiled as she commented on the Mother's generosity. He had thought their success was due to man's ingenuity, but he would not argue that point with her. What Fleet wanted to hear was what Sister Samethia had to say about the wedding. "Justin just told us that he is marrying Sister Eaglet tonight."

She smiled and said, "That's right, and we still have a lot to do. So get these horses taken care of quickly. Brother Wesley, Brother Wyatt, and Sister Alisma, once you are done, get a change of clothes and something to eat. Then I need you to gather all of the Brothers and Sisters who are with the flocks and tell them to come. I want everybody to be here." She looked at Brother Fox and then to Fleet and announced happily, "This will be the Family's first wedding."

There was no point in delaying. Once Sister Samethia had given her instructions it was best to snap to it. Justin went with them, glad to have something to do. Since he had asked Sister Eaglet to marry him, she had been in the women's quarters with Sister Mischka and Sister Samethia. Every time he had asked to see her, Sister Mischka had told

303

him it was bad luck to see the bride before the wedding and slammed the door in his face.

As soon as they were done with the horses, Kurt and Fleet put off bathing and eating to take Justin aside and talk to him away from the Family. Kurt was blunt, "Are you crazy?"

Justin was crushed by his reaction. He had been floating on his own private cloud for several days and Kurt was trying to knock him off. "I am marrying Eaglet and nothing you say will change that."

Fleet was a little subtler with his question. "Have you decided to join the Family?" He could not imagine Sister Samethia being in favor of the marriage if it didn't result in Justin's conversion to the Family.

Justin's answer was an emphatic, "No!"

"Then Sister Eaglet is coming with us to the Settlement?" Fleet asked. It didn't make any sense to him. He knew Sister Samethia would never agree to that.

"No, Sister Eaglet will stay here," Justin answered simply.

"And where are you going to live," Kurt asked. He knew Justin wasn't thinking with his head. It was another part of his body that was making the decisions.

"I'll stay in the cabin when I'm at the Settlement like always, but when I'm here I'll be with Eaglet," Justin explained.

"That's not a marriage, boy," Kurt was trying to get him to understand. "For a marriage to work the two people involved have to live together."

"Well, it's what I want. I love Sister Eaglet and I will marry her tonight," Justin said angrily. Then he looked at both Kurt and Fleet and added, "And if you can't be happy for me, then the least you can do is stay out of my way."

Fleet could tell that Justin had made up his mind and there was no point in arguing. He only had one more question. "Do you want to be released from your duties with the Guard?"

"No," Justin's answer was quick. There was no uncertainty in his mind about the Guard either. He took his responsibilities very seriously.

"Then I will be able to count on you as always?" Fleet asked. He wanted to be certain Justin knew that Fleet still needed his complete devotion to the Guard.

Justin held his left-hand palm forward as if taking a pledge and said, "You will, until the death."

Fleet looked at him, wondering if Justin realized that he would be making the same pledge to Sister Eaglet in a few hours. Fleet saw Kurt shaking his head. The irony had not escaped Kurt either. They both knew that at some point Justin would have to make a choice, but there was nothing to be done about it other than to tie him up and drag him back to the Settlement. Then he would only come running back the first chance he got. If Justin was going to have a wedding, he might as well enjoy it. Suddenly, Fleet was grinning ear to ear and he clapped Justin on the shoulder, "Well then, if we're going to have a wedding, we had better get the groom ready." He winked at Kurt and said, "I think he needs a bath. What do you think?" Before Justin knew it, Fleet grabbed him under the arms and Kurt took his feet. They carried him kicking and cursing all the way to the lake then threw Justin into the icy cold water.

While Fleet and Kurt were doubled over with laughter, Justin pulled himself up the muddy bank and grabbed Fleet by the ankle, catching him unprepared. Next thing he knew, Fleet was in the water and Kurt was backing away, keeping well out of their reach before he ended up in the drink, too. Fleet looked angrily at Justin who was holding out his hand to help him out of the water. When Fleet ignored his offer to help and scrambled up the bank on his own, Justin said, "It's not so funny when you're the one in the water." Then looking at his muddy clothes he added, "Now what am I supposed to wear?"

"Don't worry, we'll take care of that," Kurt said. Then looking at Fleet, he added, "We all need to clean up and get something to eat."

They spent the rest of the afternoon washing themselves and their clothing. Justin presented a problem. The only shirt he had was the homespun shirt with the bloodstain on the shoulder. Despite Justin's protests that he wanted to wear it, Fleet and Kurt refused to let him and insisted that the groom needed to look respectable. It took some urging on Fleet's part, but he finally convinced Justin to wear a white shirt that belonged to Brother Eldar. It was long sleeved and had little wooden buttons up the front. Brother Eldar was quite proud of the buttons, telling Justin at some length how he had carved them himself and he had made the shirt as well. He was so pleased by the fact that Fleet

305

wanted Justin to wear his shirt that he insisted it would be his wedding present.

They spent the whole time in men's quarters waiting for their clothes to dry and watching Justin pace the floor like a nervous cat. Every few minutes he would go to the door and look outside then check his trousers to see if they were dry yet. Fleet and Kurt were lounging on the floor enjoying the fire and the fact that for the first time in a week they were not on the back of a horse. They were also enjoying a flask of Brother Eldar's homemade wine.

"Aren't you going to give me some?" Justin asked when he saw that they had only two cups.

"We're not getting married," Kurt said as he poured the wine then held his cup above his head to make a toast, "To the groom." Then he and Fleet emptied their cups.

Fleet held out his cup for more and after Kurt had filled it, Fleet made his toast. "To the bride," and they emptied their glasses again.

"Would you please sit down," Kurt said as he refilled the cups. "You're making me nervous." He set out a third cup and said, "If you sit down, I'll let you have one cup of wine."

Justin left his watch at the door and sat next to Kurt. He took the cup from him and after only one small sip, looked back at the door again. Fleet laughed and said, "Don't worry, they won't start without you. So try to relax a little, you're supposed to be enjoying yourself."

"How can I enjoy myself? I want to be with Eaglet, not you two," Justin said sharply. Fleet and Kurt exchanged glances. It was great fun teasing the prospective bridegroom, but they knew when it was time to back off. Justin drank the rest of his wine and looked down at his two companions. "There is something that I want," he was smiling now, "You can call it your wedding present."

Fleet looked at Kurt and then to Justin before asking, "What is it that you want?"

"I want an extra day," Justin said. "We don't have to go back tomorrow do we?"

Fleet couldn't say that he was surprised by his request, but they had already been gone too long. Sadie would be expecting them home and the longer they delayed the frostier Fleet's reception would be. He wanted to keep to his schedule, but he couldn't refuse his young friend's request. "A honeymoon?" Fleet laughed, he was drinking his third cup of wine and was starting to feel the effects. Brother Eldar made a powerful brew. "I suppose we could work something out." Justin smiled and went back to pacing, but his step was a little lighter now. Fleet and Kurt continued with their drinking. All they were waiting for was someone to let them know when they were ready to begin the ceremony.

Brother Fox arrived shortly before nightfall. Fleet and Kurt were still lounging in front of the fire wearing nothing but their underclothes with the empty flask beside them. It was obvious that they were intoxicated. Brother Fox grinned at the men and said, "Brother Kurt, Brother Fleet, why don't you get dressed now and join the others waiting outside. I would like to speak to Brother Justin before we begin the ceremony."

Fleet got up and as he began to pull on his trousers said, "We might as well join the party outside. We're all out of wine." They both dressed quickly and headed outside.

Before he closed the door, Kurt looked back and said to Justin, "We really are happy for you Justin." He was able to say it with a little more conviction than earlier. The wine had helped lighten his mood.

Once they were gone, Justin looked at Brother Fox. He was much taller than Justin and was standing with his arms folded. His expression was solemn as he said, "Sit with me for a moment." Once Justin was seated and facing him he asked, "How old are you Brother Justin?"

Immediately, Justin was on guard, "What does that have to do with anything?"

Brother Fox held his hand up and said, "I mean no insult." Then he started again. There was something he wanted to say, but was not sure where to begin. "A little over a year ago, the world was a different place Brother Justin. I was like everyone else. I had a job, a house, a family, but after the evacuations everything changed. I was living alone here at the lake when Sister Samethia came to me and told me about her Family. Together we brought together the Brothers and Sisters. A few were older like Brother Eldar and Brother and Sister Treblki, but most of them were quite young. Sister Samethia and I love them all like our own children." He paused for a moment. It was a difficult thing for Brother Fox to talk about what he was feeling. He was a man of action, not words. "Sister Eaglet is very young. She is only sixteen and I would guess that you are not much older. Marriage is nothing to be done lightly or without careful thought and consideration." Justin opened his mouth to speak, but Brother Fox said, "Please, let me finish." Justin remained silent and watched Brother Fox warily as he continued, "I have spent the afternoon with Sister Samethia discussing this decision. I was in favor of postponing this wedding until the two of you had time to think about what you are doing," he paused and took a breath before adding, "but Sister Samethia has assured me that she approves and has given her blessing. I want to hear from you now, Brother Justin. Why do you want to get married now?"

Justin met Brother Fox's stubborn glare with one of his own. "You mentioned what life was like before the evacuations. I remember, too. I lost my family, my friends, and my home, too. For the last year, I have had to fight every day to stay alive. When Fleet chose me for the Guard he gave me a purpose in my life, which was what I needed. But there was something missing, I didn't know what it was until I met Sister Eaglet." Justin paused for a moment searching for the words, wondering how he could explain the emotions that had been in command of his actions since he arrived here at the camp. "I know that it is too soon. I know that this has all happened in a matter of days, but now that I have found Sister Eaglet, I can't let her go. It makes me happy just to sit beside her, to know that she is there. I knew that I loved her and wanted her to be with me for the rest of my life when I stopped thinking in terms of what I would do and began thinking about what we would do with our lives. I can't explain it or tell you when that happened, but I couldn't help it. When I think about where I will be in a year or two or twenty, Sister Eaglet is with me."

Brother Fox smiled. He was pleased with the explanation that Brother Justin had given him. He had asked Sister Eaglet the same question and had gotten the same answer. Love was a strange thing. With some people it grew slowly over time and with others it was like being hit by a bolt of lightening, sudden and electrifying. He stood and said, "They're ready for us." He held out his hand and when Justin clasped his hand, Brother Fox pulled him to his feet, but he did not release his hold. He held Justin's hand in both of his for a moment and said with a smile, "I'm supposed to give the bride away and now I can do that with a clear conscience. Take care of my little Sister, Brother Justin."

"I will," Justin answered and then turned the tables. "And I will entrust my wife to your care when I am away. Keep her safe for me, Brother Fox."

"I will, Brother Justin," he said as he released his hold and turned to leave with Justin right behind him.

Outside the celebration was underway. One of the six large bonfires had been lit and Brother Fox indicated that was where Justin should go. As Justin walked across the muddy ground toward the fire, the Brothers and Sisters who were gathered there cheered, clapped, and whistled their encouragement. The wine had been flowing freely and everyone was in high spirits. When Justin reached the fire, he found Sister Samethia waiting for him. Fleet and Kurt were standing nearby. When they saw Justin, they both nodded and smiled.

When Sister Eaglet appeared at the doorway of the women's shelter with Brother Fox at her side the group became silent. It was the moment for which they had been waiting. As silence descended the only thing Justin could hear was the thunder of his heart pounding in his ears and the crackle and hiss of the fire behind him. His eyes were riveted on Eaglet. She was an angel in white, his angel. Sister Eaglet walked through a corridor formed by the Brothers and Sisters holding torches high in the air and came to stand beside him.

Justin looked at her. Eaglet was more beautiful every time he saw her. She was wearing a simple white dress with small flowers embroidered around the neck and bodice. Her golden hair was not braided and the long tendrils flowed over her shoulders and the small curls around her face danced with the breeze. There were flowers in her hair, a braided chain of small white clover and dandelions. Weeds from the garden, but on Eaglet they were a crown of precious jewels. Justin reached out and took her by the hand and they stood side by side waiting for Sister Samethia to begin the ceremony.

Sister Samethia raised her arms above her head and held her open palms toward the sky and said, "The Mother created the earth from the fires of heaven." As she said the words the Brothers and Sisters threw their torches into the unlit bonfires and they sprang to life with a rush of flame and heat. "She gave us the earth, water, and wind." Almost as if it were waiting for its cue, the wind gusted and whipped the fires even higher. It seemed that Sister Samethia had commanded it. Then she lowered her arms and looked at Justin and Sister Eaglet, "These are the Mother's gifts to her children, but her greatest gift is the gift of love." She looked at Sister Eaglet and said, "The love of a woman for a man is a marvelous thing but with pleasure there is always pain, with joy there is always sorrow." Then looking to Justin she said, "The love of a man for a woman is wondrous thing, but with the bliss there is the burden, with the ecstasy comes the anguish." Sister Samethia reached out and took Sister Eaglet's and Justin's hands in hers and said, "Are you ready to accept the Mother's gift of love with all its joys and all its burdens?"

In unison Sister Eaglet and Justin answered, "Yes, we are."

"Then may the Mother bless this union and bestow upon you her gifts of love, children, and a long life together," Sister Samethia said as she released their hands and motioned for them to turn around to face the others. "Brother Justin and Sister Eaglet, from now until the end of time your spirits will be one in the Mother's love as you begin your new lives as husband and wife." Justin did not wait for anyone to tell him to kiss the bride and as he took Sister Eaglet in his arms a cheer erupted from the Brothers and Sisters who were watching. When he kissed her, Justin ceased to hear the noise surrounding him for the moment he was blissfully unaware of anything or anyone other than Eaglet.

Chapter Twelve

Kyla was in the kitchen helping Agatha cook the noon meal. When Kyla had first offered to help, she'd been a little suspicious. The kitchen was her domain and Agatha didn't want anyone telling her what to do, especially not the newest member of the Guard. However, when she realized that Kyla wasn't a threat to her authority, Agatha had gladly accepted the help, even if she couldn't get Kyla to do the laundry. At first all she had trusted Kyla to do was stir what was in the pots, but before long they were working side by side. Besides, Kyla liked to cook and it was nice to do something useful rather than just hanging around the house waiting her turn on duty at the shelter house in the Settlement.

The other pastime that she had taken up was hunting. Everyday since Fleet had left with the others, Kyla had taken a rifle and riding Brownie, she'd found that the game was more plentiful the further she went from the Settlement. On horseback she was able to travel further than the men on foot and could carry back more game, too. But she didn't take what she shot to the cabin; everything went to the Settlement. She was working on doing what Armand had advised her to do her first night on duty at the shelter house, to make friends with the people at the Settlement. Providing food with no strings attached had gone a long way toward achieving that goal.

The first day when she brought back a dozen rabbits and began distributing them to the people who happened to be standing in front of the shelter house, Kyla almost started a riot. Before things got too far out of hand, she fired a shot into the air to get everyone's attention. Once the arguing stopped, she let them know that there would be no food tomorrow if the fighting continued. Then there was Armand's reaction when he found out what she had been doing. At his insistence, she had to take someone with her when she left the farm.

Kyla had surprised them all when she asked Carleen to accompany her, and of course, Carleen was more than happy to be released from her duties in the garden. On their first day out together, Kyla discovered that Carleen was a better shot than she was and they soon doubled the amount of game that they brought back in a day. On their third day hunting together, they found a herd of deer and they both managed to bring one down. When they returned to the Settlement with two deer, they were cheered like conquering heroes. This time there was enough for everyone. The only request that Kyla made when they dropped the two deer on the ground in front of the shelter house was that they give her the skins from the deer. Kyla hadn't really expected to get them back, but that evening when she went to the shelter house, she was pleasantly surprised. One of the women who had been there when they left the deer made a great show of presenting the skins to her while the rest of the people in the shelter house sat silently and watched. It had been the first time that Kyla had seen everyone so quiet and orderly. Even, Armand had been impressed by the show of respect and after that her hunting trips had his full blessings.

Fortunately for Kyla, Agatha was now her friend and she was allowed to store the rolled skins in the freezer. Kyla didn't know how to tan the skins, but the Family did. She was going to take them to Sister Eaglet as soon as she had a chance. It was the first step toward her repayment of the debt that she felt she owed the Brothers and Sisters. She had been thinking about the Family and worrying about Fleet, Kurt, and Justin over the past few days. Even Sadie had seemed concerned, but when James had suggested that they send someone to look for them Sadie had been firm in saying, "No." Fleet had been clear about his wishes in that regard. No one was to be sent if they did not return.

Kyla was busy in the kitchen when Armand opened the door and said, "They're back." The bread that she had been kneading was forgotten and without bothering to wash her hands or brush the flour from her apron, Kyla rushed out the door after him.

Once outside she could see the riders coming down the lane, three riders and several horses. That was a surprise. Fleet had said nothing about bringing back more horses when he left. When they saw Kyla and Armand coming to meet them, the men urged the horses to a faster pace. Once they were in front of the cabin, Fleet jumped off his horse and smiling broadly said, "It's good to be home."

"We were worried when you were gone so long," Kyla said as she reached the end of the walkway.

Fleet was still grinning when he looked over his shoulder at Justin and said, "We were delayed an extra day visiting with the Brothers and Sisters."

The look that passed between the three men left no doubt that there was more to the story than they were telling, but something else caught Kyla's eye. She went to the white horse that Fleet was leading next to his. Kyla touched the white mare's soft nose then patted her on the neck. "She's magnificent," Kyla said, as she looked the horse over. "Where did you get her?" Then she looked at the saddle and ran her fingers over the silver trimming the leather, "And this is a show saddle. I know the Family didn't make this."

"If you like her, she yours," Fleet said graciously. Until that moment he hadn't thought about who might want the white horse.

Kyla's reaction was immediate and heartfelt. She wrapped her arms around Fleet's neck and planted a kiss on his jaw and said, "Thank you, she's a beautiful." When she felt him stiffen slightly, Kyla realized what she was doing and let go. Then as she stepped back, she saw that Fleet's black tunic was now covered with white flour. Kyla began trying to brush off the white powder, which was only adding to his embarrassment.

Fleet grabbed her by the wrists and pushing her hands away, said, "Don't worry about that. I have to change anyway," and began to brush himself off. Kurt, Justin, and Armand were all trying to keep from laughing. Fleet glared at them with a look warning them to keep their comments to themselves. Then turning the conversation back to the mare, he smiled at Kyla and said, " Maybe if you're riding this one, she'll be able to keep up. Not like that old brown nag you have been riding." That was the reason he gave, but Kyla's reaction had pleased him more than he was willing to admit, even to himself. She was changing. In the time they had been gone, Kyla had begun to flesh out a little and she no longer looked like a skeleton with skin. Her hair was growing back, too. He could see that she truly was an attractive woman and Fleet always felt that a beautiful woman should have beautiful things.

"Don't call Brownie a nag," Kyla scolded, but she had already forgotten about Fleet and was looking at the horse and saddle. "I can't use this saddle. It's much too nice to use everyday."

"Well, then you had better learn to ride bareback, because the saddle goes with the horse," Fleet answered. "Besides, we don't have enough saddles for all the horses as it is." Saddles and bridles were a problem, but once the word was out that they needed some, the scavengers would go to work. It wouldn't surprise Fleet if saddles started showing up tomorrow.

As she stroked the horse's neck Kyla said, "I'll bet she runs like the wind. A horse like this should have a name."

"Call her Flour," Justin offered. When the others looked at him like he was crazy, he added, "You know Flour. She's got flour on her hands." Then he said, "Forget it. It's not funny if you have to explain your joke."

Kyla looked at Justin and smiled, "That's what I would expect from some one who calls his horse Bung Ho'." She was glad to see the three men back. Although Kyla had made friends with many of the others at the farm and the Settlement, she felt a close bond with Justin, Kurt, and Fleet after their trip to Spring's farm.

It was Kurt who spoke up and said, "There was a strong north wind the night Fleet found her. Why don't you call her North Wind?"

"I like that," Kyla said looking at Kurt. She liked the name, but she also liked his choice of words in explaining how Fleet had acquired the horse. Kyla knew that Fleet had not found the horse and saddle. He had stolen them from someone. She also knew that it hadn't been Cole Spring. Somehow, she was going to have to pry the story from them, but that would have to wait for later, Sadie was coming down the walkway to greet the men.

Sadie had heard Armand's announcement and was in the library and watching as Armand and Kyla ran down the walk. As soon as Sadie laid eyes on the white mare and it's expensive saddle, she knew it would bring trouble. When she saw Kyla kiss Fleet and begin to brush off the flour, Sadie started toward the door. As she glided down the steps and the walkway, Sadie was not hurrying. That was something she would never do. Her bearing was always reserved and in control; something that she was finding a little difficult to maintain at the moment. Already, it was obvious that Fleet had given the horse to Kyla. That in itself was an irritation, but once she reached the small gathering, Sadie ignored the horse and looked at Fleet. "I would give you a hug to welcome you home, but I see that someone else already has," Sadie said in her most indifferent tone of voice. Then looking at Kyla she said, "I prefer to leave the flour in the kitchen."

Kyla fought her first response, which was to apologize and run back to the kitchen. Instead, she looked at Sadie and said, "Fleet gave me this horse. Isn't she beautiful?" Kyla was well aware of what Sadie's reaction would be, but she didn't care. The three men looked at the women uncomfortably, waiting for the explosion, but it never came.

"That was very generous of Fleet," Sadie said indifferently. Then turning her back to Kyla, she shifted her attention to Fleet. He was expecting her to say something sharp, but to his surprise Sadie took him by the arm and said, "Let me take you inside where you can clean up." Then with one last look to Kyla she said, "Will you tell Agatha to send some hot water to my room. Fleet will want a hot bath and clean clothing, too." As Sadie led Fleet away, Kyla felt as if she had reached out and slapped her in the face.

Kurt watched Sadie and Fleet walking toward the house and shook his head. If there was one thing that Sadie was good at doing, it was handing out an insult. All the while being so polite about it that you had to say thank you when she was done. Kurt wondered what Fleet saw in her other than the obvious physical attraction. Sadie was an elegant woman what Kurt would call a classic beauty. Today she was wearing her long brown hair up in a knot on the top of her head with the curls hanging down the back. Something special for Fleet's homecoming he suspected. Kurt knew what Sadie wanted and that was to keep Fleet at home. He had lived with both of them long enough to know when Sadie was going out of her way to be nice to Fleet. She hadn't said one word about where they had been or what had taken them so long. Her only concern had been to get Fleet alone and away from the rest of them, Kyla in particular.

He looked at Kyla who was standing beside her horse and glaring angrily at Sadie's back. Kurt had been surprised by Fleet's impetuous gift. The horse and the saddle were probably something that Sadie would have wanted or in Sadie's case, expected to be given to her. Still, she had forgiven Fleet's insult and taken her vengeance out on Kyla. The other thing that had surprised Kurt was Kyla's reaction. For a split second, he had seen Fleet move to return her embrace and then stopped

315

himself. Kurt wondered if Fleet would have stopped if Sadie had not been just inside the house. Which brought the realization that Sadie must have been watching. Judging by the look on Kyla's face, Kurt was beginning to think that Sadie might have met her match.

It was Armand, who broke the uncomfortable silence by saying, "I'll tell Agatha to take the water and clothes for Fleet."

As Armand walked back to the cabin, Kurt said, "Kyla take Fleet's string." Then they continued on their way to the barn. Before they reached it, they saw James and Riley coming from the opposite direction.

Riley was walking so fast that she was nearly running in effort to arrive at the barn at the same time as the men with the horses. "There's not enough room in the stables for all these horses," she exclaimed. "Where are we going to keep them all?"

"It's good to see you too, Riley," Justin said as he slid off his horse.

"I'm sorry Justin," she said a little embarrassed to have seemed so insensitive. "I'm glad to see you home safely. I was just so surprised to see so many horses. Fleet didn't mention anything about bringing home more horses when he left." Then she noticed the white horse that Kyla was leading and added, "Especially, one like that." She eyed Kurt suspiciously and said, "Where have you been?"

Kurt was the last one to dismount and he had to grin a little at Riley's amazement. All he said was, "We'll tell the whole story later. Right now we have some work to do." When James finally caught up with them, Kurt said, "We're going to need to do some repairs on the fences, James."

"I can see that," he said. Then he went to each of the horses and looked them over from head to tail. "I wish Fleet would let me know in advance what he plans to do. We could have had the pens ready when you got back."

"It was something that came up while we were gone," Kurt answered. He knew the reason Fleet had not said anything before they left. They both suspected that someone had tipped off Cole Spring about their first raid and then told him where to find Eddie and Dylan. Even Kurt hadn't known what Fleet had planned until they were on their way to the Family's camp. Given the success of their latest trip, Kurt was as certain as Fleet, that someone had betrayed them.

James pushed the large wooden door of the barn open, allowing the horses to be led inside. "I'll go get some men to start work on some kind of pen to hold them until we can repair the fences on the stock pens." He was referring to the fenced area just outside the barn. Inside, the barn had six large stalls for horses on one side. The other side was divided into two pens that were meant for cattle. There was a large door from each of those pens leading to the fenced area outside which was also divided into two. It was the fencing outside that was in need of repair with several boards broken or missing.

The first chore was to decide which horses were to go in the stables. Reluctantly, Riley led her Guernsey cow from one of the stalls and took on the task of deciding which horse went where. There was no question that Fleet's black stallion and the white mare would be kept in one of the stalls. While Kyla took North Wind into the stall that Riley indicated, the curly haired woman was busy evaluating the horses that were the current occupants of the stalls. Next she went to the ones on the leads. Finally she made her decision and Kurt and Justin were having a hard time keeping up with her instructions as she told them where each horse should go.

Riley had been looking at the horses and judging their value as breeding stock. Six geldings included Justin's gray and the bay that Kurt had been riding would go in one pen. They were good horses for riding, but useless for breeding. She was pleased that most of the new horses were mares. Out of the twelve there were only two geldings and one colt. He was a buff color with a white mane and looked to be the same high quality stock that the white horse was. All of the horses that Fleet had returned with were in excellent condition. She had hoped to double up the horses in all the stalls, but Fleet's black stallion kicked and reared every time they tried to put another horse in its stall. North Wind did the same. So Riley ended up with the ten best horses in the stalls, six geldings in one pen and two mares in the other pen with the cow.

They couldn't let the horses out of the barn until the fences were repaired. So for the time being they had to tie each lead to the manger on one side of the pen. When James returned with some men carrying tools and materials to begin working on the fences, Kurt and Justin excused themselves and went to the cabin to bathe and change their clothing, too. Kyla followed them out the door.

"I'm glad you're back," she said. "How is Sister Eaglet?" Justin jumped like he had been stung by a bee and gave Kyla the strangest look.

"She's wonderful," he said wistfully. Then with a look from Kurt, he snapped to attention and added, "They're all fine. Sister Samethia said to give you her regards." Justin was bursting to tell Kyla about himself and Eaglet, but Kurt and Fleet had convinced him that the marriage was best kept a private matter for now.

Kyla saw the look that passed between Kurt and Justin. She was sure that if she got Justin alone for a few minutes he would tell her what was going on. He looked like he was ready to explode from the strain of holding whatever it was inside. She changed the subject for now. "Where did you get the horses from?"

Kurt looked at Kyla and frowned at her questions. He was tired and not in the mood for explanations right now. "I'll tell you everything later. Right now what I want is a bath and something to eat," he snapped at Kyla. Kurt was also a little put out at Fleet for not coming to help with the work of settling the horses in the stables. Still when he thought of Fleet with Sadie, he was sure that Fleet had his hands full right now.

Kyla knew Kurt well enough by now to know that she would have more luck getting her questions answered once he'd had a change of clothes and his stomach was full. She smiled and said, "I'm sorry. I forgot that you just got home. I'll get some hot water ready for you and Justin." Then she ran ahead to get things ready for them. Maybe a hot bath would help soften Kurt's mood. Kyla would get the answers to her questions later.

That day the noon meal was the liveliest that it had ever been during Kyla's short time at the Settlement. It was also the first time all twelve members of the Guard were present. While they were eating the conversation focused on Justin and his time with the Family. As he told them about the Brothers and Sisters and their camp, Kyla still felt he was leaving out something. She had a hunch that something had happened between Justin and Sister Eaglet. Every time Kyla mentioned her name Justin either smiled like he was recalling some pleasant memory or grimaced like he had lost his best friend.

As Agatha was clearing the empty plates and dishes from the table, Sadie began the formal part of their gathering by saying, "It is good to see all the seats at the table are filled." Then looking to Fleet at the opposite end of the table, "We had some excitement here while you were gone." With a nod to Armand, Sadie let him know that she expected him to give the report.

The big man coughed as he choked on a piece of bread. He had expected Sadie to tell the story and had just decided to eat the last roll. His mouth was full when she had called on him. Armand swallowed and took a drink of water before beginning. "The night you left we had a visit from a pearl trader calling himself Slick and two thugs that he brought with him. It wasn't until later that we realized what they were really after was the horses. Slick handed out enough pearls that night to start a riot. While all the Guard was up at the shelter house trying to keep things from getting out of hand, Slick's two buddies were sneaking down here to steal the horses." Armand paused for a moment before adding, "If it hadn't been for Sadie and Riley, they would have succeeded."

"I never thought I would shoot a man for stealing horses, let alone two," Sadie interjected. "Two men died that night trying to steal some horses. It's distressing to think that we have come to that."

"Three men died that night." It was Kyla that interrupted Sadie. She looked at Fleet as she said, "The next morning we found the old man named Orin near the Settlement. Someone had slit his throat from ear to ear. It was horrible." When she finished, Kyla looked to Sadie. Every time Sadie talked about what had happened that night she always forgot to mention Orin's murder. Like it didn't matter as much as the other events.

Sadie nodded and said, "We think the pearl trader was responsible for that, too." It was annoying that Kyla kept bringing up the subject of the old man. Sadie would prefer that everybody forgot about the strange little man.

"I would like to discuss something else, while we're on the subject of what happened that night," Armand said. He looked to Sadie for her permission. When she nodded, he continued, "I would like to

319

formally request that Kyla be given her black bead. I am satisfied with her actions that night and her work since then. I think that she should be recognized as a member of the Guard with full status."

"I agree," Moon said as he held up his arms and showed the red welts on his arms. "If she hadn't fired the rifle when she did, I don't think I'd be here today."

"She's also done a lot for morale in the Settlement," Armand said. Then with a grin he added, "She has them eating out of her hand."

Kyla was becoming embarrassed by the praise. She was only doing what she thought was right. "Firing a warning shot that night in the shelter house was the only way to get the attention of the mob and feeding the hungry is something I have to do. It hasn't been that long since I was hungry, too," she explained simply.

"Providing food for the people in the Settlement certainly is commendable," Sadie began, "but I wonder if giving them food so they don't have to do anything to help themselves is best in the long run." She was not as anxious as the others to heap praise on Kyla for her humanitarian efforts.

"Once you've missed more than your supper, then you can tell me what it's like to be starving," she shot a burning look to Sadie. "When you get to the point when all you can think about is your next meal, if you're lucky enough to find it, you can't think about anything else. I'm hoping that if their stomachs are full for a few days they will start looking for long term solutions to their problems, instead of hanging around the shelter house looking for pearls and moonshine." Everyone at the table was staring at Kyla. There was no one who could disagree with what she had said and she had spoken with the passion of some one who had knowledge that came from personal suffering, but she had taken Sadie to task. Not one of them would have dared to speak to Sadie in that tone.

Fleet had been listening without comment. He had also been watching Sadie's face as Kyla spoke. Her expression had not changed one bit, but her eyes were becoming colder by the second. Before Sadie could respond Fleet said, "There is no harm in feeding the people at the Settlement." Then to smooth Sadie's ruffled feathers he added, "But we need to make sure that we encourage them to take on more responsibilities at the same time."

He wanted to change the subject, too. "I think we should go back to Armand's request for Kyla to receive her first black bead and I have to agree. Kyla was an invaluable member of the team when we went after Eddie and Dylan." Fleet looked around the table and his eyes stopped when he came to Sadie. "If no one has any objections, we'll do it at the next Gathering." The only objection would come from Sadie. Looking from Sadie to Kyla, Fleet was realizing that the two women would always be at odds with one another. They were both strong willed and spoke their minds without much thought to whose toes they stepped on.

No one spoke up, though Fleet could tell that Sadie wanted to say something. After a brief silence he said, "Well, now that's decided. I guess you want to know about the horses." Fleet smiled and leaned back in his chair, stretching his long legs out in front of him. He was relaxed and happy. Things had gone well retrieving the guns, stealing the horses, and the wedding celebration had put him in a good mood and nothing was going to spoil it now. Even the decision to give Kyla her promotion, he viewed as a personal triumph. His hunch about her had been right on the mark. Now he was ready to tell the others his story.

"We went back to get the guns and ammunition at the covered bridge," Fleet looked around the table to gage everyone's reaction. Judging by the surprised looks from the ones who had not been with the six at the bridge, Fleet was satisfied that Eddie, Dylan, and Kyla had not been talking about the hidden guns. "We gave them to the Family in exchange for taking us to the stock farm where they were getting their horses." He paused for the murmurs and questions.

"Where is it?" Rod asked the question that was on everybody's lips. His eyes lit up and he stroked his beard thoughtfully as he considered the possibilities.

His question was forgotten when Sadie said, "You did what?"

Fleet didn't move a muscle, as he answered, "I gave twenty guns and all the ammunition to the Family." He smiled broadly. Even Sadie's ill will toward the Family was not going to interfere with his good mood. "I haven't changed my mind and we have discussed this before. The Brothers and Sisters are the only allies that we have. They're armed now and they're between the Settlement and Spring's farm. I don't know about you, but I sleep better at night knowing that."

Sadie was not ready to give up, "They certainly are armed, thanks to you Fleet but I am still not fully convinced that their interests and ours are the same. If the men from Spring's farm threatened the Settlement, I'm not so sure that the Family would be willing to come to our aid. They seem to only care for themselves."

"That's not true," Justin spoke out as if he had received a personal insult. When everyone turned to look at him, he was compelled to add, " They're good people. I know they would help us if we needed it and we should do the same for them."

"Let me finish," Fleet said. The discussion was straying from the point he was trying to make. "I have promised Brother Fox that we will not go to the stock farm without the Brothers or tell anyone its location. What I can tell you is that it is big. Still, the more I thought about Spring's farm and the stock farm, I came to the realization that there must be many more farms and compounds where food and other necessities have been stockpiled. I plan on trying to find settlements like ours, and if there are any more compounds operated by Manjohnah's men in our area. We need to know who our friends are and where our enemies are located."

Sadie couldn't believe her ears. Fleet had not spent one night at home and already he was making plans to leave again. She had to do something to keep him at the cabin or at the very least influence the direction that his next venture would take. "I think whatever we do that it should be with the intention of making friends not enemies. Perhaps we should change our tactics and go as ambassadors of good will rather than as thieves in the night." Her tone was pleasant and her point well taken by all seated at the table. Sadie's next bit of information came as a surprise to everyone. "Which brings to mind something that the man named Orin mentioned. According to him there is a large settlement west of here on the outskirts of the city. He says it is quite large. Perhaps that would be a good place to start."

Armand perked up as she mentioned the location. "I came here from the west and I don't remember any settlement, but there were people." His confrontation with the gang that had threatened him and Ruth came to mind.

"Things can change with time Armand," Sadie answered patiently. "Even the Settlement has grown since you arrived."

Fleet liked the idea and could see himself as an ambassador as Sadie had said. The last thing he wanted was another enemy to his west. With the stock farm located to the south, Cole Spring's farm to the east and Manjohnah's operations in the north, west was the only direction left to explore. "That sounds like a good possibility, but we have plenty of time to decide what to do. I don't plan on going anywhere for a few days."

Sadie's sigh of relief was almost audible, as she said, "One thing we need to do is make sure that when you leave this time there are enough men to keep order left at the Settlement. I don't like the farm left unguarded."

That was a subject on which James wanted to elaborate. "I think we need armed patrols here every night, especially now that we have so many horses. They'll continue to be a temptation for every drifter who comes to the Settlement. Besides, I don't like the idea of Sadie and Riley being here without protection."

As he looked at Riley and Sadie, Fleet could not imagine either one of them needing protection. He had not been surprised to hear that they had dealt with the horse thieves as they had. Sadie had always impressed Fleet as the type of person who would shoot first and ask questions later. Still, he agreed with James. They could do a lot to improve the security of those living at the farm. "That brings us to another problem that I wanted to bring up. Twelve Guard members are not enough to keep order here and at the Settlement. The number of people in the Settlement has doubled since we started the Guard. We need to increase our numbers."

"No, the number is twelve and it will remain twelve," Sadie's response was immediate and clear that she was not willing to discuss the number.

It was the reaction that Fleet had expected and he was ready with his compromise. "I agree, the number of the Guard should remain twelve, but that doesn't mean we can't get some of the others to help. There already are some men we can count on when we need help."

"Like Tom and Captain Frye," Dylan offered the two most obvious choices.

"Exactly," Fleet agreed, "and there are others we can trust to help." Then as he looked at Sadie he said, "That would go a long way toward getting the people at the Settlement to start thinking of themselves as human beings again, instead of acting like animals." Fleet had plans for the future and peace, order, and enough food for everyone were his goals.

"Just how many people do you plan on adding?" Sadie asked warily. The idea was not totally unworkable, but she didn't want to change the number of the Guard. The inner circle should remain unchanged.

"Four people to start," Fleet said and he looked around the table. "Does anyone have objections with Tom or Captain Frye?" When there was no answer Fleet continued, "I would like to know of any other men that you could recommend."

Kyla only hesitated for a moment before saying; "Carleen has been helping me since you left. She's a good shot and rides like she was born on a horse."

Fleet considered Kyla's suggestion for a moment. Another woman was not what he had in mind. "We might be able to use her," Fleet said cautiously, "but I would like to talk to her first. I don't know her very well." There were no other suggestions, so Fleet finished by saying, "We should all think about this for a few days. Tomorrow at lunch I want some names from each of you. Then we will interview each person and make a decision as a group, Tom and Captain Frye included." With that said Fleet stood, for him the meeting was over. He strode confidently from the room and across the foyer to the hallway that led to his quarters.

As everyone began leaving Kyla caught up with Justin as he was going out the front door. She had not forgotten about her plans to get the whole story. Fleet's version at lunch had been somewhat lacking in details. "Do you mind if I walk with you?" she asked as she followed him out the door. Kyla didn't know how to bring up the subject so she asked, "When are you going back to see Sister Eaglet?"

Without thinking Justin answered, "Soon, I hope." Then with a look at Kyla, he asked, "How did you know about that?"

324

"Just say it's women's intuition," Kyla laughed. She hadn't really known, but she'd had her suspicions since this morning. Justin had only confirmed them.

He took her by the arm, dragging her down the walkway and away from the others who were coming out of the cabin. Once they were far enough away so they could not be overheard by anyone, Justin said, "I have to tell someone and since you know Eaglet," he paused and looked over his shoulder. "We're married. Sister Samethia married us two days ago." His face was positively glowing with pride.

It was all Kyla could do to contain her excitement, too. She couldn't think of a better match for Justin. "I'm so happy for both of you," Kyla said. "But tell me when will you be going back?"

"I'd leave right now if Fleet would let me," Justin answered. He hadn't had the nerve to ask Fleet yet.

"Well, tell me before you go," Kyla said. "I have something for Sister Eaglet." As she left Justin, Kyla headed for the barn. She was pleased that Justin had told her about his marriage. Now if Kurt would do the same, Kyla would be up to date on all their activities, but Kurt would have to wait until later. Carleen would be ready and waiting for her. Kyla thought about riding the white horse, but decided against it. North Wind seemed a little high-strung and Kyla didn't want to try shooting from her back, not yet.

~ ~ ~

Fleet was sitting in a large armchair in front of the fire in Sadie's room with his feet propped up on a footstool, doing something that he hadn't done for many weeks, nothing. He wasn't riding, discussing plans, or working in anyway. For a change he was sitting and enjoying a few quiet moments alone. Even Sadie was gone, but it was getting dark outside and she would be returning soon. Fleet was not planning on leaving the room tonight. He had Agatha bring a tray with sliced cheese, cold chicken, and bread and Fleet had a flask of Brother Eldar's homemade wine. He was sure that Sadie would find it a refreshing change from their usual routine.

He wanted tonight to be special. Fleet had been thinking about what he wanted ever since Justin's wedding. In a way he envied the young man, Justin had seen what he wanted in life and grabbed hold when the opportunity presented itself. Since then Fleet had been thinking about his own life and he was ready to move forward with his plans. He had plans for the Settlement. Every time Fleet visited the Family, he was impressed by their willingness to work together. He was certain that he could turn the Settlement around and make it a place where young men could bring their wives without fear. Fleet had been pleased to hear about Kyla's efforts to feed the hungry. The horses made it possible to travel to places where game had not been over hunted. It was good to see that someone had the good sense and initiative to take advantage of that fact.

The plans for the Settlement were only half of what he had been thinking about. Fleet had plans for his personal life as well. He wanted a family of his own. For the last year there was not a day or an hour that went by when Fleet did not think of his wife and son. He had wanted to find them after the leaving his unit, but by then they were long gone. Now he was thinking about the future, he wanted children and he was certain that Sadie would feel the same way. Sadie had been especially attentive today and Fleet was enjoying every minute. He knew she was pleased with his success. When he heard the door to the anteroom open Fleet was on his feet smiling, waiting for Sadie.

When Sadie entered the room and saw the platter with food and Fleet standing in front of the fire waiting for her, she was relieved. She wasn't even in the room and Fleet was already trying to please her. That meant it would be easier for her to bring him to her decision, which was that Fleet should stay at the farm and let someone else go exploring next time. She smiled sweetly and went to Fleet. As he put his arms around her she frowned and said, "I miss you when you're away and it seems like you're never home anymore."

"Well, I'm home now," he answered and kissed her pouting lips.

Sadie let out a deep throaty laugh and pushed him back, "We have all night for that. I want to talk to you. We haven't had a moment alone in weeks."

Fleet let her go. He knew she would let him know when she was ready. Sadie always liked to be the one who decided when it was time to make love. Fleet left it at that, as long as they got around to it sooner of later, he was happy. Besides tonight he wanted to talk to Sadie, too.

Fleet went to the table where the platter was sitting and as he picked up the flask he said, "I have a little surprise for you, some of Brother Eldar's wine." Fleet poured two glasses full of the sweet red wine and handed one to Sadie. In the clear crystal goblets it looked as red as blood. If it lacked the clarity of some wines, it did not lack potency.

Sadie took a cautious sip and said, "It's not bad." Fleet smiled. He knew she would not be able to compliment the wine too much knowing that it was from the Family. Fleet drained his glass and poured another while Sadie sipped hers thoughtfully and asked, "What does Brother Eldar use to make this."

"Beets," Fleet said as he took another drink. "I don't think I could ever say I liked beets before tasting this wine."

Before he could finish his second glass, Sadie brushed close to him and said, "Don't drink too much you will need a clear head tonight."

He smiled and drained the glass. Sadie was like a cat stalking its prey, teasing and moving on. Only Sadie was no farm cat after a mouse, she was a tigress and her favorite prey was man. It was all part of the game that she liked to play when they were alone. She put her glass down on the table and went to sit on the bench in front of her dressing table. It was an old vanity with a large oval mirror. As Sadie began to pull out the long pins that were holding her hair on top of her head, Fleet stood behind her and looked at their reflection in the mirror. He watched silently as she loosened her hair and began to brush it. He was lost in the pleasure of the moment. The scent of her perfume seemed stronger with every stroke of the brush.

Finally, Sadie put down the brush and looked at him in the reflection. "What are you thinking?" the look on Fleet's face seemed to be far away. Sadie wanted his thoughts to be focused on her.

"I've been thinking about the future," Fleet said. He had been waiting all day to tell Sadie about his vision of their life together.

Sadie smiled at him as she stood and turned to face Fleet asked, "What have you decided?"

"I want to start a family with you," Fleet said. "We should think about having children."

At first Sadie laughed. Then she realized that Fleet was quite serious. "Where did this come from? We have never discussed children before."

Fleet was not sure what to think about Sadie's reaction. "I've never mentioned it because I wasn't ready until now," he explained.

Sadie walked across the room to stand in front of the fire before she turned and faced Fleet again. "What makes you think that I am ready?" There would be no discussion on the topic of children. Sadie was trying to find an explanation that Fleet could understand. Finally she said, "Do you think the Settlement is any place to raise a child?"

"It's getting better every day," Fleet said defensively. Sadie's flat refusal to talk about the possibility of a family bothered him, but he tried to smooth things by saying. "I am talking about the future. We don't have to make any decisions today." Fleet would drop the subject for now, but he would not forget it. He went back to the table and filled his glass with wine again then sat in one of the chairs and watched Sadie as she came to the table and sat in the chair across from him.

She took one of his hands in hers and said, "I wanted to talk to you, too." Then with a smile, she added, "but not about children." Fleet returned her smile with a half hearted one of his own and Sadie continued, "I want you to let Kurt take charge of looking for settlements to the west. You need to stay home more often."

Fleet's reaction was immediate as he leapt to his feet and exclaimed, "What are you thinking? If anyone goes, it'll be me." Fleet was finding the whole conversation frustrating. No matter what they discussed, it always seemed that he and Sadie ended up in disagreement.

"How can you talk to me about starting a family and having children on one hand and then tell me that you plan to continue running around the countryside like you have no responsibilities here?" Sadie was willing to use whatever leverage she had with Fleet. His mention of a family was only a convenient excuse that she could use against him. Sadie had no intention of ever having a baby with Fleet or anyone else for that matter. Sadie watched as Fleet filled his glass again and drained it. Sadie knew he was angry. After spending the whole day trying to make sure that tonight would go well, she had had no luck influencing him at all.

Sadie went to stand behind Fleet and she wrapped her arms around his neck and whispered, "I'm sorry, Fleet. I didn't want to fight with you tonight." Slowly, she untied the lacing at the neck of his tunic and slipped her hands under his shirt. As she ran her hands over the hard muscles of his chest and shoulders, Sadie smiled contentedly. Sadie truly took pleasure from her time with Fleet, he was a very attractive man and the fact that he lived his life on the edge was exciting to her.

Fleet relaxed a little and rested his head on her bosom as she massaged his shoulders. Sadie could be loving and sweet-tempered when she wanted. He closed his eyes and let her work the tension from his muscles until he'd had enough. He stood and stripped off his tunic then pulled her close to him. Sadie smiled at him. It was that self-assured look that he knew so well. "At least there is one thing I can count on with you," he said.

"And what is that Fleet," Sadie asked. She was tracing the line of his jaw with her fingers. Then running her hands along his arms, she began pushing him backward toward the bed. Seducing Fleet was not difficult, but that didn't mean that it wasn't pleasurable.

Fleet was backing up, pulling her with him as he went, "After an argument, I get the pleasure of making up with you."

As he sat on the edge of the bed Sadie stepped back and laughed. "If you spent more time at home it's a pleasure you could enjoy more often." Now that Fleet's attention was all hers, she loosened her own clothing. As she let her blouse and skirt fall to the floor, Sadie ran her hands along the curve of her breasts and her firm belly and hips. Sadie loved to watch Fleet as he admired her body. She was well aware of the fact that she was a flawless beauty and enjoyed the fact that men stared at her. The thought of her body swollen with pregnancy was repugnant to her, but if Fleet wanted children there were other ways.

Chapter Thirteen

Despite her best efforts, Sadie was only able to keep Fleet at home for three weeks. During that time Fleet had been busy putting his plans to add four new people to their security force into place. Captain Frye and Tom had everyone's support but there had been considerable discussion concerning the other two. Sadie had suggested Lipsky, but Fleet managed to sidestep her suggestion by pointing out that Lipsky already had an important position as the gatekeeper. Eventually, the group accepted Carleen, who had been Kyla's nomination and another young man, named Garrett. There had been an announcement made at the Gathering concerning the addition of the security force. The only problem was that no one knew how they should refer to them since they had agreed that the number of Guard members would remain twelve. It was solved the next night when people at the shelter house began calling them the Citizen's Patrol and the name had stuck.

Another new addition to Fleet's plans for increased security was to send a scout to keep an eye on Cole Spring's activities. Despite the fact that Cole seemed to have no interest in coming after Fleet and the others, he certainly had sufficient reason to want to retaliate. Fleet could not rely on the fact that he would stay at home and needed information concerning his men's activities. The best way to do that was to establish regular contact with the Family. The Brothers and Sisters could be his eyes to the east. Justin had been the obvious choice for the job and as soon as Fleet had mentioned his new duties, Justin had wasted no time in preparing to leave. Fleet instructed him to report back to the Settlement every seventh day and made it clear that he expected a complete and detailed report when Justin returned.

The next decision to be made was how many people would go with Fleet when he left and who they would be. Fleet had decided that the number would be four. There had been no question in anyone's mind that Fleet would be one of the four. Even Sadie had not argued the point, at least not publicly. Armand had been the first to ask to go with him. They would be going to the city that had been near his home and Armand was hoping to find someone he knew still living there. It had been difficult for Fleet to agree to take him. He needed Armand at the shelter house to keep order, but Armand wouldn't have asked if it hadn't been terribly important to him. Under the circumstances, Fleet couldn't refuse his request. The only other person he would trust to keep order at the Settlement was Kurt and the thought of leaving Kurt behind made Fleet uneasy.

The other two members of the party were the subjects of lengthy discussion. Everyone wanted to go. Everyone but Justin, he already had the assignment that he wanted. When it finally came to making the decision, it was up to Fleet. When he announced that he was taking Kyla and Carleen, the objections started flying. Sadie was especially adamant that they should not go, but Fleet had made his choice and refused to discuss the matter other than giving two reasons. First, he hoped that they would seem less threatening with women in their party. Fleet wanted to avoid all appearances of being an armed gang. Second was the fact that both women had spent the last month hunting on horseback. With a rifle in their hands, the two were equal to any member of the Guard.

It had taken a week for Fleet to make his decision, which gave the others two weeks to get ready to leave. Armand's preparations began when he started accompanying Kyla and Carleen on their daily expeditions. Fleet had agreed that Armand could go, but demanded that he spend some time learning to ride before they left. The day after the announcement when Kyla went to the barn to prepare for her hunting trip, she found Armand and Riley waiting for her. Riley had selected the sturdy gray gelding that Justin usually rode for Armand and was busy showing him how to put on the bridle and saddle when Kyla arrived.

Carleen breezed through the door right behind her. "If your legs were any longer they'd be dragging on the ground," she said as Armand was mounting the horse. The gray was long legged horse, but Armand still looked too big for the animal.

There was no answer from Armand. He was too busy listening to Riley. "Now remember," she was saying, "a slight pressure to the flanks and he'll go. Pull the reins in the direction that you want to go and back to stop. Gentle but firm, let the horse know who's in charge."

It only took a few minutes for Kyla to get North Wind saddled and ready. As she led the white mare out of her stall, Kyla looked at Armand and thought that Riley had left out one important thing. Kyla swung up into the saddle and smiled at Armand. "Relax," she said, "you might enjoy yourself."

Carleen led her horse from the stall. A black and white pinto with a black spot on one of his eyes, it was a spirited little mare that Carleen had named Buckeye. As she mounted her horse she said, "Come on Armand. I'll race you to the fence." Then without another word she kicked Buckeye in the flanks and they tore out of the barn.

Armand was hesitating, but Riley slapped the gray on its rump and the horse was in motion before Armand was ready. Swaying stiffly in the saddle, he immediately pulled back on the reins and the horse stopped before it got out of the barn. Kyla rode North Wind next to the gray and took hold of the reins and led Armand and his horse out of the barn. "Give the reins a little slack, Armand," Kyla said as she released her hold. "Watch and we'll show you how its done." Kyla nudged her mare ahead and put North Wind through her paces, showing Armand how to guide the horse using gentle pressure on the reins and flanks. The white mare was well trained and a pleasure to ride and Kyla was not above showing her off a little as they rode in circles around Armand and the gray. Fortunately, Armand was a quick study and by the end of the day he was a little more at ease on the horse. It took several days to get him to ride the horse any faster than a trot, but by the time they were ready to leave, Armand was ready.

When the day finally arrived, a strong breeze was blowing from the south. Kyla was lying in her bed listening to the sound of the wind. The window was opened a crack and the air flowing through it was quite warm. There was a soft perfume of green grass and newly sprouted leaves in the air. Spring had finally arrived. It was Kyla's favorite time of year and a ride in the countryside would be a welcome change from the routine at the Settlement. She had been counting the days and was actually looking forward to the trip. It promised to be a pleasant outing. Hopefully, the people living to the west would be as friendly as the Family was.

There was no point in lying in bed. She was too anxious to sleep. Kyla lit the candle that was on the small nightstand at the end of her bed and began to dress. When she pulled on her tunic, Kyla absently fingered the shiny black bead that had replaced the white one. She had not been the only one to receive a bead at the Gathering. Fleet had been given another one, as well as Kurt and Justin, the whole party that had gone to Eddie and Dylan's aid.

Once she was dressed Kyla decided to repack her saddlebags. Taking the contents out, she laid everything on her bed to make sure she hadn't forgotten anything. Although she had gone through the same process the night before, Kyla was doing it again. There was one extra set of black trousers and tunic. She had debated whether or not to pack her thermal underwear, remembering the late season snowstorm, but had decided against it. Lately, the black tunic was more than warm enough by itself, but she was taking the black cape. The only other clothes she had were changes of underclothes and stockings. Her personal belongings were few. She had decided to take the handcuffs. They were her good luck charm. She still had the two knives that Rod had given to her the night the pearl trader had visited the Settlement. However, she had made leather sheaths for both of them and now she could slip them into her boots without worrying about cutting herself on the razor sharp blades. The larger hunting knife that had come from Sister Eaglet was also securely sheathed and she kept that out of sight under her tunic. Kyla had learned that one could never have too many knifes and it was best to keep them with you.

In addition to her clothing she also had blankets, towels, and soap for bathing. Hopefully, they would be able to take time for luxuries like washing and campfires and cooking. At the thought of cooking, Kyla quickly repacked her personal items and hurried to the kitchen. She intended to finish packing their food supplies, but when she arrived in the kitchen Agatha was there already. As Kyla started poking through the bundles of supplies, Agatha sailed across the room and rapped her on the knuckles with the wooden spoon she was holding. "What's the matter, don't you trust me?" she said tartly.

Kyla left the bundles alone and didn't answer. She had spent enough time with Agatha to know when it was best to keep out of her way. As the tall blond woman went back to her work, she was talking. "It just isn't right if you ask me. Fleet shouldn't be taking you and Carleen with him." Kyla wasn't sure if Agatha was talking to her or not. It seemed that she wasn't waiting for a response as she continued, "Who knows what could happen?" Agatha shot a look at Kyla as she repeated, "It's just not right."

Despite her prickly manner, Kyla knew that Agatha was concerned about their welfare. "Don't worry," Kyla finally said as she picked up a corn muffin and began to eat. "Carleen and I will make sure nothing happens to Fleet or Armand."

Agatha shot her a heated look. "Don't make jokes," she said. "There is no good reason for anyone to go anywhere." She looked at the door and added in a soft voice, "It's that Fleet. I think he's crazy. Like he's looking for trouble. It's bad enough that he has all those young men following him, now it's you and that other girl, too." She shook her head and narrowed her eyes as she looked at Kyla. "Just look what happened to Marta. Where is she now?" Agatha had made her point and she bustled off to the laundry, leaving Kyla standing alone in the kitchen.

It was the same thing that Kyla had been hearing for the last two weeks and she wasn't going to let Agatha discourage her anymore than the others. Kyla left the kitchen and paused for a moment in the foyer. She could hear voices coming from the direction of Sadie and Fleet's rooms. It was impossible for her to hear exactly what was being said, but she knew they were arguing. Apparently, Agatha was not the only one unhappy about the fact that they were leaving. Kyla quickly exited through the front door. She didn't want to be around when Sadie decided to come out of her room. Whenever she argued with Fleet, and that was often, Sadie would generally take her frustrations out on the first person that was unlucky enough to get in her way.

The light was beginning to grow in the east. As she stepped outside, Kyla heard Agatha beating on the side of the metal drum. It was time for everyone to rise and as soon as breakfast was over they would be leaving. She picked up her pace and was running by the time she reached the women's dormitory. Once she arrived, Kyla found Carleen up and ready to go.

When she saw Kyla coming across the farmyard, Carleen rushed to meet her. "I couldn't sleep either," Carleen said, adjusting the saddlebag slung over her shoulder. Carleen was packed and ready to go. Without another word, the two women began to walk toward the dining hall. Kyla was going to eat breakfast with Carleen instead of at the cabin with the Guard. Sadie had refused to let Carleen eat with the Guard, so Kyla decided to eat breakfast with her. They were too early and the food was not ready when they arrived. Kyla and Carleen got a cup of hot coffee and sat down at one of the tables to wait. The coffee wasn't really made from coffee beans. Agatha had told her that it was made from something called chicory. Still, it was hot and Kyla smiled as she thought about her first breakfast at the Settlement. The coffee had been the best thing about the meal.

Things had changed a lot for Kyla since that day. First, there was the uniform that she wore. Once people started to arrive for breakfast she could hear the whispers, but Kyla ignored the fact that everyone was staring at her. Other than the usual comments about her unusually quick acceptance to the Guard, there were some over loud inquiries about why she was eating in their dining hall. It was unheard of for a Guard member to eat in the dining hall, but people were beginning to get used to the fact that Kyla did many things that the other Guard members wouldn't. Carleen was enjoying the attention and her new found notoriety. As soon as the food was ready, she jumped up and went to the front of the line.

When she returned with two bowls of lumpy, gooey oatmeal, Kyla said, "I see the menu hasn't changed."

Carleen laughed and gulped down her breakfast, "I won't miss the food here. That's for sure."

"You never know," said Kyla, "this oatmeal might look pretty good after a couple of days. You never know what might happen."

"Now, don't you start on that subject, too," Carleen groaned. She was ready to get away from the Settlement. Carleen had never realized how much she hated being isolated from the rest of the world until she had been given a chance to leave the farm. If Fleet changed his mind and decided to leave her behind, Carleen would steal one of the horses and follow them anyway. The short hunting trips with Kyla had been just a sample of the independence that Carleen wanted. Freedom was just a few hours away and she couldn't wait.

Going with Fleet had been all Carleen talked about for the last two weeks. The promise of adventure had her fidgeting like a cat on a leash, but Kyla had been with Fleet on one of his forays and knew it wasn't all fun and games. She wasn't so foolish to be unprepared for the possibility that they would run into trouble. The fact that Fleet was going was enough to guarantee a certain amount of excitement. It didn't take a genius to figure out, as Agatha had so eloquently stated, Fleet was looking for trouble. Or the converse could be true, that trouble was looking for Fleet as Sister Samethia warned, putting anyone who was close to him into danger, too. For a moment, Kyla considered telling Carleen about Sister Samethia's readings, but decided it would be better to remain silent on the subject. She didn't think Sister Samethia intended for everyone to know what she'd said about Fleet. Besides, Carleen would probably think that she was crazy for believing in a fortuneteller.

Kyla said nothing more on the subject. They wasted no time eating and were leaving the dining hall while most people were on their way in the door. Going to the barn they met James, who was beginning his day with a trip to the dining hall looking for new arrivals. It was part of the routine that had seemed so foreign to Kyla a few short weeks ago. "You're up early," James said. He was about to say something else and for a moment, Kyla was certain that he was ready to add one last objection to the long list of reasons why they should not be going with Fleet, but he didn't. Instead, he said, "I'll see you later," and with an effort added, "before you go."

"I thought he was ready to give us another lecture," Carleen said with a sigh of relief. "I don't know what they're all so worried about anyway." She was swinging her arms as she walked and began to whistle. Carleen didn't whistle songs, as Kyla had discovered. Instead, she began going through her extensive repertoire of birdcalls. It was a game that she had introduced to Kyla when they were hunting. Carleen would whistle one of the bird songs and Kyla had to guess which bird it was. It was a rather one sided game, since Carleen was the only one really having fun, but Kyla didn't mind. It helped pass the time and it had helped Kyla remember the names that went with the sounds. The sad thing was the absence of some calls in the woods and meadows. Many migratory birds had not been seen this year even after the weather warmed and the ones that had returned were few and far between.

When they arrived at the barn, Riley was there before them. "Good morning," she said briskly as Kyla and Carleen entered. "I don't know if I'll ever get this horse ready before you leave." She had Brownie tied to one of the posts and was busy brushing her shaggy coat. Now that the weather was warmer the horse was shedding and hair was flying everywhere around Riley. Even though Kyla was not riding Brownie, the horse was going with them. She was back to being the pack animal.

Kyla scratched the brown mare's nose and said, "Well, I'm glad she'll be going. Brownie's an old friend." It was funny to think of a horse that way, but she had known the horse as long as any person at the Settlement, Fleet included. The horse was one little piece of her fragile pile of consistency as Kyla began rebuilding her life. Then as she turned to Carleen, she said, "Let's go to the cabin and start carrying the supplies out here." If there was one thing that Kyla hated, it was standing still and doing nothing. Until they were on their horses and riding away from the farm, she wouldn't be able to relax.

When they walked in the front door of the cabin, Kyla and Carleen ran right into Fleet and Sadie on their way to breakfast. It was the very thing that Kyla had wanted to avoid. Fleet nodded and mumbled, "Good morning," and walked toward the dining room.

However, Sadie paused to look at the two young women who had stopped like startled deer to stare back at her. These two were the subject of her argument with Fleet that morning and every day since he had made his ridiculous announcement to take them on his trip west. The idea that Fleet wanted Kyla to go with him was particularly infuriating. Sadie looked at Kyla, examining her critically from head to toe. What Sadie really couldn't abide was her attitude. Kyla had started out rather meek and Sadie had hoped to make her into another Riley. Instead she had become willful and stubborn and would take on responsibilities without consulting anyone first. Her hunting trips were a good example of her disobedient behavior. Although Sadie would probably have approved her activities, it galled her that Kyla felt no compulsion to consult her about anything. "You know I am against you girls going with Fleet," Sadie said stiffly, emphasizing the word 'girls'.

Kyla ignored her obvious attempt to start an argument and answered, "Fleet has confidence in our capabilities." She stood straight like a soldier at attention because that was how Sadie always treated her, as if she were under inspection by a superior. When Kyla saw her shift her attention to Carleen, she said, "Don't worry, we already ate breakfast. We were just going to start carrying supplies to the barn. So, if you will excuse us, we had better get to work." Then grabbing Carleen by the sleeve, she pulled her past Sadie and they made a hasty exit to the kitchen where the reception wasn't any warmer than it had been earlier that morning.

Fleet was shaking his head as he walked into the dining hall. Sadie had kept him up half the night arguing and then she had started again this morning. She hadn't stopped her harangue until they ran into Kyla and Carleen in the foyer. Call him a coward, but when they distracted Sadie, Fleet seized the opportunity to leave her behind. He only hoped that Sadie wasn't taking her anger out on them right now, but she was only a few steps behind Fleet and came through the door before he had a chance to take his seat. When she entered the dining hall, she had changed to her public persona, cool and totally under control. That was not the side that Fleet saw in private. He had received the full fury of her stormy temper last night.

After Sadie took her place at the opposite end of the table from Fleet, breakfast was served and eaten in silence. The tension flowing between Sadie and Fleet was enough to dampen any conversations. Fortunately for Fleet, Kyla was not there. He had finally realized that Sadie's main objection to the women going was not out of concern for their safety, but due to her hostility toward them and Kyla in particular. The whole idea was nonsense. Sadie had never objected to Riley or Marta being included in his plans. Fleet couldn't understand why Sadie disliked Kyla so vehemently. The only reason that he could think of was Kyla's connection with the Family.

Fleet wolfed down his breakfast and as he rose to leave he said, "I am going to take my things to the stable. Armand meet me there when you're done." Then without a word to Sadie, Fleet turned and strode out the door and down the hall. When he heard the door open and close behind him, Fleet turned with a smug smile on his face, certain that it was Sadie hurrying after him. His smile faded when he saw Kurt instead of Sadie. Fleet should have known that it was too much to hope for an apology from Sadie before he left.

Kurt fell into step beside him and walked down the hallway with Fleet then followed him into his quarters. Once they were inside Kurt closed the door and said, "I want to talk to you before you leave."

Fleet sat down on the bed and said wearily, "Why should you be different from everybody else? What do you want to tell me that I haven't already heard?"

Kurt walked to where Fleet was sitting and stood looking down on him. "I am holding you personally responsible for the welfare of those two women. If you can't bring them both back here unharmed, don't come back yourself."

Fleet stood and looked Kurt squarely in the eye. He couldn't remember his friend ever threatening him before now, but he wasn't going to let his challenge go unanswered. "There are twelve members of the Guard and I must use each one according to his or her strengths or weaknesses. Now, how much help would Kyla be wrestling drunken men at the shelter house? Not much, but she can ride and shoot as well as you. Now where would you say she could be the most help?" Fleet paused for just a moment and when Kurt didn't have anything to say, he finished his explanation by saying, "And I'm taking Carleen for the same reasons."

"I don't care what your reasons are," Kurt said flatly. "And I know that nothing I can say will change your mind, but I meant what I said."

Fleet sighed and sat back on the bed. "I'm counting on you to keep things under control here." What Fleet really wanted to say was that he wished Kurt were going with them. It was the first time that Fleet would be without Kurt there to back him up.

"I hope Armand is up to his job," Kurt smiled now. He could read between the lines. "He has his work cut out for him if he's going to keep you out of trouble."

Picking up his saddlebags, Fleet looked at his friend and said, "I never go looking for trouble."

"There is no need to take unnecessary chances. That was all I wanted to say," Kurt said. It was true that Fleet didn't look for trouble, but he never ran from it either.

"Don't worry, I'll bring the ladies back without a scratch," Fleet said as he held his hand over his heart as if he was making a pledge. "I promise." As he walked to the door with Kurt following right behind him, Fleet was hoping it was a promise he could keep without Kurt there to help him.

Fleet and Kurt had to have been the last people in the Settlement to arrive at the barn. People were milling around like they were waiting for a parade. As they walked through the crowd, Fleet was smiling. He was supposed to be the ambassador after all. That was ridiculous enough, but people had gotten the idea that Fleet was looking for some sort of promised land. Once he found it, Fleet would return and lead them to it. What Fleet really expected to find was another link in Manjohnah's chain of armed fortresses. When they stepped inside the barn they found a crowd inside, too. Every member of the Guard, except Justin, was there and the members of the new Citizens Patrol.

Agatha was there. She had actually left her kitchen to come and supervise the process of packing the packages of corn flour, rice, and beans. Kyla had told her that they could hunt for game along the way, but she also was packing several large packets of dried meats and salted fish, two large cast iron skillets and a pot for coffee. Packets of her chicory coffee and herbal teas, salt and honey, Agatha hadn't left anything out. Everything was loaded into the large leather panniers on Brownie's back. Besides the food, she carried several large rubber bladders filled with drinking water. They were never sure when they could find a deep water well that was still working and they could not trust that the water in the rivers would be unpolluted. Added to that were bags of oats and corn for the horses and Brownie had all she could carry.

Someone had already saddled his horse and Fleet threw his saddlebags across the horse's rump. His rifle was in the case and smaller leather bags with ammunition were resting just in front of the saddle within easy reach. Every thing was ready for him and everyone was waiting. All he had to do was say the word. He looked at each member of the party. First there was Armand. Although he had been the first person to ask to go, he seemed to be uneasy about leaving. His sister Ruth was hanging on his arm and Armand was patting her hand to comfort her. The young girl was having a hard time accepting the idea that Armand was going without her.

Next was Carleen, who was busy tying and untying the lacing holding her blankets in place. She was wearing a bright red and black plaid flannel shirt and a pair of jeans tucked into dark brown leather boots that went almost to her knees. Everything about her was neat and trim. Her wavy black hair was cut short around her ears. She had dark eyes, almost black and her skin was a golden tan. There was a mischievous quality about her and when she caught Fleet looking at her she grinned broadly before she looked away and went back to checking the contents of her baggage.

Kyla was also occupied with checking her bags. Fleet was pleased to see that she was using the saddle trimmed with silver. Although she never used it when she went hunting, today she would be riding in style. Fleet felt a certain amount of personal satisfaction when he looked at her. No one had thought much of the bony skeleton that he had brought back with him almost two months ago, but looking at her now it was hard to remember Kyla that way. She was blossoming like springtime. Her hair was growing back and it was about the same length as Carleen's was. Soft little ringlets of chestnut brown hair covered Kyla's head now. The old woolen hat was a thing of the past. Her black tunic, which had hung loosely when she first started wearing it, was now a little snug and in all the right places, as Fleet observed with an appreciative smile.

They were ready. Fleet was ready. There was one person who was not present; the one person for whom Fleet was waiting and that was Sadie. In his heart he knew that Sadie would not let him leave without saying good-bye. Even Agatha had stopped fussing with the packages on Brownie. Everyone was waiting for Fleet to say something. After a few uncomfortable minutes without any sign of Sadie, Fleet finally took his horse's reins and led him past the others and outside. Without saying a word Armand followed him leading his horse, then Kyla and finally Carleen leading her horse and Brownie, too.

When they came outside, the crowd that had gathered parted to make way for the horses. Everyone inside the barn followed Fleet and his party as he led them toward the cabin. Once they were at the end of the walkway leading to the front door, Fleet mounted his horse and looked toward the cabin, Sadie's shadowy figure was visible standing just inside the library window. She would see him leave. Fleet would make sure of that.

Once he turned his attention from the window, Fleet saw that the others had followed his lead. The party was mounted and ready to go. The crowd following them seemed to be expecting something, perhaps a speech to fuel their great expectations. Fleet didn't like speeches and speaking of grand visions for the future. That was Sadie's talent. Still, he knew they expected something. "I know you have all heard rumors about where we are going. There is a good possibility that we won't find anyone," Fleet paused to let the murmurs die down. They didn't want to hear the negative side. Everyone was counting on Fleet to perform miracles. He raised his voice above the commotion and continued, "And if we find someone, there is no guarantee that they will be better off than we are." Fleet stopped speaking. It was useless. Everyone in the crowd was talking at once. Instead, he waved his arm above his head and like the trail boss at the head of the cattle drive he stood up in his saddle and said, "Let's move 'em out!"

Carleen didn't have to be asked twice. She gave a loud whoop and kicked Buckeye in the flanks. The little black and white pinto took off at a full gallop down the lane. This time Armand was right behind her racing his big gray against her little quarter horse. Kyla and North Wind followed with Brownie in tow. Fleet brought up the rear, watching over his shoulder all the way down the lane. Only when they were out of sight of the cabin did he give his full attention to where they were going. Until the last moment, he had hoped that Sadie would come out to see him leave.

~ ~ ~

After leaving the Settlement behind they had ridden the whole day without seeing another living soul except for the occasional rabbit or squirrel. Once they had even surprised several pheasants roosting in a clump of dried grasses. Carleen had been ready with her rifle and managed to shoot one of the birds. Kyla kept telling her that she had been lucky; while Carleen insisted that it was skill and boasted that next time she would bring down two birds with one shot. For the two women spending the day riding had become their daily routine, but tonight they would not be going back to the Settlement.

For the first part of the day both Armand and Fleet had been quiet and moody. Leaving Ruth was not easy for Armand, even though he knew she would be cared for if something happened and he didn't return. What was really bothering them was the fact that this was the

343

first time that they had been separated since the city they lived in had been destroyed. Fleet's problem was no secret. The tension between Sadie and Fleet had been obvious. Add to that her failure to say good-bye to Fleet, and it didn't take much imagination to know what was troubling him. Kyla and Carleen rode together trying to enjoy the beautiful day despite their doleful companions. Neither one of them was leaving anything or anyone behind. They were satisfied with whatever lay before them and their hopes were for something better yet to come.

The breeze that had been blowing from the south all morning had died out as the heat and humidity rose. Even though the sky was still cloudy they could feel the effects of the sun. By midday the temperatures were soaring and Fleet, Armand, and Kyla were sweltering in their heavy black tunics. Their sleeves were pushed up as far as they would go and the lacing at their necks left untied so the shirts hung open, but perspiration was rolling off their foreheads and dark wet spots grew on the backs of their shirts. Fleet was the first one to give in to comfort and peeled of his shirt saying, "I can't stand it." It was only a few minutes later when Armand removed his shirt as well.

Carleen held out for a few more minutes before she said, "Well, I don't want heat stroke either," and she took off her flannel shirt. Under that she wore only a lightweight cotton undershirt. As she rolled up her shirt and stuffed it into one of her bags she fanned her face and said, "I feel better already." Then she smoothed her hair back and looked at Kyla. "You had better do the same. Your face is already flushed."

Kyla removed her tunic. She was wearing a cotton undershirt like Carleen's. They were the standard issue at the farm. There was no denying the fact that she was cooler, but she was definitely not more comfortable. Fortunately, Fleet and Armand were riding in front of them. She felt a little embarrassed wearing nothing but the thin undershirt. Even though Kyla didn't want the men staring at her, she had no problem watching Fleet. She had never seen him without his shirt. Looking at his broad shoulders through the fabric of his tunic was not the same as seeing his well-defined muscles and easy graceful movements as he rode uncovered from the waist up. She didn't realize that she was staring so blatantly until Carleen leaned close and asked,

344

"Enjoying the view?" then leaned back and laughed loudly at her joke. Before long Kyla's face was turning red. Only this time the heat showing in her cheeks was not caused by the warm weather. Fleet and Armand both turned to see what was so funny, only to shake their heads in bewilderment.

Once Fleet and Armand had turned their attention forward, Carleen guided Buckeye nearer to Kyla and whispered, "Fleet's the pretty one, but I like my men big like Armand. I could ride him all night."

Kyla looked at the dark haired woman riding next to her. She was studying Armand like a horse trader at a stock auction. "Really, Carleen," Kyla said with all the propriety she could muster, "you can be so crude." If there was one thing that Kyla had learned in the last few weeks, it was the fact that Carleen usually said whatever popped into her head.

"Really, yourself," Carleen said in return, "You can't tell me that you never think about it. Besides, I know that the only reason that you wanted to come was so you could be with Fleet."

"Where did you get such a crazy idea?" Kyla was outraged. She had thought the rumors about her and Fleet had been forgotten.

With a scoffing laugh, Carleen answered, "I'm not blind. I can see the way you look at him when he walks into the room. You're in love with him and if you don't know it, then you're the only one. Why do you think Sadie was so hot?"

"I don't know what you're talking about," Kyla said as she shifted uncomfortably. "Fleet saved my life and brought me to the Settlement. I consider him a good friend and nothing more." She was trying to sound outraged, but her denial sounded a little less than emphatic even to herself.

Carleen laughed again. "You just keep telling yourself that, and maybe you'll believe it."

Fortunately for Kyla, the movement of a rabbit in the brush distracted her. In an instant, Carleen had her rifle out of its case and was firing. When she rode to retrieve it, Kyla could breathe a sigh of relief. Once Carleen started on a subject, she didn't drop it until something else drew her attention. The subject of her feelings toward Fleet was something that she was not prepared to discuss. She couldn't deny that she found him very attractive and he was always smiling and teasing her, but Fleet acted the same with everybody, especially women. Fleet had no trouble attracting women. Then there was Sadie. Kyla would have to be crazy to try to come between her and Fleet. As far as Sadie was concerned, she owned Fleet, body and soul. Kyla had no doubt that she was capable of doing anything to keep him.

The sound of the rifle being fired brought Fleet's attention back to the women as he turned to look at Carleen galloping after her latest kill. He had to admit that she was quick with her gun and accurate, too. Fleet had yet to see Carleen miss her mark. She wouldn't waste the ammunition if she couldn't get a clear shot. With the pheasant from this morning and another rabbit that she had bagged earlier, they would certainly not be hungry tonight. Fleet was beginning to wonder if he would have to remind her that she was not feeding the entire Settlement tonight.

He had been riding all day listening to the women riding behind him chattering and laughing. He was glad that someone was enjoying themselves. It was a beautiful day and they had been riding at an easy pace. There was no hurry to arrive anywhere and no hurry to return. As he thought about returning to the Settlement, he thought of Sadie again. When she hadn't come to see them off, Fleet had been deeply disappointed. The fact that they spent most of their time together arguing, was not a problem for him. Sadie was a strong woman and the same passion that she employed in her arguments was what he looked forward to in their lovemaking. No matter how much they disagreed, Sadie had always supported him in the end. Until today, that is.

He shook his head as he thought about Sadie. He couldn't blame her for being angry, but she wanted something that he couldn't give, a promise that he would stay at the farm with her. There was only one thing that drove Fleet and that was his desire for revenge. Someday he would find Manjohnah. What he would do when that day came was only a nebulous plan at best. How could he exact vengeance for millions of people from one man? As his thoughts went from Sadie to Manjohnah, Fleet's mood grew darker by the minute.

When Carleen came trotting back with her rabbit for Fleet to see, he snapped, "I think you've done your job for the day. Why don't you give your rifle a rest?" He was not in the mood for pleasant conversation.

Carleen shrugged and said, "Why don't you give that nasty attitude a rest, too. It's too nice a day to waste your time worrying about that nasty witch back at the farm. If she cared about you at all, she wouldn't have let you leave without saying something." Then she abruptly wheeled the black and white pinto around and trotted back to ride beside Kyla, smiling to herself, as she looked first at Fleet and then Kyla. If those two idiots were stupid enough to ignore each other, this trip would give Carleen plenty of time to work on getting them to take notice. She rode without saying another word. Having planted her first two seeds, all she could do was wait to see if they took root.

Armand couldn't believe that Carleen had said what she did, but there was no denying the truth of her statement. He didn't know whether to scold her for being so blunt or thank her for the same reasons. If love was blind, it had to be deaf and dumb, too. Fleet ignored all the bad things about Sadie, because they were usually directed toward someone other than himself. Even though they argued constantly, Sadie had always treated Fleet with deference and respect. Today Fleet had found himself on the receiving end of Sadie's indifference and had been embarrassed in front of everyone from the Settlement. No one had missed the fact that Fleet had been looking for her. Then when he stopped in front of the cabin and Sadie stayed inside, it had been uncomfortable for Armand, too. He didn't like to see anyone treated so callously.

"I know it's early, but I see a line of trees just at the horizon," Armand said as they came to the top of the next hill. "If it's a creek or river with water for the horses, why don't we stop there for the night?" He didn't want to admit it, but he was not used to riding for so long and wanted a chance to get out of the saddle.

"We'll see," Fleet answered absently. He was in favor of taking a break. A few minutes of privacy were all he wanted right now.

Armand's suggestion turned out to be a unanimous decision when they arrived at the bank of a wide, but very shallow river. It was a pleasant setting, with willows and cottonwood trees lining the banks and little bits of white fluff from the cottonwoods dancing in the breeze and floating in the slow moving water of the river. As they led their horses to the water, they had to push aside the long golden branches from the willows. It was a peaceful and serene setting and even Fleet was having difficulty maintaining his bad mood in such a beautiful place. He gave his reins to Armand and said, "I want to take a look around. Call if you need me."

As he walked away Armand watched him go, wishing that Kurt was here. Whenever Fleet was troubled, it seemed that Kurt knew what to say to him. Hopefully, a few moments alone would be all that Fleet needed to get his mind back on task. Today had been nothing more than a lark and it didn't matter that he was distracted, but Armand wanted Fleet to be ready when they needed his full attention. He took the black horse and leading it with his own went to join the women, who were already walking upstream looking for a place to camp.

Carleen found the perfect place at the bend of the river. There was a high bank and a path leading down to a wide sandbar, the water flowed in a narrow channel nearly a hundred yards away at the other side of the riverbed. It was not a path made by men. The only tracks to be seen were the ones left by deer and raccoons and Carleen pointed them out on the trail and in the sand. There were large piles of deadwood just before the sharp turn in the river's course, the remnants of trees that had grown too close to the edge and had been washed away in high water to end up in a twisted mass along the banks.

After looking it over thoroughly, Armand said, "It'll do." He nodded toward the horses tied to the branches of the trees at the top of the bank. "I'll take care of unloading the horses. You and Kyla get a fire started."

It took Armand nearly as long to unsaddle all four horses and tie them to a line strung between two trees as it did for Kyla and Carleen to gather the wood for a fire. It may have been plentiful, but much of it had been wet or too green to use. They did managed to get a fire going, but had to add dried grasses and leaves to start it. When Armand joined them at the bottom of the bank the fire was blazing and a dark column of smoke was rising into the sky. Carleen was still gathering more wood while Kyla kept adding more dry material to keep it going.

After a few minutes, Fleet appeared above them and said, "I saw the smoke." Then he looked away from them, back to the east. A concerned frown appeared on his face and he said, "There's a rider coming." As the other three were scrambling up the bank to see for themselves, Fleet was looking for his pack. "Where are my binoculars?" he shouted at them.

Kyla was the last in line so she went back for the binoculars. Fleet met her halfway up the trail and took them from her. Without a word of thanks, he turned and hurried back to higher ground. Putting the binoculars to his eyes he looked in the direction that he had seen the man on horseback, waiting for him to come back into view again. As the rider came to the top of a rise again Fleet quickly brought the field glasses into focus and saw who was following them. "It's Lipsky," he said as he lowered the binoculars. Sadie had sent her spy to follow him, only this time he wasn't bothering to stay hidden. Lipsky was riding hard and was obviously trying to catch up with them. So they stood silently and waited for him.

Lipsky's horse was covered with lather and breathing hard when he pulled it to a stop in front of them. The wiry little man jumped down off his horse. The first words out of his mouth were "Are you people stupid?" He pushed past them and scurried down to the fire and began to kick the logs away and throw sand over the burning leaves and grasses. They had followed him and were listening as he continued his tirade. "I didn't need a smoke signal to find you, but I can guarantee that anyone within twenty miles knows exactly where you are now."

"Who are you hiding from?" Carleen retorted smartly.

"I'm not hiding from anybody," Lipsky snapped back, "but I'm not going to advertise my whereabouts either. That's like inviting trouble."

For once Fleet had to agree with Lipsky. He had been ready to tell them the same thing. The rare moment of agreement did nothing to lessen his suspicions. "Why are you following us?"

"Sadie sent me," he answered. He grinned boldly and took an envelope from a pouch hanging from his belt. "This is for you." Then reaching into the pouch again he took out a rather large silver broach and as he placed it in Fleet's outstretched palm, he said, "and this, too." A smile came to Fleet's face as he took the letter and walked away from the others. Lipsky watched him with satisfaction. Fleet's reaction had been what Sadie had hoped for. Lipsky knew his mistress played Fleet like a fish on the line. She would let him run then jerk him back and set the hook. Lipsky was enjoying his part in her little game.

As he looked at the letter with its old-fashioned wax seal on the back, Fleet was relieved to have received some word from Sadie, even if she had sent Lipsky to deliver it. Fleet tore open the envelope and looked at her letter. It was a short note written in a graceful flowing hand, although Fleet could not remember ever seeing anything that Sadie had written, there was something familiar about her style of writing. He dismissed that for the moment as he read what she had written.

My dearest Fleet,

I am sorry I missed you this morning. I feel badly that our last words to each other were spoken in anger. You are always in my thoughts and I will not have a moment without worry until your safe return.

All my love,
Sadie

P.S. I have sent Lipsky to help you. I'm sure you will find some way that he can be of use.

The contents of Sadie's love letter couldn't have been more formal and her postscript left no doubt to her true motives. The note was nothing more than a feeble excuse for Sadie to send her spy. Fleet knew she sent Lipsky to follow and report on his activities. That was an annoyance at the worst and Fleet put up with it, but this was an insult. He looked at the broach as he turned it absently in his hand. It was nothing that he had ever seen Sadie wear. If it was supposed to be a token to evoke her memory, then she should have sent something more personal. It had a large oddly shaped stone that was roughly oval in shape and a cloudy white color. It might have been an uncut diamond, but it looked more like a piece of ice. It was set in a small silver crescent, which nestled inside a larger silver crescent. An unusual piece of jewelry, but it was a woman's broach and Fleet had no use for it. He shoved it deep into the pocket of his trousers. When his hand touched a crumbled piece of paper at the bottom of his pocket, a flash of recognition crept into his mind and he pulled it out.

Fleet unfolded the little scrap of paper that he had been carrying for the last month. It was the note he had taken from Clovis on which the words 'North by Northwest Road' were scrawled. As he compared the note to Sadie's letter, Fleet felt as if someone had reached into his chest and was tearing his heart apart. The handwriting was the same. Looking now for a place to sit, his head was swimming with accusations and denials at the same time. He had to think before he jumped to conclusions. Finally, he found a fallen tree trunk and sat down to look at the two pieces of paper again. Fleet didn't want to believe what he was seeing. Even though he was no expert at handwriting, there was no mistaking that the same person had written both notes.

The realization was slow sinking in only because Fleet didn't want to believe it. That would lead him to the next conclusion, which was unthinkable. If she had told Cole where to find Eddie and Dylan, had she been the one to warn Cole Spring about his first raid? It was all too much for him to believe. His head told him to trust his eyes, but his heart was telling him to trust Sadie. Fleet fought the urge to jump on his horse and gallop all the way back to the Settlement, to Sadie, but what would he do when he got there? Confront her with the accusation; ask for an explanation? As he got to his feet Fleet folded both pieces of paper together and thrust them into his pocket. He wanted them both out of his sight and wished he could get the doubts out of his mind as easily. Maybe Sadie had done him one small favor. She had sent her sneak out into the open and he would keep an eye on Lipsky. It was the other snakes, the ones still hidden, that Fleet worried about.

Armand was surprised when Fleet's mood seemed even blacker when he returned. The contents of the note from Sadie must not have been good news. The party had ended when Lipsky appeared. Kyla and Carleen were sitting side by side on a log that was half buried in the sand staring sullenly at the ground. Lipsky was leaning against another large tree trunk a few feet away from them, leering at the two women who were doing their best to ignore him. Fleet stopped a few feet away from Lipsky and said, "Since you're the expert here, why don't you build a fire that doesn't send out too much smoke. I want something hot for supper tonight." Then finding his pack in the pile of supplies that Armand had carried down the hill, he took out his shirt and pulled it over his head. "It's starting to cool off a little, don't you think?" he asked as he looked at Kyla and Carleen. He was not trying to be subtle and they scrambled for their packs.

As they were putting on their shirts Lipsky said, "I wasn't trying to spoil your fun boys." He was lying back with his legs stretched out in front of him and a smug grin on his face.

Armand and Fleet both glared at him angrily. "What is that supposed to mean?" Fleet was the one who spoke. Lipsky was a mean spirited man. It wasn't any wonder that he had no friends.

"You figure it out," Lipsky said as he stood up and stretched. "But as far as the fire goes, you'll have to make that yourself. I'm not one of your recruits and I take my orders from Sadie and no one else." There wasn't any anger or boastfulness in his voice. He was stating the facts as he saw them. "But something hot for supper does sound nice. Now, why don't you send one of your girls up there to take care of my horse while I take a nap? You can call me when its time to eat." Then he walked arrogantly to the pile of supplies and grabbed one of the blankets that was lying on top and walked up the path to the top of the bank as he looked for a place to lie down and sleep.

Fleet had to physically restrain Carleen from running after Lipsky, since it was her blanket that he had taken with him. "You can have mine," Fleet muttered to her under his breath.

"Who does he think he is," Carleen was livid. Her black eyes were almost smoldering with the heat from her fury. "Send him back." She was looking at Fleet like all it would take was one word from him to send Lipsky running home. As Fleet looked at her, he was sorry that he had stopped her from going after Lipsky. The thought of her thrashing Lipsky, brought a smile to his face; which only sent her temper flaring even higher. "I don't see anything funny about this," Carleen said as she crossed her arms.

"Sadie sent him and we'll have to put up with him," Fleet said flatly. The smile on his face had disappeared. "We'll treat him with respect whatever our personal feelings might be." He was not any happier about Lipsky's presence than the others. "And we will do it, whether he deserves it or not," he added the last more as a reminder to himself than the others.

Kyla was the first to speak up, "I had better see to his horse. He certainly isn't going to do it." Lipsky's unexpected arrival bothered her, and Fleet was certainly troubled by the note that Sadie had sent. So far the scrawny little man had managed to do nothing but stir up disharmony. She did agree with Fleet's statement. If they were going to be burdened with Lipsky, they might as well try to make the best of it. Still, the idea of spending the next several days performing menial chores for Lipsky was not her idea of fun.

~ ~ ~

As they traveled west the wooded areas were becoming fewer and far between. They had been riding along the side of the highway where it was easy going for the horses. After a year of neglect and disuse the roads were beginning to show some signs of deterioration. Freezing temperatures had caused the concrete and asphalt to disintegrate in places and weeds and grasses were quick to fill in the cracks caused by the forces of nature. A few more years and there would be nothing left of them.

The next day began even warmer than the first and before midday everyone, Lipsky included, had stripped off their heavy winter clothing in an attempt to remain cool. Actually, Lipsky's arrival had proved to be only a minor irritation. Other than the fact that he expected someone else to cook for him and take care of his horse, once they were on horseback it was easier to ignore him. They rode as they had the day before with Fleet and Armand riding together followed by Kyla and Carleen. Lipsky brought up the rear listening to the two women talking as they went.

Kyla and Carleen were all too aware of their big eared shadow and kept their conversations low and of a non-personal nature. Carleen was entertaining them all with her birdcalls and even Lipsky had gotten caught up in the game as he offered a guess to one of them. When Carleen glared at him and told him that his answer was wrong, he went back to riding in silence.

"You could try to be civil," Kyla said in a low voice. For her suggestion, Kyla received a glare that was just as sharp as the one Lipsky had received. After that even Carleen rode in silence. Kyla was watching the sky above them. The clouds were so dark that they appeared black and they boiled furiously overhead. The wind had picked up considerably as the day wore on and by noon a strong wind that whipped their hair was blowing in strong gusts across the open fields.

Kyla handed Brownie's lead to Carleen and kicked North Wind to a trot so she could catch up with Fleet and Armand. "I think we're going to be in for a storm before much longer." They were at the top of one of the long ridges and they could see for miles in every direction. Kyla was looking at a patch of especially dark clouds along the horizon to the southwest. "We should think about finding some kind of shelter before it hits."

Fleet looked around the empty countryside. There had been few houses visible from the road they where following but none at that particular moment. "I'm open to suggestions," he said. The wind gusted so strongly that it seemed to blow the words away as he spoke.

As Kyla looked around for someplace to go, the wind was becoming even stronger and when she saw bolts of lightening striking the ground a few miles away, she began to feel a certain amount of urgency. The lightening had gotten Carleen and Lipsky's attention and they hurried to join the others. Armand's sharp eyes spotted the only shelter for miles. There was bridge about a mile away where another road crossed over the one they were following. It wasn't much but they could use it for shelter from the wind and lightening. As they pressed the horses to a gallop, everyone knew they were racing to reach the bridge before the storm did.

The first few drops of rain began falling before they reached the shelter of the overpass were followed by large pellets of ice, in the form of hail, pelting them and stinging their exposed skin. When they finally reached the bridge, it didn't provide much shelter from the wind, which was blowing so hard the rain no longer fell down but sideways. Everyone kept a firm hold on the horses as they led them up the embankment to huddle close to the concrete piers supporting the bridge over their heads. It was miserable and everyone was soaked to the skin.

There was nothing to do but wait for it to blow over. The storm front with its gusty winds and lightening passed them by in a matter of minutes, but the torrential rain did not let up. After several minutes they decided to continue despite the rain. The wind had also ushered in much cooler air and before leaving their refuge under the bridge everyone was wearing their heavy clothing and cloaks once more. The change in the weather had been so severe and drastic that it reminded them how tenuous the late spring's arrival had been.

As Kyla pulled the hood of her cloak low over her face in an attempt to keep the rain from blowing in her face, she was thankful that they'd had at least one day of pleasant weather. It was like Lipsky's arrival had jinxed the entire journey. She smiled at the thought, now she was blaming him for the weather, too. There was no point in dwelling on the unpleasant aspects of their journey. The rain would end eventually and Lipsky was only as irritating as she allowed him to be. As the party slogged along through the rain, they were forced to keep to the roads now. The ditches were full of water rushing into the streams and creeks at the bottom of every ridge and they were pouring into the rivers, forcing them to cross on the bridges, since fording the swollen rivers on horseback would have been impossible.

They rode until well after dark that night, hoping that the rains would stop and finally, they were forced to take shelter at another crossroad, under another bridge. There was no wood for a fire, even if they could have started one in the pouring rain. Wet and cold, they all ate some of the dried meat that Agatha had so wisely insisted on packing and huddled miserably in their blankets.

Chapter Fourteen

They spent the third day riding in the rain. It wasn't the torrential downpour that it had been the previous day, but there didn't seem to be any indication that it would end soon. The first two days they had followed the highway west. Toward the end of the third day, they came to the high wooded bluffs that bordered the flood plain of the river, one of the main arteries of the continent that carried all the runoff from the plains on its way to the ocean to the south. Once they crossed the bluffs and descended into the valley, they came to the end of the road. It could go no further west. They had come to the river.

The highway they followed now was six lanes of concrete running north to south, with three lanes on each side of the grassy median. It would lead them directly into the heart of the city or rather what remained of it. Armand had told them there was nothing there when he left, but things could change over time. Fleet knew that they were chasing after a rumor, but curiosity had brought them this far and tomorrow they would reach the end of their journey.

Once more they decided to camp underneath one of the bridges that crossed over the freeway. It wasn't because they couldn't find any buildings to use. There were several close to the road, but the fields surrounding them were all flooded. The roadbed rose above the water like a long narrow island and Fleet was becoming concerned about the rising floodwaters. The flood level could rise another five of six feet before the pavement was under water, but Fleet didn't know how high the river was running beyond the levees just to the west of their camping spot.

Armand had decided that they would have a fire that night and after the horses were settled he took the hatchet from his saddlebags and began walking toward a wooded spot on some high ground east of their campsite. He returned with some lengths of pine and dead wood. It took some effort, but they finally achieved a sputtering flame using the damp firewood. Once Armand was satisfied with the progress of the fire, he returned to the woods again and this time Carleen went to help. While they were gone Kyla began cooking supper. She made a simple mixture of dried beans and rice and began simmering them in one of the skillets by placing it directly on the fire. By the time Carleen and Armand had made their third trip to the timber, the food was ready and they had enough wood to keep the fire going all night.

Lipsky, as usual, had done nothing to help. He spent his time complaining first about how the fire was inadequate, and then changing to the fact that supper was taking too long. After he had eaten, he griped about the lousy food. He did nothing to improve his situation and made sure that everyone around him was sharing his misery. After three days of listening to his criticisms everyone responded by ignoring him. Fleet was less vocal about his dissatisfaction but wasn't any more helpful than Lipsky was.

Kyla had been watching Fleet for the last two days, wondering what it was that was eating at him so badly. Ever since Lipsky arrived and delivered the note, Fleet had been troubled and was always muttering to himself as he rode. After they were done with their supper, he had started pacing back and forth on the roadway below them. No one had asked Fleet what was wrong and he hadn't volunteered an explanation to anyone.

Once the rice and beans were gone, Kyla had mixed up a batter of corn meal and water then poured it into one of the hot skillets to make a pancake like fried bread. When she cut it into quarters and poured honey over it, she gave a piece to Armand and Carleen who ate the treat with grateful smiles. Lipsky didn't ask for any, but when Kyla offered him a piece he ate it greedily. For once he didn't complain, perhaps he had a weakness for sweets. The last piece Kyla carried to Fleet. It was an excuse to talk to him. Someone had to bring him back from wherever his mind had been. Tomorrow they would need his full attention. Kyla was remembering the night when Justin had been shot. The day leading up to the mad dash across the road, Fleet had been preoccupied, but this was different. Something was truly wrong and Kyla wanted to find out what it was.

Fleet was standing in the rain staring into the darkness toward the river. They hadn't seen it yet, but they knew it was close. When Kyla walked up behind him, Fleet seemed startled by her presence. His mind had been far away. Kyla offered him the piece of the cornbread she'd brought for him, but he only waved his hand absently. "You need to eat, Fleet," she said, "You hardly touched your supper." Kyla was not going to let Fleet dismiss her so easily. He refused to acknowledge her, just like he had been ignoring them all for the last two days. She wanted to grab him by the shoulders and shake him until he responded, but first she tried a more gentle approach. "I can tell something is bothering you, Fleet. Is there a problem with going to the city?"

Fleet gave her a look that Kyla could only describe as tortured amusement. He was laughing when he said, "No everything is great."

Obviously, things were not 'great' and Kyla was not going to accept that as his answer. "If something is bothering you, you need to let someone know. We're here to help you. You can't carry the weight of every decision by yourself."

Fleet finally turned and looked at Kyla. She was wearing her black cloak with the hood pulled over her head, but he could see the worry and concern that filled her eyes. He wanted to put her mind at ease and tell her everything would be fine, but he couldn't. All he could think about was Sadie and his suspicions of her betrayal. He had thought he loved Sadie, but how could he love someone who was capable of such treachery. What was preying so heavily on his mind right now was the fact that the trip to the city had been Sadie's idea. Thousands of scenarios had played through his mind over the last two days as to what might happen when they reached their destination, but each one had a common thread. He was wondering what surprises Sadie might have waiting for them. Then there was the proof of his suspicions, two rain soaked scraps of paper hidden deep in his pockets. He fought the urge to pull them out and show them to Kyla. Fleet desperately wanted someone to tell him that he was wrong, but what stopped him from showing Kyla was the fear that she would agree with him.

Kyla watched Fleet's face. He was staring directly at her but he didn't seem to see her at all. It was as if she could see him thinking, weighing the choices in his mind. Every time she thought he was about to say something, he stopped himself. There could only one thing bothering Fleet and she knew that it had to have something to do with Sadie. Fleet's problems with Sadie were a subject Kyla had avoided like the plague, but she had to ask. "What did Sadie write in her letter?" As soon as the words were out of her mouth Kyla shifted uncomfortably as Fleet came back to attention.

His brows came together in an angry frown. He knew she was guessing, but her suspicions were too close for his comfort. He almost laughed when he thought that Kyla was thinking that Sadie had written something that upset him. He knew she wasn't going to leave him alone until he had given her some kind of explanation, so he skirted the issue. "The letter is personal."

She was getting nowhere with him and Kyla was wishing Kurt were here. Fleet would talk to him. As she watched his expression turn from a scowl, to amusement, and then back to pained indecision, she couldn't stand it anymore. "Fleet something is obviously bothering you. Whatever it is you owe it to the rest of us to tell us what's wrong." As Kyla spoke she did grab his arms and forced him to look at her and really see her this time. "Fleet, you have to trust somebody," she was pleading with him and finally, she got through.

Fleet looked at the three people lying by the fire. No one was watching them. Shaking himself free from Kyla's grasp, he turned and motioned for her to follow. Then he started walking up the earthen embankment to the roadway passing over their heads with Kyla scrambling after him. When she reached the top of the muddy slope, Fleet was waiting for her. "You're right," he said, "I've got to tell somebody."

Relief flooded Kyla's mind. Fleet was finally going to unburden himself, but as she waited he remained silent. His indecision wasn't gone. Fleet was going to make her drag it out of him. Kyla was ready to say, 'Just tell me', but Fleet spoke first.

"I can trust you," Fleet said. Kyla thought the tone of his voice was odd as he continued, "You're one of the few people that I know I can trust."

He was repeating himself. Kyla wasn't sure he was ready to tell her anything, but she tried to reassure him. "I won't tell anyone else, if that's what you want." Kyla was grasping for anything that would help Fleet feel more at ease.

Fleet shifted uneasily as he finally came to the point. "Do you remember your first day at the Settlement and the meeting after dinner?"

Kyla nodded. "Yes, I remember," she said slowly. She wasn't sure what that had to do with their present situation.

"Do you remember what we discussed?" Fleet asked.

The questions seemed pointless to Kyla. She couldn't see where Fleet was going, but she patiently answered, "We talked about your raid on Spring's farm and about how I fit into the picture." Then as an afterthought she added, "We talked about Marta being shot." Perhaps that was what was bothering Fleet. Kyla thought she had discovered what he was worrying about. It seemed the logical thing. Everybody had criticized Fleet about his decision to take Carleen and herself. He must be worrying that the same fate might be awaiting them. "What happened to Marta was not your fault. Carleen and I both know that there are risks involved every time we leave the farm. We're responsible for our decisions, not you. Neither one of us would have come if we weren't willing to take the risk." Fleet waved his hand impatiently as she spoke, forcing Kyla to fall silent. Finally, losing her patience, she demanded, "Well then what is it? I'm all out of guesses. You're going to have to tell me."

"We also discussed the possibility that someone had warned Cole Spring and told him we were coming," Fleet wanted to go slowly. He wanted each piece of information that he gave to Kyla to have a chance to sink in before he added another. When he saw the light of recognition on her face he continued, "I think I know who it was."

Kyla's mind leapt to the obvious conclusion. "Lipsky?" she asked in a hushed whisper, remembering that he was nearby.

Fleet smiled grimly. He was sure that Lipsky had had some part in it, but that wasn't the point he was desperately trying to make. "No, not Lipsky." Then he stopped and looked at Kyla, Fleet couldn't make himself say the words. He felt uncomfortable telling Kyla that Sadie, the woman he loved, had betrayed him. He was confessing more than just a betrayal of his trust. It went deeper. He had loved the woman, still loved her. How could he tell another woman about something like that? But he had gone too far to stop; he forced the words from his mouth. "It was Sadie."

Kyla felt a knot growing in her belly. The shock that Kyla was feeling was more in sympathy for Fleet than surprise at the suggestion that Sadie was not to be trusted. No wonder Fleet had been acting like he was being torn in two. Still, she had to wonder about his statement. Sadie surely wouldn't have written a confession in her letter. Kyla knew

361

Sadie well enough to know that she wasn't foolish or stupid and she could only ask, "How did you find out?"

Now that the subject had been breached Fleet could discuss it, as long as he didn't have to say Sadie's name. "The note that I took from Clovis and the letter that Lipsky delivered, the handwriting is the same."

"You have them both?" Kyla wished that she could look at them and see for herself. Handwriting comparisons were usually a matter of opinion. Still, the fact that Fleet's suspicions were so strong, made Kyla believe that he must have had other deeper doubts about Sadie's love and devotion.

"That doesn't matter," Fleet wouldn't have shown the letter to Kyla even if it had been daylight. "It just makes me wonder if we are being sent into a trap."

"We don't have to go into the city," Kyla offered. As soon as the words were out of her mouth and she saw the reaction from Fleet, she knew that was not one of options Fleet was considering.

He ignored what she said and told her his plans. "Armand and I will go across the river alone."

"If you go, I'm going too," Kyla stated firmly. She had ridden through two miserable days of rain to get here and she was not going to be left behind.

"You just said that you didn't want to go," Fleet answered. His tone was flat and unemotional. He'd made up his mind.

"I said, 'We'," Kyla answered. "I am one of your Guard, when you go, I'll be right behind you." She wanted to add that even if she were not a Guard member, she would still follow, but left the words unspoken.

Fleet startled Kyla as he reached out suddenly and pushed back her hood. He stood with his hands resting on her shoulders looking down as Kyla tilted her head to look up and meet his gaze. Her short hair was blowing in the wind and she was frowning stubbornly at him. For the first time in days, Fleet felt like a burden had been lifted from his shoulders and he smiled. "Suit yourself," he said lightly then turned abruptly, leaving Kyla standing alone with the wind whipping around her and the raindrops running down her face.

It was a few moments before she could move. All Fleet had done was touch her and she had suddenly felt weak in the knees. She knew what Carleen would tell her. Her friend had been quite outspoken on the subject of Kyla's feelings toward Fleet, which left her wondering if she really was that transparent. She didn't know if love was the right word to describe her feelings toward Fleet. Kyla worshipped him. Like her personal savior, Fleet had plucked her from the pits of doom and brought her into the center of his life. He was the light that she followed and Kyla felt herself tied to him more tightly than any other person in her life. At first she had attributed her feelings to the gratitude that she felt after her rescue, but they had grown since then. Every thought that she had in some way revolved around Fleet. When would she see him? What would she say? Then when he had announced that he was taking her on this trip, she had been in heaven.

Her only reluctance to say something to Fleet had been his ties to Sadie. No matter how she felt about Fleet's confession of Sadie's betrayal, Kyla couldn't help feeling a certain satisfaction that Fleet was finally seeing Sadie for what she really was. Nor could she deny that she was jealous of Sadie, who had what Kyla wanted and that was Fleet's love. The longer she had lived in the house with Sadie, the more Kyla had wondered what Fleet could possibly love about her. Sadie was a vindictive, manipulative shrew that used Fleet just as surely as she used everyone who came in contact with her. Kyla had never felt that Sadie loved Fleet and now she was sure of it. What she would do with the knowledge was another thing, but Kyla would keep her promise to Fleet and what he had just told her would remain between them. If Fleet wanted to tell the others, it was up to him to make that decision. All Kyla could do was wait and see what would happen next.

When she had finally gathered her composure, Kyla walked back down the bank to the roadway below. She was suddenly struck by the loneliness of the place. They were surrounded by cold hard concrete above and below and silence was everywhere. Only a few miles to the north were the remains of one of the largest cities in the region and the freeway where they were camping had once been crowded with vehicles night and day. No one traveled these highways anymore and from what they had seen there was not a soul living in the area between the Settlement and the river. If there were people living in the city on the other side of the river, that remained to be seen.

When Kyla returned to the fire Fleet was talking and smiling, acting like the man they were used to seeing. Carleen caught Kyla's eye and gave her a smile of approval. She clearly credited Fleet's sudden change to something that Kyla had done. As she came to stand next to Fleet, he looked at Kyla and said, "I was just about to go over my plans for tomorrow." His tone was all business. "The only information that we have is based on what Orin said."

Lipsky spat on the ground when Fleet mentioned the old man and said, "You're nuts if you listened to anything that crazy bastard had to say."

Fleet ignored his crude behavior and continued as if Lipsky had not interrupted, "He said that there's only one bridge left intact with armed guards patrolling it night and day. If they let us pass then we can go across, if not then we look for another way. According to him there are people living just across the bridge in what used to be the zoo."

"Now that's what I call a plan," Lipsky said derisively. "What are you going to do ride up and say 'Pretty please'?" He laughed at his joke. There was nothing that gave Lipsky more pleasure than criticizing every word that came out of Fleet's mouth.

Fleet smiled in return. Only there was nothing pleasant about the look that he gave Lipsky. "Yes, something along those lines. I am going to ask for permission to visit their settlement. We are supposed to be on a friendly visit to our neighbors, now aren't we?" Fleet's challenge to Lipsky went unanswered. For once the scrawny little man held his tongue.

Then Fleet turned his attention to the others as he added, "It is simple and straightforward. No tricks, we all go together and we hope for the best."

Armand nodded solemnly and said, "I'm ready, but I don't want to go unprepared. We should have a watch tonight and send a scout ahead tomorrow. I'd feel more comfortable knowing what to expect before we get there."

"Who wants first watch?" Fleet's question was his way of affirming Armand's suggestions.

"I'll be first," Carleen jumped to her feet and went to get her rifle from its case. As she slung the rifle over her shoulder, she strutted past the others. She was ready for some action. Riding in the rain was not her idea of a good time, and the sooner they were on their way tomorrow, the better. She was itching to see what was on the other side of the river.

Lipsky snorted in disgust as he grabbed a blanket and said, "Wake me up when its time for breakfast." No one expected his help or trusted him enough to want him to take a turn at watch, so they let him go without a word.

Fleet was next to take his blanket and lie down. It seemed that he was asleep as soon as he closed his eyes. Kyla was relieved to see him sleeping soundly. He'd had less rest than any of them had over the past few days. When she turned her attention away from Fleet's sleeping form, she became aware of the fact that Armand was staring at her.

"I have never seen corn cakes and honey have such a strong effect on a man before," he was smiling as he said it. Kyla felt her face warming as she blushed and was embarrassed that she had no control over that aspect of her physiology. It always revealed her true emotions. "What did you say to him?" Armand asked as he pressed her for details.

"Fleet has something on his mind that he has to sort out for himself, Armand." Kyla was choosing her words carefully. Armand was as concerned as she was about Fleet's state of mind and she needed to reassure him that Fleet was back on track. "All I did was remind him that we need him." She hoped that would satisfy him for now.

Armand was still smiling as he lay back on the cold hard concrete and cupped his hands behind his head. "I don't know what you said or did, but just keep it up." When Armand closed his eyes and tried to rest, he was thinking about Fleet. The man had been moody and useless for two days after receiving a letter from a woman. Now after fifteen minutes alone with another woman, he was back to normal. It was only logical that if one woman had sent Fleet into the depths of misery, that it would take another to bring him back. The thought was not a comforting one. Armand didn't like depending on a man who couldn't seem to keep his mind on the business at hand. Fleet was in the middle of a tug of war between two women and Armand wondered if Kyla had any clue of what could happen to her if Sadie thought that she might come between Fleet and herself. As he drifted off to sleep, his thoughts were troubled as he worried about what might happen tomorrow.

Kyla was still sitting by the fire after everyone else had gone to sleep. The only sound was the heavy breathing of her companions while they slept and the wind rustling about them. Occasionally, she heard soft footsteps as Carleen paced the road overhead. She crept quietly to the pile of saddlebags and took the last blanket. They had been one short since Lipsky came. Then selecting a place near Fleet, she removed her cloak and rolled it up to make a pillow for her head. When she lay down, she put her head on the cloak and pulled the blanket over her. After a moment on her back, Kyla turned to her side, so she could see Fleet.

No one was there to see her watching him as he slept and Kyla studied his face as she fought to keep her eyes open. His brow and face were no longer wrinkled with worry as he slept peacefully. Fleet looked so young, almost childlike as the slept. Long golden brown curls with light blond streaks, beautiful long tresses that any woman would love to have, fell into his face. Kyla smiled when she thought of Fleet battling with his hair everyday, pulling it back into a ponytail and smoothing out the curls. She often wondered why he just didn't cut it off, since it seemed to bother him so much, but Kyla was glad he didn't. She thought it suited him, just a little unruly and beyond anyone's control. With a sigh she rolled over on her back and closed her eyes. With all the talk from Carleen, Kyla was thinking like a teenager with a crush, but as she fell asleep she was thinking about Fleet.

Kyla may have been thinking of Fleet when she fell asleep, but she was dreaming of wolves and riding North Wind across an open prairie. All around them were the sounds of wolves howling. In her dream the white horse panicked and whinnied with fear as she galloped on and on. She didn't know where they were going and never saw the wolves, but with every hoof beat the howling was growing louder and closer. When someone touched her shoulder, Kyla sat up suddenly still gripped with the panic from her dream. It took her a moment to realize that the howling was real. Fleet, Armand and Carleen were already busy and it was only a second before Kyla was on her feet and helping them bring the horses closer to the fire. Armand was trying to start two more fires to make a ring around them. Even Lipsky shed his blanket and began helping Armand with the fires. Apparently, he was willing to help when his life was in danger, too.

Their only protection was the concrete at their backs. Everything else was wide open. The howling was coming from every direction, a mix of coyote yips and dogs howling. The coyotes were bad enough, but the thought of wild dogs running with the pack made it worse. Everyone was on their feet, rifles in hand. No one had said a word. There was no need. Everyone was focused on watching the darkness for any sign of movement. Carleen fired the first shot when a mangy gray hound slunk cautiously out of the darkness. At the sound of the shot and the yip of the dog as it bolted away, the horses began to pull at the ropes.

"Armand," Fleet shouted, "get hold of the leads. Don't let them bolt." He knew Armand was not comfortable with the horses, but he needed someone strong enough to make a difference. The women were useless there.

Hesitant at first, Armand slung his rifle on his shoulder and went to try to keep the horses under control. He watched the situation carefully. If they lost a horse, it would be too bad. Armand would let them all go if he was needed. Lipsky took over with the fires and their meager supply of wood was shrinking with his efforts to keep the flames dancing. Fleet, Kyla, and Carleen kept their rifles ready, shooting at the shadows circling their fires. It started with the bolder ones charging their circle and each was greeted with a bullet. Sometimes it was a coyote, others times a dog, or some kind of mix, but they were all half-starved and crazed with hunger. The smell of the horses had drawn them and the scent of man was no deterrent. Even though there were now three dead animals lying within sight, they kept coming. Then there were the sounds of fighting each time a wounded animal managed to run away, the animal screaming as the pack turned on it. There was no doubting the vicious nature of the mixed breeds.

As the attacks continued the animals became bolder, coming two or three at a time and trying to slip behind the shooters to get to the horses. At one point all three were shooting and reloading constantly, trying to keep up with the onslaught as the pack began closing in on them. Lipsky finally left the fires and began re-loading their guns.

Keeping one loaded and ready, then handing it to whoever was out of ammunition. It was hard to admit, but if Lipsky hadn't been there to help, they wouldn't have been able to keep up. Kyla didn't know how long the attacks continued, but after a point they noticed that the sound of howling was dying down. When they couldn't see any shadows skulking just beyond the light, everyone began to breathe a little easier. The horses were still nervous, but Armand could finally leave them when they stopped trying to break free of the leads.

No one tried to go back to sleep. Everyone sat silently watching the fires die as the light began to grow with dawn. The morning was gray and cloudy, which was what they expected, but at least the rain had stopped. There was no wood left for a fire to cook breakfast or warm water for washing. Armand had wanted to go after some more wood, but Fleet said no. He was anxious to be gone. The ground was littered with dead animals and the carnage was beginning to draw crows and buzzards that squawked noisily as they fought over the carrion.

Despite everything, Fleet insisted that each member of the party wash and put on a fresh change of clothing. He wanted everyone to look presentable when they asked for entry to the settlement on the other side of the river; a small attempt to appear civilized, despite their circumstances. Within an hour of first light they were all scrubbed and changed, horses saddled, baggage packed and ready to go. Fleet was the first to mount his horse. He watched the others as they swung into their saddles and waited for him to give the word to go. Kyla smiled at him and pointed to her collar. She had noticed that he was wearing the arrow pin that Sister Samethia had given to him.

As Fleet looked at Kyla dressed in her black tunic, with her cape draped over her shoulders. He was struck by how elegant she looked riding her snowy white mare seated on the ornate silver saddle. There was only one thing that she needed. Fleet reached into his pocket and pulled out the silver broach with its large translucent white stone. He guided the black stallion to where she was waiting and held the broach in his open hand, offering it to Kyla.

She was dumbfounded by his offer. They had all seen Lipsky give it to Fleet and Kyla knew that the pin belonged to Sadie. "I can't take the pin, Fleet," Kyla stammered as she looked at the others. Armand was neutral. Carleen was beaming. Lipsky shot her a look that made Kyla shift nervously.

If Fleet noticed or cared about their reactions, he didn't show it. He took the pin and reached out to fasten it on her cloak. As he leaned close and started to push the pin through the fabric, he stopped and whispered, "I promise that I won't stick you like you did me." He looked in her eyes for a moment and smiled warmly at their private joke.

As he leaned closer, she could smell his scent. Kyla felt like she was going to melt when he touched her throat, slipping his fingers under the fabric of the tunic just as she had done when she had fastened the arrow pin on Fleet's tunic that night at the Family's camp. It was all she could do to keep her composure in front of the others. When the pin was fastened, Fleet sat up tall in the saddle and looked at Kyla. He was obviously pleased with the results. "Thank you, Fleet. It's beautiful, but I can't keep it," Kyla repeated her objections, but Fleet never heard a word that she said. He was already gone, galloping down the road. Everyone else scrambled after him, Kyla last of all. She trailed behind them, pulling Brownie with her. She had been worried about Fleet last night, but now Kyla was having doubts that she would be able to keep her mind focused.

~ ~ ~

Fleet was in a hurry. Now that his destination was so close, he was anxious to reach it. He would never have slowed their pace, if Armand hadn't reminded him that he wanted to scout the area first, so they stopped at the first signs of the ruin and devastation that had once been a thriving city and the home of thousands of people. Kyla had heard the stories about the destruction of the cities at the Gathering, but nothing could have prepared her for the shock of seeing the desolation that spread for miles before them. There was nothing left of the buildings and structures. Nothing that was big enough to be considered rubble. Everything had been reduced to fine pulverized sand and grit. It was truly a desert. The road they had been following ended where the sand was blowing and drifting across it.

369

That was where they stopped to wait for Armand. There was not much scouting to be done. They could see him riding across the gray landscape until he disappeared into the low area leading down toward the river. A few minutes later he returned at a gallop. When he stopped before them he said, "The bridge is just ahead and it is guarded." He looked at Fleet and said, "I just went to the top of the next rise. I don't think they saw me, but there's no cover. They'll be able to see us coming from a mile away." Fleet looked at Armand and then turned his gaze in the direction from which Armand had just returned. Without looking back, he kicked his horse and urged him forward into the sand. The others followed in silence. Even Lipsky seemed subdued.

It was not easy going for the horses. The surface was soft and with each step their hooves sunk into the sand. At times it felt as if they were slogging through mud. As they reached the top of the first rise, the ground was a little firmer and Fleet tried to keep to the higher ground. Once they came to the top of the next hill, they could see the bridge in the distance with six men visible from their vantage point. Fleet paused to look for only a few moments before he began to lead the party forward. He didn't head directly toward the bridge, but began to circle slightly to the north. It wasn't until he called for them to halt and form a line at the top of the ridge, that Kyla realized what he was doing. Fleet had brought them around to a point where they were clearly visible to the men on the bridge, but still well out of range of their rifles.

They watched as the men on the bridge began to wave and point in their direction. Fleet was watching through his binoculars. When the men guarding the bridge had all moved to their side of the river, Fleet put down the binoculars and said, "It looks like they're ready." He nudged his black stallion forward and led the way slowly down the hill. Kyla went next, followed by Carleen, then Armand with Lipsky following a good distance behind at the rear of the column. Everyone was watching the guards on the bridge, who, in turn, were watching them. Suspicion was apparent from both groups. When Fleet came within a few yards of the bridge, one of the men walked forward with his rifle shouldered. He was a young man with short dark hair and dressed in a jacket and trousers that were gray like the sand that surrounded them. "You've come close enough," he said warily, keeping his gun pointed at Fleet while he looked at the four others following him.

Fleet put out his hand in a friendly gesture and said, "You can lower your gun, friend. We only want to cross the bridge. We're not looking for any trouble."

When Fleet's horse moved toward the bridge, the man jumped nervously and tightened his grip on the trigger. "No one goes across. You might as well turn around and go back now," he shouted. The young man was trying to make a good show of being fierce, but fear was evident in his voice.

Fleet immediately brought his horse to a stop. Watching the nervous young man with his gun, he was afraid that he would fire if he twitched. "You can see that we mean no harm. We have women with us."

The young man didn't lower his gun. "It makes no difference to me who you have with you. You're just as dead if a woman shoots you, as you are when it's a man." He eyed Carleen for a moment. When he looked at Kyla, he seemed surprised about something, but quickly recovered as he said, "I've given you warning. If you all turn around now, we'll hold our fire."

Fleet could see that the direct approach was not going to work. He smiled and said, "Fair enough, we're not looking for a fight." He pulled the reins and wheeled the black around. This time Fleet brought up the rear as they retreated back up the rise.

Once they were out of sight of the bridge, Lipsky started swearing. "God damn, Fleet, you are the dumbest son of a bitch that I ever met. Is that it? We came this far to turn and run like a bunch of women because some little whelp says no?" He'd been unusually silent all morning and now he was ready to make up for lost time.

"I don't remember anyone asking you to come," Fleet answered. "You're free to leave anytime."

"It's a good thing Sadie sent me to nurse maid you children," Lipsky snapped.

"What would you have us do?" Fleet asked, trying to keep his temper in check. Lipsky was an irritation he could have done without. "Gallop in there with guns blazing and force our way across the bridge?" He pulled sharply on the reins causing the black horse to rear

371

back as Fleet took his anger out on the animal rather than Lipsky. "I'm not ready to commit suicide," Fleet almost spit the words at Lipsky. The sight of Fleet scowling angrily with the black horse rising up before him was enough to intimidate Lipsky into silence. He continued to grumble under his breath with obscenities flowing in an unending stream as the rest of the party tried to ignore him. "There has to be another bridge somewhere," Fleet said and he started to ride south.

They weren't very far from the edge of the debris, but they were much closer to the river. As they tried to make their way south of the city, the flooding from the river blocked every route they tried to take. Their only choices were to backtrack and follow the freeway south or they could ride along the top of the earthen dike next to the river. Fleet didn't want to go near the bridge again so they followed the levees. The river had risen to flood level and the current swirled and eddied as it passed through the wooded ground next to the river. It was unnerving to ride with the rushing water so close at hand. In some places the water had eroded parts of the earthen wall and they had to force the horses forward when the path narrowed. They had continued in that manner for nearly two hours when they heard a voice hailing them.

Fleet stopped immediately and everyone turned to see whom it could be. It was a few moments before they saw a man wading through the standing water on the eastern side of the levee. "You on the horses," they heard him shouting. "Wait." He was carrying a shotgun above his head. At that moment his main concern was getting through the water, which was as deep as his waist in some places, not firing at them. Everyone waited anxiously. This was the first potentially friendly face they had seen in days. When he finally reached the spot where they were waiting, the man began to try to climb up the side of the levee, but slipped back into the water.

Armand jumped down and offered the stranger his hand, pulling him up to level ground. "Thanks buddy," the man said as he squinted through his round wire-framed glasses at the riders and their horses. He was wearing hip waders and a flannel shirt. On top of his head he had a fur cap made from the pelt of an opossum, beady eyes and all. He was a memorable sight. "I don't know where you're headed, but it isn't safe to ride on the levees. One of them washed out south of here last night."

"We can't go back. We've already been to the bridge," Fleet answered.

The stranger grinned knowingly and rubbed the beard on his chin. "I can see your problem."

"You seem to know the area," Fleet said, "do you have any suggestions?"

The man was still grinning when he said; "I think I can help you there." He pointed in the direction they had been travelling and said, "There's a road that's still above water. It's just a little further. I would recommend that you take it."

"Thank you." Fleet was glad to find someone who was willing to help. "We were wondering where the next bridge is."

The man let out a hearty laugh as he said, "How far do you want to go?" When he saw the puzzled looks, he explained. "I've traveled both directions for days and couldn't find one. You need a boat."

"I don't suppose you happen to have one?" Fleet was joking with the man. He didn't expect the response that he got.

"Well, now that you mention it, I do happen to have a boat," he was grinning ear to ear.

As Fleet looked at him he could have sworn that the opossum was smiling, too. How on earth could they have been lucky enough to stumble onto someone who had a boat? It was too good to be true, and the man seemed to be friendly. It would be easy to see if he was boasting or telling the truth. Fleet was ready to play along. "So what is the fare for a ride across the river and back?"

The man eyed the packhorse and then looked up at Fleet. "It seems you and your friends have plenty of supplies. The wife and I are getting a little tired of 'possum, if you get my drift."

"Show me the boat and we can discuss a deal," Fleet was hopeful that whatever the man had, it would be bigger than a rowboat. He didn't like the look of the swirling currents.

"Why don't we take the ladies to my house first. The old lady will be thankful for someone besides me for company. We live near the road I was telling you about," he started to walk past the horses to lead the way, his rubber waders squeaking as he walked.

As Fleet rode slowly behind him, he said, "What's you name, friend."

"You can call me Liam," he answered turned to look at Fleet. "And while we're doing the introductions, what might your names be?"

"I'm Fleet and this is Kyla, Carleen, Armand, and Lipsky," Fleet pointed to each member of the party as he named them.

"Well, it's a pleasure to met someone friendly. Those folks across the river are a snooty bunch. They don't let anybody over the bridge and they never come across the bridge either," he looked at them again. "You're the first people I've seen for ages that I didn't have to shoot." Liam was chuckling to himself as he walked, apparently enjoying his joke. Fleet thought the statement had the ring of truth to it.

They followed Liam as he took them past a bend in the levee where they saw the gravel road leading to the east. As they went past a grove of willow and ash, Liam stopped and pointed, "There it is. Home sweet home." What he was pointing to was not what they had expected. His home was a mobile home raised twenty feet above the ground, or water, under the present circumstances. Eight sturdy poles supported the dwelling and a wooden walkway led to it, but how they would get to the front door was not immediately evident. "Come on," Liam said as he waved at the riders and walked down the pier to stand below the trailer. "Shawnee, we have quests," he shouted above the sound of the rushing water. A woman with long brown hair appeared at the doorway with gun in hand and sighted on Fleet and the others. "It's okay. Let the ladder down. They're coming up," Liam called out and stepped back in anticipation of her next action, which was to kick a long rope ladder with wooden rungs out the door. After unrolling to its full length, the ladder started to swing back and forth. Liam caught it and looked at them. "The ladies can go up first."

Kyla and Carleen were both looking at the slender rope ladder then back to Fleet who was already halfway off the black horse. Armand was looking at the ladder, too, and he said, "I'll watch the horses."

Kyla and Carleen slid out of their saddles. "I think you made the best choice," Carleen said as she handed her reins to Armand.

Fleet waited for the two women to go first before he stepped on the wooden planking. The current appeared to be quite strong, but the pier was well constructed and there was no swaying or motion as they walked toward the end where Liam was waiting. What worried him was the fact that the water was only a few inches under the pier. "I wouldn't want to get trapped up there if the river rises," Fleet said. Judging by the watermarks on the tall wooden poles, the river had risen much higher in past floods.

"Don't worry, the river crested last night. It's been going down since then. Besides it wouldn't be the first time, it's happened before." Liam looked at the women and asked, "Who's first?"

Carleen stepped forward and put her foot on one of the rungs of the ladder. "Might as well get it over with," she mumbled under her breath, but still loud enough for everyone to hear.

Kyla watched as she started to climb. Despite the fact that Liam was holding the end of the rope, it still twisted and wobbled wildly as Carleen climbed. Once she was at the top Shawnee reached out the door and helped pull her inside. As Carleen disappeared inside, Liam called, "Next," and looked at Kyla who stepped forward and took hold of the ropes. It may have been a ladder, but it was not easy to climb. With each step Kyla had to try to balance on the rungs as the ropes twisted back and forth. From above she could hear Carleen shouting, "Come on, its easy." After what seemed like an eternity, Kyla knew she had reached the top of the ladder when she felt two pairs of hands grab her under the arms and pull her inside.

Kyla's head was swimming and her knees weak from the climb. It had not been very far, but she'd struggled every inch of the way. Once she caught her breath, she started to look around the room. It was crammed with all kinds of odd contraptions and there were animal pelts everywhere. She was on her feet by the time Fleet's head appeared. As Carleen and the woman named Shawnee grabbed the back of Fleet's tunic, he slid in on his belly and tried to stand. The rope seemed to have the same effect on Fleet as it did Kyla and he swayed slightly as he stood. Lipsky was next up the ladder followed by Liam. Kyla wondered how he managed to get up the rope without anyone holding it steady at the bottom, but apparently he was used to it. When he scrambled inside, he pulled the ladder up and waved to Armand who was waiting happily below.

"I brought guests," Liam said as he wrapped one arm around Shawnee, beaming proudly. "Now, I'm not very good at remembering names, so correct me if I'm wrong." He pointed as he named them,

"Fleet, Kyla, Carleen, and Lipsky." Then leaning back a little and pointing out the door, he said, "And the big guy down there is Armand." He had taken off his waders before climbing the ladder and after he made his introductions, hung them on a hook by the door. Next he pulled off his fur cap and tossed it into the corner. There was not a hair on the top of his head. He was totally bald except for his long ponytail. As he gave his wife a hug he said, "This is my old lady, Shawnee."

Shawnee hit him playfully on the shoulder and said, "I told you not to call me that in front of company." She stood about average height and her long brown hair was rather bushy. She was dressed in jeans and a flannel shirt like Liam, but it was her vest that was unusual. It was covered with feathers that had been sewn onto the fabric in fanciful patterns and stripes made by using different colored feathers. Shawnee saw them staring at her vest and shrugged as she said, "I had a lot of time on my hands last winter."

"And a lot of feathers, too," Liam teased. Then as he gave Fleet a hearty clap on the back he said, "Let me show you around the place."

Fleet looked around the room. There didn't appear to be much to see, but he followed Liam as he went to open the door at the end of the room. When Fleet looked inside he had to squint at the bright light shining in his eyes. As he eyes adjusted, he could see that the room was lined with foil and filled with tomato plants. "This is the garden. Shawnee's the botanist." He grinned at Fleet's surprised look and closed the door. Without moving he said, "The kitchen's right behind me." Fleet could see that the kitchen consisted of a small wood stove and two shelves with dishes, pots, and pans lined in neat rows. Liam reached out, flicked a switch behind them, and turned on the lights.

"Where do you get the electricity?" Kyla asked. She couldn't hear the sound of a generator.

"It's wind power," Liam said with pride. "Didn't you see the windmill before you came up?"

Fleet looked out the door at Armand waiting below with the horses. Even though he was not anxious to climb back down the ladder, he said, "I don't want to leave them too long. Is there any place nearby where we can take the horses?"

Liam and Shawnee looked at each other, but it was Shawnee that answered, "The tennis courts." Liam was nodding as she continued. "They're about a quarter mile from here. The fences are in good shape and it should be above the floodwater."

"We definitely need something with a fence," Fleet answered. "We had quite a time with a pack of coyotes and wild dogs last night."

Liam laughed as he said, "I wondered if it was you folks that were doing all the shooting last night."

Fleet hadn't thought of it until now, but they had traveled far enough to the south to be close to their camping spot of the previous night. "Do you have a lot of problems with the coyotes?"

Liam's answer was indirect, but his point was clear when he said, "We're living twenty feet in the air aren't we?"

"Why don't we bring the packs up here before you go," Kyla suggested. "I'm sure we could have something ready to eat by the time you get back. We'll be happy to share what we have, " She wouldn't say anything to insult their hosts, but given Liam's mention of eating opossum and the abundance of small gray pelts in their home, there was little doubt that they ate it often.

Their hostess took the suggestion gratefully and said, "I could go for something different. There's only so much you can do with 'possum and tomatoes."

Until then Lipsky had been quiet, but he voiced his objections, "If I go down that ladder, I'm not coming back up."

Fleet smiled and said, "Good, because you will be with Armand watching the horses." He expected an argument or sarcastic comment, but for some reason, Lipsky was on his best behavior. It could have been that he was trying to make a good impression on their hosts, but Fleet doubted that was it. Whatever the purpose, it would be to Lipsky's benefit and no one else's. He was sure of that.

It took a few minutes for them to climb back down the ladder and haul the panniers up into the trailer. Once they were done bringing all their supplies into the small living space, there was not much room left to move around. The men left with the horses while Kyla and Carleen started going through the bundles of food and supplies. Although Fleet had promised to give them some of their food after they saw the boat, the two women were more than generous in giving Shawnee portions of the dried beans, rice, and corn flour.

What really thrilled her was the salt. Shawnee found a small glass container to hold some of it. As Kyla poured the salt into it, Shawnee said, "You never know what you'll miss the most until you have to do without it."

"How long have you been living up here?" Carleen asked. Judging by the jumble of odds and ends and pieces of machinery lying all about them, it had to have been a long time. No one could have collected such an assortment of junk unless they had been at it for awhile.

"We've been living out here in the woods ever since," she paused and looked at the two women then nodded toward the north to where the ruined city was, "well you know." It was hard for her to put a name to the destruction. She turned and busied herself looking for another container to hold some of the rice, talking as she searched. "We were on a camping trip, canoeing down river when it happened. If we'd been at home that day I wouldn't be talking to you now. Here put some in this," she said presenting a plastic container with a lid. "I've been saving this for something special."

"So all you eat is 'possum and tomatoes?" Carleen handed the container filled with rice back to Shawnee. She couldn't contain her curiosity any longer.

Shawnee had a light almost lyrical laugh and she regarded Carleen with an amused smile. "I've eaten plenty, but don't worry tonight we're having something different." Then going to the woodpile beside the stove she picked up four plump ducks. "Where do you think all the feathers came from?" Then tossing one to Kyla, she said, "You'd better get busy plucking if you're going to have something ready when those men come back. Put the feathers in that bag by the door." Then giving the others to Carleen she said, "You help her while I start a fire in the stove. We'll be eating duck stuffed with rice tonight."

When Fleet returned with Liam the aroma of the duck roasting welcomed him before he was inside the door. This time when the ladder was pulled inside Liam closed the door. Fleet looked around the room for a place to sit and chose a spot on the floor near the packs where he could watch Kyla and Shawnee preparing the food. Carleen was not helping. There wasn't room for three people in the small kitchen area. It was just as well. Fleet had tasted a sample of Carleen's cooking on the first night out. As he leaned back against their pile of baggage and stretched his long legs out in front of him, Fleet said, "It smells wonderful. What's for supper?"

Shawnee smiled and answered, "Roast duck stuffed with rice, cornbread, roasted cattail roots, and a salad of greens."

"No 'possum?" Fleet asked. He was looking at Liam's cap as the spoke.

Liam laughed heartily and took of the cap. "No, this big fellow was the last one." With a look to Shawnee, he said, "The 'possums are kind of a private joke with me and Shawnee. When we first decided to move into this place, it was already occupied. There were 'possums everywhere. After we chased them out and cleaned the place up, they kept coming back. We plugged every hole we could find, but they kept finding or making new ones. The only way to get rid of them was to kill them." With a shrug he added, "And waste not want not, we ate every last one of them, skinned them and tanned their hides. But this big guy was too smart for us. Every night for weeks, he climbed the poles and got into the food that we were trying to store. We would hear him scratching around but he was always gone before we could catch him."

"It was a battle of wits between the 'possum and Liam," Shawnee took up the story at that point. "I told him if he ever caught the 'possum that I'd make him into a hat. So you can guess who finally won. Personally, I miss Mr. Whiskers." It was then that she opened her large roaster and announced, "Supper's ready."

Shawnee and Liam only had two plates, one for each of them. So Carleen went to their packs and got their platters and eating utensils. "What about Armand? He won't get anything to eat." She wasn't worried about Lipsky.

"You can take something to them if you want," Fleet said. He wasn't worried about Carleen walking alone to the place where the horses were penned. He had spent quite some time looking around with Liam on their way back to the trailer. Most of the area was flooded and the only way to reach this place was along the levee like they had done. He had also seen Liam's boat. At first when he had seen the rowboat tied to a tree, Fleet had been a little disappointed. Then Liam had told him to get in and they rowed to the place where he had a larger one hidden. It was a pontoon boat with a large outboard motor. Liam also showed him a drum filled nearly to the top with gasoline. He was more than satisfied with Liam's boat and Liam had been more than happy to agree to ferry them across the river.

Fleet was feeling more cheerful than he had in days and as he took his plate and held it for Shawnee to fill, his stomach growled loudly. They had hardly eaten anything that day and when everyone looked at him, he laughed and said, "You can take Armand something if there's anything left when I'm finished."

It was like a feast. Liam was especially enjoying the cornbread and honey. "I can't remember the last time I tasted anything so good. Did you make this Shawnee?"

"No, that was Kyla," Shawnee answered.

"It wouldn't have been as good if Shawnee hadn't given me some eggs. I made some last night without eggs and it just crumbled into pieces," Kyla said. She wanted to give their hostess some credit for her contribution.

"Eggs," Fleet said with a surprised look. "I didn't see any chickens around."

"They're goose and duck eggs," Shawnee explained. "There's a marsh a few miles from here where they're nesting; thousands of them, more than I can ever remember seeing in the spring. Usually, they go further north." No one commented on Shawnee's observation. There were many things different about the arrival of spring that year other than the fact that it was late in coming.

There was plenty of food left to send to Armand and Lipsky. As soon as they were done eating, Carleen put what was left into a large pot that Shawnee gave her to use. Carleen and Liam went down the rope ladder and Shawnee carefully lowered the pot in a large wire basket tied on the end of a rope. It was something that they had made for that purpose. Obviously, carrying loads up and down the ladder would have been difficult otherwise. Liam went a short distance with Carleen and once he had her headed down the right path, he returned to the trailer.

He picked a spot on the floor next to Fleet and leaned back on one of the large bags that were filled with feathers. Then putting his hands behind his head, Liam relaxed with a big sigh. "Where did you folks come from? If you don't mind me asking."

Fleet hesitated for a moment, but decided there was no harm in telling Liam about the Settlement. It was difficult to put aside the suspicions that had become second nature to him when talking to strangers. "There's a community a few miles east of here that we call the Settlement. If you include the people living at the Settlement and the area around it and the farm where we live, there are over one hundred people living there." He didn't mention the Family or Spring's farm. There was no point in giving more information than he had been asked to give.

"If you wanted you could go back with us," Kyla offered. "There's work at the farm and food for those who stay there."

Liam smiled and looked to Shawnee, "No thanks, Shawnee and I are heading south on the river once the flooding stops." He turned back to Fleet and was looking at the pile of supplies that they had hauled up on the ropes. "May I look at one of your weapons?" Fleet took one out of its case and almost stopped to unload it before giving it to Liam, but decided not to do it. It was Fleet's indirect way of saying that he trusted Liam. "I have some shotguns, but I ran out of shells a long time ago." He stood and held the gun to his shoulder looking down the sights, "These are military issue. Aren't they?" Liam saw the look on Fleet's face and chuckled softly as he said, "Don't worry. I won't ask where they came from." He lowered the gun and was still examining it when he asked, "Do you have any automatic weapons?"

Fleet shook his head and answered, "No, but we could've used one the other night with the coyote pack. It was all we could do with three people shooting to keep up when they rushed us."

That was all the encouragement Liam needed and he said, "Well, I can help you with that." He laid the weapon on the floor in front of Fleet and went to the far side of the small room. Once again, he had sift through the piles of junk to find what he wanted, but it was only a minute before he found his toolbox and went to work on the gun. Fleet watched him as he dismantled the gun and made a few adjustments. Fleet knew it was possible to make a semi-automatic into a full

381

automatic, but he had never seen it done before. Once he was finished, Liam rose and pushed the door open. The sound was deafening inside the tiny room as he fired the gun out the door, showering the trees with a hail of gunfire. After completing his demonstration Liam handed the converted weapon back to Fleet saying, "Be careful. She's got a greasy trigger now. Do you want me to do the others, too?"

Fleet unloaded the gun before returning it to its case, unsure just how 'greasy' the trigger might be. "No thanks," Fleet said. "One will be enough. Besides I don't have enough ammunition to waste with automatics, but it's good to have one if we need it." He didn't want to insult Liam, but the thought of Carleen with an automatic weapon was not comforting. He would keep the converted rifle for himself.

Liam shrugged. It made no difference to him one way or the other. "We're going across the river tomorrow," he said, changing the subject.

Shawnee didn't look surprised by the news. "You have friends over there?" she asked casually. She hadn't asked as many questions as Liam had.

"No," Fleet answered. "I guess you could say we're on a fact finding mission. Anything you can tell us would be helpful."

Shawnee looked at their guests. She hadn't said much, but she had been watching them. They were wearing black uniforms similar to the ones that the sentries guarding the settlement across the river wore. Then there was the pin with the two crescents. If it had been up to her, they wouldn't have made it in the door, but Liam was a good judge of character and they seemed friendly enough. "I've only been inside their compound once and never went back. It seems nice enough, but Liam and I like our freedom. We don't like anyone telling us where we can go and what to do." She looked at Kyla and said, "They might let you in, but not the others."

Kyla wasn't sure what Shawnee meant by that. "We heard that they're living in what used to be the zoo." She wanted some information that they could use.

"That's right," Liam answered. "It's in a low spot next to the river surrounded by high bluffs. I guess that's the reason it escaped the destruction. Whatever leveled everything else must have passed right over it. I could drop you right off on the shore, but I don't want to come that close. I would prefer that no one saw me bring you over. They know that Shawnee and I are living out here and they leave us alone. I doubt they would continue to do that if we started dropping visitors off on their doorstep."

"You can't take the horses across," Shawnee said. She knew that Liam and Fleet had been discussing their plans while they were gone. Now she wanted all the details.

"That had occurred to me, too," Fleet answered. "Liam said we could leave the horses at the tennis courts. The only ones going across will be Kyla, Armand, and myself. We'll be leaving Carleen and Lipsky here to watch the horses. We won't be staying long. Liam will meet us tomorrow evening to bring us back. Then if we can impose on your hospitality one more night, we'll be on our way home day after tomorrow."

"What time are you leaving in the morning?" Shawnee asked.

"Early, I want to be across the river and back before dawn," Liam answered.

Shawnee rose from where she had been sitting and said, "Then as soon as your friend Carleen gets back we'd better get some sleep." She went to one corner of the room and began handing out pillows and blankets. "This is where Liam and I sleep," she explained. "The back room is for the plants. It'll be a little tight with five of us tonight. I just hope none of you snore as loud as Liam does."

Chapter Fifteen

Shawnee had not been exaggerating about Liam's snoring or the fact that the sleeping arrangements would be rather cozy. Fleet was awakened in the middle of the night by Liam's cacophony of snorts and whistles as he breathed in an out. As he lay awake, Fleet realized that Kyla was curled up next to him. He could feel her body against his and feel her hair brushing softly against his chin as they lay together. Her fragrance was a mingling of smells from cooking and of course the horses and leather, but there was also a softer perfume that he had come to associate with her. He fought the urge to reach out and hold her close, but he couldn't do that. Over the past few weeks, Fleet had done everything that he could to keep their relationship 'strictly business'.

He didn't have to bring Kyla on this trip, but he had wanted to bring her. What his reasoning had been even Fleet wasn't sure. He felt comfortable with Kyla. Ever since that night at the Family's camp, he had been trying to keep her near. It wasn't something that he wanted to admit to himself. Even when he went to the stock farm, he had found himself wishing that he'd brought Kyla with them. Fleet stood up hastily.

Kyla was awakened by his sudden movement and asked drowsily, "Where are you going?"

"It'll be time to go soon," Fleet said. "I want to get Armand so he'll be ready." Fleet was lying. The real reason was staring at him with sleepy eyes. He went to the door and as soon as he opened it and let in the cool air, Liam sat up suddenly.

"It's you," he said. "You startled me." He got up quickly and went to the door. "Are you ready to go?"

Fleet had set events in motion and decided to keep them going. "We might as well get it over with. It'll be light in a couple of hours," he said as he pushed the ladder out the door with his foot, then he picking up his rifle, loaded it in the dark. With the rifle slung over his shoulder, Fleet started down the ladder without saying another word. He was in a hurry to get to the ground. Walking would clear his mind. The air was cool, but not too cold and the wind was light, perfect weather for a boat ride. Once he got close to the tennis courts Fleet called out to Armand. He didn't want to surprise them and end up being shot. He was sure that Lipsky would leap at an opportunity to shoot him by accident.

"Fleet, I've been waiting for you," Armand answered immediately. His voice sounded anxious.

Picking up his pace, Fleet hurried the last few yards and asked, "What's wrong."

"Lipsky's gone," Armand answered as Fleet came into sight. "He took off last night. Tried to take the packhorse and the some of the supplies, but I wouldn't let him have anything more than what he brought with him. Personally, I'm glad he's gone."

"There's nothing we can do about it now," Fleet said. He didn't like Lipsky tagging along either, but at least he had known where he was and what he was doing. His disappearance worried Fleet. Who knew what task Sadie had given him? Fortunately, Lipsky had not been present when they had discussed their plans, but he did know that Liam had a boat. Now he would have to warn their host about Lipsky. He changed the subject. "I didn't hear any howling tonight."

"No it's been quiet," Armand answered.

"I need you to come with me when we go across the river. When Carleen comes back with Liam and Shawnee, she'll watch the horses." Fleet hadn't had a chance to tell Armand what they had planned until now.

"And Kyla?" Armand asked the question knowing what the answer would be.

"She's coming with us," Fleet answered then turned and began the walk back to the levee.

Fleet turned his back before he could see Armand shaking his head. He was not surprised to hear that Kyla would be going with them. It took only a few of Armand's long strides to bring him to Fleet's side as he asked, "Have you told Carleen that she'll be staying behind?"

"Yes, she knows," Fleet could have elaborated, but he didn't want repeat the things that Carleen had said. She had a very colorful vocabulary and had used some expressions voicing her dissatisfaction that even Fleet had never heard before.

When he returned with Armand, the others were waiting for them. Kyla was the first to comment on Lipsky's absence, "Is Lipsky staying with the horses?" she asked hesitantly. She couldn't imagine that Fleet would trust him with something that important.

"He's gone," Armand answered.

It was Liam that spoke out next, "I'm glad to hear that. I don't want to question who you choose to travel with, but he didn't appear to be a very trustworthy sort. I really didn't want him on my boat."

"Liam," Shawnee said his name sharply.

"Don't worry," Fleet said. "We didn't bring him by choice. He followed us and attached himself to us. What worries me now is that he knows you have a boat."

Liam laughed and said, "The people in the city know I have a boat. They've tried to find it before and couldn't do it. But I would watch my back, that fellow looked like he would love to plant a knife there for you."

"That's good advice," Fleet answered but Liam wasn't telling him anything that he didn't already know. Then turning to the others, he said, "Let's get this done."

"What about breakfast?" Shawnee asked. "Don't you want to eat before you leave?"

Fleet smiled politely and said, "You can fix breakfast for us tomorrow if you like."

Liam took that as his cue to lead the way. As they followed him to the spot where the rowboat was hidden, he was wondering about his passengers. He had noticed the similarities in their uniforms and the men across the river, too. It had been Shawnee who had pointed out the broach the woman named Kyla was wearing. The symbol was everywhere at the zoo. They had it painted on almost every blank wall. What it meant neither of them knew. The puzzling thing was that their visitors didn't seem to know anything about the compound. He was curious to know what they were up to, but patient enough to know that most answers came with time.

Six people in the rowboat were a heavy load, especially when Armand got in. It would have been better to make two trips, but time wouldn't allow it. When they reached the old shed housing the pontoon boat, Liam jumped onto the wooden dock and tied the line from the rowboat to one of the posts. There was to a rickety old shed covered with rusty metal sheeting that was partially concealed by the brush and trees growing around it. When they began to climb out of the rowboat Liam warned, "Watch where you step. There are some boards missing." The planking was old and the whole structure seemed unstable. After Liam's warning everyone waited for him to lead the way, watching and following in his footsteps. No one wanted to step on a rotten board and fall into the torrent of water flowing underneath them. Opening the door, Liam stepped inside and felt in the darkness for the light switch. At the sound of the switch, the light from one weak bulb cast a dim glow around the room.

Fleet smiled at Liam and asked, "Another windmill?"

"No this one is run by a water wheel," Liam explained. "Same principal, different power source." He jumped onto the deck of the pontoon boat and the others followed. Liam went to work, checking the gas tank on the motor and passing out the long poles lying at their feet.

"What are these for?" Armand asked as he took the one that Liam handed to him.

"You're going to help me pole this thing out into the main channel. Once we get clear of the debris from the flood, I can use the outboard." While Shawnee pushed open the big doors in preparation for launching the boat, Liam was untying the lines. Once he was done, Fleet, Armand, and Liam all pushed with their poles to cast off. Kyla and Carleen watched while Shawnee used her pole to guide the craft out the door and they followed her example. "I hope everybody can swim," Liam said after they cleared the side of the building and the current took hold of the boat. "Not that it matters, no one can swim in this river, not when she's flooded like this."

It wasn't a comforting thought. The river was making the pontoon boat buck and twist as it tried to sweep them downstream. They didn't need the poles to keep them moving, but to keep the boat from being driven into one of the trees or the brush that was submerged by the floods. After a few nerve-racking minutes they were past the tangle of flotsam and Liam started the outboard. As the motor roared to life they could feel the pontoon come under control, but the rolling motion didn't stop.

Carleen and Kyla were standing side by side. They had put their poles on the deck and were holding onto the railing with both hands.

Carleen leaned nearer to Kyla and whispered, "I never thought you could get seasick riding on a pontoon boat."

If Kyla hadn't been feeling a little queasy herself, she would have laughed, but she was too busy trying to keep on her feet. If the river hadn't been flooded the ride wouldn't have been so rough. Fortunately, the channel was not overly wide at this point and the ride wasn't too long. In the darkness it was difficult to distinguish the water from the shore, but Kyla felt the jolt as the boat ran up onto the bank. Shawnee had taken over the motor and she shut it off as Liam jumped on shore with a line in hand. Before he had time to tie it securely, Armand and Fleet had already jumped off. As Fleet waited to help Kyla down, Carleen grabbed her arm and whispered in her ear. "You're not really going to leave me here with 'Possum Boy and the Bird Woman?"

Kyla turned to Carleen and said, "Who? Liam and Shawnee? They're good people. Besides, we need someone to come after us if something goes wrong." Until that moment when she said it, Kyla hadn't given too much thought to how important it was to have somebody nearby waiting and watching for them to return.

"Hurry up," Fleet said. "We don't have all night." Whatever the two women were talking about it would have to wait. He could tell that Liam was anxious to be back across the river. As Fleet reached for Kyla's hand, ready to lift her down, she jumped down on the rocky ground, avoiding his assistance.

Liam was busy giving Armand last minute instructions. "The bridge is just a few miles north of here, but I would recommend that you circle to the west to avoid it or they'll just stop you there. The old zoo is just north of the bridge right next to the river. I'll come back here after dark tonight and we'll wait as long as we can."

Kyla wanted to ask him what he would do if they missed each other, but it was understood by all that the deadline would have to be met. She was thinking again of Carleen. Her friend was not the type of person who would desert them and she could see her hounding Liam to help her. It was the only comforting thought that Kyla had as they began to walk into the wasteland of dust and grit. Behind them was the sound of the motor disappearing into the distance.

They followed Liam's advice and went west before they turned north. It had been daylight for several hours by the time they sighted the compound. If it hadn't been for one tall, green tree they might have missed it completely. When they walked a little closer they could see a tall chain link fence running around the compound. The fence reminded Kyla of the one surrounding Cole Spring's farm. Only here there was second fence just inside the other one running parallel to it and forming a corridor. They were almost to the fences before they saw a man walking inside the compound. By then they were close enough for Kyla to see that he was armed and she expected him to open fire, but instead he disappeared, probably to go and get somebody else to shoot them. Kyla was not very optimistic about their prospects.

It wasn't long before a party of armed men appeared. They continued walking just inside the fence and following as Fleet led Kyla and Armand around the outside looking for the gate. Once he sighted it, Fleet headed in that direction and the activity inside the fence increased as everyone rushed to the gate. Kyla's knees were growing weaker with every step closer to the fence. If she hadn't been with Fleet she would have turned and run at first sight of the men, but Fleet was focused on one thing only, getting inside the compound. Following him now took all the courage she had and she focused on Fleet and not the men inside the compound.

Fleet was watching the commotion inside the fence, still hoping they would be admitted without incident. As they walked up to the fence Fleet held his hands at his shoulders, palms facing outward as a gesture of their intentions. With twenty guns or more trained on them, they were definitely outnumbered. He would not risk any movement that could be considered threatening. When they were less than twenty feet from the outer fence Fleet stopped with his hands still in the air. He was close enough now to see all the men clearly. The first thing that Fleet noticed was the fact that two of them were wearing tunics similar to theirs. Theirs were dark gray in color and had buttons that ran down the left breast, but otherwise they were identical, a rather unnerving coincidence. Fleet looked at Armand and Kyla and saw that they were staring at the two uniformed men inside the fence, too.

It was the two men in uniform who came to meet them. They opened a small door-like gate in the inner fence and went through the walkway that led to the outer fence. It was enclosed on all sides as if to keep them inside, but Fleet and the others soon saw the reason for the double row of fencing and the enclosed walkway. There were tigers in the area between the fences. Two of them suddenly emerged from the brush, charging at the men walking through the corridor. The men ignored the big cats, but the visitors were visibly shocked. Using tigers like a guard dogs was bizarre to say the least. "What do you want?" one of the men dressed in gray shouted.

"We've come from a settlement east of here. My friend used to live here and was hoping to find some friends or family still living," Fleet answered.

The men inside were not moved by the request. "There's nothing for you here. You might as well go back where you came from." They were walking away when Kyla stepped out from behind Fleet and Armand and shouted, "We aren't here to cause any trouble; we just want to see if there is anyone that our friend knows."

One of the men turned to look at Kyla. When he saw her, he reached out and stopped his friend who also turned to look. They abruptly changed direction and walked back to the gate. "Where did you get that pin?" the taller man asked.

"It's Sadie's broach," Armand answered.

The two men conferred briefly and the taller man said, "Wait here." As they walked back through the corridor, the tigers were pacing on the other side, stalking the men. The taller man waited at the gate inside the compound while the other disappeared. After a few moments, he motioned for the others to lower their guns.

"What was that all about?" Armand said softly.

Fleet was just as puzzled, but he was also worried. Sadie had sent him the broach for a reason. He just wasn't sure what that was. "I don't know, but they've sent that other one somewhere. Right now I'd bet that he's telling whoever is in charge all about us." A feeling was growing in Fleet that made him wish that they could just walk away, but he knew the opportunity to do that had passed them by. When Fleet saw the messenger returning, he stood stiffly with his legs set slightly apart. He had the automatic weapon and at the first sign of trouble he was going to drop to the ground and start firing.

After receiving his instructions from the messenger, the tall man once again walked through the corridor and stopped at the outer gate. The man stood motionless for a moment as he appraised the two men and the woman standing on the other side. No matter what his orders had been, he was forming his own opinion concerning them. As he reached for the gate, key in hand, Fleet felt his heart pounding while he watched the man turn the key in the lock and push the gate open. Fleet stepped forward boldly, past the open gate to walk through the corridor. He didn't look back, trusting that Armand and Kyla would be right behind him. Instead he walked with his head held high, surveying the crowd inside that was growing larger by the minute. He had expected to be asked to surrender their weapons when they entered the corridor, but nobody tried to disarm them. Once inside the inner gate Fleet stopped and waited for Armand and Kyla. Then with the tall man leading, they followed in single file through the crowd. They were not visibly unfriendly. Perhaps wary curiosity would have been a better word to describe the mood of the people surrounding them.

They were led down a wide concrete walkway to a brick archway that had once been the entrance to the zoo. The outline of the letters that spelled out the name of the zoo was still visible, but the letters themselves were gone. In their place were three identical symbols painted on the bricks. It was all Fleet could do not to stop and stare when he saw the two crescents; a smaller one nestled inside the larger with an oval shape in the center. They were identical to the broach that Kyla was wearing. As they continued walking along the path, past one building after another, Fleet saw that the symbol was painted everywhere. Now, he understood the meaning of Shawnee's remark that Kyla would be admitted. She must have seen the symbol when they were here. Fleet had no idea what it represented, other than an obvious connection between Sadie and this place. Had she only pretended to get the information from Orin? If she had planned any treachery, Fleet had walked willingly into her trap.

They had walked some distance into the zoo when their guide finally opened the door to one of the buildings and went inside. As Fleet and the others entered with their escorts, the crowd following them stayed outside. It was dark and cool inside. Clearly, this building had housed the Arctic exhibit. As they stood in the large open space at the center of the room, they were surrounded by water and ice. Their guide walked past the empty exhibits and brought them to the end of a long corridor. When he knocked on the door, he did not wait for a response, but opened it immediately and motioned for Fleet and the others to step inside.

Fleet had no idea what to expect when the entered the dimly lit room. There was only one light burning in the room, a small lamp setting on the large mahogany desk at the opposite side of the room. Sitting behind the lamp was a dark haired man who seemed intent on the contents of a letter that he was reading and totally unaware that anyone else was in the room.

"Lazarus," the tall man said stiffly. "They're here."

As he spoke the man looked up at the three visitors dressed in black, as if he had just noticed them standing at attention in front of him. Then rising slowly to his feet he said, "Leave me alone with them, but take their weapons before you go." Fleet had expected to be disarmed sooner, but he was still reluctant to relinquish his weapon. It was a certainty that he would never get it back. Without protest, Kyla and Armand did the same. They were too far inside to have any hope of forcing their way out.

Kyla watched Lazarus as he walked around the desk and stood before them with his arms crossed, studying them one by one. He was a tall man about the same height as Fleet. It was hard to judge his age. He looked young, but there was something about his eyes as he watched them and his mannerisms that made her think he was someone who had the self-assurance that comes with age. Finally Lazarus said, "You were at the bridge yesterday weren't you?"

"Yes," Fleet answered. They had done nothing wrong and he could see no reason to deny it. He was watching, too. Trying to judge what kind of man Lazarus was. He was dark haired and had a dusky complexion. There was something familiar about him although Fleet had never laid eyes on him before. He also wore a dark gray tunic like the two men who had just left. Except Lazarus had a small pin like the one Kyla was wearing fastened on the left breast of the uniform.

"You came with a scrawny fellow who calls himself Lipsky," Lazarus continued.

The little sneak was already here, Fleet was thinking, as he answered, "Lipsky is not my responsibility. He followed us here and left us last night." He looked at Lazarus and asked him a question, "How do you know Lipsky?"

393

"He shot and killed one of my guards at the bridge this morning." Lazarus' voice was hard and cold as he answered. His manner spoke more of irritation at the loss of the guard's services, than sorrow that the man had died.

Fleet felt the knot growing in his stomach. Given Lipsky's actions, they were lucky that the men had not shot them on sight. "Where is he now?" Fleet asked cautiously. He wanted to know, but at the same time wanted to distance them from any connection with Lipsky.

"We have him locked up in the gorilla cages. Can you tell me why I shouldn't put you all in there with him?" Lazarus walked back behind the desk and sat heavily in his chair. He watched them, waiting for someone to answer.

"We are not here to shoot your men in the back," Fleet answered. Although Lazarus had not detailed the incident, Lipsky wasn't one for a fair fight. "We wanted to open lines of trade and communication between your community and ours." If he was going to be an ambassador, Fleet decided to make an attempt at acting like one.

"A peaceful mission?" Lazarus spoke the words as if he was weighing them carefully. "Then why do you come to my front door carrying weapons?"

"Surely, you realize how dangerous it is to travel unarmed," Fleet answered easily. "We had problems with coyote packs on our way here."

Lazarus didn't answer and continued to watch them. Fleet could see him weighing his options. It was an uncomfortable feeling, having your life in the hands of a complete stranger. After what seemed like an eternity, Lazarus called, "Michael come in here please." The tall man entered immediately. He must have been waiting for the summons. "Take our guests to their rooms and see that they're settled in and have whatever they need." Michael stood motionless as if he was waiting for something more. Lazarus smiled and looked at Kyla as he said, "Take them to the rain forest. I think the lady would enjoy that." Then to Fleet he said, "You are welcome to look around. Perhaps your friend will be able to find someone he knows, but I doubt it very much." As Lazarus stood to accompany them to the door, he added, "When you leave your weapons will be returned to you."

After they left, Lazarus went back to his desk and picked up the letter, folded it and put it back in the envelope. He looked at the wax seal, now broken, before putting the letter in one of the drawers of the desk. Lipsky had been carrying a letter for him. If he hadn't shot the guard, it was likely that Lazarus would never have received it. It had come from Sadie and was meant to be a letter of introduction for Fleet. Lazarus didn't know why Sadie had sent him here, but now that Fleet was within the compound, Lazarus had no intention of letting him go. As long as he didn't cause any trouble, Fleet and his friends would be given freedom to go where they wanted, but at the first sign of mischief they would all be locked up with the other one. He had little patience for their kind.

Fleet, Kyla, and Armand followed the man named Michael as he led the way out of the dimly lit room, down the hallway, and into daylight again. Most of the crowd that had followed them had dispersed, but there were a few people left to watch where they were taken. Undoubtedly, visitors were few and far between and Fleet and the others were nothing more than a curiosity. As they walked Fleet kept his eyes open, he was already looking for a way out. Winding around the walkways and trails in the zoo, they passed many cages and pens that were empty, but many were not, one larger pen was filled with bison, another with antelope. At every corner they ran across noisy peacocks with their broods of chicks following behind the females while the males showed their colorful plumage at their intrusions. It was an unusual, but beautiful place and Fleet wondered how many people were living there.

Their escort had brought them from one side of the compound to the other before walking up to a large circular structure. As they stepped inside, the first thing that hit them was the steamy heat. Lazarus had not been joking when he said to take them to the rain forest. They walked through the lobby where a few people were gathered and then down a corridor with viewing areas that looked out on the large rain forest exhibit which filled the center of the large building. As they walked past each one they could see the colorful birds, which flew freely inside the huge, domed room and hear their chatter and calls. They stopped after passing two viewing areas. Standing in the third, they waited as Michael unlocked a door and held it open. He looked at Fleet and said, "This room is for you and the lady."

Kyla was about to protest, but with a look from Fleet she kept silent as he said, "Thank you, it will be fine."

Kyla and Fleet stood by the door and watched Michael as he went a few feet further down the corridor and unlocked another door. "This will be for you, sir," he said as he nodded to Armand. "I wish you luck in finding your friends." Then he turned to Fleet and said, "There is a toilet down the hall and you can wash in the sinks. If you need a shower there is a building near the river that was used by the employees of the zoo and there are showers there, but I would recommend that you use the facilities in this building." With those last instructions, Michael walked back down the hall, leaving them alone.

Fleet bent down to whisper in Kyla's ear. "Don't worry about the sleeping arrangements," he said softly, "I'm not planning on staying the night." Then to Armand he said, "We need to talk." All three of them went into the room that Michael had assigned to Fleet and Kyla.

The room was not large and simply furnished. There was one bed and a chair but no windows and no lock on the inside. "It looks like a cell," Armand said once they were inside and the door was closed.

The first thing Kyla did was take off the broach and throw it on the bed. She didn't know the meaning of the symbol, but whatever it was she wanted to distance herself from any connection to it. "Did you see their uniforms?" she said. It was a question that needed no answer. They had all noticed the similarities.

Armand sat in the chair. It was small and barely adequate for a man of his size. "What's going on, Fleet." There had been nothing said to indicate that Fleet knew any more than they did, but Armand had a feeling that he did.

Fleet sat heavily on the bed. "It's Sadie," he said the words wearily. "She sent us here to get us out of the way."

Armand was furious as the rose out of the chair to stand in front of Fleet. "If you knew that then you should have said something before now."

"I'm sorry Armand, but until now I didn't know," Fleet said. He knew that Armand had every right to be angry with him, but arguing amongst themselves would not help their situation. Fleet changed the subject. "Did you notice the letter that Lazarus had on his desk?"

"The one he was reading when we came in?" Armand asked. He had seen it but couldn't see any connection between the letter and their current situation.

Fleet reached into his pocket and pulled out the crumbled envelope with the wax seal that contained the letter from Sadie. As he threw it on the bed beside the discarded broach, he said, "Lipsky was carrying two letters, one for me and one for Lazarus. Didn't you find it strange that he never asked our names?" Fleet looked at his companions before answering his own question. "It was because he already knew who we were."

Armand picked up the crumbled envelope and looked at it. It did look like the one that Lazarus had. "I don't know, Fleet," he said cautiously. He had always trusted Sadie. She may have been a hard woman to get along with at times, but Armand had accepted that as a part of her personality. There had been nothing in his experience that would make him think that she was not trustworthy. As he tossed the letter back on the bed, he said, "I can't believe that you could think Sadie would do something like that. You couldn't have read what was written in Lazarus' letter not from where we were standing."

Fleet knew that Armand would require more proof. He pulled out the small slip of paper and handed it to Armand as he said, "I took this from Cole Spring's son." As Armand looked at the note, he continued his explanation, "North by Northwest road is the place where Eddie and Dylan were ambushed." He could tell by the expression on Armand's face that he was still unsure. Fleet handed the letter back to Armand and said, "The handwriting on the letter and the note are the same. You can look for yourself."

Fleet watched as the big man took the letter and the scrap of paper and sat down on the chair again. As he pulled the letter out of the envelope and compared the writing, he was silent. Armand looked at the two pieces of paper for some time before he folded the letter, put it back in the envelope, and handed them back to Fleet. He was certain that the handwriting was the same but he was not as certain as Fleet was that they had come from Sadie. "Lipsky could have written the letters. I wouldn't put it past him." Armand offered a possible explanation.

"I had thought of that, too," Fleet said. "But that doesn't explain the uniforms." He pulled at the fabric of his tunic as he said, "These are Sadie's design. She had them made for us." Armand looked at Fleet as he continued, "And what about the broach?" Fleet rose from the bed and began pacing the small room. "Until we walked into the compound and I saw the uniforms and the symbol painted on every wall, I still had some reservations about my suspicions of Sadie." Fleet didn't finish the thought. There was no need. All three knew their situation.

"What are we going to do?" Kyla asked.

Fleet was still pacing. It helped him to keep moving while he thought. "Today we'll do what we came to do. It seems they plan to let us go where we want." He looked at Armand as he said, "Kyla will stay with me. I want you to look around and if you're lucky enough to find someone that you know maybe they'll know a way out. Kyla and I will be looking for the same thing. If Shawnee and Liam were able to get out of here then we can find a way, too." As Fleet thought about their host and hostess, he wished that they had been a little more forthcoming in their information about the compound, but given the fact that they were dressed like the men inside, Fleet couldn't blame them for keeping quiet. What surprised him now was that they had helped them in the first place.

They were ready to go out the door when they heard someone knock. Fleet opened the door. It was another man dressed in a gray tunic holding a flat box in his hand. "I'm supposed to tell you that the noon meal is being served below." He looked at Kyla and handed her the box. "This is for you, ma'am. It's from Lazarus." As Kyla opened the box and took out the black dress that was inside her eyes opened wide. It was an evening dress, with a halter type bodice and a plunging neckline. There was no back to the dress either. Actually, there was very little fabric above the waistline and what there was below the waist, was a thin clingy material. The messenger was speaking while Kyla looked at the dress, "Lazarus would like the gentlemen and you to join him for supper tonight."

"I can't wear this," Kyla said. She had not cared for the way Lazarus had looked at her during their brief meeting. He had stared at her in a manner that could only be described as a lecherous.

The messenger looked at her dispassionately as he said, "I would recommend that you do. Lazarus would be insulted otherwise." Then looking at all three he added, "And when Lazarus is happy, everybody is happy." His message and package delivered the man left, closing the door behind him.

Fleet took the dress from Kyla, holding it between two fingers like it was something distasteful and tossed it on the bed beside the broach. He didn't like the fact that Lazarus had sent it, but there was a part of him that wanted to see Kyla wearing the dress. He put the picture of Kyla in the skimpy dress out of his mind with some difficulty as he said, "Well, let's go eat and we'll start our explorations after that. Keep your eyes open Armand. I don't want to spend a minute more in this place than we have to."

Fleet led the way out of the room, with Kyla following close behind. Armand came last and closed the door. They walked only a short distance further down the corridor before they came to the stairway that led down to the ground floor. They stopped for a moment as they stepped out onto the wooden decking and looked around the huge open space. It was filled with tropical foliage and palm trees. Above their heads were light panels like those in the greenhouses at the farm, another coincidence or more evidence of Sadie's secret involvement with this place. As they descended the stairway, it was not difficult to find the place where lunch was being served. The smell of food cooking led them to the spot.

There were several people in line waiting for their meals. Fleet, Kyla, and Armand went to the end of the line to wait their turn. Everyone turned and looked at the newcomers, whispering and pointing. The first thing that Kyla noticed was the fact that eveningwear for the women seemed to be popular. There were no women dressed in jeans and flannel like they wore at the Settlement. Here everyone was dressed like they were on their way to a party.

Kyla was beginning to feel the effects of the sultry atmosphere. The perspiration began to bead on her face and she could feel it trickling down her body under the heavy winter uniform that she was wearing. She thought of the dress lying on the bed in the room above them. It would have been more comfortable to wear given the heat and humidity inside the building, but she would melt before putting it on.

There was roasted meat and a variety of fruits being served, bananas, oranges, apples, peaches, and grapes. All were fresh although they were not in season. As she looked around the room, Kyla could see a banana tree growing nearby with its fruits hanging from it. For a moment she thought about the orange juice that Asa had given her, wondering if this place could have been the source. As the thought of the farm crossed her mind, she was beginning to wonder if the conspiracy included Cole Spring, too. Orange juice was slim evidence just as the notes were, but putting all the little coincidences together the evidence was becoming overwhelming. Still, recognizing the fact that they were working together did not explain why.

They ate their meal sitting on the rocks under a waterfall. It was a beautiful setting and if the circumstances had been different it would have been enjoyable. No one spoke during the meal and when they were finished, Armand left. After a few moments, Kyla and Fleet followed him back up the stairway and out of the building. The temperature outside was pleasantly cool compared to the sweltering heat of the rain forest.

Fleet went back to the front gate with Kyla walking beside him. He was taking long strides in his hurry, which forced Kyla to nearly run to keep up with him. Once they were in sight of the double row of fencing, he began to follow it to the north. Kyla knew he was looking for a place where it ended or any weakness in its design that they could use. They followed it all the way to the river and could see that it was well maintained. Lounging on the rocks and under trees, the tigers watched them as they walked on the other side of the fence. Kyla felt like they were hoping that they would try to climb the fences.

The area along the river was not anymore promising. It was a sheer cliff that dropped vertically to the water below. It could be scaled, but there was nowhere to go once you reached the bottom except into the river. Without a boat, the river was not an option. They came to the fence again and followed it back to the front gate. It was the same on the south end as it was on the north, except for the high bluff that overlooked the compound on the other side of the fence. It may have been a way to get in, but it definitely wasn't a possibility for getting out. After completing their circuit around the fence, they began to wander along the numerous walkways that wound around the zoo. It was like a maze and they kept coming back to places that they had passed before.

Kyla didn't know how many miles they had walked, but she was glad when Fleet stopped and sat on a bench beside a large pond. They sat silently for a few minutes. Kyla could tell that Fleet was thinking about their situation and she was hoping that he had seen something because she hadn't. From what Kyla had observed, they had the area secured. There appeared to be no way in or out, except through the front gate.

Fleet looked at Kyla. She hadn't said a word during the entire time they had been walking. He could tell that she was worried, and expected him to come up with some solution to their dilemma. If there had been a way out, it had escaped his notice. "I'm sorry," he said. "I should have left you with Carleen. At least you'd be safe."

Kyla looked at Fleet and realized that he needed some encouragement as badly as she did. "Well, maybe Armand had better luck than we did. We should go to the rooms and see if he's back." She was trying to sound optimistic, but her attempt was weak at best.

"Let's sit here for a few minutes," Fleet answered. "I want to think for awhile." He knew she was trying to keep a positive attitude, but they had both seen that the fence was a formidable obstacle even without the tigers. After sitting in silence for several minutes, Fleet stood. "Let's get back to the room," he said wearily. "I guess we have a dinner party to go to tonight." As they began walking in the direction of the building housing the rain forest, Fleet was wondering what Lazarus had in mind for tonight.

When they returned to the rooms, Fleet checked the one that Armand had been assigned. There was no sign of him there, so they went into their room. Someone had been there and left a stack of towels on the bed next to the dress. Kyla picked one up and said, "I guess I'll go and wash." Fleet picked up the other one and followed her as she walked down the corridor in the direction that Michael had said the toilets were located. They were public restrooms with signs on the doors, one marked 'Men' and the other 'Women.'

When she opened the door, Kyla was relieved to find that she had the whole place to herself. She stripped down to her undergarments and washed quickly. Once she was dressed again and stepped out of the door, she found Fleet waiting for her. It seemed that he wasn't going to let her out of his sight. "Armand is back," was all he said before starting back to the rooms. They met him on his way to the restrooms. Armand was carrying a towel. Someone had been in his room, too. Fleet stopped him and said, "You can do that after we talk." Somewhat reluctantly, Armand reversed his course and followed them back to their room.

"Did you find out anything?" Fleet asked.

"Not much, I found a friend of a friend, and talked to her for awhile. But she didn't have much to say that we could find useful," Armand said. "They all love it here and can't understand anyone wanting to leave." He looked at Kyla and Fleet and asked, "What about you?"

"Nothing," Fleet answered. The frustration that he was feeling was evident in his voice.

Armand went to the door, but before he opened it to leave, he asked, "What are we going to do?"

"We're going to have dinner with Lazarus, and once that's over we go to the front gate and demand to leave," Fleet answered.

"Do you really think that they'll let us go?" Armand asked.

"No, but it never hurts to ask," Fleet answered. Armand was shaking his head as he went out the door.

Once Armand was gone Fleet turned to Kyla and said, "I'm going for a walk in the rain forest. Do you want to join me?" There was nothing else to do other than wait in the room so Kyla followed Fleet as he left. When they came to the observation platform with the steps leading down to the floor, Fleet stopped for a moment looking at the people roaming the paths below.

"It really is a beautiful place," Kyla said as she stood beside him.

"No matter how pleasant they make it, it's still a prison," Fleet answered sourly and began to descend the steps. When they reached the bottom Fleet waited for Kyla and they began to stroll through the gardens like they were taking a casual walk in the park. All the while, Fleet was listening to the people around them. Hoping to glean some information from their conversations, but they only talked about parties that they had gone to in the past and the one that was planned for tomorrow night.

They hadn't walked very far, when to her shock and surprise, Kyla saw a familiar face. She tried to pull Fleet in the other direction before the man saw her, but before they disappeared into one of the small hidden grottos that were everywhere, the man had spotted her. Kyla saw a look of recognition on his face as he smiled at her. "What is it?" Fleet asked, rather annoyed at being pulled off the path that he was following.

"I saw someone that I've seen before," Kyla said breathlessly. Getting Fleet to follow her had not been easy. She had expended no small amount of energy changing his course.

Fleet was surprised by the news and asked anxiously, "Who was it?"

Kyla tried to peek past one of the large tropical plants at the man and saw that he was watching them, too. She moved back out of sight as she said, "That man with the long black hair, he looks a little different without his hat, but I'd know him anywhere. He was the pearl trader that came to the Settlement while you were gone. He called himself Slick."

It didn't surprise Fleet that a pearl trader would have access to this place. It seemed a prime spot for him to do business. From what he had seen so far, the people here had no concerns other than having a good time. When he stepped back into the walkway to take a look, Fleet couldn't see anyone fitting Kyla's description. "I don't see him," he said as he looked at Kyla.

When Kyla looked again there was no sign of Slick. "He was there," she said defensively.

"Don't worry," Fleet said. He was a little amused by her dismay at the fact that Fleet hadn't seen him, too. "I believe you." He looked up at the ceiling. It seemed that the light from the panels was beginning to dim a little as they mimicked nightfall. He smiled as he looked at Kyla and said, "It must be getting close to time for supper. I guess you'd better get ready."

She looked at him with her eyes opened wide. "You don't expect me to wear that dress? Do you?" She couldn't believe that Fleet had mentioned it and the way he was smiling only added to her embarrassment.

Fleet looked at her and said, "I won't force you, but I think it would be a good idea to go along with whatever Lazarus has planned." He looked at Kyla and before she could object, he added, "Up to a point, that is. Don't worry. I won't let you out of my sight."

When they arrived back at their room, Armand was waiting for them with Michael. There was relief in Armand's expression when he saw them returning. "Lazarus is waiting for you now," Michael said. Then looking at Kyla who was still dressed in her black tunic, he added, "You were supposed to be ready."

With a look to Fleet, Kyla left the men standing outside while she went into the room to change her clothes. Under different circumstances, she would have loved to wear the dress, but not when she was being forced to do so and not for Lazarus. She had to take off everything, including her undergarments for the dress to fit properly. As she slipped it on and tied the laces behind her neck, Kyla still felt naked. The thin fabric clung to her skin and left nothing to the imagination. Once she was dressed, Kyla stood motionless in the center of the room. She could not make herself open the door to step outside.

Fleet and Armand waited patiently with their escort. It seemed to be taking Kyla a long time to change her clothing. With every minute that passed, Michael was growing visibly impatient. Finally, Fleet said, "I'll see what's taking so long." He went to the door and tapped softly. There was no answer from Kyla so he cautiously opened the door and peeked inside. When he saw that she was wearing the dress, he went in and closed the door. "What is it?" he whispered softly. He knew she was embarrassed and tried not to stare, but Fleet was finding it difficult not to look at her. Lazarus had excellent taste in women's clothing. There was no denying the fact that the dress accentuated Kyla's slender build as it clung to the curve of her breasts and hips.

Kyla was standing with the broach in her hand looking at Fleet like she was wondering where to pin it. Fleet took it from her hand and tossed it back on the bed. "Don't worry about that," he said. He would have added that there wasn't enough fabric in the dress to hold it, but he hadn't wanted to add to her distress. He smiled and with all the chivalry he could manage, Fleet held out his arm. Kyla didn't respond.

So he took her hand, with a reassuring pat, placed it on his arm, and said, "May I escort you to dinner?" As she finally came to life and moved toward the door with Fleet guiding her, he was thinking that people would be staring, but not at him. Kyla was stunning in the dress, and he knew every man that saw her would envy him tonight.

As they stepped out into the corridor, for a moment Armand looked startled as he saw Kyla, but quickly recovered his composure. Michael on the other hand eyed her openly and smiled. Kyla answered him with a cold glare. If she had to wear the dress, she wasn't going give the impression that she was enjoying it, too. There was no doubt that Lazarus intentions were to put her on public display. It was like the people living here were part of his own private zoo and for his viewing enjoyment just like the other animals.

As they strolled at a leisurely pace, people were staring. Kyla kept her head high and her eyes focused on the path before them refusing to acknowledge them. Michael brought them back to the Arctic exhibit where they had meet with Lazarus earlier. Only this time they went down to the lower level and through a long glass corridor. Overhead was the water of the exhibits above. This must have been a place to view the animals swimming in the water. Now it was empty and the place seemed cold and lifeless. At the end of the glass corridor, Michael opened a door to their right. Inside they could see a long dining table with Lazarus seated at the far end waiting for them. He rose when they entered and came to greet them.

Smiling broadly, he pried Kyla's hand loose from her grasp on Fleet's arm. Then taking her by the hand, Lazarus said, "I'm glad that you could come. I hope you enjoyed my gift." He did not take his eyes from Kyla as he led her to the other end of the table, but he was not looking at her face. Fleet and Armand followed close behind. So far, Lazarus had not acknowledged the fact that they were there, too. As he pulled out a chair for Kyla next to his seat, Lazarus asked, "I hope your accommodations are acceptable?" He was still speaking to Kyla and no one else.

"Yes, thank you," she finally answered; nervously looking toward Fleet and Armand to make sure they were still nearby. "We are all quite comfortable," Kyla added, stressing the word 'all'.

It was almost as if Lazarus needed to be reminded. "Yes, the gentlemen," he said absently as he looked at Fleet and smiled. Then turning to Armand, he asked, "Did you find your friends?"

"No, sir, I did not," Armand answered formally. Lazarus asked all the right questions and was very polite, but there was no genuine concern in anything he said.

As he returned to his seat Lazarus, said lightly, "Well, I'm not surprised." Then almost as an afterthought he looked at the two men standing behind Kyla and said, "Please be seated. I'll ring for the help." He picked up a small silver bell and it tinkled melodiously as he shook it. Fleet took the seat next to Kyla and Armand went to the other side of the table to sit across from them.

Before he was seated, the 'help' arrived. No dowdy maid or butler for Lazarus, two young women dressed in short, flowing dresses entered the room. Their apparel reminded Kyla of togas, as the dresses were draped over one shoulder leaving the other bare. Like bookends one girl stood on each side of Lazarus' chair and as they did Lazarus reached out and began to fondle their buttocks, one in each hand. It was obviously a show meant for their benefit and it was not making Kyla feel any more at ease. Lazarus was enjoying himself immensely and at her expense. Finally, he said, "This is Monica and Michelle."

As Fleet watched Lazarus and the women, he noticed how they stood impassively. He thought they both looked like they had been drugged, and wondered how many pearls it had taken to achieve this result. With every minute they spent in Lazarus' company, Fleet's desire to leave was growing stronger. He wanted to stop the display. "Is supper ready? I'm starved," Fleet said with all the enthusiasm that he could muster.

With a smile at Fleet, Lazarus released the women and said, "We're ready to eat now." They disappeared through the door at the end of the room where they had entered and within a few minutes returned with the first course.

The entire meal was a gourmet treat. Everything was delicious and expertly prepared. They had started with the soup, a clear broth seasoned lightly with chives, followed by a salad, the main course of bison and rice, then crepes for dessert and brandy after that. It had all been very formal and civilized and was without a doubt the most tedious affair that Fleet had ever been forced to sit through. Lazarus spent the entire evening talking about trivial matters. He seemed to be an expert at speaking while saying nothing. The whole time he had stared at Kyla and when he wasn't staring at her he was fondling Monica and Michelle as the served each course and again as they cleared the dishes. Lazarus acted like a lecherous old man. Fleet only drank one glass of brandy, but Lazarus had continually poured more into Kyla's glass with each sip she took. He refused to leave her alone and kept urging her to drink more by bringing out first one brandy after another and insisting that she try each one.

Before very long it was apparent that Kyla was intoxicated, although she was trying not to show it. Fleet had finally had enough of Lazarus' generosity and he stood suddenly saying, "We've had a long day. If you will excuse us, my friends and I would like to return to our rooms."

Lazarus seemed amused by Fleet's sudden decision to leave and he rose and offered his hand to Kyla. Before she could respond, Fleet pulled her chair back from the table and put his hand under her arm, helping her to her feet. He was on his way to the door with her firmly in hand as he said, "Thank you again for the meal." It was all he could do to keep the sarcasm from coming out in his words. There had been nothing pleasant about the evening.

Armand got up to follow them, but Fleet saw Lazarus catch him by the arm and the two men exchanged a few words before Armand joined them. With Fleet holding one of Kyla's arms and Armand the other, they retraced their steps through the glass corridor, up the steps and out the door supporting Kyla every step of the way. Once they were outside, Fleet looked at Armand and asked, "What did he want?"

Armand looked down at Kyla, who was trying to stand steady and said, "He asked about your relationship with Kyla."

"What did you tell him?" Fleet whispered softly. He was sure Kyla was too drunk to be listening.

"I told him that she's your lover," Armand said. He shrugged and said, "I thought it would be better if he thought she wasn't available." Then he looked at Fleet and smiled, "He also asked if I wanted Monica or Michelle to come to my room tonight." Fleet looked at Armand with a question on his lips, but Armand provided the answer, "I said, no. I don't have to get a woman stoned out of her mind if I want one." With Kyla in tow the two men began walking toward the front gate. Fleet didn't care if they had to carry her all the way to the river. The sooner they left the better.

They had no luck at the gate, which wasn't a surprise. When they asked for the gate to be unlocked, the guard refused, saying that no one could leave without Lazarus' permission. They had no choice, but to return with Kyla to their quarters. As Armand left Fleet at the door with Kyla, he smiled and said, "Good luck." Then walked the short distance to his room. When he opened the door and started to go in, he added, "Call if you need me." Fleet could hear him chuckling softly as he went inside and shut the door.

Supporting Kyla with one hand, Fleet opened the door with the other. He guided her inside and set her down on the bed. As he looked at her sitting obediently where he had put her, he decided that she would have to sleep in the dress. She was in no condition to undress herself and he wasn't going to try. He did kneel down to remove her boots. He smiled as he pulled off her boots and the knives dropped out. Evening dress and all, Kyla was still wearing the boots that Sister Eaglet had given her and had her knives.

When Fleet took off her boots, Kyla laughed and lay back on the bed. She had heard every word that Fleet and Armand had said. "What's so funny?" Fleet asked as he loosened the lacing of his tunic and took it off. It was too hot to wear it any longer.

Kyla sat up on the bed and for some reason the sight of him without his shirt was amusing. She giggled uncontrollably as she said, "Armand told Lazarus that I'm your lover. What do you think Sadie would say about that?" and fell back onto the bed holding her sides while she shook with laughter.

"You're drunk," was the only answer that Fleet had, given her present behavior. He reached across her and took one of the pillows off the bed. "I'll sleep on the floor," Fleet said as he threw it down beside the bed and turned off the light. Kyla continued giggling for some time, but it wasn't long before the laughter turned to moaning and she ran out the door. Fleet thought about following her, but she had left the door open and it wasn't far to the restrooms. It didn't take long for Kyla to leave the four-course meal and all the brandy in one of the toilets and

Fleet heard her unsteady steps as she walked back to their room. She closed the door quietly and collapsed on the bed and that was the last Fleet heard out of her that night.

As he lay on the floor beside the bed, Fleet was thinking about Kyla. He hoped he had not stared as blatantly as Lazarus, but he had not been able to keep his eyes off Kyla. Fleet was not made of stone and the sight of her in the revealing dress had definitely stirred his desires. Now that she was so close, he was finding it hard to sleep. There was only one thing keeping him from her right now. Like Armand, he preferred that the woman be in control of all her faculties. If he made love to Kyla, Fleet wanted to make sure that she would remember it.

Chapter Sixteen

When Kyla woke the next morning her head was pounding, and she was still wearing the evening gown. She remembered everything from the night before, including the part where she was lying on the bed laughing at Fleet. As she dangled her feet over the side of the bed, she almost kicked Fleet, who was sleeping soundly on the floor. Very quietly, Kyla tiptoed around him and picked up her underclothes and her trousers then taking one of the towels went out the door and walked down the dark corridor to the restrooms. She felt a little better after washing and walked back to the room where Fleet was still sleeping. Kyla didn't feel like sitting in the dark room waiting for him to wake up, so she decided to go for a walk in the gardens below. There was not a soul to be seen or heard as she stepped out onto the observation deck and looked at the rain forest.

It was quiet and pleasant. Kyla was enjoying a few moments of solitude and wandered around the paths until she came to the waterfall. She was sitting on the rocks and playing absently in the water when she heard a voice from behind saying, "I wouldn't do that if I were you. There might be piranha in there."

Kyla jerked her hand out of the water as if she had been bitten and jumped to her feet. When she whirled around to see who was behind her, she had one of the small knives from her boot in her hand. "Slick," she said.

He was laughing as she watched him warily. "Around here they call me Raphael, but I'll let you call me Slick." As he took a step closer, Kyla stepped back still holding her knife. "I remember you now," he said. "You're that girl from the shelter house who likes to play with knives. You look different with hair." He was grinning from ear to ear now as he advanced while Kyla continued her retreat until she was standing with her back against the stone wall that formed the base of the waterfall. Raphael moved quickly as he pinned her against the wall with one hand and took the knife with the other. He tossed that knife aside and said, "I remember that you had two of these," and he pulled the other one from her boot. He was leaning against her now and searching her pockets. When he found the handcuffs, he held them up and twirled them on his finger. "You and your pretty boyfriend like to

411

play games?" he asked as the handcuffs disappeared into one of his pockets. "Well, I like to play games, too. Maybe, you'd like to join me sometime." Raphael found the key in her other pocket and that disappeared, too.

Kyla thought about screaming for help, but by the time Fleet and Armand could get to her, Raphael could slit her throat and be gone without a trace. "We aren't staying long," she answered and tried to move away.

Raphael found that extremely amusing as he laughed and stepped back for a moment. He was still leaning against the wall with one hand beside Kyla's head and in the other he held her knife. As he twirled it between his fingers, he said, "If you're going to carry one of these things you need to be ready to use it. I could have killed you if I wanted to." As if emphasizing the point he was trying to make, he began to run the razor sharp blade across her shoulder and down her chest until he reached the top of the thin undershirt that she was wearing. He looked at her with amusement and said, "I'm sorry. You're bleeding." With a sly grin he reached out and wiped the small trickle of blood from her breast with his finger, then touched it to his tongue. His next expression was surprise as he felt Armand's huge hand on his shoulder.

Spinning Raphael around to face him, Armand took the knife from his hand in much the same way that Raphael had disarmed Kyla. He held the point of the knife to Raphael's throat and with his other hand, grasped him tightly on the shoulder almost lifting him off his feet, as he asked, "What is this all about, Slick?" Armand's voice was hard as he held back the urge to use the knife on the smug little man.

"I was just talking to the lady," Raphael answered, trying to sound suave and collected, but panic filled his voice.

"I don't think she's interested in anything that you have to say," Armand said as he threw him to the ground. Kyla had already picked up her other knife and she hurried past Raphael. He could keep the handcuffs. There was no way that she would spend another second talking to him. "Come on," Armand said gruffly as he took Kyla by the arm and escorted her back up the steps and to her room. He didn't say a word until he left her at the door to the room she was sharing with Fleet. "Don't go anywhere unless, Fleet or I go with you. Do you understand?"

Kyla nodded and slipped through the door. Fleet was awake when she went inside. "Where have you been?" he snapped as soon as she came in. When he had awakened and found Kyla gone, Fleet had panicked. He had been on his way out the door to look for her.

"I was with Armand," Kyla stammered. She had not expected this reaction from Fleet. Kyla was used to coming and going without checking with anybody.

"You're bleeding," Fleet said as he saw the trickle of blood running down her chest. "What happened?"

Kyla was embarrassed by her run in with Raphael and she didn't want to tell Fleet. She already felt ashamed that Armand had to come to her rescue. She quickly pulled her tunic over her head as she said, "It's just a scratch."

Fleet knew that she was lying. Armand would tell him what was going on and he stormed out of the room leaving Kyla behind. As an afterthought, he poked his head back inside and said, "Don't leave." It only took a few seconds to go to Armand's room and get the rest of the story. Fleet was furious when he returned. He came in the door and slammed it shut behind him. "Don't ever lie to me again," he shouted angrily. The thought of another man touching Kyla had affected him more than he ever imagined.

Kyla had never seen Fleet so enraged. His face was red as he continued. "How are we supposed to keep you safe if you go running off every chance you get?" The thoughts running through Fleet's mind were worse than anything that had happened. All he could think about was what Slick might have done if Armand had not followed Kyla down to the waterfall.

"I'm sorry Fleet," Kyla answered. "I didn't want you to worry about me. I can take care of myself."

"Well, you obviously need some help in that department," Fleet answered sharply. He picked up his towel and said, "I'm going to wash up now, if you think you can stay out of trouble that long."

Kyla didn't care for his tone and she sat in the chair and crossed her arms. "Don't waste your time worrying about me. I'll be fine." She turned her head and would not look at Fleet. Kyla couldn't stand to have him angry with her. His only response was to slam the door on his way out. A few moments later, Kyla heard someone knocking softly on

413

the door. She hurried to answer, hoping that it was Fleet coming back to apologize for his behavior. She was disappointed to see that it was Michael and he was carrying another box like the one delivered the day before. Kyla looked at the box and said, "Lazarus?" Michael nodded and bowed slightly as she took the box and slammed the door in his face. She was not in the mood for gifts from Lazarus today and she tossed the unopened box on the bed and went back to sit in the chair. Kyla waited for Fleet to return, arms crossed and glaring at the door.

Fleet came back with his hair dripping wet and the towel wrapped around his shoulders. It was hard for Kyla to stay angry with Fleet. As soon as she saw him her resolve started to melt. When Fleet saw the unopened box on the bed, he took off the lid and looked inside. Today Lazarus had sent Kyla a white silk camisole with tiny pearl buttons and embroidery down the front and light blue silk slacks to go with it. Not quite as revealing as his previous gift, but his insistence that Kyla wear the skimpy outfits was not making his job any easier. He'd had time to cool off and was sorry that he had shouted at Kyla. It was not her fault that the man in charge of this place treated women as possessions to be traded like chattel and apparently encouraged the same behavior in the others.

He continued to dry his hair and looked at Kyla sitting in the corner. "Are you going to wear it?" he asked. The icy glare that he received from Kyla was all the answer that he needed. "Do what you want," he said and pulled his tunic on over his head. Fleet was wishing that he had somebody bringing him a fresh change of clothing everyday. He would have liked something clean to wear after bathing. Now that they were both fully dressed, Fleet opened the door and said, "Let's go to breakfast." Kyla swept past him and walked toward the stairway. Fleet hurried after her this time, taking only a second to knock on Armand's door to let him know that they were going. She was halfway down the steps before he caught up with her.

This morning the meal was fruit again and eggs. The eggs were unusually small and when Fleet commented on the size, the person serving them had informed him that they were peacock eggs. Fleet had only shrugged and held out his plate. Eggs were eggs. It didn't matter much to him where they came from. They ate in silence. Kyla was still trying to stay angry with Fleet and Fleet was busy pretending not to care. Armand was watching them both and wondering if they had any idea how childishly they were acting. When they finished breakfast and Kyla announced that she would be going with Armand today, Armand thought Fleet was going to object. Instead, he had risen and walked away without a word to either of them.

The morning had gotten off to a bad start, but it had only served to deepen Fleet's resolve to get out of this place. The sooner he found a way, the better. He spent the day observing the activities in the compound. He watched for the men in gray tunics and counted twelve. The same number as the Guard. Only here there were no women with uniforms, which probably added to the curiosity about Kyla. He was trying to keep his mind on the business of watching the guards and learning their routines, but his thoughts kept straying and he found himself thinking of Kyla at every turn. When he came to the bench where they had rested the day before, he sat down heavily. If Kurt were here, he would have had somebody to talk over his plans. The only problem was that Fleet had no plans.

One bright point in Fleet's day was when he located the armory. He watched from a good distance away as men entered the building unarmed and came back out with rifles. It was an important bit of information and Fleet would make use of it if he could. He also spent a portion of the day walking along the shoreline of the river. He paced back and forth watching the far shore, hoping for a glimpse of Liam or Carleen. All he saw was the river. He had been there for quite some time, when one of the men wearing a gray tunic came and told him that he had better move along. From there he went on to pacing the fences. He watched the tigers inside the fence and felt a certain understanding pass between himself and one of the larger males pacing on the other side. They were both trapped and looking for any opportunity for escape.

It was nearly dark when he returned to the rain forest exhibit. When he went into his room he found Kyla waiting for him and she was wearing the camisole and blue silk trousers. "I thought we could go to the party," she said when he closed the door. Fleet didn't answer. He wasn't in the mood for a party, but she continued anyway. "It's going to be downstairs. Armand and I spent the day talking to people.

They say there will be music and dancing. It sounds like it might be fun."

This was the last thing that Fleet wanted to hear right now. Kyla was carrying on like she was ready to join these people. "You go with Armand if you want to. I think I'll stay here." Fleet lay down on the bed and kicked his boots off as if emphasizing his point.

"I think we all need to go," she said emphatically. "From what we heard everybody will be there." She stressed the word everybody. "Even the guards join in. Sometimes they even leave their posts without permission." That got Fleet's attention. He sat up to see Kyla beaming at him. "I hope you've had a productive day, too."

Fleet looked at Kyla. She seemed very pleased with her information. It was a slim hope at best, but it was all they had. Even with the guards away from their patrols, that would not get them over the fence or past the tigers. Still, he would see what happened. Any opportunity was worth consideration. He didn't want to appear too anxious, he lay back on the bed again, and put his hands behind his head, "It might be fun."

Jumping up from the chair, Kyla went to Fleet and began tugging on his hand like a child trying to pull an adult somewhere that he really didn't want to go. "Come on," she said. "The music has started." She really did want to go, and she wanted to go with Fleet not Armand. Tonight she was wearing the camisole and blue silk trousers because she wanted to look nice for Fleet, not because Lazarus was insisting. Her anger with Fleet had been because she was embarrassed that he had been right. She shouldn't have left without him. Tonight she wanted to see him enjoying himself.

Fleet sat up, pulled on his boots, and tried to keep from laughing at Kyla's childlike insistence that he go now. He enjoyed her company and her trusting nature. As long as Lazarus stayed away, Fleet thought he might be able to enjoy an evening of merrymaking. It had been a very long time since he had been at a party with music and he was having a hard time trying to make Kyla think that he was reluctant. Right now he was enjoying her efforts to get him to go. She was pulling him by his hand out the door, but as soon as they were in the corridor, Fleet offered his arm to Kyla as he had done the night before. Tonight she took hold without any prompting and he began to escort her down the hall. He almost stopped to knock on Armand's door, but didn't. For just a few minutes, he wanted Kyla to himself.

They didn't have to wait on Armand. He was already there and waiting for them. Fleet waved from across the room when he saw him, but didn't go to sit with him. He could see that Armand was busy talking to one of the young women that had been hanging around him since they first arrived. Fleet was not worried about Armand. He could take care of himself. He found a seat for Kyla and himself on a bench near the musicians. There was plenty of food, liquor, and Fleet lost count of the times that somebody came to offer them some pearls. They politely refused each time. They wanted to make sure that they would be ready to go if some opportunity presented itself.

Fleet was watching the crowd. All twelve of the men in gray tunics were there circulating through the crowd. If he had to choose which one was the senior member of their group it would have been Michael. He seemed to be directing their activities. Anytime the revelers got out of hand, with a word from Michael the men in gray tunics would quietly escort them from the party. It was similar to what they did at the shelter house. Later in the evening, Fleet noticed that some of the guards started to wander in. They wore light gray trousers and coats like the young men they had seen at the bridge.

Fleet had sat with Kyla the whole evening, but had never danced with her once. When they started what appeared to be a rather spirited folk dance for the third time, he asked her if she wanted to join them. Kyla jumped at the chance to do something. She had been enjoying the party, but wanted to participate instead of sitting and watching, which was all Fleet wanted to do. As they went to join the two circles of dancers, Kyla caught sight of Raphael standing with the others and waiting for the music to begin. He smiled and touched his finger to his tongue like he had done that morning when he tasted her blood. He was a handsome man with long black hair and a dark golden brown skin. Kyla was sure that many women found him attractive, but he made the skin on the back of her neck crawl when he looked at her.

Kyla took a place in the inside circle that was formed by the women while the men formed the outer circle. It was an easy dance and took no skill whatsoever. All the participants in each circle would link their arms together and when the music started the women moved counterclockwise while the men moved clockwise, each circle picking up speed as the music increased in intensity and tempo. The two circles would spin one inside the other until somebody either fell or let go causing both circles to break up and the participants to fall on the floor. As they started Kyla tried to keep her eye on Fleet but as they went faster it was impossible to do anything other than maintain your footing. They had only gone around a few times when one of the ladies who'd had too much to drink fell and brought the circles down. Kyla felt herself flying backward and was caught by one of the men in the circle behind her. She was laughing until she realized that it was Raphael who had his arms wrapped tightly around her.

When Fleet got to his feet and saw Slick with Kyla locked in his grasp, he moved quickly, stepping across the people still lying on the floor. "Let her go," Fleet demanded.

Raphael was still laughing, "The rules of the game are that you keep who you catch."

"Those are your rules, not mine," Fleet said as he took Kyla by the hand.

Raphael released her and as Fleet led her away, she could hear him shouting over the noise, "If you change your mind you know where to find me."

Fleet didn't stop until he had pulled Kyla up the steps and out the door into the darkness and quiet outside. He was glad to get away from the noise and the people. Leave it to them to take what looked like an innocent game and make it into something vulgar. "I'm sorry," he said, "I just had to get out of there." He felt that he owed Kyla some explanation for their hasty exit. "Let's walk along the fence for awhile," Fleet suggested. He didn't have much hope that they would find a way out, but he had to do something. He had to keep looking.

It was cool outside and Fleet was more comfortable. It was too hot in the rainforest exhibit. They walked to the place on the south side of the compound where the bluff rose high above them. It was then that Fleet finally noticed Kyla was rubbing her bare arms trying to keep warm. He stopped and she stood next to him. Fleet had no coat to offer her, so he did the next best thing. "You must be freezing," he said as he pulled Kyla close and wrapped his arms around her bare arms and shoulders. She was standing with her back to him and as she rested her head against his chest, he could feel her shivering. "We'll go back now," he started to move, but Kyla turned to face him. As she looked up into his eyes, Fleet began to bend to kiss her. As his lips touched hers, Fleet thought he heard a bird whistling in the trees behind them. With an effort his mind focused on the sound and he stood back, releasing Kyla from his grasp. No bird would be whistling in the middle of the night.

Kyla heard it, too. It was Carleen. Half of her was thrilled to hear her, but the other half was ready to throttle her for her bad timing. They went as close to the fence as they dared. In a loud whisper, Kyla hissed, "Carleen is that you?"

"No, it's a mocking bird," she answered.

It was Liam's voice that they heard next. "I've got a rope. If you can climb over the first fence, we'll pull you up."

"We can't do that," Fleet answered. "Besides, I can't leave Armand." Fleet knew they didn't have much time so he was brief, "Bring your boat and we'll meet you at the river at the same time tomorrow night. It's the only way. Can you do it?"

"We'll do our best," Liam answered. Then there was silence.

Fleet and Kyla didn't move but stared up at the dark bluff above them. Finally, Fleet said, "We'd better get back." The moment between Kyla and himself was gone, and Fleet was not certain what he should do. Right now he wanted Kyla.

When they returned to their room, Fleet deposited Kyla in their room and went to find Armand. Kyla's mind was swimming with emotions. For a few wonderful moments, Fleet had held her in his arms and kissed her. She was on top of the world and she wanted more, but when Fleet didn't return right away Kyla lay down in the bed and tried to go to sleep. It was a long time before he returned and when he did Fleet lay on the floor beside the bed without a word. As he did, Kyla sighed softly and turned her back to him. She couldn't understand Fleet. Kyla had never known a man who could run hot and change to cold so quickly.

Fleet had found Armand and was able to fill him in on their plans in a matter of minutes. He had spent the rest of the time pacing the corridor hoping that Kyla would be asleep when he returned. Fleet knew that if she had been waiting for him when he went back to the room that he couldn't have stopped himself from taking her in his arms and making love to her. He was still thinking about that brief moment when his lips had touched hers. He had thought of nothing else as he was walking the hallway, but he had decided that he had to be free of Sadie before he could feel comfortable with another woman. Thankfully, he would not be sharing a room with Kyla another night. Fleet wasn't sure if he continue to do the honorable thing when the object of his temptation was so close at hand.

The next morning when Kyla awakened Fleet was already gone. It was becoming painfully obvious that Fleet was trying to avoid her since kissing her. She dressed quickly and when she opened the door to her room found Armand waiting for her outside. Although she tried not to show it, her disappointment that it was Armand and not Fleet waiting for her was obvious.

Armand was not blind. He knew that he was not the person that Kyla wanted to see, but Fleet had come to his room early that morning and told him to keep an eye on her today. "Good morning," Armand said warmly. "Fleet had some things he wanted to do today. I guess it's you and me together again." He was trying to sound light hearted, but he was tired of being caught in the middle of whatever it was that was going on between Fleet and Kyla. The attraction between the two was no secret to him or anyone who saw them together. Armand found himself wishing that they would admit it to themselves and just get it over with. He was tired of Kyla's dejected moods and Fleet's avoidance of the situation.

As they walked down the stairs to eat breakfast with the others, Kyla was trying not to let Armand know that she was miserable, but she knew that she wasn't doing a very good job. Armand's jaw was set and his whole body spoke of the fact that he was uncomfortable. All the way down the steps, Kyla was looking for Fleet, hoping he would change his mind and at least eat breakfast with them, but there was no sign of him. Thankfully, there was no sign of Raphael either.

Armand was very attentive and polite. They spent the day talking to the people living in the compound just as they had done the day before. Most people had the same story. After the evacuations Lazarus and the men in gray tunics, whom they called the Defenders, had told them that they could live here and that food was plentiful. There was no doubt that they were all well fed, but anytime they brought up the subject of leaving they were answered with laughter. Nobody wanted to leave. Why would anyone want to give up paradise for a hard life of scrounging the countryside for food?

The time for lunch and then supper passed and there had been no sign of Fleet. Armand waited with Kyla in the room assigned to Fleet and herself. As the minutes and hours ticked by, Armand was becoming concerned that something had happened to Fleet. Who knew what he might have been doing? It was well after midnight when Fleet slipped in the door and said, "Are you ready?"

Kyla wanted to jump up and shout at him for keeping them waiting and worrying for hours. Instead, she nodded without saying a word.

Armand was on his feet in a heartbeat. "Let's get out of here," he said in response to Fleet's question.

"Kyla you come with me," Fleet said. Then to Armand, "You follow in a couple of minutes. We'll be waiting outside." Fleet checked the corridor to make sure that it was still deserted before stepping out the door. Kyla was right on his heels. Cautiously and quietly, they crept down the corridor. Security was non-existent inside the buildings, but they didn't want to run into anybody who might wonder why they were roaming the halls in the middle of the night. Once outside the main entrance, Fleet guided Kyla to some bushes and they hid behind them while they waited for Armand. Within minutes Armand came through the door and Fleet stood and motioned for him to join them. As soon as Armand was hidden with them, Fleet began to hand them both ropes to carry. Fleet had two burlap bags and a crowbar, too. He had spent the day scrounging for the supplies that they would need for their escape.

With Fleet in the lead they began to make their way from one patch of shrubbery to the next as the crept down the winding pathways of the zoo. They hid in silence, afraid to breathe, every time one of the guards passed by them. Finally, Fleet led them to one of the buildings and as they crept up to the door in the back, Armand whispered, "What are we doing here?"

Fleet stood and began to use the crowbar on the padlock on the door. "It's the armory. I want my gun," he answered.

Armand was not pleased. "We don't have time for this Fleet. Forget the guns, we have others."

"We need them to get home," Fleet answered. He was thinking about the packs of coyotes in addition to the two-legged packs that would be looking for them if they were successful. He was still pulling on the crowbar when Armand stood and took it from his hand. For a split second, Fleet wasn't sure what he was going to do, but with one quick motion Armand had broken the lock and pushed the door open. Once inside, Fleet took a flashlight out of one of the bags then handed the bag to Kyla. "Start filling that with ammunition," he ordered. Armand left the door open just a crack and stood by it watching for any sign that they had been discovered.

While Kyla began filling her bag, Fleet was searching for his gun. The weapons on the racks lining the walls were all identical to the ones that they carried and he could have taken any of them, but he wanted the one that Liam had converted to automatic. It didn't take him long to find three rifles standing against the wall in the corner and he picked them up, giving one each to Armand and Kyla. Fleet was ready to leave when he noticed a locked cabinet next to the door. Taking the crowbar from Armand, he used it on the metal cabinet and forced the door open. Smiling as he saw what was inside, Fleet deposited two items in the sack that he was carrying and said, "We've got a ride to catch."

The armory was in the middle of the compound. They still had a little way to go before reaching the river. The bag full of ammunition was too heavy for Kyla to carry and keep up with the men, so Armand took it from her. When they finally arrived at the river, Fleet left Armand and Kyla hiding in a grove of trees near the edge of the cliff as he crept forward cautiously. He was looking for the pontoon boat, but when he didn't see it he began to call softly, "Liam. Carleen."

It was a few moments before he heard Liam saying, "Hurry up, we're down here."

As Fleet motioned for Armand and Kyla, he asked, "Where's your boat."

"It's right here," Liam called softly. "I brought the rowboat; couldn't risk taking the other one under the bridge. They'd see it for sure."

Working quickly, Fleet tied one of the ropes to a tree near the edge of the bank. Kyla was right beside him as he wrapped the rope around his waist. "Have you ever gone rock climbing?" When she didn't answer he said, "It's easy, just let the rope out slowly and use your feet to keep yourself off the rocks. I'll go first, you watch." Then he scrambled over the edge and started to lower himself down.

As Kyla watched she could see it was anything but easy. She was terrified at the thought of falling onto the rocks or into the river raging below. Armand had the second rope tied and ready. "Just do your best," he said as he wrapped the rope around her and urged her toward the edge. He would have tried to lower her on the rope, but he was afraid that they were running out of time. After Armand had started Kyla on her way, he lowered the two burlap bags and the guns on the end of the second rope before untying it and throwing it down to Fleet who had already reached the bottom. Then he went back to check on Kyla.

Kyla had made it down the first few feet without much trouble, but when she got to the bottom of the rock ledge at the top of the bank suddenly there was nothing solid for her feet to rest on and she was hanging in mid-air. Armand was lying on his belly looking down at her, "Let the rope slip through your hands slowly and lower yourself down." Armand was hearing voices from the direction of the armory. They were still far away, but their break-in had been discovered and it wouldn't take long to find them. "Hurry, they're coming," he hissed urgently to Kyla dangling on the rope below him.

Kyla panicked and loosened her hold on the rope and she began to drop rapidly. She tried to grip it tighter, but the rope was burning her bare hands. Before she knew it, Kyla had lost her hold on the rope completely and was falling. She missed the rocks and the boat and fell into the water. The strong current caught her immediately and swept her downstream, away from the boat. Fleet saw Kyla falling and heard her splash into the water. He was still holding the rope in his hands and without giving it a moment's thought, pressed one end into Liam's hands and holding the other dove into the water after Kyla.

Fleet felt the water swirling around him and struggled against the strong undertow trying to sweep him away. He could hear Kyla thrashing in the water just out of his reach as he swam with the flow of the water trying to catch hold of her outstretched hand. It was only a matter of seconds, but to Fleet it seemed like an eternity before he felt his hand make contact with Kyla's and he latched on to her and held her wrist as tightly as possible. Fleet was being stretched in two directions. One hand was holding Kyla and the other the rope. It was all he could do to keep his head above water. He could feel Liam pulling on the rope, but he was only able to keep them from going further downstream. It wasn't until Armand reached the bottom and leant a hand that Fleet could feel that they were being pulled back against the current. Fleet felt Armand's strong hands pulling him out of the water and into the boat and Liam was doing the same with Kyla. Carleen was pushing the rowboat away from shore and once she was in the boat they let the current take them down the river.

Fleet was exhausted from battling the currents, but he pushed past Liam to get to Kyla who was in the bow of the rowboat. Without a word, he sat down next to her and wrapped his arms around her. As they huddled together, both of them soaking wet, Kyla laid her head on his shoulder. Fleet's heart was still pounding. He thought he had lost her. Behind them was the sound of voices shouting, but soon they were too far away to hear. The current was carrying them faster than any of them could row. Within seconds the boat was in sight of the bridge, all they could do was hope that no one would see them in the darkness.

Thankfully, no one patrolling the bridge looked down or they might have seen the little boat. Once they were out of sight of the bridge, Liam pulled out the oars and he and Armand began the task of bringing the boat to the eastern shore of the river. When they came to the shed that housed Liam's pontoon boat, Shawnee was waiting for them. Liam was the first one out of the boat. Shawnee didn't give him a chance to tie off the line for the rowboat before she embraced him and said, "Thank god, you're back." As they helped the others out of the rowboat, Shawnee ushered them all inside the boathouse. When she saw that Kyla and Fleet were soaking wet and shivering with cold, she said, "Carleen, go get their dry clothes out of the packs."

Carleen and Armand disappeared out the door and began rowing toward the levee where the horses were saddled and ready to go. As they waited for them to return Fleet looked at the pontoon boat that was loaded with Liam and Shawnee's possessions. "You're leaving?" Fleet asked.

"We were planning to go sooner or later," Liam said as he shrugged his shoulders. "After tonight we figured that sooner would be better. They've left us alone up to now, but I don't think they'll appreciate the fact that we helped you escape."

"I'm sorry," Fleet said. He hadn't meant to drive them from their home. It was quite a price to pay for helping them.

"Don't worry," Liam said with a rather grim smile, "I have a feeling that if the shoe had been on the other foot, you would have helped us."

In a few minutes Carleen and Armand returned with two bundles of dry clothing. There was no place or time for modesty and as Fleet and Kyla began stripping off their wet clothing, Shawnee and Carleen used their bodies as a screen for Kyla. When Kyla got the black tunic and trousers off and Carleen saw the white camisole and blue silk trousers that she was wearing underneath, she smiled as she whispered in Kyla's ear, "I'll bet there's a story behind that outfit." Why would Kyla have gone to such lengths to bring it with her? Carleen was curious, but there was no time for explanations. After Kyla peeled the clingy fabric off her body, Carleen rolled them inside the rest of her wet clothing.

Once they were dressed, Liam was urging them out the door. "We want to be underway before dawn," he said. They all piled back into the rowboat for one last trip and rode silently as Liam rowed them to the levee. When the reached the muddy bank, Fleet picked up the bag filled with the ammunition and was ready to toss it ashore when Kyla said, "Wait." Then she opened the bag and began to drop box after box of shotgun shells on the bottom of the boat. "I thought you might find a use for these," she said to Liam.

"Thank you," he said. Kyla couldn't see him clearly in the darkness, but she could tell by the sound of his voice that he was pleased.

Everyone was out of the boat except Fleet. When he turned and held out his hand, Liam returned his gesture by grasping Fleet's hand. "We can never repay you for what you've done for us today. I just want you to know that we had no idea," Fleet paused before finishing, "We are not like them."

"I figured that much," Liam said and released Fleet's hand. As he rowed away and disappeared into the darkness, Fleet heard him saying, "Whatever it was that you went for, I hope it was worth it."

Fleet was standing and staring into the darkness. What had he gotten for all his trouble? He had jeopardized himself and the safety of those with him, but he had gained in knowledge. Fleet still had many unanswered questions, but he knew more than he had when they left the Settlement six days ago. It was Carleen tugging on his shirtsleeve that brought him back to the present.

"Come on," she said urgently. "We have to go. The water's down on the east side of the levee and Liam showed me how to get to the road." He followed her to the horses and with Carleen leading the way they followed the levee for awhile before heading the horses down a muddy path that two days before had been under water. Once they reached the high ground where the freeway was, Fleet took the lead and they galloped with all the speed that the horses possessed away from the city and Lazarus. No one followed them. Fleet knew they wouldn't. Lazarus knew where they had come from and he would know where they were going. Fleet wanted to reach the Settlement before any messenger sent by Lazarus could arrive.

Chapter Seventeen

It had been two days of hard riding with Fleet pushing them and the horses every step of the way and it was well after nightfall on the second day when the party returned to the farm. There was only one light on in the cabin and that was in the library. At the sound of the horses galloping down the lane, someone turned on the bright spotlight that illuminated the whole farmyard and people started spilling out of the cabin to meet them. Kurt was the first and when he reached Fleet's horse, he was just in time to catch the reins as Fleet dismounted and strode quickly up the walkway then in the front door without a word to anyone. Kurt could tell by the mood of those who had returned that something was wrong. There was no joy in their homecoming and everyone slid wearily from their saddles, but no one made a move to go into the cabin. From where they were standing they could hear shouting from the library as Fleet found Sadie.

For two long days, Fleet had rehearsed exactly what he wanted to say to Sadie when he saw her, but he never got a chance. As soon as he stepped into the library, Sadie, who was standing at the door, slammed it shut behind him. "Where's Lipsky?" she said in an accusatory voice.

"Don't worry. I didn't hurt you spy," Fleet spat the words in her face. "He's securely locked up."

Fleet had been ready to mention Lazarus, but Sadie cut him off, "You left him?" She was nearly screaming when she said, "I can't believe that you came back here without him."

Fleet was furious. He couldn't believe that all she was concerned about was Lipsky. Sadie pushed past him and went out the door. "Riley," she was still shouting. Then opening the front door she shouted, "Riley, saddle two horses. We're leaving."

Fleet followed Sadie as she went into the kitchen and started throwing open cupboard doors and slamming bags filled with dried goods onto the table. The racket awakened Agatha who came running to the kitchen. She stared wide-eyed with terror at the sight of Sadie wrecking her kitchen. When Sadie caught sight of her standing in the doorway, she said, "Start packing supplies. Riley and I are leaving tonight."

Fleet caught hold of her arm and said, "You're crazy. That snake isn't worth the trouble."

Sadie looked at him and Fleet immediately released her arm from his grip. He had seen her angry before, but Sadie had gone beyond anger. If she had had a weapon in her hands, Fleet was certain that she would have used it on him. "I should have left you to die when I found you. It would have saved me so much trouble," she hissed. Fleet could feel the venom in her words. Then she disappeared out the door.

Fleet stood motionless in the kitchen while Agatha flew around him trying to get supplies together as Sadie had ordered. Fleet was stunned. He had expected his confrontation with Sadie to become ugly, but he hadn't even mentioned one of his suspicions. All this was over one worthless little man who had gotten what he deserved. When Riley came into the kitchen to get the supplies, Fleet went to her. Surely, she would be reasonable.

"Don't go with her," Fleet was pleading with her. "You have no idea where you're going. If you go your life will be in danger." Riley stared back at him, her eyes wide with fear. When she heard Sadie calling for her from the foyer, Riley picked up the bundles of food and went to the door. With one last look at Fleet, she went through the door. Fleet knew that right now she was more frightened of Sadie than any unknown danger that could be waiting for her.

Shaking himself into action, Fleet pushed open the door in time to see Sadie and Riley going out the front door. He was following them down the walkway calling after them, "I am telling you not to go. It isn't worth it."

Sadie spun around to face him. "You do not tell me when or where I may or may not go. You are nothing without me." Then she continued toward the end of the walk where Riley had two fresh horses saddled and ready to go.

Armand tried to talk to Riley. "You should wait until tempers cool," he said. "There is no reason for anyone to go anywhere tonight." Armand wasn't worried about Sadie. He didn't want Riley to go with her, but he knew he was talking to the wrong person. He had never seen Sadie loose control like she had tonight. Her temper had been so quick and volatile and given what he already knew, there was more going on than met the eye.

Sadie mounted one of the horses. Her dress was not made for riding, her long skirt was bunched up around her hips, and her legs were bared. As she pulled at the reins, she looked at Riley who scrambled up onto the other horse. Without speaking another word to those who were gathered Sadie began riding toward the end of the lane in the direction from which the others had just come. Before reaching the end of the lane one of the men from the Settlement flagged them down. Sadie paused for just a moment to speak to him before continuing on and disappearing into the darkness.

It was then that James came running from the direction of the trail that led to the Settlement. "What's going on? Where's Riley?" he was shouting as he saw the people gathered in front of the cabin. "Someone told me that she's leaving with Sadie."

"They just left," Kurt answered. He was still staring blankly down the dark lane.

"Why didn't you stop them?" James turned and shouted accusingly at Fleet.

"He tried to," Kyla answered. When James turned and glared at her she added, "Sadie wouldn't listen."

James was usually an even-tempered man but his temper was flaring as he turned to the men standing in the crowd and said, "Let's get these horses stabled." Then turning to Fleet he pointed at him and said, "You! Get inside. I want to know what's going on."

Fleet turned and stalked back to the cabin with James close behind. The crowd began to disperse as the men charged with caring for the horses led them to the stables and the remainder of the Guard members headed to the cabin. A few people remained standing at the end of the lane and before going inside Kurt turned and said, "There's nothing more for you to see here tonight." Then he turned off the yard light.

Fleet was exhausted physically, emotionally, and mentally as he led the way into the dining room and collapsed in his chair at the end of the table. James, Rod, and Kurt were the only members of the Guard present besides the ones who had just returned. Carleen came in, too. Although she was not a member of the Guard, she was one of the Citizen's Patrol and a member of the returning party. There was no way they would discuss what had happened without her being present.

429

As everyone seated themselves at the table, Agatha entered with hot tea and cups for everyone. No one moved as she set the cups around the table. Once she was gone everyone turned to Fleet. They depended on him for guidance and no one, James included, was ready to take his place. As he looked at the faces around the table, all of them watching him, hoping that he had the answers, Fleet weighed the options in his mind. How much could he say and to whom should he speak. He couldn't make a decision. All he wanted to do was crawl into his bed and sleep. Maybe he could sleep and tomorrow wake up to find that everything that was weighing down on him now, crushing him, would just turn out to be one long bad dream. He was so tired that everything around him had a certain surrealistic quality about it. Finally, he looked at James and said, "We tried to stop Riley from going with Sadie. It's not Sadie that I'm worried about its Riley."

Fleet's words were no comfort. "Where have they gone?" James asked. "I'll go and bring them both back."

Kyla looked at James and then to Fleet. She couldn't stand to see the men at odds with one another. "If anyone can get in and out of the compound at the zoo, it will be Sadie. If you go after her James, you'll be in danger, too."

Fleet looked at her angrily. Kyla had already said more than he wanted to reveal right now. Anything that was said about Sadie had to be handled delicately. Too many people owed their lives to her, and would not listen to anything negative, no matter how overwhelming the evidence was. "Kyla," Fleet said her name sharply like calling a dog to heel.

James had only one thing in mind. "I'll stop them before they get there." He rose to leave but stopped when Fleet jumped up to stand in his path.

"I can't stop you from going, but Kyla is right. Riley stands a better chance of coming back if she's with Sadie." Fleet didn't want James to end up a prisoner with Lipsky. He wasn't so sure that Sadie would do anything to help James. Riley on the other hand was someone that Sadie depended on. "Please sit down until you've heard what I have to say." James returned to his seat, but continued to look anxiously toward the door like he expected Riley to come running back any moment. Fleet looked at Kyla as he began to pace the length of the room. The look in her eyes was pleading with him to tell the others what so far only she and Armand knew.

"We went to the city and there was a community of people there, living in what remains of the zoo," he said slowly. Fleet wanted to tell them but he needed to explain his reasons first. "We noticed that there were a lot of similarities between them and us."

"What kind of similarities?" Kurt asked. He knew that Fleet would talk in circles if someone didn't bring him to the point.

Fleet looked at them. As he formed the words in his mind he realized how crazy it all seemed. Their uniforms were the same. There were twelve Defenders and twelve Guards. The symbols on the walls being the same as the broach that Sadie gave them. The fact that Lazarus knew who they were. What could Fleet say to make them understand the gut feeling that he had? How could he show them the letters, now nearly illegible after being soaked in the river?

A small voice was calling him. Someone was saying, "Fleet, you have to tell them and start from the beginning. Like you told me." It was Kyla.

She was right and Fleet knew it. He sat down and told them all just as he had Kyla, starting with the meeting when he had first brought Kyla to the Settlement. Rod nodded as he spoke of it. He had been there, too. Then he showed them the note that he had taken from Clovis and Sadie's letter. Everyone looked at them and passed them on. He told them about Lipsky, the broach, and the symbols painted on the walls. Then he told them about the compound at the zoo and Lazarus and Lipsky and the letter. Everything; including their escape with Liam helping them, up to the point where they headed for home. When he was done, everyone sat silently, taking in the implications of what he had said.

It was James who said, "What we have just discussed goes no further than this room." He looked around the table at each person seated there.

"Are you going after them?" Armand asked.

"If what Fleet says is true, there is nothing that I can do but wait," he looked at Fleet. "When Sadie returns, we will all speak to her."

"When Sadie returns, I will speak to her," Fleet said in a tone that left no doubt that he had more at stake than any of them did. "When I'm done, you can say whatever you want to her." He pushed back his chair and rose abruptly. "Now if you will me excuse. I'm tired." Fleet turned and left the room.

As Sadie rode down the lane she had stopped to take care of one last detail. The plans had been in place since Fleet left over a week ago. The fact that Fleet had returned without Lipsky was just a convenient excuse for her to leave. Sadie could make the plans and give the order, but she didn't have the stomach to be present to see he results of her actions. Besides, it would do her good to get away from the Settlement and the farm. She had been isolated for so long and a trip to see Lazarus could be a pleasant change from her regular routine.

~ ~ ~

The next two days the farm seemed like a different place. With Sadie gone, it seemed that no one had confidence that life would or could go on without her presence. There had been enough people present to see and hear the words that Sadie had with Fleet. Many people blamed Fleet for her departure and to a certain extent; he felt that the members of the community had ostracized him. People who would normally be following him or asking for advice openly avoided him. The fact that people were avoiding him was actually a blessing in disguise because he wanted to avoid them, too.

One person in particular that he avoided was Kyla. There was no other person whom he wanted to see more than Kyla, but he was afraid that association with him at this time could prove dangerous for her. None of the people, who were present at the meeting where he revealed his suspicions of Sadie's betrayals, had come to him and expressed either their support or their doubts. Fleet felt more alone than he could ever remember. He fought the urge to go to the Family and find solace with them. Their camp was one place where he could go to escape the storms that seemed to swirl around him everywhere he went. But he couldn't go; he had to wait for Sadie's return. Then he planned to leave.

It was after the noon meal, which he had made a point of missing, when Fleet saw Kyla. She was with Carleen and they were mounted and ready for hunting. It seemed that Kyla had fallen right back into her daily routine without missing a step. When Kyla saw him and began to ride in his direction, Fleet had ducked into the woods and gone the other way.

Kyla tried to see where Fleet went, but he had disappeared as soon as she saw him. She wanted to be with him and talk to him. The way people were acting toward Fleet wasn't right. They were judging him without knowing all the facts. She sighed audibly as she turned North Wind to follow Carleen and Buckeye. Kyla didn't want to go hunting today, but Carleen had insisted that they should continue especially now that Sadie was gone. It was important that everyone had confidence in the dedication of those who were still there.

"Don't worry," Carleen said as Kyla caught up to her. "He just needs time to think." She was trying to do her best to keep Kyla busy and to keep up appearances that nothing had changed. Until two nights ago when she had heard the whole story from Fleet, she hadn't known about what happened inside the compound. Carleen had been shocked to hear about Sadie. Like everyone else at the farm, she had viewed Sadie as a generous benefactor. The thought that there was a conspiracy with Lazarus and Cole Spring had led Carleen to suspect that Sadie had ties to Manjohnah as well and she wondered if any of the others felt the same.

"I know," Kyla said. "I just wish that I could talk to him for a few minutes." She had wanted to say that she wished he would stop avoiding her, but she didn't have to say it. Carleen understood what she meant.

"I think he's trying to keep you from getting hurt," Carleen said. She'd had plenty of time to observe Fleet and knew that putting distance between himself and Kyla was his way of protecting her. There were plenty of people who would take what Sadie had said to heart. She had announced for everyone to hear that Fleet was nothing without her. Many people would take that as their cue to move against Fleet, and Carleen was not sure that Kyla realized the danger that he was in.

Kyla didn't understand. All of her thoughts revolved around Fleet, and she couldn't imagine anything hurting more than being cut off from Fleet right now. "When we get back tonight, I'll track him down and set him straight about that, too," Kyla said as she kicked North Wind in the flanks and galloped ahead. The sooner they got their hunting done the

433

better. Today, what had been a joy before their trip west was a chore to be dispensed with as quickly as possible.

They returned shortly before dark and left the day's kill at the shelter house. They had been moderately successful returning with several rabbits and squirrels, but no big game, Carleen had shot them all. Kyla had been unable to focus on the task at hand and was of no use except to carry what Carleen killed. The whole day Carleen had not complained that her friend was no help. She had put up with Kyla's sullen and sulky mood, but when they were stabling the horses and Kyla had made some comment that Fleet didn't care for her, Carleen had had enough. "If you are ever going to be of any use to that man then you had better stop sulking like a baby. Who was it that went into the river after you without a thought about himself? Fleet has a problem bigger than you right now. What he needs is some understanding and if that means he needs time to himself then you will have to give it to him." Once she had her say, Carleen slammed the door to the stall shut and stalked out of the barn, cursing as she went. As Kyla watched her leave, she did feel ashamed. She was only thinking of herself. She loved Fleet and Carleen was right when she said that Kyla would have to give him the time and room that he needed to sort out his problems. Hopefully, that would not take too long. Every hour spent without him seemed wasted.

It was nearly dark when Kyla came out of the barn and started toward the cabin. She caught sight of Fleet walking away from the cabin and fought the urge to run after him. She had been thinking about what Carleen said and she would wait for Fleet to make the next move. Slowing her step, she watched him walking with his head lowered and her heart went out to him. His whole manner spoke of someone who was deeply troubled. As he began walking through the wooded portion of the path to the Settlement, she lost sight of him as he rounded a turn in the path. It was then that Kyla thought she saw someone else, a shadow in the darkness moving in the direction that Fleet had gone. Unconsciously, her course changed as her feet began taking her toward Fleet. Kyla was still some distance away when she rounded the turn in the path. The shadow materialized into a man and she saw him wrestling with Fleet. Her step quickened as the struggle continued, until she was running. When she saw Fleet stand straight and the other man fall to the ground her heart was racing. Then from the other side of the path, behind Fleet another figure appeared.

As the second man approached Fleet from behind, Kyla screamed, "Fleet. No!" and began running as fast as she could. She was right on top of them with the large knife that Sister Eaglet had given to her in her hand. As she saw the man strike Fleet over the head, Fleet fell forward and the man bent down over him as if to finish him off. Kyla jumped on the assailants back with her knife in hand and used the weight of her body to drive it in. At first she could feel the resistance but with the force and momentum of her body falling on the blade, she felt it slide in deeper until it was buried nearly to the hilt in the assailant's back. From somewhere, she found the strength to throw the man to the side and off of Fleet. As she saw the face of the man she had just killed, she was horrified to see that it was Raphael. Her only thought as she saw him lying dead was that he had told her that she should use her knife if she was going to carry one.

Right now, Fleet was her only concern. It was too dark to see, but when she knelt beside him, Kyla could feel the blood streaming from a wound in his side. She was screaming, "Kurt, oh my god, Kurt. Somebody help me," over and over again. Using her hands to hold pressure on Fleet's wound, Kyla was trying to stop the bleeding with her hands, as she waited for somebody to come. It was only a few moments before Kurt and Armand were there, lifting Fleet and carrying him to the cabin. All Kyla could do was ask, "What took you so long?" as she followed them holding Fleet's hand as they hurried him into his room.

Once he was on his bed. Kyla began taking off his clothing to see how badly he was hurt while Armand went for help. Once she had removed his shirt they could see that the knife had pierced his left side, just below the ribs. It was a long jagged wound and still bleeding profusely. When Kurt returned from the bathroom with several towels and they used those to press against his wound trying to slow the loss of blood. Before Armand returned with Agatha and Sara, Kurt and Kyla had to use a second towel, because the first one was already soaked with blood.

Agatha was carrying a basin and a kettle filled with hot water and Sara had her sewing kit. Kyla looked at the two women and said, "He doesn't need his shirt sewn up."

Sara came to the bed and pushed Kyla aside. "I used to be a nurse, honey," she said bluntly and removed the towel and began to swab the area with hot water.

"How bad is it?" Kurt asked as Sara examined the wound. The bleeding had slowed a little by then, but it was still flowing.

"I can't tell for sure, but he was lucky. It looks nasty but it's not too deep." Next she looked at the place on his head where he had been struck. She swabbed at the blood that was flowing from the abrasion and tried to rouse him. "Fleet, answer me." She shook her head as she shook him gently and spoke again. "Fleet, let me know if you hear me." She took his hand in hers and said again, "Squeeze my hand if you can." Sara looked at the others. "I can't tell how bad it is, but he will have a headache when he wakes up." She did not say if he wakes up, not wanting to add to the distress of those watching. As Sara took out one of her needles and threaded it she said, "I have to try to close the wound. I've done my best to sterilize the thread and needle, but I can't make any guarantees. Infection is my biggest worry after the blow to his head."

"Hold him," she said to Kurt and Armand. To Fleet she said, "I don't want to hurt you any more than I have to, so hold still and it will all be over soon." There had been no need to tell him. Fleet was oblivious to everything. By the time Sara was done, Agatha had returned with fresh bedding. They stripped the bed hospital style, moving Fleet from one side to the other as they removed the bloody sheets and blanket. As Sara left she said, "All you can do now is wait."

After Sara was gone, Kyla sat on the bed next to Fleet, holding his hand. Armand had begun building the fire and Kurt was pacing the length of the room when James entered. "There were two of them. One was a regular at the shelter house. The other man looked familiar but I couldn't place him. We also found the horse that Lipsky took tied to a tree at the end of the lane but there's no sign of him." James went to the bed and looked at Fleet and then turned to Kurt and said, "I don't know how Fleet managed to kill both of them."

"I killed the second one," Kyla said tiredly. "It was Slick. Lazarus must have sent him." The three men looked at her in amazement and then at Fleet lying on the bed.

~ ~ ~

When Sadie was finally ushered into Lazarus' office she was already steaming. It had taken two days of hard riding to get here and then he had left her standing outside the gate for an hour before giving his men the order to let her into the compound. Now he didn't even have the good grace to be in his office when she arrived. When Riley started to follow her into the office, Sadie snapped, "Wait for me outside." Once the door was closed Sadie began to look around the room. Lazarus was the same as always. He had expensive tastes and liked to surround himself with luxuries. She ran her fingers along the edge of the massive mahogany desk and was looking at the papers lying there when Lazarus entered the room.

"Sadie, it really is you this time," Lazarus said as he sat in the large leather chair behind the desk. "I'm honored by you visit. Won't you have a seat? Perhaps something to drink?"

Sadie knew he was only paying her lip service. Lazarus cared only for himself and respected no one. "What do you mean by this time?"

His amusement irritated her as he said, "Another woman with dark hair wearing a broach with the Commanders seal came here trying to pass herself off as Sadie." Lazarus opened one of the drawers in his desk and took out the broach. As he tossed onto the desk he continued, "She was with your friend Fleet. What was her name? Kyla, that's it. When I asked the big man, Armand, about her he told me that she was Fleet's lover."

Her composure slipped for a split second. Sadie had to watch herself with Lazarus. If he found any weakness, he would go for her throat like a wolf making its kill. Still, the thought of Kyla pretending to be her was galling. The rest of it was complete fantasy. If there was one thing she could depend on it was Fleet's sense of honor. He would not have taken another woman into his bed while he still thought that she loved him. "I didn't come to discuss them. I am here because you have my man. I want him back."

"Your man," he said coolly, "killed one of my guards. He's lucky that I didn't have him killed."

"Then why didn't you?" Sadie said as she came to stand in front of his desk.

Lazarus laughed and said, "Then you wouldn't have wanted to make that long trip to pay me a visit and I have been wanting to talk to you. Now why don't you stop pacing and sit down? You're like one of the tigers on the perimeter."

With a sullen scowl, Sadie took the seat across from Lazarus. "What could you possibly have to say that I would find interesting?"

"What were you thinking when you sent that man Fleet to my doorstep?" Lazarus came right to the point.

"I didn't think that you would actually let him inside," she said dismissing his question as trivial. "It was supposed to be a little adventure. Something to keep him out of trouble."

"Trouble?" It was Lazarus who was on his feet now. "That man has been nothing but trouble and you have done nothing to keep him under control. From what I can tell, you actually encourage his activities. He has been a constant irritation to Cole Spring. The man can't do his job when his men are out chasing after your rabble. You could have a little more respect for your neighbors and keep your pets on a leash."

"Cole Spring is an inept fool." Sadie's contempt for the man was evident in her voice. "It has never failed to amaze me that he cannot catch a few men on horseback when he has so many men and weapons at his disposal. I have even told him when they were coming and he still can't manage to defend himself." In a way she felt a personal satisfaction that Fleet had always managed to beat the odds. She had found it exciting. Even Lazarus with his high fences and tigers could not hold onto Fleet. Her only regret was the fact that Fleet had outgrown her control.

"Cole Spring is a farmer. He's not supposed to have to defend himself." Lazarus circled the desk and came to hover over her menacingly. "If it were me, I would have come to the cabin and pulled him out of your bed." Now it was Lazarus who was pacing. "Then there was the horse." Lazarus paused and looked at Sadie, as she rolled her eyes. "He stole one Manjohnah's private breeding stock. Took it out of the barn and then burned it down."

Sadie had known the horse would be trouble when she first laid eyes on it. Manjohnah probably had thousands just like it, but he would hold her personally responsible. Again, the thought of Fleet giving the horse to Kyla pricked the back of her mind. Another irritation added to the growing list of offenses that she could attribute to Kyla. She turned her full attention to Lazarus. "You don't need to worry. I have made arrangements to take care of the problem before I left." Sadie found it difficult to say that she had arranged Fleet's assassination before she left. It was something that she truly regretted having to do. Fleet was her only source of amusement and she would truly miss him, but he had forced her to do it. If he had only listened to her when she told him to stay at home, things would have turned out better.

"I have made my own arrangements as well," Lazarus said and he sat down again leaning back in his chair.

"I am capable of handling my own affairs without any interference from you," Sadie said. Her voice was beginning to betray her irritation with Lazarus' overstepping his authority.

"I'm not so sure that you are." Lazarus was blunt. Then changing the subject he added casually, "A messenger from Manjohnah arrived here yesterday. I imagine that he was on the way to your farm when he left here." He watched while Sadie's face stiffened and he could see her knuckles turning white as she griped the arms of her chair. Finally, Lazarus had been able to shake her resolve. Not being home when a messenger arrived would not look good for Sadie. Especially since he knew the purpose of the visit was to call her back, but Lazarus was not going to be the one to tell her that. Sadie would have to find out through the proper channels.

It was Sadie's turn to change the subject. "What about Lipsky? He's been very useful in the past and it's hard to find someone you can trust." Her choice of the word trust hardly fit her relationship with Lipsky. She could trust him as long as he remained in terror of what she could do to him. Then she tried to turn the tables on Lazarus. "Your man, Raphael, has been to the Settlement. I had to deal with them trying to steal the horses."

"Raphael has a job to do. We have to make sure there are plenty of pearls to meet the demand. Now don't we?" Lazarus was smiling with satisfaction as he continued, "How does it go? Keep them happy. Keep them fed. Take the ones you like to bed. I'm sure you will find replacements for both Lipsky and Fleet if you put your mind to it."

Sadie rose to her feet. She couldn't believe that Lazarus had repeated the rhyme. She had heard it before, but it was in extremely poor taste. She had thought that Lazarus would be above such boorish behavior. "If you could have someone show me and my companion to our rooms now, I am ready to rest from my journey." Her words bristled with the contempt that she felt for Lazarus.

Riley heard Sadie coming and barely had time to move away from the door before she came sailing out. She had heard every word and was terrified that Sadie would know she had been eavesdropping. Ever since they left the farm, Riley had been suspicious of Sadie's motives for the trip. She found it hard to believe that Lipsky was of such importance to her. Now that she knew the truth, she was more frightened than ever. How could Sadie be capable of such a heinous betrayal of their trust. Everyone at the Settlement had followed her blindly, never questioning where the food came from or the strange lights for the greenhouses. Sadie could always manage to get everything they needed. Everything that she offered had been accepted with gratitude. As she followed Sadie down the long corridor, Michael met them at the entrance to the building and escorted them through the maze of paths to a low circular building. Once inside, Riley saw that it had been the rain forest exhibit at one time.

As they followed Michael down the corridor they saw three women standing near one of the observation windows. They were all dressed in eveningwear, like they were on their way to a party. When Sadie saw them she approached the women. One of the women was wearing an unusual dress with an intricate pattern cut in the back revealing her skin underneath. The bronze fabric of the dress seemed to shimmer as she moved. It was the woman in the bronze dress that caught Sadie's interest. "I want that dress," Sadie said or rather commanded.

The women and her friends laughed, and the woman wearing the bronze dress retorted, "You have no use for this dress where you come from."

When she started to turn away, Sadie stopped her and produced a small silver dagger hidden in the tightly rolled coils of fabric that formed the belt around her waist. Pressing the point against the woman's throat Sadie replied, "No, I believe it is you who will have no use for the dress."

The woman's eyes were wide with terror and she looked to Michael who was standing and watching impassively. As the woman understood that Michael was not coming to her aid, she quickly stripped off the dress and handed it to Sadie. Then the woman and her friends made a hasty retreat, watching Sadie over their shoulders as they went. As she held the dress in her hand a satisfied smile spread across Sadie's face and the dagger disappeared as quickly as it had appeared. Lazarus had been enjoying himself and surrounding himself with luxuries while she was living in exile on a chicken farm. While she was here, Sadie planned on enjoying herself. The dress was just one small step in that direction.

Without a word about the incident that he had just witnessed, Michael began walking down the hallway again. When he came to the guestrooms, he unlocked the first one and Sadie looked inside. "Is this the best that Lazarus can do?" Sadie asked when she saw the small room with the one bed and a chair in the corner.

"I'm sorry, but it is all we have." Michael's tone was cold and uncaring. As Sadie went inside, Michael went to the next room and opened it for Riley. In doing so he said, "I hope this meets with your satisfaction."

"Yes, thank you," Riley said as she hurried inside. "It will do nicely." When Michael turned to leave, Riley closed the door and looked for some way to lock the door. She was upset to find that the only way to lock it was from the outside with a key. Leaning with her back against the door, Riley's heart was pounding with fear. She wasn't sure which was more terrifying, the people living at the zoo or Sadie. How she wished that she had listened to Fleet and Armand. She could never have imagined that Sadie would put her in such a precarious situation. As she closed her eyes Riley was praying that she would make it safely back to the farm.

~ ~ ~

Kyla was sitting in a chair next to Fleet's bed. At times she thought he was coming round as he talked and mumbled in his stupor. Every hour that passed with Fleet still remaining unresponsive to her efforts to wake him was a torment for Kyla. Her greatest fear was that he would never open his eyes and look at her again.

It was late and Kurt had come and gone just a few minutes ago. Kyla pulled her chair as close to the bed as she could and was resting her head drowsily on the edge, holding one of Fleet's hands in hers. She was nearly asleep when she felt him stirring. He began to move and was trying to sit up. Kyla was awake instantly and she moved to sit on the bed beside Fleet. His eyes were open and when he saw her, a smile came to his lips. When he began to push himself up, she put her hands on his shoulders and firmly but gently pushed him back saying. "No, lie still." She felt the tears welling in her eyes as she looked at his face. His beautiful blue eyes were looking at her, as she lovingly stroked his cheek. "I thought I had lost you," she said softly. The words caught in her throat as she spoke. His only answer was a smile and as Kyla bent down, Fleet's brought his hand to her shoulder and pulled her closer until her lips met his.

As she kissed him deeply her tears of joy and relief mingled with the taste of his lips and mouth. Kyla felt her whole body trembling as Fleet's hands began to caress her body. She had waited so long for this moment that she could barely contain her desire for Fleet. His hands moved to cup her breast and she moaned softly at his touch. In response to the sound of her pleasure, Fleet began to pull at the tiny buttons of the white camisole, his large hands clumsily trying to unbutton it as they kissed.

With a considerable effort, Kyla took her lips from his and said, "We should wait until you're stronger."

He smiled and buried his fingers in her hair as he pulled her to him again and said, "You're not going to start telling what I can or cannot do." Kissing her throat now, he continued caressing her breasts.

At that moment Kyla wanted Fleet more than anything or anyone and she could not deny the passion that she felt for him any longer. She pushed his hand aside and began to unbutton the blouse herself, kissing him on the lips and cheeks as she did. Once they were undone Fleet brushed the straps of the garment from her shoulders and as it fell he took her breasts in his hands again holding and fondling their firm roundness. His hands moved gently, bringing sensations rippling through Kyla's body with every touch.

Then he began to move his hands slowly upward. His fingers tracing the curve of her shoulders and throat until he cradled her face in his gentle grasp. Slowly, Fleet began to move her down to lie next to him. As he started to move toward her Kyla felt him gasp in pain from the wound in his side. She sat up quickly and as he laid back she smiled and untied the drawstring to the blue silk trousers that she was wearing and quickly slipped them off. As she knelt naked beside him, Fleet's hands went out to her again. She was beautiful. Her short chestnut brown hair was in wild disarray and her eyes were the clearest blue that he had ever seen. As he ran his hands across the soft curves and valleys of her breasts and hips he could feel his heart pounding as the desire for her filled his mind and body.

As Kyla pulled back the covers, she knew that Fleet was ready for her and she slowly and carefully climbed on top of him. As he filled the void in her body and soul that she had almost forgotten existed, Kyla was filled with the ecstasy that he gave her. As they moved slowly, she lost herself in the pleasure and sensations of their lovemaking. His fingers bringing tiny thrills with every touch and strong hands guiding her movements now, she thought she would die from the bliss that filled her body and mind until at last they reached the climax of their union. Kyla couldn't remember ever having felt more wonderful or fulfilled as she bent down to taste the sweetness of his lips again.

Then moving to lay beside him, she watched as he closed his eyes and the blissful expression that filled his face as he fell back to sleep holding her tightly in his arms. She could not tear her eyes from his face and her hands caressed his chest and arms and brushed the curls from his face as he slept now, exhausted and content. Loving Fleet filled her mind as she remembered the sensations that he had brought to life inside of her. As she closed her eyes, Kyla listened to the sound of his breathing and she too felt the serenity surrounding her that she had been missing in her life.

The next morning Kurt opened the door and walked into Fleet's bedroom to bring breakfast for him. When he saw Kyla and Fleet lying together naked on the bed, he quickly backed out of the doorway and shut it quietly. He smiled to himself as he thought that Fleet certainly appeared to be feeling better today. Leave it to Fleet that the first thing he would do was to consummate the passion that had been growing between himself and Kyla over the past weeks. Kurt was happy for his friend. As he had watched Fleet and Kyla when they were together, he could see that Kyla was a better match for Fleet than Sadie had ever been. Kyla truly cared for Fleet and her love for him was evident to anybody who saw the two of them together. That was what Fleet needed in his life, a woman who loved him without question. He paused for just a moment before knocking softly on the door.

Kyla was wide-awake at the sound of someone rapping on the door. As she sat up, Fleet opened his eyes. When he saw her, he smiled warmly. He had almost thought their lovemaking had been a dream, but at the sight of her he remembered and sat up to kiss her. As his lips brushed against hers, he heard the knocking at the door, a little louder this time. Kyla picked up the camisole, which had been discarded so casually the night before, and her fingers fumbled nervously as she pushed the tiny buttons through the fabric. Then as she pulled on the silk trousers, she went to the door. Fleet had lain back down on his side with his head propped up on his hand, watching Kyla as she went to answer the door.

Opening the door, she took the tray from Kurt. "Thank you," was all she said. As she carried it to the bed where Fleet was waiting, she saw that Fleet was grinning broadly, watching her as she came to him.

Kurt paused for a moment at the door. He had a smile on his face as he looked at Fleet and said, "I'm glad to see that you're feeling better." Then he closed the door behind him as he left.

Before Kyla could reach the bed, Fleet was sitting with his legs over the side and he stood up. He reached out to the bedpost for support as his knees began to give way under him. Kyla was a little shocked at first at the sight of his naked body. She had never seen him like this before and she could not take her eyes off of the smooth line of his lean and muscular body. She hurried to put the tray down and help him as he started toward the bathroom, but he pushed her gently away and said, "I'm fine." Kyla let him go and went back to the tray of food. Sitting on the edge of the bed, she nibbled at the toast and drank some tea, as she waited for Fleet to finish washing.

When he finally emerged, this time with a towel wrapped around him to cover his nakedness, he came to sit beside her and began to devour the food on the tray. She left him to take her turn in the bathroom and when she emerged washed and refreshed she saw Fleet sitting in the bed waiting for her, the empty tray and towel on the floor beside the bed. She tried to control her steps, not wanting to appear too anxious, but she found herself nearly running the last two steps as she climbed onto the bed and into his waiting arms. As they kissed, she reveled in their newly found intimacy.

Fleet kissed her hungrily. The food had satisfied only one of his needs. He felt much stronger this morning. He would never have admitted it to Kyla, but their lovemaking the night before had been draining both physically and emotionally, but this morning he was ready to make love to her. As he guided her, lying her down on the bed beside him he began to undo the buttons of her blouse. Once again she hurried to do it for him, but this time he pushed her hands away. Then using both hands he undid the buttons one at a time, kissing her softly as each button revealed a little more of her soft flesh. Each time his lips touched the sensitive skin between her breasts, a small gasp would escape from Kyla lips. As the last button was unfastened and her breasts were uncovered, Fleet was caressing and kissing them with his lips. Finding her nipples, he suckled greedily as his hands began to untie the string at the waist of her trousers.

While he began to slip them slowly over her hips and down her thighs, Fleet continued to explore her body using his lips and hands, her body vibrating and moving with his touch like a finely tuned instrument and he was the virtuoso eliciting a response with his every touch. With every sound that escaped from Kyla's lips, Fleet found his excitement growing in response to hers until finally bringing her pleasure to crescendo in their rhapsody of love. As he brought his lips to hers, Fleet thrust himself deep inside as she opened herself to him completely, Fleet taking pleasure from her body as he gave it back.

Every movement from Fleet, Kyla met with her own, arching her body to accommodate his excitement. Their bodies were joined in harmonious bliss as they forgot everything except the passion that brought them together. At the final moment as their gratification was complete, Fleet collapsed, all his weight pressing down on Kyla. He could not remember having ever felt such rapture as Kyla had transported him past happiness to feelings of joy and delight that he had never experienced with any other woman.

Kyla began to speak and as the words, "Fleet, I have never..." escaped from her lips. He kissed her gently, not wanting words to spoil the enchantment of the moment. He lay motionless now, enjoying the feeling of her body, her legs still wrapped around him, as they remained joined in love. Finally, he began to move from her, knowing that he had to be crushing her with the weight of his body, but she only held him tighter refusing to let him go, not wanting their lovemaking to end. As he propped himself up on his elbows and looked into her eyes, what he saw was blissful contentment. Kyla touched his face tenderly and said, "I love you. I knew it the first moment when you reached out to me and took my hand," remembering the night that Fleet had snatched her from certain disaster.

Fleet only smiled and kissed her again. He had no words to describe the feeling in his heart. He knew that he had found the love that he had been searching for and more. Kyla had filled the emptiness in his life so completely that he felt he would explode from the sheer joy of knowing her. Now that he had found happiness, he would never let it go. He nuzzled her throat and nibbled ears playfully as they lay together, listening to Kyla as she spoke. "Fleet," she said his name softly. "You know that I am married."

He stopped his ministrations for a moment and looked at her. Her face was serious and he could see that she was worried about what his reaction might be. He smiled reassuringly as he stroked the line of her cheek and jaw. Then placing his finger on her lips as if to silence her, he said, "I was, too. For nearly two years, I have mourned for the loss of my wife and son, but they're gone just like your husband. I'm ready to start a new life and a new family and I want to do it with you." Fleet felt his heart leap as the smile returned to her face.

Kyla searched his eyes and as she held his face in her hands, she knew that she had found what she wanted. She wanted Fleet and his children, without that her life would be empty and meaningless. She laughed lustily as she said, "If its children you want then you had better get to work," then she began to move her hips against him to emphasis her eagerness.

Fleet returned her smile with his own. "I thought you were worried that I wasn't strong enough for this," he teased as he felt his body responding to her.

"I will wear you out before I'm done with you," Kyla answered as she kissed him on the lips. As Fleet responded and began to make love to her once again, she could not remember a time in her life that she had ever felt greater contentment than she did at that moment.

Chapter Eighteen

Fleet couldn't believe it when Kyla told him that he had been unconscious for several hours. As soon as she had gone to begin her chores for the day, Fleet decided to do the same. He had a pounding headache and when he stood he felt a little unsteady as he had when he rose earlier that morning. He rubbed the bump on the back of his head. It was a little tender to the touch, but other than the headache, he was fine. The cut on his side was more bothersome. Looking under the bandage at the long gash, Fleet realized just how lucky he had been. He remembered the first attacker coming out of the woods. The man was a clumsy fool and had practically fallen on his own knife, but he never saw the second one. The fact that it had been Slick was unsettling. Lazarus had impressed him as a dangerous man and the attack was proof. He would have to be more careful in the future.

The thought of Kyla having killed Slick was even more disturbing. It was a paradox in his mind. He had been able to accept her killing a man when they ambushed Cole's men, but this attack had been on him. That made it a personal matter and he could not dismiss the possibility that he would be attacked again. What if Kyla was the target next time?

His relationship with Kyla was going to present a problem. Her safety concerned him more than his own did. He had tried to protect her by placing himself at a distance from her both physically and emotionally, but he could not do that now. His first thought was to keep his relationship with her secret, but knew that would be impossible. Kurt knew. Fleet had seen the grin on his face when he brought their breakfast. Although he wouldn't tell anyone, it would only be a matter of time before everybody knew. The Settlement was too small for secrets. Nor would he ask Kyla to sneak to his room, their love was something he wanted to celebrate. He would not cheapen their relationship by clandestine meetings, which by their very nature would brand them as less than honorable

His public image was tied to Sadie and his private one as well. She truly believed that Fleet was nothing without her and he realized now that his relationship with Sadie had been one of mutual convenience. The difficult thing would be to break his connection with her in the minds of the people living at the Settlement. It was something that would have to be handled with delicacy, but he had already been giving that problem some thought.

When Fleet left his room he found Kurt waiting for him in the hallway. As Fleet reached the spot where he was standing, his friend fell in to step beside him. "When I saw Kyla go into the kitchen, I knew you wouldn't be far behind." Kurt looked at him out of the corner of his eye as they walked, watching Fleet's reaction.

Without looking at Kurt, Fleet shrugged and said, "Things change. I have plans for a lot of changes around here."

As they reached the library, Kurt put his hand on Fleet's shoulder and pointed toward the room. "We need to talk," he said and went through the door.

Fleet followed and closed the door as he said, "I'm glad you were waiting for me because I need to talk to you, too." It was as if Kurt had read his mind.

Kurt crossed the room and looked out the large window. With his back to Fleet, he said, "With Sadie gone and then the attack on you, things have been a little strained around here. I think we should have a sentry at night from now on."

"What good will one man do?" Fleet didn't care for the insinuation that he needed to be protected. Nor did he want to give people the impression that he was frightened. No matter what, Fleet had to continue to project an image of confidence. "I have something different in mind."

Kurt turned around and saw Fleet standing beside Sadie's empty chair and he was smiling. Only Fleet could find humor hidden in a situation where his life was in danger and the chain of command at the Settlement was in serious doubt. "Whatever it is, we have to be careful. No matter what we know or think about Sadie, we can't just try to dethrone her. We would have a riot on our hands," Kurt said. He did not choose his words lightly. Sadie was Queen of the Settlement and she had ruled them all, holding generosity in one hand and deceit in the other.

"I know," Fleet said. He had one hand resting on the back of Sadie's chair. "I've been thinking about that, too. We can't get rid of her and I have no doubt in my mind that she will be back and soon."

Kurt was watching Fleet as he stood next to the chair and for a moment he seemed unsteady on his feet and clutched the back of the chair for support. It was a subtle movement, but Kurt saw it. He frowned and walked closer, studying Fleet's face carefully as he asked, "Are you sure you're alright? Why don't you sit down?" Kurt knew Fleet should be resting if the blow to his head was bad enough to leave him unconscious.

An angry glare was all he received for his concern as Fleet snapped, "If I need to sit down I will." He walked away from the chair and said, "The next Gathering is in two days and if we're lucky Sadie won't be back by then. If she pushes the horses it would be two days to ride out and two days back. They'll have to spend at least one day at Lazarus' compound. It should be just enough time."

"What is it that you have planned?" Kurt asked.

"I tried to think who we could get to replace Sadie without making it look like we were trying to get rid of her." He looked at Kurt and asked, "Who do they trust?" Fleet wanted Kurt to understand how he developed the plan. "Do they trust me?"

Kurt was surprised by Fleet's question, but he answered truthfully, "Not everybody. Especially if you try to take over while Sadie's gone."

"Right," Fleet replied. "It can't be me or any other member of the Guard or the Citizen's Patrol."

"Well, then who would it be?" Kurt asked impatiently. Fleet hadn't left many options open.

"One of them," Fleet answered beaming. It was not only a solution to his problem with Sadie, but a step in the direction that he wanted the people at the Settlement to begin moving. Fleet still wanted to make the Settlement a real community with people working together.

"An election?" Kurt was smiling now, too. It was inspired and it was the right thing to do. "What kind of power will this person have?"

"The same as Sadie. Whoever it is will sit in Sadie's place when the Guard meets. They will be able to join in any discussion and decisions that are made." Fleet paused slightly before adding, "But only in Sadie's absence. That should take the wind out of any objections that she has. We just want to make sure that the person is selected before she returns. That way Sadie won't have any influence in who is elected."

"It might work." Kurt was hopeful in regard to that problem, but there was another one that was on his mind, too. He cleared his throat nervously before asking, "What are you going to do about Kyla."

Fleet could have been angry but he wasn't. Kurt was concerned as he was about Kyla's welfare. He met Kurt's gaze squarely as he answered. "She'll be moving in with me tonight and if she'll have me, we'll get married as soon as possible." Fleet was thinking about asking Sister Samethia to perform the ceremony.

It was the answer that he expected, but Kurt was considering the repercussions. He was sure that Fleet didn't need to be reminded either, but it didn't make him any more comfortable about the situation. They could not continue to occupy the bedroom next to Sadie's after she returned. Sadie would have to drive them out and make a show of doing it. It was going to be ugly and whatever damage was done to Fleet; he'd had a hand in making the mess. Kyla hadn't done anything except have the bad luck to fall in love with Fleet.

Fleet's train of thought had already returned to the plans he had been making. "I think we should make the suggestion to the others at lunch today," he said as he paced the room. His words flowed with his steps, spilling out quickly as he said, "Not everyone in the Guard knows about Sadie and I don't think this is the time to discuss it. The reason I will give for the election is the fact that people have been worried about who is in charge when Sadie is gone. If we present it to them like that, I don't think there will be any objections." He finished abruptly and turned to Kurt. "What do you think?"

"I'm behind you," Kurt answered. "But when Sadie comes back, then your elected representative has no power."

"The power is in the importance that we place on their right to have a voice in their lives," Fleet answered. "Sadie is a petty despot ruling a world of self perpetuating squalor. If we begin to raise people's expectations, I'm hoping that they will rise to meet it." It was the first time that Fleet had discussed his vision for the future with Kurt and the first time that Sadie had not been present to control the outcome of his plans. There would be no arguing with her and no compromises.

As he looked at Fleet, Kurt was hoping that he could do what he wanted. He was a dreamer with plans and ideas that were beyond the realm of most men's imagination. His greatest asset was the ability to take those ideas and use them to start a small fire, but before he was done Fleet would fan that tiny flame into a raging wildfire. The trick was to keep it from growing out of control. They would have to wait and see what the others had to say at noon. "What are you planning on doing this morning?" Kurt asked. He wanted to suggest that he take it easy, but Fleet had already made his feelings clear on that subject.

As he walked to the door Fleet answered, "I think I'll take a walk and let people see that I'm still around."

Kurt followed him out the door and said, "I'll go with you."

Fleet stopped so suddenly that Kurt almost ran into him. He turned and giving Kurt a level gaze replied with only one word, "Alone," and strode out the door.

Kurt was shaking his head when the door closed. Fleet was too stubborn to know what was good for him. When Kurt saw Peach coming down the hallway from his room he called, "Peach, I need you to do something."

The blond haired young man quickened his step when Kurt called and asked, "What do you need?"

"I want you to follow Fleet today," he said softly. He didn't want anyone else to hear. If Fleet found out, he would be furious. "Whatever you do, don't let him see you. Do you think you can do that?"

Peach nodded and asked, "Why?" If Kurt was asking him to spy on Fleet, he wanted to know the reason.

"We've had enough accidents around here. Just keep your eyes open and let me know if you see anyone hanging around that's suspicious." Kurt watched as Peach hurried out the door. After he was gone, he wished that he had told him to take a rifle.

~ ~ ~

As Kyla left the cabin after the noon meal, she was elated. Fleet's idea had met with unanimous approval from all the Guard members. He hadn't told her about his ideas for the Settlement and she was caught up in the vision that he had shared with them today. It was

453

exciting to think about being a part of building a real community. Throughout the entire discussion, she had been watching Fleet. His face came alive when he talked about his plans and if it was possible, she loved him even more than before. When she went into the barn, Carleen was waiting for her.

Buckeye was saddled and ready to go and Carleen was busy putting the saddle on North Wind. "You're late," she said, as she pulled the cinches tight and patted North Wind on the rump, Carleen looked up at Kyla who was standing right beside her now, grinning from ear to ear. She stood up straight and looked Kyla in the eye and said, "You have that, 'I've just been laid' look." As Kyla's face turned red, Carleen laughed and handed her the reins.

"Really, Carleen, you can say the silliest things," Kyla said as she put her rifle into the case attached to the saddle. Then she mounted North Wind and this time she was the one who galloped out of the barn with Carleen scrambling to catch up.

Carleen was right behind her, but Buckeye could not catch North Wind until Kyla slowed her to a walk at the end of the lane. As she brought her horse beside Kyla's, Carleen said, "I didn't hear you denying anything." She watched Kyla, but another grin was her only response. There was no point in continuing direct questions. Kyla would tell her in her own way, so Carleen changed the subject, but only slightly. "So how is Fleet?"

Kyla's smile turned to a concerned frown as she said, "I'm worried about him being up so soon. I begged him to stay in bed."

"I'll bet you did," she laughed heartily. Carleen couldn't resist the temptation to tease Kyla.

"Stop that," Kyla said. She was trying to be angry but she was finding it hard not to laugh with Carleen because the same thought had crossed her mind, too. "I'm trying to be serious."

"I know," Carleen said, trying to get her laughter under control. "I'm sorry. He looked fine when I saw him. He was up in the Settlement talking to everybody." They rode silently for a few moments before Carleen voiced her next concern. "What are you going to do if Sadie comes back?"

"You mean, when Sadie comes back," Kyla said. There was no doubt in her mind that she would be back and soon. "I don't want to be living in the cabin, that's for sure."

"You're not thinking about moving back into the dormitory are you?" Carleen asked.

It was Kyla's turn to laugh. "We can't live in the dormitory," she said, stressing the word 'we'. It was as close as Kyla would come to telling Carleen about Fleet and herself. She had been giving the problem of where they could live quite a bit of thought. She wanted to put a little distance between them and Sadie, but not enough that they were living outside the Settlement. They were riding on the gravel road that led past the lake and the Settlement. Just past the bridge at the entrance the road turned sharply to the right and ran west past the steep tree covered hill where the Settlement was located. It was not the way they would usually go when they went hunting, but Kyla had a reason to be riding this way. Less than a quarter of a mile down the road was the lane that led to the rock-cut, the fishing place at the nearby river.

When they came to a small building along the way, Kyla stopped North Wind and dismounted. After tying her horse to one of the small trees growing next to the old structure, Kyla went to get a closer look. According to a plaque hanging next to the door, it had once been a one-room schoolhouse. As Kyla peered in the windows, Carleen jumped down and said, "You're not thinking about living here?"

"Why not?" Kyla asked as she walked to the steps. When Kyla put her weight on the first tread, it gave way underfoot with a brittle snap.

"Well that's one reason," Carleen said. She left Buckeye with North Wind and went to stand beside Kyla.

"I know it needs some work," Kyla said undeterred. She stretched to step over the broken stair to reach the stoop. It creaked a little, but nothing broke. As Kyla pushed the door open, it squealed on rusty hinges. Before going in she looked at Carleen and asked; "Are you coming?" then disappeared inside.

Scrambling onto the stoop, Carleen followed. It was dark inside despite the fact that there were two windows on the east and west walls. They were covered with such a thick layer of dirt and dust that it made the light coming through them dim. Carleen watched as Kyla walked around the empty room brushing aside cobwebs as she went. "You can't really be serious about this place. It'll be cold and drafty in the winter."

"It's only temporary," Kyla answered. Fleet's speech at lunch had been about his vision of the future, but Kyla had her own ideas about what she wanted. Fleet didn't know it yet, but they were going to build a cabin. Nothing big or elaborate like the one Sadie lived in. All she wanted was a place to call her own.

"If Sadie and Riley hustle they could be back tonight. It takes two days to ride to the river and two days back." Carleen was thinking about how much time they would have to clean this place. Whatever Kyla had in mind, she knew that it was going to mean work for her, too.

Thinking of Sadie at the zoo compound brought to mind a picture of Sadie and Lazarus together. It was not a comforting thought and she tried to put it out of her mind. Kyla said, "Even Sadie has to rest and the horses, too. I don't think she'll be back before the Gathering. That gives us two days."

"One day you mean," Carleen corrected. "Today is half over already and we still have to do some hunting."

Kyla was only half listening. She was looking at the wall opposite the front door. There was a chimney but no fireplace. "We'll need a wood stove for heating and cooking," Kyla said.

"Great," Carleen replied, "and I suppose you want me to find it and carry it in for you?"

"Don't worry, we'll work it out," Kyla was getting excited. She couldn't wait to see Fleet and tell him about her plans. As Kyla went outside again and mounted North Wind she said, "I'll come back tonight and get started."

As Carleen swung into her saddle, she said, "I'm having a hard time believing that." Kyla was certain to be busy tonight and that would leave tomorrow to get the place cleaned and bring in some furniture. They would need some help, and given the fact that Kyla's head was in the clouds, it would be up to her to arrange it. They way Carleen looked at it, Kyla was going to owe her a really big favor someday.

Their hunting was moderately successful. They brought back one deer. It seemed that they could never repeat their success of the day that they brought back two. Once again Kyla asked for the deerskin. She had sent every one with Justin for Sister Eaglet. Someday, Kyla would ask Sister Eaglet to show her how she tanned the skins. They returned to the barn just before nightfall. Carleen had to hurry to settle Buckeye into her stall if she was to get to the dining hall before supper was ready. Kyla had told her that she would get her something at the cabin, but she had refused. After she hurried out Kyla stayed behind to curry North Wind and comb the burrs from her tail.

When she heard the door open behind her she smiled warmly when she saw Fleet. His step quickened when he saw her and he picked her up off her feet as they embraced. Then he kissed her before setting Kyla back on her feet. Still holding her close, he said, "I've been thinking about you."

"When do you find time to think about me when you're so busy making plans?" she asked mischievously. She wanted to tell him about the house, but she was going to wait to surprise him tomorrow after the Gathering.

He laughed and said, "You're in the center of all my plans." He released her from his embrace and waited while Kyla quickly put the horse in its stall.

"Where do I fit into your plans," she asked when she returned.

Fleet put his hand in his pocket, took out the tiny arrow pin, and looked at Kyla. "I don't have a ring," he started, "but I wanted to give you something." She was watching him, waiting for him ask the question that she was hoping to hear. "Will you marry me? I want you to be my wife," he said softly. Fleet thought he knew the answer but his heart was beating faster as he said the words.

As Kyla reached out to take the tiny pin from his hand, her words were gushing as she said, "Yes, but who would marry us?"

"Sister Samethia," Fleet answered as he took the pin from Kyla's hand and started to pin it on her tunic. As he slipped his fingers under the fabric, Kyla could feel his hands trembling slightly. She wasn't sure if it was because he was nervous about asking her to marry him or if it was the head injury making him shaky. When he slipped and pricked her with the pin, she didn't say a word.

~ ~ ~

It was the middle of the night when Fleet sat up suddenly in bed and awakened Kyla. "What's wrong?" she asked as Fleet started to pull on his trousers.

"I heard voices in the hall," Fleet said. He looked at the door, and then turned to whisper, "There they are again. Don't you hear them?" Fleet picked up his rifle that he had loaded and set beside their bed earlier that evening.

Kyla was sitting quite still and listening, but she didn't hear anything. She looked at Fleet as he started to open the door and said, "I don't think there's anybody there."

Holding his finger to his lips Fleet slipped out into the hall. It was pitch-black in the hallway and he made his way along the wall listening for any sound as he went. Fleet thought he heard something in the foyer, but when he got there it was empty. Quietly, Fleet went to Kurt's room at the end of the hall and rapped softly on the door. Within seconds Kurt was at the door asking sleepily, "What is it?"

"It's me," Fleet whispered and Kurt opened the door. "I thought I heard somebody in the house."

Kurt left the door slightly ajar. When he returned a moment later wearing his trousers, he had his rifle in hand. "Let's go," he said and they walked back down the hall pausing in the foyer to listen. Next they went into the kitchen and washroom and still found nothing. When Fleet stood by the door that led to the dining room he motioned to Kurt. They stood beside the closed door for a moment before Fleet said, "Did you hear that?"

"What?" Kurt was straining to hear, but there was nothing.

"I heard somebody whispering in the other room," Fleet pushed open the door with his gun ready and turned on the light as he rushed into the dining room, only to find an empty room. The sound of the doorknob turning brought both men to attention and they whirled around ready to fire on the intruder. When they saw it was Kyla, Fleet lowered his rifle and said angrily, "You should have stayed where you were. We almost shot you."

"I'm sorry," Kyla answered. "I checked the rooms in the other wing. I couldn't find anybody." She looked at Fleet and her face showed her concern as she asked, "Fleet are you sure you're alright?"

Fleet scowled and said, "I'm tired of everybody asking me that."

"Fleet, if everybody is asking you the same question, then there must be some reason for it," Kurt said. Fleet was obviously hearing things and they had been chasing shadows.

"I know what I heard," Fleet was stubbornly sticking to his story. "They must have gone out. Maybe we should check outside."

Kurt walked past him and said, "You need to go back to bed." Then he left the dining room grumbling all the way back to his room.

Fleet started out the door and Kyla caught his arm and stopped him as he passed by her. "Fleet, it's a common thing for someone with a severe head injury to hear sounds that aren't there. You have to give yourself time and take it easy for a few days."

He pulled away from her and said, "I'm going outside. You go back to bed and wait for me there." He would not be able to sleep until he had looked thoroughly. When he stepped outside into the cold air, Fleet felt his knees go weak and he stumbled slightly going down the steps. He wasn't going to tell anybody about his dizzy spells or the headache that was still pounding in his head, not even Kyla. There was too much to do and he couldn't afford the luxury of resting in bed. Still, as he walked around the house he was certain that he had not been hearing things. After searching the cabin outside and inside, Fleet returned to his room to find Kyla sitting in the bed waiting for him as he had asked. She looked slightly peeved as he entered, but when he removed his trousers and slipped back into bed, she nestled close to him.

As she lay next to Fleet with his arms wrapped tightly around her, Kyla was thinking that she would have her hands full married to Fleet. If she wasn't worrying that someone else would kill him, then she was worrying that he was going to kill himself. He was being stubborn. She had noticed the moments of unsteadiness and had seen him holding his head when he thought she wasn't looking. Every time she had brought up the subject of rest he had become irate. There was nothing that she could do but watch and try to help him if she could.

~ ~ ~

Fleet was pacing the foyer. It was late in the afternoon and he was anxious to see what the response would be to the changes that he had

459

announced for the Gathering. He had spent the day posting notices and talking to people at the farm and Settlement, letting them know about the election. At the same time he had changed the time for the Gathering. It would be in the afternoon, before nightfall. He wanted this meeting to reflect the changes by avoiding the dark and gloomy atmosphere that Sadie created with her candlelight and fires. Fleet would bring hope and light to the affair. Everything was ready. The meeting room was opened. The chairs were set on the hearth as always. Even Sadie's chair had been placed in its usual place. Justin had returned around noon with his report from the Family, so all twelve members of the Guard were present. The only thing missing right now was the people from the Settlement. Fleet went into the library and stood at the window waiting and watching.

He heard someone enter the room behind him and turned to see Kyla. He smiled despite the fact that he was worried. There were so many things beyond his control. He had received mixed responses when he posted his announcements. There was always the possibility that they would reject the idea. Then there was Sadie. Whatever happened at the Gathering, he still had to deal with Sadie when she returned. He had been steeling himself mentally for the confrontation that was coming.

Kyla stood beside Fleet and put her hand gently on his arm. "Don't worry," she said, "everything will be fine." Kyla looked into his eyes, which were filled with uncertainty. Absently fingering the tiny arrow pin on the neck of her tunic, she stood with him watching silently as people began to gather at the end of the walk. They were arriving one or two at a time, and within a few minutes there was a crowd of people milling about in the farmyard, but so far nobody was coming to the door.

Fleet was watching, too. Then looking at Kyla, he wondered if it was the sight of them standing together in the window that had stopped the people from coming inside. Slowly he backed away from the window drawing Kyla with him. Once they were out of view, he pulled her close and kissed her deeply. Fleet needed to feel the happiness that she brought by her very presence. It was one last indulgence of his love for her and it would have to sustain him for awhile. It was time for him to finish what he had started. "You wait with the others," Fleet said.

"I'm going out to talk to them." Fleet had brought the population of the Settlement this far and it appeared that it was going to require a little push to get them moving into the cabin. As Kyla turned to leave the room, Fleet caught her hand. When she looked back at him, he said, "I love you." She smiled and left without a word. Fleet watched as she crossed the foyer and went into the dining room to wait with the others.

Stepping up to the front door Fleet put on the biggest smile that he could manage and opened the door. He strode confidently onto the front stoop and down the steps, focused on the crowd before him. He could hear the hushed tones of their voices as he approached. "I'm glad to see everybody here," he called out loudly. "We're ready if you would like to come in now." He stood for a few moments longer but no one responded or moved. Fleet turned and began to walk slowly back to the cabin. He hadn't gone very far before he heard the sound of footsteps behind him. This time Fleet wasn't hearing things and he didn't need to turn around to make sure.

When he came to the front door, Fleet stepped inside and greeted each person as they entered. With every friendly face he saw, his confidence was growing. The mood of the crowd was apprehensive but positive. As the room filled to capacity and the line at the door dwindled, Fleet went to the dining hall. When he stepped into the room, everyone rose to their feet, ready to get the procession started. The Citizen's Patrol went first. They were wearing their new uniforms, which were simply black vests worn over a white shirt. As Garret, Carleen, Tom, and Captain Frye took their places at the back of the room opposite the hearth and fireplace where the Guard would be seated, the Guard members began to file out of the dining hall. Kyla led the procession, with Fleet and Kurt walking together at the end of the line as they always did. The only thing different was the fact that it was Sadie who was missing this time.

The whispering died and there was silence in the room as the Guard took their places on the hearth. There was no fire behind them this time, no candles to cast long threatening shadows. It was, as Fleet had wanted. They were standing before the people they protected and he did not want them to fear the Guard. It was the first time that Fleet would start the Gathering. That was Sadie's domain, but Fleet had been thinking about what he would say and do when the time came.

He paced slowly from one end of the stone hearth that formed the stage upon which they were all standing, to the other, and then walked to the center again. All the while he was looking at the faces of the people gathered there. Every one had their eyes trained on him, anxiously awaiting a word from Fleet. Stopping in front of Sadie's chair, he said, "Many of you have been worried by Sadie's absence these past few days, and I understand your concerns. We are all concerned about her welfare and safety." Fleet paused slightly and motioned for the Guard to sit. When they were seated, Fleet remained standing and once again he began to pace the length of the hearth. Looking at the people seated around the room, he continued to speak; "I have faith in the fact that she will return unharmed. We all know Sadie to be a very resourceful woman and if I was able to make the trip to the west and return, then Sadie will, too." He paused again as if thinking about what he wanted to say, but Fleet knew the silences were as important as the words.

"Even so," he finally continued, "it has made us wonder about what would happen to our community if something did happen to Sadie." As soon as the words were out of his mouth the room filled with murmuring and people shouting angrily that they would never let anything happen to Sadie. Without waiting for the commotion to die down, Fleet stopped in front of Sadie's chair and shouted above their voices, "Sadie is no different from the rest of us. Who knows, she could become sick or be injured. There are no guarantees that something like that won't happen." Then Fleet stood patiently until some of the voices from the crowd began to echo his thoughts.

Once again he began to pace the hearth, but now his strides were more forceful as he began to speak passionately, "We need to maintain the integrity of our community. We need to make sure that we are not so dependent on one person that their absence would bring the rest of us to disaster. We need to build a structure of government that will allow our community to grow in the future." Fleet kept stressing the word 'need'. They had to understand the necessity of the actions that he proposed.

"You all noticed that I didn't start the Gathering by speaking of the past and asking for testimony. For over a year we have met on the eve of the new moon, talked about the past, and mourned for the lives

462

that we lost. It is time to stop looking backward and to spend our time more productively and use the Gatherings to plan for progress and prosperity. The election of a representative tonight will be just one step in that direction." Fleet stopped and looked at the faces in the crowd as he heard clapping and whistles and other sounds of support from the crowd. He had been so wrapped up in the words that he had almost forgotten about his audience. At that moment, he was standing in front of Kyla and out of the corner of his eye he could see the pride that filled her expression while she watched him.

Her confidence and the encouragement from those assembled made Fleet's spirits soar. "This is just the first step," he said repeating himself. "The fields have been planted and a good harvest looks likely. There will be plenty of food to store for the winter, but we need to begin building better shelters. If people spend another winter living in tents and shanties, there will be fewer of us next spring. We must all work together to make a better life for everyone." Fleet walked to his chair. The sound of clapping and feet stomping was deafening. As he sat down, Fleet leaned back with one arm draped over the back of his chair and beamed at Kurt. He had done his part, now it was up to Kurt and the others to complete the process.

Kurt had his work cut out for him as he rose and held his hands up to try to quiet the crowd. It took him a couple of minutes before he had their complete attention. "We are going to open the floor to nominations. Remember, the person you choose today will be asked to fill in for Sadie as the citizen's representative on the Guard. It must be one of you. The members of the Guard and the Citizen's Patrol cannot be nominated," he was shouting to be heard above the buzz of conversation. "After receiving all nominations, you will be asked to fill out a ballot with the name of your choice. Once everyone has voted we will count the ballots. If you wait, we'll announce the outcome when we're done." As he spoke the other Guard members were busy making preparations. A chalkboard, on which they would write the names of the nominees, was brought into the room. In the foyer, Peach and Moon were bringing in a small table. Dylan had a large box that was to be the ballot box and Rod brought pencils and scraps of paper for the voting. Once the flurry of activity had died down, Kurt looked to the people of the Settlement and the farm and said, "Do I hear any nominations?"

The room was suddenly quiet as people looked at each other. It seemed no one wanted to be the first. Finally, Wolf, the young man that Kyla had seen with his bag of fish her first night on duty at the shelter house, rose and shouted defiantly, "I think it should be Fleet."

The suggestion brought cheers of agreement as well as angry shouts against it. Fleet jumped to his feet and called for quiet. Once they were listening, Fleet explained, "I already have a position of importance with the Guard, I cannot perform the duties of two people." He had anticipated the possibility that someone would want to nominate him and had the answer ready. "I know that any one of you is capable of providing your opinion whether you're asked or not." There was laughter at his statement. "That is all we are asking and you are all qualified to fill the position." He sat back in his chair and watched. It was up to them now.

A slim young man that Fleet knew as Tyler rose and looked around the room. "I think it should be Andrew." Everyone in the room turned and looked at the young man next to Tyler.

Kurt looked at Kyla who was standing next to the chalkboard and said, "Write Andrew on the board." Then turning to Andrew he said, "Will you please come and join us on the hearth?" Everyone watched as the young man stepped past the people seated on the floor and made his way to the steps that led to the hearth. Andrew was dressed like everyone else with a flannel shirt and jeans and there was nothing about him that set him apart from any of the others. As he stood next to Kurt, he nervously brushed the hair from his face and stood looking at the crowd.

"Is there anyone else?" Kurt asked looking out over those assembled.

Next to rise was a young woman named Tamara who lived outside the Settlement. "I want to nominate Sara." She looked at the seamstress who had been a nurse. Everyone knew that it was Sara who had helped the girl when she was sick last winter and nearly died from pneumonia. Sara rose slowly and she began a slow deliberate walk to stand with the others. She was a tall woman, nearly standing eye to eye with Kurt. Her blond hair was pulled back into a neat bun and as she stood proudly next to Andrew, she was smiling confidently at the crowd.

As Kurt heard the sound of Kyla writing Sara's name on the board, he was saying a small prayer of thanks to himself. Two nominees, at least now they could have an election. There were two more nominations shouted out almost at the same time. A rather small, black man that everyone called Charlie and Martin, one of the older men at the Settlement. As their names were added to the list, they made their way up the steps to the hearth. "Anyone else?" Kurt asked loudly. He searched the room, looking for any sign that there was. When no one spoke up, he said, "If there are no objections, the nominations are closed."

Once again Fleet rose and said, "The four people who you have nominated are your friends and neighbors. You know them. It is now your duty to choose who will represent you. If there is a tie between two or more of them, we will eliminate the others and vote again. Please form an orderly line. Peach and Rod are waiting in the foyer where you may cast your vote." He turned to the four waiting on the stage and said, "You can have a seat while they vote."

Immediately, a line began to form. There was some pushing, as it seemed everybody wanted to go first. The whole process took less than an hour. When the votes were counted it was Martin who was elected. After Fleet made the announcement the room erupted in applause and some people began chanting over and over again, "Martin! Speech!"

With a little prompting from Fleet, Martin stepped forward and held up his hands and started by saying, "Quiet, please." He was in his thirties and of average height and build. His hair was prematurely gray and he wore it cut short in front but let it hang long down the back. He seemed to be a man with confidence as he stood, head held high, facing those assembled in the room. "I'm honored by your trust in my ability to make a contribution. Though I have to admit that I don't know what will be expected of me, but I will always remember that I am representing all of you in whatever I do."

Fleet smiled as Martin spoke. If he had written the speech himself, it couldn't have done better. He knew Martin and was pleased with the outcome. When Martin finished his short acceptance speech, Fleet made his final announcement. "We have planned a celebration. If you will all stay for awhile longer, we will be serving cake and tea in the foyer." There was no need to ask twice. It had been a long time since any one had had cake and being invited as quests was a treat. No one other than the Guard had ever been served food in the cabin. It was yet another small and subtle change from Sadie's rules. An additional gesture was the fact that it was the members of the Guard and the Citizen's Patrol who were serving the cake and tea. Then collecting the empty cups and glasses after everything was eaten. They were serving the people as they served them by protecting them from harm. It was a pleasant afternoon party and everyone was enjoying themselves thoroughly.

Some of the people had wandered outside and Justin had followed them out. He was on his way back to the front door with his hands full of dirty dishes when he heard the sound of horses galloping down the lane. He hurried up the steps and in the door where Kurt was talking with Martin. Justin interrupted Martin in mid-sentence as he said, "Excuse me. Kurt I need to talk to you now."

The urgency in Justin's words was obvious and Kurt stepped aside to let Justin whisper in his ear. "It's Sadie." The words weren't needed. No sooner than Justin spoke them, Kurt could see Sadie and Riley come into view as they dismounted and started up the walk.

"The party's over," Kurt said. "We'd better start clearing the house. I'll introduce Martin to Sadie." As Justin hurried to his task, Kurt returned to Martin and smiled diplomatically as he said, "Sadie's back." Undoubtedly, Martin was thinking that he had served the shortest term in elected office, ever. Kurt then looked at Fleet who was still standing with Kyla serving the last of the cake.

Chapter Nineteen

As Sadie approached the cabin, a surprising sight greeted her eyes. The door to her cabin was wide open and everyone from the Settlement was there. When she pulled the horse to a grinding halt in front of the walkway, she slid out of the saddle and began to walk toward the house. She had driven the horses to exhaustion to return before the Gathering. It seemed that even though it was not dark, that she was already too late. Physically exhausted from the hard ride, Sadie felt that she was in a daze and the sight of everybody eating cake and drinking tea on her front lawn was infuriating. It was difficult to maintain a cool and detached composure, but Sadie smiled and acknowledged each person who welcomed her home. When she stepped inside, Fleet was waiting for her.

"We're glad to see that you and Riley are home," Fleet said. "Your sudden departure had some people worried." Sadie was standing stiffly just inside the doorway with Riley cowering behind her.

Once she sighted Fleet, Sadie's feet refused to move. Her face grew as cold and white as ice as he spoke. For the first time that she could remember, Sadie was speechless with shock. It took her a moment to regain her composure and she said, "I am tired from the long ride. Fleet, will you please come with me and you can fill me in on what is happening here."

As Sadie began to head toward the hall, Fleet cut her off and gestured toward the library. "Armand bring Sadie's chair," Fleet called. Sadie still had not moved toward the library and was openly staring at him. "Please," Fleet said as Armand hurried to place her chair back in the library. With a slight nod to Armand as he hastily exited the library, Sadie walked stiffly into the room. As Fleet followed, he closed the door behind them, for the moment he had the advantage. He steeled himself as he turned to face Sadie.

She did not sit in the chair or make any movement to do so. Sadie was fussing with her dress, trying to brush the dust from it and complaining, "I would have preferred to change into some clean clothes." With every word she felt an overwhelming rage building inside of her. She had been certain that her plans would be successful. Fleet was not supposed to be standing here. From all appearances, he didn't have a scratch on him. "What is going on here?" she demanded angrily. "The Gathering should not have started for hours."

"We have elected a citizens' representative to take your place." Fleet paused just long enough to see the anger flicker in her eyes before adding, "But only when you're absent." He could tell she was tired and was hoping it would work to his advantage. They both warily circled the real issue. Fleet continued by saying, "Where's Lipsky?" Sadie shot him a hateful glare and continued brushing her skirt, but more firmly than before. "You couldn't get Lazarus to let him go. Could you?" Fleet laughed derisively as he spoke. Still, Sadie didn't reply. After waiting a few moments, Fleet said in a hushed voice, "I know about your connections with Lazarus and Cole Spring."

Finally, Sadie spoke or rather shrieked with laughter, as she said, "And what do you know, Fleet? Just tell me, what brought you to such a conclusion." She was laughing as she sat down heavily in the armchair.

"I have a note that you sent to Cole Spring, that said 'North by Northwest road, telling him where to find Eddie and Dylan," Fleet had not moved and was still standing just inside the door. His head was pounding again. The anger that was welling inside him was causing his pulse to beat loudly in his ears and it echoed in his head.

"I did no such thing," she denied vehemently. She was watching Fleet with interest. He stared blankly at her for just a moment, but it passed quickly.

"It was your handwriting," Fleet said coolly, "and I took it from Clovis Spring."

"He took it from Eddie or Dylan, I can't remember which one I gave it to," she lied convincingly. She continued to scrutinize Fleet.

Fleet might have believed her if he hadn't been to the compound at the zoo and met Lazarus. He strode aggressively across the floor then bending over her put one hand on each arm of the chair, which brought him face to face with Sadie. "I know about you and Lazarus. I've seen the symbol." He stood and watched her smugly.

"And Lazarus knows you," she hissed the words at him. "They all know you Fleet. They know it is you when you go to Cole Spring's farm. They knew it was you when you went to the stock farm." When Fleet showed surprise at the mention of the stock farm, it only added fuel to Sadie's tirade. Sadie rose now, looked directly in the eyes and said, "You are a dead man. If you aren't dead by the end of today, you will be tomorrow." She delivered the sentence dispassionately and pushed Fleet aside as she walked to the door ready to leave.

Fleet caught her by the arm and prevented her from opening the door. "I know that you are working for Manjohnah." He said the words in a low voice, as if it were something too horrible to say out loud.

She laughed again, her entire body shaking with mirth as she tried to keep the laughter inside. "What if I am? What are you or any of your miserable friends going to do about it?" She stepped back from the door pushing Fleet with her as she moved. "My friends are powerful. They know you and they know where you are. Every moment that you remain here, your life and those of anyone near to you are in danger. I have done everything I could to prevent you from doing this to yourself." She was smiling now as she turned the tables on Fleet and backed him up, literally, to the wall. "They will pursue you wherever you go. If I were you, I would be careful whom I consider a friend. Manjohnah's men are everywhere, as you have seen."

As Fleet shook his head to clear his thoughts all he could hear was the pounding in his brain and Sadie's voice. He tried to remember what he had wanted to say to her, but now all he could do was listen. "I will give you a chance to leave, but you must go tonight." She was smiling as she made her terms quite clear. "You must go alone." As Fleet gave her a pained look, Sadie was radiant, her victory in sight as she said, "Don't worry, I won't have Kyla killed. I will promise you that. If you promise to never return, I will make sure she lives a long life, but I will kill you both if you return for her." When Fleet collapsed into one of the chairs that lined the wall, she knew she had won. Fleet had never given in with so little argument. It had barely been a fight. Something was obviously wrong with him. Sadie could see that he was weak and seemed confused. Apparently, one of the assassins had inflicted some damage. Then she turned and went to the window, saying, "Now get out of my sight before I change my mind." As she heard him put his hand on the doorknob then the click of the latch, she added, "And don't go to the Family. I will find out and then I'll have to destroy them, too."

When Fleet left the library, slamming the door behind him, Sadie allowed herself to collapse wearily in the chair. She had not expected to have a confrontation with Fleet upon her arrival. It had been the farthest thing from her mind. The most expedient thing to do would have been to kill him herself. She had her knife and he would never have expected it, but she was not in the mood for messy complications. When Fleet died, the blood would not stain her hands. Sadie wanted him gone from the Settlement and he would not come back when the penalty was his death and Kyla's. Sadie fully intended to keep her promise to make sure that nothing happened to Kyla. She wanted the skinny little whore to pay for her transgressions. Fleet belonged to Sadie and the thought of him with Kyla had sickened her. How Fleet could have wasted his time with an obviously inferior woman was beyond her understanding. Sadie wanted to make her suffering last longer than the time it took for a knife to cut her throat and her life to flow out with the blood. Sadie wanted to make Kyla's pain last a lifetime and Fleet would be the knife that she used.

The foyer was empty when Fleet emerged from the library. As he turned into the hallway leading to his room, Fleet nearly ran over Kurt in his rush. He was taking long hurried strides down the hallway to his room, with Kurt right behind him. As soon as he was in his room Fleet picked up his pack from beside the door and began stuffing his possessions into it.

"What's going on?" Kurt demanded. "Where are you going?"

"I'm leaving," Fleet answered. He went to the cabinet and took out the burlap bag that he had brought from Lazarus' compound. He pulled out two infra red scopes and gave one to Kurt then wrapped the burlap bag around the other again and stuffed it into the pack along with his binoculars.

While Kurt watched Fleet emptying the ammunition from the cabinet and filling his saddlebags until they could hold no more, he was asking, "Tell me what she said."

Fleet stopped for a moment and said, "She just reminded me of the fact that I am a dead man. Lazarus won't stop until I am dead." Then pausing for just a moment he added, "Manjohnah won't leave me alone until I am dead and everyone around me is, too."

"Don't go," Kurt argued. "You can't just give up. We need you to help finish what you started here." Kurt felt like he was talking to a madman as he followed Fleet watching him tearing the room apart as he searched for the things that he wanted to take. Finally, he stepped in front of Fleet and took his shoulders in his hands, forcing his friend to look into his eyes. "What about Kyla. Should I go and get her?"

"No," Fleet shouted with distress at the mention of Kyla. "She said that Kyla would be hunted, too, if she went with me."

"You can't just leave without talking to her, man," he was shaking Fleet hoping to bring him to reason. "You can't leave me to tell her." Kurt could not believe that Fleet would not want to say something if he was leaving.

When Fleet looked to Kurt, his eyes were begging Kurt to understand why he couldn't see Kyla before he left. His heart was being wrenched from his chest, if he had to see Kyla or speak to her, he wouldn't be able to leave her behind and he truly believed that taking her along would be like signing her death warrant himself. Fleet couldn't do it. When he had everything he needed, Fleet turned his back on Kurt and left the room without answering his pleas for reason. Kurt was hot on his heels every step of the way.

Kurt pushed through the front door ahead of Fleet, trying to physically block him, but Fleet only stepped to the side and ignored him. Once outside, it was as if they were racing to the stable, but there was no one to see them. Even though only minutes earlier the farmyard had been crowded with people, as soon as the shouting started in the library everyone had scattered. When he got to the barn, Fleet threw the pack and saddle bags on the floor, and began to bridle and saddle the black stallion.

"Where will you go?" Kurt asked. He had been Fleet's friend for some time and couldn't understand Fleet's insistence on going alone. "We can come and join you in a few weeks when things have settled down."

"Where can I go?" I've gone north, south, east and west and everywhere I turn all I find are Manjohnah's men," he paused only slightly before adding bitterly, "and women." As he finished tying his bags to the back of the saddle, Fleet mounted the horse.

Kurt came to him and grasping his leg said, "I have never asked you to change your mind before but I am begging you now to stay. Don't leave like this. You're not thinking clearly or you wouldn't be acting like this. Please, Fleet, stay and we will all fight Sadie with you."

"They would just send someone to replace her. Maybe someone worse," Fleet answered thinking of Lazarus. "You know about her now and you'll be able to protect yourself." He started the horse moving forward, but stopped as he turned and said, "Please, watch Kyla for me and tell her that I am truly sorry for everything that I have done to her. She deserves better. Tell her that I love her." Without another look back, Fleet spurred the horse to a gallop and headed down the lane for the last time. He purposely looked away from the cabin as he rode or he might have seen Kyla come running out the door when he passed by.

At the sight of Fleet riding away, she ran for the stables and was met by Kurt who caught her as she ran into him. She started to pull away, but he held her tight in his arms. "Let me go," Kyla said angrily as she struggled to break his hold. "I have to catch him." She struggled harder, but Kurt wouldn't let her go.

"You're not going anywhere," Kurt said. He had lost Fleet and he wasn't going to let Kyla follow him on whatever self-destructive course he had set himself to this time. Kurt let Kyla hit him and kick him, but he still wouldn't release his hold on her. It wasn't long before she had exhausted her anger and hurt and she collapsed and laid her head on his shoulder. He could feel the wetness from her tears as she sobbed now as uncontrollably as she had been hitting him only moments before. Kurt's heart was breaking, too. He loved them both and it was up to him to pick up the pieces left in the wake of Fleet's hasty departure. Not only was Kyla his responsibility, but also the Settlement and that little ray of hope that Fleet had kindled in every one's mind. Now Kurt would carry the weight of the vision alone.

"He'll be back," Kurt said. It was as much to console himself as Kyla.

~ ~ ~

As soon as Sadie disappeared into the library with Fleet, Riley had gone directly to James and nearly dragged him down the hallway to her room. Once they were both inside she looked to make sure no one had followed and closed the door, then locked it securely. Only then did she run to James and throw her arms around his neck. "I thought I would never make it back here alive," she exclaimed as she shivered at the thought of what she had overheard between Sadie and Lazarus. When she released James and began to walk about the room Riley was talking and gesturing emphatically with her hands. "I had no idea," she looked at him and said. "You had to be there to really understand the feel of the place. That man Lazarus is evil, pure evil. If you think Sadie is bad, she's nothing compared to him." Riley was almost speaking randomly as her thoughts came into her head and spilled out in her anxiety and rush to tell James everything.

"Slow down and start from the beginning," James said as he took Riley by the hand and led her to sit on the edge of her bed. He sat next to her and waited for her to compose her thoughts.

Riley looked at James' hand holding hers and she felt safe and secure for the first time since she had left the Settlement with Sadie. "I was listening at the door when Sadie spoke to Lazarus." She looked at James. Her big brown eyes were full of fear as she said, "He sent someone to kill Fleet."

"We know," James answered. "The day after you left, two men tried. Fleet killed one and Kyla killed the other."

"Well, Lazarus only sent one," Riley replied. "Sadie sent the other. But that's not all that was discussed. They both work for Manjohnah. I heard Lazarus implying that Manjohnah was unhappy with Sadie. It was all about Fleet causing trouble for them."

"Did you hear anything else?" James probed for more information. Riley had done well, but the thought of what would have happened to her if she had been discovered was frightening.

"No," she answered thoughtfully. "It was mostly about Fleet. They won't leave him alone. They're going to keep trying to kill him." She thought for a moment before saying, "There is one more thing. Something that Lazarus said. 'Keep them happy. Keep them fed. Take the ones you like to bed.' It gave me the creeps, like they're operating feeding stations to keep us under control. That's why they have to get rid of Fleet. He's not under their control and that's what bothers them most." Before she was done Riley was speaking angrily and she added, "We can't let them control our lives. Now that we know how can we keep pretending that everything's fine?"

James was thinking. "Sadie doesn't suspect that you know anything does she?"

"No," Riley said quickly. The fear had returned to her voice.

"Good," James was whispering as he spoke. "You know she will want you to stay with her now that she and Fleet have ended their relationship," his choice of words was mild considering the situation. "If you haven't slept with a knife in your hand before, do it now. Don't be afraid to use it on anybody, and I do mean anybody." He wanted to say to use it on Sadie if necessary, but Riley understood his meaning. As James stood to leave he added, "I am moving into your room tonight. If Sadie leaves during the night, I want you to come and get me. Don't follow her yourself. Do you understand?" He looked at her sternly, knowing that Riley was headstrong and would do as she pleased no matter what he said. All James wanted was to impress upon Riley the fact that he was quite serious.

Riley looked at James. He was so strong and earnest and she trusted him completely. It was not the first time they had discussed James moving into her room. Especially after Marta was gone, but they had not done so before out of respect for Sadie's wishes. Now they were making plans for James to move in out of fear of what Sadie might do. Things had changed drastically for them in just a matter of days. Riley knew that Sadie was a problem that would have to be dealt with sooner or later. "Do any of the others know about Sadie? Does Fleet know?" Riley asked. Fleet had been to Lazarus' compound. He had to know, too.

"Some of them do," James said, "and it is time for them all to know, but we have to be careful now that Sadie is back." As James unlocked the door to go out he said, "Clean up and rest for now. We'll talk later." Before closing the door, he said, "Lock the door when I leave." He hadn't needed to tell her, she was already at the door and the lock clicked into place before he released the doorknob.

~ ~ ~

It was mid-morning when Sister Samethia heard three shots fired one right after the other. It was the signal that someone had passed the sentry without stopping. Within moments Brother Fox and Brother Eldar were standing beside her with their rifles ready to fire, waiting to see who it was. When they saw the long legged black stallion and his black suited rider, they lowered their weapons. It was Fleet, but it did not excuse him from stopping when the sentry called. Brother Fox was visibly agitated when Fleet galloped into the camp. When he saw that the horse was lathered with sweat and blowing hard, Brother Fox called to Brother Wyatt who was coming from the direction of the stable, "Come and take this horse." Then to Fleet who was jumping out of the saddle, he said, "What's wrong?" It had to be bad news if Fleet had ridden his horse to the point of nearly killing the animal.

Fleet looked past him at Sister Samethia and said, "I have to talk to you." As he stepped past Brother Fox, Fleet took her by the arm and said, "Where can we talk in private?"

With a look over her shoulder to Brother Fox, Sister Samethia answered, "We'll go to my shelter. We can talk there." She could tell by Fleet's voice and face that he was extremely disturbed about something. As they began walking toward the small earth shelter Sister Samethia and Brother Fox shared, Brother Fox was following them.

Fleet turned and snapped, "I need to speak to Sister Samethia alone."

Brother Fox gripped his rifle tightly, fighting the urge to use it on Fleet. He was acting like a mad man. The look of desperation in his eyes was something he had never seen in Fleet before today. He stopped following only when Sister Samethia turned just before reaching the door to their home and said, "Don't worry." Then she turned to follow Fleet into the shelter. It was nearly dark inside. Sister Samethia had let the fire burn low that morning. They did not need it for the heat. She went to the hearth and stirred the embers then added a few small pieces of wood to make a small flame that provided some light. Fleet came to fire where she was sitting and knelt beside her.

"Sister Samethia, I need your help. I want you to do another reading. I need you to tell me what to do." Fleet was begging her to perform some magic.

As Sister Samethia rose slowly, she placed her hand on Fleet's head while he continued to kneel before her. She could feel the bump on the back of his head, but more than that she could feel pain, confusion, and sorrow as strongly as she had ever felt in one of her readings. She dropped her hands, afraid to touch him again. She could not help Fleet as he wished. "I have already told you everything that I know. Another reading will not tell me anything new," Sister Samethia tried to explain, but he did not want to listen.

"What good are your powers if you can't tell me what I need to know? You told me that I am the arrow to pierce the heart of my enemy, but you never told me how." Fleet turned and looked at the fire. "Sadie and Lazarus tried to kill me once and they'll try again. Both of them are taking orders from Manjohnah. That's why I need you to tell me how to find Manjohnah. I must kill him before he does the same to me."

"I don't know how Fleet, what I know is hard to describe. It is a feeling of certainty, not specific events," she said, then motioned to the rugs in front of the fire. "Please sit down while we talk. I can see that you're tired." As Fleet collapsed heavily on the floor, she filled a cup of wine and gave it to him. Fleet poured the red liquid down his throat without tasting a drop. Refilling his cup, Sister Samethia said, "I'll try to help you if I can."

He looked into her eyes and asked, "How do you know when it's the Mother telling you what to do?" Fleet had always been a non-believer, but he desperately needed to believe in her prophecies now.

Sister Samethia considered him carefully. "It is like being tossed by the wind, first being pushed in one direction, only to be snatched up and pulled suddenly in the other. Sometimes, I feel that events are beyond my control no matter how I try to change the course of my actions."

"Yes, that's it exactly," Fleet said as he jumped to his feet and stood in front of her. He took Sister Samethia by the shoulders and squeezed her so tightly that she wanted to cry out, but couldn't. As he laid his hands upon her, she was caught up in the emotions flowing through his mind. Fleet's gaze riveted her and she couldn't move. "I never truly believed until now. Isn't there some clue? Some small thing that could help me?" he asked as he released her.

Sister Samethia gasped with relief as Fleet removed his hands. Then she lowered her eyes. She did know more than she had told Fleet. "Where is Sister Kyla?" she asked.

"What does Kyla have to do with me killing Manjohnah?" Fleet asked angrily. He wasn't sure why Sister Samethia had picked this moment to inquire about Kyla.

"I never said that you would kill Manjohnah. I said that you would pierce the heart of your enemy. You are the one who named Manjohnah. Whatever you do, you won't do it without Kyla. The arrow is useless without the bow to propel it. Kyla is part of the bow and there is another. All three parts will have to work together to pierce the heart of your enemy."

"I couldn't bring Kyla with me," Fleet answered. Then he looked questioningly at Sister Samethia and asked, "And who is the third?"

"I don't know," Sister Samethia answered, "but I'll know when we meet. I knew Kyla when I first saw her." She picked up the cup of wine and gave it to Fleet. "Drink this and you'll feel better. If you truly feel that the Mother is guiding you, then leaving Kyla may be the answer that you are looking for. If she's not with you, then where you are being propelled is not your final destination. The Mother can guide you down many paths before she sets you on your final course."

Fleet drank the sweet red liquid, but it had a bitter aftertaste. It must have been the dregs from the flask. As he set the cup beside the fire, Fleet felt a little peace already. Then sitting cross legged next to the fire, he watched the flames dancing and quietly contemplated his next move. Sister Samethia had answered some of his questions, but Fleet could not stay with the Family or Sadie would take her vengeance out on them. Still, he needed to rest for a little while.

Sister Samethia began to massage his temples, speaking softly, "Fleet, you need to rest. When you wake up your headache will feel much better."

As he felt the tension and worries drain from his body, Fleet closed his eyes and slowly lay down. The pounding in his head had stopped and he answered drowsily, "Yes, but I can't stay too long."

Fleet had hardly said the words before his head dropped and he was sleeping. Sister Samethia went to the door and motioned for Brother Fox who was standing just outside.

When he saw Fleet lying by the fire sleeping soundly, he asked, "What's wrong with him?"

"I gave him something to make him sleep," Sister Samethia answered. "He needs to rest. He's had some kind of injury to his head. Fleet told me that Sadie and someone named Lazarus are working for Manjohnah and that they are trying to kill him."

Brother Fox looked at Fleet again, considering what to do. Fleet was a danger to them all, but he could not send him away when he so obviously needed their help. "What should we do?" Brother Fox whispered.

"Let him sleep," Sister Samethia said. "Fleet will know what needs to be done after that." She turned to leave with Brother Fox following. Whether Fleet believed that the Mother was guiding him or not, the decisions that he made were Hers now. Sister Samethia could feel that Her power was strong within Fleet now.

They left Fleet to sleep and he remained in blissful slumber the entire day. He was still sleeping soundly by the hearth when Brother Fox and Sister Samethia retired for the night. However, the next morning they woke to find Fleet was gone. He had left without a word, but Brother Fox was more concerned about Sister Samethia. After waking to find Fleet gone, she had seemed melancholy and unresponsive to his attempts to cheer her. When she had finally told him what was wrong, it brought him no comfort. Sister Samethia had had a dream that night. All she would say was that they would not speak to Fleet again for a very long time.

~ ~ ~

Kyla returned to the cabin early in the morning. When Kurt had finally released her, she had run to the old schoolhouse and spent the night in the bed that she had meant for herself and Fleet. She had not spent much time sleeping and when she had her dreams had been disturbing remembrances of Raphael attacking Fleet. Then in some versions it was Raphael attacking her. Even though he was dead

Raphael was haunting her dreams. She felt wretched when she walked in the door. If there had been anywhere else to go, she would have, but now her life was tied to this place. Kyla could not leave for fear that Fleet would return and find her gone. As she headed toward her room, Sadie emerged from the library. Dressed in black and moving quickly toward her, Kyla was reminded of a spider. She was in no mood for a confrontation with Sadie.

"Kyla, I have been waiting to speak to you," Sadie said in her sweetest voice. She despised Kyla and it was difficult to maintain a pleasant expression.

Without turning, Kyla continued walking toward her room and said, "It will have to wait. I am tired."

Sadie's voice became hard as she said, "I am afraid I must insist." She watched smugly as Kyla stopped in her tracks and turned to face her. At first Kyla did not move, so Sadie said, "In the library if you don't mind. This is private," then waited as Kyla stalked angrily into the library. She followed more slowly. Sadie was in no hurry. Closing the door as she stepped into the library, Sadie said graciously, "Won't you have a seat, my dear? You would be much more comfortable."

Kyla stood where she was. Her impatience came out as she said, "Say whatever it is that was so important it couldn't wait."

"I want to apologize for Fleet," Sadie said doing her best to sound genuinely concerned. She was walking slowly around the room, looking at the books and running her fingers along the shelves as she spoke casually. "Fleet is a man with," now she paused and glanced at Kyla, "strong physical appetites. You are just the latest in a long list of women that Fleet has used." Sadie turned now to look at Kyla. She wanted to see her eyes. "I don't why I put up with his infidelities for so long. You and I are the victims." It was difficult not to smile as she planted the seeds of doubt in Kyla's mind.

Kyla stared straight ahead, refusing to meet Sadie's eyes. Her attempt to turn Fleet into the villain was transparent at best and the thought of Sadie as the victim was laughable. She was tempted to respond with an insult of her own, but Kyla kept her silence. Anything that she said would be ammunition for Sadie to use against her. The best way to deal with Sadie was to refuse to react to her taunts.

The stony face that Kyla was wearing was only more incentive for Sadie to try to make her crack. "I can see that you are upset," Sadie cooed softly, "so I will be brief." As she came to stand before Kyla, forcing her to look into her eyes Sadie held her gaze for a moment and the hate that she saw in those blue eyes staring back at her only made Sadie more determined. "Did Fleet ask you to bear his children?" She saw a spark of recognition flash in her eyes, as Kyla felt the point of her knife. Sadie continued, "He asked me to do the same thing the day before you left for the west." As she thrust her point home, Sadie could see a reflexive twitch in Kyla's composure and was walking away as she said, "Fleet had a driving need to spread his seed. It was all he thought about." Sadie finally crossed the room and sat in her chair. As she looked at Kyla who was now shaking with the effort to control her emotions, Sadie said, "You can go now. That is all I wanted to tell you."

Kyla turned slowly. It took all her effort not to run from the room. As she hurried across the foyer, she ran into Kurt and Justin who were standing near the door. The two men could see that she was near tears and watched as she disappeared into her room. It was no surprise to either of them to see Sadie come to the doorway of the library to watch Kyla go.

When Sadie saw them, she said, "Justin, I'm glad that you're still here. You can give me your report." It was time that she regained control over all the members of the Guard. Justin's scouting trips to the east were the next thing that she was going to stop.

Justin looked at Sadie then to Kurt. With a nod from Kurt, Justin headed out the door. Before Sadie could object, Justin was gone. Kurt walked to where Sadie was standing. "Justin has already reported to me," he said coolly. "I will be more than happy to answer any questions that you might have." Kurt waited, standing stiffly at attention before Sadie. When she said nothing, Kurt nodded to her formally and said, "Nothing? Well, if you'll excuse me then. I have work to do." As he turned and walked away, Kurt could feel her eyes on his back. He couldn't shake the feeling that Sadie would have liked to kill him, too.

Sadie watched Kurt walking away. He had never been rude and disrespectful before now. She wondered what Fleet might have said to him about his suspicions of her involvement with Manjohnah. Kurt would have been the logical choice to replace Fleet as the new leader of the Guard. Perhaps all he needed was a little friendly persuasion. It had worked with Fleet. Once she had taken him as her lover, Fleet had been very cooperative. But Kurt was different; she was not too optimistic about the possibility of grooming Kurt for the job. There was always James. He was steady and dependable, but the thought of James brought another small twinge of irritation to mind.

He had moved into Riley's room and neither of them had asked her permission. It was still her house and everyone living here was her guest. She had only been gone for five days and it seemed that everyone had turned against her. It was all Fleet's doing, but he was gone. If he had managed to turn them against her in five days, then she could win them back in less. There had been some damage to the trust that she had worked so hard to create, but it was not gone completely.

As she walked back to her room, she was thinking of James. He was not as physically attractive to her as Fleet had been nor was he as dynamic a personality, but he would serve her purposes nicely. James would be easier to influence and she would not have to worry about him leaving the farm. It was his life and at this time that was what suited her assignment. Of course Riley would be upset if she made advances toward James, but Riley would adjust. Riley was always able to accept what she did without question.

The rest of the Guard would fall into line with James or she would have them replaced. If she couldn't dismiss them, there were other ways to create vacancies. Sadie had only promised to make sure that nothing happened to Kyla, but her assurances didn't apply to Kurt or any of the others. They would follow her without question or meet with an untimely accident. To Sadie, it didn't matter one way or the other. She was going to take back control of the Settlement and she had to do so quickly.

Chapter Twenty

Fleet had been wandering the countryside for weeks. After leaving the Family's camp he had headed south and away from Manjohnah. With no destination in mind, he let the horse choose their direction in most cases. The day after speaking with Sister Samethia, he had felt better. Despite her insistence that she could not help him, she had done more to bring peace to his mind than she would ever know. When he'd awakened in the middle of the night to find that his headache was finally gone, he was comforted by the belief that although Kyla was not with him now, that she would be again. She was with him every step that he traveled, for he held her in his heart and thoughts.

The solitude of his journey was what he had needed. So many things had happened in his life in the short span of a few weeks and Fleet had needed the time alone to think about what he should do. He spent a lot of time thinking about Sister Samethia and her Mother. She told him that the Mother would guide him in the direction that he should go, so he let chance guide his path. Fleet had traveled east until he came to another great river that was even larger than the one to the west. There was no way to cross. Every bridge had been destroyed and there was no helpful person like Liam with a boat, ready to ferry him across. Fleet had continued south until he came to the union of the two great rivers, traveling to the very point were they joined together and continued as one mighty river to the sea. The way south was blocked to him. He could have tried to build a raft to float across, but there was no way to take the horse and no guarantee that he would make it across alive. It seemed that the Mother was guiding him and he was forced to turn north again.

As he traveled north, now following the river that formed the western border of Fleet's world, a feeling of serenity and confidence filled his body and soul. Fleet had actually felt something when he held Sister Samethia by the shoulders that day, and it had filled him with wonder and awe, finally understanding what she had been trying to tell him. No matter what action Fleet took, powers beyond his control were controlling his destiny.

When Fleet came to the ruins of another large city along the shore of the river, nearly two hundred miles south of the one where Lazarus' compound was located, he stopped in a grassy meadow on the edge of the destruction and tied the horse so it could graze. Fleet had traveled without sighting anybody for weeks, but now he was following a hunch. There was nothing to indicate that anyone was living in the ruins, but something in the back of his mind was nagging at him, telling him to look further. Fleet decided to put Sister Samethia's Mother to the test. He would follow his premonition and see where it led.

As he hid his belongings under some brush, Fleet looked at the horse and hoped that it would still be there when he returned. He began to walk toward the wasteland and shrugged to himself. If someone did steal the horse, it wouldn't be the first time that he'd had to walk. Fleet picked up a long stick to use to test the ground as he walked. He had passed through enough of these artificial deserts to know that in places the ground was unstable. Fleet was alone now. If he slid into a hole there would be no one to come to his aid.

After walking through the waste for an hour, Fleet stopped and looked at the light gray dust and sand that surrounded him. Then on the horizon to the north, he saw a dark speck moving quickly over a small ridge and then it was gone. Immediately, Fleet picked up his pace heading in the direction where he had seen movement. It could have been a wild dog, but he was betting that it was a human. It was hard to tell where he was headed, since every rise looked like the next on the horizon, but when Fleet reached the spot where he had sighted the dark figure, he paused briefly. There was nothing. Fleet rushed forward again, nearly falling into a deep pit that opened before him on the other side of a steep pile of sand. It was all Fleet could do to prevent himself from sliding into the hole. As he skidded to a stop just short of the edge, Fleet saw a ladder on the other side of the pit that led into the hole. Cautiously, he skirted the edge and began to climb down the ladder into the darkness.

The first thing that greeted Fleet was the stench of human waste. It hit him so hard that it almost took his breath away. He was ready to climb back out when a voice from below called out, "You there. What do you want?" It was unbelievable that anyone could stand the smell, but Fleet climbed down the rest of the way. As soon as his feet hit the ground, Fleet held his arm across his mouth and nose, trying to breathe through the fabric and hoping it would block some of the smell. When his eyes finally adjusted to the dark, he could see who had greeted him. A small and bent old man was sitting on a chair next to the ladder. He had a strip of cloth tied across his face. Fleet had no doubt that its purpose was to lessen the stench and not to hide his identity.

"Pay the toll," the man said tiredly as he held out his hand. He was thin and bony and had only a few tufts of white hair around his ears. His jeans were stiff with dirt and his shirt, which had probably been white, was grimy and gray.

Fleet had no idea what the toll might be. He searched his pockets for something that he could give the old man. The only things he had were some small green apples he had picked earlier in the day, intending to give them to the horse. When Fleet held one out to the man, he snatched it greedily and devoured it core and all before pointing toward the darkness beyond him saying, "Go on."

As he walked in the direction the man had pointed, Fleet felt as if he were being swallowed by darkness. Looking back to the hole where he entered it seemed to be a bright spot where only moments before it had seemed dim. As he looked toward the light, Fleet was able to see that this place had been a parking garage with huge concrete columns that supported the ceiling. Fleet had no idea where he was going, but as he left the entrance behind him the light faded and he saw another dimmer light just beyond him now.

The sound of his footsteps echoed hollowly as he walked but when he came closer to the stairwell that was the source of the light, Fleet could hear the sound of people talking. Cautiously he descended the stairway and came to a level of the garage that had been filled with shops. The place had an eerie and surrealistic quality about it with the only illumination provided by the lighted signs on the fronts of the shops, which were now the homes of the people who survived the destruction. He walked past people sitting on benches and leaning from the doorways and they watched him with curiosity. No one spoke to him or inquired about his business, nor did they welcome him. Fleet was glad they kept their distance. Everyone looked pale and sickly. It was not surprising, given the fact that they lived underground with their only source of fresh air polluted by their own sewage. Even though the smell was fainter now, it still permeated the place. Fleet knew that he would not be staying long. As he wandered the narrow walkways, Fleet was looking for something and hoping he would recognize it when he saw it. When he rounded a corner, Fleet was met by a young girl.

She smiled when she saw Fleet and said, "I'll bet you're thirsty." Then she began to push him toward a door at the end of the walkway. "I'll bet you have something to eat. Do you want a woman, too?"

Fleet looked at her. She reminded him of Kyla when he had first seen her. She was painfully thin, but she was definitely not a woman. His heart went out to the young girl. When he gave her one of his apples, her eyes lit up as if he had given her a precious jewel. Unlike the man at the entry, the girl didn't devour the apple on the spot, but shoved it into her pocket. At the same time she had led him to the door, as she pushed it open, she said, "My name is Angel. If you want anything ask for me."

Stepping through the door brought Fleet into another level of darkness. The light in the room was almost non-existent. A single small lamp burned on a counter. Behind the counter stood a man who could only be the bartender. "What do you have to drink?" Fleet asked as he walked to the bar.

The man looked him over and asked, "What do you have to trade?"

Fleet took out one of the small green apples and laid it on the counter. When the man snorted in disgust, Fleet laid another beside it. He hoped it would be enough. If he had known that he was going to use the apples for barter he would have filled his pockets. Right now, Fleet was running out. Apparently, two apples were enough, and the man turned and filled a glass. When he set it in front of Fleet, he started to grab the apples but Fleet covered them with his hand, then picked up the glass and sipped cautiously. The brew they made at the Settlement was bad, but this was worse. Fleet turned and spit the liquid out on the floor. When he turned back to the man behind the counter, he said, "Surely, you can do better than that."

As the man began to reach under the counter, Fleet let go of the apples and quickly pulled his rifle off his shoulder and pointed it at the man. When the bartender raised his hands and stepped back, Fleet climbed onto the counter and looked to see what was underneath. He didn't see a gun, but there was a bottle of real liquor. Picking it up, Fleet grinned at the man still standing with his hands up and said, "Now, that's better." Then leaving the apples on the bar, he took the bottle and picked a seat where he could see everything and everyone from the moment they came into the establishment. Fleet had let fate guide him here to the very bowels of hell, but he wasn't any closer to understanding why.

Sitting quietly, he was almost invisible in the darkness as he watched the people who came into the bar. He saw the girl named Angel several times. She didn't appear to be doing anything other than hanging around waiting for someone to take her up on her offer. A pitiful old man had come in and spent quite a lot of time and energy trying to beg the bartender for a drink. When the man wouldn't leave another larger man called Mano, had come and thrown him out the door. Two other men entered and bartered for drinks. They drank the foul tasting drink that the man served and left. It all seemed rather pointless. Fleet had nearly drained the bottle of liquor and was ready to leave when another man entered the establishment.

There was something about this man that interested Fleet. He was dressed in a long black coat and Fleet could have sworn that he actually heard the sound of metal clanking under it and wondered what he was carrying. The second thing that caught his attention was the fact that this man did not belong here anymore than he did. His face was not pasty and pale like everyone else he had seen, and the man seemed in good health. Fleet watched him as he stepped up to the bar.

"I haven't seen you in awhile Scav-man," the bartender said. By the tone of his voice, it was easy to tell that the name 'Scav-man' was not meant to be complimentary.

The man in the long coat removed his hat and rubbed his hand through his short sandy colored hair. As he set the hat on the counter, he reached into one of his pockets, pulled out a can, and placed it on the bar. The bartender did as he had done with Fleet. He picked up the can and said derisively, "Cat food? You must have something better," then slammed it back on the counter. When the man picked up the can and started to leave, the bartender changed his mind quickly. "If that's all you've got, I'll take it," he said as he grabbed at the can.

"Make it the good stuff," the man said before he let go of the can, "I don't want any of that poison that you serve the locals." The bartender reached grudgingly under the counter and gave him a small bottle and a glass. It had been a costly day for him with two men insisting on real liquor. Hopefully, Mano would not find out and if he did, then he would give him the apples.

The man sitting at the counter looked around the room and took note of Fleet sitting in the corner. Then he turned and took a drink from the bottle, leaving the glass where it sat. It was too dark to tell if it was clean and most probably it wasn't. He had only been sitting at the bar for a few minutes when the girl who called herself Angel came in. She went directly to the man sitting at the bar and sat on the stool next to him. "What do you think you're doing?" he said angrily when he saw her. "Does Doc Dawson know you're here?"

"Do you have something for me?" she asked, ignoring his questions. Angel was smiling at him as she began rummaging through his pockets.

He stopped her by grabbing her by the wrists and said, "If I give you something to eat, do you promise that you'll go home?" The girl nodded enthusiastically. She would agree to anything as long as she got what she wanted. As soon as the man placed one of his cans in her hands, Angel whirled around and hurrying to the door, she ran into Mano, who was on his way in. When Mano saw the can in the girl's hand, he took it from her and pushed her out the door as he said, "Get back to work. You're going to have to do better than this if you're going to get any." The man named Mano was a broad and strongly built man, but he was not very tall. He looked at Fleet sitting in the corner. Then he walked to the man sitting at the bar and looked directly into his eyes, challenging him to do something.

"You had no right to take that from her. I gave it to Angel, not you," the man said as he rose from his seat. When he stood, he towered over Mano and glared down at the top of his head.

Mano stepped back slightly, while two men entered through the door and came to stand behind him. "Angel works for me and what she earns belongs to me," he said it without emotion or anger. Mano was just stating the facts.

"She's just a child," the man said. "Surely, you can find someone else." The man was standing quite still now with his arms held stiffly at his sides. "Return the can to Angel. It was a gift."

"I can't do that Scav-man," Mano answered. With a look to the other men, they all began to converge on him at once.

As Fleet watched, he saw the man suddenly swing a long handled sledgehammer that he had hidden under his coat. He brought it upward and connected firmly with Mano's testicles. The big man dropped immediately. Before Mano hit the ground, Fleet was on his feet with his rifle aimed at Mano's two friends. When they saw Fleet with his weapon pointed at them, the two men retreated through the door. The sandy haired man glanced at Fleet standing behind him, then reached back and took his hat and the bottle. The hammer had disappeared back under his coat. The way he had been swinging it made Fleet think that it was tied to his belt. As the man made a hasty exit, Fleet followed him out the door and had to jump back to avoid being hit by the hammer as he tried to go out.

"Don't follow me," he snapped as he watched Fleet warily. "I didn't ask for your help."

Fleet slipped the rifle on his shoulder and held his hands up. "I liked what you did. He deserved what he got."

The man turned and began to hurry away. When Fleet started after him, the man turned again and asked angrily, "Why are you following me?"

"I think we can help each other," Fleet offered. He didn't know why he was following him either.

The man looked at Fleet, eyeing him critically as he asked, "What's your name?"

"Fleet," he answered, then added quickly, "and if you know a good way to get out of this place, I'm with you."

"Well, Fleet, you can do what you want, just don't get in my way," he said and ducked down a dark passageway between two of the shops.

Fleet was right behind him as he whispered, "What's your name, friend?"

"I'm Daniel, Daniel Wallace," he answered quickly. He was busy looking for more of Mano's men. It wouldn't take long for them to return with help.

"Well, Wally," Fleet said, "Maybe you can tell me where we're going?" Daniel didn't respond to the question. He was already in motion. As he made his way through the dark passageways, Fleet was following only a few steps behind him. Eventually they came to another stairway leading up to the level where Fleet had entered. This stairwell was also much closer to whatever it was that was causing the stench. The smell was so strong that it made Fleet feel ill. When they emerged into the light only a few feet from the ladder leading out, he saw Daniel covering his face, too. They hurried up the ladder, refusing to stop when the old man called to them.

Once they were above ground Daniel started to head north but Fleet caught his arm and said, "Come with me. I left my things south of here."

Hesitating only a moment, Daniel said, "I hope you have ammo for that gun, because I can hear them coming up the ladder," and started running south.

They hadn't gone very far, before they heard the voices of the men shouting at them as they came out of the hole. Fleet had his rifle ready. When he heard the men following, he whirled around and fired some rounds into the air over their heads hoping to scare them off. It was luck that none of them were carrying guns, Fleet was outnumbered four to one. Taking a few steps back, he turned and ran after Daniel who already had a good lead. Fleet continued looking over his shoulder, expecting someone to be following.

When he finally caught up with Daniel, he said, "Apparently, we aren't worth the trouble."

Daniel finally slowed to a brisk walk as he said; "They'll just be waiting for me when I go back." He eyed Fleet critically. "I've never seen you around before."

"I'm just passing through," Fleet answered. "You don't live in that hole, do you?"

"No, I don't," Daniel answered warily. If there was one thing that he had learned, it was not to trust anybody, friendly or not.

Fleet was no less cautious about Daniel, but he was the one who had initiated the contact. Now he had to be the one to offer some information. "I've been traveling in the area southeast of here. I hadn't seen a soul until today."

"As far as I know there isn't anyone else," he said and looked at Fleet. "I've never run into anybody outside the Hole. Where did you come from?"

"I live north of here," Fleet replied, "at a place called the Settlement. You could come back there with me."

"So, are you trying to recruit me for your army?" Daniel asked. Fleet's black tunic with the long strand of beads hanging down the front appeared to be a uniform, but not like any he had seen before now. When Fleet turned and looked at him, he added quickly. "We don't see too many strangers around here, not dressed like you anyway."

Smiling now, Fleet said, "I guess you could say that I'm recruiting you, but I don't have an army, unless you call twelve people an army." He could understand Daniel's suspicions after the evacuations; anyone wearing a uniform was suspect. It was one thing to wear the uniform, and quite another to see someone else wearing one. Still, as he looked at Daniel, Fleet could tell by his expression that he was uncertain whether he could trust Fleet or not. "You can come with me or stay here. It's your choice," Fleet said, leaving Daniel behind as he picked up the pace. Now that he had mentioned the Settlement, he was becoming anxious to return.

Daniel walked silently behind the man that had introduced himself as Fleet. It was curiosity more than anything that made him decide to continue to follow him, that and the fact that there was nothing here other than sickness and death. Although the man in black seemed to be sincere, he was definitely not telling him everything either, Daniel would not let his guard down for a moment.

~ ~ ~

Kyla was in the kitchen making bread. It was the same thing that she had done every morning for many weeks. As she mixed and kneaded the dough, it gave her time to reflect on what was happening in her life. Nearly six weeks had passed since Fleet's sudden departure and things had been changing at the Settlement. It was impossible to have a meeting with all the Guard members without Sadie present. Still, they had managed to share information concerning her involvement with Lazarus, Cole Spring, and ultimately Manjohnah without her knowledge. At least, they hoped that she had no idea the Guard members were discussing her activities. Their experiences with Lipsky had made them all suspicious of Sadie and her spies.

Riley had shared her experiences at Lazarus' compound with Kyla, who had in turn told her about her own narrow escape with Fleet and Armand. Riley had become one of the most important links in their chain of information concerning Sadie's whereabouts and activities. Every morning Riley would come to the kitchen while Kyla was working, and tell her what Sadie had been doing. Then Kyla would report to Kurt who would pass the information to the others. It was their little underground information network.

This morning Riley entered the kitchen right on time. Agatha had just left to go to the storage rooms in the basement. Thankfully, she was a woman with a daily routine so rigid that you could set your clock by her actions. As soon as one door closed behind Agatha, Riley swept in through the other. Looking around the room, just to make sure they were alone, Riley approached Kyla cautiously. If Sadie entered unannounced, she would have to make up some excuse for being in the kitchen. Riley took a small piece of the raw dough and tasted it. Then she whispered, "Sadie had a visitor last night."

Kyla turned to look at the doors before asking, "Who was it?"

"We don't know," Riley answered. "James followed her to the greenhouses. After she went back to the cabin, he stayed to see who was there with her. It wasn't anybody that he knew from the Settlement."

"Was it one of Cole's men," Kyla asked.

"James tried to follow him," Riley answered, "but he lost him in the dark." She looked around nervously one more time before adding. "Whatever it was about, Sadie was in a foul mood when she came out of her room this morning. If I were you, I'd stay out of her way." Riley looked at Kyla sympathetically, as she gave her the last bit of advice. It was no secret that Sadie had been making a point of seeking Kyla out on a daily basis and talking to her about Fleet. Then without another word, she hurried out the door that led to the dining hall.

She had only been gone a few seconds when Sadie entered the kitchen. Seeing Kyla at work, she stalked to where she was standing and demanded angrily, "Have you seen Riley?"

"No," Kyla lied. She did not look away from her task or acknowledge Sadie's presence in any way.

"I know I saw her come into the kitchen," she said harshly. As she looked at Kyla standing with her hands and clothing covered with flour, Sadie noticed that Kyla seemed to look a little sickly. Her face was almost as white as the flour. That seemed to give Sadie satisfaction and she decided to take a little time out from her search for Riley to speak to Kyla. "You look pale," she said bluntly. "I thought you would be done crying for Fleet by now. Even you must know that he won't be back."

Kyla looked at Sadie now. She had been putting up with her insults and innuendoes for weeks and had never replied with any of her own, but today Kyla was not feeling well and her nerves were on edge. As she turned back to her work, she said, "I know he'll be back." She paused for just a moment before adding, "But I am not the one who has to worry about what will happen when he does return. What do you suppose Lazarus would say if he knew Fleet was still alive?" Kyla was only taking an educated guess concerning Lazarus' knowledge of the situation, but he was the only person she knew who might cause Sadie to be concerned.

Kyla's question was irritating, but nothing more. Sadie was tired of the attitudes of the Guard members since Fleet's departure. She had hoped that once he was gone she would regain her influence, but the opposite had happened. The Guard members thought they were so clever with their whispered messages and secret meetings, but Sadie knew what they were doing and after last night she didn't care anymore. "If he is stupid enough to come back, I will deal with him," she answered with a thinly veiled threat. Then changing her voice and tactics, she said sweetly, "Perhaps, I'll agree to take him back."

Slowly, Kyla wiped her hands clean and looked at Sadie. She was a tall woman and towered over Kyla physically. "He wouldn't have you. He knows you tried to have him killed," she said coolly. Kyla wasn't

493

done. She put her hands on her hips and continued, "You once told Fleet that he was nothing without you, but the reverse is true. You are nothing without him. The only power that you had in the Settlement disappeared with Fleet. We know who you are and what you represent. Even if you kill us all, it will not stop what is happening. Already you have no real say in anything," As Kyla pushed past Sadie to go into the foyer, she knew that Kurt would be angry with her for speaking so openly to Sadie, but Kyla didn't care. She was tired of skirting the real issue.

Her promise to Fleet forgotten, Sadie hissed, "I will have you killed for saying that."

"Then do it," Kyla said contemptuously. "Follow through on your threats for once." She pushed open the door and left Sadie standing in the kitchen. As she walked away, Kyla could hear Sadie haranguing Agatha when she returned. Kyla was sorry that Agatha had to suffer the consequences of her actions, but that was the way Sadie usually reacted when something upset her. She would make the next person that she happened to see just as miserable as she was.

Kyla was taking off her apron when she went out the front door and carried it with her as she went to the barn. She had left the unfinished bread dough on the counter, which was something that Agatha would be sure to complain about later. Especially after Sadie vented her anger on Agatha rather than Kyla. Right now, Kyla didn't care about whether or not Agatha would be angry with her. She needed to find Kurt and tell him Riley's latest report. When Kyla pushed open the barn door, she found that Carleen was there, but not Kurt. She had hoped to give him her report and return quickly. Now, she would have to wait and Kyla was not in the mood for idle conversation.

Carleen saw Kyla come inside and hesitate at the door for a moment. "Good morning," she said, "how did you get Agatha to let you off work this morning?" Carleen watched as Kyla walked toward her. Ever since Fleet left, Kyla's moods had grown gloomy. Today she looked pale and tired.

"I just left," Kyla answered. She didn't mention the argument with Sadie. Kyla didn't have the energy for long explanations. Then she was suddenly hit with a wave of nausea that sent her running for the door. As she knelt just outside the back entrance of the barn her stomach heaved but there was nothing there. She hadn't been able to eat that morning.

"Are you alright?" Carleen asked. She had followed Kyla to the door and was standing right behind her now. "You were sick yesterday, too." As soon as the words were out of her mouth Carleen realized what was wrong. When Kyla rose to her feet, Carleen pulled her back into the barn and said, "You're pregnant. Aren't you?"

Kyla sat down heavily on the floor and put her head in her hands. "Yes," she answered wearily. "Don't tell anyone, please." Kyla knew that it was the kind of news that Carleen loved to spread and it wouldn't take long for the word to reach Sadie.

"It's not the kind of thing that you can keep a secret for long," Carleen answered. She looked at her friend sitting on the floor and said, "Don't worry, Fleet will be back. My old granny used to say that all men have a snake in their pants and they want to slither away, but they always slither back." Carleen gave her best impression of her shaky old grandmother, trying to get Kyla to laugh. She had also added the last part about slithering back. Now that she knew what was wrong, it explained a lot of Kyla's behavior. It was bad enough that Fleet had left without a word to Kyla, now she was pregnant and had no father to help. Fleet had better come back and when he did Carleen would have a few words to say to him.

"I hope you're granny's right," Kyla answered half-heartedly. Carleen knew her too well by now for Kyla to keep anything from her attention. Once Carleen had realized her condition, the conversation would have to turn to Fleet and whether or not he would return. Her heart believed that he would, but with every day that passed her mind was filled with doubt. It was something that she had tried to put out of her thoughts, but the pregnancy had brought it back to center.

"What are you going to do?" Carleen asked. She wanted to add, if Fleet doesn't come back, but didn't.

"I don't know," Kyla answered, but the truth was that she had already decided. She couldn't have Fleet's child and live in Sadie's house. That left only one place that she could go. She would have to live with the Brother's and Sister's, which was an option that had grown more appealing over the past few weeks.

Their conversation was interrupted when Kurt almost stepped on Kyla and Carleen when he came through the door. When the two women jumped up suddenly, it was obvious that he had just interrupted something. "What are you doing?" he asked.

"Nothing," Carleen answered Kurt and headed out the door. Then with a level look at Kyla she added, "I'll talk to you later."

Kurt was still suspicious. He didn't care for secrets and the two women were definitely hiding something. "What was going on here?" he asked Kyla after Carleen left. "What were you two talking about?"

More explanations! Kyla was not in the mood to tell Kurt what they were discussing. So she gave him an answer that was sure to make him want to change the subject. "We were talking about Fleet," she said flatly.

Kurt lowered his eyes and ran his fingers through his dark brown hair. If he had thought about it, he should have been able to guess. Kurt wished that he could do something to ease Kyla's mind, but he was not good at giving advice concerning matters of the heart. That kind of consolation he would gladly leave to Carleen. He cleared his throat nervously and asked, "What did Riley have to say?"

"Sadie had a visitor last night but James didn't know him," Kyla answered. She was relieved that discussion had returned to the business that brought her out to the barn.

"That makes two in less than a week," Kurt said thoughtfully. "I wonder what she has going on?" The clandestine meetings had him worried. There was no telling what she might be planning.

"Whatever it is, apparently she's not happy about it. She's been in a bad mood." Kyla looked at Kurt before adding, "I don't think I can live in the cabin much longer." She was looking for a good way to tell him what she had said to Sadie.

"I need you there," Kurt said without thinking. As he spoke the words, he realized what he was asking. It had to be a trial for Kyla to stay in the same house with Sadie.

"She said that she'll have me killed," Kyla said flatly, "and I dared her to do it. I just can't take her insults and threats anymore." She watched Kurt's reaction as she told him. His dark eyes almost disappeared under his brows as he frowned thoughtfully.

"That's why I need you to stay near the house," Kurt answered. There was nothing surprising about what Kyla had said. He knew that Sadie wouldn't keep her promise to Fleet and leave Kyla unharmed. His only hope of keeping her safe was to keep her close and under observation at all times. With Riley to watch during the day and Kyla's room next to his at night, Kurt felt that the cabin was the safest place. "I don't care what you said to Sadie. All I care about is keeping you unharmed."

Then smiling at Kurt, Kyla said wearily, "She's not going to do anything. It would ruin her fun. Who would she have to torment if I was gone?" She meant it as a joke, but it was entirely too close to the truth to be funny.

Kurt didn't return her smile or reply. He was standing with his arms folded across his chest and scrutinized Kyla carefully. Women were a mystery to him and Kyla was no different. He knew that there was something that she was hiding. She had not been lying to him, but she was not telling him everything either. "You know, Fleet is not the only person who cares about you," he said softly.

Kyla looked up suddenly, surprised by Kurt's statement. This time her smile was genuine as she said, "I know. I don't know what I would have done without you over the past few weeks. I've never even said thank you." Without another word, Kyla stood on her toes and kissed Kurt on the cheek then hurried out the door and back to the cabin.

As he watched her leave, Kurt was shaking his head. Fleet had asked him to keep an eye on her. Well, he never said how he was supposed to do that nor for how long. His mind was full of questions as he exited the barn in the opposite direction from the one Kyla had taken. What was Sadie going to do? When would Fleet come back? Then there was the question that was always in the back of his mind. What would he do about Kyla, if Fleet didn't come back soon? It was too much to think about and more than he cared to have riding on his shoulders, but somebody had to fill the void that Fleet had left.

~ ~ ~

Sadie was standing in the library watching Kyla when she returned from the barn. A few moments later she saw Kurt leaving from the other door. If they didn't want her to know about their spying, it would be wise to make it less blatant. Normally, she would have found their covert meeting an irritation, but today she didn't care. Whatever they were discussing, it would no longer be her problem. Tonight she would meet her escort and begin her trip north. She was going back to join Manjohnah in his compound at the northern lakes. It was like she was returning from exile. At Manjohnah's compound she would be able to live in comfort. Life at the chicken farm, as Lazarus so colorfully referred to the Settlement, was tedious at best; even more so now that Fleet was gone. He had been her one source of enjoyment and once he left there had been nothing to fill her time or excite her senses. Provoking Kyla was no challenge and it was a hollow victory at best. As much as Sadie hated to admit it, she had lost, too. Her only consolation was that Fleet had left Kyla, too, so much for love.

Chapter Twenty-one

It was a beautiful day. If the sun had been shining, Fleet would have called it perfect. The day suited his mood. He was in sight of the Settlement and after having been away for weeks, it was hard not to gallop the horse the rest of the way. Daniel was riding behind him and both men were taking in the sights that greeted them. As they rode down the lane to the cabin, they could see the crops in the fields. Men were working in one of the fields raking straw into rows. It wasn't long before someone saw Fleet and recognized him. There were a few shouts and waves to Fleet and he raised his arm above his head and waved back.

When they reached the cabin, there was no one in the farmyard to greet them. It seemed that every available hand was in the field working. Fleet waited for Daniel to dismount after he stopped the horse then he slid off and stood beside him. For just a moment, he looked at the cabin and the window of the library wondering what his welcome would be. He gave the reins to Daniel and said, "Wait here. I'm going to see who's home." Striding quickly up the walk, Fleet knew there was only one person he wanted to see. He opened the front door and stepped into the foyer.

The room seemed dark and quiet. It was after mid-day and as far as Fleet could tell there wasn't a soul in the house. "Is anybody home?" he called out. It only took a few moments for a response. Kyla and Riley came through the door from the dining room. Nearly flying across the room, Kyla went to Fleet and threw her arms around his neck. Without a thought to who else might be coming, Fleet embraced her and kissed her deeply. There was no other thought in his mind other than Kyla and the fact that he was holding her once again. What he wanted was to be alone with her and make love. Over the past few days he had thought about doing nothing else when he finally returned, but that would wait until later. There were a few things that he had to take care of first. With some effort, he released Kyla and stepped back. Still holding her by the shoulders, he gazed into Kyla's eyes. It was as if he were afraid that she would disappear if he looked away. "Where's Sadie?" he asked. His voice was hard but his heart was soaring.

Kyla looked at Riley, then back at Fleet. She smiled and said, "She's gone." Kyla couldn't believe that Fleet had come back and only a week after Sadie had left. It was too good to be true. "I knew you would be back," Kyla said as she reached up and softly stroked Fleet's cheek. Her emotions and her heart were racing at the sight of him standing before her. She had to touch him again to make sure that she wasn't dreaming.

The news about Sadie was unsettling to Fleet. While he was glad that she wasn't here, he also knew that her absence was no assurance that he would be safe. "Where did she go?" he asked warily.

It was Riley, who answered, "We don't know. She left alone in the middle of the night." Riley was a little uncomfortable discussing Sadie. Fleet was still standing like a statue, holding Kyla by the shoulders and staring at her. "I should leave you alone," she said awkwardly and started toward the dining room.

"Wait," Fleet said, suddenly remembering that he had left someone standing outside. He released his hold on Kyla, but was still watching her intently as he added, "I want you to meet my friend Wally." He grinned broadly as he opened the door and let the two women go out before him.

Kyla was walking backwards as she went outside. It was impossible for her to look at anything other than Fleet. "I'm so glad you're back," she said again and once more hugged him around the neck, kissing him on the jaw. She walked with her eyes on Fleet every step of the way and hanging on his arms. They had reached the end of the walkway before she finally turned to see whom Fleet had brought home. When she saw the tall sandy haired man standing by the horse and staring at them, Kyla stopped suddenly. There was no thought of anything else. Her reaction was instantaneous. "Oh my god," she gasped and threw her arms around the stranger. "Daniel, it's you. I can't believe it." Her eyes were filled with tears and she was laughing as her hands flew about him, touching his face and stroking his hair and shoulders. All the while she was babbling a steady stream of exclamations of surprise and joy. "I thought you were dead. I thought I would never see you again. Oh my god, its Daniel." As she repeated the words over and over, Kyla was suddenly aware of the fact that Daniel hadn't said a word. He was standing stiffly and staring at something behind her or more accurately someone. Kyla stepped back and looked, too. Daniel was staring at Fleet, who was staring at her. She had been so caught up in the surprise of seeing Daniel alive that she had forgotten what she was doing. The longest and most uncomfortable silence that Kyla had ever experienced followed. It was up to her to make some explanation. She looked at Daniel then at Fleet. How she ever managed to say the words, Kyla didn't know. "Daniel is my husband," she said. Although Fleet's expression didn't change, the look in his eyes was like a knife piercing her heart. To say that she was torn in two was an understatement. Kyla's mind was reeling as she tried to grasp the reality of her situation. Fleet, the man she loved had returned with her husband.

Fleet had watched Kyla's reaction and hadn't needed her to tell him who Daniel was. He could tell just by looking at the man. Fleet couldn't believe his luck. This was another in the little series of pushes that Sister Samethia had described. Ever since talking to her, Fleet had let fate guide his choices and this is what he had achieved. With one blind action he had driven a wedge between himself and Kyla that he would never be able to budge. There was only one option left. "I imagine that you two have a lot to catch up on," Fleet said stiffly. He took the reins from Daniel's hands and began to walk toward the barn. He didn't have to look to know that both Daniel and Kyla were watching him every step of the way.

Watching as Fleet disappeared into the barn, Daniel continued to stand in silence. He was still in shock. There had been nothing to prepare him for the surprise of Kyla being the first person he met. Every day that he had ridden with Fleet he knew they were coming closer to his home, but he had never mentioned it or that he was hoping to find his wife. Now he could only wonder what Fleet's reaction would have been if he had. Seeing Kyla with Fleet had been unsettling. She was still staring at the barn where he had gone. It was definitely not the reunion that he had imagined.

Riley had watched the whole incident and was as surprised as anyone was. It was nothing short of a miracle that Kyla's husband had found her. The fact that it was Fleet who had brought him to her was truly a bizarre coincidence. As she looked at Daniel and Kyla standing together, she knew that she would have to do something. Neither one of them was going to move. "Kyla, why don't you take Daniel to your room? You can have some privacy there."

It was the first reasonable suggestion that had been made and it brought Kyla back to her senses. "Yes," she said as she took Daniel by the hand. "We need to talk." Kyla started to lead him up the walkway. Every step of the way she was wondering what she was going to tell him.

Daniel let Kyla pull him along. He was taking in everything about the place as they went and his questions were mounting. He wanted to know about the uniforms, the fact that Kyla and the other woman were wearing uniforms like Fleet's had not escaped his attention. The large cabin that they entered was also a mystery. The idea that Kyla was living here was unbelievable. Compared to the places where he had been living, this was a palace. Kyla took him through the foyer and down a long hallway. When she entered the room at the end, he followed her inside. It was a small room. The only furnishings were a bed with a small nightstand. As he closed the door, Daniel was finally able to speak. He reached out and gently stroked Kyla's cheek as he said, "I never thought I would see you again." Her lips trembled slightly and her eyes began to fill with tears again, but she didn't say anything.

Daniel slipped off his coat and untied the sledgehammer that he still carried on his belt and tossed them both into the corner. Then sitting on the bed, he motioned for Kyla to join him. As she sat next to him, Daniel put his arm around her and pulled her close. He didn't know what to say. The picture of Kyla walking down the walkway with Fleet filled his mind. When Kyla rested her head on his shoulder, Daniel was filled with a familiar feeling of comfort and bent to kiss her softly on the lips.

As Daniel kissed her, Kyla pushed him back gently. She was not able to pretend that things had not changed in the years since she had seen him. "I'm sorry," she said softly. "I'm not the same person that you knew." Kyla wasn't sure how she felt. For months, she had prayed for Daniel to return, but after Fleet had brought her to the Settlement her life had changed. For the first time in years, she had tried to move forward.

"Everyone has changed," Daniel answered. "Just look at me. I carry everything I own in my pockets. All I want to do is go home." He was not going to give up easily. Seeing Kyla had brought back his hopes of going back to the way things had once been, when his life had been less complicated. "We can go back to the farm together. If these people can grow crops, we can, too."

"We can't go home," Kyla answered. "Cole Spring wouldn't allow it." Kyla was studying Daniel's face. His features were the same as she remembered, but his expression was hard and uncompromising. He was wearing his hair trimmed very short and it looked like he hadn't shaved for days. His clothing was worn and had holes in several places. Daniel looked like all the other scavengers and drifters that eventually found their way to the Settlement. He was just another stray that Fleet had brought home with him, just as she had been.

"What does he have to do with anything?" Daniel asked angrily. All he wanted to discuss was how they could begin to rebuild their life together and each time Kyla responded with the negatives.

"He controls the whole area now," Kyla knew that her responses where not the ones that Daniel wanted to hear. She pulled away from him suddenly and stood to face him. "I want to hear about you," she said, changing the subject. "Where have you been living? Why didn't I hear from you before the evacuations?" There was so much that she wanted to know. So much time that had passed since they had gotten married, more time than they had ever spent together.

"I can't understand how Cole controls my property. It's my land not his," Daniel was agitated by her attempt to change the subject. He wasn't ready to talk about what he had been doing. He wanted to know about Kyla and their home.

"I don't know where you have been, but nobody lives outside of armed compounds now. Cole has men and weapons plus the supplies and support he needs to keep everyone out of his territory. He's claimed hundreds of square miles of land," she answered.

"That's not possible," Daniel scoffed. He couldn't believe that a man who had been his neighbor all his life could deny him the right to return. The land Daniel called home had been in his family for generations. "We'll go back together. He won't do anything. The land belongs to me." Daniel was standing now, as if he was ready to leave that moment.

"We can't go back," Kyla said firmly. She took his arm and guided him back toward the bed and once he was seated again she continued, "Cole was going to send me to Manjohnah. After everything that's happened in the past few months, I believe that Cole would just shoot me on sight."

Kyla might as well have been speaking a foreign language. Nothing she said was making any sense. "What are you talking about?" he asked. "And who is Manjohnah?"

Smiling for just a moment as she remembered how strange everything had seemed to her only a few months ago, Kyla sat on the bed next to Daniel. "I don't know where to start," she said. "I was living in the woods for months, hoping that you would come back. I spent the whole winter in a root cellar and nearly starved. When I tried to sneak into Cole's farm for food they caught me and were going to send me to Manjohnah. He's the one who organized the evacuations and the one who gives Cole the men and supplies to keep what they've stolen." She stopped for a moment, unsure what Daniel would think when she told him, "We know of four compounds in this area that Manjohnah operates and there are certain to be many more. The Settlement is one of them."

Was she trying to tell him that she worked for Manjohnah, too? "Is that what the uniform is for?" Daniel asked. He wasn't sure what to think about Kyla's confusing explanation.

"Yes and no," Kyla answered ambiguously. "We are members of the Guard and we're the people responsible for keeping order at the Settlement, but it wasn't until a couple of months ago that we learned about our connection with Manjohnah's network."

"What have you gotten involved in?" Daniel didn't care for anything that Kyla was telling him. First she implied that Cole was dangerous because of his involvement with Manjohnah, and then she said that she was connected with the same man. Her whole appearance seemed strange. Kyla had always had long hair; and now she had it cut short, and the black uniform bothered him more with every word she spoke. He could not imagine her as a member of any type of security force. Daniel was wishing that he had asked more questions of Fleet when he'd had the opportunity.

"It's not what you think," Kyla was suddenly defensive. "We didn't know that the woman who owned this house was involved. The Guard worked with her, but we didn't know what she was doing." She knew he wasn't going to approve of her involvement with the Guard and that included Fleet. It was not in Daniel's nature to be trusting and he questioned everything. Kyla was certain that his experiences over the past years hadn't done anything to change him. "She's gone now. Sadie left a week ago and we don't expect her to return. Right now we're waiting to see if Manjohnah sends a replacement or just someone to round us up like cattle."

Daniel couldn't believe what she was saying. "The evacuations have been over for a long time."

"Are they?" she asked, "or have they just started a new phase? One where they gather up the stragglers with offers of food and an easy life."

"Is that what you think they're doing here?" Daniel was incredulous. He had a suspicious mind, but Kyla was talking about things that were impossible to believe.

"I know it," Kyla answered. "I've been to another place like this one that's west of here. They're doing the same thing there." She wasn't going to elaborate about Lazarus' compound. Their experiences and Riley's account left no doubt in Kyla's mind what the compound and the Settlement were meant to accomplish.

"If it's that bad then you should leave with me now," Daniel said. There was no doubt in his mind that this place was dangerous. If the fantastic stories that Kyla related to him were true, then it was doubly so.

"We can't go," she answered stubbornly. "There's nowhere to run to anymore. We either give in or we fight them. We've already decided that we will fight if anyone comes for us." Kyla wanted Daniel to know that she was a willing participant. It may have been chance that brought her to the Settlement, but it was her choice whether she would remain or not. As she spoke to Daniel, Kyla was realizing where her life was heading. Her path and Daniel's had separated a long time ago, through no choice of their own.

Daniel regarded Kyla warily. To say that she had changed was an understatement. He remembered the young and devoted girl he had married. Now, he was sitting with a woman who was telling him about deceit and subterfuge like it was an everyday occurrence. "You seem to have everything figured out," Daniel said dryly. He was ready to place blame for his disappointment where it belonged, with Fleet. "I suppose I should be leaving. It doesn't seem that I fit into your plans."

As he stood abruptly, Kyla jumped to her feet. "No, please don't go," she pleaded. "I'm sorry, but I can't change the way things are. I know this is not what you expected." Kyla didn't know what to say to him.

"No, I didn't expect to see you with another man," Daniel's tone was harsh and accusing. "I didn't expect that we would be talking about anything other than how happy we were to see each other again." Nothing that Kyla had said to him had done anything to ease the pain and loss that he was feeling. While he felt like he was talking to a stranger, Daniel was focused on his longing for the happiness that he had once known. Meeting Kyla again under these circumstances was worse than when he believed that he would never see her again.

"I'm not going to tell you that I can go back to the way it was before Daniel," Kyla said softly. She knew he was angry and in many ways she still loved him. "I wish things were different, but my life has changed so much." Kyla hesitated before adding, "I love Fleet. We're planning to get married." She could see the pain in Daniel's face as she repeated the words, "I can't go back." There was no way that she could tell him that she was carrying Fleet's child. It would be too much.

Daniel didn't have anything to say in response to her revelation. He was not surprised having seen her with Fleet. As he reached for his coat, she stopped him again. "Please stay, at least long enough to rest. You can wash in the bathroom and I'll have Agatha bring you some clean clothes and something to eat." Daniel's glare was cutting but she asked him again. "Please, let me do that much for you."

Daniel stood up straight and looked at Kyla coolly. "I'll stay for awhile. I'd like to see for myself what's going on before I head home." No matter what Kyla said, he was determined to go home. Now that he was so close, he would go, with or without her.

Relieved that she had gained some time to deal with Daniel, Kyla knew that there was someone else that would need an explanation. She needed to find Fleet. "I'll leave you alone for awhile," she said, making her excuses to Daniel. "I'm sure that you need some time to decide what you want to do." As she stepped out of her room and closed the door, Kyla breathed a small sigh of relief. Daniel's unexpected appearance was the last thing that she needed in her already complicated life. She walked down the hall and into the foyer. When she went to the kitchen, she saw Agatha and said, "There's a gentleman in my room who needs some clothes and towels. He's about Kurt's size."

"Who is it?" Agatha asked. She had seen Fleet come in and then Kyla taking the stranger to her room. If she was supposed to wait on him, the least she wanted was an explanation. She crossed her arms and waited for an answer.

"His name is Daniel Wallace. He's my husband," Kyla said as casually as possible, then left while Agatha was still staring at her with an open mouth. There was no doubt that Daniel's presence would be awkward, but there wasn't any point in lying about who he was. Now that Agatha knew, everyone in the Settlement would know before sunset.

~ ~ ~

Fleet led the black stallion to the barn. It was the only thing that he could think to do at the moment. He couldn't stay with Kyla. The sight of her joy and relief when she saw Daniel was more than he could stand. It was as if a piece in Samethia's puzzle had just fallen into place. Fleet was certain that Daniel was the third person, the one that Sister Samethia had predicted would come and help send him to his final confrontation with his enemy. Fleet's life was headed in a direction that did not allow for love and family and it was time that he accepted it. In one way Daniel's presence would make things easier. Although he had planned to take Kyla with him, it would be easier to leave her behind now that he had reunited her with her husband. He was almost laughing at the irony of the situation when he entered the barn and ran into Kurt and Justin.

Kurt had just finished giving Justin his instructions before he left for the Family's camp when he saw Fleet. The sight of a smiling Fleet was a relief. It seemed that his time away had done some good.

507

Apparently, he was in good spirits. "Welcome home," Kurt said as he went to greet his friend.

"It's about time you came back," Justin called out as he grinned broadly. The news of Fleet's return would be a relief to Sister Samethia and the others.

Fleet smiled broadly. At least with these two, he knew where he stood. "It's good to see you, too," Fleet answered. Looking at them standing together in the barn, Fleet had a strange feeling. Everything seemed so familiar and at the same time Fleet felt that he didn't belong here anymore.

As he reached the spot where Fleet was standing, Kurt took the horse's reins and led him to the stall while Fleet stood by the door. "Have you seen Kyla yet?" Kurt asked. If he had been looking at Fleet when he asked the question, Kurt would have seen the anguish in Fleet's face.

Justin was watching. "What is it?" he asked. "Is something wrong?" At the mention of Kyla, it was as if a dark cloud had passed over Fleet.

He was still smiling, but it seemed forced and out of place as he answered, "Yes, I've seen her." Then when Kurt turned to look at him, too, he added, "She should be a very happy woman. I brought her husband back with me." He had tried to sound as if he had done Kyla a favor, but the bitterness came through in the tone of his voice.

As he let out a low whistle, Justin said incredulously, "You're kidding." Unfortunately, for Fleet, Justin knew by the look on his face that it wasn't a joke.

Kurt hadn't commented. He was slowly taking the packs and saddlebags from the horse. He knew that he should be happy for Kyla. It was the first time he had known of anyone being reunited with someone from their past, but his mind was reeling with shock. Part of what he felt was in sympathy for Fleet. Another was all his own. "Where are they now?" Now Kurt knew why Fleet had shown up at the barn alone.

"In the house," Fleet answered. He looked at Justin now, who was staring at him with his mouth open. "How is Sister Eaglet?" As he asked the question, Fleet was wondering if the young man knew how much he envied him right now.

Realizing that he had been gaping, Justin shut his mouth and looked down nervously, before answering. "She's fine. Everyone at the camp is well." Hoping to change the subject he looked up. Maybe discussing something else would spark some interest in Fleet. Justin smiled brightly as he added, "I've been watching Cole and his men like you wanted. They've kept on their side of the highway. I even went to the farm a couple of times. They've been busy all summer, planting crops and farming."

"I can see that everybody has been busy while I was gone," Fleet answered unemotionally. It was as if any enthusiasm that Fleet had ever had was gone. He made the plans, but others had put them into action and followed through. Any success that they had in his absence was in spite of him, not due to anything that he had done.

Kurt had finally finished removing the saddle and bridle from Fleet's horse. He had to move one of the other horses to make room for it to have a stall by itself. Once he was finished moving the horses, he turned his full attention to Fleet who had not moved an inch since Kurt took the horse. Standing as if he were rooted to the spot, it appeared that it was taking every bit of Fleet's concentration to maintain a calm and detached demeanor, but Kurt could see that he was ready to explode. "Did you hear that Sadie is gone?" Kurt was not going to return to the subject of Kyla's husband, not yet.

"Yes, Riley and Kyla told me," Fleet answered flatly. One other thing for which he was thankful, there would be no confrontation with Sadie.

"She left without a word," Kurt told him. "We knew that she had been sneaking out of the cabin and meeting with someone in the middle of the night. It seems that she had been planning her departure for a few weeks." Kurt watched Fleet, hoping that the news about Sadie would help ease some of his worries.

Where would Sadie go? The question filled Fleet's mind. To Lazarus or perhaps to Manjohnah himself, Fleet knew that he was not finished with Sadie. "She won't forget her promise," he said the words out loud as he thought. Fleet hadn't meant for Kurt or Justin to hear his thoughts.

"What promise?" Justin asked. He had no idea what Fleet was talking about.

509

FALSE WINTER

"Her promise to have you killed?" Kurt asked. "Is that what's worrying you?" He looked at Fleet who seemed to be focused on something that only he could understand. "Once we knew what she was doing, we left her out of any real decisions. She couldn't do anything to stop us. We let her live in her house, and keep up appearances that nothing had changed, but she knew that it was because we allowed it." If there was one thing that Kurt claimed as his own victory, it was the battle of wills that he had waged with Sadie after Fleet disappeared.

Finally, Fleet reacted with some emotion as he glared angrily at Kurt. "I am not worried about Sadie. There are others that concern me more than her." No matter what the discussion, Fleet's focus was not going to change.

Kurt could tell that Fleet's anger was floating just below the surface. It might be that an explosion was what was needed to release the pressure that was building inside. "What are you going to do now?" Kurt asked bluntly.

When Kurt asked the question, Fleet smiled. He knew the answer and without a moment of hesitation he said, "I'm going to head north. Manjohnah's compound is somewhere north of here and I'm going to look until I find it."

Kurt had expected that his question would cause Fleet to finally burst with frustration, but it had had the opposite effect. He was smiling enigmatically and looking at him as if he should have known the answer to the question before asking, but it was the first time Kurt had heard Fleet mention going to find Manjohnah's compound. "You just got home," Kurt said. "Don't you think you ought to discuss this with the others before we leave again?"

Once again, Fleet was filled with blissful confidence. "There is no 'we' this time," he said as he looked at Kurt. His friend wouldn't understand that this was something that Fleet would have to do alone. "Sister Samethia told me that I would pierce the heart of my enemy. This battle is not for you my friend."

At the mention of Sister Samethia Kurt looked aside to Justin, who was still standing beside his horse, listening to everything that was being said. Justin shrugged slightly, but Kurt knew that he was not surprised by what Fleet had said. He turned back to Fleet and said, "What kind of crazy notion has she planted in your head?" Kurt had spent enough time with the Family to know that they all believed that Sister Samethia had the ability to predict future events, but he had always thought that Fleet had the good sense not to believe in such nonsense.

Fleet almost laughed at Kurt's choice of words, because he felt like Sister Samethia had planted something in his brain the night that he had gone to see her. Everything that had happened since that day had only served to reinforce his conviction that her prophecy was true. He also knew that no matter what he said that Kurt could not believe, comprehend, or understand what had happened to him, not until Kurt experienced it for himself. "There is nothing crazy about it, Kurt," Fleet answered. He was finally moving. As he went to his friend and put his hand on his shoulder he said, "Everyone has a purpose in life and Sister Samethia has told me what mine will be. At first I didn't believe her either, but I have spent the summer running in every direction except the one that I am supposed to go. Kyla will stay here with her husband and I will find Manjohnah and fulfill my destiny."

Kurt watched as Fleet left the barn without looking back or saying another word. As soon as he was gone, Kurt looked at Justin and said, "If you know anything about this you had better tell me now."

"Sister Samethia did a reading for Fleet," Justin began slowly. "She won't tell me anything about what she said to him then or about what happened when he came to the Family after he left here. Everything I know, I had to drag out of Eaglet." The whole story was hard to believe, but after seeing Fleet just now, Justin was beginning to wonder.

"Well, am I going to have to drag it out of you, too?" Kurt asked impatiently.

"She told him that he is supposed to pierce the heart of his enemy," Justin repeated the same thing that Fleet had just said. "She also said that two other people would help him by propelling him on." He looked at Kurt before adding, "Kyla is supposed to be one of the two. As far as Eaglet knows, Sister Samethia doesn't know who the third person is."

As he rolled his eyes, Kurt looked at the door where Fleet had been standing only a few moments before and saw Kyla coming in. He rubbed his hand through his hair and looked at Justin. Fleet had only been home for a few minutes and already the confusion was mounting.

"Where's Fleet," Kyla asked. When she looked from Justin to Kurt she knew that they had seen him.

"He just left," Kurt answered. Kurt knew that he should tell Kyla how happy he was to hear that her husband had returned, but he didn't. It wouldn't have been the truth. When Kyla crossed the barn to go out the other door, Kurt stepped in front of her and blocked her from leaving. "It might be best to let him have a few minutes alone," Kurt said diplomatically. He wasn't trying to shield Fleet from Kyla as much as he was afraid of what Fleet would say to her.

Kyla looked at Kurt. "Move out of the way," she said emphatically. "I need to talk to him."

"I know that you do," Kurt answered, "but not right now." His eyes were pleading for her to understand. As she backed up a step, he asked, "Where is...?" His question trailed off unfinished. Kurt couldn't ask Kyla about her husband.

"Daniel, his name is Daniel," Kyla said impatiently as she completed the sentence for him. Of course, Fleet would have told them about reuniting her with her husband. "That's why I have to find Fleet, I have to talk to him." She pushed past Kurt and went out the door.

Alone with Justin once again, Kurt turned to the younger man and said, "You ride to the Family's camp now and bring Sister Samethia back with you. I don't care if you have to tie her up and drag her to the Settlement kicking and screaming. This is her mess and she's going to help me clean it up." Justin was still standing by the horse staring at the door when Kurt shouted at him, "Move and I mean now."

After Justin scrambled into the saddle, he said, "I don't think she'll come with me."

Kurt walked to the horse and said, "You tell her that Fleet is leaving to go north to find Manjohnah and he needs to talk to her before he goes. If she's like any other meddlesome woman, she'll come."

"You know the Family all believe in her prophecies," Justin said as he looked down at Kurt. He was remembering the night when the Family had come to their rescue. They would not have been there at all if Sister Samethia had not told them where to go. "Maybe what she told Fleet is true. Don't you believe just a little bit yourself?"

"It doesn't matter what I believe or anyone else for that matter," Kurt answered. "Haven't you ever heard of a self-fulfilling prophecy? What matters now is what Fleet believes." As he smacked the rump of the horse, Kurt said, "Get going now and maybe you'll get her back here before he leaves again." As Kurt watched Justin go, he was thinking about his question. Kurt didn't know what to believe when it came to prophecies and destiny. His feet were firmly planted on the ground and he believed in what he could see and what he knew.

~ ~ ~

Kyla spent the next hours searching for Fleet. It seemed that she was always just a little bit behind him no matter where she went. Just before nightfall, she finally caught up with him at the shelter house. It was still a little early for the crowds to start gathering, but Armand was there when Kyla walked into the dark building. A fire was burning in the hearth and it provided the only light. When Armand saw Kyla, he nodded toward the corner where Fleet was sitting with Rollo and another man. As she crossed the room, all three men were watching her as they sat back in the chairs with their feet propped up on the table. No one said a word as she came to the table and looked at them.

There was a jug of Rollo's moonshine setting on the table in front of them, but as Kyla looked at the three men grinning at her, she knew that there was something more than the liquor that was behind the serene good humor. It was not the way she had wanted to start her conversation with Fleet, but she was shocked to find him this way. "Do you have pearls?" she asked as she looked directly at Fleet. Kyla had seen the effects on other people but seeing Fleet this way was unnerving.

Fleet grinned at the men sitting beside him before holding out both hands palm upward to show Kyla that he wasn't holding anything. It didn't matter. They were gone now anyway. Then crossing his arms across his chest, Fleet watched Kyla. He didn't have anything that he wanted to say to her, not now.

"I need to talk to you," Kyla said flatly. She knew Rollo, but the other man sitting with Fleet was no one that Kyla had seen at the Settlement before. No doubt he was the one with the pearls. She looked at Fleet again and added, "Alone."

Fleet looked at Kyla and grinned broadly, "I'm just relaxing with my friends. Whatever you want, it'll have to wait until later." He put his feet on the floor and reached for the jug of moonshine. After taking a drink, he handed it to Rollo as he attempted to ignore Kyla.

Kyla put her hands on the table and leaned forward trying to get as close to Fleet as possible. "Please, Fleet, this is important," she hated pleading with him, especially in his present state of mind.

The stranger looked at Fleet and asked, "Is she your old lady?" He had a deep gravelly voice and his face was almost entirely hidden behind a bushy gray beard.

Fleet laughed so hard he almost doubled over as he answered, "No, but she ought to be satisfied. I brought her husband back for her today. I think that is above and beyond the call of duty, don't you?" Despite the effects of the pearls, Fleet's words were as sharp and cutting as he had intended. Deep in his heart he knew that what he had done was not anything that Kyla had asked of him, but the frustration he was experiencing had to go somewhere.

Kyla stood up and looked at Fleet. She had never thought that he would ever hurt her intentionally, but his tone was hard and cruel. Once again she said, "I'm not leaving until you talk to me alone." She was fighting to keep her emotions under control. After waiting weeks to see Fleet again, he was doing everything possible to drive her away.

It was Rollo who ended the impasse when he leaned over and whispered loudly enough for Kyla to hear, too, "I don't think you're going to get rid of her until you talk to her." Then he looked at Kyla and added, "Alone." He started laughing at his joke and the stranger joined in as they pushed the reluctant Fleet to his feet and toward Kyla.

Kyla was both humiliated and angry at having to force Fleet to come with her. She went to the door and waited while Fleet took one last drink then sauntered slowly to where she was standing. Daylight was fading fast when they came out of the shelter and a few people were beginning to gather for the nightly ritual of bonfires and revelry. Kyla led the way to a secluded spot near the woods. When she stopped

Fleet immediately sat on the ground and leaned back on the trunk of one of the larger trees.

As she knelt beside him Kyla asked, "Why are you doing this?" She needed Fleet's full attention and he was trying to shut her out. "Nothing has changed about the way I feel. I love you."

Fleet looked at Kyla. If it was possible, she was even more beautiful than when he had left. His heart was breaking as he said, "I love you, too. But can you tell me that you don't love Daniel." Fleet was fighting to think, struggling with the fog that was clouding his mind. When Kyla didn't answer, he wagged his finger at her and said slowly, "I thought that's what you'd say."

"When you asked me to marry you and we talked about having a family, I meant what I said," Kyla answered. "Didn't you mean it, too?"

"You married another man first," Fleet said in a subdued voice. "Didn't you mean what you said when you married him?"

Nothing that she said was getting through. Fleet, it seemed, had already made up his mind. "You're not being fair," she said angrily. "I've changed since I married Daniel. Everything has changed since then. My life is different. I need you Fleet. I can't imagine living without you."

Fleet could see the desperation in Kyla's eyes as she pleaded with him. He reached out and touched her cheek. He wanted to hold her and pretend nothing had changed, but he couldn't. "How can I be sure that I'm the one you love if you don't give yourself time to decide?"

How could Kyla make him understand that time was not going to change the way she felt? How could she tell him about the child now? There was no point in talking to Fleet anymore in his present state of mind. Right now he wasn't listening to a word that she said. "I don't need time to decide," she said as she stood. "I know what I want. You're the one who has to make up your mind. I love you and I'll follow you wherever you go, if that's what it takes to prove it to you. Promise me that you won't do anything until we have a chance to talk again." Her worst fear was that Fleet would leave again before she could tell him about the baby.

With an effort, Fleet got to his feet. He had never wanted anything or anyone more than he wanted Kyla at that moment. He wrapped his arms around her and drew her close one last time. He felt a craving for her touch as he kissed her tenderly. She had asked for a promise that he couldn't keep, but he wanted to see her happy so he lied. "I promise that I won't do anything before I talk to you again." Before he released Kyla, Fleet looked at her trying to memorize the color of her eyes and the curve of her lips. He wanted to remember Kyla as she was now, while she still loved him.

As Fleet kissed her Kyla knew that she would never be happy without him. Even now, she couldn't be angry with him. When he promised that he wouldn't leave, in her heart she knew that he was lying, but she wanted to believe him. All she needed was a little time and Fleet would understand that her place was with him. Sister Samethia had told her that her path was intertwined with Fleet's and she knew it was true. Slowly, Kyla backed away from Fleet watching him as she went, fearing that he would disappear. "Remember, you promised. You won't go anywhere." Kyla turned her back to Fleet and walked to the path leading back to the cabin. When she stopped and turned to look back one last time, he was gone. It was all she could do to keep from running back and looking to see where he had gone, but she didn't. Fleet had to make a choice, too. He was the one who had left her for six weeks. Kyla had done everything including getting down on her knees and begging him to stay. If that wasn't enough, she intended to keep her promise. Kyla knew what she wanted and she was willing to do whatever she had to do to stay with Fleet.

Fleet didn't move as he watched Kyla backing away. It wasn't until she finally turned that he began to walk back to the shelter house. There were a few more people gathered inside than when he had left a few minutes earlier, but Rollo and his new friend were sitting where he had left them. Fleet quickly crossed the room and sat in the seat between them. Then turning to the stranger with the bushy beard, he asked, "Do you really know where Manjohnah's compound is located?" Fleet wanted to get right back to the conversation that Kyla had interrupted.

"I already told you that I do," he said in a hushed voice. "That's why I'm here. My people have been doing everything that we can to disrupt his operations, but we need help. We need more men." The stranger took another drink from the jug of moonshine and asked, "So what do you say? Are you coming with me?"

"Yes, definitely," Fleet's eyes were bright with anticipation. Another piece of the puzzle had just fallen into his lap and he had to take the opportunity that was presented. "How far is it?"

"It's up north in the lakes, right on a point of land that juts out like a spearhead into the water," the stranger said. "We can make it in two days riding on my cycle. That is if you can get me some gas. My tank is empty."

"That's no problem, but it won't be enough to get us that far," Fleet said, becoming more excited as they discussed the plans. "Do you know a place to get more fuel on the way?"

"You never know," the man said as he laughed. "If we don't then I guess we'll be pushing the cycle the rest of the way. It won't be the first time I had to walk my wheels home."

Fleet pushed his chair back and asked, "How soon do you want to leave?"

"I'm ready to go as soon as I get some gas," the man answered. "The sooner the better as far as I'm concerned." He looked at Fleet and smiled as he added, "But I can wait if you need to say good-bye to your lady friend."

Fleet wasn't smiling as he replied, "I've already done that." He looked at Armand who was sitting across the room from them and trying not to be obvious about watching Fleet. "Give me an hour to get some things together and I'll meet you up the road at the town."

The man rose slowly and held out his hand. As Fleet clasped his hand, he shook it heartily and said, "Whatever you say. I'll be waiting."

Fleet followed him out the door and headed back to the farm. As he walked quickly down the hill and across the dam at the end of the lake, the mist was beginning to rise off the water as the air around it cooled. Fleet had walked the path thousands of times but tonight something was different. It wasn't the smell of new mown hay drying in the fields or the fog that lay heavy in the low places. Instead it was Fleet who was changed. Things that had once seemed familiar were now strange and distant.

It was quite dark when he reached the farm. As Fleet came from the woods and approached the barn, he could see the lights in the window of the cabin. Fortunately, there was no one outside to see him as he opened the door and slipped into the barn. Kurt had piled his pack and saddlebags on the floor and Fleet was hoping they were still there. Making his way carefully through the darkness, Fleet heard someone moving just ahead. "Who's that?" he called out, his knife already in hand. There was no time for hesitation. Fleet was not going to fall victim to another attempt on his life.

Kurt lit the lantern that he was carrying. "It's only me," he said quickly when he saw Fleet only a few inches away with the knife ready to strike.

"What are you doing sitting in the dark?" Fleet asked even though he knew the answer. Kurt's pack and saddlebag were on the ground next to his.

"I knew you would be wanting to leave," Kurt answered. "I'm going with you this time."

Fleet looked at Kurt standing with his arms crossed against his chest and a determined frown on his face. It was the stance that Kurt always took when he was digging in for an argument. Smiling as he said, "Not this time. I need to do this on my own," Fleet bent down to pick up his pack.

"Whatever it is that you have planned, you don't have to do it alone," Kurt countered quickly. "When we went for the horses, you wanted enough so everyone in the Guard could ride. Let us all go with you." He reached out and grabbed Fleet by the arm as he added, "You need someone to watch your back."

"If I do what I plan, I won't need anyone to watch my back," Fleet answered. There was no room for compromise in his mind. "Sister Samethia said that I was the one who would pierce the heart of my enemy. I'm going after Manjohnah and I won't be coming back."

As he let go of Fleet's arm, Kurt ran his hand through his hair. He was pacing now while he spoke. The mention of Sister Samethia's prophecy was causing his patience to wear thin. "I can understand fighting against Manjohnah's organization, but what makes you think that killing Manjohnah will accomplish anything? He's just one man."

"I want them all to know fear, Lazarus, Sadie, Cole Spring, and all the others that serve Manjohnah. If I kill Manjohnah, then the rest will fall with him," Fleet answered calmly. He knew their tactics now and would use them for his advantage. There was no anger in his voice as he said solemnly, "Assassination is the only thing that they'll understand."

Watching Fleet as he spoke, Kurt found his calm demeanor disconcerting considering the subject he was discussing. "What you're planning is suicide," Kurt argued. "You'll never get to Manjohnah. Even if you did and you were able to kill him, you'd never get back out alive." Kurt felt as if he were fighting for his friend's life.

Fleet stared directly into Kurt's eyes as he answered, "I know." The discussion with Kurt was every bit as difficult as the one he had with Kyla. Today Fleet would say good-bye to the two people that he cared for most. "I know you don't believe in Sister Samethia's prophecy. I didn't believe in it either, not until I went to see her when I left six weeks ago." Feeling a serene confidence as he spoke, Fleet tried to explain his transformation. "When I left that night, I was confused and in pain." When he paused, Kurt started to speak but Fleet continued, "I went to see Sister Samethia and asked her to help me." With a smile that seemed to light his eyes with wonder, Fleet said, "She said there was nothing that she could do, but when I put my hands on her shoulders, I felt what she had told me."

Kurt looked at Fleet with disbelief, "What do you mean you felt what she told you?" He remembered Fleet's state of mind when he left very well. For Fleet to say that he was confused did not begin to describe his incapacity for rational thought at that time. The more he talked to Fleet, the less certain Kurt was that anything had changed since then.

"It's hard to describe," Fleet said. "It was like Sister Samethia was the conduit for some current of energy that came through her and passed into me." Fleet stopped for a minute and looked at Kurt whose expression had changed to something between shock and skepticism. "I know you think that I'm crazy." Fleet said with a laugh. "I think that I'm crazy, but I know what I felt. After that, she put her hands on my head. It was like she drew the doubt and confusion from me. I felt the pain fading and then it was gone." Fleet hadn't told anybody about what had happened to him that night, not even Sister Samethia. "I don't know what she does or how, but Sister Samethia is guided by something. She calls it the Mother. I don't know what it is, but I believe in it now."

Fanaticism was not something that Kurt knew how to dispute so he tried to use it to his advantage. "Then wait for Sister Samethia. I sent Justin to bring her. She'll tell you what to do." He was hoping the suggestion would buy him a little more time. If Fleet would only put off his plans for a day or two, Kurt was certain that at least he could persuade him to take some of the Guard. When Sister Samethia arrived, perhaps Kurt could reason with her, too.

"I can be at Manjohnah's compound in two days," Fleet answered. "It will take that long for Sister Samethia to arrive. That is if she comes. I've never known her to leave the Family's camp." Fleet had his packs in hand and looked toward the door. He had agreed to meet his friend in an hour. His time was running out and he still had to get the gasoline. "I have to go Kurt," he said as he began to move toward the rear door of the barn.

"Did you tell Kyla that you're leaving?" Kurt asked sharply. "She was looking for you earlier." He didn't want to be left to make explanations for Fleet again.

"I talked to Kyla." Fleet stopped and looked at Kurt as he said, "She deserves better than the kind of life that she would have with me. Her husband is back now. She'll be fine." Fleet wasn't sure who he was trying to convince, Kurt or himself.

As Fleet put his hand on the door to open it, Kurt said, "I wish you would reconsider. We need you here Fleet."

"You don't need me, Kurt," Fleet answered. "I can't think of anyone who is more capable than you are."

Kurt shook his head and his eyebrows lowered in a troubled frown. "I do what has to be done," he answered gruffly. Kurt could not remember ever having dissuaded Fleet once his mind was set.

"That's all I am doing, too," Fleet answered. "I have to go now. My ride is waiting." As he looked back at Kurt, who was standing with his feet set slightly apart and his arms crossed over his chest, Fleet smiled as he said, "Good-bye, maybe I'll come back this way again sometime."

Kurt answered, "You do that." He was uncomfortable with farewells, especially when he disagreed so strongly with the reasons that Fleet had given him for leaving. Fleet hesitated slightly before going out the door as if there was something he had forgotten, but then disappeared without another word. It seemed that his friend had no further use for him or anyone else at the Settlement. Kurt was angry with Fleet for leaving and even more so for having refused his offer to help. As he struggled with the urge to follow Fleet and try to convince him to stay, Kurt, for the first time since meeting Fleet, felt powerless to help his friend.

Chapter Twenty two

Kurt walked in the cool darkness of the night for hours after Fleet left. He needed some time to think. Unlike Fleet, Kurt had no great vision of the future. He was firmly rooted in the present and knew that he would continue as he always had, taking each day as it came. When he finally returned to the cabin, the lights were burning brightly in the windows. Opening the door, Kurt found Kyla anxiously pacing the foyer.

As soon as Kurt entered through the front door Kyla asked, "Where's Fleet? Have you seen him?"

"Yes, I saw him about a few hours ago," Kurt answered hesitantly. "He said he had talked to you." Kurt had stopped when he entered, but Kyla was still pacing and looking out the window each time she came to the door.

"Yes, I talked to him for a few minutes," Kyla answered. She hadn't really looked at Kurt when he came in the door. All of her attention had been focused on Fleet and what she wanted to say to him when he came home. When she finally noticed the set of his jaw and the lines in his forehead, Kyla knew something was wrong. "Where is Fleet?" she asked again, more forcefully this time. Kurt knew something that he didn't want her to know. His expression told her that much.

"Fleet's gone," he answered simply.

"Gone?" Kyla's voice was raised in distress, but she didn't stop her pacing. If anything, she quickened her pace and without taking her eyes from Kurt she began talking. "He promised that he wouldn't leave until I talked to him again. How could he do that? How could you let him leave?" It was hard to discern whether she was talking to herself or Kurt. Suddenly she stopped and stalked across the floor. When Kyla came face to face with Kurt, she demanded, "Where did he go?"

"I don't know," Kurt stammered uncomfortably. He had never seen Kyla like this before. Last time Fleet had left, she had cried on his shoulder. The determination that he saw in her eyes as she stood staring up at him was definitely not what he had expected. "He said that he was going north."

"After Manjohnah?" Kyla finished his sentence. Once again she was pacing. "He knows that I have to go with him. Fleet needs me. This time he's not going to leave me behind." With every step that she took and every word that she said, Kyla's voice was rising until she was nearly shouting.

It brought Daniel, who had been sleeping in her room, running into the foyer. He was wearing only his trousers and rubbed his eyes as he asked, "What's going on out here?"

Kyla gave Daniel the same agitated glare that had greeted Kurt. "Fleet's gone," she said as she walked down the hallway and began to pound on one of the doors. When Peach came to the door, Kyla didn't waste time on apologies or explanations as she said, "Get dressed and go find Rollo. I need to talk to him." When Peach craned his neck around the door and looked at Kurt as if wanting him to confirm the request, Kyla said sharply, "Don't look at Kurt, I'm the one asking you. Please, go find Rollo and bring him back here. It's important. I need to talk to him." Peach went back into his room and Kyla continued down the hallway to her own room.

Daniel looked at Kurt standing by the door then followed Kyla to her room. He couldn't say that he was dismayed by the news of Fleet's departure, but as he looked in the door, he found the sight of Kyla hurriedly stuffing her clothing into her pack distressing. "You can't be thinking of going after him," he said incredulously. It was obvious to him that Kyla had lost all sense of reason.

Without turning to look at Daniel, Kyla answered, "That is exactly what I am doing." It took only a few minutes for Kyla to stuff her few belongings into the pack. Once she was finished, she pushed her way past Daniel who was standing in the doorway staring angrily at her and then almost ran into Kurt who was behind him in the hallway.

"You can't go after him alone," Kurt said as she swept past him. He turned to follow Kyla and almost ran into her as she whirled around to face him.

"I can and I will," she said fiercely her blue eyes burning with resolve. "There is nothing," and she paused slightly to look at both men as she added, "and no one who can keep me here." Then she turned again and continued down the hallway, pausing only to rap on Peach's door again. The blond haired young man opened the door now fully dressed. Kyla said, "Please hurry," as he started down the hallway in front of her. Then she headed toward the kitchen with both Kurt and Daniel following close behind. Once Kyla was in the kitchen, she went to the cupboards and began to stuff more supplies into her pack.

Kurt was standing in the center of the room watching her. "You can't be thinking of leaving tonight."

Without stopping what she was doing, Kyla answered sarcastically, "You seem to know a lot about what I can and can't do, Kurt."

It was Daniel who went to Kyla and grabbed her by the arms, forcing her to stop her packing. He looked into her eyes and said, "Don't leave." It was as close to pleading as Daniel could get, but his request sounded more like a demand.

"I managed for a long time without you Daniel," she answered. "I have to go." In her heart she regretted having to leave Daniel like this, but she couldn't let Fleet go this time. As she returned to her packing, Agatha entered the kitchen. The commotion had awakened her, too.

It didn't take her long to decipher the situation. Taking her turn now, Agatha went to Kyla and demanded, "What do you think you're doing?" Then setting her hands on her hips, she waited for Kyla's explanation.

"I'm going after Fleet," Kyla answered simply. Her pack was full when she turned to see Kurt, Daniel, and now Agatha all watching her wordlessly. It seemed that they were waiting for some further explanation. She knew that everyone thought they had her best interest at heart, but she still found the attempts to stop her irritating. "I don't expect any of you to understand," she said as she faced them, "but Fleet needs me." Then walking past the three, Kyla went out the door into the foyer, continued out the front door of the cabin, and headed toward the barn.

Kurt and Daniel were staring at the door after Kyla disappeared, neither one moving to follow her further. It was Agatha who set them in motion again as she commanded, "You two better go after that girl and talk some sense into her if you know what's good for you." When the men only turned and looked at her, Agatha waved her hands like a mother scooting two reluctant children off to do their chores, "I said go. Now!"

They both sprang to life at the same time as they hurried to leave. It was a race to see who would reach the door first. Kurt pushed past Daniel and was out the front door of the cabin just in time to see a dim figure in the distance. It had to be Kyla going into the barn. He was down the steps and nearly running when Daniel caught up with him. They matched each other's pace step by step crossing the farm yard and burst through the door of the barn together. Kyla had lit the lantern that hung on the wall and was leading North Wind from her stall when they arrived. She only looked at them for a second before returning to the task of bridling and saddling the horse.

"You don't even know where Fleet went," Kurt said as he walked to stand next to Kyla.

"I will as soon as Peach gets back with Rollo," Kyla answered. "I have a feeling that he'll know where Fleet is heading." Every move that Kyla made was done with forceful determination. As she was putting the blanket on North Wind's back, Peach and Rollo, both panting and out of breath, came into the barn and stood just behind Daniel. Two steps behind them, was Carleen. As soon as she saw Rollo, Kyla forgot what she was doing and went directly to where he was standing. Although, there were several people watching her every move, Kyla had only one person in her field of focus and that was Rollo.

Kyla planted herself in front of the broadly built man and with her hands on her hips asked, "Where did Fleet go?"

Rollo looked around the barn. He was a little apprehensive after having been herded down from the Settlement at top speed by Peach. Also, it was late in the night and he was more than just a little groggy from the effects of the moonshine that he had consumed that evening. His only answer to Kyla was a half-hearted shrug.

Kyla reached out, touched him gently on the arm, and said, "No one is upset with you, Rollo I saw you talking to Fleet and the stranger earlier today and I know that you can tell me where they went." She paused for just a moment and added, "Please, it's very important."

Once again Rollo looked nervously at the people who were all watching him now, and waiting for his answer. "I told him not to go with him," Rollo began slowly. "That fellow with the cycle was heading back north to the lake country." He smiled groggily and his mind wandered as he added, "It's too cold and snowy up there for me."

"Did he say which lake?" Kyla asked. She knew that it was going to take some effort to keep Rollo focused.

"I don't know," Rollo answered with a frown. All the questions were too much for him right now. He was having enough trouble just standing and wobbled slightly as he tried to remain upright.

"Please, Rollo," Kyla said as she leaned closer to whisper in his ear, "I need to know where Fleet went. It's very important to me."

Perhaps it was the tone of her voice, but something finally got through to Rollo and he realized that her request was of a personal nature. In his mind it was one thing to answer questions about a conversation that he happened to overhear, but quite another to help a lady find her love. He smiled broadly and put his arm over Kyla's shoulder as he whispered so only she could hear, "The man's name was Jack and he came from a place up north where they're fighting Manjohnah's men. Fleet went with him, you know, to join the cause. They left earlier tonight on Jack's cycle. He said it would only take two days to get where they were going."

"But where did he go?" Kyla whispered back. The lake country to the north covered thousands of square miles. There was no way she could search it all. "I need to know where to go," she said emphatically.

"I really don't know," Rollo answered as he looked at her sympathetically. He had tried to help and had told Kyla everything he could remember. Finally, he recalled one more detail and he added, "Jack said that Manjohnah's compound is built on a point that juts out into one of the larger lakes." He paused slightly before adding, "I swear that's all I know."

"Thank you," Kyla said gratefully. She did believe that Rollo had told her everything that he could. At least he had been helpful, she thought as she looked at Kurt and Daniel who were making no effort to hide their disapproval.

As she turned to go back to packing, Daniel said, "What did he say?" His tone was impatient and demanding. Kyla turned and shot a scathing look at Daniel, refusing to answer his question. Instead she went back to her horse and began to put on the saddle.

Finally, Kurt said, "If you're going after Fleet, then I'm going with you." He looked at Kyla and was relieved to see her look of gratitude at his offer. "But I am asking that you wait for Justin to return, before we go."

"What does Justin have to do with anything?" Kyla said quickly. For a moment, she had thought that Kurt was going to help her, but now she felt that he was only trying to delay her departure.

"I asked him to bring Sister Samethia to the Settlement," Kurt answered. "Besides, if they're on a motorcycle, you'll never catch up with him on horseback. Waiting a day isn't going to matter when they have that much of a lead."

"It matters to me," Kyla answered. Now that her mind was made up to go, she couldn't wait a second longer than necessary.

Kurt looked at the others who were standing in the barn and then at Kyla again. "You aren't the only one who cares about what happens to Fleet. We also care about what happens to you. You need to ask the members of the Guard if anyone else wants to go. You owe them that much. All I'm asking is that you wait until morning, so we can have time to prepare. If you're going, don't be reckless about the way you do it."

Kyla stopped and looked at the others who were watching. She could see the concern on their faces. A few hours would make no difference and if Kurt would come then she could wait that long for him. Slowly, she said, "Alright, I'll wait until tomorrow, but anyone who is going with me had better be ready. I'm leaving at dawn." As she began to take the saddle off the horse, Peach and Rollo were the first to leave.

Kurt put his hand on her shoulder and as she looked at him, he felt a rush of emotions filling his mind. The thought of Kyla leaving had made him loose all his good sense. He couldn't believe that he had promised to help her find Fleet. "I'll talk to the others," he said. Then with an effort he let go of her and walked to the door feeling the heat from Daniel's glare with every step he took.

Daniel was struggling with his choices. Now that Kurt had promised to help Kyla, it was certain that she would go after Fleet. For a few minutes he had hoped that Fleet was out of Kyla's life, but he could see now that Fleet was not his only competition for Kyla's attention. The dark haired fellow named Kurt had made it impossible for him to persuade Kyla to stay. That left him only two options, stay here without her or go with them. If he could not stop Kyla from going after Fleet, then he would make sure he was there when she did find him. Better still, he would be there when she had to give up her search, which was the outcome that he wanted. It was not a choice that he made willingly, but Daniel said sharply, "I'll be going, too." Then without another word or even a look in Kyla's direction, Daniel stalked out of the barn.

That left only Carleen, who had been standing quietly behind the others. Now that they were alone she finally spoke. "I can't believe you're going after him, not after he left you again. Especially after you told him about the baby," Carleen said. When she received no response, Carleen gave Kyla a hard look and added, "You did tell him didn't you?"

Kyla was standing with her back to Carleen. She couldn't look at her when she answered, "I didn't get a chance."

Carleen quickly crossed the few paces that separated her from Kyla. Then putting her hand on Kyla's shoulder, she pulled her around to face her, as she demanded, "You talked to Fleet didn't you?"

"Yes," Kyla said. She was having difficulty meeting Carleen's accusing glare.

"Then why didn't you tell him," Carleen demanded incredulously. "He has a right to know."

"I know that he does," Kyla answered. She was becoming angry and defensive. "I couldn't tell him. He wasn't in any condition to think rationally when I saw him."

"Good, god," Carleen exclaimed, "if he was breathing, you should have told him. It's easy. You just say, 'Fleet, I'm pregnant,' or 'Fleet, you son of a bitch, you knocked me up.' Take your choice."

Kyla watched as Carleen walked across the barn and put her hand on the door to leave. "Surely you understand why I have to go. I have to find Fleet and tell him."

Looking back at Kyla, Carleen shook her head and said, "You and Fleet are the sorriest pair that I ever saw. He's like a jackrabbit hopping from one place to another and you can't get up the nerve to tell him what he needs to know. You two deserve each other."

Despite the angry tone, Kyla knew that everything Carleen had said was true. That was one of the things that she liked about her. Carleen had the ability to speak the truth, whole and unvarnished. "I'm going to miss you, Carleen," Kyla said. "You've been a good friend."

Carleen looked at Kyla thoughtfully before saying, "When we left here to go west, I thought that I would find something better. Now I realize that everything I need is right here. If I want a better life, I'm going to have to make it myself." She opened the door to leave and added, "You and Fleet both seem to be searching for something and I hope you find it. Good luck to you. You're going to need it." Then pushing the door open, she disappeared into the darkness leaving Kyla alone.

It would have been easy for Kyla to leave, just as Fleet had done, without a word to anyone, but she couldn't do that to Kurt or Daniel. They had both said that they would accompany her in her search for Fleet. Kyla was truly relieved when Kurt had offered to go. Although she was still prepared to go alone, she knew that she would need some help. The fact that Kurt had offered to go was not a surprise, but Daniel's announcement had been unexpected. Even so, Kyla had no problem guessing what his motive might be. She was certain that he would be trying to convince her to give up the search every step of the way.

After settling North Wind back in her stall, Kyla sat on the floor just outside and began to sort through the things that she had packed. If there was one thing she could count on, it was Kurt's good sense. She had not been thinking clearly and hadn't taken many items that she would need, especially, if they were going north to the lake country. She hadn't packed any real snow gear and had only one blanket. When Kyla left tomorrow morning, she would make sure that her supplies were adequate. Nothing could go wrong. Finding Fleet was too important.

As she sat thinking about the things that she needed to pack, Kyla was becoming sleepy. It was quite late, but when she began thinking about where she could go, Kyla decided to stay where she was. Daniel was sleeping in her room. Which left Fleet's room or Sadie's; Kyla couldn't bring herself to go to either one. So she picked up her blanket and using her pack as a pillow, lay down on the floor. It was no harder than the ground that would be her bed for the next few weeks, so she might as well get used to it. Sleep was slow in coming as Kyla thought about Fleet and the well deserved scolding that Carleen had given her. Then there was the question that kept rolling around in her head. Would Fleet have gone if he knew about the baby?

~ ~ ~

Kyla slept little that night and was up well before dawn. When she started back to the cabin to complete her preparations, the lights shone brightly through the windows. Somebody was already awake. When she entered the foyer, Kurt was in the center of the room, standing amid piles of supplies for their expedition. It appeared that Kurt had been working all night. There were blankets, tents, food, winter clothing, cooking utensils, weapons and ammunition. Everything that Kyla could have thought to take was already there packed and ready to go.

"Good morning," Kurt said, relieved to see Kyla coming in the door. He had not seen her come back to the cabin and had been afraid that she would disappear into the night just as Fleet had done. "The others are in the dining room," he added cheerfully, "Agatha was kind enough to get up early and fix breakfast before we go."

"Thank you," Kyla answered softly. She wasn't referring to the offer for breakfast and she went to Kurt and gave him a warm hug as she added, "Thank you for everything," before going to the dining room to join the others.

It was a small gathering at the table. Daniel was there, looking more like Kyla remembered now that he was dressed in new clothes and freshly scrubbed and shaved. Peach was there and Dylan, too. Kyla wasn't sure whether she was relieved or disappointed that there weren't more people willing to go after Fleet, but she realized that like Carleen, many of the others would be unwilling to leave the Settlement for any length of time. It was their home and the only hope they had for surviving the winter.

As she sat down and began to pour some tea from the pot, Agatha came through the door with a plate full of eggs and fried venison steak. She set the plate down in front of Kyla. "It's about time you got here.

531

The others are done with their meals," she said briskly then disappeared into the kitchen with a handful of dirty dishes from the table.

Kyla ate quickly as the others watched. It seemed that they were ready to go and only waiting on her to finish. When her plate was empty, Kyla stood and began to leave. The three men seated at the table got to their feet to follow her. No one had said anything to her yet. So before going out the door, Kyla turned to face them and said, "I want to thank you for deciding to go with me."

Peach smiled as he said lightly, "It beats staying at here. Things have been a little dull around here lately." He slipped past Kyla and looking into the foyer said, "I'd better help Kurt carry the supplies to the barn."

Dylan only smiled and nodded as he also went past Kyla to the foyer. "Fleet came for me when I needed him," he said as he looked at Kyla. His dark eyes were keen and piercing as he stared back at Kyla. The dark haired young man was reserved, but Kyla knew that he was someone that she could count on when needed.

That left Daniel who was standing with his head cocked to one side eyeing Kyla thoughtfully. She shifted uncomfortably as she said, "I'm glad you're going, Daniel, but you don't have to come. I can take care of myself." She still wasn't sure what to think about his decision to accompany them.

"I know," Daniel answered, "but I want to go. What are my other choices?" He didn't wait for Kyla to answer and went into the foyer to help the others.

Kyla was ready to follow when Agatha came into the room. "Who's going to bake bread for me when you're gone?" she said sharply.

Smiling now, Kyla looked at her. She knew that was Agatha's way of telling her that she would be missed. "I'll be back before you know it," Kyla answered.

"Love must be deaf, dumb, blind, and stupid," Agatha said. "I always thought that you had more sense than to go chasing after a man."

"I have to go," Kyla answered. "I hope you can understand." As she opened the door to leave, Kyla looked back one last time and saw Agatha disappear into the kitchen, shaking her head as she went.

In the foyer the men were busy gathering up the bundles and carrying them to the door. Kyla picked up some of the packages of food and followed them to the barn. After carrying the first load, Kyla began to get the horses ready while the others went back for more. She had North Wind and the bay that Kurt rode saddled and ready by the time the men returned with another load of supplies. Next, she selected two of the faster horses for Peach and Dylan. It was Fleet's black that she saddled for Daniel to ride. By the time she had the five horses ready, all the supplies had been piled in the center of the barn.

As he stopped and looked at the pile on the ground, Kurt said, "I think we had better take two pack horses." They all worked together in silence as they loaded the two horses that Kurt tied to one of the poles that supported the loft above them. It was growing light outside by the time they had the horses ready.

Kyla was tying her saddlebags and pack behind North Wind's saddle when Riley and James entered the barn. "I'm glad you came to see us off," Kyla said as Riley stood next to her.

Riley looked around the room. It was a terrible loss of resources in her eyes, in terms of both men and animals. "I wish that you would all reconsider. It's bad enough that Fleet is gone. We can't afford to loose anymore of the Guard."

"I can't speak for the rest, but I'm going," Kyla answered flatly. Nothing Riley could say would change her mind. "As far as the Guard is concerned, you'll have to replace me." Kyla looked to the men who had volunteered to help her and seeing that all were ready, she mounted North Wind. As she did, Kyla was reminded of all the times that they had followed Fleet. Just as they waited now, for her to signal that it was time to leave. In a way, it made her feel she truly was following in Fleet's path.

Kurt was the next to climb into the saddle, but before the others could do so, Armand appeared in the doorway and announced, "There are riders coming down the lane."

Kyla looked at Kurt then nudged North Wind to the door. Armand opened it wider so the horse could pass through. As she rode out and headed down the lane, Kyla was hoping that it would be Fleet returning, even though she knew that was not likely. Still, when she reached the walkway in front of the cabin, Kyla was not disappointed.

At that point she could see who was coming and pressed her heels into the horse's flank to bring her to a gallop as she rode to meet them.

Justin and Brother Fox were riding at the head of the party. Right behind them was Sister Eaglet and Sister Samethia. There were also three other Family members who Kyla did not know, two young men and a young woman. When Justin saw her, he called out, "I went to get Sister Samethia and they met me halfway. Where's Fleet?"

As Kyla came to the riders, she pulled North Wind to a halt and Justin and the others stopped, too. "He's gone," Kyla said. "We were just ready to leave and go after him."

Sister Samethia and Brother Fox exchanged a brief glance. Then Sister Samethia turned to Kyla and said, "It's good to see you again Sister Kyla."

"And it's good to see you Sister Samethia and the others, but I'm sorry you came all the way for nothing," Kyla said. "It's a long ride, especially if you have to turn around and go right back."

"We're not going home," Sister Samethia answered as she dismounted. "We'll be going with you."

Kyla felt her heart leap at her words. To have Sister Samethia and the Family accompany her was more than she had hoped for. Kyla jumped to the ground and hugged Sister Samethia as she said gratefully, "I have never been happier to see anybody in my life." As she released her and looked at Sister Samethia, Kyla could see that she was prepared for travel. Instead of the long brown dress that was her usual attire, Sister Samethia was wearing trousers and boots that went to her knees like the ones that Brother Fox wore.

Sister Eaglet climbed off her horse and joined them. "Sister Kyla," she said, "I'm glad to see you looking so well." Then brushing her hands playfully through Kyla's shaggy growth of dark brown hair, she added, "I guess you won't be needing a hat now."

"I see you put the deerskin to good use," Kyla said as she smiled at Sister Eaglet who had also shed her brown homespun dress and was wearing buckskin boots and trousers.

Brother Fox and the other Family members had dismounted when Kurt walked up leading his horse behind him. Daniel, Peach, and Dylan were right behind him each leading their horse. Dylan had also brought the packhorses. Bringing up the rear were James, Armand and Riley.

It made a small crowd, which was beginning to draw curious onlookers as people began coming out of the dining hall after breakfast. The people from the Settlement watched the Family members with curiosity and some apprehension.

As Kurt reached Brother Fox, he held out his hand and greeted him. "It's good to see you. How did you get here so soon?" Then he smiled as he recognized the others in the group and called out, "Brother Wesley and Brother Wyatt and Sister Alisma, you've come, too." As he looked at Justin who was standing next to Sister Eaglet, Kurt asked, "How did you manage to ride to the camp and back in such a short time?" Looking at the horses, Kurt expected to see them ready to drop from exhaustion, but they seemed well rested. He watched as Justin looked nervously at Sister Samethia, then back at him.

"They met Justin," Kyla answered the question and could see the skepticism in Kurt's expression.

"How did you know when to come? Did you have a vision?" Kurt asked. His tone was mocking but even he was finding it hard to dismiss their arrival as coincidence.

"No, not exactly," Sister Samethia answered smoothly, ignoring Kurt's derisive attitude. "I knew that Fleet had come back." She looked at Kyla and then toward the north. "I could feel him." The awareness of Fleet, pulling at her subconscious, was as powerful as the connection she experienced with Fleet at their last meeting.

If anyone else had made that statement, Kyla would have thought that they were mentally unstable, but she believed Sister Samethia. "Sister Samethia, I need to speak to you in private." So far, Kyla had not told anyone else the sketchy information Rollo had given her.

Sister Samethia considered Kyla with a satisfied smile. The young woman had changed dramatically since she had seen her. No longer frail and timid, her confidence and determination shone like a beacon to Sister Samethia, confirming her belief that Kyla was integral to Fleet's success. Putting her hand on Kyla's shoulder, she guided the young woman to a spot just out of earshot of the others. The crowd stood in awe of the tall woman in the strange clothing and gave them a wide berth as they passed. When she stopped, Sister Samethia turned to Kyla and asked, "Do you know where Fleet has gone?"

Speaking in a low voice, Kyla answered, "I don't have much to go on. All I know is that Fleet has gone north to find Manjohnah's compound. Its in the lake country on a point of land that juts out into one of the lakes." Kyla shook her head and looked down as she added, "It could be anywhere."

"Look at me," Sister Samethia commanded. When Kyla raised her head, Sister Samethia stared deeply into her pale blue eyes. Kyla had confirmed her suspicions and she hoped that she might find some clue if she searched further. Still holding Kyla's gaze with hers, Sister Samethia placed her hands on Kyla's shoulders as Fleet had done with her. After her experience with Fleet, Sister Samethia wondered if she would feel the same current of energy flowing through Kyla, too. Slowly, she began to speak. "Last night I dreamed of a place surrounded by water on three sides with many buildings and a high wire fence." When Sister Samethia closed her eyes, she saw the images that had flowed through her mind. "I saw Fleet. At first I wasn't sure but then I saw him clearly in the light of a fire. There were so many images of places that I had never seen before, the river and the old bridge. I saw the tall timber with the water sparkling in the distance and a long gray ribbon of road stretching out before me in a land covered in snow." She stopped and released Kyla.

The connection was broken when Sister Samethia dropped her arms to her side and suddenly stared past Kyla. For a moment, Kyla wondered if Sister Samethia had spoken at all. The images were imbedded so deeply in her mind. "It's not Fleet's time, is it?" Kyla asked. She didn't have to elaborate. Sister Samethia knew what she meant.

"No," Sister Samethia answered, "but Fleet needs our help. I can feel the desperation that is driving him." She turned to look at the riders waiting for them and the small crowd that surrounded them.

Kyla had noticed the growing crowd, too, and said, "I think that we'd better leave soon." She had hoped to slip away without a big commotion, but that wouldn't be possible now. As the two women returned to their horses, Kurt and Brother Fox were deep in their own conversation as they discussed the direction that they would take that morning.

Once she was back in the saddle, Kyla looked at the Guard members and the others who were standing in a circle around the riders. She knew that some explanation was expected. This time she would make the announcement. "Fleet has gone north to looking for Manjohnah's compound," she said loudly enough for all to hear, "and we're going to join him." Kyla wasn't good at inspirational speeches like Fleet was. "I don't know when we'll be back," she added. A murmur of whispers passed through the crowd, but no one commented out loud. Still, it seemed that they expected more. Kyla looked to the others in her party for help but like the others, they were waiting for Kyla.

North Wind pranced nervously, as if she could sense Kyla's uneasiness. The wind was blowing from the north that morning and as Kyla felt the icy chill to the air, she said, "Our enemy lies to the north. We can no longer sit and wait for him to come to us. Fleet knew that and in our hearts we all know that he is right." Kyla's long black cape was whipping in the wind as she spoke and her dark hair blowing across her face. Looking at the faces in the crowd, she continued, "Not everyone will carry a gun in our fight. You will be doing your part here when you harvest the crops and help your friends and neighbors through the next winter. Every person who lives to plant and harvest again will be fighting against Manjohnah and what he represents." With a gentle nudge, Kyla turned North Wind toward the end of the lane and looking now to Kurt and Brother Fox, asked, "Are you ready to go?"

The men nodded in agreement and without waiting for further good-byes or speeches, Kyla pressed her heels into North Wind's flanks and she jumped to a gallop, leading them away from the cabin and the Settlement. It had been her home for the summer, but the warm weather was waning. The chill in the wind was signaling that winter would soon be at hand. With the change of seasons, Kyla's life was changing again. Ever since Fleet had gone, the Settlement hadn't seemed like home. No matter where he went Fleet would carry the feeling of completeness that Kyla needed. The place didn't matter to Kyla. She felt no ties to the land. Despite any distance that Fleet traveled, she could feel the strings that bound them together pulling her after him. If only she could unravel them and find the way.

Chapter Twenty three

It was a company of twelve that traveled north with each member of the party having their own reasons for being there. The first day while traveling north the group had become acquainted with each other. Kurt felt at home with the Family members. He'd spent enough time with them that he didn't notice their unusual beliefs. Daniel, on the other hand, had never heard of the Family and spent most of the day riding to the side of the group. When Kyla had introduced him as her husband, the reaction from the Family members was restrained surprise. They said little, but there was a mutual suspicion that passed between Daniel and Sister Samethia after that. Daniel's plan was to keep his eyes open and his mouth shut until the time was right. He still hadn't figured out what had passed between Kyla and Sister Samethia back at the Settlement, but he intended to find out.

Dylan and Peach were quite curious about the Family and questioned Brother Wyatt and Brother Wesley about everything, which had earned them a rather lengthy explanation concerning their beliefs about the Mother's power. Still, the young men seemed to enjoy each other's company. Dylan and Peach listened intently as the young Brothers told them about their exploits with Fleet at the stock farm. Then they recounted their tales of their brushes with Cole Spring's men. The discussion turned to hushed whispers as they explored the possibilities of adventures that might lie ahead.

According to the plan discussed by Kurt and Brother Fox, they headed directly north after leaving the Settlement for one full day before heading east. They hoped to avoid all contact with Cole Spring and his men or any others like him that they might discover along the way. The land to the north of the Settlement was nearly flat. In between narrow bands of trees growing along the streams and shallow rivers, gently rolling hills stretched for miles in every direction. Tall grasses and weeds covered the fields that had once been filled with crops. Occasionally, they would find patches of corn that had gone to seed from the previous years. They were small spindly plants, but the small ears of corn were gathered as they went. They also hunted small game as they traveled, but Kyla and Sister Samethia kept pressing them forward, setting a steady and determined pace.

Kyla rode by herself most of the time, stopping on the tallest ridges, where one could see for miles in every direction. The dark greens and browns of late summer stretched unbroken from one the horizon to the other. Although Kyla knew she would not find Fleet so soon, any sign of human activity would be important. They were riding cross-country and avoiding the roads, which meant they often had to stop and cut through the fences. Kyla complained about the time wasted and wanted to ride on the roads, but both Kurt and Brother Fox had argued against it. They wanted to avoid any eyes that might be watching. Still, Kyla kept looking for signs of anyone traveling the roadways and in the first day they saw no one.

That night they camped on the shore of a small river. Everyone knew they still had a long distance to travel. Kurt had estimated that it would take nearly two weeks to reach the lakes and no one knew how long after that to find Fleet. As they prepared for the night Kyla insisted that they gather a plentiful supply of firewood, enough that they could build a ring of fires around the camp if necessary. All the horses were tied to a line stretched between two trees near where they would put their tents.

What Kurt had brought were small one-man tents, which were made from canvas and barely big enough for one person. "If you need somewhere to sleep," Kurt said to the two young Brothers standing beside him, "it would be a little tight, but we could probably fit two people in one of these."

Brother Wesley and Brother Wyatt smiled knowingly at each other as they each took a bundle from the pile of supplies they had brought with them. When they unrolled it, it turned out to be tent made from skins stitched together. Inside the bundle were the poles that were cut into sections. The Brothers fit those together to make longer poles. It took only a few minutes to assemble the poles and erect the tent, which was big enough for two people to occupy comfortably. They repeated the process and soon two small skin tents were up and ready.

It was Brother Wesley, who grinned at Kurt and said, "You didn't think we slept out in the cold when we're watching the sheep, did you?" Then he picked up his pack and Sister Alisma's and tossed them into one of the tents.

Peach jumped up from where he had been sitting and looking at Kurt's tent said, "You wouldn't mind trading tents with me would you, Brother Wyatt." The ones that the Family brought were definitely roomier and looked like they would be drier, too.

The lean young man laughed and said, "We brought enough tents for everybody if we share. You can join me if you wish, but you have to thank the Mother for her gift."

Peach wasn't sure if Brother Wyatt was serious or joking. "I'll thank whoever you say, if it keeps me warm and dry," he answered thankfully as he gathered his belongings to put them into the empty tent.

"If you want, I can give you one, too," Brother Wyatt offered as he looked at Kurt.

For a moment, Kurt considered if his pride was worth sleeping in the drafty little tent. As he began pulling the stakes from the ground, Kurt said, "I think I'll take you up on that offer." Within a few minutes, they had another one of the Family's tents up and were starting on the fourth. Soon all six tents were up and the last details of whom would be sleeping with who were worked out. Justin and Sister Eaglet, Brother Wesley and Sister Alisma, Brother Wyatt and Peach, Kurt and Dylan had already made their choices known, which left Sister Samethia and Brother Fox and Kyla and Daniel.

Sister Samethia felt the tension between Kyla and Daniel as they faced the possibility that they would share a tent. "I will share with Sister Kyla," she announced quickly. Her reasons were not limited to an attempt to save Kyla from embarrassment. There were still many things that she wanted to discuss with Kyla, not the least of which was the strange connection that they had shared for a few brief moments before departing the Settlement.

Daniel felt even more the outsider when the decisions of the sleeping arrangements were made. He picked up one of the remaining blankets and one of the rifles. Then walking outside the circle of tents, he said, "You'll need someone on watch. I'll go first." Kyla watched as he stalked away and almost followed him, but she didn't. Not now, anyway, Kyla would talk to Daniel later when no one was watching. It would be a long trip if Daniel remained sullen and unfriendly.

Now that the tents were up, it was time to think about supper. They had been foraging the whole day as they rode. This time of the year, there were usually apples and peaches in abundance, but most trees were barren. The late frosts had killed most of the blossoms. Still, some of the hardier varieties managed to produce a modest crop and they picked what they could. The best were packed and stored for leaner times, while they cut the others and cooked them with honey for a sweet and chunky applesauce. They roasted several rabbits and the two pheasants that Kurt had shot along with some fried bread for what seemed like a feast after a long day in the saddle. Once the meal was done and the horses watered and checked for the night, it was time to prepare for bed.

Kyla went with the Sisters to the river to wash. They walked a little way from the camp looking for a place where they could climb the bank to the water easily. Both Kyla and Sister Alisma carried rifles. Even though they had not seen anyone, they considered everywhere they went to be potentially dangerous. Finally, they came to a place where the bank was level with the river and they were able to walk on a small spit of sand that led to the water. It was not much of a river. Very little water was flowing through it. Not much rain had fallen in the past few weeks and it would have taken a long rainy period to fill it to the banks, but there was more than enough for washing.

Kyla watched as the Sisters quickly shed their clothing and began to wash in the cool night air. She hesitated to do the same, knowing the women would recognize the signs of her pregnancy. When Sister Eaglet looked at her standing by the river, she laughed and said, "You don't have to be shy."

Kyla laid her gun down slowly and began to undress. As she went to the water and began to wash, Sister Samethia looked at her swollen breasts and the small roundness of her belly and announced loudly, "You're pregnant."

Kyla smiled as she nodded. There was no use trying to hide anything from Sister Samethia. "The others don't know yet," she said as she continued washing. When Kyla heard Sister Eaglet laugh suddenly she looked at the young woman. "What is it," Kyla asked, wondering what was so humorous about the situation.

Sister Eaglet smiled enigmatically as she said, "It seems our children will be born at about the same time." She looked to Kyla waiting to see Kyla's reaction when she realized what Sister Eaglet meant.

"Then you are, too," Kyla said as she raised her eyebrows in surprise. Kyla had been too absorbed in her own thoughts to notice that Sister Eaglet was showing the same signs as she was. It was a happy coincidence, but her joy was compromised as Kyla thought about the fact that Sister Eaglet had Justin to share in her happiness. Once again she asked herself if Fleet would have gone, knowing about the child. The question had taken possession of her mind in waking and sleep.

Sister Samethia looked at Kyla and wondered why she hadn't noticed Kyla's condition before now. It should have been obvious, but it had not been the focus of her attention. In all her visions of Kyla and Fleet she had not seen a child, but the Mother did not show her everything. "None of us will tell your friends," Sister Samethia said. "That's up to you, but don't wait too long." She smiled at her small joke.

Sister Alisma was the first to dress. She put on a pair of buckskin trousers like Sister Eaglet's. Her boots were lined with a thick gray fur and there was a fur lining on the leather jacket that she wore. As she picked up the rifle that she had carried with her, she said, "We had better get back. Unless you want to wait for the coyotes."

"You would like that, wouldn't you, Sister Alisma?" Sister Eaglet laughed as she pulled on her trousers and boots. "You could use some more fur for a lining in your coat."

Sister Samethia and Kyla were soon dressed and the four women started back to the camp where the small fire could be seen clearly in the darkness. Walking a few paces behind Sister Eaglet and Sister Alisma, were Kyla and Sister Samethia. When Sister Samethia stopped, Kyla turned and looked at the taller woman waiting to hear what was on her mind. "Before we go back, I want to know," she said. "Is it Fleet's child?"

Kyla felt her face flush with embarrassment. She had assumed that Justin had told the Family about her relationship with Fleet, but perhaps he hadn't. "Of course," she stammered. Kyla had never thought that anyone would doubt that Fleet was the father, especially not Sister

Samethia. "You didn't know, did you?" she asked with sudden realization. Kyla had assumed that Sister Samethia knew everything that would happen.

"I only see small images," Sister Samethia explained patiently. "I could have seen a child and not known what it meant." She wished that there were some way to control the power that flowed through her mind. Sister Samethia had begun to think that her ability to see images of the future was stronger when she formed a link with someone else that the Mother had touched. Fleet was one person who had magnified her link and with Kyla she had also felt something. It was not a numbing surge of power through the earth like Fleet had commanded, but a gentle and subtle awareness of something flowing around her, surrounding her heart and mind. The same phenomenon that pulled her toward Fleet was flowing through Kyla and even now she could feel it.

"I want you to tell me everything that you have seen," Kyla said as she looked into Sister Samethia's eyes. "I want to see them, too." She looked at Sister Samethia who was nodding and smiling slightly as she understood what Kyla meant. Before she was done, Kyla would try to extract every memory that Sister Samethia carried inside her head and she focused all her attention on the tall Sister.

"You felt it, too," Sister Samethia said, her voice hushed with awe of the power that she didn't fully understand. "I felt the same thing with Fleet when he asked me to help him. Only with him the power came as if it were lightening flowing through my body. I have never known anything like it." Sister Samethia looked at Kyla with her eyes wide with wonder as she recalled the moment. "I could feel his pain and his thoughts. His mind was a flood of emotions raging against himself." Sister Samethia stopped suddenly. With a wary look at Kyla, she said, "We'll have many hours to discuss everything." Sister Samethia was suddenly uncomfortable as she realized that she had already revealed more about her last meeting with Fleet than she had intended.

After their brief exchange, Kyla and Sister Samethia walked in silence. When they reached their camp, Kyla excused herself by saying, "I'll go give Daniel a break at watch." Then with her gun still in hand she walked past the ring of tents to the spot where she had last seen Daniel. He was still there, sitting on a fallen log and watching as the light dimmed in the west. As Kyla sat beside him, Daniel didn't take his eyes off the far horizon.

"If you watch the sunset, sometimes you can catch a glimpse of the sun just before it disappears," Daniel said as she sat down.

Kyla sat quietly watching and waiting, but tonight there was no glint from the sun only growing darkness. They sat for some time without speaking. Finally, Daniel said, "It would make my life much easier if you would not introduce me as your husband." Kyla looked at him and was about to protest, but he cut her off by saying, "You don't treat me like your husband, so don't tell people that's what I am. Why don't we just consider ourselves divorced or the marriage annulled. Whatever you want to call it, let's end it here and now."

It wasn't until then that Kyla truly understood the consequences of her actions. She could see it in Daniel's eyes. "I didn't mean to hurt you," she said. "Why did you come, if it's so hard to be near me?"

Daniel stood up abruptly. He couldn't stand to sit so close to Kyla and not be able to touch her. How could he tell her that he had come because the love that he still felt for her was all that he had? Instead he said, "I'm going to take a break. Are you my replacement for the watch?"

Kyla stood and with her rifle in hand said, "I am." The fewer words, the better. In time she hoped that she could learn to talk to Daniel without feeling that she had let him down. It would definitely be a test for both of them as they adjusted to the change in their relationship.

They next day they headed east. There was nothing different about the land that they passed through. Everything looked the same as the day before. Three days and nights passed without any change in the landscape and they rode silently and quickly through the empty countryside. On the third day, they skirted to the north of a ruined city. Although all eyes were searching for signs of life, other than the wild game that flourished in abundance, they still saw nothing. It wasn't until midday on the fourth day of their journey that the hills began to grow steep and rocky. The trees grew in larger and larger groves until the land around them was entirely wooded. Soon they found themselves riding under the boughs of tall, long-needled pines and winding around the smaller brush that crowded around their trunks.

The smell of pine as the needles were crushed under the horses' hooves was refreshing. Kyla was enjoying the beauty of the wooded bluffs, when Brother Wyatt returned from scouting the trail ahead. "There's a settlement about a mile from here. It's right on the river," he reported with excitement. It was the first report of any human activity that they'd had for days.

Daniel kicked the black and it leapt closer to Brother Wyatt's shaggy brown mare. "Where is it?" Daniel asked. He was as excited as the young man was by the news. "Show me," he demanded.

Before Brother Wyatt could comply with Daniel's request, Brother Fox said, "Let's not go rushing into anything, Brother Daniel." Although, he was older, Brother Fox was learning that Daniel needed to be reined in, much as the younger men did. "What else did you see?" he asked as he turned back to Brother Wyatt.

"It's a fenced compound on the river," Brother Wyatt answered. "They have it built around the lock and dam. It looks like there's a working power plant there, too."

Kurt joined the conversation as he said, "Now, I'd like to see that." The report had aroused his curiosity, too.

"We don't all need to go," Brother Fox said as he looked at the party. He could see the excitement was contagious as everyone looked expectantly in the direction from which Brother Wyatt had come.

Kyla had never stopped North Wind. As the others were talking, she had been riding the white horse in circles around the group. "Who do you propose to leave behind?" she asked in response to Brother Fox's statement. Then without waiting for Brother Fox to answer, Kyla turned to Brother Wyatt and said, "Show us the way."

Brother Wyatt sat up straight in the saddle and pushed his long hair behind his ears, as he looked first at Kyla and then to Brother Fox, who nodded grudgingly. No one would have agreed to be left behind and Brother Fox had to accept that Kyla was right. "Let's at least go quietly and in single file," he ordered gruffly. He was used to Sister Samethia giving orders to the Family members, but not Sister Kyla. What surprised him even more was the fact that Sister Samethia had allowed her to do so. It seemed that Sister Samethia and Sister Kyla were always deep in some private conversation and neither one would tell the others what they were planning.

As he rode at the end of the line of riders, Brother Fox was watching the men from the Settlement. The young man with the light blond hair, the one called Peach, was riding behind Brother Wyatt. His horse was a shaggy dun mare with a black mane and tail. He seemed to have a reckless nature, always trying to convince someone to race or jumping his horse over fences when it wasn't necessary. Still, he had seen that the young man had a good eye and could shoot with accuracy. He was one that Brother Fox would keep his eye on.

After Brother Peach was the other young Guard member. Brother Dylan was riding a dark chestnut brown horse with a silky black mane. With its long legs and a long stride, the horse and rider seemed a good match for Dylan who also had dark brown skin and sleek black hair. Trailing behind his horse were the two pack animals that they had brought form the Settlement. Every few minutes Dylan would turn to check the horses, his movements were graceful and he rode the horse with seemingly no effort at all. Brother Fox had seen Dylan at the skirmish with Cole's men earlier in the summer. The young man seemed to be able to handle himself while the bullets were flying. He liked knowing that Brother Dylan could be counted on to keep his head.

Next in line was Sister Kyla. She had changed so much since he had first met her that she seemed a different person. There was no doubt in anyone's mind that this was Sister Kyla's quest. If it were not for her, Fleet would have gone without a ripple in the pond. As she rode the white horse that she called North Wind, Kyla was always focused on the object of her search. Brother Fox wondered how long she would be willing to continue. Given the look of determination that she wore on her face, he estimated that it would never end.

Next came Sister Samethia. Brother Fox had thought that she would never leave the camp and her watch over the Family, but she had insisted that they follow Fleet to the North. He watched as she drew close to Kyla and saw the two women exchange a knowing glance. When Kyla nodded, Sister Samethia fell back into line behind her. It was irritating to Brother Fox, knowing that the women were keeping secrets.

Following Sister Samethia was Sister Eaglet who was riding a small gray mare with a white face. She nudged the horse closer to

Sister Samethia who turned to speak to her briefly. Sister Eaglet nodded so vigorously that her long blond braids were swinging with the motion. It seemed that she was a co-conspirator with the other two women. The young girl had blossomed into a confident woman over the course of the summer. At first Brother Fox had been against her marriage to Brother Justin, but he had seen that the two young people were devoted to each other and had enjoyed watching their relationship mature and grow. He found it gratifying that Brother Justin was riding right behind Sister Eaglet. Watching every move that she made and keeping an eye to the left and right, he was always alert and ready for anything. Brother Fleet had made a good choice when he had sent Brother Justin to scout Cole Spring's operation.

Next in line was Sister Alisma riding her brown appaloosa mare. She was only a year older than Sister Eaglet was and in many ways the two young women were alike. Yet they had very different skills and served the Mother in very different ways. Sister Eaglet preferred hunting with a bow and refused to carry a gun, even for protection. Her talents lie in her skill with healing herbs, which she was learning from Sister Samethia. Sister Alisma spent her time with the shepherds and had joined in fighting against Cole's men when they harried the sheep. Brother Fox counted Sister Alisma among those that he could count on in battle.

Riding after her was Brother Wesley on his black and white pinto. The high spirited horse was not as long legged as the others were, but it had beaten Brother Peach's horse when he had challenged Brother Wesley to a race. Like the horse Brother Wesley seemed small, but the spirit within him was strong. It was Brother Wesley who had been the first to volunteer to go with Sister Samethia when she said announced that she was going to search for Fleet. The young man was devoted to Sister Samethia and would follow her wherever she led. It was something that Brother Fox could understand, as he too was following Sister Samethia.

Daniel was riding the black stallion and he had the place just in front of Brother Fox. During the past days, Brother Fox had tried to speak to the sullen, sandy haired man and had received only rude stares or was ignored altogether. He appeared to be a capable man and Brother Fox had no doubt that he was fearless in a fight, but he wasn't sure that he could trust him. Daniel had no loyalties to either the Guard or the Family. He was the unknown factor in Brother Fox's tally.

Brother Fox was having a premonition of his own and he urged his small bay mare to a faster pace and passed the riders in line before him. When he came to Sister Samethia, he slowed and guided his horse close to hers. "If there is something about this place that I should know, it is time to tell me," he said as he looked into Sister Samethia's eyes searching for some clue to the secret that she was guarding.

She smiled only slightly as she said, "I have seen this place in my visions, but I don't feel any danger surrounding it." There were times when she felt that Brother Fox knew what she was thinking, but then he had been watching and knew her well enough to guess what she had been discussing with Kyla.

Not entirely satisfied by her answer, Brother Fox once again spurred his horse to a loping gallop and caught up to Brother Wyatt just as they reached the rise that overlooked the compound at the river. As Brother Wyatt stopped and dismounted, the others did the same. It was a large company of people and horses and Brother Fox hoped that no one would be watching. Such a large group would be easily visible. They tied the horses to some low brush and everyone crept cautiously to the crest of the ridge to look at the valley and the river below.

There was a lock and the dam stretched across the wide river. On the far bank they could see the remains of another city. It was dust and sand just as the others they had seen. Looking down river, they saw what remained of the bridge that had once spanned the river. Only one of the towers that had formed the support and a portion of the roadway remained intact. The other tower was a small island of rubble in the channel. On the western bank of the river was a large fenced compound surrounding the area where the lock was located. Several long buildings similar to the ones they had seen at Cole Spring's farm were erected in rows at the southern end. They were too far away to see the activities of the people in the compound clearly, but they could see the trucks with empty flat bed trailers that entered the compound and trucks leaving the compound with full loads.

As he watched and wondered what they were hauling, Brother Fox looked down, toward the road that ran at the foot of the bluff where they were standing. When he saw Daniel making his way down the rocky slope, he was ready to call out to him, but Kurt put his hand on his arm and said, "I'll go get him."

As he scrambled down the hill, Kurt was cursing softly to himself. Daniel had acted without regard for the rest of the party. Now, it was up to him to bring Daniel back since he had come with the Guard, not the Family, and Kurt felt a certain responsibility for his actions. He had to watch closely to see the direction that Daniel took. The sandy haired man in the long black coat was nearly invisible, as he kept low in the brush, making his way quickly down the hill. It wasn't until they were almost at the bottom that Kurt realized where Daniel was headed. Parked at the base of the hill, was a truck with a full load. Whatever it was that they were bringing out of the compound was hidden under the tarpaulin.

Kurt finally caught up with Daniel when he crouched at the crest of a ridge just above the truck. They watched the driver jump out of the cab and walk to the back of the truck. It seemed that he had some trouble with one of the tires as he bent to examine them closer. Again without a word to Kurt, Daniel moved quickly and quietly down the slope. Kurt was right behind him when he left the cover of the trees and crept around the back of the truck. Before Kurt or the driver knew what was happening, Daniel had used the butt of his rifle as a club. With one forceful blow to the head, the driver was down and Daniel was dragging him off the road. Then he produced a length of rope from one of his pockets and Daniel began to tie the man's hands behind his back.

Exasperated by Daniel's disregard for their attempt to pass without notice, Kurt snapped, "What do you think you're doing? We could have ridden right past this place without anyone knowing that we were here."

Daniel ignored Kurt's question as he finished tying the man then began searching his pockets. Everything he found, Daniel stuffed into one of the large pockets inside his coat. Once he had emptied the man's pockets, Daniel stood and looked at Kurt with a satisfied smile. "Don't you want to see what's under the tarp?" he asked as he climbed onto the back of the trailer and began to cut the straps that held the tarpaulin down.

Curiosity got the better of Kurt and he scrambled onto the trailer to help pull back a corner of the cover, revealing several long pieces of what appeared to be metal webbing for a transmission tower. It was nothing that could be of any immediate use, so Daniel jumped down from the trailer and went to the cab. Kurt followed and watched while Daniel began going through the papers sitting on the passenger seat and searching the sleeping area behind the driver's seat. Once again, everything went into one of his deep pockets. Including a handgun and a box of ammunition he found under the seat. When Daniel put it in his pocket, he grinned at Kurt and said, "That fellow should have been carrying his gun."

"Just what are you looking for?" Kurt asked as Daniel started looking through the cab again. He looked anxiously down the road and added, "Someone could be coming any minute."

Daniel smiled grimly at Kurt as he explained, "I don't like following two women who are being guided by visions. I'd like to find a map or something a little more reliable, if you know what I mean."

It was the first thing Daniel had said that Kurt could agree with. He would have preferred something more tangible, too. "We'd better get back," he said urgently. Time was ticking and they would have to hurry if they were to be gone before the driver and truck were discovered.

Daniel jumped down out of the cab. He had found a gun, but there was nothing else that made any sense. None of the papers mentioned any specific location, only lists of supplies. Ones to be picked up or dropped off, Daniel didn't know what they meant, nor did it matter. He knew he had taken a big risk by searching the truck, but it would certainly be their only chance to see what the trucks were hauling. As Daniel followed Kurt back up the rocky slope, he was wondering if all the trucks were carrying the same thing. Once the two men reached the top of the hill, the others were mounted and ready to go.

As Daniel climbed onto the black stallion's back, Kyla rode close to him and hissed angrily under her breath, "You had no right to endanger us all with your reckless behavior." She glared at him as she waited for his response.

Daniel sat tall in the saddle and looked down at her as he answered, "I saw an opportunity to search one of their trucks and I took it." The others were already on the move and Daniel kicked the black horse to follow them.

Kyla had to press North Wind to catch the black stallion, but when she caught up with Daniel once again she chastised him by saying, "Next time you might want to discuss what you plan to do with the rest of us."

Daniel slowed the horse and caught hold of the reins to Kyla's mount. Then stopping both horses he said, "There wasn't time," in a calm and even tone. Then he looked at Kyla. The fury that flared in her eyes was part of the new Kyla. He could not remember her ever having reacted with so much anger and passion. Only the smallest upturn of his lips revealed his amusement with her bristling temper as he added, "I thought you could trust me enough to know that I wouldn't endanger you or your friends."

Kyla eyed Daniel with obvious agitation and replied, "I know that I can trust you, but you have to trust us, too." Then pulling North Wind's reins from Daniel's hand, she looked in the direction the others had gone. "We'd better go." With one last fiery glare in Daniel's direction, Kyla dug her heels into North Wind's flanks and the horse took off, running like her namesake.

Daniel was smiling as he followed close on the heels of the white horse. He still hadn't given up hope. There were many long days ahead of them and the chance that they would find Fleet in the lake country was not good. Eventually, Kyla would have to give up her search and he would be there when she did.

Chapter Twenty four

Fleet reached the top of the hill, then stopped and looked back at Jack who was trailing behind him and still at the bottom of the hill. Pushing the motorcycle kickstand into place, Fleet let go of the heavy machine and sat down on the road to wait. Even though he was the one pushing, Fleet still had to stop and wait for the big man to catch up with him. When Jack finally reached the top of the hill, he collapsed onto the pavement beside Fleet. "I need a drink," Jack said as he reached into on of the bags tied to the back of the cycle. The gasoline may have run out but Jack still had a good supply of Rollo's moonshine. He took a drink from his flask and offered some to Fleet.

"No thanks," Fleet said as he smiled to himself and wondered how much moonshine was left. Jack might be in more of a hurry if he didn't have anything to drink. While the old man remained seated, drinking deeply from the flask, Fleet stood and put his binoculars to his eyes. Looking down the road in both directions, he said, "I'll bet we haven't traveled over sixty miles in the last three days." Then he lowered the binoculars and looked at Jack. "We could make better time if we left your cycle behind." Fleet was tired of pushing the metal monstrosity.

"We're not leaving my cycle behind," Jack answered stubbornly. He was tired of the subject. Fleet brought it up every time he stopped to rest. "You can go whenever you want." He took another drink and looked up at the tall blond man dressed in his black uniform. Jack had never met anyone quite as impatient as Fleet was. The younger man was driving himself and wanted him to keep the same pace. For some reason, he was obsessed with reaching Manjohnah's compound as quickly as possible. Standing and taking one more drink, Jack tucked the flask securely in his pack. Then he laughed, slapped Fleet on the back and said, "Don't worry my young friend, my people will be along any day now and then we'll ride."

"You've been saying that for three days," Fleet answered as he put the binoculars back in their case. "So far I haven't seen anyone on this road."

"Don't worry," Jack said. "They use this road all the time, but so do Manjohnah's men." He grabbed the handlebars of the cycle and said,

"I'll take a turn pushing now," as he sat on the seat and began coasting slowly down the hill.

"Now you take a turn," Fleet shouted after the older man as he hurried to catch up with him. "After I push that thing up the biggest hill for miles."

"No one ever said life was fair," Jack laughed as he left Fleet behind.

Fleet slowed to a walk and watched Jack rolling to the bottom of the hill. This time Fleet decided not to hurry. He would catch up with Jack on the way up the next hill.

As Fleet walked, he thought he saw a snowflake and by the time he reached the bottom of the hill a light but steady flurry of tiny white flakes were blowing in the wind. It was only late August. Even this far north it was a little early for snow. Fleet looked at the trees in the forest that surrounded the highway on both sides. Most of them were dark green pine and spruce, but there were a few hardwoods scattered among them. The oaks and maples had not begun to turn to their fall colors before the snow started this year. He hoped as everyone else did that this winter would not be as long and cold as the last, but after a cool, cloudy summer, now it seemed that fall would be cut short by an early winter.

Fleet knew they had to be getting close to the big lakes. The hills were more rugged, almost small mountains. The land between the ridges was low and marshy and every few miles they saw small lakes. This region of the country was known for its mosquitoes as well as the lakes. As he thought of the mosquitoes, Fleet was thankful for the snow. He preferred a light snowfall to swarms of the biting insects. When he caught up with Jack who was already puffing with the effort of pushing the cycle up the next rise, Fleet shoved Jack out of the way and said, "I don't know how you'd get this thing anywhere if it wasn't for me." He chuckled at the old man who smiled gratefully when Fleet took over the burden. Both men knew that Fleet was right. Without Fleet, Jack would have to sit with the cycle and wait for his friends to come by and give him a ride. It was Fleet who was in a hurry.

As they reached the top of the next rise, Fleet stopped even though Jack had managed to keep up with him. He almost dropped the motorcycle in his rush to get his binoculars out of their case. Jack caught the bike before it hit the ground and asked, "What is it?"

"Can't you hear the trucks?" Fleet said as he began pushing the motorcycle off the road and into the cover of the trees.

"It might be my friends," Jack said, looking back in the direction from which they had come. It was impossible to see who it was. The last ridge they crossed hid the approaching vehicle from sight.

After ditching the motorcycle, Fleet came back and pulled Jack into the trees saying, "I'm not going to stand in the middle of the road waiting to find out." They had just reached cover when Fleet saw the first truck coming over the top of the ridge just behind them. It was followed closely by two other trucks, forming a small convoy. A few seconds later the first truck sped by the spot where Fleet and Jack were hidden. As soon as it was past Jack ran out to the road waving and shouting. The second truck had already gone by, but the driver of the third began to slow. It traveled several yards up the road before coming to a complete stop. Jack was running after it with Fleet following right behind him every step of the way. The drivers of the other two trucks, seeing that the third had stopped, were now backing down the road.

The driver of the last truck jumped out of the cab with his gun ready. He was wearing a white jacket with the hood pulled over his head with trousers and boots that were also white. As Fleet watched the snow falling around him, he realized that here white clothing was necessary for camouflage. The man watched them warily and stood by his truck.

"Am I glad to see you boys," Jack shouted happily. Before he reached the truck Jack had to stop to catch his breath, running wasn't something he could do for any length of time.

As he stood next to the wheezing old man, Fleet asked, "How could you tell it was them?" The trucks had passed so quickly that Fleet hadn't been able to see anything.

Jack looked up at Fleet and said, "Didn't you see the arrows?" He pulled up his sleeve and showed Fleet a red arrow shaped scar on his wrist. "There are red arrows painted on the trucks." He smiled and added, "That's the mark for the Expendables. They mark you with the red arrow before they send you north."

All the days they had walked together, this was the first time Jack had told him anything about himself. "Send you north for what?" Fleet asked, but never got an answer to his question. Jack was walking toward the young man with his arm bared. For a moment Fleet stood where he was. When Jack motioned for him, Fleet quickly joined Jack and the young man dressed in white. The drivers of the other trucks were standing beside the first man and the trio watched Fleet with some trepidation as he approached. They had seen similar uniforms at Manjohnah's compound.

At the same time Fleet was assessing them. All three were young, wearing identical white hooded jackets, trousers, and boots, and they were all heavily armed. First they looked at the scar on Jack's arm then at him. Fleet could feel their indecision. It was clear that they didn't know what to do.

"He's come with me to join the rebels," Jack explained. "My cycle ran out of gas. If you have some to spare, we can go the rest of the way ourselves."

The tallest of the young men in white, pushed back his hood as he considered what to do. He had been driving the third truck and it seemed the others were looking to him to make some decision. He had dark brown eyes and a strong square jaw. His hair was shaved close to his scalp except for the top of his head. There his hair was quite long and he wore it in a long dark braid that hung down his back. "We can't do that," he finally announced after a lengthy period of indecision.

The other two young men lowered their guns and pushed their hoods back, too. Fleet was surprised to see that their hair was cut and braided in the same fashion as their friend. The uniforms and identical haircuts made them appear even more like soldiers. It was becoming apparent that they did not consider him or Jack a threat and were now getting to the business of deciding what to do with them.

"We aren't supposed to take riders, either," the young man with white blond hair and blue eyes argued.

The third one to voice his opinion was the driver of the first truck, a youth hardly in his teens with tousled brown hair and dark brown eyes. He looked earnestly at the tall young man who had been driving the third truck. "If he's an Expendable then we have to help him." He looked at Fleet and added, "We should take anyone who's willing to help."

The driver of the third truck looked at Fleet and the old man. "My name's Jabe," he said as eyed them with suspicion. "What are your names and who do you serve?"

The old man grinned as he answered, "My name is Jack and this young fellow with me is called Fleet. We serve mankind." He knew the answer the boys wanted. Then just to make sure they knew he was serious, he added, "We're heading to my friend's house. His name is Oley." The three of them nearly fluttered with excitement at the mention of the name. It seemed that Jack at least knew the right names to drop.

The young man who had introduced himself as Jabe looked at Fleet and said, "You can ride with me." Then to Jack he said, "We can't give you gas. We hardly have enough to get home ourselves, but you can ride with Knute," and pointed to the young man with the blond hair. Then to complete the introductions, he added, "And that's Quint driving the first truck. You can ride with him, but I wouldn't advise it."

"He can hardly see over the steering wheel," Knute teased the youngster and cuffed him playfully on the side of the head as they headed back to their trucks.

Jack looked at Jabe and said, "I can't leave my cycle."

Fleet rolled his eyes impatiently. He had been listening to that same excuse for too many days. "We can send someone back for it later. Your ride is here, so let's go." He didn't want to be left behind because Jack refused to leave his cycle.

"Isn't there room in one of the trucks?" Jack asked, refusing to drop the subject.

"They're already full," Jabe said as he looked at the three small panel trucks parked in the road. "I don't think we could get a motorcycle in one of them even if it was empty."

Jack looked at Fleet and said, "You'll have to go without me. Just have them take you to Oley and don't forget to send someone back with gas." Then without giving them a chance to respond, Jack turned and started jogging back down the road to where Fleet had hidden the motorcycle.

Fleet looked at Jabe and said firmly, "Don't leave without me." When the young man nodded, Fleet ran after Jack. Before he caught up with the gray bearded old fool, he was shouting, "Wait, you said that you would take me to the rebels."

Jack turned and looked at Fleet, "I did. Who do you think those boys are? They're not dressed up for trick or treat." He stopped and said, "You don't need me. I'm an old man. I did my job bringing you here." Jack eyed Fleet critically as he added, "I have a feeling that you can shake things up where ever you go. Good luck to you, Fleet. It's been a pleasure to know you." He turned and walked away whistling a tune as he went. It was a familiar old song and when Fleet had been a young boy, he had heard his grandfather whistle the same tune, but Fleet had forgotten the name of the song. It was something about a bird and freedom.

Fleet ran to the motorcycle ahead of Jack and took his pack and weapon. As he hurried to return to the truck where Jabe was waiting for him, Fleet felt his hopes soaring again. He looked at the red arrow painted on the doors of the truck when he climbed inside the cab and wondered why he hadn't seen them. It seemed fitting that the rebels used an arrow for their symbol. He thought of the arrow pin that he had given to Kyla and wondered if she ever wore it. The regret that he felt whenever he thought of Kyla nearly overwhelmed him and he fought to push her memory to the back of his mind. Instead, he would focus on his goal, which was so near at hand that he could taste it.

"How far is it," Fleet asked as he jumped into the truck and it began rolling down the road. He had no idea where they were going, but that was only a start to the questions that he had.

"Only two hours," Jabe answered and turned on the wipers for the windshield. "The snow is getting heavy," he commented absently.

"Jack said, that I should ask you to take me to Oley," Fleet said, sitting back and watching the trees as they sped by them. It was definitely much better than walking with the motorcycle. What the truck could travel in two hours would have taken several days on foot and at least two on horseback and Fleet definitely preferred riding in the truck to riding a horse.

Jabe shifted gears and as the truck began pulling up the steep grade of another long slope, he laughed and said, "Don't worry. Oley will insist on it." He wondered about the motives of the man dressed in the black tunic. Some of the men in Manjohnah's compound wore the same uniform; only the color of theirs was deep blue.

"Who are the Expendables?" Fleet asked. "Is that what you call the rebels?" He glanced at the wrists of the young man driving the truck, trying to see if he had a red arrow on his wrist like Jack's.

Jabe considered him with renewed interest. Fleet's questions were about things that he considered common knowledge. "The Expendables are the ones sent north to the work camps. The rebels are not Expendables." It seemed strange to Jabe that someone dressed as Fleet was, would not know that simple distinction. He smiled as he added to Fleet's confusion by saying, "But many of the rebels used to be Expendables." He pulled back the sleeve of his white jacket to reveal a red arrow on his wrist. "Only those of us who have been sent north have the scars."

"Why?" Fleet asked. "I don't understand what you're trying to tell me."

Jabe looked briefly at Fleet, and then returned his eyes to the road. "I've already said too much. Oley will answer all of your questions. You'll have to wait until then."

Fleet turned his attention to the road ahead. The snow was starting to accumulate, but the road remained a thin gray ribbon in stark contrast to the white snow that was covering everything else. They had only traveled a few miles further before the road turned to the north. Every once in awhile Fleet could see the dark water of the lakes through the trees when he looked to the east. Like an inland sea, the water of the huge fresh water lake stretched to the horizon and beyond. He was almost at the end of his journey and Fleet was becoming increasingly anxious with every mile.

Jabe, true to his word, kept silent for the rest of the journey. It was just after midday when Quint stopped the truck he was driving in the middle of the road. Knute and Jabe also came to a halt and all three vehicles idled noisily. Just as Fleet was about to ask why they were waiting, a group of people dressed in the white hooded uniforms appeared from the cover of the woods. Fleet watched as they pulled back a screen of camouflage, which concealed a rough dirt track leading into the woods. Once the way was cleared the trucks turned onto the bumpy road and they began to travel deeper into the forest. Fleet watched in the rear view mirror as the camouflage was put back in place and those guarding the entrance took their places once again. Even though he knew where they were, Fleet could barely see the rebels dressed in their white uniforms and crouching in the snow.

The path through the woods seemed to stretch on forever. After half an hour bouncing around inside the cab of the truck, Fleet finally caught sight of what looked like a tall concrete wall, painted white. When they came closer he could see that it truly was a fortress with walls that Fleet estimated at twenty feet tall with towers at the corners and covered with the same camouflage netting used to conceal the entrance. It struck Fleet as being very medieval in its appearance, but he had no doubt that the wall was very effective in keeping people in or perhaps this time it was to keep them out. Something Fleet was sure that he would know in a very short time.

The three trucks came to a halt outside the gate to the fortress. Fleet saw Quint and Knute jump out of the cabs of their trucks. Jabe turned to Fleet and said, "This is as far as we go," then opened the door and jumped out of the truck.

Fleet got out and with his pack and gun in hand, waited beside the truck, wondering what he was supposed to do next. The three young men were heading toward a doorway in the wall and Fleet hurried after them. Before they were inside, three other men had jumped into the empty trucks and began to drive them further down the lane and into the woods beyond. Jabe was waiting for Fleet at the doorway. "It was our job to get the supplies this far. From here they'll go by boat to the ones fighting north of here."

"When will you take me to meet Oley?" Fleet asked as he stepped inside the doorway. Once he was inside, Fleet stopped short. He had not been prepared for the sight that greeted his eyes. There were dozens of people inside the large walled complex. All of them were wearing white hooded uniforms with their hair shaved at the bottom and long braids on top. Men and women were all dressed alike and all carried automatic weapons. It was truly and armed camp where everyone was ready for warfare.

"Who wants to meet Oley," a voice behind Fleet inquired loudly.

When he turned around, Fleet saw a squarely built man with brown hair. He looked like a man who had spent his life working outside. His face was tanned and deep laugh lines appeared when he squinted his eyes and grinned at Fleet. He was dressed in the same white uniform as the others, but his head wasn't shaved and he didn't have a long braid like everyone else. Fleet wasn't sure what to say, so he asked, "Why don't you wear your hair like the others?"

Oley laughed and said, "The kids do that. I'm a little old for long hair and braids, don't you think." Then turning suddenly serious, he said, "You know who I am. Now, don't you think you ought to tell me who you are and what you want?"

"I've traveled almost a thousand miles to get here," Fleet answered. "A fellow with a bushy gray beard named Jack said that you could tell me where I could find Manjohnah's compound."

Oley considered the stranger in the black tunic and said, "I know Jack." He was still looking at Fleet as if he was weighing his options. "We had better find a place to talk in private," Oley said and began to lead the way through the crowd of people milling around the open ground in the center of the compound. Fleet followed Oley to a low domed building that reminded Fleet of an igloo made from stucco and painted white. When he followed Oley through the doorway Fleet rubbed his hand along the smooth, almost glasslike surface of the building. It was not like any building material he knew. It wasn't wood, concrete, brick, or stone.

Noticing that Fleet was staring at the material used to make the shelter, Oley said, "We have borrowed a few of their better technologies for our own use." He motioned to Fleet, urging him to step inside then pulled the door closed behind them. The inner surface of the structure was just as smooth and brilliantly white as the outside had been. The small lantern burning on the table in the center of the room was the only light necessary as the glow reflected off the walls illuminating the tiny room. Fleet was still standing with his mouth open, gaping in amazement when Oley said, "Why don't you sit down."

The shelter was sparsely furnished with only two chairs and a small table between them. Fleet sat in the empty chair across from the one where Oley was seated. "Do you live in these things?" Fleet asked.

"We can if we have to," Oley answered the question, and then abruptly changed the subject. "Now, what is your name and why are you looking for Manjohnah's compound?"

"My name is Fleet," he answered. Then he lowered his voice as he leaned closer to Oley and said, "I have come here with only one purpose in mind. I am going to kill Manjohnah."

The man's statement took Oley by surprise. This one was certainly not afraid to come to the point. "You're crazy. No one can get close to him," Oley laughed at Fleet's naïve assertion. Then as quickly as the laughter had come, it stopped and the look that Oley gave Fleet now was deadly serious, "Now tell me, what is someone who is wearing the uniform of the Commander's servant really doing here in the heart of my stronghold?"

Fleet had never thought about what the black tunic might mean to the rebels. "I am not a servant to anyone," he answered defiantly. "If you find my clothing unacceptable, then give me something else to wear."

Laughter was Oley's answer. "Where did you come from stranger?" he asked. Fleet was something of a puzzle. "You're not like any of the men that Manjohnah keeps around him."

"I'm from a place called the Settlement southwest of here," Fleet answered. "But I know what you mean, I've been to another compound run by a man named Lazarus. His men wore uniforms like mine, only theirs were gray."

Oley frowned thoughtfully as he said, "I know Lazarus."

It was Fleet's turn to be surprised and he asked, "How do you know Lazarus?"

"I used to work for Manjohnah," Oley answered in matter of fact tone. He said it casually as if he were telling Fleet the time of day. "I've met most of Manjohnah's men at one time or another. I was a builder and they needed somebody to help them put up the fences and buildings in their compounds." Oley watched for Fleet's reaction, before he added, "They offered me a pretty good deal. I could keep my home and my family. As long as I did what they said, I was useful. To them people are just tools to be used and discarded when they're finished. They call the ones they send north to the work camps Expendables, because they aren't expected to come back. When they sent me north to help with the first of the towers, they let me come back, but it didn't take me long to figure out that sooner or later I would be an Expendable, too."

"You've met Manjohnah?" Fleet asked; his voice hushed with awe of the man and the knowledge that he had.

"Yes, and that's how I know that you'll never get close enough to scratch him," Oley answered. "If you want to fight Manjohnah, you're welcome to join us. We're doing everything we can to disrupt his operations and flow of supplies. He has a lot of men and every week convoys of trucks loaded with supplies travel the road that you came in on today. We intercept what we can." He looked at Fleet with curiosity as he asked, "Who was Commander at your Settlement?"

The question took Fleet by surprise. The thought of Sadie as a Commander was unsettling. "I was at Sadie's compound," he answered cautiously.

With a broad smile and knowing wink, Oley said, "If I had to choose one of them, it would have been her. A pretty package, but she's just as cold as the rest of them."

As he thought of Sadie, Fleet lowered his eyes with embarrassment. The more he learned of what she represented, the more Fleet regretted his involvement with Sadie. Still, he had been more than willing where Sadie was concerned. Anxious to change the subject, Fleet said, "You mentioned the work camps and Jabe did, too," He paused before asking what he really wanted to know. "What are they doing in the north?"

"Manjohnah's building towers for his Masters." Oley was a little uncomfortable discussing the subject. Even though he knew the truth it was still hard to believe and even harder to explain. "They're building a forest of towers above the Arctic Circle. They're using them to change the weather patterns around the poles. Each one has to be precisely placed in a grid pattern. The more complete the grid the colder it gets. They say it will take twenty-five years to complete a permanent climate change. "

Fleet looked at Oley and said, "You called me crazy!" He laughed and said, "I suppose that Manjohnah's Masters are aliens from another planet." Fleet had heard the stories, but he never believed them.

"I've seen them myself," Oley answered. His face and voice were deadly serious. "It was only at a distance, but I saw them when I went north." As he leaned back in his chair, he said, "They're up there, my friend, and Manjohnah and his people are helping them change our planet's weather to suit their needs. Now if that doesn't make the hair on the back of you neck stand up then I don't know what will. It gives me the creeps every time I think about it."

There was nothing that Fleet could say. He had traveled north searching for Manjohnah and the truth about what had happened. Now that he had heard what Oley had to say he wasn't sure that the truth was what he wanted after all. One thing was certain, Oley was telling the truth. There was something about the look on his face that convinced Fleet of his sincerity. Something had to explain the drastic change in the weather, the constant cloudiness, but the explanation was too fantastic to believe.

It seemed that his host had a great deal of knowledge about the Commanders and their alien Masters. There was one other question that had plagued Fleet for months, ever since he had seen the people in trains going into the tunnels. Hoping that Oley would know the answer, Fleet asked hesitantly, "Do you know what happened to the evacuees?" Fleet stumbled over the words, but he managed to spit out the question.

"Now there's the million dollar question," Oley answered with a grim smile. "They're the Expendables." He looked at Fleet, wondering if he was ready to hear the whole story. Clearing his throat and looking directly into Fleet's eyes, Oley continued his explanation. "You see these Commanders and their Masters are a very efficient bunch. They have millions of potential workers in the deep freeze just waiting to be thawed out and sent to the north to work on their towers."

"Deep freeze," Fleet scoffed at the idea, "you can't just freeze someone and thaw them out later."

"We can't, but they can," Oley answered patiently. "They call it artificial hibernation." He watched the blond haired stranger, as he tried to grasp what he was hearing. Oley had told dozens of people the truth about what was happening to them. Most of them reacted the same way as Fleet. No one wanted to believe what he said, but no one could deny that it was true.

"I don't know what to think," Fleet was shaking his head. "I want to think that you're crazy or lying to me, but you seem to be sane and I believe that what you said was true," Fleet paused before adding, "or at least you think its true."

"You believe what you want," Oley answered. "Most folks don't believe at first." He grinned again and rose to leave. "Come with me," he said and opened the door.

As they stepped outside, Fleet asked, "Can you get me a white jacket and trousers like you wear?"

A young red haired woman was standing just outside the door. Her long braid whipped against her cheek as she turned her head abruptly to look at Fleet. After giving him a thorough head to toe assessment, she wrinkled her nose with disdain and said, "You'll need some boots, too." Then turning crisply back to Oley, she said, "We're ready when you are."

It was obvious that the young woman was anxious to be off to the task she had waiting, but Oley wasn't in a hurry. "Fleet, this is Elle," he made the introduction and looked on with amusement waiting for her reaction.

"It's nice to meet you," Fleet said, trying to be polite even though the young woman was ignoring him.

Elle gripped the weapon that she had slung over her shoulder and faced Fleet with a furious glare. "I'm sure it is," she answered tartly and turned back to Oley. "Your truck is ready. Do you want to go now?"

"You're always in a hurry," Oley said as he put his arm around Elle's shoulder. The young woman gave him an exasperated look, but she didn't argue with him. Seeing that she was ready to listen, Oley said, "Now, since you have expressed an interest in our guest's boots, why don't you take Fleet and get him some new clothes?" Elle looked at him as if she was ready to protest, but Oley gave her a look that silenced anything that she might have said. "I won't leave until you get back with Fleet. So the sooner you're done, the sooner we'll leave."

Elle immediately stalked off and stopped a few paces away from where Fleet and Oley were standing. She put her hands on her hips and demanded, "Well, hurry up. I haven't got all day." Then with a flick of her head that sent her braid whipping around her shoulders, she turned and stalked away from the men.

"What was that all about," Fleet asked. He couldn't help being a little amused watching Oley tease Elle.

"They're all young and in a hurry," Oley answered. "Elle is supposed to go with my patrol tonight." He looked at Fleet with a mischievous gleam in his eye. "I'm just trying to teach them a little patience." Then Oley nodded toward Elle who was watching from a distance, her arms crossed and her toes tapping impatiently, and said, "If you know what's good for you, you won't let her wait too long."

With a nod to Oley, Fleet left him and went to join Elle, who had started walking as soon as she saw Fleet coming toward her. He had to hurry a little to keep her in sight as she made her way through the jumble of trucks parked inside the walls. There were dozens of young men and women, all dressed in identical white jackets, but Fleet had focused on her long red braid. The color set her apart from all the others. Finally, they came to a shed at the back of the compound. Fleet followed Elle inside. The moment he stepped inside the door, Elle began throwing clothing at him.

"Wait a minute," Fleet said as he picked up the jacket and trousers off the ground. "You don't even know what size I wear."

"I know enough," she answered and looked at him with narrowed eyes. "You can change in here." Elle opened the door and tilted her head back haughtily. "I'll wait for you outside," she snapped and slammed the door behind her.

Fleet looked at the baggy trousers and jacket that Elle had given him. Without bothering to undress he pulled the pants on over his black ones and tightened the drawstrings at the ankles and waist. Then he pulled the jacket on over his head. He tried to put on the boots, but the ones Elle had given him were too small. Rather than risk her wrath again, Fleet looked on the shelves and found a pair that was large enough for him. He picked up the black boots that the Family had given him and went outside.

Elle tried to grab his boots when he came out, saying, "We can burn those and your clothes." She craned her neck and looked past him into the shed. "Where'd you leave your clothes?" she asked.

Fleet lifted up his jacket and showed her that he was wearing them under the white uniform. "I think I'll keep what I have."

His answer was apparently not the one that Elle wanted to hear. "I should have known," she sniffed. "Your kind can never change."

"My kind?" Fleet responded tersely. "Maybe you shouldn't be so quick to make judgments, especially, when they're based on things that you know nothing about." His patience was wearing thin with Elle. Youthful exuberance did not excuse bad manners. She was still staring angrily at him, when Fleet said, "I thought you were in a hurry to get somewhere."

The fact that Fleet had reminded her seemed to add to Elle's growing dissatisfaction. "I will go when I'm ready," she said defiantly. Then waiting only a few seconds, she turned and said, "You'd better hurry if you don't want to be left behind," as she sprinted away. Fleet ran after her while Elle did her best to loose him. He reached the door where he had entered the fortress, just in time to see her run outside. Only a few seconds behind her, Fleet burst through the doorway and almost tripped over Elle who had stopped just on the other side.

Oley had been waiting for them. "She's got you rushing around, too," he laughed as he opened the door of a battered old pick-up parked just outside the entrance. Four young men and two women, which included Elle, who was climbing into the back of the truck, were armed and ready to go. "Jabe put your things in the truck," Oley said as he climbed into the driver's seat. "You can ride up front with me."

As he walked around the back of the truck to get to the passenger side, Fleet looked at Elle whose burning gaze followed him every step of the way. The others watched him with curiosity. No one else seemed as openly hostile as Elle was. When he climbed onto the seat of the pick-up and closed the door, Fleet looked over his shoulder. It was as if Elle's eyes were burning into the back of his neck. She was still staring at him. "She's a real sweetheart," Fleet said sarcastically.

Oley glanced back at Elle as he started the engine. "Elle?" he said with a smile. "She likes to make a show of being tough, but once she gets to know you, she's a real pussycat."

"More like a mountain lion," Fleet said. "I think that she'd like to tear me apart."

"You should be so lucky," Oley laughed as he put the truck into gear and it lurched into motion. They were continuing on the same rutted path that the trucks had taken when they first arrived. Only now they were going deeper into the woods.

"Where are we going?" Fleet asked as he braced himself between the seat and dashboard.

"To Manjohnah's compound," Oley answered casually, as if it was an every day occurrence.

Fleet felt his heart jump and suddenly he understood why Elle had been so impatient. Now he too felt the anticipation surging through his mind and body. Fleet had come so far and had waited so long for this moment and he couldn't believe he was finally so close to his goal. In a flight as true as an arrow that was let loose from a marksman's bow, he had come directly to Manjohnah. Sister Samethia's vision was unfolding before him and all Fleet had to do now was wait for the Mother to show him the way to his final destination.

Chapter Twenty five

Fleet was sitting beside the fireplace in Oley's small hunting cabin. Several of the young men and women who were members of the rebel forces Oley commanded were also there. He had spent three days with them and so far had not been able to get close to Manjohnah's compound. Each night the rebels would surround the compound and shoot at anyone foolish enough to come into range. It was nothing more than organized harassment and in Fleet's opinion, wasted effort. Still, Fleet had been accepted by most of the people in Oley's little army. Even Elle's attitude had mellowed somewhat and she had taken a personal interest in converting Fleet into a full-fledged member of their rebel group.

This evening Elle was sitting on the floor near Fleet, sharpening a long hunting knife that she carried in addition to her automatic weapon and a pistol. As she finished her task and put the whetstone into her pack, she looked at Fleet. "Why don't you let me cut your hair like ours?" she asked as she tested the edge of her knife with her thumb.

"I'll keep my hair," Fleet said with a grin. "Besides, even if I did let you cut my hair, I wouldn't let you anywhere near me with that knife."

Another of the young women, a dark haired girl called Sherie, stood behind Fleet and took his ponytail in her hand. She smiled sweetly as she leaned close and whispered, "I'll cut your hair and I promise to be gentle."

Fleet looked at the young girl. Her hair was shaved and braided like the others, but the short hair around Sherie's face curled in little ringlets like a dark brown halo around her face. If it weren't for the knife and gun that she carried, she would have looked angelic dressed in her white uniform.

Jabe was lounging in one of the chairs with one leg swinging over the arm. He was sitting close enough to shove Elle with his foot as he said, "Why don't you two leave him alone. Fleet said that he doesn't want his hair cut."

Elle put her knife away and looked at Jabe when she answered, "Most men don't know what they want until a woman tells him."

One of the others, the blond haired young man named Knute laughed, "You could fit what you know about men into a thimble, Elle."

It was pleasant spending time with the young people, listening to their playful chatter, but Fleet was not ready to forget the real reason that he had traveled so far. "I'll tell you what I want to do," he started cautiously knowing that what he was about to suggest was not allowed. "I would like to go back to Manjohnah's compound for a closer look."

Oley was not at the cabin that night. When he left he had placed Marshall in charge of the others. A serious minded young man with mousy brown hair and dark brown eyes, he was well suited for the job. "I don't think that Oley would approve," he said eyeing Fleet with suspicion. Just mentioning something that was so far outside the parameters of their rules was disturbing for Marshall.

Fleet looked at the young man and said nonchalantly, "It was just a suggestion." Then he looked around the room at the faces of the others, wondering if he would have any nibbles on the proposal. He had learned that once Oley was gone, discipline was virtually non-existent. The others would follow Marshall's orders only if they agreed with him. The first person to catch his eye was Jabe. The dark haired young man grinned slyly and inclined his head toward the door. Fleet wasn't surprised that Jabe was the one who wanted to go. In the three days that he had been with Oley's rebels, he had seen the young man take on any task that his friends could dream up. On a dare he had gone swimming in the icy cold water of the lake, just because they said that he wouldn't. Good natured and fearless, he could be a real asset to Oley if he could just channel his abundant energy toward more practical activities. If he went along, Fleet would make sure that the time was spent productively.

Marshall was still watching and Fleet didn't want a confrontation. So he waited until his attention waned. After awhile, Fleet got up and stretched. Then he looked at Jabe as he picked up his pack and rifle and went out the door. Marshall turned to watch as he went out, but said nothing. Fleet hoped that Jabe had the good sense not to come right after him. All the sneaking made him feel a little foolish, but Fleet had to get a closer look at the compound if he was going find a way to get inside. He also needed someone with a key to one of the trucks to drive him the twenty miles to the compound and that was Jabe.

After waiting in the cold for several minutes, Fleet was beginning to wonder if Jabe was coming. He was about ready to go back to get him, when he came through the door. Without a word to Fleet, his young co-conspirator threw his pack and rifle into the back of one of the pick-ups parked beside the cabin while Fleet hurried to get in on the other side. Only he kept his pack and weapon with him. As Jabe started the engine, the door to the cabin flew open and Fleet was certain that it would be Marshall coming to stop them.

Instead it was Elle. She ran to the truck and opened the door just as Jabe began to pull away from the cabin. Pushing at Fleet, she ordered, "Move over. I'm going, too." Then she tossed her pack to Fleet and jumped into the moving vehicle.

There wasn't much that either Jabe or Fleet could say. If they stopped to put Elle out of the truck, Marshall would have a chance to protest. They rode in silence for a few minutes with Fleet in the middle, straddling the gearshift. It was an uncomfortable place to sit and as they bounced over the rough trail, it was all Fleet could do to hold onto his pack and Elle's. He had to brace his feet under the seat to keep from sliding. As far as Fleet was concerned, Elle was an unwelcome addition to the mission.

"I don't know why you're going," she said to Fleet. "There's nothing to see in the dark."

Fleet pushed Elle's pack at her as rudely as she had thrown it at him. Then opening his own, he said, "That's why I brought this," and took out the infra-red scope stolen from Lazarus' compound. During the time that he had traveled on his own, Fleet had experimented with the scope and now felt very comfortable using it.

"Where did you get that?" Jabe asked and tried to grab the scope from Fleet.

"Keep your hands on the wheel and watch the road," Fleet said as they hit an especially large rut in the road that jarred his whole body. "And don't worry about where it came from," he added. It was difficult with the bouncing and swaying motion of the truck, but Fleet somehow managed to attach the scope to his rifle as they rode.

"What do you have in mind?" Elle asked suspiciously.

"I just want to do a little night hunting," Fleet answered. Jabe laughed, but when Fleet looked at Elle he recognized something in her eyes. The girl had a fiery passion for the cause. He should have known that she wouldn't allow herself to be left behind.

"I don't thing you're the type that hunts raccoons," she said, watching Fleet out of the corner of her eye. Elle tilted her head and smiled knowingly. She knew what Fleet was hunting before she asked, but had wanted Fleet to confirm her suspicion.

"Tell me about the scar on your wrist," Fleet said to Jabe instead, not wanting to discuss what he hoped to do with Elle.

Jabe shrugged his shoulders and said, "There's not much to tell."

"You showed me a red arrow scar on your wrist," Fleet said. Not really sure how to broach the subject, Fleet asked, "What was it like?"

"I never went north," Jabe answered simply. "I'm one of the lucky ones. Oley and his rebels intercepted the truck I was riding in. This is as far north as I ever went."

There was one last thing Oley had mentioned which was on Fleet's mind. "Were you frozen in artificial hibernation?" It was such an incredible question that Fleet felt uncomfortable asking.

"I guess I was," Jabe said. "I don't remember anything about it. I went to sleep and I felt a little stiff when I woke up, but I didn't know that I'd been out for a year." They rode in silence for the remainder of the trip. Just the mention of Jabe's experience was enough to make all three contemplate what it was that they were fighting. Fleet was glad for the silence. He was preparing himself mentally for the task that he had set for himself.

Oley's rebels had gone to Manjohnah's compound every day just before sunset. As far as Fleet could tell, the people inside could set the time by their appearance. He was hoping if he went back later there might be more activity inside the fences. All he wanted to do was scout the perimeter of the fence and try to find a way to get inside. If he were lucky maybe Manjohnah would come outside. As Fleet thought about Manjohnah, he realized there was one thing he had not asked Oley. He should have asked him for a description of the man, but it didn't matter. There was no doubt in Fleet's mind that when he saw Manjohnah, he would know him.

They drove the last few miles with the lakeshore to their left. A strong north wind blowing off the water roared overhead and whipped the water into frothing white caps. The sound of the waves crashing against the rocky shore was loud enough to be heard over the truck engine. Less than a mile from the fence surrounding the compound, Jabe pulled the truck into a grove of cedars and turned off the engine. "We'd better walk the rest of the way," he said, trying to sound as casual as possible, but the slight hesitation in his voice revealed his apprehension.

When Elle got out of the truck, she put up the hood of her jacket and turned her back to the wind. "Do you want me to lead the way?" she volunteered. Now that they were at the point, she was anxious to get down to business.

Fleet shouldered his rifle and answered, "I know the way." He looked at Jabe and Elle, and then said, "I'd tell you to wait here for me, but I know that you'd follow anyway." It was dark and impossible to see their faces, but Fleet saw them exchange glances. "All I ask is that you stay down and stay out of my way." Fleet realized that he was shouting to be heard over the wind and waves. He gladly turned and started to make his way into the shelter of the trees. In the woods the wind was not quite so strong, but the sound of the trees creaking and moaning was added to the roar of the wind. It was a wild and windy night as Fleet stumbled blindly through the underbrush. The only way that he could be sure of the direction was to keep the sound of the waves close to his left. Slowly, the three worked their way up the rocky shoreline until the were nearly on top of the fence that stretched across the narrow point of land from the western to the eastern shore, marking the southern border of Manjohnah's domain. When they stopped behind a large pile of boulders near the shore, they could hear the sound of the boats bumping and grinding against the dock just to their left.

Even though there was snow on the ground, the trees and rocks outside the fence were quite dark. Fleet's objective was to make his observations and remain unseen. Tonight he would be looking for any weakness he could find. Tomorrow he planned to return alone and penetrate Manjohnah's defenses. Fleet began to take off the white jacket and trousers. Underneath, he was still wearing his black uniform. He even had his old boots in his pack and he put them on, too. Then for a final touch he reached down, scooped up a handful of moist black dirt, and rubbed it on his face. He wanted to be invisible in the darkness.

Elle watched as he took off his outer layer of clothes and was dismayed that Fleet had shed the rebels' white uniform. To do so was the same as treason in her mind. "You're anxious to return to the old uniform I see," she whispered fiercely in Fleet's ear.

"You two stand out like a couple of spooks dressed in white," Fleet whispered back. He didn't want any noise or conversation. The less said the better.

Jabe was searching his pack and produced a dark colored knit cap then handed it to Fleet without a word. He understood what Fleet was doing. As soon as Fleet pulled it on to cover his hair, he was ready. Only a narrow strip of trees separated them from the open area next to the fence. Fleet crouched low and crept closer with Jabe and Elle right behind him. Just before he came to the edge of the trees he turned and caught Elle by the arm and motioned in the darkness that they should wait for him. Then Fleet got down on his hands and knees and crawled under the pines. The lowest branches brushed his back and the needles crackled softly as Fleet inched his way through them. Finally, he reached the last of the trees. Although, he was unable to see the fence in front of him, Fleet knew that it was only a few short feet away.

Using the infra red scope, he began to search the perimeter of the fence for signs of activity. It was a few minutes before he saw the glowing image of a man walking inside of the fence. It was only the sentry. Fleet waited and a few minutes later the sentry made another pass along the same area. It was cold and Fleet's fingers were growing numb, but after almost an hour of watching the man walk back and forth, he was finally rewarded for his patience.

Another man joined the sentry Fleet had been watching. When the second man walked toward the shoreline, Fleet was watching every move he made as he let himself out a gate in the fence and began walking toward the area where the boats were docked. After a few minutes, the man returned and went back into the compound. Without a word to the other sentry, the second man went along his way. It was all Fleet could do to keep from shouting out in his excitement. He had just found his way into the compound. A man with a key to the compound, outside the fence and alone was the kind of opportunity that he had been hoping for.

It was nearly midnight when the sentry finally stopped pacing the length of fence that Fleet was watching. He waited a few more minutes, wondering where the man had gone and was almost ready to leave when he heard an especially strong gust of wind pass overhead. First he looked upward, following the sound, but when he turned back toward the compound, Fleet saw something glowing faintly just inside the fence and two figures bent over the source of the light. As the figures straightened to standing, Fleet could see their faces illuminated in the weak light. He gasped audibly when he recognized Sadie. Standing next to her was a bald man dressed in a dark tunic who appeared to be much older than Sadie. Fleet was fixated on the sight as he tried to recover from the shock of seeing Sadie inside Manjohnah's compound.

Now, he could see a third figure kneeling between them. A slender young man dressed in black clothing rose slowly to stand with them. Fleet could see that he was holding the source of the light in his hand. It had to be a very small lantern and the light it gave out was growing weaker and seemed about to flicker out completely. Suddenly, coming to his senses, Fleet began to fumble for his gun, which he had dropped in his surprise. The light was fading fast and as Fleet focused on the three figures using his scope, he was surprised to find that he couldn't see them clearly with the infra-red device. All he could see were two indistinct blurs, only the shadows of an image, like they had moved and now the scope was picking up the traces left behind. Without using the scope, he could still make out the figures but just barely. Fleet could see three people but when he looked through the scope, he only saw two shadowy figures.

There had to be something wrong with the scope, Fleet thought. Still, it had worked just minutes before. Maybe it was something about the light the man was holding, but the scope was useless. Fleet tried to sight on the tall, bald man but the light was gone and he had missed his chance. When he looked through the scope again, he saw nothing, not even the shadow of an image. Fleet was furious with himself. He had been given the perfect opportunity and had hesitated. The scope had malfunctioned but that was no excuse. He had not fired a single shot.

Fleet heard a rustling in the trees behind him and turned with his rifle aimed toward the sound. When he saw Jabe coming through the trees, he tried to pull him down, but it was too late. Fleet didn't hear the shot. He saw Jabe look down and then the red blood staining the chest of his white uniform. As the young man fell to his knees, he said, "Did you see the light?" and then collapsed. Fleet could hear the commotion inside the fence and knew it was time to leave. He crawled back toward the spot where he had left Elle, dragging Jabe as he went. He didn't know if he was dead or alive, but Fleet couldn't leave him behind. Elle met him halfway. Fleet gave her the gun and pack and hoisted Jabe onto his back. Then they began to make as hasty a retreat as possible with Fleet carrying such a heavy and awkward load.

If anyone had decided that they were worth chasing in the dark, they never would have made it back to the truck. Obviously, the men in the compound felt no fear of the rebels safe inside their fence. Fleet's mind was reeling with the consequences of his actions. How could he face Oley when he was responsible for the death of one of his young men? If only he had stayed with Elle, Jabe would be alive. It had all been for nothing. Fleet had failed, but instead of feeling discouraged, his resolve only increased. He would be back and next time he would either be successful or die trying.

~ ~ ~

Kyla reached the top of the hill and reined North Wind to a halt then turned to look at the others following behind her. Kurt was the first one to catch up to her. Kyla had been pushing the horses and everyone else harder every day. He watched as she looked expectantly toward the road ahead. A light snow was falling and the wind was from the north.

"We need to take a break so the horses can rest," Kurt said and dismounted to emphasize his point. He wouldn't admit that he needed to rest himself, instead he said, "You look tired, too." He caught North Wind's reins and held them while Kyla climbed down slowly. His concern was genuine as he added, "Kyla you can't keep up this pace forever. We need a day to rest. We've been riding for twelve days without a break."

Kyla looked at Kurt for only a moment before turning her attention back to the road stretching before her. "We're close now, Kurt. Look," Kyla said as she pointed east.

Squinting at the far horizon, Kurt could see the dark blue lake in the distance. He shook his head slowly and said, "We've come to the first lake, but we're no closer to finding Fleet than we are to finding a needle in a haystack." Kurt was relieved to see they had come to the end of their eastward trek, but they could spend the rest of their lives searching thousands of miles of shoreline for Fleet. "We've never talked about what we would do if we can't find him," Kurt cautiously broached the subject. The snow falling around them only served to remind him that winter was close and they could not survive the harsh weather living in tents.

His words brought Kyla's attention from the lake in the distance. When she turned to Kurt again her eyes shone with determination and she said firmly, "We will find him. I know it." Ever since finding the old railroad bridge hidden in the woods and crossing the river, Kyla had been like a woman possessed. The bridge had been exactly the same as the image that Sister Samethia had planted in her mind. It was something that had no reasonable explanation. Even Sister Samethia could not explain why Kyla could remember the things that Sister Samethia had dreamed. Ever since the first day at the Settlement, the two women had tried to repeat the strange phenomena they had experienced, but to no avail. Still, what she had learned from Sister Samethia that day was enough. She had recognized the bridge and now here was the image of a long gray road stretching into the distance with the lake shimmering in the distance. For Kyla the sight of the lake was a shining beacon leading her to the end of her journey.

As Sister Samethia approached, Kurt made a hasty retreat. "We'll talk later," he said as he went to join Brother Fox. He had heard all about the visions and images that Sister Samethia and Kyla were searching for and he was tired of the subject. Kurt would have given anything for a map, something that he could see and believe.

Kyla was nearly bursting with excitement as she pointed to the lake in the east. "Do you see it?" she asked with wonder and awe. "We're here at last." She was ready to climb back into the saddle and gallop on North Wind until they both collapsed from exhaustion.

Standing still and waiting for the others to rest took all the restraint that Kyla possessed.

"It's one step in the journey," Sister Samethia said confidently, "but not necessarily the end." She was as excited as Kyla to see another of the images become reality, but she knew that it was only a small piece of the visions she had seen. She sighed audibly as she looked at the deep blue water to the east. Sister Samethia struggled to understand the power that surged through her body. Her ability to transfer an image to Kyla had been a miracle, one that she could not reproduce. Sister Samethia had tried to gain control of the power. She wanted to be able to command it at will, but she was learning that she didn't control the Mother's powers. The Mother controlled her and the gift was not hers. It was something the Mother gave her only when it was needed.

After standing for a few minutes in silence, Sister Samethia looked at Kyla and said, "Kurt's right, you need to rest. You've eaten very little and I can't remember the last time that you slept for more than a couple of hours." She leaned closer so no one could overhear and said, "You have someone other than Fleet to worry about now. If you don't want to loose the child you had better take care of yourself."

Kyla looked at Sister Samethia, her eyes suddenly wide with fright as she said, "Have you seen something? Is there something wrong?" All of her attention was focused on her search for Fleet, never once had any doubt entered her mind concerning the child she carried.

"I don't need a vision to know that you need to take care of yourself," Sister Samethia answered.

Looking at the others and back to Sister Samethia, Kyla said, "We'll ride until nightfall and rest tomorrow." Then she turned back to the east. The sight of the lake in the distance had her full attention.

Kurt and Brother Fox watched the two women conferring. Both men were following for now, but there were limits to their patience. "I told Kyla that we need a day to rest," Kurt said.

Daniel was watching Kyla and Sister Samethia, too. As he joined Brother Fox and Kurt, he commented sarcastically, "They seem to have found another 'image'."

Brother Fox considered Daniel briefly before saying, "Don't mock what you can't understand." He had never known Sister Samethia to be wrong where her visions were concerned.

"I understand that Kyla is running herself to death and the rest of us with her," Daniel said, "and I'm going to put a stop to it." He started toward Kyla and Sister Samethia.

Before he could go to Kyla, Kurt put his hand on Daniel's shoulder to stop him. "I have already discussed that with her. We'll rest tomorrow, no matter how much they object." He nodded toward Sister Samethia and Kyla, but it wasn't necessary. They knew who he meant.

Daniel brushed Kurt's hand from his shoulder. There were times when he felt as if Kurt was trying to keep him from Kyla. Leading the black horse behind him as he went, Daniel strode to where Kyla was standing and staring like someone in a trance at the eastern horizon. He shot a burning glare at Sister Samethia. After Fleet, Daniel blamed her for Kyla's irrational behavior. Then placing his hand on Kyla's shoulder, he said, "I need to talk to you alone." Stressing the word alone, Daniel once again looked at Sister Samethia, waiting for her to leave.

"Whatever you want to say, you can say in front of Sister Samethia or any of my friends," Kyla answered. The fatigue was evident in her voice, but never once did she turn to look at Daniel. Her eyes remained glued to the road to the east.

"You're not well," Daniel began, "I can tell just by looking at you." He moved to place himself in front of Kyla, forcing her to look into his eyes as he spoke. "And I'm not just talking about your physical health." He looked at Sister Samethia, who was watching and for once remaining silent.

Every day without fail, Daniel had come to her and asked Kyla to give up the search for one reason or another. She smiled, as she lightly touched Daniel's cheek and said, "We're almost there."

It was not what he wanted to hear. "Tell me what is wrong," he pleaded. Kyla couldn't have changed this much. Deep in his heart, he knew there had to be something more than just the search for Fleet and the visions that she told him about. Instead of an answer Kyla looked at Sister Samethia and shook her head when the other woman eyed her critically. Daniel was bursting with frustration when he growled, "I'm tired of your secrets. We all are," and stalked away angrily, unsuccessful once again in his attempt to crack through the wall that Kyla kept between them.

Sister Samethia followed Daniel. "Wait," she said as he hurried after him. Grudgingly, Daniel stopped while Sister Samethia caught up to him. Sister Samethia didn't understand why Kyla refused to tell Daniel and Kurt about her pregnancy. At this point in the trip they were the only ones who didn't know. She had told Brother Fox, of course and Sister Eaglet and Sister Alisma had told Justin and Brother Wesley, who had told the other young men. It was becoming increasingly uncomfortable for them to keep her secret, but Sister Samethia respected Kyla's wishes although she couldn't understand them. "Don't be so hard on her," Sister Samethia said. "You don't understand everything."

"I don't like secrets," Daniel answered. "If she would tell me then I might understand." He eyed Sister Samethia hopefully and added, "Or you can tell me." She had come after him; maybe the elusive Sister was ready to enlighten him, too.

"Kyla has to tell you," Sister Samethia answered uncomfortably. This time she agreed with Daniel.

"Well, when you have something to say, you know where to find me," Daniel said with obvious irritation. He left Sister Samethia standing alone as he led his horse to the side of the road to join the rest of the party. Daniel enjoyed the company of the younger men. Their motives were easier to understand. They had come on the journey out of loyalty to Sister Samethia and Fleet. All they were looking for was a little excitement, but like him they were becoming weary of the journey.

Brother Wyatt was busy building a small fire in an attempt to provide some warmth. The wind from the north not only brought an icy chill, but it also brought snow, big puffy flakes that covered the leaves on the trees, which had been green when the snow started falling a few days ago. Now they were frozen in place on the branches, never having a chance to fall. There had been no chance for autumn to make its appearance as the cool summer slipped directly into winter.

"What did they say," Brother Wesley asked as he returned with an armload of deadwood for the fire. He brushed the hair from his eyes as he dropped the wood and looked at Kurt and Brother Fox.

"I guess, we're resting tomorrow," Daniel answered as he squatted next to pile of wood and poked at the weak flame with a twig.

"Good," Justin said looking at Eaglet. "We all could use a day to rest." Although, Justin said 'we', he really meant Eaglet. Then he looked at Kyla still standing in the middle of the road. She needed rest more than any of them. "We'll probably have to tie Kyla down to keep her in one place for a whole day."

Everyone laughed at Justin's comment. Everyone except Eaglet who gave Justin a disapproving look as she said, "I'm going to talk to her."

Daniel almost called out 'Good luck', but kept his mouth shut instead. Sister Eaglet was almost as fanatical as Sister Samethia was. He looked at Justin and shook his head. Eaglet was his wife and Daniel was sure that the pretty young girl was going to grow into a mule headed woman. All the indications were there. Still, he was thankful to see that Sister Eaglet was successful in coaxing Kyla out of the middle of the road.

As Kyla came to stand with the group around the fire, all conversation ended. It was as if they had all forgotten how to speak. Nine people huddled in silence around the small fire. The only sounds were the wind blowing overhead and the horses rustling as they grazed on the dried grasses at the side of the road. Brother Fox, Kurt and Sister Samethia eventually left the watch on the road and joined them.

Brother Fox looked at the dirty, tired, and ragged little group. They didn't look anything like they had when they left the Settlement. "Kurt and I think that we can reach the lake tonight, but we may have to ride after dark to do it," Brother Fox said. As those seated at the fire groaned in unison at the mention of another long day, he added, "But we'll rest by the lake tomorrow."

"Plenty of water for a bath," Peach said as he pushed Dylan. "The odor's been getting a little strong lately." The mention of a day off his horse had brought back his sense of humor.

Dylan's dark glare was turned to Peach as he retorted, "I don't know how you can smell anything over your own stink."

Sister Alisma looked at the two young Guard members with impatience and said, "You both stink. Now can we change the subject?"

Brother Fox smiled. It was good to see them back to friendly bickering. Just the promise of a day to rest had brought back some of their enthusiasm. Then he brought up a subject that he knew was going to receive a protest from Kyla. "We also decided to start traveling off the road again," Brother Fox paused slightly and looked at Kyla. "The ground is not as swampy and soft here."

"We can make better time if we stay on the road," Justin exclaimed. Brother Fox had just said they were going to ride to the lake before stopping for the night. Riding through the woods would only make the journey longer.

A little surprised and relieved that it hadn't been Kyla who objected, Brother Fox gave his explanation. "If we are as close to Manjohnah as Sister Samethia and Sister Kyla believe then it would be best if we kept out of sight." Brother Fox scanned the faces in the circle around the fire looking for any indications that someone might object to the plan, but everybody stared silently at the fire.

Suddenly, Brother Wyatt jumped to his feet and started to put out the small fire. "Then we had better get going," he said kicking the branches away as he tried to erase the traces of the fire. He picked up the unburned wood and loaded it on one of the packhorses. If they had gone to the trouble of gathering it once, he wasn't going to do it again later. The others knew that he was right and reluctantly made ready to ride. The sooner they got to the lake the better. At least they all had a goal in mind, one that everybody could see.

Chapter Twenty-six

It was the evening following Fleet's ill-fated trip to Manjohnah's compound. Fleet was standing by himself watching the preparations for Jabe's funeral. The remorse and grief he felt was overwhelming. The young man had been alive and his life full of promise yesterday. Now because of Fleet's reckless attempt to scout the compound, he was dead. Oley had been furious as he expected, but hadn't ordered him to leave. Like any man in command of an army, he knew that young men and women died. It was part of the life that they led. Still, Fleet knew that when someone died unnecessarily, it was more than a waste of life. It was a crime. That was how Fleet felt. He was responsible for Jabe's death, just a surely as if he had pointed the gun at him and pulled the trigger himself.

Elle was with the group standing at the shore. When she saw Fleet standing alone on the rocks above them, she began to climb up to him. For a moment she stood in silence beside Fleet, looking out over the water. "It wasn't your fault," she said solemnly. "Jabe shouldn't have exposed himself like he did." She had seen him stand behind Fleet, a large white target in the darkness.

"If it wasn't for me, he wouldn't have been there," Fleet answered without looking at the young woman standing beside him. He wasn't willing to accept the excuse she offered.

Elle looked at Fleet. She had been suspicious of him at first, but even though she had met him only a few days earlier, Elle knew him as well as she knew herself. "You're wearing the black uniform tonight," she said accusingly. Elle hated to see him wearing the clothing that she associated with Manjohnah. She knew now that Fleet shared the same blinding passion that she did. Elle wanted to see Manjohnah dead and everything that he had built destroyed. She couldn't understand why Fleet would wear their uniform. Suddenly she was pleading, "Why don't you join the rebels? We need someone like you to lead us."

"You already have someone to lead you," Fleet answered. He wasn't sure whether to be flattered or amused by her proposal. "I have something else that I need to do."

"You're going back tonight," Elle whispered.

As he looked into her eyes, Fleet could see the excitement growing. He would have to be careful if he were going to slip away without Elle following him. "No, I'm not going tonight," he answered. A little white lie might save her life.

Watching as Fleet turned his attention back to the preparations by the lake she smiled knowingly. His words meant nothing. She could see that he was ready to go. Every motion, the look on his face, and even his silence, told Elle the truth. Fleet was going back to the compound tonight and he was going to try to kill Manjohnah. He had never said that was what he planned to do, but she knew it was so. He hoped to catch a glimpse of Manjohnah and assassinate him. Why else would he creep up to the edge of the compound dressed in black with a gun equipped with a night scope? She also knew that he would try to sneak off without anyone knowing, but it would take someone more clever than Fleet to loose her. Elle wanted to be there when he shot Manjohnah.

Fleet was watching as six of Jabe's friends carried him to a boat they had pulled onto the rocky shore. They laid his head in the bow of the boat. Then each of the six placed one of Jabe's possessions into boat with him. Once that was done, they began to load firewood on top of Jabe's body until it filled the small boat. Oley poured gasoline over the pile of wood. The six men who had carried Jabe's body then began to push the boat into the water as Oley gave a short eulogy.

"He was a good man and too young to die," he said loudly enough that even Elle and Fleet could hear his words clearly. "I saved him from death once, but it seems that death caught him this time." As Oley reached out and pulled one of the torches set into the sand on the beach, he added, "I hope you found what you wanted." He threw the burning torch onto the boat and the gasoline blazed high into the air above the boat. The six men pushed the burning craft until they were up to their necks in the freezing water. Finally they released it and slowly the currents began to push the boat further down the shore. As Fleet watched the young men swimming in the cold water, he thought that Jabe would appreciate the irony of their actions. They were the same friends who had convinced Jabe to go swimming in the icy water. Now they were doing the same thing in tribute to him.

Fleet and Elle stood together and watched in silence until the boat had either finally burned itself out or disappeared into the distance. By then it was almost totally dark as night fell around them. "Is this what you always do when someone dies," Fleet asked. The ceremony had been moving, but it was unusual.

"No," Elle replied, "It was what Jabe wanted."

~ ~ ~

The party had spent a pleasant day by the lake. Even Kyla had to admit that she felt better, but now that they were on horseback again, she was pushing just as hard as she had any other day. After struggling for most of the day, Brother Fox had been forced to give up his idea of riding in the woods. Following the shoreline and the rocky ground near the lake's edge was impossibly slow with the horses. Once they returned to the road they had ridden hard until late in the afternoon and had come to a point where it veered away from the shore. The woods towered overhead and in places the branches on one side of the roadway almost touched the branches of the trees on the other side. They were riding through a shady stretch of road when Kyla noticed some small red arrows painted on the pavement. As she slowed suddenly to look at one of them, the rest of the party passed by her. Finally, when she had come to a complete stop, the others stopped and Kurt turned his horse and returned to see what she was doing.

As she saw Kurt riding toward her, Kyla pointed at the pavement. Then he saw the red arrows, too. They were small, but they were there and they were all pointed in the same direction, like they were pointing the way to something. Kurt turned and both he and Kyla rode together following the tiny red arrows. By then the rest of the group had also looked down and noticed the arrows, too.

The whole group was milling about in the center of the road when someone in the woods shouted, "Get those god-damned horses out of the road." Suddenly, they saw six men clothed in white with hoods and ski masks covering their heads and faces. They emerged from the woods waving their hands and pointing their guns at the group. They were surrounded before they knew what had happened. One man who wore no mask appeared behind them and with his gun also pointed

585

toward the group on horseback, he ordered, "Get down now!" Quickly, they all dismounted while still more men dressed in white with their faces masked appeared and began dragging the horses off the road. "Get your hands on top of your heads and move. Now!" he ordered as his men began pushing them to the side of the road and into the woods. The man, who wore no mask, was obviously the commander. He walked behind them cursing as they went. "Damn kids and their arrows."

As they pushed them through the woods, Kyla tripped and fell onto her knees. Before she could stand the guard following her pushed her and knocked her down again. Brother Fox was right behind them and he struck the guard and growled fiercely, "Leave her alone."

Brother Fox received a blow between his shoulder blades for his actions and a sharp warning, "Next time you try something, I'll shoot you," the masked guard said as he bent to help Kyla to her feet.

The voice sounded young, but there was not a doubt in Brother Fox's mind that the threat was genuine. "Just be careful of the women," Brother Fox mumbled as meekly as possible, but his voice carried a threat just as real as his captor's.

"Quiet," the man who was in command said sharply. A few yards from the road they reached a small clearing. "Secure the prisoners," he ordered. Then to the group of strangers, he said, "If I hear a sound out of any of you or your horses, they'll shoot first and don't worry. I won't have any questions later."

"Get down on your knees," one of their guards ordered gruffly. Then one by one, all twelve had their hands pulled behind their backs and bound with plastic strips that were cinched tightly into place. Once they were securely bound, four of the original six guards returned to the others waiting near the road, leaving only two watching the prisoners. The two who remained walked behind them and pushed their heads low as they went by, until all were bent down with their faces as close to the ground as was physically possible. No one dared to move. They could hear the two guards pacing nervously behind them.

Justin was between Kurt and Daniel at the end of the row. Out of the corner of his eye, Kurt could see the two guards standing together at the other end of the line. Very softly, he whispered to Justin, "Why would Brother Fox do that? He could have gotten us all killed."

"Because Kyla's pregnant," Justin whispered back. He turned his head slightly and looked at Kurt when he heard the sound of his surprise. "You didn't know?" The words were barely out of Justin's mouth before both he and Kurt received a kick from the guards.

After kicking Kurt in the head, the guard bent down and whispered, "Are you just stupid or don't you understand? Shut up!"

Kurt was a little surprised that the voice behind the mask belonged to a woman, but he didn't have much time to think about it or what Justin had said. At that moment the sound of trucks coming down the road had his complete attention and Kurt listened intently as they came closer. When the trucks were about to pass, the sound of gunfire erupted in the woods around them. He was suddenly glad that they were bent low, as return fire from the trucks on the road tore through the branches above them and hail of twigs fell on their backs. Even their guards were now crouched low beside their prisoners as the battle began.

Except for a few rounds being fired in their direction, the battle appeared to be rather one-sided and was over in a few minutes. As Kurt heard the cheering from the guards and the others hiding in the woods when the shooting ended, he heard the commander shouting orders and within moments the trucks were roaring down the road again, undoubtedly with new drivers and a new destination. He still wasn't sure if they should be happy that their captors were the victors or not.

When the guards gave the order to rise, Kurt got to his feet and looked to the man who now commanded their future in addition to his army. If he had been in the same position, Kurt wasn't sure what he would have done. He knew that deciding what to do with prisoners was a dilemma for a man in his position. Prisoners would slow him down when he needed a speedy retreat. The easiest solution would be to shoot them all right now. Instead, he said, "Get them moving."

"What have you done with the horses?" Brother Wyatt demanded angrily. He stood and looked defiantly at the commander, waiting for an explanation.

"Don't worry, son," the man said casually. "If I decide to let you leave, you'll get your horses back. But right now, I don't have time to talk. Now all of you keep quiet and hopefully, we'll get where we're going without anyone getting hurt."

With one of their guards leading the way, the other with the woman's voice ordered, "Single file." As they fell into line, the man leading them began to run through the brush and trees, with the prisoners following close behind him. The woman at the end of the row kept urging them to go faster, saying, "Hurry up, hurry."

After a short distance, Kurt said, "We could run better if you untied us. It's hard to keep your balance on the rocks without your hands free."

She moved up quickly, tripped Kurt with her foot, and then used the butt of the gun to hit him across the back. "You're a trouble maker, aren't you?" she said as she pushed him toward the others after he stood. "Now move your ass, they're loosing us." The woman continued to urge him faster with a string of obscenities that flowed with every step.

He wasn't sure how far they had run through the woods, but Kurt was certain it had been a mile or more. When they finally came to an open field, he saw several pick-up trucks already filled with people making their way across the field and disappearing into the woods on the other side. Only two trucks remained and Kurt and his guard were the last to emerge from the woods. The twelve in their party were all herded together and loaded into to the back of one of the waiting trucks. Kurt was last and the woman who had been following him pushed him toward the truck.

"Why don't you make it easy on us and just cut off these straps," he demanded as he turned to the woman.

She pushed back her hood and took of the ski mask that covered her face. "And why don't you stop complaining and do what you're told?" she said. As she leaned close to Kurt and stared up at him, she pushed him into the back of the truck and slammed the tailgate closed. Then with a snap of her head, her long red braid almost caught him in the face as she turned to hurry to the other truck.

The girl had kicked him in the head, tripped him and hit him with her gun then cursed him every step of the way, but when Kurt saw her face and smelled her scent as she stood close, he felt his heart race. It had nothing to do with fear. He had every reason to dislike the woman even though she was the most exceptional woman he had ever seen. Instead there was something about her intensity that intrigued Kurt. As the truck that he was riding in began to speed across the open field, Kurt turned to face the rear of the truck and craned his neck to see the other vehicle that carried his fiery red-headed guard, hoping to catch a glimpse of her. When he finally saw her, Kurt realized that she was looking directly at him and returning his gaze. Even after she looked away, he couldn't take his eyes away. He watched until they reached the trail that took them through the timber. After that the other truck was following right behind them and all Kurt could see was the driver.

For nearly an hour they bounced and slid around in the bed of the pickup truck. Every inch of the way Kurt wished that his hands were free. There was no way to brace against the motion of the truck on the rough track. The only thing that saved the group from receiving more bruises than they did was the fact that their twelve bodies crammed together, filled the back of the truck. When the pick-up finally stopped, Kurt looked over his shoulder and stared in surprise at the tall white walls towering behind them. The commander strode to their truck and said, "Cut them loose." He stood and watched as they climbed out of the truck one by one. The guard cut the bindings as each person's feet touched the ground. None of them spoke, not even Kurt, who wanted to ask why they were cutting them loose now, after the bumpy road.

Looking at the twelve people, the commander knew what they wanted. "My name's Oley," he announced. "Who wants to speak for the group?"

Almost in unison, Kurt, Brother Fox and Daniel said, "I will." Followed by objections from Sister Samethia and Kyla.

When the whole group began talking, Oley held up his hand and let out a sharp whistle. Once he had their attention and silence, he said, "Surely, you can agree on one person without an argument." He still wasn't sure what to think about the group. He recognized the black uniforms. They were identical to the one that Fleet had worn, but the others were unusual to say the least. Six people dressed in skins and clothing that was made of roughly woven fabric. The fact that they had been riding horses and just happened along, right at the time that he had planned his ambush was unnerving. How his scouts missed them he didn't know, but someone was going to explain. Oley watched impatiently as they exchanged looks up and down the line. "You'll all get a chance to speak, but right now I just want to talk to one of you. I have a very small office." Finally, they all looked to a small dark haired woman standing to one end of the line. She was the only woman dressed in the black tunic, and the only woman that Oley could remember seeing wearing such a uniform. He wondered if she was just as ignorant as Fleet had been.

Kyla saw everyone staring at her now. Without hesitation, she stepped forward and said, "I'll speak for the group."

"Great," Oley said, relieved that the decision had been made. He took hold of Kyla by the arm and started to lead her away as he said, "Watch the others." Twenty young men and women immediately surrounded the remaining eleven prisoners. They were all dressed in identical white uniforms and wore their hair shaved at the bottom with long braids that hung down their backs and each one had a gun, which they held ready to use if one of the prisoners gave them the opportunity.

Kyla looked over her shoulder and saw her friends being surrounded. "We don't mean to cause any trouble," she said. "The guns aren't necessary."

"If they don't cause any trouble, then you don't need to worry," Oley said lightly. When Kyla looked at him, she saw that he was smiling at her. Something about the look on his face made her think that he had already guessed what she wanted. Before they had gone through the door that took them into the fortress, Kyla said, "You've seen Fleet. Haven't you?"

It was hard to keep a straight face. Oley wanted to laugh, but instead he said sternly, "We should wait to talk until we get inside."

Kyla's heart was racing as she followed Oley. He led the way to a small white building in the center of the bustle of activity inside the walls. Kyla saw dozens of young men and women watching her with curiosity. They all wore white uniforms, but she was searching for someone among them dressed in black. Kyla was standing just outside the door staring into the crowd. Oley had to get her attention by saying loudly, "Come on in."

Startled from her search, Kyla followed him inside and sat in one of the two chairs that were sitting beside a table in the center of the small white building. After closing the door Oley sat in the other chair and looked at the woman. She had short dark hair that curled wildly in every direction, like it was wind blown and she hadn't used a comb on it for days. It was her eyes that caught his attention. They were a light, crystal blue and she was staring at him with an intensity that made him want to turn away. "You asked about Fleet," he said as he watched her now.

Kyla reached out and grabbed Oley's hands. "Is he here?" she asked anxiously.

Oley could see that she was frantic, but instead of answering her question he asked, "Tell me who you are and why you're looking for Fleet."

Almost trembling when she spoke, Kyla said, "My name is Kyla." She hesitated slightly before adding the why. Rather than a lengthy explanation of visions and shared destinies, Kyla gave Oley a reason that she was sure he would understand and accept. "He's the father of my child."

Oley was skeptical. He had seen her working out the story in her head. Besides, why would eleven other people come with her, if that were all there was to it? "I saw no children with your party," he said impatiently.

"I'm pregnant," Kyla said softly. She was hoping that Oley would be more willing to cooperate if he knew that she was looking for Fleet for personal reasons.

Oley stood and looked at Kyla angrily. "I don't doubt that, or that Fleet's the father. But you're not telling me the truth about why you've come here." He crossed his arms and said, "I can smell a lie from a mile away."

Kyla stood and faced him. "All I want from you is an answer. Is Fleet still here?"

"No, and good riddance, too," Oley said sharply. "He left last night, but not before getting one of my men killed."

Kyla sat down heavily. She had come so close. If they hadn't stopped to rest yesterday, she would have been here in time to catch Fleet. As she put her elbows on the table, she held her head in her hands as she began shaking it in disbelief. As she did, she was saying, "I shouldn't have stopped," over and over again.

Oley watched as the young woman began weeping and shaking her head. After listening to her say, 'I shouldn't have stopped' for the twentieth time he was wishing that they had picked one of the men as their representative. "Please, stop," he pleaded softly. He couldn't stand the chattering or the crying. Comforting women in distress was not his strong point. Oley opened the door and for once he was relieved to see Elle standing outside. "Get in here and talk to this girl," he said gruffly. "See if you can get anything out of her. I'm going to talk to the others."

As he stalked off in a huff, Elle gladly took his place and she slipped inside and closed the door quietly. She had been standing nearby when the woman mentioned Fleet. She gently placed her hand on the woman's shoulder. Until then the dark haired woman hadn't seen her. "My name's Elle," she said. "What do they call you?"

"Kyla," she said as she sat up straight. Kyla was ashamed that she had started crying in front of Oley, and now he was gone had sent in one of the women to watch her.

The girl with the long red braid took the seat across from Kyla and eyed her with curiosity. "You know Fleet?" Elle asked.

Immediately, Elle had her full attention. "Yes," Kyla answered with anticipation. "Do you know where he is?" When Elle looked at her and nodded solemnly, Kyla thought she would burst with joy. "Can you tell me? Can you take me to him?" The questions tumbled one on top of the other.

Elle was a little hesitant to answer but finally she said, "I followed him to Manjohnah's compound last night and saw him go in." Then Elle reached across the table and taking both of Kyla's hands in hers, she looked directly into Kyla's eyes and added, "No one knows where he went except me. Not even Oley."

Kyla's reaction was immediate as she moaned, "He can't go without me. I'm supposed to be with him in the end."

What the strange woman meant, Elle didn't know, but she understood her anguish. She was like a woman possessed. She was like Fleet. "I waited until morning, but he never came out," Elle finished her tale as if she were pronouncing that Fleet was dead. Kyla's only reaction was to squeeze Elle's hands so tightly that she left marks from the pressure.

Oley gladly left Elle with the woman. He would be certain to get more useful information from the others. He needed a place where he could talk to them all in private. The only place big enough would be the hunting cabin that he called his home when he was at the fortress. As he went out the doorway in the wall, Oley motioned to one of the young men and said, "Go get Elle and tell her to bring our guest out here. We're going to my cabin." Then as he approached the group of prisoners, he said, "Everybody back in the truck." With their armed guard watching, they obediently climbed back into the truck.

"Where's Kyla," Daniel demanded angrily, as he stood in truck and looked at Oley.

Oley eyed the sandy haired man warily. He was the only one who didn't seem to fit with the others. He didn't wear a uniform or any skins. It was a strange collection of people and he was sure that once he heard it, he would find their story very interesting. "She's coming," he answered as patiently as possible.

Daniel refused to sit and watched the gate, waiting for Kyla. When she finally appeared with the red headed guard following her, Daniel turned back and looked defiantly at Oley. He might have twenty men with guns pointed at him, but he would have gone after the man if he thought that Kyla had come to any harm. When she got to the truck, Daniel stepped over the others to help her up. As soon as Kyla looked at him, Daniel said softly so only she could hear, "Why didn't you tell me?" Kyla looked at him with surprise. She could tell by the look on his face that someone had told him about her pregnancy. Only it was not the time or place to discuss anything and she sat on the bed of the pickup next to Sister Samethia. Kyla watched as Daniel sat down and continued to watch her, his expression was one of disbelief mixed with concern.

Once everyone was sitting, Elle closed the tailgate. "Can I go, too?" she asked as Oley climbed into the driver's seat.

"I don't care," he said tiredly. There was no point arguing with Elle. The only surprise was that she had asked, instead of just jumping into the cab like she usually did. As the young girl slid into the cab, she turned and began staring at the man with dark hair who was wearing the black tunic. "So did she say anything?" Oley asked. He knew he hadn't given Elle much time, but he was hopeful that Kyla had made some confession.

"No," Elle answered absently. "She's just someone looking for Fleet."

Oley eyed her suspiciously. He had never known Elle to be evasive before now. As he turned the key and started the engine, Oley vowed that he would get to the bottom of the whole mess before the night was over.

As they bounced around in the back of the truck, Kyla told them the news that Fleet had only left the night before and that he had gone to Manjohnah's compound and not returned. The news was distressing to all concerned, except Sister Samethia who said, "He's still alive. I can feel him stronger than I ever could before."

"How can you say something like that?" Daniel was furious. "How can you say that he's still alive, because you can feel him? I for one, want no part of this foolish venture of yours."

Sister Samethia returned Daniel's heated looks with her own placid self-assurance. "There are many things in the world that you can't see or hear, but that doesn't make them any less real." She was used to his doubts, and nothing Daniel said would ever shake her confidence in the Mother's gifts. "You have become a part of our venture, whether you like it or not Brother Daniel." Even though Daniel did not respond, Sister Samethia knew that she had not won the battle of wills that waged between them.

By the time the truck stopped and they had arrived at Oley's cabin it was quite dark. There was already a fire burning in the hearth and hot coffee and soup simmering over the fire. Someone had been there before them to make preparations. "It's about time you got here," a young brown haired woman said as she came from a room at the back of the cabin. She stopped short and stared in surprise as Oley entered with his guests.

Oley quickly pulled off his jacket and kicked off his boots as he came in the door. "This is Sherie," he said as he went to the fire and began to fill one of the cups lined up on the mantle with hot coffee. He sat down heavily in the only padded chair in the room and put his feet up on the footstool. It was his cabin and the master was home. "Guess we're having company tonight," he said to the young woman who was still staring at the strange group that entered with Oley.

Kyla looked at Elle and Sherie standing together, and Oley watching from his seat beside the fire. "We're grateful for your hospitality," Kyla said graciously. Although the only hospitality they had received was a jarring ride in the back of a pick-up.

"Help yourself to whatever you want," Oley said. "Then after you've eaten maybe we can get down to names and someone telling me why you're here." He cast a sideways glance at Kyla to let her know that he still had doubts about her reasons.

"Thank-you, sir," Sister Samethia said coolly, "My name is Sister Samethia, perhaps we could start the introductions with your name."

Oley looked at Kyla, who blurted his name out quickly, "Oley. He told me his name is Oley." Then turning to the women, she said, "And that is Elle." Then almost as an afterthought she looked at Sherie and said, "I'm Kyla." Now that she had started, Kyla continued to say their names until everyone had been announced.

"Why do you call each other Brother and Sister," Elle inquired of the strangely clad visitors.

"We're part of the Family," Brother Wesley volunteered and seemed ready to start into a lengthy explanation.

Oley interrupted him by saying, "Eat first, explain later." Then looking at Sherie and Elle he said, "Get some spoons and bread." When they disappeared, Oley urged the others on by saying, "Just use one of the cups for the soup. The ladle's hanging next to the hearth."

Dylan didn't need any further urging as he went to help himself to the thick broth bubbling in the pot. Before he had his cup filled, Peach was right behind him saying, "Hurry up, I'm hungry, too." By the time Elle returned with spoons nearly everyone had filled their mugs, but they waited for Sherie to pass out the bread and before they ate and for Sister Samethia to say the blessing.

"Before we eat we must thank the Mother for all of her blessings." The Family members standing around the fire lowered their heads. Sister Samethia began the chant and as they had done the first time Kyla ate with them and before every meal on their long journey, the Family members chimed in on the chorus of the chant.

"The Earth is our mother. She gives us life."
"Bless the Mother."
The Earth is our Mother. She gives us food."
"Bless the Mother."

The Earth is our Mother. She gives us shelter."
"Bless the Mother."
"As Mother cares for her Family, so do we care for her."
"Bless the Mother."
"As mother cares for her Family, so do we care for each other."
"Bless the Mother."
"So keep the Mother. So keep each other."
"Mother keep us in the end."

Trying to be a gracious host, when they had finished, Oley repeated, "Mother keep us in the end," and smiling warmly, held his mug up as a toast. Sister Samethia returned his smile and nodded formally. She wasn't ready to let down her guard, not yet. They still had much to discuss with this man before she would trust him with the reason for their visit.

Once they had finished eating, Oley looked at Sherie and said, "Maybe our guests would like something to drink." Without a word, the dark haired girl disappeared and returned with a bottle of brown liquor and several cups. If there was one thing that would help to loosen someone's tongue, it was a cupful of bourbon. As Oley offered the drink, he was not disappointed when Brother Fox, Kurt and Daniel all accepted with relish. "Kyla said that you are looking for Fleet," Oley said as he decided it was time to get down to business. He was sure to refill any cup that was emptied. "He never mentioned any of you when he was here. Why are you looking for him?" he added when no one jumped to answer his first question.

Sister Samethia was standing behind Brother Fox and she answered by saying, "We believe that he is in danger."

Oley laughed and emptied his glass. As he refilled his glass, he held it up and looked at the clear brown liquid as he said, "I can't imagine a man like him not being in danger." Through the glass, he caught sight of Elle. When the talk had turned to Fleet, she had begun moving closer and now she was standing behind Kurt, blatantly eavesdropping on the conversation. Oley was beginning to think Elle knew more about Fleet's activities than she had told him, so he let her listen and watched her as she did. He turned his attention to Kurt and said, "Fleet never got around to telling me exactly what he was planning to do." It was a small white lie, but right now Oley was fishing for answers. The statement was bait and he was waiting for a bite. Only it was Elle who took it and she wasn't the one that Oley wanted to hear from right now.

The young woman almost jumped on Kurt's back in her excitement to get the words out. "They know why Fleet came here and we know why Fleet came here," she announced loudly. "So why don't we all stop pretending and get down to business. Fleet went after Manjohnah and they want to go after Fleet."

Oley looked at Elle and said, "How do you know that Fleet went to Manjohnah's compound."

"I followed him, but he didn't know that I was there," she said in defense of Fleet. "Fleet went into the compound, but he didn't come out. I waited until morning for him." Elle looked at Oley defiantly, waiting for his censure. She had broken the rules twice now, but she would never say she was sorry for what she had done.

"He's a dead man if he went inside," Oley said, his voice devoid of emotions. He wasn't sure if he was happy or sad about Fleet's certain demise.

"He's not dead," Sister Samethia announced. Her tone was every bit as certain as if she had said that fire was hot and ice was cold.

"How can you be so certain?" Oley looked at the strangely dressed woman, struck by the voracity of her statement.

Before she could answer Daniel rolled his eyes and said, "Here we go again." He stood up suddenly and looked at Oley. "Don't listen to her or any of them for that matter." Daniel was tired and he pulled at the hair on top of his head trying to keep his arms from flailing with exasperation as he continued, "They're all crazy. I have spent the last two weeks with them and you're the first sane person I've seen in all that time." Daniel turned back to Oley and without another word, started taking folded papers out of the pockets inside his jacket and dropping them into Oley's lap. "Maybe you can tell us what this all means," he said hurriedly as he rushed to empty his pockets and ask the questions that were preying on his mind. "We searched a semi truck at the lock and dam. It was loaded with materials for building a transmission tower or something like that. We saw dozens of trucks going in and out." Daniel watched Oley as he looked through the stacks of paper.

Oley didn't have to look through the entire mess, he had already seen what he wanted in the stack of papers that Daniel had so generously laid in his lap and was holding onto one piece of paper tightly in his right hand. No one would take it from him. He grinned broadly knowing the young man had given him the key to the Manjohnah's compound. "Maybe we can help each other," he said. "Elle get back to the fort and see if you can find a truck that don't have red arrows painted all over them." He leaned back in his chair laughing at his good fortune. "We're going to drive right into Manjohnah's compound."

"What do you mean," Kyla asked eagerly. She had been standing in the corner watching and listening while the others talked. Now she was hovering over Oley, trying to see the paper that he had clutched so tightly in his hand.

"Your friend has a requisition for supplies," Oley said. "It's all official, signed and sealed. They're just waiting for somebody to come and pick the stuff up."

Brother Fox crossed his arms and eyed Oley suspiciously; "You make it sound like it's easy." The idea of taking his men into Manjohnah's compound was unsettling and he would need more assurances that it could be done. More importantly, a plan to get out of the compound needed to be discussed as well.

"Don't get me wrong," Oley said solemnly. "Nothing is simple when you're dealing with Manjohnah or without danger." He looked around the room and said, "There is no reason for everyone to go. The less who do, the better." Before he continued, Oley looked up at Elle and said impatiently, "Didn't I tell you to go?"

As the young woman turned and left the cabin, Kurt's eyes followed her out the door. She had been standing just behind him and the scent of her was still strong where she had touched him. It was all he could do to stop himself from following her now, but Oley was talking and he should be listening.

As Kurt watched Elle, Oley was grinning at he dark haired man. Everyone noticed Elle. It was hard not to notice her. Still, they had a lot to discuss and he needed his full attention. "Kurt," he said. Then again and more forcefully, "Kurt."

When Kurt finally looked back, he lowered his eyes, embarrassed by the fact that now everyone had noticed him staring at Elle. When he looked at Kyla, she was laughing at him, too. "I'm sorry," he mumbled. "What did you say?" Kurt listened carefully as Oley explained how they could use his stolen truck and uniforms to drive to the compound. Men driving trucks came and went every day and no one would question them if they had the proper identification. Daniel's rash behavior had been their salvation it seemed. Sister Samethia was quick to point out the real reason for their good fortune. It was obvious that the Mother had guided all of their actions, every step of their journey, right down to the red arrows on the pavement.

As Oley told them about the Commanders and their Masters, some stared at him in disbelief, but not Sister Samethia. With every word that he spoke her focus remained on his eyes, until Oley became so uncomfortable under her gaze that he had to look down at the floor to avoid her blatant stare. Still, there was more. He explained about the towers and the Expendables. Then he told them about Fleet's brief visit and Jabe's death.

Once he was done speaking, Sister Samethia said, "I knew it." Her words were said softly and meant for no one else, but they all heard her triumphant affirmation. "I've seen so many things that didn't make any sense before now." As she looked at Brother Fox and then to the other Brothers and Sisters, she said, "The Mother told me that the ice was coming. She showed me in a vision and told me to bring together the Family." Then to Kurt she said, "We have to find Fleet before it's too late. He can't accomplish what he wants without the help of others. He can't do it alone. The Mother has shown me the end. Fleet, the rebels, and the Expendables, each had adopted the arrow as the symbol of their cause, whether by choice or chance." As she looked at each person in turn, she said, "Are you ready to become a part of the end?" Sister Samethia asked the question a dozen times and no one delayed in answering. Not Kurt, Kyla, or the other Guard members, not any of the Family or even Oley. Only Daniel hesitated before answering.

"I'm not someone who makes a promise lightly," he said. "I'll promise to be a part of the end, but I don't believe your prophecies," Daniel said as he looked at Sister Samethia. Then as he turned to Oley, he added, "And I don't believe in your aliens. I believe in men fighting and dying together. That's a promise that I can make. I'll die, before anyone takes what belongs to me."

Oley was the one to put an end to the discussion by saying, "Well, hopefully no one will have to die tomorrow." He sat back in his chair and looked at the people in the room. At least now he knew who he was dealing with - fanatics and zealots, a potentially dangerous combination.

Chapter Twenty seven

It was not long after Jabe's fiery funeral when Fleet finally slipped away from Elle and began his trek to Manjohnah's compound. He had miles of shoreline to traverse before midnight and he began running. Nothing would stop him this time. Fleet was going to enter the compound and if he found Manjohnah he would kill him or if he failed, he would die trying. His greatest regret was not for himself or the life he had wanted. Fleet still carried the weight of Jabe's unnecessary death on his shoulders. It was another in a long list of regrets, which included his ill-advised relationship with Sadie, and his betrayal of Kyla's trust. As he ran, he could forget the ghosts of his past. Instead he concentrated on the sound of the waves crashing on the rocks along the shoreline and the icy cold wind. Each breath and every step became a conscious effort as he continued to run, refusing to stop and allow his body time to rest. There was no time to worry about the fact that his feet were so cold that he couldn't feel them anymore. No physical weakness would delay his progress.

Only when Fleet heard the sound of the boats bumping against the docks, did he allow himself to stop and he collapsed with fatigue onto the rocks. Every breath burned in his chest as he breathed in the cold air. Immediately, he pulled his night scope out of his pack and positioned himself so he could watch for the guard. Before Fleet had time to rest for even a minute, he saw a figure coming down the walkway toward him. Fleet put down the scope and drew his knife. Then creeping quickly but silently, he moved in the direction where he had last seen the man. Just as he had reached the end of the pier and was turning to go back, Fleet emerged from the darkness. He seized the man by wrapping his arm around his neck, choking the breath out of him with one arm and with the other he thrust his knife deep into the man's chest. He had moved with deadly efficiency and as Fleet released his hold, the man fell to the ground without ever uttering a sound.

His half-frozen fingers fumbled with the fastenings as he removed the dead guard's uniform and stripped off his own clothing. So far everything had gone as he planned, but when he tried to put on the uniform he ran into his first major problem. The guard was a much smaller man than Fleet was and there was no way that he could wear the clothes. It was a minor irritation, but at this point Fleet would have gone naked. He wouldn't have been able to hide his identity for long wearing the blood stained jacket, so it mattered little what he wore. He only regretted the time that he had wasted in undressing and dressing again.

Searching the dead man's uniform, Fleet found some keys in one of the pockets and put them in his own pocket. Then after dragging the dead man and his pile of clothing into the woods, Fleet picked up his rifle and pack and began to walk toward the fence. He didn't try to hide his presence as he walked boldly to the gate and let himself in using the guard's key. It was so easy that Fleet couldn't believe that he was inside. The only problem was, now that he was in, Fleet wasn't sure which way to go.

He knew that the southern end of the compound was filled by rows of buildings identical to the ones he had seen at Cole Spring's farm and again at the compound Jack has shown him by the river. It was the only part of the compound that was visible from outside the fence. He quickly crossed the distance between the fence and the first row of buildings. As Fleet walked through the narrow corridor between two of the buildings, he stopped and listened when he came to the end of the building before going on. It reminded him of the night that he had stumbled over Kyla. If the Mother had been guiding him that night, surely She would come to his aid now.

Finally, after winding his way through the maze of corridors, Fleet reached the end of the last building. Here he found a large open driveway lit by a harsh yellow light on a pole in the center. Staying in the shadow between the buildings, Fleet watched while a man in a dark blue uniform similar to his, appeared out of the darkness. He had come from one of the large brick buildings on the far side of the drive. There was no sound except the man's footsteps on the gravel as he crossed the open area just in front of him. Fleet was certain that the man would hear his breathing and his heart pounding. The sound was so loud in his own ears that it had to be audible to others. Despite his fear, the man walked on his way without giving any indication that he knew anyone was hiding in the shadows.

Remaining in the darkness between the buildings, Fleet turned his attention to the building across the drive. An old brick structure, it was three stories high with rows of large windows. There was something sterile and unfriendly about its appearance and it reminded Fleet of a hospital or some similar institution. Fleet skirted the area carefully, keeping out of the light and creeping cautiously from one shadow to the next. When he went past the building, another just like it came into view directly behind the first. Like the first building it was three stories of dark windows, looming over Fleet as he made his way deeper into the compound.

Behind the second building Fleet found a narrow band of trees. He knew that he had to be nearing the end of the point of land. The sound of the waves crashing on the shore could be heard clearly on both sides now. When he came through the trees, Fleet knew that he had found what he was seeking. Just beyond the spot where he was standing was a small island or it was nearly an island. A narrow pile of rocks was the only thing that connected the island with the tiny peninsula. On the island, Fleet could see a house lit up like a beacon in the night. It would have been visible for miles to any ship sailing on the lake.

Like a moth to a flame, Fleet was drawn to the bright light. There were boats on the beach but he ignored them. Instead, Fleet stumbled across the rocks, the waves crashing around him as he went. Before long he was drenched to the skin, but Fleet ignored the freezing water. His only concession to the water was that he was careful to keep his weapon above the waves. That, at least, would remain dry.

After crossing the short distance to the island Fleet paused for a moment to consider his next step. He had been amazed that no one was guarding the island. It seemed that Manjohnah felt very secure on the little island, but Fleet would not let himself be fooled by the ease of his penetration into Manjohnah's stronghold. Even now he had the uncomfortable feeling that he was being watched and moved into the deeper shadows of the trees.

Fleet took shelter under one of the pines before beginning to creep slowly toward the house. It was a large two-story structure, a mansion actually. As he approached from the wooded side of the island, he could see only a small portion of the building rising above the trees. He had gone only a few hundred yards before he came to the end of the timber and found himself on the edge of a rocky slope and sitting at the top of the incline was the house. More than a simple dwelling to Fleet, it was a fortress of luminescent white light that dominated the tiny island.

He only paused for a few seconds in the shadows at the edge of the woods. The culmination of his destiny was at hand and he began to scale the steep rocks that led up to the mansion. The wind whistled and howled about Fleet as he climbed, scouring him with a stinging mixture of water and grit. The rocks, slippery with the spray, caused Fleet to loose his footing and he slid back down the slope with a clatter of stones. For every loss of ground that he suffered, Fleet forced himself to climb again. He felt his bloody and torn fingers only vaguely, as if he were dreaming. Nothing seemed real, except the shining light above him.

Finally, Fleet reached the top and drug himself to his feet just to the left of the front entrance. It was a grand portico with tall columns and everything was covered with the same white, glass-like substance that Oley's fortress was. He no longer made any attempt to hide his presence. If anyone were going to stop him, they would have come by now. His greatest fear at this point was not that he would be captured or killed. He was afraid that the reason no one had come to stop him was that he was wrong. That Manjohnah was not inside.

His body was heavy with weariness as he placed his foot on the first step and then the next. Every leaden motion brought him closer to the front door, which was standing slightly ajar. Fleet pushed the door with one hand and it swung open easily. As he stepped into the foyer, it seemed that the place was deserted and he stopped just inside the entry and looked around the room. Inside and out the whole place was finished with the white material. The brilliant white and icy blue shadows inside the room were cold and foreboding. Slowly, Fleet walked into the grand entry and his footsteps echoed loudly as he crossed the white marble floor. He went past the stairway and a hallway that led from the room. Instead his focus was on an open doorway at the back of the room. Fleet paused just outside and listened.

No conversation, nothing to make a rational person think that the room was occupied, but Fleet had left rational thought behind. His actions were controlled by a reasoning much deeper than conscious thought. Fleet raised his weapon to his shoulder and took a deep breath.

With a cry of rage that rose from the very depths of his soul, Fleet burst into the room ready to fire on whoever might be inside. In the split second that it took to pass through the door, out of the corner of his eye, Fleet saw the man who had been with Sadie, the bald man dressed in the dark tunic. He wheeled around. The man was in his sights and his finger tightened on the trigger. Then Fleet felt a jolt as a surge of energy ran through his body and he stopped as surely as if he had run into a wall. As he fell to his knees and dropped his weapon, Fleet felt something pressing down on him. It was as if the weight of the world had fallen on his shoulders. He lost all control of his body and his gun fell to the floor. The room began to spin and darkness was closing in around him, but just before he lost consciousness, Fleet saw the face of the man and he was smiling.

Whether it had been a few minutes or hours, Fleet didn't know, but when he awakened he was seated in one of the chairs in the room he had burst into. As he tried to move, he found that he was pinned in place. He felt the same weight upon his body that he had before he passed out, but he couldn't see anything holding him. For a moment he thought he was alone in the room, but a man's voice from behind Fleet said, "We were waiting for you."

Fleet tried to turn his head to see who it was, but he couldn't. "Who are you?" he demanded. At least he was allowed to move his mouth to speak.

Fleet heard the footsteps as the man walked to sit behind the desk in front of the chair where Fleet was seated. He was a tall man with a broad and muscular build. There was no hair on his head and the skin was smooth and showed none of the creases and wrinkles that come with age, but Fleet could tell that he was not a young man. As he looked at the man's dark, almost black eyes, Fleet felt the gaze of somebody who was truly ancient. With an amused smile, Manjohnah replied to Fleet's question, "I think you already know who I am." He paused and put on a pair of small silver framed spectacles that were held in place by two small bows that pressed against the side of his temples. It was the only sign of human frailty that the man showed. "Very resourceful," he said. "The guard at the pier was careless, but even one of my men failed to detect you."

Fleet couldn't move to respond, but every muscle in his body flexed against the unseen bonds. They had seen him and were just waiting for him to come to them, like spiders waiting for the fly and now he was caught. "Release me," Fleet's face was red as he strained to rise.

Manjohnah laughed as if Fleet had just told a joke. "Now why would I want to do that?" Then looking behind Fleet, he added, "I can see why you like this one. He is amusing."

Manjohnah's answer only served to increase Fleet's fury. Struggling even harder, he shouted angrily, "Who else is there?" He hated not being able to move or see who was in the room. When Sadie came from behind his chair to stand next to Manjohnah, Fleet felt every muscle in his body go suddenly weak. If it had not been for the restraint that held him in place, he would surely have fallen out of the chair. Even though he had seen her with Manjohnah two nights ago, Fleet still felt the shock of seeing her with him now. For a few moments, Fleet was almost happy to see Sadie. She had been his lover and he still felt a deep attraction for her, but she was like a luscious fruit with a rotten core. Once he remembered the blackness within, Fleet felt sickened as he looked at her and said, "How can you serve them?"

Sadie didn't answer. She stood silently as Manjohnah said, "You are asking, how can we serve the Masters? We have always served them. No matter where they go, we serve them and they care for us." Manjohnah's voice was without emotion. He was stating a simple fact and nothing more.

"Why do you call them the Masters? Surely they have a name," Fleet asked. He could not move. So he watched them both, staring at them defiantly, as he demanded to know the name of the creatures that had come to conquer his world.

Manjohnah regarded him with barely concealed amusement, "The Master's language is not something that can be reproduced with human vocal capabilities. They are so far above you in terms of evolution that I'm sure you would find it hard to comprehend. It is the language of the universe and it is felt rather than heard." Still, Manjohnah smiled and continued as if talking to an inquisitive child, "But if you must have a name. Then you might call them g'Narm."

Fleet listened as Manjohnah said the name. It sounded like he swallowed the word as he spoke. "g'Narm," Fleet said as he tried to duplicate the sound. Again Fleet looked at Sadie as he said, "But you didn't say why. Why destroy everything?"

Manjohnah smiled at Fleet's feeble attempt to speak what Manjohnah could feel. "The Masters are travelers of the universe. Your planet is one of their favorites, with its ice and water. The last time we came here, it was a pristine paradise and your kind were simple creatures playing with sticks. The Masters were quite disappointed when they returned to your planet and found it infested with vermin, the waters and atmosphere fouled with your filth," Manjohnah answered. His voice filled with disgust and contempt as he recalled the g'Narm's reaction upon their arrival.

"Vermin," Fleet almost spit the word out in his fury and frustration. "They killed millions of people when the cities were destroyed. How can you sit there and act like they were justified in doing that?" Fleet was sickened by Manjohnah's smug superiority and he would have torn his heart out of his chest with his bare hands. That is, he would if the man had a heart, but Fleet wasn't so sure that he did.

Manjohnah could feel the man struggling against the bonds that he had placed around him. The blond haired man that Sadie called Fleet was truly a simple creature and had no comprehension of the powers that bound the universe; the powers that the g'Narm commanded and allowed Manjohnah to use in their service. Nothing that Fleet could do would break his restraint, but he continued to fight. It was one of the things that he found amusing about his kind. He stood and walked to the other side of his desk and stood hovering over Fleet, observing him more closely. "How many times have you stepped on an anthill and destroyed it without a second thought? Do you mourn for the ants when you step on them?" Manjohnah asked.

"It's not the same," Fleet answered, but he understood the analogy. There was something else that Manjohnah had mentioned. "You said you came here before?"

"Your literature calls it the Age of Ice or is it the Ice Age," Manjohnah said absently. The tone of his voice left no doubt that he was beginning to grow weary of answering Fleet's questions. "Last time your kind were anxious to help. They considered us gods and were more than happy to die in our service."

He paused only slightly before continuing. "Your life is so short," Manjohnah said as he turned and crossed the room to stand beside Sadie. "The Masters have known life since the beginning of time. Your existence is less than a grain of sand on the beach, nothing, insignificant." When he turned to face Fleet again, Manjohnah's smile was gone and he said, "With the Masters we will live forever. Even if you had been successful in destroying my body, the Masters would not let me die. I am too important, too useful to loose. I am the one who prepares for their arrival. Before they came, I had already secured this planet. I have seen thousands like you. You should have stayed at home. There you would have been allowed to live your short life in comfort."

Manjohnah had already started walking toward the door when Fleet responded. "You're right," he said coolly. His anger was gone and Fleet felt at peace with himself as he continued, "There are thousands of people like me." Manjohnah passed him and Fleet heard him go out the door and his footsteps echoed as he passed through the cavernous room. As Manjohnah's footsteps faded, Fleet continued to raise his voice until he was screaming the words, "I didn't succeed but someone will. I don't believe that you can't be killed. You and your Masters will receive justice for what you have done."

Manjohnah was gone but Sadie remained. Fleet had no choice but to look at her as she stood motionless and silent behind the desk. After what seemed like an eternity for Fleet, he finally asked, "What will he do now, have me killed or will I just be slowly crushed where I sit?"

"No, if you were to be killed, it would have happened when you tried to come in the gate," she answered. Her voice seemed strained as she spoke. Seeing Fleet sitting helpless under the restraint seemed strange and unnatural. It was not how she wished to remember him.

Fleet could hear the distress in her voice. Hoping that he might still have some influence with Sadie, he asked, "Can't you release me?"

He saw her eyes look past him into the other room. It was only a fleeting glance, but Fleet saw indecision that was there for one brief moment. "Only Manjohnah is allowed to use the Master's power," she answered. Once again in control, her voice had no trace of emotion as she said, "I have already done what I can to save your life. You will be sent north with next group of workers. You're a strong man, I'm sure you'll be up to the challenge."

"You're telling me that I'm expendable?" Fleet's statement was also a question.

"No, I'm telling you that you have a chance," Sadie answered. She had argued with Manjohnah for many hours about what was to be done with Fleet. Luckily for Fleet, Manjohnah truly felt that he was insignificant. If she hadn't convinced Manjohnah that Fleet was nothing more than an amusing nuisance, he would not be alive and talking to her now. "You really don't understand, do you?" she said as patiently as possible. "I have been trying to save your miserable life since the beginning. I begged you to stay at the Settlement, but you couldn't be happy with what you had. You were safe and fed." Then she paused and lowered her eyes before she smiled and added, "And I believe you were treated very well."

As Fleet stared at her, finally he understood. Sadie actually believed that was all that was necessary for happiness. "Keep them happy, keep them fed. Take the ones you like to bed," Fleet said the words derisively. "Where do I fit into that?" The realization that Sadie would live thousands of lifetimes to the one that Fleet was allotted gave a whole new meaning to the nasty little rhyme. In her mind, she was helping him by controlling his life.

Sadie's searched her memory, wondering where Fleet had heard the rhyme. Lazarus came to mind immediately, but she knew he would not have told it to Fleet. She had been alone with Lazarus when he said it to her, but Riley had been outside. Despite everything, Sadie was surprised by the realization that Riley had betrayed her trust. Manjohnah had been correct when he warned her not to become emotionally attached to her people. Sadie was glad to be rid of the responsibility of running the Settlement. She did not crave danger as Fleet seemed to do and she no longer wanted to live outside the safety of a fenced compound. Let Lazarus assume the responsibility of her unfenced feeding station and good luck to him.

There was nothing more that she wanted to say to Fleet, but there was one last thing that she could do for him. As she walked toward the door she stopped to stand beside Fleet. Slowly, she reached out and placed her hand on his head. His eyes followed her motions, wild and frightened like a trapped animal, but he did not speak. His hair was still wet and she could feel that his body was cold as she lowered her hand and covered his eyes. Sadie could feel the sleep entering his mind and she hoped that it would last long enough. Fleet would not want to know what was going to happen to him next. Soon, he would be even colder than he was now.

~ ~ ~

Sleep was impossible for Kyla. Oley had graciously offered his own bedroom to Kyla after Sister Samethia had pressured him into doing it. After almost two weeks of sleeping on the ground, she should have had no problem falling asleep, but all Kyla could do was toss and turn as she worried about Fleet. Every minute that they delayed made it less likely that they would find Fleet still alive, no matter what Sister Samethia said. Kyla knew that Fleet might already be dead and she tried to prepare herself for that possibility. It was long before first light when Kyla got out of bed and put on the white rebels uniform that Oley had provided for her. Only five people would go to the compound and she would be one of them. It still seemed incredible. She had had to argue with everybody before it was agreed that she would be allowed to accompany Oley, Kurt, Daniel, and Sister Samethia when they went. If it hadn't been for Kyla, none of them would be here. It was her place to go after Fleet not theirs.

The plan was simple. Oley would drive one of his stolen trucks to the compound and with the requisition form in hand they would be admitted without question. Since all drivers were required to travel with armed guards, Daniel would ride with him in the cab. As Kyla thought of Daniel, playing the part of the armed guard, she was certain that he would give a convincing performance. Sister Samethia, Kurt, and Kyla would be smuggled into the compound in the back of the truck. Since the guards would search the truck, Oley had told them that they would be hiding inside a false wall that they had built into the back of the truck. He assured them that they had used the truck for smuggling weapons and ammunition and it had never been detected, but he didn't seem quite as certain when he told them that they would be able to squeeze into the narrow space. Once they were inside the compound, Daniel and Oley would have to find some way to release them without being seen. With Sister Samethia and Kyla wearing the rebel uniforms the three men would pretend they were taking prisoners to the lock up. Oley had knowledge of the buildings in the compound and knew where the prisoners were kept. They would use the time that it took to load the truck to search for Fleet. It would have to be enough.

When Kyla entered the front room of the cabin, she almost stepped on Dylan who was still soundly asleep on the floor just outside her door. Kurt was standing with the door open a crack and looking outside. When he saw Kyla, he turned away and stepped outside. Kyla crossed the room quickly and carefully avoiding the sleeping bodies that covered the floor. A rush of cold air greeted her as she opened the door and slipped outside where Kurt stood waiting for her.

"Why didn't you tell me that you're pregnant?" he said suddenly. Then without waiting for her to answer he added, "I can't believe that Fleet would leave knowing about the baby."

"He didn't know," Kyla answered.

"Why didn't you tell him?" Kurt asked. He couldn't believe Kyla had kept her pregnancy a secret from Fleet, too.

"I don't know," Kyla answered impatiently. She had asked herself the same thing, a million times and the answer was always the same. She had the opportunity. There was no reasonable explanation for her silence and she was sick of the question. "I don't know why anything happens like it does. Why did I have to stop for a day, when I was so close to finding Fleet?"

"If you hadn't stopped then Oley wouldn't have found us and we wouldn't be here now," Sister Samethia said as she came through door behind them. "If you had told Fleet, it would have changed what he planned to do. The Mother guided us here and only She knows what purpose we will serve."

Kurt was not pleased with Sister Samethia's interruption. Now that he had spent some time with her, Kurt was certain that her constant ravings had turned Fleet into a raging lunatic and now she was working on Kyla. "I have only one thing in mind and that is to find Fleet, dead or alive and put an end to this madness," he said firmly. There was no anger in his voice but his conviction showed in his eyes. He set his jaw firmly and lowered his brow as he stared at Sister Samethia. Kurt had decided to keep a close eye on Kyla today. He didn't want her to spend a minute alone with Sister Samethia. For the first time since they had decided Kurt would hide with the women behind the false wall in the truck, he was glad that he would be there.

Daniel and Oley came out the door right behind Sister Samethia. They were wearing the uniforms that the workers inside the compound wore, light gray jackets, caps, and trousers with black boots. Kurt was also dressed in the same uniform. Oley looked at the group and said, "It looks like we're ready to go." As he turned and began to walk to the truck Oley was still talking as he went. "That's what I like. Get an early start and get it over with. We'll be back for lunch if we're lucky." When he reached the truck and saw the others still standing by the cabin, he called, "I thought you were in a hurry."

Together, they walked the short distance to the truck. Oley opened the door to the back of the trailer and Kurt jumped inside. He held out his hand and helped Sister Samethia up into the trailer. Then he held out his hand to Kyla. Before she could take hold of Kurt's hand, Daniel lifted her up and set her inside the trailer. He looked into Kyla's eyes briefly and without saying a word, he turned and walked toward the cab. Oley jumped into the trailer with the other three and walked to the end where a section of metal had been removed to reveal a small empty space within. Not only was the space narrow, but also they would have to kneel once they were inside.

Oley was holding a flashlight and he watched their reaction when they looked at the hiding place. "We won't seal you inside until we get to the highway. It'll only be twenty miles that you'll have to ride in there. It shouldn't be more than a half-hour at the most." He gave Kurt the flashlight and walked to the back of the truck. Before shutting the door to the trailer he said, "Hold on. It's going to be a bumpy ride."

True to his word, as Oley drove them to the main road, it was a wild ride. Still, it was better sliding around the empty trailer, than it was after they were crammed into the tiny smuggling compartments. Once Oley replaced the metal panel and fastened it into place, Kyla felt like she was sealed in a coffin. Even though they were now driving down the highway, they were all afraid to make a noise. At any moment, Manjohnah's men could stop the truck and demand to search

612

it, but it never happened. Despite Oley's promise that the trip would be short, it felt like an eternity before Kyla felt the truck slow to a stop. The next sound she heard was the door of the trailer opening and footsteps just outside their hiding place. There were voices, too, but they seemed muffled and far away. The door closed and slowly the truck began to move forward again.

As Daniel climbed back into the cab of the truck, he looked at Oley. Even though it was cold outside, drops of perspiration beaded on his lips and forehead. As he wiped his face with his hand, he was shaking when he said; "I thought that guy was going to start pounding on the sides of the trailer when he jumped inside like that."

"You did fine," Oley said, as he put the truck into gear and began to pull through the gate as the men inside opened it. "Just remember, as far as they're concerned, you're just like them. So do your job, keep your mouth shut, and don't ask any questions." As they drove slowly up the drive Oley was giving Daniel his final instructions, "When I give my requisition form to the man at the supply office, I'll keep him busy. While I do that, you get the others out of the truck and try to stay out of sight. Keep you're guns pointed at the women if anyone asks you what you're doing just say that you're following the Commander's orders. I'll find you when I'm done."

Daniel nodded and looked at the rows of storage buildings on their left. Further up the drive he could see some larger, brick buildings. Behind the buildings were the woods again and somewhere beyond that the end of the tiny point of land. There weren't very many people to be seen; perhaps it was the early hour. They hadn't gone very far when Oley stopped the truck in front of one of the buildings. There was nothing to distinguish this building from any of the others except over the door to this one there was a strange symbol; a smaller crescent nestled inside a larger one and an oval at their center. Oley jumped out of the cab and went into the building, while Daniel walked to the back of the trailer. After checking to see that no one was watching, Daniel opened the door and climbed inside. He worked quickly to remove the screws that held the panel in place and once he removed it all three inside tumbled out gasping for fresh air. Without a word, Daniel put the panel back into place and secured it tightly. On the way out they wouldn't be able to use the same hiding place, since Oley's payment for his help was a full load of supplies.

Once he had finished, Daniel jumped out of the back of the trailer. There was not a soul to be seen as he helped Sister Samethia and Kyla to the ground while Kurt jumped down beside them. Then as Oley had instructed, they held their guns pointed at the women and disappeared into the maze of corridors between the buildings. They had no idea where to go from there. Without Oley, they could wander aimlessly for hours and never find Fleet.

They had to wait only a few minutes before Oley found them. Smiling when he sighted them, Oley strode confidently to where they stood. Still grinning, he pulled Daniel and Kurt's caps low, concealing their eyes. "Keep your eyes on the women and don't look at anybody. The trick is to make everyone believe that you're not anyone they want to question." Then with Oley leading, they started toward the brick buildings just beyond the storehouses.

Kyla watched as Oley strutted confidently before them. If she hadn't known, she would have thought he owned the place. They passed another man wearing a uniform identical to the ones that Oley, Daniel and Kurt were wearing. Without so much as a glance in their direction the man went on about his business. When they passed a man wearing a dark blue tunic, he slowed to look at them. Kyla felt his gaze long after they walked by him, but even he did not stop to inquire about their activities. They followed Oley past the first building and then to the back entrance of the second. When Oley tried to open the door it was locked.

"Don't worry," Oley said as he began to search the top of the door and the area around it. Finally, he found a key hidden in a small opening of the wall at the bottom of the stoop. As he used it to open the door, he said, "If they're such an advanced race, you'd think that they would be able to find a better place to hide their keys." As he let them in he added, "Their only problem is they rely too much on humans and sometimes we forget our keys."

Once they were inside the building, Kyla was struck by antiseptically clean appearance and smell of the corridor where they stood. "Is this a hospital?" she whispered. Although Oley seemed at ease, she was still very much afraid that they would be discovered at anytime.

"In a way," Oley answered. He had told them he knew where the prisoners were kept, but he hadn't told them what Manjohnah did with them. "This is where they prepare the prisoners for artificial hibernation. A frozen popsicle is a low maintenance prisoner. No food. No trouble. They're very practical about things like that." As they followed Oley down the corridor, they tried the doors as they went, but they were all locked.

"So you think that they froze Fleet?" Kurt asked when they reached the end of the hallway.

"If they didn't kill him," Oley answered and pushed open the door to the stairwell. He had his gun ready as he cautiously stepped inside and looked up the steps. The others followed moving as silently as possible.

They had not yet opened the door that led to the corridor on the second floor, when Sister Samethia, who had been silent the whole time, suddenly announced, "They're both here."

"Who," Kyla whispered, "Manjohnah and Fleet?"

"No," Sister Samethia answered her eyes wide with surprise, "Sadie and Fleet." Ever since she had been released from the metal compartment inside the truck, Sister Samethia had felt the vibrations that emanated from the ground upon which they stood. More powerful than anything she had experienced before she had found the focus that she had been seeking. It was no vague feeling that she felt. Sister Samethia knew that Fleet and Sadie were in one of the rooms nearby. She felt them and pointed the way, "Follow me," she said and pushed past Oley into the hallway. Kyla was right on her heels and the men scrambled after them, trying in vain to maintain the pretense that they were guarding them.

They walked past two rooms with large glass observation windows. Inside the rooms they could see large metal storage cabinets lining the walls and an examination table in the center of each room. It was cold in the hallway; so cold they could see their breath as they walked. When they came to the third door, Sister Samethia burst into the room. Upon seeing Sadie, she was horrified but not surprised. "I knew it was you," she said, her voice barely a whisper as she faced the embodiment of evil.

Kyla was right behind her and seeing Fleet lying motionless on the examining table, she shouted, "What have you done to him?"

Daniel and Oley entered right behind them, running as they entered the room. "I have prisoners ready for preparation," Oley blurted out, still hoping that Sadie would believe Kyla and Sister Samethia were under his command.

"It seems that you almost lost your prisoners," Sadie said sharply. Then she looked at Oley and asked, "Don't I know you? You look familiar."

"Yes, ma'am," Oley answered obsequiously, "I've been working here a long time. Perhaps I can be of service to you." He grinned at Sadie. She was a beautiful woman, but he didn't doubt that he would be dead if she remembered his face. Instead, he hoped she might send him away as he added, "Anytime day or night is fine with me."

There were so many men in the compound and they all looked the same in those lumpy, gray uniforms and acted the same way. Sadie couldn't remember where she had seen this one before and she didn't care for his disrespectful manner. "Wait outside," she ordered. "I want to speak to the prisoners."

Daniel began to protest by saying, "We shouldn't leave you with these prisoners." A look from Oley told him that he should have kept his mouth shut.

Sadie turned on him like a viper and hissed, "I am the Commander. Leave, now, and wait outside until I call for you." As the door slammed shut behind Oley and Daniel, she turned and looked at Kyla who was standing next to Fleet's motionless body and was about to touch is face. "Keep your hands off. Don't touch his skin," she nearly screamed the words. Her anger with the guard was still fresh and she was ready to unleash her fury on Kyla. It was incredible luck that the guards had brought both Kyla and Sister Samethia to her before Manjohnah saw them. Sadie was not surprised to see them. Kyla had always impressed her as a loyal type and like the faithful dog that she was she had followed Fleet. Now they could both share Fleet's fate. Only, unlike Fleet, Sadie would make sure that they were never awakened.

Sadie walked to Fleet and placed herself at the top of the table with Kyla standing to her right. Sister Samethia had not move or uttered a word since she came into the room. Sadie smiled at her knowingly, then turned to Kyla and said, "He has been prepared for hibernation and the heat from your skin might damage him now."

Kyla's mind was reeling with disbelief. "He looks like he's dead," she said softly. Then she looked at Sadie. "If you ever loved Fleet, how could you do this to him?"

"He has not been harmed in any way," Sadie answered. Her tone was cold and unfeeling.

"How can you say he hasn't been harmed? It's unnatural," Kyla looked at Sadie and saw that the word unnatural applied to her as well. "You're just like us. How can you help aliens take over our world and change our lives like this?"

"You assume that I am like you, but I am not," Sadie answered. "We are what the g'Narm have made of us. Our seed was gathered here long ago. We appear to be like you, but beyond that the similarities end." Sadie looked at Sister Samethia and smiled as she said, "But Samethia is like us. Maybe at some time in her past her mother and mine were the same."

Kyla looked at Sister Samethia then back at Sadie. The women were similar in height and build and could have been sisters, but there was nothing else that they shared as far as Kyla could see. "Why did you pretend to help us? Why go to all the trouble of the evacuations? Why not just kill us all and be done with it?" Kyla's questions were hurled at Sadie like accusations.

"The Masters don't want to totally eradicate your species, but the population was out of control," Sadie said. "We still needed a work force and now we have one in hibernation. The feeding stations were for the stragglers. We put out the food and you came in droves. With the pearls to keep everybody happy, it's a perfect world for everybody."

"You can't keep everybody happy with pearls and the promise of an easy life," Kyla said with disgust. For Sadie it was so simple. "You can't control people that way."

"We can and we do so very successfully," Sadie answered smugly. "Besides, pearls are not intended to keep the population happy.

The euphoric effects only serve to make them more appealing and assure that everyone will want them."

"What other use could they possibly have?" Kyla was growing tired of Sadie and her superior attitude.

"To sterilize the population," Sadie answered. It was a bit of information that she was sure Kyla and Sister Samethia would find interesting. "We have all the workers that we will ever need. There is no reason to add the burden of more mouths to feed." Pleased by the shocked looks on their faces, Sadie continued to explain the effects in greater detail. "It works best on women. One use and they are no longer able to reproduce. With men, it takes more exposures and may wear off in time, but with women there is no reversal. It's very effective, wouldn't you say?"

Kyla looked at Sadie and for the first time in days she wanted to laugh. Still, she didn't even crack a smile as she thought of the child that was growing inside her. Sadie and her kind thought they were superior and clever with their plans to end the many generations of humans who had lived on earth with hers. "Nothing will ever end the human race," Kyla said with a confidence that was growing as surely as the life within her was. "We are the strongest most adaptable species that exists on this planet or anywhere in the universe. We will continue to fight you and after us, if necessary, our children will fight against you. It will never end."

"Yes, that's what Fleet said," Sadie said cruelly, " and you can see where he is now. Soon, you will both join him." She was bored with the conversation and the company. "Guard," she shouted. When Daniel entered, he waited silently.

"Can I have a minute alone with Fleet?" Kyla asked. Daniel's eyes shifted to her and Kyla could see that he was anxious to be done and gone.

Sadie smiled and said, "Take the other one out." Daniel complied, took Sister Samethia by the arm, and pulled the catatonic woman out the door. "I'll allow it if you promise not to touch him," Sadie said and went into the hallway where the others were waiting. As she went through the doorway, Sadie looked back at Kyla standing beside Fleet. It was a moment of weakness on her part, but in a way she shared something with Kyla. They both loved the same man.

As soon as the door closed, Kyla reached inside the jacket she was wearing and unfastened the tiny pin that she always wore near her heart. Carefully, she undid the tie on Fleet's tunic and fastened the arrow pin inside where it couldn't be seen then tied it back in place. It was the only way that she could let Fleet know that she had come for him. That she had been there. As she took her hands away, Kyla heard footsteps behind her.

Before she could turn Oley was there and had taken hold of her arm. "You can't do anything for him now," he said under his breath. "So lets get the hell out of here, now. Before she figures out what's going on." Oley pulled Kyla out the door as Sadie came in and he felt as if he were caught between two cats that were ready to pounce. As Oley continued to drag Kyla down the hallway and away from the observation window, they both continued to stare at each other until Sadie finally was out of sight. Kurt and Daniel were already at the end of the corridor with Sister Samethia standing between them.

Without a word they hurried down the stairway and left the building by the same door where they had entered. There were more people in the compound and although they tried to maintain the same charade that they were simply escorting prisoners. It seemed that their group attracted more notice heading away from the buildings, than they had going toward them. They had almost reached the storage sheds when one of the men wearing a dark blue tunic called for them to halt. It was still too far to try and run to the truck, so Oley stopped and faced the man.

"What are you doing?" he said as he considered Oley and the others critically. "You're taking your prisoners in the wrong direction."

"I'm just following the Commanders orders," Oley answered.

"Whose orders?" the man asked.

"The woman Commander, Sadie," Oley lied quite convincingly. His answers were all delivered promptly and without hesitation. "She is going to meet us at the perimeter so the prisoners can show her how they gained access to the compound." Then just to make sure it all sounded believable, he added. "I don't want to be late, sir. I believe that she would make me an Expendable if I'm not there waiting when she arrives."

The man hesitated for a moment as he looked at Oley and the others. There was nothing extraordinary about any of them. It would be easy enough to check his story. No reason to suspect a lie from the simple man following orders, but he didn't trust Sadie. Since her arrival, she had tried to circumvent every order Manjohnah gave. She was definitely not one to play by the same rules that he and the others followed without fail. "Wait here for me," he ordered.

"I won't be held responsible when Sadie finds out," Oley called out as the man walked away.

"We can't just stand here and wait for him to come back with Sadie," Kurt said anxiously.

"Just be patient," Oley said as he watched the man disappear behind the first building. As soon as he was out of sight, he said, "Let's go. Quickly."

They were only a few feet away from the rows of storage sheds. Once they reached them they began to run. By the time they reached the waiting truck, they could see the man returning and shouting as he spotted them, too. "Get in," Oley said as he opened the door to the cab and began shoving Kyla and then Sister Samethia inside, before climbing in himself. Without waiting for Kurt or Daniel to get to the other side and climb into the cab, Oley started the motor and put the truck into reverse. The passenger side door was open and Kyla and Sister Samethia pulled up Daniel first and then Kurt as Oley continued backing the truck down the driveway.

When the guards at the fence began shooting, they were already at the gate. Oley backed right over it and rammed through the barricade outside. Then he turned the semi and headed down the highway traveling as fast as the truck could go. As they sped down the road, Daniel was shouting with jubilance, "We did it. I can't believe that we got in and out of that place."

No one else was ready for celebration. "We didn't do anything," Kyla said. "Fleet is still in there." She had failed in her attempt to rescue him and he was condemned to a fate as final as death in Kyla's mind.

"It's not over yet," Oley said as the truck skidded around a curve. The trailer swerved behind them, threatening to jack-knife. "They'll be right behind us in a minute." He slowed the truck to a stop and abruptly ordered, "Get out here." His tone was one of a man used to being obeyed without question. "If you follow the shoreline you'll find our base," he said quickly. "Now close that door and get out of sight." As Oley pulled away, the others hurried into the woods.

"I can't believe he left us like that," Daniel said when they had reached cover. He still felt the flush of excitement after their narrow escape. He would have gone with Oley if the man had given him a chance. The words had barely escaped his lips when several vehicles zipped past the spot where they were hidden.

"He did what he promised," Sister Samethia said.

"Now, you have something to say," Daniel said. "What was wrong? You acted like you were in a walking coma." He hadn't been especially concerned about Sister Samethia's uncharacteristic silence while they were inside the compound, but he had to wonder about her strange behavior.

"A walking coma?" Sister Samethia repeated his words. "It was more like a waking dream." She was surprised that Daniel had been the one to mention her reaction to their visit to the point of land where the compound was built. "As soon as I set foot on the ground, I could feel their power." She looked at Daniel and said, "I don't expect you to understand or believe, but they chose that point of land for a reason. It's a conduit for energy. I could feel it vibrating under my feet and ringing in my head as clearly as a bell. It was stronger than anything I have experienced." Then looking at Kyla, she said, "I'm sorry that I wasn't any help."

"It doesn't matter," Kyla said. "Manjohnah and Sadie may have won this battle, but we will win the war. It isn't over yet." She smiled and without thinking her hand cradled her belly where even now she felt the tiny movements of the life growing inside her womb. "They think that they can seduce us with promises of an easy life and eradicate our species at the same time, but they're wrong. We will triumph, and survival is the only weapon that we need." Kyla's pregnancy was a small victory, but Sister Eaglet was expecting a child, too. If two women were pregnant, then there would be others. The human spirit and the ability to adapt had served the human animal for eons, and there was nothing that could diminish their will to live.

Epilogue

After Kyla was gone Sadie returned to the room and looked at Fleet lying on the table. It was a terrible waste. Soon, he would be sent to the storage rooms underground. After that, Sadie would not see him again. In her own way, Sadie had loved Fleet as much as she loved anyone. If he had listened to her and stayed at the farm, she would have stayed there with him. After he left, there had been nothing to keep her there, nothing to hold her interest. Still, the things that had caused Fleet's downfall were the very things she admired about him most. His untamed spirit and craving for danger and excitement were the things that she loved.

There was one thing that Sadie could do for Fleet. He had wanted a child that would carry his lineage into the future. Although she would not submit herself to the primitive practice of using her body as an incubator for his offspring, she would produce a child that was a combination of both Fleet and her best qualities using the same methods that had been used to create Sadie and the others. She had already collected the genetic material from Fleet that she would need.

Although she had never performed the procedure herself, she knew others been able to recreate the process that the g'Narm used. Sadie was living proof of that. Manjohnah had created her in the same way. Sadie was his daughter, a mixture of his genetic material and that of a woman who had sparked Manjohnah's interest during his last visit to this planet. It was impossible for Manjohnah to deny her the same indulgence that he had allowed for himself.

She had decided that the child would be male. He would possess Fleet's lean muscular build and look like him, except that he would have her dark hair and eyes and the tawny golden skin. The child would be stronger than a human child and all the genetic defects that still plagued the inhabitants of this planet could be avoided. He would possess all the knowledge that the g'Narm had given them. Most important of all he would have Fleet's irrepressible appetite for life.

There was one last thing that made her triumph all the sweeter. It would be her child and Fleet's not Fleet and Kyla's. Kyla would never be able to do what she planned to do. Now that both Fleet and Kyla

623

were under her control, she would be able to make sure that they never saw each other again.